Templar Scholar

The Renaissance Army Series

Renaissance Calling (2017)

Templar Scholar (2019)

**

Visit www.RenaissanceArmy.com for
background information on
the Renaissance Army series.

Templar Scholar

Michael Bernabo

First Printing, 2019

ISBN – 10:	Hard Cover	0-9986993-5-7
	Paper Back	0-9986993-6-5
	Kindle	0-9986993-8-1
	ePub	0-9986993-7-3
ISBN – 13:	Hard Cover	978-0-9986993-5-6
	Paper Back	978-0-9986993-6-3
	Kindle	978-0-9986993-8-7
	ePub	978-0-9986993-7-0

Impending Imagination, LLC
St. Paul, MN

www.michaelbernabo.com

Dedicated to:

My parents, for giving me their love of stories in all their forms.

My friends, for the stories we tell each other through our games.

My readers, who asked me when the next book was coming out.

Author's Note

When I started to write a book in the spring of 2011, I had no idea it would be any different from a hundred other books I'd started to write. I certainly didn't think I would get so inspired as to write an eighty thousand plus word rough draft in six weeks. But I did, and I had my first rough draft.

Even then, I had a hunch I was going to have to cut it into two books. Not because of length, but because there was so much going on, I didn't think I could do it all in one book. A second draft (that was twice as long) and several alpha readers later, I divided the book in two.

The first part became *Renaissance Calling*. That was a rather simple process. Take the written chapters, workout a new ending, and write away.

The second part became *Templar Scholar*. That proved to be an entirely different process, for two reasons.

First of all, when I considered what I wanted the book to cover, I expanded the story to last a whole year. That presented an issue of pacing. A book covering a whole year at the pace of *Renaissance Calling* would be more than four hundred thousand words. Far too long.

To solve it, I wrote this book from both ends to the middle. From writing the end I figured out what Sasha needed to know, and from the beginning I could direct the flow towards those lessons.

The second reason was because of Kickstarter. To fund *Renaissance Calling* I completed a successful Kickstarter campaign, and allowed backers of a certain level the opportunity to create a character for Book 2. With the success of the campaign, I now had to add the new characters to the book.

Working with the backers to create the characters was a fun experience. Some backers came to me with a role they wanted their character to fulfill, and it was up to me to build the character who would do it. Others came to me with a character, and I found a role for them in the story. From some backers I got a few sentences, from others several paragraphs of notes.

In the end I had fourteen new characters to add into the story. Some of the characters were easy, fitting into roles I was already planning to have. Others required a lot of planning to fit in. Afterall, I wasn't going to reward a special backer with a character who shows up for one page, says 'Hi!', and leaves.

It took a while, but in the end, I got all fourteen in there. Do they all work? The list of them is at the end of the book, so you can check. Who knows? Maybe some of them will surprise you.

In any event, it took a lot longer to bring *Templar Scholar* to publication than I'd hoped. But after a lot of work, a lot of re-reading, and a lot of re-writing, I'm finally ready to tell the next chapter of Sasha Small's story.

Enjoy.

-Michael Bernabo

Acknowledgements

*Thanks to my editor, Brittany, who has worked
with me to bring Sasha's story to print.*

*Thanks to my artist, Courtney, for her talent of
crafting a cover that fits the story I'm telling.*

*Thanks to the alpha and beta readers who gave me their
time and advice over all the drafts.*

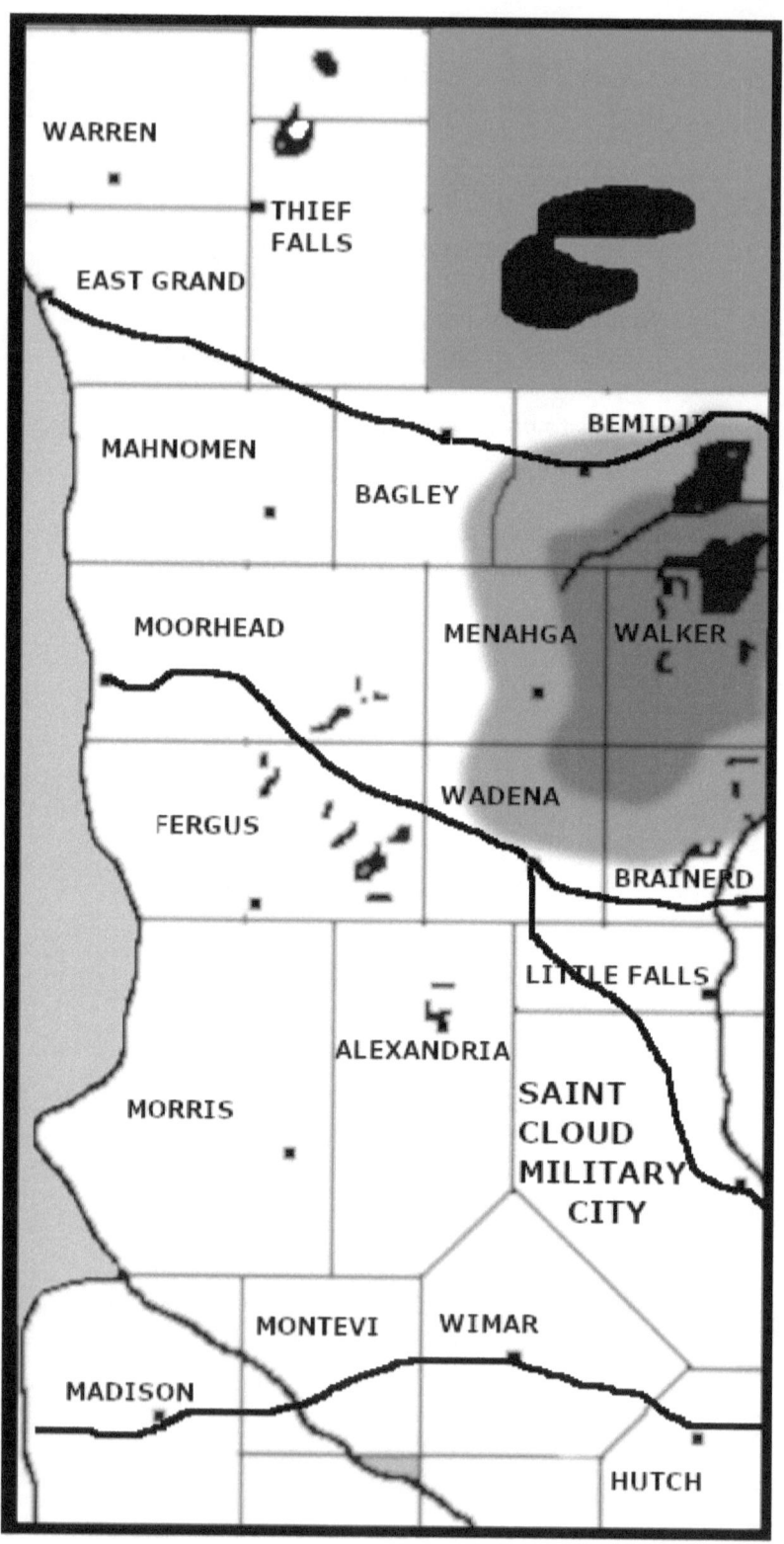

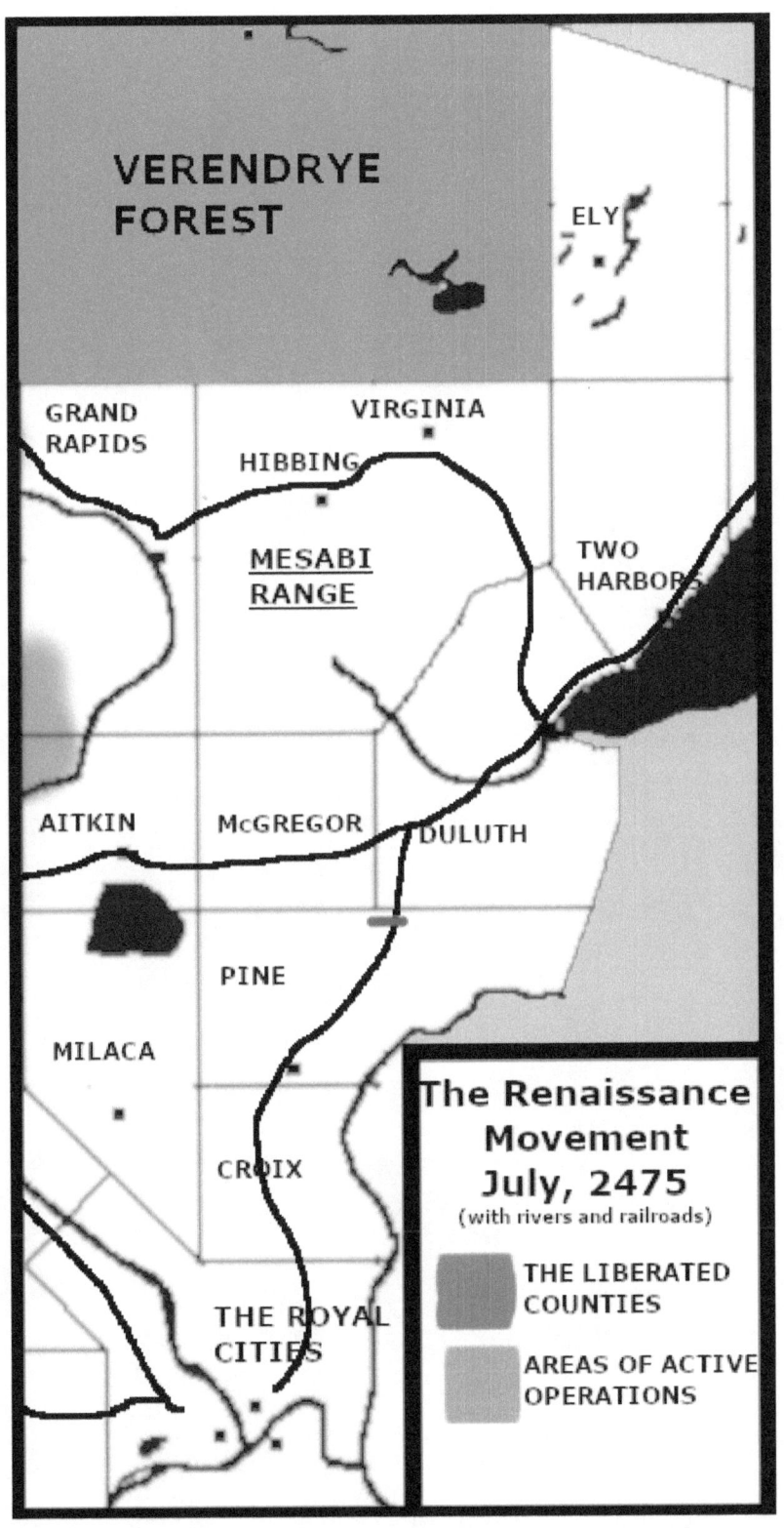

Prologue

'I WAS A GENERAL!'

Vittorio Montessori, Count Walker, screamed at the painting. It depicted him as a young major, leading his battalion into the maze of trenches around Tripoli. He had been at the prime of his life, years younger than other battalion commanders, with a fire in his eyes that rivaled the fires of hell. His attack earned him the notice of the general of the siege, and a medal from the Great Emperor himself. And the attention of young woman at the Eastern Court in Sarajevo. And a year's income from estates around Ankara. What a lion he had been at that age.

And now, what was he? Fat and wallowing in an ill-fitting uniform. The count of a small, poor county, in Minnesota of all places, populated by lazy peasants who did not understand their place. They were supposed to work and provide goods for him to profit from. That was the way of things. He had proven his worth on the field of battle, and he had earned the sweat of their brow.

But no, they did not see it that way. Instead they grumbled. They complained. And then, they fought back.

That was not the way of the world. Peasants did not control their fate. The whole Before Time had fallen because they thought they could. No, peasants existed to toil. Some might be worthy of marching in uniform, others might be capable of pulling themselves out of servitude, but for most of them, that was their life.

And why should they want more? Power and responsibility were heady things, and not everyone was meant to wield them. He was, of course. Born into a powerful family in Milan, he had grown up around authority. He and his siblings learned command from the nursery. Even he, as a younger son, not expected to inherit, was bathed in the rules and forms of leadership.

He was drawn to the Imperial Commonwealth to earn position denied him by birth, and he had done well. Yes, he was annoyed that the Commonwealth did not award nobility for life, but twice had earned the income from estates. Three times he was awarded the Imperial Cross. He had lost count of how many times he had been welcomed enthusiastically at courts across the world.

And now.

He pushed himself out of his chair and lurched towards the windows of his tower.

He had been a General of Division, commanding the Seventeenth Odessan Grenadiers. He led twelve thousand men, some of the finest to ever fight for the Commonwealth. They crossed the Atlantic, making landfall in Quebecois ports and marching to the front. For months, his grenadiers held their part of the front near Albany, defeating two offensives as the Commonwealth assembled their forces and prepared for their own campaign.

The great day came, and the Commonwealth armies launched their offensive. And he ran right into the Red Redoubt.

He cursed the Red Redoubt. A sizable citadel outside of Albany, perfectly situated to control miles of front lines. Two corps made the attack, four divisions, of which his was the only one to make it to the walls of the defenses. At horrible, horrible cost.

And who suffered? The generals who failed to push their men forward? No, he became the scapegoat. He took the most losses because he had gone forward while others held back, and the others dragged his name down. Now, the best life he could work out for himself was this lousy, minor title of nobility.

Damn them all! He ambled from one window to another. Damn the generals. Damn the king. Damn my peasants who refuse to keep to their station!

He thought of his wife. She had died some time ago, after building the cathedral, overseeing the redesign of Walker Town, and developing the beautiful gardens. For her, this was a place to build as a resort, for proper cultured people to come and spend their time resting and relaxing away from their stresses. The gardens, extensive and well planned, had taken up more than a square mile just south of Walker Castle, from lake to lake. She loved those gardens.

Now, they were ruined. The gardens were marred by a trench line, extending across the entire property, with bunkers and redoubts built in, to maximize the limited number of troops and weapons he had available for defense. Whatever else he was, he knew how to build a strong fortification.

Beyond the trenches was the forest, and within it, the enemy. The Renaissance Army, the Mardurers, whatever name they chose for themselves. Traitors! No other name made sense.

He turned and started down the stairs to the Great Hall, which had become the headquarters of his defense. He wanted to look at the map, to reassure himself of the state of his city.

If nothing, Walker looked well defended. Sitting on an isthmus, the town could only be approached from the west and south. The western approach had

2

long ago been cultivated as a wide, difficult marsh, spanned by two bridges, both of which sat broken and burned. The southern edges were protected by the long trench line, anchored by the castle on the west and a redoubt on the east. And if they did try to land by lake, they could not do so except under the view of guns mounted in the cathedral.

Manning the defenses was a bit more difficult, but not impossible. Montessori had started with fifty yeomen. He'd hired many more after the rebellion began, and after casualties and cowards still have almost eighty chased into the walls with him. Not the best soldiers, but loyal. Another hundred or so were veterans and their sons, men who followed Walker to try their hand at farming outside the city. More men were conscripted, pressed into service against their will. That gave him almost three hundred men to defend the city, and by using the fortifications, he made that number work.

The war room was dominated by a large map of Walker and its defenses. Montessori's son, Giulio, sat in his own chair, staring intently at the map. Though his leg had been amputated only a few short months earlier, Giulio had refused to spend long in bed, instead becoming Walker's second officer, organizing the men and supplies and keeping the town in order.

'Any change?' Montessori asked in Italian.

'No, Father,' Giulio said. 'Nothing new, as it has been for weeks. No shots taken, no skirmishes or sorties. It is all quiet.'

'They are still out there,' Montessori growled. 'They will not run.'

Other officers assembled. A tall lieutenant from his yeomanry, an aged veteran from his farmers, and a civilian who commanded the conscripts. Montessori listened to their reports, his son translating for them.

'And our supplies?' Montessori finally asked.

Giulio looked at the figures. 'We did stockpile enough to keep us through the winter,' he said. 'It will not be an easy winter, but we can make it.'

'Assuming these rebels are still here this winter,' Montessori said. 'Watch, Son. A harsh winter will drive them from their foxholes, and Minnesota winters are harsh indeed.'

'Which would be more of a comfort if the people in those foxholes weren't from Minnesota,' Giulio said.

Montessori scoffed but changed the subject. 'Any word from the outside?'

'No, but we have some men willing to try. Stealthy men, who can make it to Brainerd undetected.'

'Ready them,' Montessori said. 'We must ensure the king knows we fight on.'

'Yes, Father,' Giulio said. He turned to make the preparations.

The veteran officer spoke in Odessan. 'What if they come while we wait?' he asked.

'We make them pay,' Montessori said. The officer nodded, as if he had heard such bravado before and dismissed it as such.

Montessori hid a smile. It was not bravado, no idle threat. Let them come, and I'll teach them a lesson they won't forget.

Chapter 1

Sasha Small looked at her reflection in the pool and smiled. She was proud of the changes she saw. She gained muscle in her legs and arms, and she felt her body was leaner. She sported a few small scars and bruises, enough to prove she was an active participant in several battles. And the face that looked back was one of a confident and happy young woman.

I am a warrior woman, she thought to herself, flexing her arms. I should ask if there's a word for that.

Finally, Sasha stopped staring and waded back to a rock the edge of the pool. She pulled her hair into a ponytail and considered its length.

'Do you think I should cut my hair?' she asked the woman sitting on the rock.

Able Medical Officer Mary, the regimental surgeon, looked up. 'Short to your scalp, or just shorter?'

'I don't know,' Sasha said. 'I don't think I'd like being bald.'

'It would help keep lice and such away,' Mary said. 'What did you do with the soap?'

'I handed it off,' Sasha said, 'and if I was bald, I wouldn't have to worry about keeping my hair out of the way during a firefight.'

'Many practical reasons to shave it all off,' Mary said.

'Then why does no one do it?' Sasha asked. The Third Minnesota Field Regiment had, between regulars and local militia, more than two hundred souls serving. To Sasha's knowledge, no one purposefully shaved their head, though a number cut their hair very short. Lieutenant Colonel Snow, their commanding officer, kept her hair only an inch long.

Mary shrugged. 'I don't know, and I'm not particularly worried. So long as we keep our hygiene up, it shouldn't be an issue. Now, are you ready?'

Sasha nodded. 'Yes, ma'am.'

'Any issues you want to tell me about?'

'No.'

'Problems walking, lifting, sitting or standing up?'

'No.'

'No problems with breathing or diet?'

'No.'

'Any trouble sleeping, dealing with other people, reactions to loud noises?'

'No,' Sasha said.

Mary took out her stethoscope and gestured for Sasha to step forward. She listened to Sasha's heart and lungs and took Sasha's pulse. She made notations in her book. 'Okay, you're good.'

'Thanks,' Sasha said and turned to move back to the bank of the pool where the rest of the women were waiting.

The pool was a broad, shallow expanse in a flowing creek that Third Field Regiment had chosen for their bathing area when they moved into Brainerd county three months earlier. The terrain allowed the pool to remain secluded, away from spying eyes, and the regiment had worked to make the pool deep enough for those bathing to immerse themselves completely by sitting down. As they were bathing, they took the chance to do their laundry as well.

Presently, almost twenty women from regiment were using the pool. Some were doing their laundry, others washing themselves. Some were on guard duty, and some were taking a nap or conversing on the edge. The women had several hours at the pool, and no reason to rush. It was a chance to rest for most of them.

Sasha was always one of the first to bathe, so she made her way to the laundry section to clean her clothes. Much to her surprise, she found her clothes already hanging on the lines, along with the clothes of several other women Sasha knew had not done their laundry yet.

'Harriet,' Sasha shook her head.

The woman appeared from behind a hanging blanket. 'Oh, stop complaining.'

'It's not your responsibility to clean my clothes.'

'No, it isn't, but I do it anyway,' Harriet shrugged. The woman was a few years older than Sasha, a civilian wife of one of the first rifles to join in Brainerd County. She had come out with him several months earlier, fleeing the yeomen, and became part of the regiment, all while being very pregnant. Not a fighter, she worked hard to earn her keep with the regiment, doing laundry and cooking and other camp duties. After giving birth to a son a month earlier, she was working her way back to what she considered her normal duties.

'Harriet,' Sasha said, 'it's not right for someone else to do my chores.'

'Okay,' Harriet replied, 'toss them in the mud and get to cleaning.' She crossed her arms and looked at Sasha expectantly, successfully reminding Sasha of her own mother.

Sasha did not move.

'I didn't think so,' Harriet said after a few moments. 'Your clothes are mostly dry, though I'd give the coat some more time. Enjoy your break.'

'Thank you,' Sasha said. She pulled on her blouse and pants, decided to leave the clunky and annoying boots and her bodice until later. She picked up her backpack, rifle and utility belt to take with her.

Sasha made her way to the watch post, where Sergeant Winnie and Rifle Margarite stood guard. The men currently stationed at their base camp were restricted to its confines while the women were at the pool, as the women were restricted when the men bathed. But even if the men would respect the privacy of the bathing pool, a patrol of county yeomen would not, so a watch was set.

'Done already?' Winnie asked when Sasha stepped up.

'Harriet got to my laundry before I did,' Sasha said.

Winnie chuckled. 'If it's one less thing to worry about, I say let her do it.'

'I'm certainly not going to fight her over it,' Sasha said. 'And I do get more reading time.'

'Of course,' Winnie said with another chuckle.

Winnie was Sasha's sergeant and friend, though the friendship had not come easily. The two had sparred early after Sasha's arrival, with Winnie threatening to beat Sasha from the regiment. It was only after the regiment's first battle, ambushing a bandit company moving through their territory, that the two had become friends. Both of them had proven their worth in that battle, and Winnie had to concede Sasha was indeed a good addition to the regiment.

'I'll take your spot,' Sasha said, 'go get clean.'

'I might just take a nap,' Winnie said, getting up from her position.

'Whatever you want,' Sasha replied, sitting down next to Margarite. She laid her rifle next to her, the belt next to it, and leaned back. 'See anything?' she asked.

Margarite shook her head. 'No, Corporal.'

'Good,' Sasha said with a smile. Margarite was a timid young woman who had joined the regiment only a few weeks before. Sasha was unsure of her,

7

thinking she was not good fighter material, but Winnie had become a sort of mentor to her. A very different approach than she had done with Sasha.

Maybe Winnie sees something in Margarite that reminds her of me? Sasha asked herself.

'Just let me know if you see anything,' Sasha said and opened her book.

She was only a few words in when Margarite spoke. 'Is that a new book?'

'It is,' Sasha said.

'You finished the other one?'

'I did,' Sasha said, trying not to let her annoyance show.

'What was that one about?'

'It was about the American Revolution, from the Before Time,' Sasha said. 'This is a biography of Field Marshal Rudolph Imperian, from the war with Iowa.' She settled down to get to reading, making it through several paragraphs before Margarite spoke again.

'Where do you get the books?'

Sasha sighed. 'Grandpa Middlestedt. After his son lost the debate to General Prince, he took his family south to Brainerd, but his father stayed behind. And Grandpa Middlestedt had a decent number of books.'

'And he lets you read them?'

Sasha nodded. 'He does.'

'Any books of children's stories?'

Sasha chuckled. 'No. All ancient books. Histories and such.'

'Oh,' Margarite said. 'I like children's stories.'

Sasha did not respond, trying to concentrate on her reading. She was no more than three pages into the next chapter when Margarite tapped her shoulder.

'Corporal?

'What is it, Margarite?' Sasha asked, trying not to let her annoyance show.

'I think there's someone out there.'

Sasha looked up and glanced over the lip of the incline. She quickly slipped the silk bookmark into place and slid the book into her backpack. Picking up her rifle, she started watching.

Out in the forest, she saw a figure moving through and between the trees. It was still a way off, and Sasha was not sure if it was heading towards the bathing pool or not. The noise from the pool was not loud, but it was not quite silent either. A hum of conversation was common.

'One of the men from the camp?' Margarite asked.

'Colonel Snow would come down on them pretty hard if they tried, assuming we left them alive to be punished.'

Margarite chuckled nervously. 'What do we do?'

'We wait,' Sasha said. 'If they move by, we can follow them.'

Someone from the pool had come up behind them. Margarite whispered to her, then she moved back to tell everyone around the pool. The conversation from the camp died down, and Sasha heard rustling. She turned and saw the women arming themselves, many in various degrees of undress.

Margarite shrugged. 'I guess we'll fight naked,' she said.

Sasha turned her attention back to the figure. It was not moving directly towards them, but rather at an angle. She did not think the figure knew they were there.

'What do we do?' Margarite asked.

Winnie was at her side, her automatic ready. 'Yeoman?'

'No,' Sasha said. 'I'd guess a kit, but I can't see yet.' A kit was a courier from the Special Services Group. They were called kits after their commander, Major Fox. They often traveled alone, carrying dispatches and letters from one county to another.

'Don't shoot him if he's friendly,' Winnie warned.

'No, really?' Sasha replied sarcastically. The figure was close enough for Sasha to see a face, had a large hat obstructed her view.

Please don't make me shoot you, please don't make me shoot you.

The figure paused and looked up, trying to figure out his position. Sasha saw his face, and leapt up, startling several of the women.

'HOLD!' she bellowed. The figure stopped and stared at the woman now standing before him. 'Unless it is your desire to be killed by a company of naked women, stop where you are.'

The figure looked at her, and a broad smile crossed his face.

'My dear Sasha Small,' Major Fox said, 'of all the deaths I have ever been threatened with, that is by far the most appealing. Were I not on a duty for General Prince, I might entertain such an ending.'

Sasha could not help but smile.

Major Fox. The man who had changed her life. A friend.

'What does he want?' Winnie prompted.

'What is your purpose here?' Sasha asked.

'I come bearing dispatches for Lieutenant Colonel Snow. Would she perchance be back there?'

'Snow is not here,' Sasha said, then paused as Winnie tugged on her pants.

'Tell him to go to the camp,' Winnie growled. 'We will be there when we finish.'

'Can you make your way to the camp?' Sasha asked. 'We are in no position to welcome you as we are.'

'Of course,' Fox said. 'I shall see you there.' Fox turned and made his way towards the camp. Now that he knew where he was, he knew where to go.

'I wonder what he wants.' Winnie said. Then she turned to the women who looked at her expectantly. 'Ladies, please don't dawdle. 'We are still part of an army, and we still have responsibilities to tend to. Plus, I want to get back to camp before the boys eat all the food.'

The women laughed and went back to their chores.

Sasha sat back, pulling the book back out of her backpack. She stared at the closed book, lost in thought.

Sasha Small used to be a very unhappy girl. Her hometown, Penelope's Haven, had considered her trouble, constantly fighting with the mayor's son, Samuel Cartier. That Samuel was a bully and she was simply defending herself did not matter to them. Her family practiced Alvanism, a belief system known for its pacifism, and never supported her in her fights to defend herself. Yet Sasha refused to let herself be bullied and continued to fight. For that, the town called her trouble.

Then came Major Fox. The first time she met him, he rescued her from a fight. He complimented her. Ultimately, he started her on the path that led her here.

The second time, he brought her to an intellectual conversation with General Prince, the leader of the Renaissance Army. That had turned out to be an enjoyable experience, one that left Prince impressed with her.

What does he bring this time?

***

The camp was a small ravine in the middle of the woods. When the Renaissance Army sent Snow and the Third Field Regiment into Brainerd County, it was their first home. They cut alcoves into the walls for sleeping and supplies, constructed defenses, and organized the rocks into a fire pit. It was the perfect size for the first sixteen men and women of the regiment and continued to work as the regiment grew.

Sadly, it was no longer their home. The camp was now where squads came to rest and relax, to bathe and rearm. Small tents and lean-tos dotted the forest around the original ravine, which now contained two fire pits and a tarpaulin covered area with logs for sitting. Several roughly made tables sat in the middle, currently being used by several rifles reloading ammunition. Some took naps, taking advantage of what the lazy day offered. And some of them debated the news of the latest broadsheet.

The Tribune was printed by the generals for distribution to the units of the Renaissance Army. Fox had brought the latest printing, along with a kit's normal load of letters and dispatches. Sasha took one from Margarite and scanned through it, scouring it for information. Her family was being held hostage in Walker Town, long under siege from the Renaissance Army, and Sasha read each broadsheet thoroughly to see if she could glean any information about what was happening. As usual, Walker Town was barely mentioned.

Sasha went to her sleeping den, a small alcove she had dug out herself some months earlier. She used to share it with Mary and Beth, another friend of hers, when this was the Third Field Regiment's main encampment. Now Beth had a bed in Arrowhead, and Mary took over the colonel's old sleeping den, leaving Sasha this one all to herself. She was thankful; sleeping with another person was annoying enough, but even worse than that was the season's mosquitoes. She thought about dealing with both of them at once and shook her head. *No thank you.*

Sasha went back to her book, focusing on the words. It was a shame that there were so few books to read in this age. Sasha knew she was lucky to have anything beyond Bibles and short books of children's stories and folk tales, but she was frustrated.

The conversation with General Prince had convinced her she enjoyed reading and learning. She wanted to read everything she could get her hands on, as limited a selection as that was, and she wanted to use her knowledge to help the regiment. She had even asked Snow to consider her for a regimental warrant, to make her an officer within Third Regiment. She had no problem fighting, but she wanted to learn to use her mind as well as her weapons.

That led to her ambitious reading program. She read whenever she could between patrols and skirmishes, exercises and guard duties. Times like this, where she had several hours to really get into a book, were rare, and she could only enjoy them because Winnie let her.

'Let everyone else refill ammunition and stand guard,' Winnie said the first time Sasha had protested the lack of assignment. 'You prepare yourself to be an officer. Read and read again.'

Sasha was secretly grateful for that, and if anyone else complained about it she had yet to hear of it. Almost everyone seemed to agree that she was going to get her warrant someday. It was a question of when. And if that was the case, she was going to work like crazy to prepare herself.

She read for several hours, lost in the life of Rudolph Imperian, until Winnie kicked at her foot.

'We are heading back to Arrowhead tonight,' she said.

'What?' Sasha asked. They were not supposed to head back until the morning. 'It'll be dark before we get there.'

'I know, but Fox's message can't wait.'

Sasha grabbed Winnie's hand. 'What's going on?' she asked nervously, getting to her feet.

'The generals are coming,' Winnie said. 'Both of them.'

Chapter 2

Arrowhead had once been a village of a hundred souls; now it was a town of over four hundred. Most of the growth came from the liberation of northwest Brainerd County a few months earlier. Arrowhead was the most defensible of the villages, so many of the civilians were moved for their protection. Those who stayed behind did so to tend crops that would be needed come winter.

Some of the members of the regiment hated Arrowhead, including Winnie. It was not that they thought the civilians should be left defenseless, but the Third was a field regiment. Their mission was to go into a county and take the county away from the noblemen through unconventional warfare, ambushes and raids and such. A town tied down resources the regiment needed elsewhere. The best protection was to keep the fight away from the civilians.

Sasha understood, but did not completely agree with her sergeant. The resources that Snow put into defending the town were weapons too big to be easily carried and manned by men and women not physically ready for the warfare she needed to wage. The groups Snow could send out were lighter and well trained in the fighting that Snow needed them to fight.

Besides, Sasha could easily find places to stay up and read in Arrowhead.

Winnie dropped off most of the followers in Arrowhead, taking Fox and a few younger rifles along with her to see Snow at the small cabin outside town she used as her post. Sasha had a late dinner and read until she was roused by a night patroller and sent to a tent. It was going to be an early morning, he warned.

It was. The sergeants roused everyone before dawn for a quick meal of porridge, then assembled everyone before Master Sergeant.

Master Sergeant was the oldest member of the regiment, with greying hair and a well-worn look, which reminded most of the regiment of their grandfathers. He still walked tall and looked as if he could wrestle a bear. And yet, he was a calm individual, experienced and more than willing to work hard for the regiment and his colonel. And no one knew his true name.

He was also the regimental sergeant, the senior non-commissioned officer, or noncom. Undoubtedly, he was a veteran of the Minnesota Army from the time of the Republic, but no one knew what he did with them. When the regiment was in its darkest hour, he had been the rock on which it survived. Now, he worked with Beth to train those who volunteered for service in the regiment, and the emergency militia who would defend Arrowhead in the event of an attack.

Today he trained everyone on parade marching. Even the officers were involved, learning the commands and orders to give. Thought she had no experience with marching, it was obvious to Sasha that the regiment was clumsy. Marching in step was difficult, some concentrating too hard on their pacing they missed commands, turning the wrong way or marching off and away from their units. At one point, the third company veered right instead of left, splitting the regiment in half and marching in opposite directions.

The civilians of Arrowhead enjoyed the spectacle. Among them were children, laughing at the display and marching sloppily alongside their parents. Friends and loved one shouted encouragement and jokes at those they knew.

Watching from a more subdued quarter were the headmen, leaders of the liberated villages. Many of them had been rescued from the clutches of the count by Third Field Regiment at the Battle of Kimble. While they had no intention of surrendering to the nobleman who ordered their arrests, they were old enough to understand what was still coming their way.

The regiment's practice stopped before lunch. The town had taken to the festive atmosphere and made a much better meal than they would normally have eaten, and the regiment sat around the village eating and talking. They had finished and wondered what was coming next when word spread through the ranks: riders had just arrived. Sasha joined Winnie, standing on a porch to see over the heads of the crowd, and recognized them immediately.

Olympians.

Olympians were the personal guards of the generals, wearing distinct green and black striped uniforms and wielding the black carbines. There were four of them, speaking with Snow and Fox in the distance. After a moment, one of the Olympians waved his hat at the tree line to the north. Figures began to emerge, approaching the village at a decent pace. Several wagons followed close by.

There were numerous riders, three or four dozen. Most looked to be Olympians, others armed civilians, and several uniformed officers. Sasha looked for officers she would recognize.

She saw Able Staff Officer Bellona, General Prince's blonde aide-de-camp. Her long golden hair flashed in the sunlight. Next to her was another staff officer, one with fiercely red hair. Sasha did not recognize her but shrugged it off. If Bellona was there, then he was somewhere in the crowd.

There! She recognized Prince, firm in his riding posture, riding behind the aides. She smiled. Prince was a handsome man, with a commanding but kind presence. She watched him defeat a royalist mayor in a debate some months earlier; in fact, she had helped deliver the final argument. He planned the battle that freed more than a hundred prisoners, and took time to care for the wounded, even the enemy wounded. Sasha was grateful for fighting in Snow's regiment, and she only had that chance because Prince started the Renaissance Movement.

The riders entered the town. The Olympians and some of the armed civilians moved to the side, silently watching for threats. The adjutants and several other sergeants, the general's staff, stayed with them. Three of the civilians rode forward with General Prince and one other officer, whom Sasha recognized almost immediately.

General Caesar, the other general of the RAM. Sasha had only met him once, after the ambush that brought her freedom. He was quiet, and appeared almost embarrassed to speak with her, but he was also intelligent. He had briefly debated her father, an Alvanist pastor, on pacifism in the Bible. For that, he had earned her respect.

But Sasha knew little else about him. Caesar had not come up much in discussions. Many of the Mardurers didn't even know he existed. Most of the rest did not know him at all, except that he was intimately connected with the training and building of the army. They remember seeing him here or there, but rarely did he speak.

Some of the officers knew more. Lynx, one of the regiment's warrant officers, knew him as the officer who blocked her commission on the grounds that Lynx had difficulties with letters and reading, but Lynx was not bitter about it, as Caesar had also given her exercises to practice with, and encouraged her to try again in the future.

Of anyone in the regiment, it was Colonel Snow who knew Caesar the best. She spoke of him as being an intelligent but bashful officer, who was well suited to building the Renaissance Army from nothing. Sasha believed Snow knew much more, but her colonel refused to say anything. When pressed on Caesar's position, Snow simply commented that he was 'right where he needed to be.'

Snow greeted the generals and their guests with the headmen standing behind her. Sasha could not hear the words, but soon enough the lot of them had disappeared into one of the houses. Some of the guards remained, while the rest went to take care of the horses. The wagons stopped, and more civilians stepped out. One looked like a simple carriage, carrying a man and several more armed men. Another was a large wagon, with the words 'Hamline Family Theater' painted in bright gold letters. A half-dozen men and women sat on

15

top, waving at the crowds.

The excitement over for now, the crowds began to disperse. Sasha and Winnie stood still, waiting for the crowds to thin a bit. Mary made her way through the crowd to Sasha, Beth following in her wake.

Beth had been a common rifle when the regiment first made its way into Brainerd County, known for her relationship with another rifle named Rick. When Rick died fighting bandits, Beth had responded by becoming the regiment training instructor, teaching others to fight and survive on a battlefield. Shortly after, Snow gave her a warrant, making her Training Officer Beth.

'Wonder who those civilians are,' Winnie said, looking at the house.

'A civil government, I think,' Beth responded. The women all looked at her. 'Snow told me about them. General Prince asked some headmen and mayors to form a council, to represent the people and provide direction.'

'And the armed men?' Sasha asked. Sasha noted they were all men, while the Olympians at least had a handful of women in their ranks.

'Civil guards. Trained, but not military, and not answerable to Prince or Caesar.'

'I guess that makes sense,' Sasha said. 'The civil government is guarded by civilians and not the military.'

'It's a division of resources,' Winnie said curtly. 'I get why they do it, but do we really need another guard unit snatching up people and equipment?'

'Someone disagrees with you,' Beth said.

'No surprise there,' Sasha smiled.

'And the wagons?' Winnie asked.

'Teachers,' Beth said. 'From Walker. To begin educating our own civilians.'

Winnie sighed. 'I guess that's why we're practicing drill? To march and show off for civilians?'

Everyone looked at Beth, who finally nodded. 'Yes.'

'Swell,' Winnie said.

'Oh, do try to look on the bright side,' Sasha said. 'Some of the books I read show pictures of huge flags. At least we don't have any of those.'

***

Much to Sasha's surprise, they did have flags.

Sasha did not see them until the next morning, when the regiment assembled for their parade. Some of the older rifles, men who had served in the Iron Republic Army and knew the proper cadence for such things, led the regiment with a pair of them.

The first flag was the flag of the Renaissance Army of Minnesota, the white field with the blue diamond in the middle. Sasha had seen that one before, flying over the prison camp after its liberation. It was, Sasha later learned, the same flag that had flown over the camp. Prince had given it to Snow and the regiment as a gift.

The second was the flag of the Third Field Regiment. This was a forest green field with three white snowflakes stitched into it. It was a gift to the Third Regiment from the liberated people of Arrowhead. This was the first time Snow displayed it.

Both flags led the regiment through Arrowhead, accompanied by an honor guard and two drummers. There was a festive spirit in the air, a celebration that Sasha had not expected. The people cheered them, some seeing their loved ones marching, others just cheering for the whole unit. As clumsy as they were, the crowd was still enthusiastic.

The center of town had been cleared of the clutter from normal life and prepared for the display. At one side stood Colonel Snow, along with the generals, their civilian guests, and the local headmen. They watched the regiment march into the square in four companies, marching past a wagon covered with a wooden deck and stairs up both sides, then around the edge, coming to a halt on command with only a few members stumbling forward then quickly jumping back into formation.

The regiment now formed a rough square. To the north was the wagon and the civilians. To the west was Beth and her trainees. To the right was Militia Captain Babbage and his militia. And to the south was Weapons Officer Erick with his Weapons Company, and Winnie leading the rifles, including Sasha.

It was almost a shame none of the other officers were here, otherwise Winnie could march with the rest of her company and not apart from it. As it was, First Lieutenant Buck, the regiment's other commissioned officer, and Field Officer Lynx, were both on extended operations to the east.

Sasha saw movement across the field. One of the civilians moved forward. It was the woman Sasha had noticed earlier. She had brown hair, already streaked with grey, and wore a green dress with a leather vest. She walked with a strong gate and stood tall. She climbed the wagon and looked out over the men and women around her.

'Third Field Regiment,' she began, speaking loud enough to be heard by everyone assembled, 'civilians of Brainerd County, and Elected Headmen. My name is Anna Templeton. I am one of the elders of Walker County, elected by popular vote to the Civil Council, and I was asked to come speak with you here today.

'The last time there was an election was almost twenty years ago, just before the Imperial Commonwealth swept in and turned our world dark. Most of us here did not vote in it. We were too young, too poor, too uninterested to guide the course of our country. And when it was gone, we believed that we would never see it again in our lifetime.

'When General Prince arrived in Walker County, he claimed he was fighting for a return to democracy. I did not believe him, but I learned that he meant what he said, that this is not just the Renaissance Army, but the Renaissance Movement. I learned it when the first teachers arrived in our town to educate my grandchildren. I learned it when he requested a civil council, elected by all adults regardless of their sex or wealth. I learned it when Prince addressed our first meeting and outlined his desire for a civil government.

'To the civilians, I'm sure some of you have learned that lesson from the actions of this regiment. Soon you will see it in the teachers. You have your own council already, and I'm glad to call them fellow representatives. And I'm looking forward to adding more as we continue forward.

'Third Field Regiment, I have heard from your officers and your representatives, about what you have done; how you have fought for them, sacrificed for them, and asked for so little in return. Whatever it is about this Renaissance that brings out that notion in you, I hope it keeps. We need more of that in this world.

'Thank you,' she said and stepped back, to the applause of some of the civilians.

'Are we supposed to clap?' Margarite asked Sasha.

'I have no idea,' Sasha replied.

General Prince climbed the wagon now. He surveyed the regiment and the civilians, all watching him intently. All of them knew he was a Dawson, a member of the family that founded the Iron Republic centuries ago when the old world fell. The Iron Republic which became the Minnesota Republic. Of all those assembled, he was the only one who would never be extended a pardon by the king.

'I am willing to believe there is one question on all your minds,' he said. 'What does marching in unison have to do with ambushing the enemy?' He paused. 'The answer is, nothing. I've seen Third Field Regiment in combat. Now, I just wanted to see how Lieutenant Colonel Snow's regiment could handle a real challenge.'

Sasha laughed with the rest of the regiment.

'I have had several debates over the merits of drill. Some say it is a waste of time. Others say it is important to instill discipline. I see the merits of both, but I will say this: it is damn impressive when a regiment marches by. Especially a regiment that I have fought with, with rifles I admire and a colonel I respect.'

Some of the regiment cheered. Sasha was one of them.

Prince waved them quiet. 'But I do know the importance of ceremony, for both military and civilian organizations. For me, a ceremony is a specific act that announces something. We held a ceremony for the first meeting of the Civil Council. We hold a ceremony whenever we graduate a class of rifles. We hold a ceremony to bury our dead, to celebrate a birth, to make sure that the importance of the moment is not simply lost in the flow of life.

'We are gathered here today for a ceremony, one which I'm very proud to oversee.

'The Renaissance Army was founded with a system of awards in place. Many of you know of them from your training in Walker County. Some of them are simple ribbons, awarded for service to the army. Others are awarded for specific actions. I'm speaking, of course, of the three crosses.'

He raised his hand, raising one finger for each cross mentioned.

'The Crimson Cross; awarded to those wounded in battle.

'The Renaissance Cross; awarded to those who find an inventive solution outside of combat.

'The Colonels' Cross; awarded for heroism in combat itself.

'To be awarded such a medal, you must be nominated by your colonel, and supported by other officers. The Crimson Cross is simple enough; a letter from a surgeon will suffice. The Renaissance Cross is much trickier. How does one define inventive? How difficult must the problem being tackled be? But I want to support fresh thinking, so the Renaissance Cross was born.

'The Colonel's Cross can be difficult. Anyone who has seen combat under our banner has seen heroism. How do we determine who deserves it, and who does not? I would give it to every soldier under my command, but that would devalue the times the award is warranted. The Combat Wreath, worn by those who have seen battle, must suffice to that end.

'So why am I speaking of medals? After our battle at the prison camp, I received a letter from Lieutenant Colonel Snow nominating one of your own for a Colonel's Cross. So sure was she that this nomination was deserve that she included not one, not two, but four letters from other commissioned officers supporting her nomination. Five letters, all equal in their praise. When one officer speaks, I should listen. When five speak, I must pay attention.'

He gestured to Bellona, who started to climb the stairs behind him. 'Those of you who learned of the crosses, you know that the three of them are not the highest award I can give. You know that there is something more.'

'The General's Star,' someone whispered behind Sasha.

Bellona opened a box. Prince lifted out a long cut of dark blue ribbon with a metal star hanging from it.

'The General's Star,' Prince said. 'The highest award the RAM can give. No one has ever won this award, so high an emphasis do we place on it.

'Which means today will be the first.'

A wave of whispers rolled through the crowds. Sasha looked around, smiling, wondering who it could be.

Prince returned the star to the box and took a folded paper from Bellona. He did not look down at the paper, already knowing the name. He turned to the regiment and called.

'Sergeant Winnie, front and center.'

Winnie glanced about, shocked by her name. Snow waved her forward. 'Go on, you!'

'Go up there!' Sasha smiled.

Winnie found her feet and walked forward. She moved to stand below Prince's wagon, but he gestured for her to climb the stairs. She came to a stop before Prince and saluted.

'At ease,' Prince said. He opened the letter.

> *'On Tuesday, the 22nd of May 2475, during the Action at Bonnie Lake Internment Camp, both the Third and Fourth Minnesota Field Regiments were engaged in a fierce fight south of the camp with B Company, Fourth Rochester Rifle Battalion of the Royal Army of North Mississippi. Sergeant Winnie, of the Third Minnesota Field Regiment, did single-handedly engage, clear, and capture an enemy mounted machine gun. She then used the machine gun to disrupt the enemy offensive, exposing herself to*

great enemy fire. When the gun was finally rendered inoperative, Sergeant Winnie continued to fight, holding the wagon train until commanded to fall back by her superiors.

'*Sergeant Winnie is nominated by Lieutenant Colonel Snow, of the Third Minnesota Field Regiment, her commanding officer. Her nomination is seconded by Lieutenant Colonel Wild, of the Fourth Minnesota Field Regiment. And is thus confirmed by General Prince, Renaissance Army of Minnesota, Commander in Chief.*'

He handed the letter to Winnie, who looked at the words. Prince said something and she stiffly turned around.

Prince took the medal out of the box in Bellona's hands. He stepped forward and placed the medal around Winnie's neck. It hung several inches below her neckline. It looked like someone had guessed her neck size well.

Finally, Prince stepped back. 'Third Field Regiment, assembled representatives, and all civilians present. I give you Sergeant Winnie, First Recipient of the General's Cross, Hero of the Renaissance Army of Minnesota.'

The crowd, civilian and soldier alike, cheered, Sasha loudest of all.

Chapter 3

The Hamline Family Theater constructed a small stage from their wagons. They made deals with local children; bring them chairs and benches and blankets for an audience to sit on, and they would get candies as a treat. Soon they had a respectable set of seating available, which was mostly full as they played their parts.

Sasha got back from her perimeter check to see only Bill Hamline and his mother on stage, a large sign to the side proclaiming 'SCENE: SKY CASTLE'. Bill, the tall leader of the family, stood in a large black robe, with a black mask and a large sword in his hands. His mother, an elderly woman, stood across from him, wearing a brown robe and a large fake beard, also wielding a sword. The rest of the family was hiding behind the curtains, hidden from the audience's view.

Bill, speaking in a booming voice, stood tall and laughed. 'Oh, Old Man, your age is showing. When you were my teacher, you were indeed a master of the sword and the arts, but now, frail and weak, you are hopeless. I am the master now!'

'Only a master of darkness, Dark Lord. Of the arts, I am still your master,' his mother responded, speaking as an old man might.

'The arts do not help us here,' the Dark Lord laughed. 'In my sky castle, the arts work for none but me. It is how I knew to find you, as you snuck back to your airship as a thief in the night.'

The two actors leapt at each other, swords flashing. They moved across the stage, dancing with the blades.

Two more actors appeared from the curtain. Bill's children, the son in armor, the daughter in a dress, stared at the fight.

'We must help them!' the son said, but his sister pulled on his arm to keep him back.

'No, Sir Knight! You heard the Dark Lord. In his castle, only his art works, and if the Old Man cannot overcome that obstacle, neither can you.'

'Then what do you suggest, Princess? That we run like cowards?'

'You are not here to defeat the Dark Lord, Sir Knight,' the Princess said. 'You are here to rescue me, that I may bring my knowledge of their plans to the rebels. That is the mission. Running away to complete the mission is not cowardice.'

The brother sighed. 'You are correct, Princess, and I am sorry I yelled. Come, let us skirt this fight. Perhaps the Scoundrel has made his way to his machine, and we can prepare our escape.'

They walked behind the stage, taking care to avoid the pair fighting in the foreground.

Sasha glanced over her shoulder as Mary arrived, holding a pair of apples. 'What did I miss?'

'I have no idea.'

The crowd gasped as the Dark Lord struck the Old Man's arm and his sword dropped.

'Your castle cannot control all arts,' the Old Man said. 'Strike me down now, and I shall return more powerful than you could possibly know.'

The Dark Lord laughed. 'You mock me, even now? Your friends fly from my keep, you at my mercy, and you mock me still? Old Man, even if you came back a hundred times more powerful, I would still best you.'

He lashed out and the Old Man fell. Somewhere in the audience, a girl started crying.

Another figure appeared at the side of the stage; Bill's wife, wearing a proper military jacket and a monocle, rigidly marched onto the stage. She stood over the body of the Old Man and nudged it with her foot.

'He is dead?'

'He is, General. The old fool had no hope yet fought anyway. Some may call it valor, but not I. What of the craft?'

Bill's wife cleaned the monocle. 'Escaped, as you wished. I risk much by letting such a prize as the princess go. Your spell will work?'

'My arts have not failed me yet,' the Dark Lord boasted.

'Then we wait, and amass our troops for the decisive battle,' the General said. 'Come, Dark Lord. We have much to do!'

The two turned and marched off stage. The Old Man suddenly stood up, causing a few children to cry out in terror.

> *'Yes, my friends, I have died. But cry not for me.*
> *My death has bought precious time for everyone else to flee*
> *And yes, the Dark Lord cast upon the plane a spell,*
> *Once it made a safe landing, the place he would instantly tell*

So, give us ten minutes of rest And I promise we shall return
For there is much about this story That you should like to learn.'

She bowed, earning applause from the audience, then disappeared behind the side curtains. 'Do you want to see the end?' Mary asked. 'I think Winnie gets out soon.'

'Let's see what she's up to,' Sasha said. She did want to stay, but she wanted to hear about Winnie's lunch with the generals even more. Besides, rumor had it the family would be in town for some time. She may see more shows yet.

They found Winnie shortly afterwards, saying goodbye to several of the civilian leaders. She tried to get through to them as quickly as possible, but Sasha and Mary still waited ten minutes for the sergeant to extricate herself.

'Let us see it!' Mary said. Winnie took it off, showing the General's Star to her friends. Sasha noticed she was extremely careful about handling it. The star was metal, maybe real gold, though Sasha did not know how to find out. The ribbon was dark blue, except at the front where the medal hung; that was white with the blue renaissance diamond.

'Congratulations,' Sasha said.

'Thanks, but I don't think I deserve this,' Winnie said.

'I agree,' Sasha said with a laugh. 'At least Third Regiment will stand out now. "See how dumb and lucky our sergeants are!"'

'Says the woman who didn't win the first General's Star in the Renaissance Army,' Winnie said and stuck her tongue out.

Mary leaned forward and sniffed at Winnie. 'You're drunk,' she said.

'I am not drunk!' Winnie proclaimed. 'I am moderately befuddled. Perhaps, intoxicated, but drunk? Never.' Winnie put on a stern face, turned on her feet, and promptly stumbled. 'But perhaps we can find a place to sit down? They were not miserly with the wine.'

The three made their way away from the theater performances, finding one of several fire pits around the town. Some militia were vacating one as they approached, offering congratulations to Winnie. As they left another figure appeared; Beth, carrying a tray of food and a bottle of wine. 'I thought I heard you guys coming this way,' she said. 'Hope you don't mind some company.'

'The more the merrier,' Winnie slurred a little. Beth sat down the food, then handed a paper to Mary.

'Is that the newest *Tribune*?' Sasha asked. It looked different from the one Fox brought only yesterday.

'Yes,' Beth replied. 'It's got the detailed report on the prison fight.'

'Finally!'

Sasha sat next to Mary and looked at the sheet. It was about a foot wide and a foot and a half long, with three columns of texts. Each article had a bold headline, and a single picture sat in the middle. It looked to be a pair of RAM soldiers.

'Who're they?' Sasha asked.

'Says they're a pair of scouts from First Field Regiment, helped clear out some civilians ahead of a yeoman raid. Saved a lot of lives.'

'Good for them,' Winnie said. 'Where's me?'

'This one,' Sasha pointed to one headline. Mary started reading.

PRISON CAMP LIBERATED

-Brainerd County, Third Field Regiment

After LTCOL Snow, Commander of 3FR, located a secret prison camp within her area, elements of several units descended on the location to liberate its prisoners, under the command of GEN Prince.

'That's one way of describing it,' Mary said with a chuckle.

The force engaged a Royal Army rifle company, some one hundred and fifty or so soldiers, who fought their way into the camp, taking several prisoners from 3FR with them. An attempt at negotiation between LTCOL Snow and the enemy captain failed to produce a solution.

Sasha nodded. She remembered escorting Snow to that meeting. She also remembered liking Captain Lewis, the army captain. If they had come to an agreement, there was no doubt in Sasha's mind that he would have followed it.

That night, RAM forces assaulted the camp, while the Royal Army Company attempted a breakout to the south, taking important prisoners with them.

To the north, Pioneers and Marines led the assault group. The group overcame engineered bunkers and minefields. They secured the prison camp guards and yeomen defenders, securing the facility as quickly as they could.

Sasha laughed. The pillboxes were remarkably weak, no more than a single

25

inch of concrete backed by wooden boards. And there was one minefield, no more than thirty feet across. Whomever wrote this article was embellishing the danger.

> *To the south, both 3FR and 4FR fought against the breakout. Seizing an initially defensible position, both regiments held on while outnumbered more than two to one. They eventually captured the wagons of prisoners, liberating them from their prison.*

> *Total casualties for the RAM forces were less than ten dead, with another thirty wounded to varying degrees. Thirty or so royalist forces were killed, along with fifty wounded. Six civilians died in the battle, and three royalist men were executed for murder committed during the confrontation.*

> *Special mention is given to Sergeant Winnie of 3FR, who single-handedly captured an enemy heavy weapon and used it to disrupt the rifle company's attack on both field regiments.*

'Damn right I did,' Winnie said. 'I even got interviewed for the next broadsheet. The first Hero of the Renaissance!'

'Anyone else from Third Regiment mentioned?' Beth asked. Such articles usually mentioned soldiers who did things of note during the battle.

'Let's see. Other individuals of note,' Mary scrolled down.

> *Rifle Sasha, 3FR, for holding the defensive position alone for some time.*

'"For some time"? It wasn't even a minute,' Beth said.

'Felt longer,' Sasha replied.

> *MedOfc Mary, 3FR, who continued her duty while captured.*

'That's it from us,' Mary said.

'Nothing about Sonja or Jim?' Sasha asked. The two of her friends died in that battle, and she was disappointed they were not being noticed.'

'Nothing,' Mary said.

'There's limited space,' Beth pointed out.

'But they got the important ones,' Winnie said, jumping to her feet. 'Cheers!' she thrust her wine bottle out, stumbling forward. Sasha jumped up to catch Winnie before she fell over.

Sasha got her sergeant sitting down. 'Drink some water,' Beth said, handing her a canteen.

'I will trade you,' Winnie replied, taking the canteen and handing a bottle of wine to Mary. 'I drink, you drink.'

Mary took a drink of wine as Winnie took a swallow of water. Mary handed the wine to Sasha, who drank her own mouthful. Sasha handed it to Beth, who took her own. Winnie matched each drink.

'Well,' Winnie said. 'Now I'll throw up water in addition to everything else.'

'Well, if you need to throw up, face that way,' Beth said. She and Mary sat on either side of Winnie, as Sasha moved the food to the other side of the fire and away from a potentially sick Winnie. Sasha turned to watch them get water into Winnie's stomach, and did not notice the figure approaching until the voice spoke.

'Is she going to be okay?'

Sasha looked over and saw the red-headed staff officer who rode next to Bellona. She turned to salute but the officer waved her down. 'I'm surprised there was enough alcohol to affect her so. Is it common in Third Regiment to drink so much?'

'Special occasions warrant special stores,' Beth said.

'And the civilians made me,' Winnie said. 'Kept toasting me, and I didn't want to be rude. Now, I drink with my friends.'

'Do you need any assistance?' the officer asked.

'If she needs it, I'm here,' Mary said.

'Good,' the redheaded officer smiled.

The officer continued to watch Winnie and made no move to leave. 'Was there something else, ma'am?' Mary asked.

'Hm? Oh, yes, I'm sorry. I am looking for Corporal Sasha.'

All four of the women looked up at the major. Then three of them looked up at Sasha.

'I'm Corporal Sasha,' Sasha admitted.

'Oh, good. I'm First Staff Officer Saxon, aide-de-camp to General Caesar. I was asked to bring you to him.'

'General Caesar wants to see me?' Sasha asked in disbelief.

'General Caesar, General Prince, and Lieutenant Colonel Snow.'

Beth looked up at Sasha. 'What did you do?'

'Nothing!' Sasha exclaimed. 'When do they want to see me?'

'As soon as possible,' Saxon said. She smiled, but it was obvious that she meant now.

Sasha stood. 'Yes, ma'am.' She risked one last glance at her friends before she followed Saxon.

On a hill overlooking Arrowhead sat an old plantation house. General Prince had used the building as his headquarters when he came down for the prison battle. As such, it had been renamed the War House, and any Mardurer units that came to Arrowhead camped on the empty fields around the building. It was only a short walk up to the porch. Again, in the presence of an officer, Sasha was unchallenged.

The front hall looked remarkably different from the last time. The stairs had been repaired, the cobwebs swept out and a new coat of paint layered on. Curtains still hung as doorways, and a table still sat as a desk. And again, Officer Bellona sat at the table.

Sasha stiffened; glad she had not drunk too much that afternoon. Bellona was not a woman Sasha cared to interact with; in the few minutes she had spent with the woman a few short months ago, Bellona had proven to be curt, arrogant and dismissive. In this case, however, the two officers just exchanged a look without speaking, and Bellona ignored Sasha.

Instead of heading straight through to the fireplace, Saxon turned right into a room Sasha had not been in before. It was simple, holding only a single table with three chairs. A curtain made up the fourth wall, dividing this room from the rest.

Saxon gestured to one of the seats. 'Please, have a seat, and do not leave.'

Sasha nodded, still curious about what she was doing there. Saxon went through the curtain into the main room.

A minute later, Snow came in. Sasha stood. 'Colonel, what....'

'Sasha,' Snow interrupted. 'Have a seat.'

Sasha did so, looking up at her commanding officer. Lieutenant Colonel Snow was a fine role model, a strong woman who accepted Sasha as she was and pushed her to be better. Well into her twenties, with short hair, her most distinguishing feature was her scarred face. A portion of the right side showed burns, received, she said, when she was a teenager.

Sasha first met Snow when Snow was passing through Penelope's Haven and intervened in a fight Sasha was losing. She later rescued Sasha from yeomen who were taking her to Walker Town as a hostage. Snow led the regiment into

Brainerd County, established their base, and befriended the civilians. She destroyed a bandit company and returned their stolen goods, only to be betrayed by some of those she had just helped. She refused reprisals, continuing to defend the civilians, even those who worked against her, from the yeomen and slowly earning their trust.

There was no one Sasha admired more.

'Sasha,' Snow said, pausing. She looked conflicted. Sasha squirmed in her seat, wondering what had her colonel so unnerved. 'Remember a few weeks ago, when Major Fox brought you here and to converse with General Prince and Colonel Aristotle?' Sasha nodded. 'General Caesar would like to speak with you, along the same lines, I believe.'

'Why?' Sasha asked.

Snow started to speak but stopped. Finally, she rested both hands on Sasha's shoulders and looked into her eyes. 'Do you trust me, Sasha?'

'Yes, Colonel, I do.'

'Then trust me now. There is nothing you could do here that would disappoint me. Just speak with Caesar as you did with Prince.'

'Yes, ma'am,' Sasha said. Snow smiled and left. Sasha was once again alone.

Caesar wants to speak with me as Prince did. Sasha took some deep breaths. That had been an enjoyable conversation, between her, Prince, Fox and Colonel Aristotle, the director of the Medical Group? Would she have just as much enjoyment with General Caesar?

A few minutes later, General Caesar came into the room.

Caesar was not the charismatic leader that Prince was. He was a timid-looking man, with a well-trimmed beard and a receding hairline. He did not smile, did not try to make her feel comfortable. Instead, he looked at her with intense eyes, eyes she remembered from the April Fool's Day Ambush that rescued her from the yeomen and brought her into the Renaissance Army. *Like I'm a book and he's going to read me.* Sasha looked down at her hands in her lap.

'Are you okay, Rifle?' he asked.

'Yes, sir,' she said. She had forgotten about his accent: that strange, sharp phrasing that sounded so foreign and yet so easy to understand.

'Have you been drinking alcohol?'

'Sir?'

Caesar shrugged. 'It is not unusual to celebrate with alcohol, although some people might say you are too young to drink it.'

'Some people might say I am too young to fight,' Sasha said.

'True,' Caesar agreed without familiarity. He stared at her, awaiting an answer to his question.

'I had a single drink of wine, General,' Sasha admitted, 'but I am not drunk. I don't like to drink that much.'

'Why not?'

'The first time I had alcohol, I got drunk. And I suffered for an entire day, and into the next.'

'When was this?' he asked.

'Just before I was rescued by the Mardurers.'

Caesar frowned at the name Mardurer. Not every officer liked it. Instead of saying anything, he pulled out a chair and sat down, gesturing for Sasha to take a seat opposite him. He laid open a book, an ink fountain and a pen.

'After you were rescued, your father rode in and attempted to remove you from our custody. I exchanged words with him, regarding pacifism and the Bible. Do you remember?'

'I do.'

'Do you feel any anger towards me about that exchange?'

Sasha was surprised at the question. 'No, sir, I don't. If anything, I was impressed.'

'How so?'

'Well, most people don't challenge my father. And those that do usually just insult him. I don't know that anyone has argued the Bible with him seriously.'

'Do you know the differences between the Alvanist and Lutheran Bible?'

'No,' Sasha admitted. The conversation was not close to what she and Prince had exchanged, but curiosity was getting the better of her.

'On Saturday, May Fourth, of this year, Third Field Regiment engaged and destroyed a bandit company moving through Brainerd County. Did you plan the battle?'

'No,' Sasha said, 'not exactly.'

'Explain.'

Sasha thought for a moment before continuing. 'I had two books I was reading. One was *The Art of War*, and the other was *The War of the Three Fools*. I was trying to learn the lessons of the first by reading examples in the second. Snow knew this, and when the bandits came, she asked my opinion; she also asked Beth and Erick their opinions. My idea just happened to be similar to what Snow was planning.'

'You fought and were promoted, even though you were made a rifle in haste.'

'I worked hard before and after I was made a rifle, sir.'

Caesar made some notes. 'What did you feel about Rifle Rick's death?'

Sasha felt a lump in her throat. 'At the time, I was angry. I killed the man who killed him, but I was still angry. Then I was sad,' she started tearing up, 'and when I heard Beth crying, I cried with her. She was my den-mate, sir. I'd gotten to know her pretty well. She really liked Rick.'

Caesar pressed on, ignoring her tears. 'Did you like killing the bandit?'

'No,' Sasha said.

'Are you saying that because you think that is what I want to hear?'

Sasha looked at Caesar sharply. 'I'm not a killer. Major Fox called me that once, and I'll tell you the same thing. I'll fight and kill if I have to, but I don't enjoy it.'

Caesar did not get angry or defensive. He wrote a note and turned the page. Sasha watched him and realized what they were talking about.

Me. We're talking about me. Not the Art of War *or any other book. We're talking about me!*

'Why did you assault Kimble?'

Sasha blinked, thinking back. 'Snow had taken the regiment out to find and fight the yeomen who were collecting civilians. Snow was going to ambush them, and I realized there were yeomen still in Kimble, and when Snow launched her ambush, they could threaten the civilians living there. I thought that if I could keep them focused on me, I could protect them.'

'I understand. So, you attacked without orders and without support?'

'I knew that I had to get in there fast,' Sasha said.

'How many people did you kill there?'

'Two or three, why does that...?'

'And then you stopped Sergeant Winnie from executing a yeoman.'

'He had raped and murdered a ten-year-old girl, Rain. He was naked and still had her blood on his hands.'

'And you stopped her?'

'Yes,' Sasha said. 'He had surrendered. He was a criminal, but he surrendered.'

'And you were part of the firing squad that shot him?'

'Yes, why?' Sasha asked heatedly. She understood she was getting upset, more upset than a rifle should when speaking with a general, so she clenched her fists and took a deep breath. How strong was that wine?

'Why is it, Rifle Sasha, that you can kill two men in the morning and a third that evening, and in between stop your friend from shooting a man who, everyone believed, was all but guaranteed to be executed for his crimes?'

Sasha thought for a moment. 'When I first started training with the regiment, I had to learn all these rules and creeds. I asked why, and I was told, "the yeomen don't have rules, so we do." I learned about discipline. When Winnie was about to shoot him....I wasn't protecting him, I was protecting her from being like him. If that makes sense, sir.'

Caesar said nothing. More notes. Another page. 'Tell me about Sun Tzu.'

Sasha grasped for a thought as the topic changed suddenly. 'A Chinese general from thousands of years ago. Wrote a book called *The Art of War*. Snow has a copy.'

'And you have read it. Once?'

'Several times.'

'Why did you ask for it?'

'I didn't. I asked for something to help me catch up. It was Snow's decision to give it to me.'

'What do you think of it?'

'It is a good start,' Sasha said, 'but it has to be read cautiously. Every rule in there has an exception or alternate. You can't fight by those rules alone. That must be why they call it art,' she chuckled.

Caesar did not smile. He continued writing.

'Can you think of anything from *The Art of War* that you believe is wrong?'

Sasha thought for a minute. Caesar watched her, waiting for a response.

'Sun Tzu wrote that "by discovering the enemy's dispositions and remaining invisible ourselves, we can keep our forces concentrated, while the enemy's must be divided." I understand what he's saying, but there's something about it that doesn't make sense to me in terms of what the Third Regiment is trying to do. If we want the yeomen to be spread out defending a number of different places, then we have to prove we can attack a number of different places. Easier to do that with smaller parts than the whole. Now, I do believe we need to keep the regiment and our main attacks invisible, and we can't let the enemy regain the initiative, but if it takes a small squad, operating alone and causing problems to make that happen, then that would be breaking the rule, sir.'

'Sun Tzu is talking about invisibility. Your enemy will have to defend every place because they do not know where you are.'

'That seems too passive, sir. Better to harass them and keep them guessing where we will hit next than to hope they'll do what we want. Also,' she said suddenly, 'with Arrowhead, they know where some of our forces are always. We can't make all of them invisible, so we have to spend some effort to keep them guessing.'

Caesar wrote down what she said. 'You had a discussion several weeks ago, with General Prince, Colonel Aristotle and Major Fox. What did you talk about?'

'*The Art of War* in relation to the American Revolution and the War of the Three Fools.'

'What did you think of the conversation?'

'I liked it,' Sasha said. 'I was nervous, but they all listened to me. They helped me get my thoughts out. And....'

A moment passed. 'And?' Caesar prompted.

'And I realized that I was enjoying myself. I didn't have to explain the facts we were talking about or worry about being judged. We were just talking.'

Caesar wrote down a few more notes, then closed the book and looked at Sasha.

Sasha met his gaze, and a thought blossomed in her mind.

Several years ago, when Sasha still lived in Penelope's Haven, a man had come through looking for work. He had stayed a few weeks, helping in exchange for food, before moving on. Old Man Sanchez had said the traveler was 'someone whose gears barely turn.' It took her a few questions to understand it meant the person did not think much, comparing his head to a clock that did not work. It was a curious expression that Sasha had remembered.

Caesar was the opposite. She could tell, somehow, that he was a man who was constantly thinking. If he had been a clock, the hands would be spinning so fast as to be almost a blur. Sasha almost felt dizzy. What alcohol she did consume did not help.

'One last question,' Caesar said. 'You requested a meeting with Lieutenant Colonel Snow, during which you put your name forth for consideration for a regimental warrant. Why?'

Sasha thought for a moment before answering. 'When I first joined the regiment, I was accepted by most, but not really trusted. Winnie, who is now my friend, tried to beat me from the regiment. Even Snow had me attacked to show me it wasn't going to be easy.

'I earned their trust and respect, throwing off the limits that I had learned in Penelope's Haven, but I don't think I've learned what my new limits are. My friends all say I should be an officer, that I'm smart enough, respected enough,' she shrugged. 'I guess I just want to know if I can.'

'I understand. That your friends think that of you is good, of course, but what about you? Do you want to be an officer?' Caesar asked.

'I do,' Sasha said.

'Why?'

'Because I want to be the best I can be. And I think I could be a good one.'

'Compared to Officers Beth and Erick?' Caesar asked. 'Or do you compare yourself to Officer Lynx and Lieutenant Buck?'

Sasha paused before answering. She was friends with both Beth and Erick, but they were very much officers given their warrants to fulfill a need, Beth as a training officer, Erick in command of the heavy weapons won at the prison camp. She liked them, but they were both doing their best in jobs they had not been trained for.

Lynx and Buck were different. Both had been trained as officers in Walker County. Buck had gotten his commission and even promoted to First Lieutenant before he was sent to Third Field Regiment. He was an aggressive and competent officer, and Sasha enjoyed learning from him.

Lynx she knew less about. The woman's warrant was from Colonel Snow, on the recommendation of General Prince. She only missed out on a commission because she had issues reading. Sasha had interacted with her only a few times and had never been out on a mission with her. But those who had worked with her in Walker and in Brainerd all agreed she was a good officer.

'I compare myself to Colonel Snow,' Sasha finally replied, 'and Buck and

34

Lynx.'

'Someone who has taken the time to learn the job properly, instead of fulfilling a need at the time?' Caesar pressed.

Sasha nodded. 'Yes, General.'

Caesar looked at her for another moment, then stood. Sasha followed suit. He turned to leave, and Sasha asked a question of her own.

'Sir, what is this about?'

Caesar looked at her and she wondered if he was going to answer, or if he had moved on and was thinking about something else.

'It's about the Renaissance, Corporal Sasha,' he said. Sasha saluted, he responded, and he left.

Sasha sat back down, wondering what Caesar meant by that. Her discussion with Prince had been to showcase what she had learned from the books; this had been an overview of everything she had learned since joining the Renaissance Army. It was less a discussion and more of an interview.

General Caesar just interviewed me. Sasha smiled to herself. Interacting with a general did not happen every day in the Renaissance Army. She had been proud just to have the chance to speak with General Prince for a short time during the prison camp campaign. But to be sought out? To be specifically asked for by the generals? That was something else indeed.

A minute later the curtain parted, and Snow walked in. She had a canteen, which she handed to Sasha. Sasha took a long drink, then looked up at Snow.

'Why did General Caesar just order me to sit for an interview?'

Snow sat down. 'You haven't done anything wrong, Sasha, if that's what you're worried about. It's about your request.'

'To be an officer? But you don't need a general's permission to give me a warrant, you only need it to . . . ,' she stopped. 'Oh. You want me to get a commission?'

Snow smiled. 'I thought you might figure it out.'

Sasha smiled back. She took another drink. 'Why a commission?'

'Sasha, do you know the difference between a warrant officer and a commissioned officer?'

'A warrant officer specializes, a commissioned officer generalizes,' Sasha repeated.

'In detail, Corporal,' Snow said sternly.

Sasha blinked at the sudden shift in tone. 'A warrant officer is granted authority within a regiment to fulfill a specific role. The authority is derived from the commanding officer of that regiment, and is applicable to that regiment, and that role, only. Other commanding officers may or may not follow that authority, as they see fit.

'A commissioned officer is granted authority within the entire Renaissance Army. Their authority is derived from the generals and is respected by everyone else in the army.'

Sasha paused. 'Why is it like that?' she asked.

'We worked out the system over a couple of years, long before the Renaissance Army was an actual army. We needed a way to put talented people into a leadership position, without automatically putting them in position to command the army itself. I personally think the requirements are too harsh, but General Caesar was adamant that we commission only the most qualified. And, even if I disagree, I trust him to know.'

'So, they want to give me a commission?' Sasha asked. She liked the sound of that.

'Not exactly,' Snow said. Sasha was surprised that her colonel looked nervous. Snow stood, looking out a window at the camp beyond. It was late afternoon, the sky just beginning to darken, but the men and women under her command and her protection were still visible.

'Caesar had this idea, from many years ago. The idea was to gather a pool of exceptionally talented young people and put them through a rough course to make them into exceptional officers. He argued that regimental warrants and battlefield commissions were sufficient to provide officers in the short term, but he wanted a program that thought long term, to build officers of higher quality, future leaders of not just the army, but the movement.

'Many of us agreed with him in principle, but we felt that with defeating the yeomen and training up an army, trying to create a whole new class of officers would be too much.'

'But you've changed your mind,' Sasha said.

'I have. So, has almost everyone who originally opposed it. Those who still oppose it do so for other reasons; they have their own agendas that the Templar Project doesn't fit into.'

'The Templar Project?' Sasha asked.

'That's what Caesar calls it,' Snow confirmed.

'And they want me?' Sasha asked. 'Why?'

Snow smiled as she turned back to the table, taking a seat across from Sasha.

'General Caesar has four things he looks for in a potential candidate.

'First, he looks for competence. In four months, you went from an untrained farmer from a pacifist family to a respected junior noncom in a field regiment and a member of the First Squad. You've seen action several times and kept your calm every time, despite a wide variety of situations.

'Second, he looks for physical ability. You proved that along with the first, through your training and actions.

'Third, he looks for mental ability. You read and try to understand everything you can, which, given our limited resources, is difficult. You impressed General Prince during the Middlestedt debate and that evening when he spoke with you in private, and General Caesar a few minutes ago. I told him how you trade books with Grandpa Middlestedt, and how quickly you read now.

'Fourth, he looks for a strong sense of morality. When you stopped Winnie from shooting Yeoman Davidson, you proved that you have a strong moral compass. Fox's story of you fighting those bullies probably helped as well, as did mine.'

'And all this makes me an exceptionally talented possibility?' Sasha asked.

'Yes. '

'Did Prince have this idea after our chat?'

'No,' Snow said. 'I demanded Prince take you.'

'What?' Sasha started.

Snow gave Sasha a serious look. 'Sasha, I can train you to be a field rifle, a noncom, even give you a warrant, but I cannot exercise that mind of yours. And a curious, interested, and thirsty mind like yours is a rare thing in this Dark Age. You have the potential to be another Prince or Caesar. And we need as many of them as we can get. So, after you asked to be considered for a warrant, I told Prince that I wanted you to be trained by someone else. By this group. By General Caesar.'

Sasha looked at her colonel. 'Ma'am, are you telling me to go?'

'Sasha, I cannot tell you to go. You must want to go. It will be a long, rough, and difficult process, but if anyone can pull out your full potential, it's the generals. And I believe that if you don't go, you are ultimately failing yourself.'

Chapter 4

'So, what do I do?' Sasha asked.

'Are you seriously asking that question?' Winnie snapped. Between the alcohol and the attention, she was obviously exhausted, but refused to go to bed until Sasha returned. There was a fire going now, the glow illuminating everyone's faces as dusk came.

Sasha nodded. 'Of course, I'm asking.'

'It's a terrific opportunity,' Mary said. 'Colonel Aristotle mentioned it once or twice. The Templars, I mean. He liked the idea.'

'If I get commissioned, I'd outrank you,' Sasha said.

'My warrant is equivalent to a first lieutenant, Sasha, and unless they commission you a captain, you wouldn't,' Mary said sternly, then smiled. 'At least, at first.'

'Imagine what a feather in our cap that would be,' Beth said. 'Third Field Regiment providing the first General's Star and one of the first Templars.'

'Cadet Sasha!' Mary exclaimed.

'I haven't accepted anything yet.'

'You damn well better,' Winnie said. She drank some more water, glaring as Sasha. 'You wanted to break your limits, and you did, but you haven't found the new ones yet, have you? Do you really think you should pass up the opportunity?'

'That would leave you the only enlisted woman in our little group here,' Beth said.

'Any good army needs good sergeants to keep the officers in line,' Winnie growled. 'I'll be a first sergeant by the time you get back, at least.'

'When will that be?' Mary asked.

'Snow said I'll be back next June,' Sasha said.

'It's almost August now,' Beth said. 'You'd be gone almost the whole year?'

'It would start in September,' Sasha said. 'I'd graduate and be commissioned in early June, return to the regiment then.'

'Unless they send you somewhere else,' Mary said.

38

Sasha blinked. 'What? Why would they do that?' she asked. 'My place is with Third Regiment.'

'Sasha,' Mary said, in the tone of someone who was about to give an important lesson, 'the fact is, we are in an army. And though the Renaissance Army is making significant efforts to avoid stepping on the toes of the civilians, it's still an army. Yes, all of us volunteered to join the Third Regiment, but there were plenty who volunteered and were sent somewhere else. Just because you want to come here, doesn't mean they'd send you here.'

Winnie looked up. 'And if General Prince was to tell you that he needed your talents elsewhere, you damn well will listen to him. Understood?'

Sasha looked at Winnie in shock. Winnie shrugged.

'Sasha, get it through your skull, will you? This rebellion is not just Third Regiment in Brainerd, or the generals in Walker. It's the Renaissance Army. Hell, it's the whole Renaissance Movement! And I remember what Prince said when he debated Mayor Middlestedt, what he was fighting for. He's giving up a lot to fight this war, and we damn well can't endanger that because we're comfortable where we are, can we?'

Mary and Beth both nodded. Sasha realized she was nodding too.

'When do you have to decide?' Beth asked.

'After dawn. General Caesar is riding back to Walker and I'm to go with him, if I say yes.'

'Say yes,' Winnie said.

'I'll think about it,' Sasha said, and turned to walk in the night.

'Think fast,' Beth called.

***

Sasha walked through Arrowhead. The darkness allowed her to skirt the crowds, avoiding anyone she might know. She did so unintentionally, so lost in thought avoiding the crowds was automatic.

All her friends were correct. She had been so quick to run away from her father and her family into the arms of the Third Regiment to find herself, but what if she was meant for more than this? Growing into her role here had involved more than a few fights, and the project sounded even more difficult. *Could I leave the comfort of Third Regiment? Would I ever forgive myself if I didn't?*

Sasha found herself in an area of new buildings, small huts and cabins built to accommodate new inhabitants. She turned a corner and found herself before one of the wagons that came with the generals. Two of the armed civilians guarded it, one sitting in the driver's seat and the other standing in the bed. Both looked bored in the torchlight and ignored her as she approached.

Sasha paused, as she wasn't sure what to do. Did they have a rank? Did she need to salute them? She honestly didn't know.

Just then the door of the small building next to them opened and a man stepped out. He looked to be seventeen or eighteen, a year or so older than Sasha, with jet black hair. He was dressed in clean clothes, but not the same fine-looking clothes that the councilwoman and her like had worn. He looked up at the guard standing in the bed.

'Could you help me carry my box inside?' he asked.

'Look, son, my job is to protect the Representative's kit, not help you haul your damned books all over the countryside.'

'Since I'm here, it'll be the last time you have to haul anything,' the younger man said. The guard simply chuckled and stood, crossing his arms and staring down at the man. The driver was smiling and shaking his head.

Sasha stepped forward. 'I'll help,' she offered.

The man turned and looked at her; in the torchlight, she saw him blush and smile sheepishly. 'Thanks,' he said. The two guards laughed at him.

Sasha stepped forward while he grasped a handle for a moderately sized box, maybe three feet long and two feet wide. 'It'll be heavy,' he said. She nodded, and together they lifted the box off the wagon bed. It was in fact very heavy, and Sasha used both hands to keep it upright as she moved it into the small cabin.

'Thanks,' the young man said when it was on the floor.

'Did I hear it's full of books?' Sasha asked curiously. There wasn't any light inside, so she had no idea what the man's reaction was, but a harsh voice called out through the open door.

'Hey, lass, how about you come take a drink with me?'

Sasha grimaced. 'No, thank you,' she called back. Before she could ask again, the voice called out.

'Oh, come on, girl. I'll make it worth your while.'

Sasha sighed. 'Hold on,' she said to the man. She stepped to the door, hearing the man follow her. She stood in the torchlight, looked up at the man who grinned down at her. She tapped a finger on the chevrons on her jacket sleeve. 'It's not girl or lass, mister. It's Corporal.'

'Oh, excuse me!' the man said in an exaggerated tone. He stepped off the wagon and stood right in front of Sasha, a foot taller than her at least. 'I didn't know this regiment had gone so far as to give girls chevrons. And here you are, a corporal.'

'A sergeant – a woman – just won the General's Star,' Sasha said.

'And I'm sure she earned it in battle,' the man taunted. Sasha's fists tightened with anger. 'Come, lass, don't expect to match me. I've been at this longer than you've been alive. And I've actually killed someone.'

'Really?' Sasha asked, seeing the pride in his face. 'Only one?'

The driver laughed at his companion, whose grin turned to a scowl. 'What's that? "Only one?" she asks. Tell me how many you've killed, lass?'

'Me?' Sasha asked. She held up a finger. 'I bayoneted a bandit during the river ambush, that's one. I shot two yeomen at Kimble, then was part of the firing squad that executed a third for raping and murdering a ten-year-old girl. I don't think I killed anyone when the rifle company pushed us off the road to the prison, but I killed at least three more during the night battle. If we assume I haven't killed anyone I don't know I killed, then that's seven, but more likely, it's higher. Let's say twelve, to be safe.'

Sasha didn't like bragging about killing men, but she was in no mood to be polite to a bully. She smiled a bit as her words hit home. The guard turned red.

'Bullshit!' he said. 'Not possible.'

'Yeah it is,' the driver said. 'I told you, Jay, Third Regiments got some fights in its belt. And not just against yeomen.'

Jay gritted his teeth. 'So? I guard an elected representative. I deserve respect.'

'Except when your actions bring shame upon yourself,' Sasha said. 'Then you deserve nothing.'

Jay balled his fist. 'Don't toy with me, girly. I will fight you.'

'Go ahead,' Sasha said. 'I've finished every fight I've been in. Every single one.'

The driver whistled at him. 'Come on, Jay. We don't got time for this, and the Cap'n will have you on charges if you get into another fight.'

Jay glared at Sasha for a minute. 'Fine,' he muttered, turning and jumping back into the wagon. He sat down. The driver smiled, tipped his hat to Sasha, and started the wagon again.

Sasha watched them go. Then she heard a soft cough behind her.

'Did you really do all that?'

Sasha looked back. He stood in the doorway, a sad look on his face.

'I did,' Sasha said. 'I don't like bragging about it, but I also don't like bullies.'

'Okay,' he said. He held out his hand. 'I'm Adam.'

'Corporal Sasha,' she took it. 'So, books?'

'Yes, books,' Adam smiled. He brought her into the shack and lit a candle. With a key, he unlocked the chest and opened it.

Sasha saw books, lots and lots of books. She picked several up and looked at the spines. *An Introduction to Mathematical Principles* in one hand and *Surveying the Fields of Science* in the other. They were all old things, worn and weathered. Knowledge bound and always on the edge of disappearing.

'What are you here for?' Sasha asked.

'I'm a teacher,' Adam said. He pulled out some more books, organizing them on the tabletop. 'I've been asked to set up here in Arrowhead and teach those who want to learn.'

Sasha smiled. 'A teacher?'

'Yes,' Adam said. He paused. 'I take it you never had one before?'

'No,' Sasha admitted. 'My family instructed me only on what they wanted me to know. I've had some instruction since I joined Third Regiment.'

'In fighting?' Adam asked.

'Yes,' Sasha said, 'but not just fighting. I've learned a lot from some of the few books we do have, but that's been all me teaching myself. Third Regiment doesn't have an instructor for anything other than fighting.'

'Well, I'm to make myself available to Colonel Snow,' Adam said, still pulling books from the chest, 'so if you want to learn anything, I can get you started.'

'What sort of things can you teach?'

Adam shrugged. 'I've had instruction in a number of topics. Science, math, history, literature.'

'Isn't literature just stories?' Sasha asked.

'That's one way to put it.'

'But aren't stories just for children?'

'They most certainly are not only for children,' Adam said with a laugh. 'Books written to entertain adults, novels and anthologies, can convey important ideas just as well as serious writing. I take it you've never read a work of literature?'

'I've read everything I can, but there's not much selection,' Sasha admitted. 'But I would like to read more, if I could.'

'That's a healthy attitude,' Adam said. 'I'm not allowed to lend books out, at the moment, but when you are in town, come here and I will let you read. I'll even start you with a good fiction book, get your brain working.'

'That sounds fun,' Sasha said, thinking suddenly of the choice before her. 'Where did you get these books?'

'From the generals,' Adam said. 'I don't know where they got some of them, but they've assembled and impressive collection, of which this is a small part.'

'So, they must have more,' Sasha wondered.

'Many more,' Adam put down the last books. 'I am no fan of fighting, Corporal, but it makes me glad to know that the men who lead the Renaissance Army put so much worth in their books. It brings me hope that this movement of theirs is more than just a sudden expression of violence.'

'I agree,' Sasha said quietly. She looked at the books in her hand. She understood most of the words on the covers and the spines, and she had a longing to read each book over and over until she understood every word on the pages as well.

'Is something wrong?' Adam asked, suddenly worried he had offended his guest.

'No,' Sasha shook her head. 'But I do have to go.'

'Did I offend?'

'No, Adam,' Sasha smiled, 'I just have to go, but I will take your advice about the books. I will read as many as I can.'

'Good,' Adam replied. 'Have a good night, Corporal Sasha.'

'You too, teacher Adam.'

Sasha left, suddenly feeling the need to be alone. She walked towards the forest, exchanging pleasantries with a sentry. She sat at the base of a tree, looking out over the campfires and town lights.

Templar Scholar

No one has any question that I should do this, she thought.

She thought back to her conversation with Winnie, after the attack on the prison camp. 'If you are not an officer, then this regiment is not the best it can be,' Winnie had said. The woman who once tried to beat her out of the regiment, now saying it was a waste for her not to be an officer.

Sasha accepted her friend's word back then, had spoken to Snow that very night. If she still trusted Winnie – and she really did – she should trust her now.

What happens if I don't go? Sasha asked herself. *Stay here and get a warrant. Read the books that Adam has, or that I borrow from Grandpa Middlestedt? Trust that I can teach myself what I want to know?'*

She thought of Adam's words. The generals had hundreds of books. She imagined several chests worth, each one full of books, each one open for her. She imagined debating and discussing topics with other officers, as she did with General Prince that one night. She thought of the words of Winnie and Mary and Beth. She thought of Snow writing letters on her behalf, coming to Prince specifically for her.

Everyone thinks I should be a part of the Templar Project, Sasha thought. *Every person I trust, every person I admire. They all agree.*

She wrapped her coat around her and leaned against the tree.

I think they're right.

***

The sky was turning blue when Sasha woke up. She found herself covered in a fine layer of dew and shivered a bit. It was unusually cold for a July morning.

She stretched and stood, looking out over the camp. Only a single lantern, on the porch of the War House, still burned. The campfires were dead, surrounded now by tents and bedrolls. A few sentries milled about, pacing or standing guard. Overall, Sasha looked out over an idyllic scene.

I'm going to miss this, she thought to herself.

She started towards the camp, careful to stay in view of the sentries, so they would not be surprised by her approach. Sure enough, she was challenged before she got amongst the tents.

'Who goes there?' the voice asked. Sasha recognized it.

'Corporal Sasha, Third Regiment. Stay awake tonight, Cassie?'

The young woman sighed and shook her head. 'It's been rough, Sasha, but

I've stayed awake. I'm looking forward to sleeping through the morning.'

'As long as someone doesn't call a drill.'

Cassie chuckled, then looked worried. 'They wouldn't do that, would they?'

Sasha laughed and patted Cassie on the shoulder. 'They might. They might not. Try to be ready for either.'

Cassie groaned, and Sasha continued. A light was burning in a window in the War House, and Sasha wondered which of the generals was up. Or if only one was up. Maybe both were. Snow, Sasha knew, often had short nights of sleeping, and she was only a colonel.

As if summoned, Sasha saw Snow making her way slowly through the tents towards the War House. She was not far from the place where Sasha had waylaid her to put her name forward for a warrant. *That was an odd coincidence,* Sasha thought.

Sasha moved quickly towards Snow. Snow was yawning, covering up her mouth and eyes closed, and did not see Sasha until Sasha was right in front of her.

'Colonel,' Sasha said.

Snow looked up in surprise. 'Sasha. Have you slept?'

'A little, ma'am. I sort of dozed off in the forest.'

'Oh?' Snow looked tired.

'I had a hard decision to make, and I had to make it alone.'

Snow nodded. 'Did you make it?'

'I did,' Sasha said. She took a deep breath. 'Colonel, I want to go to the Templar Project.'

Snow smiled. 'Good. May I ask why? Was it me or Winnie?'

'No,' Sasha shook her head. 'I am proud of what I've done here, Colonel Snow: the bandits, Kimble, the prison camp. I've fought well, over and over again.'

'You have,' Snow agreed.

'But,' Sasha paused, struggling with her words. 'But, ma'am, I don't want to fight. I'm willing to fight, and when I fight, I want to win, but frankly, I don't want to. I want to be smart. I want to find ways to win without fighting. I want to make people's lives better, to teach them how to be better. Even if that means I don't come back to Third Regiment, I want to do it.'

45

Snow smiled and stepped forward, embracing Sasha. 'Good, Sasha. Good. I'm glad.'

Sasha smiled, tearing up. She wiped one away. 'What do I do now?'

'We'll get to that,' Snow said. 'But there is one thing I want to ask you.'

'Of course,' Sasha said.

'You know, Sasha, that most officers have a renaissance name. I do, the generals, Buck, Saber, Mary. All of them have the names they use in their professional sense within the Renaissance Army. Beth and Erick don't yet, but that will change soon enough.'

'I know,' Sasha said.

'You're going to need one for the Templars.'

'Oh,' Sasha said. 'I guess Bobcat.'

'Bobcat?' Snow blinked in confusion, then chuckled. In battle, Sasha tended to scream when she attacked. It had earned her the nickname of Bobcat from some of her fellows.

'No, Sasha, I don't think that would work. Not if you want to be the woman you just described to me a minute ago. In fact, it's a name I've had for you since before you asked to be considered for a warrant.'

Sasha smiled. 'Okay,' she said. 'I'd be honored.'

'You don't even know what it is.'

'I don't care,' Sasha said. 'If you give it to me, it'll be good.'

Snow said, 'Come with me.'

She led Sasha up to the War House. Officer Saxon sat at the entryway, standing up when Snow and Sasha walked in. 'Colonel, corporal. Good morning.'

'Anyone in this house get some sleep?' Snow asked.

'Yes, ma'am, I think we snuck in a quick nap somewhere around two this morning,' Saxon said. They laughed, some bond of friendship between them. Sasha smiled at the camaraderie.

'Are the generals up?'

'Of course,' Saxon said. 'Go on in.'

Snow led Sasha through the curtain. The two generals sat at the table, reading books, a pot of steaming liquid sitting between them, surrounded by several metal cups. Both looked up at the two women.

'Ladies,' Prince said. Caesar looked on quietly, sipping from a hot cup. Sasha smelled the strong aroma of coffee. A different smell than she was used to; a different coffee.

'Generals,' Snow said, 'after a long night of consideration, Sasha has come to a decision. Sasha?'

Sasha took a deep breath. 'I accept the offer of the Templar Project.'

Prince stood and smiled. 'Excellent,' he said, holding his hand out. 'Congratulations, Sasha.'

Caesar also stood, awkwardly holding his hand out. 'Congratulations, Cadet.'

Sasha shook their hands. 'Thank you, sirs.'

Snow smiled. 'You'll do well,' she said.

Prince sat back down. 'Sit down, have some coffee. Sergeant Tou?'

A sergeant stepped in from the back. 'General?'

'Two more for breakfast.'

'Yes, sir,' he said and disappeared.

Sasha and Snow took seats, opposite the two generals. Prince was beaming and smiling. Caesar went back to reading his book.

'Ready?' Prince asked Sasha.

'I don't know. What do I bring?'

'Nothing,' Prince said. 'Everything will be provided.'

'Do you have anything of your own?' Caesar asked, looking up from his book again.

'Soldier's bits, for sewing uniforms. A pistol, 'cause I'm in First Squad.'

'Any books?' Prince asked.

'None that are mine. Borrowed from others.'

'Return the books,' Caesar said, 'and return the scroll to Major Fox. Bringing the soldier's bits would be beneficial, as you will still be soldiering, but you cannot bring the pistol. Weapons will be provided during the training.'

'Yes, sir,' Sasha said. Sergeant Tou brought in two plates of various foods. It looked and smelled incredible. A benefit of rank, she realized.

'Corporal Sasha,' Prince said as the sergeant withdrew, 'if I may ask, what made up your mind? I'm just curious, and please feel free to refuse to answer.'

Sasha sniffed the coffee as she thought. 'I thought about books and about fighting. I thought about your debate with Mayor Middlestedt and the conversation we had at the fireplace. In the end, sir, I just realized I want that. To be smart and solve problems with words, if I can.'

'You've never been in organized education before,' Caesar said.

'No, sir, but I love books, and I enjoyed the fireside chat. I was so proud to have been even a part of the debate with Mayor Middlestedt, and the thought that I could do that on my own? I want this, sir, and I'll learn whatever I have to learn to do it.'

Prince smiled. 'I think you'll do fine,' Prince said. 'Right, Caesar?'

Caesar looked at Sasha once more and returned to his book.

***

Snow quietly assembled some of her regiment to say goodbye. Sasha's friends were there, Mary and Beth and Winnie, as was Master Sergeant.

'I'm glad you were smart enough to say yes,' Winnie said.

'Just think, when I get back you can be my sergeant,' Sasha said.

'That'll be the day,' Winnie smiled, then stepped forward and embraced Sasha. 'Do our regiment proud, alright?'

'I will,' Sasha promised.

Mary stepped forward and hugged her as well. 'I've been through my own training,' she said. 'If you get overwhelmed, take a step back, go for a walk, do something to stay level. Do not get lost out there.'

Beth handed her a napkin with several biscuits in it. 'Take this chance to learn without distraction,' she said.

'I will,' Sasha promised again.

Master Sergeant smiled at her, a rare occurrence. 'I will echo Mary's advice,' he said, 'and say to you, "Do not look back".'

'Yes, Master Sergeant,' Sasha said, not understanding yet.

Snow took her elbow and started walking down towards where the horsemen were waiting. Fox sat closest, holding the reigns of her horse.

'What did he mean?' Sasha asked. 'Do not look back?'

'It's something some veterans say,' Snow replied. 'If you look behind you, you're looking to get home. If you're looking forward, you're looking to win.'

'Oh,' Sasha said. She looked at Snow. 'Any advice from you, Colonel?'

Snow pondered the question. '"No problem can withstand the assault of sustained thinking."'

'What does that mean?' Sasha asked.

'You'll find out,' Snow smiled. 'You'll be fine. It will be tough, but you'll be fine. And I'm writing to some friends who may be available for you to lean on if you need to. Please, ask for help if you need it. We all want to see you succeed.'

'Okay,' Sasha said. She stepped back and saluted. 'Goodbye, Colonel.'

'Goodbye, Corporal Sasha.'

Sasha turned and walked to the waiting horse. Fox was looking at Snow, then looked down at Sasha.

'Ready to go?' he asked.

'I don't know,' she said. 'But we're going anyway.' She climbed into her saddle.

Fox looked at her. 'You know, you will need a renaissance name.'

'I have one,' she said. 'Snow gave it to me.'

'Did she?' he smiled. 'So, when we get to our destination, who am I introducing?'

'Cadet Scholar,' Sasha said. She smiled.

Fox's laughed. 'It suits you. Cadet Scholar.' He turned the horse, leading Sasha up towards the group waiting to return early to Walker County; Caesar and Saxon, a few clerks and a handful of Olympians. Caesar nodded when the pair joined them, and Saxon called for the group to head out.

'Your friends are probably waving goodbye,' Fox said as they rode off.

'I know,' Sasha replied. 'But I'm looking forward.'

Chapter 5

Where the Mississippi and Minnesota Rivers meet sit three castles. To the north, the ornate and grandiose Highland Castle, home of King Xavier and his court. To the west, the ancient and haphazard Snelling Castle, where the military branches all held their headquarters. And to the south, Mendota Castle, the collection of towers where the heads of the civilian ministries kept their offices.

The tower of Mendota Castle closest to the rivers was the office of the Minister of War. The tall windows gave a view of the other two castles, the terraced gardens leading from the walls to the rivers, and the rivers themselves.

The office was decorated to display the power of its occupant. The walls were rich mahogany, lined with pictures and paintings, mementos of the man's life, artifacts some from the Before Time, rare things indeed. Between the view and the setting, the office was built to overwhelm any individual who came for an audience with the owner.

This time, it did nothing.

Regimental Colonel Sir Rika Miklos, Knight Commander of the Imperial Cross (Black Banner), military attaché to the Commonwealth Embassy to North Mississippi, cared little for his surroundings. He had been in this office many times over the last five years and had gotten to know its occupant well enough that he steadfastly refused to be impressed by anything the man owned. He kept himself standing at the window, looking out, waiting patiently.

The clocked chimed 12:30. The meeting was scheduled for noon. Miklos was not surprised at all. It was the petty behavior that he had come to expect.

A knock at the door, followed by creaking as it opened. 'Sir, the marshal is returning from Highland Castle now. He will be a few more minutes.'

Miklos nodded so the staff officer could retreat, then shook his head. Travel between the three castles was done by a series of wide barges that shifted from one bank to another as needed. None of them had moved in more than half an hour. The lie was as stupid as it was transparent.

The marshal never left Mendota Castle. He's making me wait to remind me of his power.

Several minutes later Miklos heard a sound of boots coming up the stairs behind him, voices muffled by the closed doors. Another few minutes passed before the door opened.

'Colonel Miklos, I'm sorry to keep you waiting,' a voice said in a tone that was not at all apologetic.

'I understand, General,' Miklos replied in an equally disinterested voice. He turned to stand across the desk as the general crossed to his seat. Miklos stood, waiting for some gesture that he could sit, but none was forthcoming.

General Lord Herschel Robinson, Duke of Hennepin, was the most powerful man in the kingdom outside the royal family. He had been a friend of King Xavier back when Xavier was a young prince who spent his time in debauchery. Based on that friendship, influence, and a military career that consisted of six years as a staff officer in a gentleman's battalion that never saw combat, he had managed to obtain two government positions.

The first was as Minister of War, a position which brought him this magnificent office.

The second was as the Marshal of the Army. The title was a conceit on his part; the Kingdom of North Mississippi was not allowed to use the rank of Field Marshal, so by titling the commander of the army 'Marshal', he could obtain the same title without breaking the law.

Miklos detested anyone who had purchased their position. He himself was the bastard son of a minor nobleman, who enlisted in the Commonwealth Army at thirteen to avoid living on the streets. He had earned his commission, and transfer to the black uniform of the Scouts, the special forces and intelligence operatives of the Imperial Commonwealth. Even at sixty, he was still in firm and fit shape, save for a right leg that protested when he ran.

Robinson finally looked up. 'I do not have a lot of time, Colonel, so please be brief.'

'I'm here about the battle at the Bonnie Lake Prison Camp, General. Margrave Khan has serious questions about it.'

Robinson sighed and shook his head, and Miklos hid a grin. The margrave was the Imperial Representative for much of Atlantic America. If he did have questions, refusing to answer them would be a mistake from which Robinson might not recover. That allowed a simple colonel to demand such things from a four-star general.

'Battle hardly seems the appropriate word for it. Skirmish, perhaps, but a battle?'

Miklos looked over the table. 'Several hundred at arms, mortar fire, assault rockets. A skirmish by importance to the world, by all means, but a battle for those who survived it.'

Robinson looked down at a folder on his desk. 'Have a seat, Colonel.' He waited for Miklos to sit. 'Your office was forwarded all the appropriate documents? The after-action reports, internal reviews, court martial records?'

'All provided appropriately, yes,' Miklos said. 'But therein lies my worry, General. After careful review, I come to a significantly different set of conclusions than your own investigation board.'

'Did you?' Robinson asked. 'And what might those conclusions be?'

'First thing, General, I take issue with the estimate that the Renaissance Army took three hundred casualties during the conflict.'

'I fail to see how anyone can have a problem with that estimate, Colonel. According to the reports, two regiments held the road south while one assault regiment attacked from the north. The northern regiment was estimated at two hundred; the regiments to the south must have similar numbers, and they only accounted for approximately sixty personnel after the battle. Three hundred is a proper estimate given those facts.'

'Except most of those aren't facts, General. By Captain Lewis' own admission, he was not only holding onto the southern line with two platoons but maneuvering to flank with his third. The enemy had taken hold of a creek bed and used the defensive position to keep him from moving south with his prisoners. Experienced soldiers report the volume of fire they felt was at platoon strength, thirty to forty soldiers. Not four hundred.'

Robinson shrugged. 'That's why they're estimates, Colonel. We're working off incomplete information. The assault regiment had three companies in it. I cannot believe that three units of forty to sixty men each would be called companies, while a unit of thirty would be called a regiment. It makes no organizational sense to name them that way.'

'That discrepancy is a clue that must be investigated, not dismissed,' Miklos pressed.

'We are continuing to evaluate information, Colonel, but we have few resources available. Civilians willing to provide information only bring with them what they knew when they were forced out of their homes. We have had no defections or prisoners taken yet, so we cannot interrogate anyone. And most yeomen who survived ambushes are not trained or experienced enough to provide the details we need.'

'I appreciate the problems, General,' Miklos said. 'But I will be asked, and I must have an answer. What is the Kingdom of North Mississippi doing in response to the Renaissance Army?'

'Well, that I do have an answer to,' Robinson said. He opened the folder, revealing two pages of typed print. 'I have here a proclamation from King Xavier, confirmed by the Council of Nobility and himself, as Prime Minister of the Kingdom.'

Miklos hid a groan. King Xavier acting as his own prime minister was legal under the Charter under which the kingdom operates, but it was believed around the embassy that his inexperience at politics had frustrated the progression of the kingdom. Without any political conflict at the higher levels, government offices and organizations tended to be unevolved.

'The first part is the usual legal language, declaring the Renaissance Army to be illegal, establishing bounties based on rank and position, all the usual words lawyers like.'

Miklos nodded.

'The second part expands the powers of more than a dozen counts whose territories may be impacted by this uprising. It allows them to recruit more yeomen, obtain heavy weapons and other military equipment, and provides some funds to offset the costs.

'The third part directs both me and General Prince Stefan to prepare plans for a spring offensive against the Renaissance Army in any counties where it still has a presence after the winter.'

Miklos heard Robinson's bitterness toward Prince Stefan, knowing the prince to be Robinson's military and political rival. 'Hoping the winter will weaken their hold?'

'Without proper facilities, any forces this one surviving Dawson has assembled will suffer throughout the winter. Striking them early spring maximizes the impact.'

'And in the meantime, you can find and choke off any outside support they have.' Miklos said.

'What sort of support can you imagine they have?' Robinson scoffed. 'The Old Guard suffered and died after the Range Riot; what's left have thrown in their hat with the Mardurers in Walker County. No other organization exists to offer them any help and we've no indication of foreign aid.'

'You have no indication of anything; but that is no reason to assume you won't find any if you look,' Miklos said.

'The king's government has more important things to do in the meantime than look for fantasy support, Colonel. As an example, it is obvious from the reports that at least one count has lost control of his county and should be removed from his lands and his title.'

Miklos frowned at the response. 'You're going to remove Count Walker?'

'He allowed a rebellion to foment in his county, did not take appropriate steps to curb it early, and has failed to retain control of his people or his land and is now besieged in his manor. Once the Renaissance Army has been crushed, I will propose a bill in the House of Nobles calling him to account. Once it passes, Vittorio Montessori will no longer be a nobleman in the Kingdom of North Mississippi.'

Miklos made no comment at first. He was aware of Vittorio Montessori's reputation from his time in the Commonwealth Army. Miklos was one of many who thought the man to be incompetent to hold high position, but there was something about the Duke's cavalier attitude that he found annoying.

'That is, of course, an internal matter for the king and the king's government,' Miklos finally said.

'Have I answered your questions?' Robinson asked.

As much as I expect you to, Miklos thought.

'Yes,' he said. He stood. 'Thank you for your time.'

***

An hour later, Miklos sat across from another man. This time, he suffered from the man's loud and boisterous laugh.

'What did you expect?' Larbi Bennabi asked in Odessan. 'Did you think he would open his files and say, "Oh, you caught me, here are all my secrets?" Shame on you if you did, my friend.'

Miklos managed a little smile. Larbi Bennabi was a former pilot in the Commonwealth Aviation Service, fighting in numerous campaigns before he was shot down over the fields of China. He survived but lost a hand. His patrons found him a position as leader of the North Mississippi Royal Air Corps, with a promotion from Squadron Major to Major General.

In the twelve years since he took the position, Bennabi had come to enjoy a sedentary lifestyle. He had traded the lean grace of a fighter pilot for the corpulent body of a staff officer. Nevertheless, he kept his uniform immaculate, and his mind was still sharp, a necessary tool when his branch of the military was neglected by the king.

King Xavier had his family's distrust of technology. Though required to maintain an air branch of his military, Xavier spent little time or money on it.

Bennabi's corps consisted of fifty-one of the cheapest, least dependable aircraft he could buy. The budget for the mechanics and pilots needed to use the equipment was far less than it had to be, as was money allocated for spare parts, munitions and aviation fuel.

For Bennabi, the King's distrust meant a constant stream of reports and orders to use what he had efficiently. This meant campaigns to gain patrons and their support in the House of Nobles for more funding, and personal meetings with military officers, reminding them of all the Air Corps could offer, to beg for more resources. All of which made him an excellent source of information on the various branches and their inner workings, and an important contact for Miklos' other duties as an intelligence agent.

A job which now found Miklos attending a late lunch with his friend on a terrace at Snelling Castle, reserved for generals and their guests. Waited on by orderlies, drinking fine spirits and enjoying cigars, they were no more noticeable than any other party enjoying the benefits of their position.

'What do I expect?' Miklos repeated the question. 'I expect him to take this seriously.'

'He is taking it as seriously as he can,' Bennabi chuckled. 'He is in his position, and he does not see himself being taken down from it. As such, he is doing what he can to benefit from it and no more.'

'That is a poor position for a professional officer to take.'

'He is not a professional, and he has never had to be one.' Bennabi gestured for another drink. 'In serious, Rika, you know what this military is like. Most officers are in their position for advancement, not for king and country. And those who are here for their kingdom are concentrated in a few special units.'

Miklos nodded. 'I know, but to deal with this level of disinterest is frustrating.' He fumed for a moment. 'Think the Air Corps can help?'

'Officially? No,' Bennabi shook his head. 'Aviation gasoline is still being rationed. Although, one or two of our monthly flights might stray over Walker County with some cameras running. Maybe we can find something.'

'That's all you can do?' Miklos asked.

Bennabi nodded. 'You know the limitations His Majesty has imposed upon me. Every airplane gets one flight per month for maintenance and training, unless an emergency is declared. No emergency, no more flights.'

Miklos shook his head in disgust. If King Xavier was not deliberately working to be the most ridiculous monarch in the Commonwealth, Miklos was going to be greatly surprised.

'So, what shall you do?' Bennabi asked, bringing the conversation back around.

'I shall investigate on my own.'

Bennabi frowned. 'But why? General Robinson is a fool, acting above his competence at military matters, but he is an expert at the political game. He can throw up obstacles. Why does this attract your interest?'

Miklos sipped his drink. It was a fair question, and he thought about the answer.

'Something about this Renaissance Army – or the Mardurers, whatever you wish to call them by – irritates me. They are not acting as a rebellious force should. There are no great, passionate speeches about the evils of the kingdom or the Commonwealth. They let their prisoners go, with no mass executions or maiming. They go out of their way to hide their strength. Their agents seem to be pulling in a significant number of recruits, and yet we know very little about their philosophies.'

'And that means?' Bennabi asked. He was a pilot, not an intelligence officer.

'What if they're not a rebellious group?' Miklos asked. 'What if we're all starting with an incorrect assumption?'

'What else could they want?' Bennabi asked.

'I don't know,' Miklos said. 'But I intend to find out.'

Chapter 6

Sasha lay on the ground, staring up at a break in the canopy. She saw stars spinning about the sky and through the leaves of the trees. A warm breeze blew through, rustling the leaves but not the stars. The stars remained spinning.

Sasha enjoyed the view until a face appeared over her, a ponytail hanging over her shoulder towards Sasha's nose.

'Are you alright, Cadet?'

Sasha blinked and the stars disappeared. She took a deep breath and became aware of a dull ache at the back of her head.

'I'm fine, Provost Corporal.'

Provost Corporal Isabella reached out her hand and helped pull Sasha to her feet. 'I apologize, Cadet. You came at me quicker than I expected. I'm afraid I had to react even faster.'

Sasha nodded. 'I understand,' she said as she stretched. 'Please show me what you did.'

Isabella showed her, slowly, how she had grabbed Sasha's punch, pulled Sasha off her feet and threw her to the ground. Then she had Sasha slowly work through how to do that to her. Sasha paid close attention to Isabella's lessons, noting where the hands gripped her arm, how the weight shifted from one foot to another. Then she tried it herself.

Sasha's natural inclination to learn extended beyond books and battle strategies to fighting as well. She had long fought bullies in her hometown, the sort of fights teenagers had, but since leaving she had learned proper fighting. Basic fighting was practiced several times a week. In addition, as a member of First Squad, she had learned some of the basics of knife fighting from Winnie.

Not that Sasha could claim any special expertise. Three months earlier, when General Prince led a force down from Walker County to support Third Regiment, Sasha and Winnie had gotten into a fight with a pair from Fourth Regiment while visiting the quartermaster's wagons. The provost were summoned to break up the fight, and in the heat of the moment, Sasha had thrown a punch at a provost, who quickly had her on the ground in an arm lock.

The provost had been Isabella.

Sasha did not know if Isabella had recognized her. If she did, Isabella made no mention of it in their weeks of sparring.

'Now do it again, only a bit faster,' Isabella said, and threw a punch. Sasha deflected, grabbed Isabella's wrist, and turned to throw her. Gently, but faster than she had before.

Isabella looked up from the ground. 'Good job.'

A cough grabbed their attention. Provost Paul, Isabella's patrol-mate, stood with their horses at the edge of the clearing, holding a pocket watch. 'We've got to get going, I'm afraid.'

'Right,' Isabella said. Sasha helped her to her feet, and she went to grab her jacket from a nearby branch.

Sasha was often reminded of the yeomen when she looked at the provost in full uniform. The Renaissance Army did not have the support to maintain the same uniform for every member, so the standard varied from one unit to the next. The provost were the exception. They wore deep blue long coats, with gold fringe, and bright brass gorgets hanging around their necks as a badge of office. Black tricorns completed their uniforms. Each provost carried a pistol and a club, and most had a bigger weapon on their saddle, an automatic or shotgun.

But if they looked much like yeomen and had the same duties, the provost went about it in a completely different way. Provost rode about in pairs, one man and one woman. The pairs were grouped into patrols of eight to twelve and rode from town to town. They brought their own food and water with them and were as polite as they could be. They were trained to fight, yes, but their training was about subduing their opponent, not killing them.

They were what the yeomen always should have been.

'Want a ride back?' Isabella asked, climbing into her saddle.

'No,' Sasha said. 'I think I'll go for a bit of a run before I head back.'

'As you will,' Paul said before starting his horse down the path back to town.

'Good day, Scholar!' Isabella said with a wave before following Paul.

Sasha smiled and turned the opposite direction, back into the maze.

That's what the locals called them. The Mardurer's Maze, the paths and tracks that looped around towns, worn into the dirt by a company of soldiers who had long since moved on. It was nice for Sasha to get out and run, especially as it got her away from the town.

Gordonsborough. The name had meant nothing to her before Fox left her there. Almost three weeks later, Sasha was starting to think of it as a punishment.

A small village in a nice defensible position, the RAM had concentrated a dozen families there, raising and arming a militia as they often did. But the people of Gordonsborough seemed to not care about anything. Their militia practice was running from one wall to another and reloading their weapons, but no tactical practices. They had refused a teacher when one was offered, and few of them, even from the families that had moved into the town, knew anyone who has joined the RAM. It was almost decidedly a neutral town within the Liberated Counties.

What made it worse was they did not let her do anything. She was not allowed to help with chores, make food, or wash clothes. They did not have any books, other than a few Bibles, so she could not read. Even constant exercise was beginning to run on her nerves.

The one ray of hope was the provost patrol that rode through every three or four days. Provost Isabella had specifically been asked to check on Sasha's wellbeing by a superior, but she did not say by whom.

No, not Sasha's well-being. Cadet Scholar's well-being.

With little to do, Sasha had spent a large portion of her time thinking. One thought that arose early and often was the idea that Scholar was different than Sasha.

Sasha, when she was with Third Field Regiment, was a person with a history. The regiment had rescued her from her father, so they knew she was from a pacifist family. They watched her learn to fight, watched her become a respected member of their regiment, so they knew her abilities. They watched her read everything she could, listened to her finish the quote from General Prince during the Middlestedt debate, saw her protect a murderer from Winnie's anger long enough to be tried and executed, so they knew her qualities.

But Cadet Scholar was a completely blank slate. Sasha could mold her to be anyone she wanted. She could be as angry as Winnie, as compassionate as Mary, as stoic as Snow. Or Scholar could simply be Sasha with a new name.

Her leg started to twinge, so Sasha slowed to a walk. She was halfway around the track from where she had started. Between the running and the sparing, Sasha decided she had exercised enough for one day and started walking back to Gordonsborough.

The village sat on a series of small hills, connected by a five-foot wall and surrounded by light forest and a few small fields for crops. Several inhabitants were working in the fields, some waving at Sasha as she walked into the village.

When the Renaissance Army fortified Gordonsborough, they did not just add a wall. They repaired and expanded the homes and built a few more, to accommodate the families moving in. The village looked quite lively, compared to Sasha's hometown and the villages she visited in Brainerd County.

We bring the color back to people's lives, Sasha thought with no small pride in her heart.

More rooms had been built than necessary, so Sasha had been given one whole room to herself, part of the house now occupied by the Silver family. Mother Silver was busy about the small kitchen when Sasha came in.

'Oh, dear, all messy again,' she clucked at Sasha.

Sasha smiled sheepishly. Mother Silver reminder her too much of her own mother, and Sasha found herself relishing being a daughter again. Even if the same enjoyment made her worry about her own family, long ago taken from their home and imprisoned in Walker Town.

'Mess is necessary,' Sasha said.

'I'll assume you're right, and not just trying to get out of trouble,' Mother Silver said. She gestured to a pot of water. 'Fill the basin from the well, and I'll heat some water for a good scrubbing. No need to stay dirty, is there?'

'No, ma'am,' Sasha agreed.

Cleaned and fed a late lunch, Sasha removed herself to her room. It was the largest space she had ever had to herself, ten feet to a side, with four beds arrayed in two bunks, two dressers, and a small desk under a window.

Still bored, she thought.

Part of her had to wonder if this was not on purpose. Snow told her often that the generals did not do much without having a plan. Even this exile must have a purpose. Sasha could not fathom what it was, but she learned long ago she was not as smart as either of the generals.

Truth be told, as much as she was bored, Sasha was also getting nervous. The Templars were to start in September, and they were already halfway through August. Every day was one day closer to the Templars, to whatever the generals had planned.

One more day closer to seeing if Cadet Scholar is worth knowing.

Sasha lay on her bed, the lower bunk next to the door, staring at the sunlight on the floor, and once again tried to think about what might be ahead of her. Between the physical exhaustion of her exercises and the mental exhaustion of waiting, Sasha soon fell asleep.

Chapter 7

Sasha woke with a start. Looking at the position of the sun on the floor, she had been asleep for maybe two hours.

A loud knock at the door; that must have been what woke her up. 'Miss Scholar?' Mother Silver's voice came through. 'Are you awake?'

'I am,' Sasha called. She sat up in her bed as Mother Silver came through the door.

'Good. I wanted to make sure you were decent before I sent them in.'

'Who?' Sasha asked, but Mother Silver had already disappeared. Sasha stretched when the first woman came through the door.

No, not a woman. A girl, thirteen or fourteen by Sasha's guess, a head shorter than her with jet-black hair. She walked in, eyes looking over the room, fixing on the window. She rushed over to look out of it, failing to notice Sasha sitting on the bed.

The girl giggled and said something Sasha did not catch.

Another voice responded, and Sasha glanced over to see a second person enter the room. She was older than Sasha, also with jet-black hair, but without a smile on her face. If anything, she looked sad, looking at the far bunks with dismay. She continued to speak, and Sasha realized they were speaking Quebecois.

The younger girl turned and saw Sasha.

'Oh, hello!' she said. 'I'm Cadet Cardinal, this is Cadet Rose.'

Sasha stood, holding her hand out, 'I'm Cadet Scholar. Welcome to Gordonsborough.'

Cardinal shook her hand, then looked at Rose. Sasha thought she must have been about twenty or so, a few years older than Sasha at least. Rose did not move from her spot, and Cardinal said something in Quebecois. Rose shook her head, and Cardinal sighed.

'Rose would say hello, but she is having a melancholy,' Cardinal said. Her English was heavily accented, but Sasha understood her well enough. 'How long have you been here?'

'Two weeks, almost three.' Sasha said. 'Where are you from?'

Cardinal's smile faltered. 'Quebec,' she said, quietly. 'Beyond that I can't say.'

'Right,' Sasha said. 'I know how that is.'

'You?' Rose asked sullenly.

'Minnesota,' Sasha said. 'Beyond that . . . .'

'Such secrets,' Rose said gloomily. She walked over to the far bunk, looking down on it with such sadness.

Sasha glanced over the two girls, noticing their clothes. They were both wearing finer clothes, with proper leather boots and precise stitches on their jackets.

From some wealth? Sasha asked herself. Or do all cadets get such things?

'I assume you want a top bunk?' Rose asked Cardinal, dropping her pack on the bottom. Cardinal giggled and tossed her bag on the top. She climbed the ladder quickly and sat, her feet dangling off the edge.

'Bunks! How exciting,' Cardinal beamed.

'Would you like to see the town?' Sasha asked.

'I would,' Cardinal said, jumping off and landing with a flourish. Rose simply shrugged.

The tour of Gordonsborough did not last long, as the village was not too large. The population was welcoming to the two newcomers. Cardinal spoke with everyone and flashed her smile. Rose was reserved, speaking little and spending her time close to Sasha.

Someone decided to make the evening a banquet, where every house made something for dinner, and they shared it in the village center. Tables and chairs were dragged out, and some instruments played. Rose begged off with a headache, returning to their room, leaving Sasha and Cardinal.

'Is she okay?' Sasha asked.

Cardinal frowned after her companion. 'She is not happy to be here,' she said. 'It is a shame. She should be looking forward to the adventure, instead of moping about the past.'

'I'm sorry,' Sasha said. 'If there's anything I can do, let me know.'

'Oh, don't worry,' Cardinal said. 'She is a grown woman, who can handle herself or not as she wishes. I will spend little time forcing her.'

The dinner went well, with Cardinal making small talk with the villagers far easier than Sasha was able to. It was not just her age that was disarming, but her personality. She was so friendly to everyone; they all became her friends immediately.

'Don't you go getting all envious,' Mother Silver said. She had crept up on Sasha and surprised her.

'About what?' Sasha asked.

'About her being the center of attention,' Mother Silver replied.

'I'm not,' Sasha said.

'Aren't you?' Mother Silver asked with a sly smile. 'I remember what the general said when you got dropped off. You're special, meant for something important. Same with those two. Well, I doubt you are all special in the same way. So, if she's better at being the center of attention, let her be the center of attention.'

Mother Silver was referring to Fox. Sasha would have corrected her, but Mother Silver seemed to call all officers general. Instead, she asked, 'And what should I be?'

Mother Silver shrugged. 'Just be you. Anything else is fake.'

Sasha thought for a moment, watching Cardinal entertaining the children, then turned to the banquet table. She piled a plate with food and returned to the room.

The sun was moved beyond the window, and the room was lit by candlelight. Rose lay in her bed, staring at the top bunk. She did not look over when Sasha entered.

'Rose?'

Rose glanced over. 'Cadet Scholar.'

'I brought you some food. I think you should try to eat.' She walked over and set the plate on the desk, then sat down on her bunk. She looked at Rose intently.

'Are you going to stare?'

'Until you eat, yes.'

'Why?'

'Because we're both cadets,' Sasha said.

Rose sighed and sat up, glancing at the plate.

'Is this what peasants eat here?' she asked.

64

Sasha frowned. 'It's common food for these parts, yes.'

Rose sniffed and took a bit of bread. She broke off a small piece and took a bite. 'How bland. Is this what we are to eat for a year?'

'I don't know,' Sasha replied sternly. 'I don't think we'll be here too much longer. Who knows where we will be after this?'

Rose sighed and took a larger bite. She said something in Quebecois. Sasha did not understand, but she was sure it was not nice.

'Eat up,' she said. 'We've got to maintain our strength.'

'What do you know of the Templar Project?' Rose asked quickly.

'General Caesar said it was a project to train leaders of the movement.'

'And commoners such as yourself are part of it?'

Sasha blinked at Rose's question. 'Why shouldn't we be?' she asked angrily.

Rose looked at Sasha, astonished that Sasha was upset. 'To be an officer of a military force is a responsibility of great importance. One must understand the importance of decisions and their consequences. What do you know of such things?'

Her tone was so dismissive and insulting Sasha felt like taking the food away but kept herself on the bed. Rose did not even seem aware that she had been insulting.

'I know more than you think I do,' Sasha said.

'I hope so,' Rose said. Her appetite had returned, and she began eating the food provided, making insulting remarks about its quality. Sasha excused herself and left the woman to her food.

She ran into Cardinal at the front door.

'How is –.'

'Your older sister?' Sasha finished.

Cardinal looked surprised. 'How did you know?'

'Black hair, quality clothes, refined language,' Sasha said. 'But how is it you are so nice, and she is so –.'

'Arrogant? Self-obsessed? Believe me, many similar descriptors can be laid at her feet.' Cardinal shrugged. 'As with many things about our past, I cannot say. Just, give her time. Rose is not so bad, once you get past her attitude. Please give her that chance?'

Sasha sighed. 'We are all in this together,' she said, 'so I have to, if we're going to get through this project together; but, Cardinal, if she's upset to be here, her attitude will not help.'

'I know,' Cardinal said. 'Just give her a few days. I'm sure she'll come around.'

***

Four days later, the three were no longer on speaking terms.

Sasha tried to get the pair of them included in her routine, starting with a hike through the Mardurer's Maze. Rose complained so much they returned well before lunch. Sasha and Cardinal went for a run that afternoon, but Cardinal became annoyed that Sasha was a better runner.

They returned to find Mother Silver, red faced and pacing. 'That one is a right proper lady, ain't she?' Silver asked, glaring at Cardinal until the girl withdrew into the cadets' room.

'What happened?' Sasha asked cautiously.

'She asked for new food, "cooked properly," says she. She wants her clothes washed with soap, not pig shit. And she demanded, outright demanded, we gather every feather we have to make her a mattress that she could sleep on.'

Sasha sighed. 'Okay. Let me speak to her.'

'Tell her I don't want to hear from her anymore. You and the youngster, fine, but not her!' Silver shouted.

Rose and Cardinal were speaking quickly in Quebecois, both upset. It was some time before either of them turned to her.

'Mother Silver is angry,' Sasha said.

'She is not my mother,' Rose snapped.

Cardinal hushed her. 'Scholar, I'm sorry. I don't think Rose is adjusting very well.'

'What did she expect?' Sasha asked. She was genuinely curious about what Rose thought she was coming here for, and how she got there. A woman of some means in the Renaissance Army did not make any sense; a Quebecois woman even less so.

Curiosity was not what Rose heard. 'I expected the benefits of being an officer!' she snapped. 'This is not the benefit of an officer; this is of a sergeant, or worse!'

Sasha turned red. The corporal's stripes on her uniforms were clearly still there, and Rose could not have missed them. Cardinal jumped up and pulled Sasha out of the room before she could respond.

'I'm sorry,' Cardinal said again. 'I'm trying to get her to ease up. Do you think Mother Silver will help?'

'Help how?' Sasha asked.

'Cook the food better? Maybe they have better soap they can use on the clothes?'

Sasha stared at Cardinal in surprise. 'They don't have better soap, Cardinal. They have what they have.'

'Oh,' Cardinal said, her face dropping. 'I see.'

Then came two days of constant rain. Stuck indoors, the differences between the women boiled over into fierce arguments.

Rose was upset that she was in this position and blamed her sister for getting her in it. Cardinal blamed Rose for not having a better attitude. Somehow Sasha got pulled into the middle, and both got angry at her. Cardinal was upset that Sasha did not know how to improve Rose's attitude; Rose simply called Sasha 'an uppity peasant moving beyond her station'. After the resulting scuffle, Mother Silver had each one banished to a different room for the rest of the day.

The following morning was the first break in the rain, and Sasha was taking advantage of it to get out and run. Whatever Rose and Cardinal were doing, she frankly did not care. She needed the release, and to her surprise she had not seen the provost since the day the others arrived. Sasha expected she could give Isabella quite the fight.

She ran for a while, realizing when she finally came to a stop that she had run around the whole track and then some. *Maybe four miles*, she guessed.

She started walking, sweating in the heat of the summer sun. Between exercise and the weather, she was absolutely drenched, and a bit thirsty. Sasha thought she should head back to her room and get cleaned. Hopefully she could avoid the other two while she did so.

A minute later she heard hoof beats. Isabella and Paul appeared down the track, making their way quickly towards Sasha.

'Cadet Scholar,' Isabella said, 'you need to return at once.'

'Oh, lord,' Sasha said, 'what did Rose do now?'

'Nothing, to my knowledge,' Isabella said, grinning. 'All the cadets are being assembled.'

Sasha caught her smile and returned it. 'It's time?'

'Yes,' Isabella said, holding her hand out. She pulled Sasha up behind her on the horse and started quickly down the road.

They rode into Gordonsborough, and Sasha had a shock. In addition to the other provost, Mother Silver's house was surrounded by the Olympians. *Was it Prince or Caesar?* Sasha asked herself.

A master sergeant stood at the doorway, watching the provost drop Sasha off in front of him. He looked down at her – barefoot, drenched in sweat, dirty clothes – and scoffed.

'Well, get inside, if you dare,' he said.

Sasha moved past him into the main room of Mother Silver's house. The hostess was speaking with a woman in uniform, whose back was to the door. Mother Silver nodded at Sasha, and the woman turned around.

Sasha blinked in surprise.

Colonel Snow?

No, not Snow. This woman's face was unblemished by scars. Her hair was so long, she worked into a braid that hung over the shoulder and almost down to her belt. Instead of the olive-green Snow favored, her uniform was a deep brown, meticulously presented. She had a blue aiguillette on her shoulder, denoting her as an adjutant or staff officer. Instead of sewn-on cloth, her rank insignia was a brass pin, three circles. A brigadier.

Other than those differences, she looked exactly like Snow.

Snow's sister, Sasha thought, then she corrected herself.

Snow's twin.

The woman stepped forward, looking Sasha up and down. 'Cadet Scholar,' she said.

Sasha nodded, coming to attention. 'Yes, ma'am.'

'I am Brigadier Lily, Adjutant General for the Renaissance Army. General Prince has tasked me to bring you and the other cadets out of Gordonsborough.' Lily even sounded like her sister, except she sounded bored. Sasha heard none of the fire in Lily's voice.

'How much do you bring with you?' Lily asked.

'Just my common uniform,' Sasha said, 'and these exercise clothes.'

'You should clean and change.'

'Ma'am, my common uniform . . . ,'

'. . . is cleaned and drying now,' Mother Silver said.

Thank you, Mother Silver. Sasha thought.

'Ten minutes,' Lily said. 'I'll be waiting.'

Sasha rushed into her room, which was empty save for the basin of water Mother Silver must have dragged in. The hostess herself followed with a kettle of hot water and a towel.

'Work quickly, girl, she means business.'

'I will, and thank you, Mother Silver.'

'Oh, hush, and get to scrubbing,' Mother Silver said. 'And leave the laundry. I'm told you'll get new ones when you get where you're going.'

Sasha cleaned quickly and emerged from her room, dressed in her worn, olive uniform. Rose and Cardinal stood before Lily, waiting patiently with their bags. Sasha joined them.

'That is all?' Lily asked. Sasha nodded. 'Good.' She paused and looked at the three cadets. 'While you were preparing, Mother Silver has told me of the fighting. Let me be clear; you are cadets in the Templar Project, chosen by the generals themselves. I know some of you are being asked to grow up faster than you should, but you did agree to come here. Do not make the generals regret their decision. Understood?'

'Yes, ma'am,' Sasha said automatically. Lily looked at the sisters, who repeated the phrase.

Neither of them has any prior experience, Sasha realized. Why that did not occur to her before now, she did not know.

'Very well,' Lily said. 'Then come with me.'

Lily led the three out into the sunlight. The Olympians and the provost maintained their guard, and four horses stood rider-less.

'Cadet Rose, take the first mount. Cadet Cardinal, you will take the second. Cadet Scholar, you take the last with Cadet Candle.'

Sasha was surprised to hear a fourth cadet's name and walked over to the last horse. Standing next to it was another young woman, wearing worn, grey clothes that looked to be too big, tied with a rope belt. She lacked even the uncomfortable wooden boots that Sasha wore, being completely barefoot. She was taller than Sasha, with neck-length brown hair and tanned skin.

'Cadet Candle?' Sasha asked.

'I am,' she said. She had an accent Sasha could not place. Almost Minnesotan but not quite. 'I hope you know how to control this beast.'

'I do,' Sasha answered, pulling herself up into the saddle. She held her hand down to Candle, pulling the woman up to sit behind her. Candle was tall, but she was not heavy, and Sasha had no problem helping her up.

'Let's go,' Lily said, and the column started to exit Gordonsborough.

Sasha turned and waved. 'Thank you for everything, Mother Silver.'

'Be safe!' the woman called out.

The riders left the village, moving north along one of the large trails. The provost turned off down another path, Isabella sending one last wave towards Sasha before she was gone.

Moving at a calm pace, Sasha felt Candle holding onto her. The woman, Sasha guessed was a year or two older than her, was tense, probably scared to be on a horse. Candle relaxed as they moved without incident.

After about twenty minutes, she whispered in Sasha's ear.

'Are all three of you cadets?'

'Yes,' Sasha responded.

'How many total, do you know?'

'No.'

Candle looked around. 'All girls?'

'So far.'

'I was hoping for some boys,' Candle said. 'You'd think there would be a few.'

'There still might be,' Sasha responded curtly.

'Why are you cross?' Candle asked. 'Oh, do you not like boys?'

'What do you mean?' Sasha asked.

'Do you like girls?'

'WHAT?" Sasha snapped. Candle almost fell off her horse as Sasha turned around in the saddle. 'What the hell are you talking about?'

Before Candle could respond, Lily was there. 'Shut up, both of you,' she said. The two cadets went quiet. 'I don't care who or why, but the next cadet who speaks out of turn will walk the rest of the way, is that clear?'

All four cadets nodded in silence. Lily turned and led them silently through the forest.

Sasha glumly followed, Candle still holding on. *Are all the cadets like this?*

Chapter 8

They rode a few more hours until they arrived at what used to be a plantation. It must have been abandoned before Sasha was born, as the roof of the main house had collapsed, and the barn had fallen over.

Like many plantations Sasha had seen, the land was a patchwork of cleared fields and thin forests. Lily led her troop towards one particularly secured field, surrounded by trees on all four sides. Following behind, Sasha saw several buildings built into the trees.

They were long buildings, obviously built in the last few months. They extended into the woods, with tree branches and netting overhead. Lily led them to one of the buildings, where large doors opened to show a long stable. Everyone dismounted as a group of young men and women took their horses.

The four cadets gathered together, looking about nervously.

'Where are we?' Cardinal asked.

'I don't know,' Sasha said. She was sure they were still in Walker County, somewhere on the eastern side.

'It's called Athens,' Lily said, suddenly behind Rose, surprising the cadets. 'It's named after an ancient city, once known as a place of knowledge and learning. It serves as a training facility for individuals being trained in staff roles. It will also be your home for most of the foreseeable future.'

She led the cadets to the edge of that copse of woods. 'This is the supply area,' she said, 'where the horses, food and supplies are kept. That building there is the armory, for the weapons. It's always guarded.'

She gestured to another copse, with more of the long huts. 'That copse there is the cadre area.'

'Cadre?' Candle asked.

'They're the officers and instructors of Athens. Every RAM facility has personnel who maintain the buildings and keep the place running. Here at Athens they include the cooks, classroom teachers, and military instructors. As that area is their personal space, don't be there unless you have a reason to be.'

She started through the paths of the woods, the cadets following behind. 'How many of these places are there?' Candle asked.

'Three training facilities,' Lily said. 'Sparta is the combat school. Rhodes is the technical school. You may be spending time at both in the future. Other locations have been established for various reasons.'

'Where are they?' Sasha asked.

'You don't need to know.'

She stopped and stood to the side, gesturing the cadets to follow her lead. A squad of young men and women came marching by, following an older sergeant down the path. Sasha exchanged glances with a few of them. They wore dull brown clothes, a few with their own stripes of various ranks. The column continued on, disappearing around a corner.

'Staff clerks,' Lily said. 'Learning to do important work. Behind us are the classrooms, where you will be spending most of your time. Ahead of you are the barracks, where you will be living. The dividing line,' she said, pointing to a structure climbing up into the trees, 'is that bell tower. It rings on the hour, every hour, between 6 a.m. and 10 p.m. How many of you are used to schedules that work by the hour?'

Candle, Rose and Cardinal all raised their hands. Sasha did not.

'You'll get used to it,' Lily said to her. She almost looked empathetic, then she turned and continued their way through the trees.

More of the long huts. Sasha finally got to see one up close. They were made of wood, about twenty feet by fifty feet, with gently sloping roofs. Each long side had four windows, with thick parchment or hide instead of glass. Each short side had a single door.

'The huts look the same,' Candle said.

'They're called ram cabins,' Lily said. 'Built to the same specification. Each one should be roughly the same size.'

Lily led them to one of the huts. 'Here we go,' she said, opening the closest door.

Immediately a voice called out.

'That's not going to hold!' a woman said.

'Yes, it will,' a deep man's voice rumbled. 'I know ropes.'

'So, do I, and it won't hold!'

The cadets walked into the room behind Lily. Beds lined each wall, six of them, each with a small dresser at the wall. The room looked smaller; a curtain had been strung up across the room, blocking the rest of the view.

'It will hold,' the man said again, 'it IS strong enough.'

'Oh, yeah?' the woman said. Suddenly the curtain jumped and fell as the ropes came loose from the walls, revealing three people, one man and two women.

The man was black skinned, as black as Sasha had ever seen a human being. He was about Sasha's height, with big muscles and curly black hair. Like Sasha, he wore an enlisted uniform with corporal's stripes.

One of the women was standing. She was what Sasha's father called Asian stock, a little shorter than Sasha with shoulder-length light brown hair. She was wearing work clothes, without any markings or insignia on them. She had caused the rope to fall by jumping on it.

The third was a blonde woman sitting on one of the cots. She had sergeant's stripes on her khaki uniform and was currently trying not to laugh at the situation she was watching, eyes closed and biting her own knuckles.

'See, it fell,' the standing woman said, beginning to fold the curtain up.

'Well it can't hold if you jump on it,' the man grumbled.

The woman sitting down opened her eyes and saw Lily and the other cadets. She stood up. 'Attention!'

The man turned and snapped to attention. The Asian woman looked confused, then saw Lily. 'Oh,' she said, and straightened slightly. 'Hello!' she smiled and waved.

Sasha repressed a laugh.

Lily stepped to the side. 'Cadets Cardinal, Candle, Rose and Scholar. These are Cadets Swift,' the woman sitting on the bed, 'Mako,' the black man, 'and Patch,' the Asian woman.

'Are there going to be twelve of us?' Sasha asked. With the curtain down, she could see another six beds and stands, twelve total. A stove sat in the middle of one long wall, originally obscured by the curtain.

'Eventually,' Lily said.

'Any more men showing up?' Candle asked.

'Yes,' Lily said. 'Cadet Hero is around somewhere. The other four will arrive before the project begins. Now, these three here can show you around and get you acquainted. Choose a bunk, women on the far side of the curtain, men on this side. And, Cadet Mako?'

'Yes, ma'am?'

'Assume Patch will jump on your curtain again and double the rope.'

74

Mako frowned. 'Yes, ma'am.'

Lily turned and left, leaving the seven cadets. Mako turned to clean up the fallen ropes and curtains.

Patch walked up to the newcomers. 'Hi, I'm Libby!'

'Patch,' Swift giggled right behind her. 'You're supposed to go by Patch!'

'Oh, right,' Patch shook her head. 'I'm sorry, I'm new to all these rules.'

'It's okay,' Sasha said. 'I'm Scholar.'

'What unit are you from?' Swift asked.

'Third Field Regiment,' Sasha replied. 'You?'

'I'm from the First Field Regiment. Mako there is from the Naval Group.'

Rose laughed. 'A navy. Ha!'

Cardinal shushed her sister. 'So, you're a petty officer?'

Mako turned away from the pile and approached the women. 'That's right,' he said, 'equivalent to a corporal.'

'Are you going to fix that?' Swift asked. 'I'd like a bit of privacy tonight.'

'I'll need more rope,' Mako said. Patch beamed. 'Shall we take a walk?'

The cadets nodded and started filing out.

'Have you been here long?' Sasha asked.

'A week or so,' Patch said. 'Swift and Mako came in a few days ago.'

And I was stuck in Gordonsborough.

Mako led the group out into the camp. Cardinal skipped forward to walk by him. Sasha found herself walking next to Swift, while Patch and Candle walked behind them, and Rose trailed sullenly behind the lot of them.

'You're from Minnesota?' Swift asked.

'I am,' Sasha said. She could tell from her accent Swift was as well. 'Why?'

'Well, eight of us, only three from Minnesota,' that's kind of weird, isn't it?'

'Is it?' Sasha wondered.

'I mean, why are they fighting for Minnesota?' Swift continued.

'Does it matter?'

Swift shrugged. 'Maybe not. I'm just curious.'

'Not everyone in my previous regiment was Minnesotan. So long as they put their boots on the line, they're fine with me,' Sasha said.

'Sure,' Swift agreed quickly. She looked down at her feet as they walked.

Sasha blushed. 'Sorry if I snapped. I'm just nervous.' She thought for a moment. 'Who's the third?'

'From Minnesota? Cadet Hero. He's . . . .' Swift trailed off.

'He's what?' Sasha pressed.

Swift sighed. 'He arrived yesterday, kind of haughty and full of himself. Made some jokes about sharing beds with me and Patch. Several jokes. I had to give him my best sergeant's voice to get him to stop. Felt awkward sleeping last night, like he was watching me, so I asked about putting up a divider.'

Sasha frowned. That was not behavior she expected from a cadet.

They passed from the barracks to the classroom huts. Sasha saw a sign on the door of one and read it as she passed. Then she came to a complete stop, so quickly Patch walked into her.

'What is it?' Swift asked. Sasha pointed at the sign.

Burned into the wood, and painted with gold to stand out, the words grabbed Sasha's attention.

"No problem can withstand the assault of sustained thinking."

'It's a quote,' Sasha said. 'Something my colonel said to me when I left the regiment.' Sasha walked up to the door and opened it.

As a ram cabin, it was the same size as the barracks Sasha had just left, but there were no cots or dressers. There were a dozen mismatched tables and chairs spread about the room. Where the barracks had a stove, this building had a full fireplace. But it was the opposite wall that took Sasha's attention.

On the wall sat shelf after shelf of books. Hundreds of them, sitting on five shelves that ran the length of the building. Wooden signs hammered above the shelves told of topics that Sasha had heard of, and several she did not know. A treasure of information.

'Wow,' Sasha said.

'Can I help you?' a man said. There was a sergeant sitting in the corner, at a desk with a plaque stating 'Librarian.' He had one arm, and a scar on his cheek.

'Just seeing what this is,' Sasha said.

'It's the Athens Library,' the sergeant said. 'I'm First Staff Sergeant Jackson, head librarian. You are the Templar Project, aren't you?'

'Yes. How did you know?' Candle asked.

'Got a warning from General Prince we had some special students coming in. Students who might actually want to come and enjoy the library.' He gestured at Sasha, still starting at the books, and grinned. 'That's about as excited as I've ever seen anyone in this building.'

'It is nice,' Sasha said. She wanted to go and look through the shelves, but she did not want to disrespect the sergeant. If he controlled access to the books, she did not want to disrespect him at all.

'We can come here often?'

Jackson nodded. 'Use of the library is restricted to military personnel, so long as your follow the rules behind me.'

He gestured to a board behind him. Sasha read:

1. *Books are to stay in the library.*
2. *The library is a quiet place.*
3. *The librarian on duty has authority.*

'You have authority?' Swift asked.

'All the librarians are sergeants,' Jackson said. 'In the event an officer thinks they are above me, I have the full force of the camp commandant, Lieutenant Colonel Carpenter, behind me.'

'Someone tried to pull rank on him a few days ago,' Mako said, suddenly behind Sasha. The rest of the cadets had followed her into the room. 'A lieutenant wanted to pull some books out against the rules, ordered the librarian on duty to forget he was there. Spent two days in the stockade, avoided a court martial by agreeing to spend several weeks instructing classes at Sparta.'

'That's a lot of authority,' Cardinal said.

'It comes from a General Order given by General Prince. And the librarians are chosen by General Caesar himself,' Patch said.

'You don't mess with a librarian,' Mako said.

'They're just books,' someone said. Another man stood in the doorway, a little shorter than Sasha with brown hair and tanned skin. He walked in, looking at the cadets. 'They look nice, but you won't win wars with them.'

'And this is Cadet Hero,' Mako said. 'Try to ignore him.'

'Hey!' Hero said. 'I'm a cadet, same as you.'

'Hi!' Cardinal said, stepping forward and extending a hand. 'I'm Cadet Cardinal.'

Hero's eyes dropped to Cardinal's feet and swept slowly up her body. He had a leer on his face when he got to her eyes. Then he smiled, reached for her hand, bent down and kissed it, saying something in Quebecois. Cardinal blushed and smiled at him.

Sasha shivered and thought of Samuel Cartier, the bully who threatened her for years in Penelope's Haven. She folded her arms across her chest and stood tall, daring him to look at her the same way.

'You're in the Templar Project?' Rose asked with disdain.

'I am.' Hero looked at her the same way, not put off a bit by her glare. 'I got chosen by the Colonel of the Fourth Field Regiment himself!'

'Colonel Wild chose you?' Sasha asked incredulously.

Hero glared at her. 'He did. Why would you think otherwise?'

'I'm just surprised that he or Captain Tamarac had time to find someone to sponsor for the project given that they got on station only three months ago.'

'How did you know that?' Hero's eyes widened in surprise.

'I fought alongside the Fourth at the prison camp,' Sasha said. 'They were a tough group, all muscles and axes. You do not look like the type of warrior they take.'

'Well, I am,' Hero became haughty. 'And I'll prove it during the training.' He fumed and turned on his heels, exiting the library.

'Yeah,' Mako said, 'he's always like that.'

Rose said something in Quebecois. Candle and Cardinal both nodded in agreement.

Patch tugged at Sasha's sleeve. 'Were you in the prison camp attack?' she asked.

'I was,' Sasha said. 'Third Regiment held the line to the south with the Fourth.'

'Did you see the assault in the north,' Patch asked, 'with the pillboxes and towers?'

'I saw the aftermath,' Sasha said. She started wondering if she had met Patch before, if she had been with the pioneers who had breached the defenses.

'I built those rockets!' Patch said excitedly. 'The ones that destroyed the pillboxes and breached the walls and minefield.'

'You did?'

Patch nodded. 'Yes. We only had a few days to build the devices, but it was pretty clear what we needed to do. Luckily, we've been practicing for some time, so it wasn't too hard to build the final examples. We called them Sky-Snake, that's the one that cut the fences and the minefield, and Mud-ball, those killed the pillboxes.'

'Who's we?' Sasha asked.

'The Workshop,' Patch said excitedly. 'It's a place where . . . ,' she came to a stop. 'Huh. Maybe I'm not supposed to talk about it? Is that one of the rules? I can't remember.'

'Why shouldn't you talk about it?' Cardinal asked.

'Because it is classified,' another voice said, 'and should not be discussed.' General Caesar, with Saxon in tow and Olympians visible outside the library, stood at the doorway. Sasha, Swift and Mako came to attention; the rest did not.

'Sir,' Sergeant Jackson said, coming to attention.

'Sergeant Jackson,' Caesar said. 'These are some of the cadets from the Templar Project. You have been briefed on their status?'

'Yes, sir.'

Caesar looked at the cadets. 'The project has not started yet, but I wanted to take this opportunity to welcome you to Athens. I am sure you will find this a challenge, but one at which you can succeed.'

'Thank you,' Patch said, smiling.

Caesar nodded, then looked at Sasha. 'In the meantime, I need to speak with Cadet Scholar in private.'

Sasha blushed. Caesar led her out the door and away from the building where no one could hear them. Saxon stood at the library, making sure the cadets were not following.'

'Sasha,' he began, 'I understand that Colonel Snow gave you your renaissance name.'

'Yes, General.'

He nodded and paused. Sasha thought he looked a little nervous.

'It may not be apparent, Sasha, but the renaissance names taken by the officers have meaning. Snow chose her name for a reason, as did Prince, Wild, myself . . . it is important for the names to matter, since the names become a part of the officer's persona. And your name, Sasha, poses some problems.'

'What's wrong with Scholar?'

'Well, to be blunt, I would not say that you have earned it.'

Sasha's stomach tightened. 'But I've read everything available. That's why Snow gave it to me.'

'Yes, but being the Scholar of Third Regiment is a much easier task than being the Scholar of the Renaissance Army.'

'So, what does that mean? Do I have to take a different renaissance name?' Sasha asked.

'We will not decide that yet,' Caesar said. He looked at Sasha levelly. 'Consider it a challenge, Sasha. If you wish to be Scholar, and I fully endorse your desire to aim for that name, you will have to prove that you are worthy of it. Do you accept the challenge, or should we find you a new name?'

Sasha shook her head. 'No, General, I'll fight for the name Snow gave me.'

'Good,' Caesar said. He looked at her again, thinking about something. 'Do not worry about the criteria for your success, Sasha. I will sit down with you and we will discuss what you need to do to keep the name. There will be no surprises, no tricks. I will lay out what you must do, and you will meet the requirements, or you will not.'

'General,' Sasha said, sounding more confident than she felt, 'Colonel Snow wanted me to have that name, and I will not fail her. I will be Scholar.'

'We shall see, Sasha,' Caesar said. 'We shall see.'

Chapter 9

Looking at the formations taking up the field, Sasha felt a flutter in her stomach.

Since she had left home, she had not been a part of any religious services. Third Regiment did not have any sort of chaplain, just a handful of Bibles and a few individuals who would pray together on Sundays.

Athens was different. Athens had a chaplain, whose purpose was to lead services. And that was what he was doing right then, with about three hundred men and women, divided up into small formations.

Sasha watched from the side. She was a little nervous at not partaking in the services, but it had been made clear that attendance was not mandatory. She was free to do as she wished.

'The groups are the faiths, right?' Candle asked. She was also not attending the services, but Sasha knew she had been to a small service the previous morning. Sasha did not know why and had not asked. Talking about themselves was not something the cadets did easily. Except for Patch, who often had to be told to shut up.

'I think so,' Sasha admitted. 'It would explain why the platoons are uneven.'

'It's nice to see the different beliefs respected,' Candle said. There was a tone to her voice that piqued Sasha's interest, but Sasha did not ask. The prohibition on personal information was frustrating her in making friends.

'It is nice to see,' Sasha agreed.

After a moment Candle leaned forward. 'We could spend the morning in the library.'

Sasha smiled. 'Sounds good.'

The pair made their way towards the library. With the majority of camp personnel at the formation, the pathways were clear. It was a nice day, with a strong breeze. Candle jogged ahead to a stump and jumped on top, smiling up to the sun.

'Days like this, it is good to stop for a minute and enjoy the sun,' she said. 'It is a simple pleasure, but a decent one.'

'I agree,' Sasha said. 'I hope the windows in the library will be open.'

'I do too,' Candle said. Hopping off the stump, she fell in next to Sasha. 'I'll admit, I'm nervous.'

'About what?' Sasha asked.

'Our training. I've never been through much school, or anything that organized. And physical training? I've seen the training companies on their marches. I don't know that I could do that.'

'It's not too difficult,' Sasha said. 'The sergeants will probably start us off slow and work our way up to longer distances and faster times.'

'What if they don't? Doesn't *special training* make it sound like we'll be under a lot of pressure?' Candle did sound nervous.

'That doesn't mean they want us to fail,' Sasha said. 'They won't make it easy, but they won't purposefully fail us.'

'That'd be nice,' Candle said as they approached the library. 'I guess we'll finally have to wear those stupid uniforms.'

Sasha chuckled.

The day before the cadets in Athens were issued their equipment. And what a set it was.

Sasha, like the other cadets with previous experience, was used to scarcity. She wore the same clothes she was given in Brainerd County, the simple olive uniform with extra pockets, the wooden and leather boots. That was all she possessed. Most equipment was drawn from a common pool and returned when done.

It was obvious that the Templar Project did not suffer from such a limitation. The cadets had no less than three complete uniforms.

There was the exercise kit, a simple pair of shorts and shirt, padded running slippers, and undergarments. It looked flimsy and small, and Sasha was worried about wearing it in front of other cadets. Then there was the staff kit, which was the uniform Candle was speaking about; simple pants and buttoned shirt, dyed an ugly grey, real leather boots and belts. Nice, but Sasha had to agree with Candle, ugly.

What thrilled Sasha was the field kit. It was the same simple uniform with extra pockets she and the other veteran cadets were used to, only a dull grey and with extra padding sewn in at some places. Each cadet was given their own belt, with canteens, knife and compass. Hats and overcoats and an outdoor backpack for each cadet rounded out that set. Each cadet even got their own rifle, an infantry carbine that was much lighter than the full rifle Sasha was used to.

Despite the amount of supplies each cadet was being given, Command Quartermaster Stock had impressed upon them the importance of keeping their gear in good condition. 'You are entrusted with so much because we believe you can handle it,' he said. 'Prove us wrong, and the entire team suffers.'

The cadets all agreed, Sasha most urgently. She had met Command Quartermaster Stock before, when he came down to Brainerd during the prison battle. If he remembered her, he would remember her as one of several women involved in a fistfight outside of his kitchen.

Lucky for her he made no mention of it, and the cadets returned to their barracks to put their equipment away and go over cleaning instructions with a drill instructor.

But until the start of the program, they continued to wear the clothes they came in. Sasha in her corporal's uniform, Candle in the simple travelling clothes, except that she scrounged up a real belt and a pair of worn slippers. Dressed as such, the pair entered the library to find, for the first time, another patron.

He was a tall man, in his early twenties, wearing a deep brown uniform. The insignia were not sewn on, but brass pins. They showed him to be a warrant officer, and the red shoulder boards declared him to be infantry.

Sasha and Candle made their way to look at a different part of the bookshelves. Sasha looked at the man out of the corner of her eye, intrigued by the mystery. The only people she had ever seen with brass insignia were colonels and generals and their staffs. No combat officers she knew wore them. So why did this man have them?

The man glanced over. 'Can I help you?'

'I'm sorry, sir,' Sasha said, 'I was just wondering how an Infantry Officer got brass pins.'

'My regimental commander demanded it,' the officer said, with a sigh. 'I think they're a bit ostentatious.'

Sasha nodded. Candle leaned over. 'What does that mean?'

'I think it means the symbols are only being used to show off,' Sasha said. 'So, they're unnecessary, but used to make them look superior.'

'That's pretty accurate,' the man said. 'Are you students of the staff school?' He was eyeing Candle's clothing with an amused look, not as judgmental as some of the other officers.

'No, we're in the Templar Project,' Candle said.

The man produced a warm smile. 'Excellent, so am I. Cadet Elector,' he held out his hand. 'I'm pleased to meet you.'

'Cadet Scholar,' Sasha said.

'Cadet Candle,' she introduced herself. 'Shall we sit and chat?' she batted her eyes. Sasha cringed.

'Of course,' Elector said. They moved to a table. The staff sergeant at the librarian's desk looked annoyed at their voices, but as no one else was in the library, he opted not to make an issue of it.

'How many are here?' Elector asked.

'Eight others,' Candle said.

'But I think there are going to be twelve at the end,' Sasha added. 'There are that many bunks in our barrack. We're waiting on three more.'

'Two more,' Elector said. 'I came with another warrant officer; he's around somewhere.'

'So how it is you're in the Templar Project if you're already a warrant officer?' Sasha asked.

Elector started to say something, then stopped. 'I'm not sure how to answer that,' he said. 'We're not . . . .'

'. . . supposed to talk about ourselves,' Sasha said. 'It's frustrating, isn't it?'

Candle nodded. 'Yes,' she simply said. 'But who is the other one with you?'

'Oh, he's supposed to be back here soon,' Elector said. A second later the door entered and another man, dressed in a similar uniform to Elector, walked in. He was between Sasha and Elector's age, with blond hair. He had a confident aura about him. He walked up to the table.

'I'm afraid I haven't found any other cadets,' he said to Elector.

'Luckily, two of them found me,' Elector said. 'Cadet Blaze, this is Cadet Scholar and Cadet Candle.'

Candle smiled and stood, holding out her hand. Blaze eyed it with a distasteful look on his face.

'They're girls,' he said in an even voice.

Sasha's face turned red and her blood boiled at the look on his face. Elector blushed and shook his head. Candle retracted her hand and stood, arms across her chest, glaring up at him.

'So?' she asked. 'What does that have to do with anything?'

'The Templar Project is to create the future leaders of the army,' Blaze said.

'Blaze, shut up,' Elector interrupted. 'You knew there were going to be women in the project.'

Blaze shrugged. 'Yes, but I still fail to see why. Just send the girls through the Athens staff training, and they'll be ready to help real officers in the future.'

Elector covered his face with his hands. 'Oh, lord', he muttered to himself.

'Excuse me?' Candle demanded. 'I'll have you know, there are six women in this program, and five of them are combat focused!'

'That's right!' Sasha said, though she had to admit to herself she did not know that was true. She had never thought to ask others about their specialties. Candle obviously had.

'I'm sure they are,' Blaze said dismissively, 'and I'm sure one of them will make it through the training, but I doubt any of you has what it takes to stand up in a firefight. Only on the firing line can you truly become a warrior.'

'Excuse me, Cadet Blaze, but I've been in several firefights,' Sasha growled. Candle nodded emphatically, though Sasha had never spoken to her about them.

'I'm sure you have,' Blaze said. 'But you'll find that ambushing a few yeomen in the woods is different than a stand-up fight, and I think you'll learn quickly enough that it is up to men like me and Elector to win those battles.'

Sasha stood, but before she could speak a voice called out, 'ATTENTION!'

Sasha, Elector and Blaze snapped to, while Candle slowly followed a second later. With her back to the door Sasha could not see who it was. She remained uncertain until General Caesar appeared at their table.

The librarian wasn't supposed to call out to us, Sasha realized. He did it to get us to shut up before Caesar heard.

Caesar took a position at the head of the table. 'Have a seat,' he said. The four sat down, Blaze moving to sit next to Elector. Sasha ignored him.

'Cadets Blaze and Elector, welcome,' he began. 'As the Templar Project is a new endeavor, I wanted to say to both of you that I am counting on you to help the other cadets hone their skills. As both of you have prior experience commanding formations, you undoubtedly have your own lessons you can pass along.'

Elector and Blaze nodded.

'And Cadet Scholar,' Caesar said, turning to Sasha, 'your combat experience will be invaluable in the coming months. Very few individuals in the Renaissance Army have experienced such a wide variety of combat situations, particularly engaging the Royal Army in a night fight. I am counting on you to bring your experiences to the cadets and help them learn the skills they'll need.'

'Of course, General,' Sasha said. Candle sent a smirk at Blaze, who had turned bright red. Elector hid a smile.

'Cadet Candle, I know you are not coming from a military background, but that does not make your experiences any less valuable. I want to hear your outside view when it becomes necessary. Understood?'

'Yes, sir!' Candle said jubilantly.

'Excellent,' Caesar said. 'Now, Cadets Blaze and Elector, please follow me. We should get you outfitted before tomorrow.'

The two followed, Blaze pointedly ignoring the women while Elected managed a small wave. The two women watched them leave.

'What an ass,' Sasha said.

'Yes,' Candle agreed. 'Also, Blaze is a jerk.'

'What?' Sasha asked, confused by Candle's response.

Candle laughed. 'Never mind, Scholar. Never mind. What are we going to do about him?'

'Blaze? I don't know. When I first joined my regiment, one of the corporals didn't like me, and she tried to force me out of the regiment. I didn't leave, and eventually she accepted me. She even became a friend.'

'That would be nice,' Candle replied, 'but I'll be honest. When a man looks at me like he just did, like I was too far beneath him to speak to, he rarely turns out to have a heart of gold. Usually, they'll end up trying to force their superiority.'

Sasha was confused. Given Candle's flirtatiousness, Sasha assumed she wanted such looks director her way. But when she turned to the woman, Sasha saw a shadow cross her face. Sasha bit back the question and wondered what demons Candle might have in her past.

Candle shook her head and smiled at Sasha. 'But we're not going to let that happen. Did you really fight the Royal Army?'

'Twice,' Sasha said. 'We skirmished with them that morning, then fought a battle with them that night.'

'That must have been tough.'

'I lost two friends that night,' Sasha said quietly.

Candle reached up and gripped Sasha's shoulder.

She's lost people, too.

'Well,' Candle finally said, 'I know I've done some impressive things, too. And I can't think of any of the women cadets who would give in to him. So, we'll take him down a few pegs if we have to.'

'Sure,' Sasha agreed.

'Great, now let's read.'

Candle moved to get a book, and Sasha turned to her.

'Who isn't combat?'

'What?' Candle stopped and turned. 'What do you mean?'

'You said five of the women were combat. I'm trying to figure out who wasn't.'

'Rose,' Candle said.

Sasha nodded, thinking of Cardinal. She had an image of the two of them in a trench, fighting as the Royal Army advanced.

She's too young for combat.

'We all are,' Candle said.

Sasha blinked. 'Was I thinking out loud?'

'No,' Candle replied. 'But I probably had that same look on my face. We're all too young for this, but we can't wait until we get older. So, here we are.'

'Right,' Sasha said. 'Tomorrow.'

'Tomorrow,' Candle agreed. 'How bad could it be?'

Chapter 10

Sasha snapped awake, drenched in cold ice water. Then came the shouting, loud and close, forcing Sasha to focus on too many things. She jumped, trying to dislodge ice from her sleeping shirt while the voices shouted for them to get up. She was out of bed, then shouted to a position of attention.

Everyone else had been similarly awakened, drenched in water and shouted to their positions at the foot of their beds by drill instructors who now stood quietly at their side. Sasha looked across the small room at Candle, whose drenched shirt clung to her closely. Sasha worried that she was similarly affected by the water, or that the men might be looking their direction, but any attempt to move her head resulted in a hiss from her instructor. Similar noises indicated other cadets were also confused and disoriented.

At least the instructors on their half of the room were women. Sasha would have been mortified to have a man standing next to her in this situation.

A heavy footstep sounded at the far door to the barracks, where Sasha could not see. A voice called out.

'Well, it is a lovely morning for exercise, is it not?'

The cadets muttered some responses. Sasha cringed for what was to come.

Yelling. 'Cadets! When asked a question, you will respond with a loud, crisp response, and end with Sergeant Major. Allow me to enlighten. Instructors, it is a lovely morning for exercise, is it not?'

The twelve instructors bellowed in unison. 'Yes, Sergeant Major!'

'Now you are enlightened. Cadets, it is a lovely morning for exercise, is it not?'

'Yes, Sergeant Major!' twelve cadets called out, much more discordant than the instructors had called.

'Better,' the voice called, with a tone that indicated they were still found wanting. The footsteps continued as he slowly made his way down the row of cadets.

'I am Sergeant Major Ernesto Del Oso. Formerly, I was the Regimental Sergeant Major for the First Regiment, Michigan Marine Corps. The Fighting First was the meanest group of fighters you've heard of, and part of the toughest corps on the continent. For two hundred years, we fought every war asked and won every battle offered. Be it Quebecois nobility, Ohio Valley raiders, or Wisconsin hard-asses: you name them, we beat them.'

The instructor had advanced enough for Sasha to see him. He was a rather short man, but broad and muscled. He wore a finely maintained uniform, with the wide-brimmed hat worn by the instructors. His arm bore three rockers and three chevrons, with a single star in the middle. A sergeant major, the highest enlisted rank one could obtain in the Renaissance Army.

'Now, in those two centuries, the Michigan Marines had one inviolate rule. One could not obtain a commission in the corps without having served two years at the rifle. Even the staff officers, responsible for pushing papers and signing documents, served long enough to understand the consequences of their actions on the corps itself.'

Del Oso had reached the end of the room and turned back to face the cadets. 'We don't have two years. We have six weeks. Six weeks in which I get to pound you into something that resembles a soldier. I don't care who you were before you became a cadet. I don't care who your parents were, or what you did in another uniform. That was another life ago. Here, you are children. And I am the parent.'

He paused to let his words sink in, then started walking back across the barracks. 'Cadets, on the command of "fall out" you will change into the exercise kits provided. You will then make your way out the door, where you will fall into formation in front of me on the pathway. You have one minute to do so. Failure to achieve this simple goal will reflect on the squad. One fails, you all fail.' He passed the curtain. 'Instructors,' he said. The six women instructors moved, four leaving the barracks, two closing the curtain, standing guard against anyone crossing.

'Fall out!'

The cadets changed quickly, tearing off their wet sleeping clothes and dressing in the kit they pulled from the quartermaster's wagons a few days earlier. Sasha pulled the shoes on and rushed out, third of the six women out of the barracks.

The cadets were forming in two squads, men on the left and women on the right. Del Oso stood in the middle, counting on a watch. He started counting aloud with ten seconds left, calling down to zero.

Sasha had just enough time to get into line and glance about, realizing that one of the last two cadets had arrived in the night. It was a man, but she could not see more, as she was shouted to attention by one of the instructors.

Rose, Hero and a second new male cadet missed the deadline.

'Oh, cadets. That is a poor start to your careers. Seconds can count. I'll just have to run you until you understand that. Instructors, arrange them by height.'

Two women instructors stepped up from behind Sasha, rearranging the two squads by height. Then the instructors aligned the two squads into one formation, men in front and women in back. Sasha found herself standing behind Elector, with Swift to her right and Rose to her left.

Del Oso called out commands, spreading the formation out, and leading them in several stretches. Sasha finally managed to focus her mind after the confusion of their waking and felt a little conspicuous about wearing the exercise kit. She had never worn so little in a mixed group.

At least it's no less than any other cadet is wearing, she thought.

'Cadets, we are going to make for a nice, steady pace,' Del Oso bellowed. Sasha was amazed at how loud he could be without shouting. 'We will hit several stations, at which you must complete other exercises. The sooner you completed each exercise, the sooner we'll finish our run, the more time you'll have to get ready for the rest of your day.'

There was a pause as Del Oso looked for any comment. The cadets stared back.

'Platoon,' he called, 'attention! Right . . . face! Forward . . . march!'

They started marching, and it was ugly. Some of the cadets had more experience than others, and some had none. Sasha at least knew to start with her left foot, but she saw Candle, the tallest woman and the head of her squad, start with her right. Del Oso started calling out feet, 'Left, right, left, right,' in time with their marching, forcing Candle to hop to get her into the correct rhythm.

Soon Del Oso increased their pace and the formation was jogging through the early morning darkness. Their path ran on the border of the checkered fields, with forest on one side and brush on the other. It was wide enough for four people to walk next to each other, so their formation had more than enough room.

Sasha estimated they had gone almost half a mile when they first came to a stop. She heard gasping from several of the cadets; they obviously were unaccustomed to this level of effort.

Their first station was nothing more than some general calisthenics; some jumping jacks and push-ups. Again, some of the cadets had difficulty accomplishing these exercises, giving Sasha and the others time to rest. While she was glad for the extra time, she worried about how worn out some of the cadets were going to be by the end of it.

They jogged on. At the second station they did sit-ups; the nervousness of being so lightly dressed resurfaced when Elector was instructed to hold her ankles. Again, Sasha said nothing, and Elector, at least, was not one of the men who made her feel uncomfortable.

At the third they had to climb over obstacles. At the fourth they sprinted across a field and back. At the fifth they had to crawl through a muddy pit with wire strung overhead, completely muddying their clothes.

After it was all done, the exhausted cadets marched back to their barracks. Sasha felt her sore feet, worn by the running slippers she had not broken in yet. The cadets quickly grabbed their grey uniforms and marched to the showers.

The showers were thankfully separated by sex. Sasha had only experienced them for the first time two days earlier, when Swift showed her how they worked. It was an odd experience, to have water falling on you instead of immersing yourself in it, but Sasha did enjoy feeling the mud and dirt wash away.

The dirty clothes were collected in a tub and the cadets, dressed in the ugly grey uniforms, marched towards the kitchen.

Meals at Athens came three times a day, and all the formations at the school ate at the same time. If a combat training company was in the area they might stop by, but even without them, there were still more than a hundred students and a sizable number of instructors eating at the same time. The cadets moved through the line, getting a plate of eggs, bread, some bacon and an apple.

There were few tables, but many logs and rocks set about as dining areas. The cadets gathered at one staked out by some of the instructors. As they ate, Sasha saw some of the other students giving them glances.

Candle was sitting next to Sasha. 'Want my bacon?' she asked.

Sasha nodded assent, still glancing about. *What do the others know about our project?* She had not had any contact with the other students of Athens. They had their own barracks, and Sasha had never seen any around the library. She resolved to change that.

'Who are you?' Candle asked one of the new cadets, 'and what do you do?'

'I'm Penn,' he said. He was a youthful-looking man, sandy-haired and green-eyed. 'I do politics and law? I'm not sure how to describe it. I want to keep the Renaissance Army on a good path, you know?'

'Sure,' Candle said. 'And you?'

The other man, tall and skinny, dark skinned, with black hair, smiled. 'I'm Roland, future infantry officer.'

'Always use more of those,' Blaze said, ignoring the glare from the women. His attitude had not won him any friends yet.

Cardinal asked the newcomers questions, getting them incorporated into the squad over the meal. Sasha was grateful for the girl's enthusiasm, as it let everyone learn about Penn and Roland.

After their meal was done, Del Oso led them to one of the ram cabins. It was a classroom, with six tables set up, two chairs at each. The front had a blackboard, another item Swift had shown her, and a small desk. There were no instructors present when they entered. Given the size of their class, it seemed positively cavernous.

'Take a seat wherever,' Del Oso said, 'and be warned, whenever an instructor enters the room you will be called to attention, facing the front of the room. So, don't get too comfortable.'

The cadets slowly shook out to find their seats. Sasha was sitting in the front row, next to Swift. Patch and Penn sat in the next table.

At the table behind her, Candle and Cardinal sat down. Both looked sore and tired.

'Are you okay?' Sasha asked.

'That was intense,' Candle said.

Cardinal nodded. 'It was.' She glared at Sasha. 'You don't look tired. You've done that before?'

'Yes,' Sasha said, 'at my previous regiment.'

'So did ours,' Swift said. 'Don't worry, it gets easier. They're just pushing your body to grow.'

'Well, they can stop pushing,' Cardinal said.

Sasha was going to respond but Del Oso bellowed. 'ATTENTION!'

The cadets stood and faced the front. Sasha heard steps up the center aisle. General Caesar came to the front of the room. He turned and looked back at the cadets.

'Be seated,' he said, and the cadets complied. Caesar looked at each of them quickly before he began.

'Cadets of the Templar Project, welcome. This project has been a long time in the making. I am proud of what we have come up with so far, and I look forward to seeing you all finish the course of instruction.'

Caesar was speaking softly and stood rigidly at the front of the class, hands

92

resolutely by his side. Sasha wondered why Prince was not there to give this opening. Prince was a much better speaker.

'One question I expect you have asked is, "What is a Templar?" Well, I will explain.

'More than thirteen hundred years ago, a religious leader in Europe called for a military campaign to march across the continent and retake the holy city of Jerusalem. Troops from many different nations followed their lords into war, resulting in a conflict between two religions that lasted for centuries.

'This was a time before gunpowder, when warriors were clad in steel armor and wielded swords. They trained for years to master the skills necessary for war, and often did so under the direction of a nobleman who gave them wealth in exchange for their service. This system worked well in their homelands, but in the constant, low-intensity warfare of the occupied territories, it began to break down.

'What grew then was a new idea, a series of military orders whose warrior served a goal common to all noblemen, not just a single lord. They protected all the people, not just those under their banner. They had their own cultures, their own icons, their own charges and philosophies. One of these was the Knights Templar.'

Caesar looked more confident now. He began pacing across the front of the classroom, his voice louder, his hands animated.

'The Templars were so named because they were headquartered in an important temple of Jerusalem. Their initial goal was to protect pilgrims making their way towards the city. Soon they, and the other orders, became some of the most powerful military organizations of the period. In some ways, they were a more modern military organization than those warriors still beholden to a landed lord.

'And you?' he asked, looking out over the cadets. 'You are the Templars of the Renaissance. Your temple is the library. Your religion is the thirst for knowledge. You are the hope that the future is not as dark as it sometimes appears.' It seemed the special program was particularly important to Caesar; there was a passion creeping into his voice. 'Now, every one of you was selected because you can finish the program. You have proven yourselves worthy. Your actions have carried great integrity. Your histories include a search for knowledge. Each of you can complete this program, so long as you want to. At the end you will be a commissioned officer, trained to make the tough choices, endowed with the spirit of the Renaissance.

'This morning, Sergeant Major Del Oso began your instruction. This first period is the Common or Basic Phase. It will last six weeks. Its purpose is to ensure that each of you has a similar foundation of knowledge and skills on which to build the rest of your education. For those of you who are veterans of combat units, you will find the exercises familiar. Others are more used to the classroom. This period will get all of you acquainted with both. Regardless, you will complete all required activities to advance.'

He paused, as if inviting comment, but no one spoke.

'Sergeant Major Del Oso is your class sergeant. Other instructors will be involved as necessary, some of them civilians. Regardless of their rank, or lack of it, you will treat each of them with respect. One of the requirements for this project is the existence of a strong moral ethic; you can fail out for being disrespectful.

'You will also have at your hand some of the knowledge we have managed to accumulate during our preparations. Most of you have found the library. The books there represent the result of years of searching and accumulating, and many of them are older than you can imagine. Treat them with respect.

'Your position with the Templars also comes with the need for discretion. You will undoubtedly learn things that you should not share with anyone. Secrets of the Renaissance Army, if you will. Part of your learning will be what to talk about and what not to talk about. When in doubt, say nothing.'

Caesar paused. 'Finally, let me say this. I do not want excuses. This will be difficult, but I believe that all of you can succeed at this course if you put in the effort. Each of you is talented in your own way. Learn from each other. Lean on each other, if you must. Each of you is in the same position, and I expect you all to remember that. I want all of you to make it to the end and graduate successfully. Understood?'

The cadets nodded. The weight of what they were doing kept them from verbally answering.

'Now,' he said, turning to pick up some chalk. 'Let's start by going over the ranks and insignia of the Renaissance Army.'

It was something Sasha already knew, but she leaned forward anyway, eager to excel.

Chapter 11

One week into training, and Sasha was already aware that she had hardly excelled at anything. Indeed, she was decidedly average.

The best was Elector, with Blaze coming in a close second. Sasha was not surprised. Both had been warrant officers in their own right prior to the beginning of training. The only odd thing that occurred to her was that Elector never really tried. He did well enough to be considered first but did not look like someone who wanted to be there. Sasha was curious about why, but asked nothing, instead just whispering a silent thanks that Blaze was second.

But if those two were the best overall, they were not the best at some specific areas. Mako was by far the strongest, while Swift was the fastest and most athletic. Rose and Penn were the smartest, but Rose also had an attitude that Sasha thought meant she did not want to be there, which prevented her from trying her best.

The rest were average, though Sasha still could not figure some of them out. How did they possibly get into the RAM, much less the Templar Project?

Patch was flighty, always seeming distracted or inattentive, but always on top with an answer when asked. Roland was incredibly quiet, much like Mako, and yet completely different, watching everything and everyone around him. Sasha was not sure what to make of him yet.

Candle and Cardinal had become fast friends, discussing some of the men around camp and gossiping. Swift had even called them the 'Pretty Pair of Princesses' to Sasha, which Sasha now used when she thought about them. If they were not in uniform, Sasha might have forgotten that they were officer cadets, and not gossipy ladies at a ball.

If there was one cadet she did not like, it was Cadet Hero. He was more likely to crow about his own achievements, however limited they were, and tear down others' successes. He was quick to ingratiate himself with the instructors, with varying degrees of success. And he made all the women nervous, with his leering eyes and sideways smile. He never did or said anything that blatantly crossed a line, but during the second week Del Oso gave a whole presentation on harassment and comfort. Sasha expected someone had complained to the sergeants, and this was their response.

If all the cadets were too good or too bad or too annoying, the only one Sasha was disappointed in was herself.

When Sasha thought of herself in the training, she cringed. Oh, she did well enough in the squad tactics and soldier skill courses, but Del Oso had higher expectations from his Templars, and she had to push herself to keep up. At least she knew the hand signals and field movements, and how to handle her weapons safely.

But having decided to fight for the name Scholar, Sasha had to admit that her classroom activities were decidedly poor. Part of that problem, Sasha was sure, was their aggressively annoying classroom instructor.

***

'No, Cadet Hero, that is wrong,' the woman's loud Quebecois accented voice grated on Sasha's ears. 'I see that despite my repeated instructions, you continue to fail to understand the order of operations. You do not complete the sequence left to right; you must follow the outline I have put on this board every day!'

Madam Moreau slapped her cane hard against the chalkboard. She glared at them, as she always did, peering at them over slim glasses. In many ways, she reminded Sasha of her father: a stiff-necked black coat, silvered hair, and eternally disappointed face.

'Perhaps, where you are from, you do not need to count beyond ten?' she asked in a mocking voice. 'Is that because you're limited to counting on your fingers?'

Hero bristled. 'No, ma'am,' he said. His anger was evident, but his first outburst had resulted in a strong reprimand from Del Oso, and he was now cautious in his response. 'But I don't see why I should know this. 3X? 2Y? I'm here to fight, not write on papers.'

'Oh, is that right?' Moreau said. She turned to the board and wrote something beneath the equation, then stepped back. 'And now?'

She had replaced the x=3 portion of the board with x=infantry battalion.

'How many men in a royal infantry battalion?' she asked.

Blaze shot his hand up. '562,' he said.

Moreau turned and reworked the equation again. 'Y = Cavalry Squadron.'

Blaze again. '337.'

'So, Cadet Hero. This equation could mean three infantry battalions and two cavalry squadrons are on the move. In sending the information to another officer, they would do the math,' she proceeded to complete the equation, 'and figure out that the enemy force was about 2,360 soldiers. However, if you received the information, you would determine the enemy force was,' she did the equation as Hero had done, '568,856 soldiers. That is quite the disparity, isn't it?'

'Not to mention headquarters,' Blaze continued, 'support troops, extra weapons –.'

Moreau slapped the blackboard again. 'Cadet Blaze,' she said, 'that is beyond the scope of this class. We are dealing with the basic math all officers must know. Understood?'

'Yes, ma'am,' Blaze said, turning red.

Moreau sighed. 'What phase of your training are you in?' she asked

'Basic Phase,' the cadets replied.

'Then you must learn the basics. I know some of you are already experienced veterans at war, some can do this math in your sleep, and some can write poetry that will make the angels weep. That will be next phase. This phase: learn the basics! Make sure they are correct. Even if you are so bored you can't pay attention!'

She might have been speaking of Patch, who as usual was staring out the window, but her focus was on Cardinal and Rose, both of whom looked bored. Despite their shared nationality, the sisters and the teacher appeared to detest each other. Moreau came down on the sisters hard, and the sisters in turn called her what sounded like rude names behind her back.

'Well then,' she said. 'If that is all, let us move on to multiplication tables. Simple memorization, but important.' Moreau wrote the graph on the board, instructing certain cadets not to respond. Several of the cadets knew the tables already, so it was up to those who had not had such education – namely Sasha, Swift, Hero and Mako – to fill them in when asked. At least Sasha was picking this up quickly.

From there they moved into basic geography. Sasha had a better appreciation for how large the world was now, and how small their own kingdom was. 'What good is knowing the size of continents when we're stuck out here,' Hero complained under his breath, but Sasha ignored him. He always complained.

Geography led into composition. Up until she came here, Sasha had never realized how bad her handwriting was. She knew how to write, but it was never a skill she practiced. So, when Moreau first saw her lines, she pitched a fit. At least now, Sasha was getting better. Not that Moreau ever gave a compliment. She simply insulted Sasha less.

***

'I wonder if they're trying to kill us,' Penn said as he laid down on his cot. 'Isn't that some sort of teaching tool? Last cadets standing gets the prize?'

'This isn't Chicago,' Elector said. 'They wouldn't do that.'

'Though it's not a bad idea,' Blaze muttered. Sasha refused to glare at him anymore. Instead, she concentrated on their grammar worksheet with Swift. She was making too many mistakes, and she was tired of being mocked as a scholar.

'Why Chicago?' Sasha heard Cardinal whisper to Candle.

'When the Dark Age began,' Candle said. 'Chicago erupted into mass chaos. There were gladiator games, where people were forced to fight to the death as entertainment.'

'Oh,' Cardinal said. 'That's sad.'

'It's also possibly not true,' Elector said. 'Much of what we've heard from that time that was embellished or false. It's not like people were worried about keeping records while their world was burning.'

'I sure wouldn't,' Hero said. He, too, was buried in a series of grammar worksheets. 'Survival is hard. Better to get guns than books.'

'Sad for the books,' Sasha said.

'The Quebecois come from the Age of Technology,' Rose said. 'We kept some books.'

'Only some?' Sasha asked.

'Not all books were worth saving.'

'Do you think the Archives did that?' Swift asked. 'Chose which books to save and which to forget?'

'The Archives?' Mako asked. 'What are those?'

'They're small communities scattered across the world,' Cardinal said, 'that retain knowledge from the Before Time, or Technology Age or whatever you want to call it. Knowledge of engineering, medicine, science, and the like.'

'Maybe literature,' Swift interrupted. 'I've heard people wonder about that. Did they only keep practical, useful knowledge? Or did they keep some useless information?'

'Literature isn't useless,' Roland said from the window. He had been looking out it for some time, lost in thought.

'Literature is stories,' Hero mocked. 'There's no use in stories.'

'Stories contain warnings and lessons,' Roland said. He turned and frowned at Hero. 'You learned lessons as a child listening to stories. The Boy who Cried Wolf teaches you to be careful about lying. The Good Samaritan teaches you to help others. The stories we listen to as children shape who we are as adults, both for good and bad.'

'I heard those stories,' Hero said. 'Not much use, them. No good Samaritan handed me food when I was starving on the streets. And anyone who didn't lie to survive didn't survive. The Bible entertains children, but adults don't pay it much mind when they're going through their day. Waste of paper, most of it.'

'Careful, Hero,' Mako said. The cadet had a reputation for not missing a service, and even had his own small Bible on himself almost every moment of the day. Now he stared at Hero, daring the other cadet to continue insulting the book.

Finally, Hero signed and backed down. 'Whatever. I'm just saying, when you are starving and dying, you're going to be looking for food and weapons. Books are good to burn for heat, but not much else.'

'Hey, Roland,' Patch asked suddenly, 'where does your name come from?'

'Huh?' Roland asked.

'Why Roland?' I'm just curious. And if you don't want to answer, I completely under- .'

Roland started speaking in a loud and clear voice.

> *'Once more pressed Roland within the fight,*
> *His Durindane he grasped with might;*
> *Faldron Poy did he cleave in two*
> *And twenty-four of their bravest he slew'*

Roland recited it from memory, pantomiming a sword in his hand. The rest of the cadets looked at him, some smiling, some interested. Blaze scowled and Hero glared.

'It's a song my family has remembered from ages past,' Roland said. 'An army is heading home and is betrayed by a trusted general. Another general, Roland, uncovers the danger and sacrifices himself to save the army and his king. It's a story from thousands of years ago, I think.'

'So, you're named after the hero who sacrifices himself?' Hero mocked.

'He's still the hero,' Roland said, stressing the last word. 'What sort are you, Hero, that you wouldn't sacrifice yourself?'

Hero glowered at Roland. 'I'm not afraid, if that's what you're saying. I got my name righteously.'

'So, I heard,' Elector said, cutting off Roland's hot retort. 'Rescuing that girl from the bandits.'

'Aye,' Hero said, huge smile on his face. 'I wasn't going to let a little thing like her get taken. I got the drop on both of them and ended them right quick.' He pantomimed firing a pistol.

'Good job,' Blaze said. Surprisingly, he meant it.

'What about you, Mako?' Cardinal asked. 'What is a mako?'

'It's a shark,' Mako said. 'A large fish, ten feet long or so, that eats whatever it can get its teeth into.'

'Are they found in lakes?' Swift asked.

'Doubtful,' Patch said, staring up at the ceiling while lying on her bed. 'Most fish in these lakes don't get that big; they can't because the lakes aren't big enough, and fresh water doesn't support larger bulks. Lake Superior is big enough, but still freshwater. It's probably an ocean fish.'

'She's right,' Mako said.

'Why would the ocean support bigger things?' Hero asked.

'It's full of salt, adds buoyancy,' Patch said.

'Buoyancy?' Hero asked. 'Are you making this up?'

'No,' Mako said. 'She's right. There are some huge creatures in the ocean. Whales as long as a ship. Beasts with long arms. Mermaids and such.'

'If you travel to other parts of the world,' Cardinal said, 'you'd see different animals. Know what a lion is? They're not from around here.'

'There are lions in the south,' Candle said. 'In the wild.'

'Are there?' Patch asked, turning to look.

'Aye,' Candle said. 'My father said they used to ship animals around the world, so people could see animals from all over. Some of them escaped when the old world died and thrived in their new countries.'

'Odd,' Patch said, turning to look back at the ceiling. Swift looked at Sasha and rolled her eyes.

'Okay,' Candle said. 'So, Hero got his name for rescuing a girl. Mako is a fish. Blaze is always angry.'

'Hey!' Blaze said.

'Well, you are,' Candle retorted. 'Roland is from a song. Elector?'

'My family was involved in the Republic,' Elector said. 'Beyond that, I can't say.'

'Sure. Penn?'

Penn turned red. 'I was named after a hero of my people,' he said. 'I'm not sure how much more I can say.'

'A famous Quaker named Penn?' Hero asked.

Penn turned on Hero in surprise. 'How did you know that?'

'I'm the one who sits next to you during weapons training, and you never touch your weapon. That means you're a pacifist, so you're either an Alvanist or a Quaker, and Alvanists are insufferable.'

'Ah,' Penn said. 'Well, I can't say I know many Alvanists, but yes, I am a Quaker. I joined the RAM to work to keep it honest. Quakers can do that, if their conscious allows them to.'

'What good is honesty if it loses us the war,' Hero sneered.

'Without the rule of law, we are no more than criminals, and we deserve to lose.'

'So, that's the men,' Candle said, cutting off Hero. 'Now, onto the women. I, myself, was known as a light in times of darkness, so I took Candle as my name. Swift, I know you run fast.'

'I do,' Swift said. 'Also, I can think pretty quickly.'

Hero snorted, but Candle spoke over him. 'Scholar, likes books.'

'I'm surprised you got the name when you're not the best at library work,' Blaze said, accusingly.

'I'm working up to it,' Sasha said.

'Patch?' Candle quickly asked, cutting off the potential argument. 'You?'

'I solve problems at the Workshop,' Patch said. 'Got a nickname helping fix and build things.'

'What's the Workshop?' Hero asked.

'It's a facility where techno-thinkers and science-types gather to build tools needed for the war effort. Scholar saw some of them used at the prison camp.'

'I did,' Sasha said, which was not technically true. When they were used, she was fighting for her life on the other side of the camp. She did see the aftereffects the next morning.

Candle turned to the sisters. 'Cardinal and Rose? I assume there's something important about red for your family.'

Cardinal smiled while Rose scowled. 'True,' Cardinal said. 'I'm Cardinal because I can sing, and Rose is pretty, but has thorns.'

Rose had been absent-mindedly brushing her hair with her fingers. She stopped and glowered at Cardinal.

'Hey, Roland,' Swift called, 'can you recite the whole song?'

'The Song of Roland? It's about four thousand lines.'

'What?' Swift exclaimed.

'That's not a song,' Hero scoffed.

'I don't know if there is a name for what it is,' Roland countered. 'I'm sure some expert on songs could tell me, but I learned it as the Song of Roland. And I don't know the whole thing by heart. It's been written and rewritten by my family for generations.'

'Why that one song?' Elector asked.

'I don't know,' Roland said. He shrugged. 'We just do.'

'Hey, Roland,' Sasha spoke up. 'Maybe you should write a Song of the Templars.'

Roland laughed, then turned to face the cadets.

> 'The Cadets of the Templar Project,
> What men and women they are!
> They come to fight for the Renaissance
> From lands, both near and far!'

He thought for a moment. 'That wasn't too good. I'll work on it.'

'You do that,' Swift said.

Athens' time bell rang out in a sequence. Ten minutes until lights out. Rose stood to close the curtains. 'I'm going to change for bed.'

'You don't have to close the curtain,' Hero said quickly.

'Shut up, Hero,' Rose snapped, closing the curtain. 'Lights will be out soon enough anyway.'

'Right,' Sasha said. The barracks was full of sound as they put away their books and papers and changed into sleeping clothes.

'Hey, Mako?' Cardinal asked.

'Yeah?' the voice came from over the curtain.

'Do you miss the sea?'

'I do,' Mako replied. 'When you grow up with the sea in your ears, you never stop hearing it.'

'Hope you see it again, someday.'

'Me too, Cardinal. Me too.'

The bell range ten. The lanterns of the cabin were turned off, followed by the last candles at individual beds. Quiet overtook the cabin. Sasha lay back in bed, thinking over the grammar rules and lessons she was still having trouble with.

The names we chose mean so much to us, she thought. *Connections to our past, things we want to remember. I don't want to lose my name. I want to be Scholar. I want to remain Scholar.*

Sasha repeated that over and over as sleep overtook her.

Chapter 12

The second week was much of the same, and so on into the third. The cadets had paired off into buddies, who spent most of their time together. The natural pairings from the first week – Sasha and Swift, Cardinal and Candle, Elector and Blaze – became permanent, while the other three developed. Rose and Penn, both of whom seemed to be dealing with the project rather poorly, became a miserable couple. Roland joined with Hero, the two of them singing often and annoyingly. And Patch and Mako had taken to sitting together.

'I wonder if Patch ever notices Mako is there,' Swift said.

'Probably,' Sasha said. 'Not much gets by her.'

'I guess it makes sense they'd be together,' Swift said.

'Because they're both quiet?'

'No,' Swift shook her head, 'I mean they're not like us.'

'What do you mean?' Sasha asked hesitantly. She had learned from Madam Moreau the concept of race, though she put little stock in the idea that it could matter that much and was absolutely horrified at some of the extremes Moreau had told them about. Mako, being of African descent, and Patch, being of Asian, were the obviously different cadets. Elector, Candle and Penn had revealed their own backgrounds to be mixed. Sasha, for one, did not care about that at all, and hoped that Swift did not either.

'Oh, just that they're not from Minnesota,' Swift said hurriedly. She and Blaze, both blond haired and blue eyed, had been chosen by Madam Moreau as examples of northern European. Blaze took pride in that, while Swift had shrugged it off.

'Neither are Candle, Cardinal or Rose,' Sasha said.

'I know, I just . . . ,' Swift shook her head. 'Never mind. Just forget I said anything.'

'Okay,' Sasha said, hoping she was wrong about what she suspected Swift was about to say.

They left the library when the bell rang. It was an easy walk from the library to the ram cabin they used as a classroom. They took their seats leisurely. Madam Moreau came in and started rotating through their instructions. They went to work, writing, reading and reciting. All with the added sound of Hero

104

muttering and complaining from the back.

'This is stupid,' Sasha heard him whisper to Roland. 'We don't need to know the continents to know how to kill people.'

'We're not just killers,' Roland whispered back. 'We're going to be officers of the army, and leaders of the movement. That requires knowledge.'

Moreau must have heard them but did not say anything that time. They moved through mathematics, then she announced they would be starting to cycle through the various sciences.

'The point is not to know everything,' she said, 'but to know enough. Men and women can spend their entire lives studying these topics before they become experts. We just want you to know the difference between physics and chemistry, between geology and biology.'

'Why?' Hero finally asked out loud. 'This has nothing to do with winning battles.'

Moreau slammed her cane down. 'Did you not hear Cadet Roland before?' she asked, sternly. 'His answer was correct. You are the future officers of the Renaissance Army, and the future leaders of the Renaissance Movement. You must know this?'

'Really?' Hero asked skeptically.

'If someone came up to you, and asked for your assistance in creating sulfur mustard, would you help them?'

'I don't know what that is,' Hero answered.

'Exactly. You don't. And since you don't, you would be deciding on helping a man create a horribly dangerous chemical weapon without knowing what you were deciding on. Or maybe you will embarrass yourself in front of others by misunderstanding the reproductive cycle, or stating that stars are angels that circle the earth, or even by not knowing how many troops are on the other side of a battle!'

Hero looked down at his hands and turned red.

'My job as your instructor is to make sure you know this,' Moreau said. 'You must know this to advance. Now, do you want to be a Templar?'

'I do,' Hero said.

'Then you are going to help me complete this overview. And you will help me with every math overview, until I'm convinced you know it. And I will do the same to anyone else who lags behind. Understood?'

The cadets all nodded silently.

***

'What was that?' Roland asked harshly as they entered their barracks.

'What?' Hero snapped.

'That! That yelling at Madam Moreau. You know we have to finish this to move on, don't you?'

'Of course, but this is stupid,' Hero said. 'Soldiers only need to know how to win.'

'We're also officers and leaders,' Elector said.

'Most of us,' Blaze interjected, his voice just loud enough to be heard.

'What does that mean?' Hero stepped forward. He was several inches shorter than Blaze, but furious. 'I have every right to be here as you do.'

'No, you don't,' Blaze said, sneering down at Hero. 'You complain too much. The goals of the class have been set by the generals, and you spend more time bitching about them than getting the work done. Do you even want to be a Templar!'

'I do!' Hero protested.

'Bullshit!' Blaze shouted. 'How did you even get in here? You saved a girl from a couple of brigands and that's it? Some of us had to work for it. Where's your morality, your intelligence? How the hell did you show professionalism in the four days you were with Fourth Regiment before you came here.'

Hero glared at Blaze. 'I didn't just save a girl, jackass. That got me into the regiment. I served with them as a rifle for weeks, proving myself. I speak four languages. And I may not be sculpted to be an officer, but I've got stuff to offer. Besides,' he swept his hand at the women. 'What about them?'

'The women?' Sasha asked.

'No, the civilians!' Hero snapped back. 'Candle, Cardinal, Rose were civilians before they came here. How could they show professionalism if they weren't asked to be professional before? Why do I get singled out?'

'Because you're the worst here,' Swift said.

'I'm not used to this,' Hero protested. 'I want to be here, but this isn't what I'm used to. I'm used to growing up on the street, to starving two out of three days until the next cheap job comes along.'

'A job to thieve,' Blaze accused.

'I did what I had to,' Hero nodded. 'Now I want to make amends to the world, so I'm here.'

'Then why do you complain so much?' Roland asked. 'This is all stuff we need to learn to be officers.'

'Why?' Hero demanded. 'Most of this is stupid. Math and words and maps. Just show me how to fight!'

Blaze shook his head and laughed. 'Just because you don't understand why doesn't make the program stupid. It makes you stupid.'

Hero punched Blaze, a quick jab to Blaze's nose that knocked him off his feet. 'Don't you insult me,' Hero said. 'I joined the RAM by winning a fight. I can win this one too.'

Blaze jumped up and rushed Hero. Elector moved forward, trying to get between the two, but both were too much for him. Blaze got his arms up and blocked another punch, landing a hard return blow on Hero's stomach.

The rest of the cadets converged pulling the two apart. They resisted, trying to get away and lay into each other again. Sasha was pulling on Blaze.

'Hero, seriously,' Cardinal started to admonish him.

Hero found a purchase for his foot and kicked back, knocking Cardinal and Elector back. He punched out at Swift, striking her face, and moved to fight Blaze again. Mako stepped between them.

'Don't do this,' Mako said.

Sasha did not hear Hero's response, but he and Mako were fighting a moment later. Mako looked angry, snarling at Hero and he punched at him. Sasha turned to them, pausing for a moment to decide who to tackle.

Her moment cost her when the door slammed open and Del Oso appeared. 'WHAT THE HELL DO YOU THINK YOU ARE DOING?' he shouted.

His voice stopped everyone in their tracks. No one had any response, nor did they try to conjure one.

'In formation, out front, NOW!' Del Oso bellowed. They moved, getting into two lines as they did every morning, but this time, instead of leading the cadets out into the woods, he led them towards the part of Athens set aside for the cadre and the offices, which held the authority of their camp.

And possibly their program.

***

Lieutenant Colonel Carpenter commanded not only the Athens facility, but also the whole Renaissance Army Training Group. He was an older man, obviously a veteran of the Republican Army. His uniform was pristine, his mustache meticulously trimmed, and his hair cut and waxed to perfection. He spoke in measured tones, without moving or speaking quickly. As he sat at his desk, looking at the cadets arrayed in front of him, listening to the report, Sasha immediately knew that he was not going to yell at them.

No, this was going to be so much worse than yelling.

'I must admit,' he finally said, 'that I find myself disappointed. The Templar Project is supposed to collect the best and the brightest and mold them into the future of the movement. You,' he sighed, 'are quite the group of petulant young children.'

He shook his head. 'You cannot bring a group of people together, tell them they are the best, and not expect some friction. That's just common sense, but public brawling? Bar room language? Is this what you were sent here to do?'

Hero started to say something, but Del Oso shushed him, and he went quiet.

Carpenter continued. 'There's a saying I have. In war, you must think like a soldier. As a part of the Templar Project, chosen by generals, I would expect you to think like an officer. But here you are, bickering and yelling and fighting like animals. I wonder, can any of you think at all?'

He shook his head. 'The future of the movement,' he said with disdain. Then he stood tall.

'I spoke with General Caesar at length about the Templar Project,' Carpenter said. 'I did, and still do, support it. But that support is not unconditional, and General Caesar agreed with me enough to plan, even for this unfortunate outcome. Sergeant Major Del Oso, do you formally request punitive measures?'

'I do, sir!' Del Oso said.

'Very well,' Carpenter looked at them again. He looked like he had taken a bite of something sour. 'Sergeant Major, return the cadets to their barracks. I'll be handing them off to Lance.'

'Yes, sir!' Del Oso said. 'Cadets, on my command fall out and reassemble out front. Now!'

The cadets dissolved into a group, moved outside, and reformed into lines without saying a word.

Who is Lance? Sasha wondered, but no questions were asked. Del Oso led them back to their barracks. He had them fall out and stand at their bunks.

'Well, cadets, now you've gone and done it,' Del Oso said. 'We're moving.'

'Moving?' Sasha asked.

'That's right. The Templar Project is spending two weeks at another location,' Del Oso said. 'You have fifteen minutes to pack your field uniforms and equipment. Get to it.'

The cadets moved to their chests, pulling out their packs and packing their clothes.

'I wonder where we are going,' Cardinal asked.

'Probably some other hole in the forest,' Hero griped.

'Maybe we're going to Avalon,' Swift said.

'What?' Sasha asked.

'Avalon,' Swift said again. 'Never heard of it?'

'It's a myth,' Hero groaned. 'It never existed.'

'What didn't?' Candle asked. Several of the cadets looked confused.

'Avalon was supposed to be a secret base,' Elector said, 'built by the Iron Republic to command their armies in the event of an invasion by Quebec. It was a secret so Quebec wouldn't be able to destroy it in an opening move.'

'Supposedly?' Cardinal asked.

'Well, what made it so secure was that it was so secret,' Elector continued. 'So secret no one ever disclosed its location, and no one ever found it.'

'Because it was so well hidden,' Blaze said, 'the Commonwealth and the King both conducted searched for it, but none of them found anything.'

'Because it doesn't exist,' Patch said, suddenly, to Blaze's ire. 'We discussed it at the Workshop. The Iron Republic didn't have the tech know-how to build a base like that.'

'It exists,' Blaze said, 'I know it does. And it was built with the assistance of an Archive. The one in Duluth, the Red Castle.'

Sasha blinked. She remembered the Red Castle from her trip to Duluth many years earlier. She remembered it being imposing before she knew what it was.

A castle that protected lost knowledge from the world.

Blaze continued. 'They helped the Republic build it in exchange for food, or something. I don't know the details, but I know it exists. Right, Elector?'

'We've been told that,' Elector said.

'I believe it exists,' Swift said. 'It just makes sense. Quebec always had more air power than the Republic did; keeping a headquarters a secret would keep them from being able to bomb you.'

'They may have been overstating the threat,' Cardinal said.

'It doesn't matter,' Penn interrupted. 'It doesn't exist. If it did, why wouldn't the Republic use it during the war with the Commonwealth?'

'Because there were reasons of public morale not to evacuate the capital,' Blaze replied.

'It's a good story,' Roland said, forestalling an argument between Blaze and Penn, 'but I don't know if I believe it. You can't just wave the Archive at a problem and solve it.'

'How would you know what's in the Archive?' Swift responded. 'They've got so many secrets in there; they might very well be able to pull something like this off.'

'Oh, I'm sure they could,' Roland said. 'But there's no evidence, and while I like the story, I'm just not convinced it's real.'

'We don't have time to debate this now,' Mako said. 'We'll find out soon enough, where we are going to.'

'Right,' Elector said. 'Let's go before Del Oso yells again.'

The cadets finished packing and assembled with Del Oso outside. 'Ready?' he asked. 'Once we leave, we're not coming back for several weeks.'

'We don't own too much to bring with us,' Cardinal replied. Del Oso glared at her. 'Sergeant Major.'

'Good,' Del Oso said. 'Cadets, left face. Forward, march!' and he led them off.

They started into the paths around Athens, and Sasha wondered if they might not just be circling the town for fun, but Del Oso soon led them off the paths and through the forest. Del Oso motioned for them to spread out, changing their formation every mile or so. They stopped for a break, and he switched up their order of march.

110

We're going north, she knew. Closer and closer to Walker.

By afternoon the cadets were sore from their marching, some more than others. Rose and Hero were particularly upset about their predicament, though Candle and Penn were also showing fatigue. Finally, they entered another Mardurer Maze, and Sasha knew they were close to their destination.

'Cadets,' Del Oso said, 'welcome to Sparta.'

'Sparta?' Cardinal asked. 'The combat camp?'

'Yes,' Del Oso replied. 'Your attitude has been raising some eyebrows, and after this latest incident, it has been decided that you will spend two weeks here, learning how to be soldiers. If you are to be officers, you need to know how to be soldiers. You need to know what the men and women you lead are going through.'

'So, we're common rifles now,' Rose said. 'We were supposed to be exemplary.'

'You were examples, just not examples of the right traits.'

Rose scowled.

Del Oso led them towards the base. Sasha noted that like Athens, it had the ram cabins built into the trees, but not as many. She also noticed more tents. A lot more tents.

'Oh, no,' Rose whispered. She noticed it too.

Del Oso chuckled. He led them to a hut, much like Carpenter's at Athens. A sign above read: Major Lance, Sparta Commander.

Del Oso called the cadets to attention in front of the door. He turned around just as it opened, and Major Lance came out.

Lance was a tall man, and before he put on the wide-brimmed training hat, Sasha saw that he was completely bald. It made his age difficult to determine, but he had that same scowl that Del Oso had.

'Sergeant Major,' he said in the same Michigan accent Del Oso had, 'are these the cadets who have offended Colonel Carpenter so much?'

'They are, Major Lance,' Del Oso confirmed.

Lance stepped down and looked over them, and Sasha felt a pang of fear.

'I presume, cadets, that the good Sergeant Major has described to you the conditions of the Michigan Marines. No man can be considered for a commission as an officer without serving at the rifle. Well, I'll tell you a secret;

111

the Sergeant Major was my squad leader when I served at the rifle. And he was my platoon sergeant when I got commissioned. I have nothing but the utmost respect for him, and if he says you chosen cadets have managed to fuck up bad enough for me to get involved, I know he means you've fucked up badly.'

The cadets were all quiet. There was nothing to say.

'Here at Sparta, we train soldiers to fight. We do not have cots inside huts, or libraries full of books, or three hot meals a day, or hot showers, or whatever luxury you got   used to at Athens. Those are things you'll have to earn back. Here is where you suffer.

'At Sparta, the cadets will sleep in pairs in tents. Pair off, same sexes, if you will.'

Sasha glanced to her left to see Swift already coming her way. They stood next to each other while the rest paired off.

'Good, I'm glad you were able to do that without error,' Lance said. 'This is your buddy. You and your buddy will go everywhere together. Eat together, sleep together, train together. If you ever do not know where your buddy is, both of you are in trouble.' Lance whistled and two sergeants came through the door, one man and one woman.

'This is Sergeant Kayla and Sergeant Maxwell. They are your new squad leaders, Kayla for the girls' squad, Maxwell for the boys' squad. They will oversee your instruction, since you've proven you don't deserve Del Oso. They have the authority to handle you as they see fit. Do not come crying to me when they say mean things to you. Learn from them or wash out.'

The two sergeants were only a few years older than Sasha; both gave their squads evil grins. Sasha braced herself.

'Sergeants,' Lance said. 'Get them settled.'

'Girl-dets!' Kayla called, 'left face, follow me!'

Kayla started them off at a quick pace, while behind them Maxwell was calling the 'boy-dets' to follow him.

'So, I don't know what you did to get picked for special training,' Kayla said, 'or what you did to risk getting kicked out of Athens. And I don't care. I've been in training here since January, when I was nothing more than one of a hundred scared volunteers. I've spent nine months training and learning to train others. I've seen hundreds of men and women come through this training, young and old, all ready to fight. I have nothing but respect for them. And if you think you can be officers who lead them, then you damn well better take this as seriously as they do.'

The cadets said nothing. They heard Maxwell behind them, saying something similar to the men.

Kayla led them to a section of the forest. Several clearings surrounded a fire pit, and a stack of carrying packs. She picked up the first one. 'You two! Names?'

'Scholar and Swift, Sergeant.'

Kayla tossed them the first pack. 'That's your tent.' She tossed a second. 'That's your sleeping kit. You're at that clearing. Set it up.'

Sasha and Swift went to work. It was a small, simple tent, a series of stands and ropes and a single tarp. The sleeping kit was a pair of small pillows and a thick blanket.

'This is going to be close,' Swift whispered.

Sasha nodded, but she was not as worried as Swift was. She had shared a similarly sized space with two women back in Third Regiment. 'Closer once we bring our packs and rifles inside.'

'Shit,' Swift said.

The tents went up under Kayla and Maxwell's stern observations. The tents were as small as Swift had feared. 'Do all the soldiers get tents like this?' she asked out loud.

'Nope,' Kayla called. 'Most soldiers get tents that can be combined into larger tents. You all got special cadet tents. Because you're special.'

Kayla's voice mocked them with that last sentence. Sasha refused to respond.

'Okay,' Maxwell said, 'who's hungry?'

'I am!' Hero chimed in. Sasha steeled herself for the response, as she was certain their meals were going to be as special as their tents.

'Excellent,' Maxwell said, 'well, we do have food here at Sparta; it's given out by the kitchen, which is on the southern side of the camp. We're on the north.'

'However,' Kayla said, 'the center of camp is currently off limits, which means to get to the kitchen, we have to go around. It should only be about three miles.'

'And the kitchen closes in,' Maxwell looked at a pocket watch, 'forty-five minutes. So, we better run, hadn't we?'

'Shouldn't we change into exercise kits?' Hero asked. He alone, of all the cadets, did not understand what was about to happen.

'Are you slow, cadet? We don't have exercise kits. We have field uniforms only,' Maxwell smiled at him.

'And don't forget your rifles,' Kayla called.

The two sergeants led the cadets out into maze around Sparta. They hustled at a strong, steady pace, not running, but not walking either. By the time they reached the kitchens, Hero, Penn and Cardinal were falling behind.

The cadets ate, a poor meal compared to what they were used to. There was no time to complain, barely enough time to eat, before they were marching back through the maze.

'I don't know what you're used to,' Kayla called, 'but here, we learn to fight as one unit, to take care of and depend on each other.'

'We cook for each other,' Maxwell continued. 'Clean for each other. We all succeed when one improves. We all fail when one fails.'

'You've been told you're special,' Kayla said. 'One of a kind. The best. And maybe you are.'

'But an army is not one man, not one woman, no matter how special they are.'

'You can plan the best campaign you know, but it will be fought by the rifles.'

'You can build the best fort you can, but you will need a garrison to defend it.'

'You eat food you did not cook.'

'You wear clothes you did not make.'

'You may be special, but you are a part of a greater force.'

'You may be special, but this army was not built for you.'

'So, we are going to run. We are going to jump.'

'And you are going to remember that an army is only a strong as its weakest link.'

'And that will not be you,' Kayla emphasis each word.

'Not after we're done with you,' Maxwell laughed.

'Okay,' Roland huffed. 'Now they're trying to kill us.'

114

'Hear that?' Maxwell yelled. 'This one wants an extra mile.'

'Well, okay then,' Kayla said. 'Another mile it is.'

Sasha groaned, but said nothing.

None of the cadets did.

Chapter 13

Sparta was not fun. True to the warnings, there were few buildings, and the cadets were not allowed in any of them. There were exercises, weapons training, and squad formations. Food cooked in a kitchen was a luxury they were rarely afforded; often it was cooked at small campfires or eaten cold. It rained for several days, but still they stayed outside. Time was told not by bells, but by the report of a cannon. It was a martial camp, one that made Sasha feel a little uneasy.

What did you expect? She chided herself. *It's an army.*

Sasha worked hard to remain optimistic. She remembered her time after she joined the Third Regiment, when she was the lowest member. She faced so many challenges, some given by people who did not even like her. Winnie had tried to beat her from the regiment, but Sasha had stood true, and now the two were friends. Sasha swore she would endure this test too.

Other cadets were taking their training in stride. Elector and Mako were annoyingly calm about everything, Patch was also seemingly oblivious to their current position, though she spoke less than usual. Swift and Blaze tried as well, but over their first week the stress and challenges started to get to them, and they grew bitter.

The rest just suffered. Roland's songs stopped coming and Hero would complain whenever the sergeants were not listening. Rose all but stopped talking and barely ate. Candle and Cardinal lost their smiles, sullenly following instructions. Penn kept looking for a bright side, but the attitude of the cadets soured him eventually.

Sasha missed her books, and her bed. She missed being a cadet, and hated this daily reminder of how they all had failed.

***

'This sucks,' Hero said again.

'Shut up,' Swift half threatened, half begged.

'Why are we here?'

'Because we failed,' Elector said.

'Not all of us,' Blaze retorted.

'Yes, all of us,' Sasha said.

'I did nothing to fail,' Blaze scolded.

'You didn't help anyone else,' Sasha said.

'No one else is my responsibility!' Blaze shouted, glancing quickly at Elector.

'Oh, shut up, Blaze!' Rose snapped.

'You heard the sergeants when we got here,' Sasha said quickly. 'A unit is only as good as its weakest link. The Templar Project is only as good as its weakest link.'

'So?' Hero interrupted.

'So,' Candle continued,' too many of us have spent too much time worried about being the best as a person to worry about the squad.'

'Too many of us,' Sasha agreed. 'Almost all.'

'And what should we be doing instead?' Blaze demanded.

'We should be helping each other,' Sasha said.

'We should be strengthening each other,' Cardinal agreed.

Hero scowled, and Blaze crossed his arms. 'That's stupid,' Blaze said.

'And yet, here we are, being forced by others to do it because we refused to do it ourselves,' Elector said. 'Blaze, we're failing to be a unit.'

Blaze frowned at Elector, then swore.

'So, what do we do?' Mako asked.

'We help each other. Fastest runner helps the slowest,' Cardinal said. 'Best in math helps the worst.

'It's not about knowing everything; it's about knowing the right things,' Swift said. 'Efficiency. Teamwork.'

'They don't have to be mean about it,' Hero said.

'They're sergeants,' Sasha said, 'it's their duty to find weak links. My sergeant before this forced me to prove myself. And now she's one of my closest friends.'

'Your sergeant?' Penn asked.

'Yes,' Sasha nodded. 'I am a veteran of a field regiment. We had to learn to work together or we would die.'

'I don't think we will die here,' Roland said.

'Don't be so sure,' Swift joked.

'So, we work together,' Sasha said. 'It's the most basic thing a unit can do together.'

'Right, Blaze?' Elector asked.

Blazed grumped.

***

Kayla and Maxwell had the cadets fall in. 'So, does anyone want to lead the run today?' Kayla called.

'I do!' Roland responded. Sasha thought he sounded enthusiastic and dismissed it as a trick of the forest.

'Good, but be warned, cadet. Do not slack on running or cadence, or you'll all be punished.'

'Right, Sergeant,' Roland said. He took his place in the leader's spot, calling the cadets to turn and move. He had them at a calm warming up before he broke them into a run. After a short while, he started singing a cadence. He sang one line, and the cadets would repeat it.

> *When the Renaissance was born,*
> *And Prince marched off to war,*
> *He gathered here in Sparta*
> *Twelve young who wanted more.*

'That's not an official cadence,' Kayla said, but Roland continued.

> *Six men who demanded*
> *To be more than a rifle*
> *Six women who declared*
> *'I am not a trifle.'*
>
> *We are the cadets*
> *Of the Templar Project*
> *The future of the army*
> *Is ours to protect.*

Roland was stretching some of the words to make them all fit within the cadence. The cadets were beginning to respond. Sasha thought they were louder than usual.

'Sing it, Cadet Roland!' Maxwell called. Kayla chuckled.

> *Roland is a soldier,*
> *With the voice of a poet*
> *Scholar is the smartest*
> *Although she doesn't know it.*

Some of the cadets laughed.

> *Penn won't pick up a rifle,*
> *But is deadly with a word.*
> *Cardinal is quick and witty,*
> *And pretty as a bird.*

> *We are the cadets*
> *Of the Templar Project*
> *The future of the army*
> *Is ours to protect.*

Now the cadets were singing loudly and in unison. The sergeants were joining in.

> *Blaze has the standing,*
> *Of a warrior of old*
> *Patch could build a furnace*
> *To keep off the cold*

> *Hero saved an innocent*
> *And now he's here to grow*
> *Rose is quiet and stoic,*
> *There's much we don't know*

> *We are the cadets*
> *Of the Templar Project*
> *The future of the army*
> *Is ours to protect.*

The cadets were no longer just repeating the cadence. They were bellowing. For the first time in a while, Sasha smiled.

> *Mako does not say much*
> *But what he says is right*
> *Swift may not look it*
> *But she can surely fight*

Elector is the best of us,
And we will take his lead.
Candle is our mother
Giving advice we sorely need.

'Really?' Candle shouted, 'I'm the MOM!?' The cadets laughed. Even the sergeants were laughing.

Roland called out steps for a while, indicating his song was over. Then he started into one of Maxwell's favorite cadences, and the cadets continued.

***

'This,' the instructor said, pulling a swatch of camo netting away from the emplacement, 'is a mortar, specifically a heavy mortar. This is not a carry-on-your-back weapon. This is a get-an-animal-to-carry-it-for-you weapon. The entire assembly weighs over three hundred pounds, most of which is the base plate to absorb recoil.'

Sasha and the cadets were part of a group of thirty-some trainees, all standing about the emplacement. It was dug into the ground, and the people stood around it so they could see the weapon being demonstrated. In this case it was a mortar, a thick tube about four feet long, set into a heavy metal plate at the bottom, with two legs holding it at an angle. Its barrel was pointing out into an empty field.

'Who knows the difference between a cannon and a mortar?' the instructor asked.

Candle raised her hand. 'A cannon fires directly at a target, like a bullet. A mortar fires up, so it lands on top of the target.'

'Is that it?' the instructor asked, staring at Candle. 'It's not that mortars are muzzle loading, and cannon are breech loading?'

'No, Drill Sergeant. A cannon is straight, a mortar is up, and a howitzer is in between.'

The instructor stared at her with a challenge, then nodded. 'That's correct,' he said. 'Mortars fire up and down upon their target. This is useful to attack targets you cannot directly see, particularly in sieges, where the defenders are in trenches or behind walls.

'Today we are going to show you how the mortar works, and we will be testing you over the next few days. We are always looking for men and women capable of handling these types of weapons. They require teamwork to handle

120

properly. And trust me, you want to handle this one properly. Because it launches these.'

Two crew members hauled out the bomb the mortar fired. Sasha stared at it, a heavy, metal cylinder with small fins out the back. 'There are called bombs. Now, a mortar can fire several different types of bombs. This is a training bomb. It will not explode, but it will set off smoke so you can see where it lands. Other options include high explosive, to hurt the enemy; heavy smoke to blind him; flares to reveal him; even chemical, if you really want to screw with him.'

'Now, see that small shack?' he pointed out into the field. About three hundred yards away was a simple shack, no more than a wooden frame and some planking to make it visible from where they stood. 'We are going to try to hit it with the bombs. We are going to fire, and adjust, rather quickly. Watch us load, watch the round hit, watch us adjust, then begin again. Ready?'

Everyone nodded, and the crew went to work. Sasha watched them prep the round, adjust the mortar, then drop the bomb into it. There was a *thunking* sound and the bomb flew up, arcing through the air.

It landed short, with a burst of smoke. The crew adjusted, and fired again, this time, landing on the far side.

'The ideal way to adjust is to bracket the target,' the instructor called. 'When you bracket a target, you make a large adjustment and try to land on the opposite side of the target from your first shot. This keeps you from wasting ammunition with small, incremental changes. Bracket! Remember it!'

The third shot landed near the shack, not directly on it.

'Now,' the instructor commanded, 'consider that if that had been high explosive instead of training, the last shot would have been well within the explosive radius of the bomb. It would have been good enough. Do not feel the need to drop it directly on top of a target. Of course, if you do manage to do so, good job.'

The trainees laughed.

'Now that we have the range, let us see what a real mortar round can do,' the instructor said. 'Now, this is –.'

Patch interrupted. 'We're being watched,' she said, pointing into the sky.

Everyone in earshot stopped and looked up, following the woman's finger. High above them, droning in a straight line, was an airplane.

'Wow,' Swift said.

Sasha nodded. It was only the second time she had seen one, and this one was much lower.

'HEY!' a voice bellowed. One of the drill instructors shouted from the trees. 'Get out of the field and into cover, now!'

Now that someone had told them to act, sergeants began shouting and the field cleared. The instructors at the weapons pulled over the camouflage netting, hiding them from the sky.

'For those of you who don't know,' the voice boomed, 'that is an airplane. The king has plenty of them, but he doesn't like using them. If you see one overhead, it's doing one of two things. It's either looking for something to attack or taking pictures so someone else can come back later and attack. If you see one, find cover! If you see one coming right at you, find cover faster.'

Some of the trainees chuckled. The cadets had congregated together, near the magazine. The plane was droning along. If it had seen them, it did not show it.

'What kind of plane is that?' Sasha asked.

'It's a float plane,' Cardinal said with authority. 'It usually takes off and lands on water. The Royal Air Corps has a pair of them in Duluth to patrol Lake Superior.'

'What is it doing all the way out here?' Hero asked.

'Like the sergeant said, recon,' Cardinal replied. 'They can stay up in the air for about ten hours; say an hour from Duluth to here, another back, that's eight hours over Walker County, looking for us. It's probably got a dozen cameras taking pictures right now.'

Hero stepped out of the trees and made a rude gesture at the plane.

'How easy would it be to shoot that down?' Blaze asked.

Cardinal continued to educate them. 'They're slow, so it's a question of getting a weapon that can shoot high enough to hit them. If we had a plane of our own, shooting it down would be pretty easy the first time, but then they're start escorting them, and it all turns into a dog fight.'

'A dog fight?' Sasha looked over.

'That's what it's called when a bunch of small aircraft fight each other. Between the speed and the maneuvering, it can get pretty difficult and dangerous.'

'But we can't do anything about that,' Mako said, pointing at the airplane. It was slowly moving westward, getting smaller and smaller.

'Not at the moment, no,' Cardinal said.

A sergeant started yelling, and a few trainees swarmed the mortar to start hauling the ordnance back to the magazine, but many others were left milling about. Their officers had left them in the care of the sergeants for weapons demonstrations, but those appeared to be over.

Swift stayed near Sasha. 'The king has more of those.'

'So does the Commonwealth,' Sasha replied.

'We'll have to do something about them.'

'Yes,' Sasha agreed. She pulled Swift out of the way as the mortar crews came by, carrying the boxes of mortar bombs. 'But what? I can't imagine we have the resources to support airplanes, even if we knew what to do with them.'

'Cardinal seems to know,' Swift pointed out.

'She does,' Sasha admitted, wondering again how Cardinal knew that much about flying. It was the first time the youngest cadet has shown any unique knowledge.

'Well, maybe we can come up with a plan for airplanes,' Swift said.

'I'd much rather have a plan for Walker Town,' Sasha said.

'Why?' Swift asked.

Sasha leaned in. 'I have family there,' she said. Swift was surprised, so Sasha continued. 'They've been in there for several months. If Count Walker makes good on his threats, they'll be some of the first to suffer.'

'I get it,' Swift said. 'Well, let's come up with a plan for Walker, then.'

'Just us?' Sasha asked.

'Why not,' Swift said. 'Once we're out of the Common Phase, maybe we can make it a project.'

'We could ask,' Sasha admitted. She liked the idea.

'Good,' Swift said with a smile. 'Maybe to start, we should –.'

WUMP!

Chapter 14

Sasha had been standing. Now she was sitting on the ground, staring at an inferno. The half of the magazine was gone, spread out across the ground around it. The other half was burning with a ferocious intensity.

Sasha knew she was numb and slow. She felt the heat of the fire, but it seemed dull, as if there was a curtain keeping her from feeling it. She started crawling backwards, still facing the blaze.

Her mind was still trying to sort itself into order, pulling herself away from the building. Her hand fell on something soft and covered with cloth. She turned and saw her hand resting on someone's leg, draped in the familiar grey material.

'Swift,' she said, realizing who it was. She pulled herself back a few more feet, so she could see her friend. 'We need to go,' she called. Then she looked down.

Swift's eyes stared blankly across the ground. Her hair was matted, her head misshapen, and the ground around her was soaked a sickly red. Her face had already taken a white pallor.

'Oh, Swift,' Sasha said. Her brain was focusing better now, overcoming the shock of the initial blast. She reached over and closed Swift's eyes.

Something plowed into her. Arms appeared underneath hers and she was lifted off the ground, half carried and half dragged away from the fire.

'I'm fine!' she started struggling to get her feet under her.

'Are you?' Hero called. He pulled her up so she could stand on her own. 'Your head?'

Sasha ran her hands through her hair. Some pain, but the hands came back bloodless. 'Sore, but stable.' She heard a voice bellowing orders, organizing the survivors and those who came to help. 'Swift is dead,' she said.

'I know,' Hero coughed. 'Where are the cadre?'

Sasha saw people running about, responding to the voice. 'Isn't that Del Oso shouting?'

'That's not Del Oso,' Hero said, gesturing.

It was Elector. Quiet and calm Elector, bellowing commands as he started working on the wounded accumulating around him. Even though he wore no

124

rank insignia, and everyone knew from his uniform he was a cadet and had no official capacity, no one was contradicting him. Even aged sergeants were rushing to get his orders done. Wounded were carried, first aid applied, runners sent out to find anyone with authority and get assistance. He was the only one who was not stunned by the explosion.

'Let's go help,' Sasha said, making her way over. Hero slowly followed.

Elector saw them approach, looking up from a trainee who clutched a broken arm. 'The magazine exploded!' he said, somewhat unnecessarily. 'Are you okay?'

'Swift is dead,' Sasha said.

'She won't be the only one if we can't get some doctors here,' Elector growled. 'Someone is fetching the medics but they're not here yet.'

'We've only got a few hours of field medicine,' Hero said, 'but we can help.'

Sasha nodded. Part of her mind surprised at Hero's eagerness. 'What can we do?'

Elector looked over Sasha's shoulder and stood. 'Come,' he said.

Patch was behind them, supporting a stumbling Rose. Rose's head was awash in blood, and her skin was pale.

'Hero,' Elector said, 'help me get her down. Scholar, take a look at Patch.'

'I'm fine,' Patch said shakily. 'Rose needs help.'

'And Elector's helping her,' Sasha said. 'Let me help you.' Patch said nothing more, the normally distracted woman looking frightfully disoriented. Sasha looked over Patch's head, trying to see anything that looked like a head wound.

Hero was holding a bandage to Rose's head, while Elector was getting others organized to care for the wounded. A dozen people were lying about now, too wounded to move, while others with lighter injuries were helping Elector care for them.

'Oh,' Patch said, 'Roland looks hurt, too.'

Sasha followed Patch's gaze to see Mako and Roland, supporting each other, making their way to Elector.

'Go,' Patch said. Sasha stood and moved over to them.

'What hurts?'

'Everything,' Mako said.

'Look for my uniform tomorrow, you might find a grave man wearing it,' Roland said.

'You're not dying, Roland,' Mako said. 'I think he's dislocated his left shoulder, and I've broken a few ribs.

'You sure?' Sasha asked, helping Roland to lie down.

Mako nodded. 'I've done it before. Feels the same. At least I'm not coughing up blood.'

'That's good,' Sasha said, hoping it was. Elector was busy dealing with someone else. 'Roland?'

'Pain, Scholar, I feel pain,' Roland moaned. 'Does Elector know enough to set a shoulder?'

'Probably, when he turns around, I'll –.'

'Rose!' a voice called. It was Cardinal, making her way towards her sister while supporting Candle. Cardinal looked completely fine. Candle's nose was purple, and the front of her uniform was awash in blood.

'What's wrong with her?' Cardinal asked about her sister. Two trainees took Candle and moved her into their line while Cardinal moved to Rose.

'Concussion,' Hero said, still holding the bandage. 'She's still alive.'

'Here, let me take that,' Cardinal demanded, taking her sister's bandage from Hero. She looked down at her sister's wound, holding the bandage and whispering to her in Quebecois.

Sasha got Mako to sit down, though he refused to lie on his back. Roland was more than happy to be prone, tears streaming from his eyes at the pain from his shoulder.

Elector made his way back, checking all of them quickly. 'Where are Blaze and Penn?' he asked.

'I don't know,' Roland said. 'I think they were close to the magazine when it went off.'

Elector grimaced. 'Scholar and Cardinal, can you see if you can find them?'

Sasha nodded. Cardinal said some last words of encouragement to her sister and stood. They turned towards what had been the magazine. It still burned with a fierce intensity, and the trees around it were flattened for some distance. They got as close as they could to the flames.

'Let's circle the magazine,' Sasha said. 'See if we can see anyone else.'

Cardinal nodded in agreement and the pair started circling. Debris littered the ground. They made it to the other side when they found the last two cadets.

Blaze was covered in branches, unconscious. Penn was also knocked out, but he had been awake at some point. Sasha could tell because he had pulled his belt tight across what was left of his right leg. The tourniquet was set just above the knee, right where they had been taught. Little of his leg remained below the knee.

'Shit,' Cardinal said. 'Let's pull Penn out first.'

'Why him?' Sasha asked.

'Because I can see he's breathing, so I know he's alive.'

'Right,' Sasha said. She shook her head, wondering if maybe she had taken harder hit than she had originally thought. Concentrating was hard. 'Let's go.'

They pressed forward into the heat. Each grabbed one of Penn's shoulders and pulled him back. He jumped a little at their touch but was not awake.

Hero arrived with several others as they got Penn away from the magazine. 'Del Oso and the medics have arrived,' he said. 'They're organizing ambulances. We're . . . ,' he saw Penn's leg and trailed off. Then he turned and vomited.

Cardinal and one of the others took to carry Penn back to Elector. 'We still have to get Blaze,' Sasha said.

There was a resounding crash behind them as the magazine finally collapsed. The heat died down a bit as the structure became smaller.

'Let's go,' Sasha said to Hero. He reluctantly followed.

They cleared the debris from Blaze. He was breathing, barely, and his skin was pale.

'He looked dead already,' Hero said.

'But he's not,' Sasha growled. 'We're going to have to move him.'

'Don't think we're strong enough to do that,' Hero said. Blaze was a tall man. 'And dragging him might make him worse.'

'If the medics have arrived, maybe they have a stretcher,' Sasha said.

'I'll go see!' Hero said quickly and disappeared. Sasha watched him run, then turned back to Blaze. She felt for a pulse; it was weak but there.

'Come on, Blaze,' she said. She heard footsteps behind her and saw a pair of trainees carrying a stretcher, with a medic and Hero behind them.

The medic knelt next to Blaze. He checked his pulse, listened to his chest. The look on his face was grim. 'He's going to die,' the medic said.

'But he's not dead yet!' Sasha snarled.

The medic looked at her and nodded. 'Right,' he said. 'Not yet.' He pulled some gear from his bag and started working on Blaze, securing his neck with a brace. Then he directed the cadets and trainees to roll him onto the stretcher.

'Let's get back,' he said. The trainees lifted, Hero and Sasha followed them back towards Elector's assembly area.

Everyone in Sparta must have responded to the explosion. Scores of trainees stood by, waiting for the chance to help. Officers conversed, discussing how to proceed, while medics picked over the wounded. Elector waved to them; he had assembled all the cadets in one part of the field, so they were all together.

'We're getting ambulances,' Elector said. 'They're taking everyone to the hospital.'

'To Holiday?' Sasha asked in relief. Holiday was the hospital the Renaissance Army had set up in Walker County, run by Colonel Aristotle. Mary had been trained at Holiday.

'When?' Candle asked in her stuffy voice.

'As soon as we can. Mako and Penn go first; I'll put as many of the rest of you in as I can.'

'What about Blaze?' Sasha asked.

Elector looked at Blaze, and the medic who had brought him in. The medic shook his head grimly.

'We can't do anything for him' Elector said. 'Get ready to move.'

***

Wagons came. Sasha watched medics load Penn into one, his limp body moved like cargo. The stretcher took up most of the floor, and Elector looked at the benches. 'I can fit five more,' he said. 'Patch, Mako and Roland, get in. I want them to take a look at your wounds first.' Medics helped the three cadets climb in.

'What about Rose?' Cardinal asked.

'I don't want to move her yet; she's not showing any signs of bleeding or wounds.'

128

'That doesn't mean she's okay,' Cardinal snapped.

'No, but Penn is actively not okay, and those three are showing obvious wounds. Rose stays.'

'So do I!' Cardinal said.

'Absolutely,' Elector nodded. 'Candle, I want you to go too, in case that head took more than a nose wound. Scholar, ride herd on them.'

Sasha nodded. She glanced over at Hero. Hero was looking at the wagon with interest, like he wanted to argue his way on it, but he said nothing.

'Hero,' she said. 'Thanks.'

Hero blushed. 'Welcome,' he said.

Sasha climbed on board and the wagon started moving. With every jolt, Patch whimpered. Mako took slow breathes. Roland was still crying, his arm bandaged to his body.

Sitting in the wagon, finally getting a break from the consequences of the explosion, Sasha started to calm down. She took deep breaths to steady herself. She started feeling the bruises over her body, the ache in her back, and the dull, constant pain in her wrist.

Swift is dead, she thought to herself. *And she's not the first friend I've lost: Rick, Jim, Sonja, and now Swift.*

She started tearing up, both at the memories of her dead friends, and the increasing pain in her wrist.

'Ow,' she said.

Mako looked over. 'What?'

'My wrist hurts,' she said. She started to rotate it. She could not make it a full circle.

'We'll have a doctor look at it when we get to Holiday,' Mako said.

'How long until we get there?' Candle asked quietly.

Sasha looked up at the sky and frowned. 'Holiday is southeast of Sparta,' she said. 'We're heading north.'

Roland frowned. 'I thought they said they were taking us to Holiday.'

'They said the hospital,' Patch said. 'We all just assumed that meant Holiday.'

'Then where are we going?' Candle asked. Her voices sounded better, less stuffy and more like herself.

The cadets heard a voice call out in the distance, shouting out to their drivers, the words indiscernible.

The driver bellowed. 'Wounded from Sparta!'

'At least we're almost there,' Penn said.

Sasha stood and looked over the driver's shoulder. They were approaching what looked like a tent city. She saw men and women approaching, wearing several brightly colored shirts. Ones wearing bright red shirts were jumping onto the wagons and talking with the passengers. One woman approached their wagon and leapt up.

'What happened?' she asked. She sounded odd, and Sasha shook her head again, wondering if she had hit it harder than Elector had found.

'Magazine explosion at Sparta,' Sasha responded.

The woman cursed. She looked at the wounded in the wagon, taking in their wounds one by one. 'Welcome to Charity-.'

'Not Holiday?' Roland asked.

The woman shushed him. 'No, this is Charity, the civilian hospital. We are closer than Holiday, so you're coming here. I am Doctor Carissa Adams, and all of you are now under my care. What are your names?'

'I'm Scholar,' Sasha said, 'Candle has the head wound, Patch with the arm. Mako has the broken ribs, Roland the bad ankle, and Penn is on the floor.'

'For Christ's sake, how old are all of you, thirteen?' Adams asked. Sasha realized it was not her hearing. The woman had a thick voice, with a harsh accent she had never heard before. Sasha looked her over quick, wondering if she could identify the woman's origins, but she was not fast enough. The woman was already waving someone over.

A man in a blue shirt jumped up next to her. 'Get this stretcher into a surgery tent. This girl gets a full head evaluation in yellow, and check the others head to toe in green.'

'Right,' the man in blue said. Others crowded around. Sasha saw greens and blues, fewer reds.

Several men pulled the stretcher out and carried Penn towards a row of small tents. Sasha saw that many of the most heavily wounded men and women were being taken there. The rest were being led to a pair of larger tents, the left one with a green banner, the right one with a yellow.

'All the red shirts are going to small tents,' she muttered. She turned to help Patch out of the wagon.

130

'They're the doctors,' Patch said.

'How do you know?' Sasha asked.

'They're the ones acting like officers, giving commands, and there aren't very many of them,' Patch said. Her voice was flat and toneless, not at all like her normal cheerful self. Sasha studied the other cadet. Patch was unnaturally still, her eyes half-closed, her breathing long drawn out breathes.

She must be in a lot of pain.

Candle was given a yellow sash and escorted to the tent on the right. The remaining were directed to the tent on the left; Sasha helped Patch, while Roland leaned on blue shirt. Mako walked, stiffly, waving away any help.

Inside the green tent, wounded were being sat at long benches. The four cadets sat together, Mako and Patch sitting opposite Sasha and Roland.

A blue shirt arrived. She looked a little older than Sasha was. 'Who are you?' Sasha asked.

'I'm a nurse. My name is Becca. What is your name?'

'Scholar,' Sasha responded.

'That's your name?' Becca asked.

'It's the one I can give you.'

'Okay.' Becca said. 'I'm going to check on you. Do you know what happened?'

'Magazine explosion at Sparta,' Sasha replied. 'Are blue shirts nurses? Then what are green?'

'Orderlies,' Becca replied. 'Now, where are you hurt?'

Sasha went over the list of wounds again. Becca inspected them, her hands gently probing and her voice softly questioning. Other nurses were doing the same to other groups. Every so often, a nurse would put a yellow sash on someone, and they would be taken into the yellow tent.

'Yellow means bad?'

'Red means bad,' Patch said. 'Yellow means getting bad. Green means it can wait.'

'How do you know?' Sasha asked.

'It makes sense', Patch shrugged.

Sasha leaned back. She closed her eyes, but saw Swift staring blankly up, and Blaze's bruised body. Penn's shredded leg.

131

She turned to Patch. 'Did you know there was a civilian hospital as well?'

Patch nodded. 'I'd heard about it. Thought it was common knowledge.'

'Why have two hospitals?' Sasha asked.

'Civilian and military,' Patch replied.

'Why?' Sasha asked again.

'In case some people are tired of uniforms.'

Becca was before Sasha now. She looked into Sasha's eyes. 'What's my name?'

'Nurse Becca.'

She checked her wrist. 'Does this hurt?'

'It does,' Sasha admitted, wincing.

'Okay. How's your breathing?'

'Good. Maybe breathed in some smoke.'

'Okay. What's my name?'

'Nurse Becca.'

'How many fingers?'

'Three.'

'Can you feel my hand on your toes?'

'Yes.'

'What's my name?'

'Nurse Becca, same as last time.'

'Good,' Becca said. She wrote several notes down, then pinned the notes to Sasha's jacket. She moved to Patch next, asking the same questions. Sasha leaned back, still trying to get her mind on track.

'Okay,' Becca said. 'Patch, Scholar and Roland, you are hurt, but you are doing well, so I need you to hold on for me. Mako, I'm worried about your breathing, so you're moving to the yellow tent.'

'If you are sure,' Mako said. Becca was, and a green shirt helped him out of the tent.

'So we wait,' Sasha said.

'There are many who're more wounded than us,' Patch said, still speaking

132

softly. 'They deserve the better attention.'

Sasha looked around. There was one nurse for every four or five people, constantly checking this and that. Most of the wounded looked worried or stunned. Many of them were praying. Then Sasha realized Roland was speaking under his breath.

'Are you praying?'

'No,' Roland said. 'Reciting.'

'Reciting what?'

Roland looked up as an orderly came by to check on his leg. Then he sighed.

> *'Roland feels his hour at hand*
> *On hilltop he lied towards homeland*
> *With one hand he beats upon his breast*
> *"To you, O God, be my sins confessed.*
> *Every hour of my life, both great and small,*
> *To this very day, I repent of all."*
> *As he raised his glove to God on high,*
> *Angels of heaven descended on him nigh.'*

'Sounds happy,' Patch muttered.

'It's from the end of the song,' Roland said. 'Roland is going to die and repents of his sins.'

'Does it work?' Sasha asked.

'It does,' Roland admitted. 'God sends angels down to take his soul to heaven.'

'Good for him,' Sasha said.

'Or he died on foreign land and never made it home,' Patch said.

'You're not much for faith, are you?' Roland asked sternly.

'I have no issue with faith, except when it blinds you to the world around you,' Patch said. There was an earnestness to her words that Sasha had rarely heard before. 'Believe all you want but act according to principal and logic.'

'I know some people who would get angry at you for saying that,' Roland replied.

'I know people who tried to kill me for saying that,' Patch said.

Mako reappeared. 'Are you okay?' Sasha asked. Roland moved over and Mako sat between them.

'They took me into a room for some sort of picture,' Mako said. 'My ribs are broken, but they're not threatening my lungs, so there's not much they can do. Gave me a bit of medicine for my pain, but other than that I just have to keep breathing.'

'Good,' Sasha said. 'I couldn't stand to lose another friend today. I mean, Swift was . . . .' Sasha started to choke up. Tears flowed. 'I'm sorry, I don't mean to –.'

Mako put his arm around her and hugged her. 'Cry on my shoulder,' he said. 'Don't hold it in.'

Sasha leaned against his shoulder and cried until she was asleep.

Chapter 15

She woke up some time later. The tempo of people running around had fallen off. She was still leaning against Mako, who had dozed off as well. Roland was gone, and Patch's arm was now in a sling and her ankle wrapped in a blanket

'How long?' Sasha asked.

'Two hours,' Patch replied. 'Give or take ten minutes. They took me shortly after you dozed off. Took pictures – they're called X-rays, by the way, using lights we can't see to get images of bones and see if they're broken. Said my arm was dislocated, not broken. They popped it back in – that hurts, in case you were wondering – and gave me this sling. '

'The ankle?'

'Started hurting when I tried to walk over there. Sprained, they say. Currently applying some ice.'

'Roland?'

'Took him about twenty minutes ago.' Patch glanced about. 'They're pretty efficient here. I like their system. It's a good way of not wasting resources on those too far gone to save.'

'That sounds rather cold,' Sasha replied.

Patch gave a one-shoulder shrug. 'In a crisis, why waste time on people you know you can't save? All that will do is increase the chances that someone else you could save will die. Simple math.'

'Horrible math,' Sasha said.

'Agreed.'

Sasha looked about. Many of the wounded she saw before she slept were gone, with new wounded in their place. 'None of the other cadets have come back yet?'

'No,' Patch said, 'but we're about due for another round of wagons. They're coming rather regularly. I think we should be seeing some more of them soon.'

Sasha looked out towards where the wagons would be coming in, hoping to see them. Instead, she saw Doctor Adams coming in. Her red shirt was stained with something a little darker than its normal hue. She came right for Sasha; Sasha elbowed Mako to wake him. Mako hissed and she apologized before the doctor arrived.

'Cadets?' she asked, approaching them.

'How's Penn?' Sasha asked.

'Alive. I had to amputate his leg at the knee, but he's alive.'

'Oh, thank you, Jesus,' Mako said. Sasha smiled and nodded. The other cadets all sighed and smiled.

'I see you've been taken care of,' Adams said, looking at Mako and Patch. 'What about you?'

'Not yet,' Sasha said.

Adams leaned down and read the note Becca had pinned to her shirt. 'Okay, come with me.'

Sasha stood, following the doctor out the tent and into the back field. There was another large tent, with a red banner, and four smaller ones numbered one through four. Adams led her to an even smaller tent, this one set next to a large wagon. Sasha saw several jars with wires and metal bars set across them, with wires and ropes leading into the tent.

'We're going to look at your arm, now,' Adams said, opening the tent for Sasha.

'With an X-ray?' Sasha asked.

Adams blinked at her. 'What do you know about it?'

'Just what Patch told me a few minutes ago: it takes pictures using lights we can't see to determine if our bones are broken.'

'That's as good an explanation as any,' Adams said. She gestured for Sasha to enter.

Inside the tent was divided into two parts by a heavy curtain. Adams led Sasha to a chair. Once she sat down, Sasha watched as Adams and a man in a gold shirt maneuvered the chair and several stands, pulling Sasha' arm into a position between a large box and a flat panel. Sasha noticed wires leading from the box.

'It uses electricity?' Sasha asked.

'It does,' Adams confirmed.

'How? Even Walker Town doesn't have electricity.'

Adams chuckled. 'We have some friends who know some things. They're not quite military, but they're not civilians either. They play around with science.'

'The Workshop?'

'Yes,' Adams looked at Sasha in surprise. 'I didn't know it was common knowledge.'

'It's not,' Sasha said, 'but the Templar Project is full of uncommon people.'

'Right,' Adams said, going back to work. 'Anyway, they've put together some ways to have electricity for emergency situations. X-ray generators, surgery lights, pumps and all the little things that make saving lives easier. Normally, we use candles and lanterns, but when we need to, we can call on these. Then once we're done, the technicians can recharge the batteries. It's not a perfect system, by any means, but it does allow us to save lives in an emergency.'

'That's good,' Sasha said.

Adams smiled, then paused and gave Sasha a stern look. 'Scholar, Penn, Roland, Cardinal, Mako. What the hell is the Templar Project? You guys are officers of some sort? That's why you can't tell me your name?'

'Something like that.'

The man in a gold shirt brought over a heavy drape and put it over Sasha. She asked, 'Red is doctor, blue is nurse, green is orderly. What is gold?'

'Gold is technician. White is administration, paperwork.'

'Not military, Doctor Adams?'

Adams adjusted the drapes. 'No, not military. And call me Carissa. Now, any more questions before we take this picture?'

'Where are you from?'

'Some place you've probably never heard of,' Carissa said absently.

'Really?'

Carissa gave her a look. 'I'm from Boston. Know where that is?' she asked harshly.

'To the east, along the Atlantic coast, between Quebec and the Atlantic Dominion. One of the few cities to survive the Dark Age intact, it made a name for itself sweeping pirates from the sea. Somehow survived conquest without being incorporated into its neighbors.'

Carissa blinked in surprise, again. 'Where did you learn that?'

'The Templar Project,' Sasha said. 'Basic Geography started day one.'

'Okay, then,' Carissa said. 'Hold your arm still.' She stepped on the other side of a heavy curtain. A few moments later the box twitched, and Sasha heard what sounded like a deep groan. After a few more moments Adams came back out with the technician. 'We have some time before the picture is ready,' she said, as the technician removed something from the panel. She then stood there, looking at Sasha harshly for several moments, before she sighed. 'Why did I spend two hours amputating a sixteen-year old boy's leg?'

'Because a magazine exploded.'

'No, I mean why was he near it when it exploded? Why were any of you? For Christ's sake, you're all children.' Carissa was speaking fast again.

'We're cadets of the Templar Project,' Sasha said.

'Yes, I've heard, but you shouldn't be. You're too young to be cadets of anything.' Carissa sat down. 'Do you understand what war is, Cadet Scholar? It's not all good guys and bad guys, black and white. It's horrible and violent. There's nothing good about it. And the ones who tell you why you should go to war are usually the ones who send others out to die for them.'

'I know what war is like,' Sasha said.

'Okay, Cadet Scholar?' Carissa was skeptical. 'How many people have you killed?'

'Seven, at least,' Sasha said. Carissa stopped speaking in shock, and Sasha continued. 'I've made peace with the people I've killed, and that I will probably kill in the future. I have buried friends, and I will bury more. I, myself, may die, but it's for a noble cause.'

'And who told you it was a noble cause?' Carissa asked. 'The generals, who told you to fight for them?'

'They didn't tell me to fight. I asked to.'

'Why?' Carissa scowled.

'Because they saved me from the yeomen,' Sasha said. 'I don't know much about Boston, it's true, but I'm going to guess you don't have yeomen in the city.'

'No,' Carissa said.

'Then, with all due respect, Doctor, you don't have one clue what I'm talking about.' Sasha was a little angry now. 'You've never felt that fear of hearing the yeomen riding into town. Watched the families gather, silently praying that all they'll do is swagger around town and eat your food. You've never carried food and water to them, felt their eyes and hands humiliating you. Twice,

Doctor, they took girls from my village, no older than I am now, and carried them to Walker. You know what I did each of those times? I cried myself to sleep, because I was so relieved it wasn't me that I felt guilty. I prayed to God that I would stop feeling guilty for not being taken against my will, and that I would not be glad some other woman was suffering in my place.

'Then, I was in their place. My father handed me over to the yeomen, as a hostage, to warm their bed and be punished if my hometown rebelled. He did it without question. The Renaissance Army saved me. They were fighting the fight I'd been on the edge of my whole life. So, I joined.

'And they're not just sending me to fight. If they were, they wouldn't have made me a cadet. They're making me into the best person I can be.'

'The best person you can be is still fighting in a war that will cost a lot of lives before it's done,' Carissa said quietly. 'No one should be a soldier.'

'I agree, no one should be a soldier' Sasha said. 'I don't like fighting, and I don't want to fight. I'm actually annoyed at how often I have to tell people the number of men I've killed, as if I should be proud of it. I know the number, and if I never have to say it out loud again, I would be happy.'

The technician came back and cleared his throat, holding a black sheet. Carissa took the sheet and walked to the entrance to the tent, holding it up to look at it against the sunlight. She gestured Sasha over.

'See?' she said. The black sheet was shiny, and had an image Sasha recognized as her forearm, only just the bones. Carissa pointed to a small line in her wrist. 'Tiny fracture. We're going to wrap your arm, keep it from getting extended and worsening. You'll need to wear it for a month or so.'

'Wrap it?'

'In a cast.'

'A cast?'

Carissa chuckled. 'Finally, something you don't know. We keep your arm from moving in the wrong direction.'

'I thought with broken bones you're supposed to wrap them with sticks to keep them straight.'

Carissa scoffed, then blushed. 'That's good for field medicine, but here we have better materials. Make yourself comfortable.' An orderly brought out a mixing bowl and several strips of cloth. 'This will keep your arm aligned, closely, and protect it from minor accidents.' She started wrapping Sasha's arm in a light cloth.

'Doctor Adams,' Sasha began, 'if I may ask, why are you here? You don't sound like someone who supports war.'

'I don't, I support life. Unfortunately, that means different things. See that?' she gestured up to the device above Sasha. 'That's an X-ray projector. It emits particles of radiation that pass through skin but not bone. It will impact the film beneath the table here. That give us the image of your bone.

'It used to be that those machines were so common, and so small, that you didn't need to go to a hospital to find one. They, and other machines, helped keep men and women alive, through some trauma that you and I would think to be fatal. Now, even when such things are rediscovered, they're ignored or reserved for a few. The Renaissance Movement gives me a chance to help people, many people, not just a few. They're helping me re-discover what was lost. Few people want to do that nowadays.'

The orderly was dipping cloth in a mixing bowl full of white liquid, and Carissa was wrapping Sasha's arm. 'You might feel some heat. That's just the plaster setting.'

Sasha nodded, and all was quiet for a moment. Then, 'Can I ask you a question?'

'Promise it will be only one?'

'No.'

Carissa smiled. 'Sure, go ahead.'

'I heard Boston has knowledge from the Before Time. That they know more about it, the Before Time, than almost anybody. Do you know why the Before Time ended?'

Carissa chuckled. 'That's not a question I can really answer. You're asking about a problem so large, most people can barely understand how difficult it would be to get ahold of it.'

'But you have thoughts and opinions on it?'

Carissa shrugged. 'When the Dark Age started, people put away information for the future. It became our secrets. Access was hard to get, and many of those who had access didn't want to go looking.'

'Did you?'

'Have access? No, but I was courted by a man who did, and he spent a lot of time telling me about it.'

Sasha pressed. 'So, what do you think happened?'

Carissa thought for a moment, still applying wrapping to Sasha's hand. 'From what I've heard, and learned, I always believed that the Before Time ended because the world became too impersonal. Society was turning everyone into numbers and labels. You were a Catholic or not, a man or woman, part of this group or this identity. The individual stopped mattering.' She reached for another wet cloth. 'Why do you ask?'

'On our first day of the Templar Project, we were told what the Renaissance was. A time when learning and art and science took off and changed the world after the last Dark Age. I've been wondering, since then, how do we avoid a Dark Age in the future? Can we even do so?'

'Big questions for a young woman to ask,' Carissa said.

'I'm a cadet of the Templar Project, I'm supposed to ask these questions. Besides, I think you probably were asking these questions when you were my age.'

'Younger, actually,' Carissa said. 'I was eight when the Commonwealth War began. I saw the injured soldiers and sailors, and the civilians from the raids on the city. I hated it, the pain and suffering. I got into a science academy in Boston at twelve, a bit on the young side, but I was dedicated. I became a doctor, and a technician. Unfortunately, as I said, a lot of people didn't care for advancing the technology of medicine.'

'And then you came here,' Sasha said.

'It's a bit more complicated than that,' Carissa said. 'Suffice it to say, I didn't have many choices when I left Boston. Maybe, someday, I can go back.' She looked at Sasha's wrapped hand. 'How does that feel?'

'Warm, snug.'

'Not too tight?'

'No,' Sasha said.

'Good. Now, my turn to ask a question,' Carissa said. 'If you didn't feel like you had to fight, what would you do with your life?'

Sasha thought for a moment. 'I don't know. I've never really thought about it.'*

'Please, do so,' Carissa said. 'I know you feel like you have to fight now, and maybe you do, but I'd be more comfortable knowing young men and women are going to war if they had some idea what they were fighting for, other than "not this", or anger at how they've been treated. Even a perfect world won't be a fair world, Cadet Scholar. Being righteously angry over every little thing doesn't make the world a better place.'

Sasha nodded. 'I'll have to think about it,' she said. She looked at her arm, the plaster still drying. 'But first, I need to go back to the world where my friend just died.'

Carissa nodded. 'Well, you'll be here for another day or two. We'll be checking on you, all of you.'

'Thanks, Doctor,' Sasha said. She stood, smiled at the woman, and followed an orderly out the tent, into the darkness beyond. Sasha glanced up, realizing a thick carpet of clouds had rolled in, turning the midafternoon to an evening darkness. 'The clouds mourn with me,' she said to herself.

'What?' the orderly asked.

'Oh, nothing,' Sasha replied. 'Which way back to the green tent?'

The orderly led her there. More wagons had indeed arrived and left. Hero and Candle were sitting with Mako, Patch and Roland.

'We're fine,' Candle said. 'Scrapes and bruises, nothing more.'

'The rest?'

'Blaze died an hour ago. Rose was taken to the yellow tent. Cardinal went with Rose. Elector is helping in the yellow tent,' Hero said.

'We're waiting here,' Candle continued.

Sasha sat down, her arm feeling heavy in the cast. *Swift is dead, Blaze is dead, Penn lost a leg, and Rose may be severely injured.*

She had mixed feelings. Swift was a friend, and her death was painful. Penn was a decent man, though Sasha was not sure if he was a friend or not. In any event, she did not want to see him suffer.

Blaze and Rose were different. In all honesty, Sasha did not much care for Blaze. He was a good officer, but arrogant and dismissive. He might have started to turn around recently, but he had never been kind to Sasha.

But I didn't want him dead, Sasha reminded herself.

No, but I can't mourn him as I will mourn Swift.

When it came to Rose, Sasha just felt sorry. Rose did not want to be there, and it was sad to her that Rose had to suffer.

Rose coming here was like me going with the yeomen, Sasha thought. *Something you didn't have control over.*

Fatigue set in, and Sasha leaned against Mako again. Sleep came to them all, even though it was only midafternoon.

Chapter 16

The elite of the Kingdom of North Mississippi lived north of the castles, in what King Xavier called the Gold Hills. From large majestic mansions that rivals the king's estates to small townhomes rented for short periods of time, everyone who wanted influence had some presence there.

And among the townhomes and mansions, hidden from view by tall walls and even taller trees, was a gold building. No sign or coat of arms decorates its entrance, the guardsmen plain clothes.

The Golden Hotel, the preeminent brothel of North Mississippi.

Miklos sat in an alcove on the second floor, overlooking the main hall. Below him, dozens of patrons watched women dancing on stages, while others carried drinks or sold trips to back rooms. From his perch, Miklos was not so harassed: if he wished to, he could send and order for one of the women, without the crowds and the displays.

Some people looked down on brothels, but Miklos could never quite understand why. These places would always exist; at least here, everyone was protected and safe. Driving them underground would only make them more dangerous. As for discretion, well, that was up to the individual patron. Miklos, a lifelong bachelor, cared little who know he visited such places.

Except on days like today, when the visit was not for pleasure.

He arrived an hour early, welcomed by the host personally. Mister Strong kept up personal relationships with all the important patrons, offering refreshments, girls, whatever he could to keep people happy, with the expectation that they would in turn keep him in business.

Miklos had explained what he wanted, and Mister Strong was happy to comply. Miklos was left in his alcove, approached only to refresh his drink, waiting for his guest to arrive and hoping he would not be too late.

In fact, the guest arrived early, escorted to one of the second-floor rooms by an exotically dressed hostess. It was obviously the man's first time at the Golden Hotel, from the look on his face as he entered the hall, but he had a mind to keep himself from being overwhelmed. He was not here for pleasure, and he made a point of remembering that despite all the distractions.

Miklos' estimation of his guest rose again.

Soon the hostess approached him. 'Colonel,' she said with a courtesy, 'your guest has been escorted to the room and provided a drink.'

'Good,' Miklos said, handing her a coin. 'We are not to be disturbed.'

She nodded, turning to follow. Once the door was closed, she would string a cord across the door, a signal to keep out. Barring the sounds of murder, the cord would be respected.

The man inside the room stood as Miklos entered. His military bearing was unmistakable, despite his civilian clothes.

'Captain Lewis,' Miklos said in greeting.

'I am no longer an officer in His Majesty's Royal Army,' Lewis said. 'I am appropriately addressed as Mister Lewis.'

'Some titles go beyond the politics of service, Captain,' Miklos said. 'You may not know who I am –.'

'Colonel of Regiment Sir Rika Miklos, Military Attaché to the Royal Embassy,' Lewis said. 'I've seen you on the stand when we march for the king during the Coronation Day Parade.'

Miklos nodded. 'Then you know why I am here.'

'I would assume it has something to do with my recent battle with the Renaissance Army.'

'Correct,' Miklos said as he sat down.

'I also assume that the official responses have been less than satisfactory.'

'I would go as far as to say they have less than minimally adequate,' Miklos said. 'So, I'm coming to the source.'

'I could use the coin,' Lewis said. While he had avoided prison for the murder of a yeoman lieutenant, he had not avoided being removed from service. However honorable his fight, the Royal Army was working to erase him from its memory.

'Tell me everything.'

For an hour they spoke, discussing the events, Miklos interrupting only for questions. He wanted the facts first, before he discussed the meaning. Lewis did not mind.

When done, Miklos looked at the captain. 'The official record is that the Renaissance Army lost more than a hundred men and women killed in the battle.'

'That's not true,' Lewis said. 'I was at the battle, and I watched the burials.

They lost at most twenty dead. Thirty or so wounded.'

'They lost fewer troops than the king did?' Miklos asked. He wanted to be sure.

Lewis shrugged. 'Yes. The yeomen and the inspectorate troops were a large part of that number, but even against my soldiers the RAM fought well.'

Miklos pondered this. 'What are your thoughts on the Renaissance Army, Captain?'

'If I may speak freely?'

'Of course.'

'I'm impressed with them,' Lewis said. 'Their forces are made up of mostly teenagers and those in their twenties, half of whom are young women. They're trained simply, but thoroughly, for their posts. When those regiments held the creek bed, they did so quite tenaciously. The assault forces who blasted through the prison camp defenses did so thoroughly and quickly. The provost kept the peace afterwards, and they certainly put a lot of personnel into their medical units.'

'And the officers?'

'Diverse, but competent. And, largely female.'

'Really?' Miklos asked. The Imperial Forces had some women in staff and medical positions, but none in combat, and certainly not as combat officers.

Lewis nodded. 'I was surprised as well, but the first two I met were women. Officer Mary, the regimental surgeon for their Third Field Regiment. She's a warrant officer of some sort, maybe twenty years of age, but both my own medics and the yeomen doctor were impressed with her abilities. Her commander, Lieutenant Colonel Snow, was stern but fair. A very tough woman to fight. I met her before and after battle, and there is no doubt in my mind if I could have let the civilians go like she asked, she would have let me go.'

'And the others?'

'Like I said before, they spend a lot of their personnel on their medical units. We have one enlisted medical staff for every thirty soldiers, and one surgeon for every three hundred, but of the four hundred or so assembled at the camp, a quarter of them were medical staff, including half a dozen officers. Their provost officer was firm and respectful. They could have shot all of us, or even all the yeomen or troopers, but they didn't. They held quick but decent trials, found only four of the five guilty, and executed them. No drawn-out torture, just efficiency.'

'And the Dawson?'

Lewis sighed and looked down at his feet. 'I'll be honest, Colonel, it never sat right with me, what happened to his family. Yes, my family were subjects of the Republic, and we were as angry about the excesses of the citizens as much as anyone else, but a whole family!'

'I'm not ....'

Lewis cut him off. 'I know why it happened, and I don't have to like it, Colonel, but that's not the point. A Dawson who survived the annihilation of his family has many personal reasons to want to destroy the Empire, the Kingdom of North Mississippi, and every soldier, yeomen and trooper at that camp, but he DIDN'T!'

Lewis paused, realizing he was worked up. He sat back and took a breath. 'Revenge is not his goal, Colonel. He was not all fire and death; he's working towards something. Did you hear about his debate with the Mayor of Pelican Point?'

Miklos nodded. 'I did.'

'It doesn't sound like someone who is out for revenge. It sounds like a man who is building something, not like a man who is tearing something down.'

Miklos looked at Lewis and finally nodded. 'I agree, Captain. He's got something planned out, and no one in the Royal Army is asking any questions.'

'I'm very much aware of that, Colonel,' Lewis sighed.

'What are your plans now?' Miklos asked.

Lewis shrugged. 'Unlikely I'd find work to the south, their kings being related to King Xavier. Nor with the Quebecois. Maybe in Michigan or one of the Dakota cities.'

Miklos pulled a purse out of his pocket. 'Please keep in correspondence. I may have further questions, and I'd like to know how to get a hold of you.' Then he pulled a red token and left it on the purse.

'What's that?' Lewis asked.

'It's a token for a girl,' Miklos said. 'You could probably use the release.'

Lewis looked down, took the purse, and left the token on the table. 'No offense, Colonel, but it's not my style.'

'No offense taken,' Miklos said. They exchanged salutes, and Lewis was gone.

Miklos left the room, standing at the railing looking over the main floor.

146

There had been a shift change while he was with Lewis, and a new round of women were dancing. One caught his eye: a small Asian woman in a green costume. He felt the red coin in his pocket.

No reason to waste.

He motioned to one of the hostesses, who came over. 'Yes, Colonel?'

'That dancer in the green,' he said, handing over the red coin.

'Ten minutes?'

'And a bottle of whiskey, with the appropriate accoutrements.'

She nodded. Mister Strong had trained his hostesses well. 'Of course, Colonel.'

Miklos smiled to himself and returned to his room. He had a lot to think over, but first he needed a break.

Chapter 17

Three weeks after twelve cadets marched out of Athens, eight returned in the back of a wagon. Only Hero and Elector looked normal, as if nothing had happened at Sparta. Candle's nose and face were still shades of purple. Sasha had her wrist cast, and Roland's arm was in a sling. Mako was constantly wincing from his ribs. Patch had a cast on her ankle and her arm in a sling. Cardinal looked exhausted; while she was physically fine, Sasha knew the youngest cadet was having trouble sleeping.

The explosion killed eleven people, all told. What happened was unknown, any evidence of the accident was lost within the magazine and the four men and women who died inside it. Unable to learn any lessons from the wreckage, the leadership ordered magazines to be removed to remote locations and forbade individuals from loitering in the area. If another magazine did explode, fewer people were going to die.

The cart let them off in front of their barracks. They took their gear and went inside.

Someone had removed two of the cots, those for the two lost at Sparta. Blaze and Swift and nine other men and women had been formally buried under the flags and pomp of Sparta's color guard. In a final act, the two had been commissioned and buried as Second Lieutenants.

The other two were now at Holiday, moving from civilian to military hospital. Penn's leg was gone, and he had taken a fever. Rose had recovered after a three-day coma. Sasha thought she was all right, but the doctors had other worries and said they were keeping her for some time. No one pulled rank on the doctors, and Rose remained in their care.

The accident had done more than reduce the cadets by a third. It cast a shadow over the rest of their time at Sparta. Only a few of the cadets could take part in all the instructions, the rest having some injury that kept them from running or shooting. Sasha could run and partake in the squad outings Del Oso took them on, but her arm kept her from strength exercises, obstacle courses and weapons training.

It had become something of a strain for the cadets. There was just over a week before their Common Phase was done, and several of them could not physically complete the tests that they had been told they must pass to continue.

'Is this how the Templar Project ends?' Patch asked one evening. The cadets had taken their dinner and been surprised to find fresh fruit available. They sat around an unlit fire pit, sharing the fruit and talking.

'Ends? How?' Hero looked over.

'Too many cadets injured to continue,' Patch said. 'Will they keep the project going if only three pass?'

Cardinal shifted as if to say something but said nothing.

Mako spoke next, peeling an orange. 'Why wouldn't they continue?' he responded. 'The need for officers is great.'

'And those of us who don't make it,' Roland asked. 'What happens to us?'

'We get warrants, probably,' Elector said. He too had become quieter since the accident, and Sasha was not sure it was all about Blaze. The two had been friends, of a sort, and Elector had teared up at the funeral, but his melancholy looked to be deeper than that.

'A warrant would not be so bad,' Mako declared.

'No,' Sasha agreed, half-heartedly. She did not want to go back to Snow and the Third Regiment for a warrant. That was failure.

'I would prefer to go on,' Candle declared. 'I want to get to the part that will stretch my mind.'

'Do you?' Sasha asked, picking at a bunch of grapes. Candle's energetic exuberance had barely dimmed since the accident, and it had become harder and harder for Sasha to stay calm around her. Horrible things had happened, and she kept smiling.

'Of course,' Candle said. 'That is why we're here, right? One of the reasons we were chosen was our desire to learn more.'

'Some more than others,' Sasha said, realizing a second too late she was speaking out loud.

'What does that mean?' Candle asked. The rest of the cadets had gone quiet at Candle's tone.

Sasha sighed. 'I mean, Candle, you don't spend a lot of time in the library, do you? When we have free time, you're either with the armory sergeants or lazily milling about Athens.'

'What do you care?' Candle asked, her smile fading a little bit. 'How I spend my time is up to me.'

'Because you don't seem to care, Candle,' Sasha snapped. 'You giggle and flirt, do just enough to get along without pushing yourself. Some of us take this seriously enough to apply ourselves, and you just float along.'

'You think I don't take this seriously because I flirt?' Candle asked. She obviously found the idea ridiculous, which just made Sasha angrier.

'You don't! We're in the middle of a great uprising, Candle. People are fighting and dying. And what are you doing? Learning to fight? To lead? No, you spend your time with the boys. If you're not careful, you'll end up a mother, and how useful will you as a cadet then?'

Sasha glared at Candle and saw a snap in the woman's eyes. Somehow, Sasha had just crossed a line with Candle.

Candle looked coolly at Sasha; her smile gone. 'I take this seriously, Cadet Scholar, and you speak of things you do not understand.'

'No, I take this seriously. Mako and Elector and I, who spend our time bettering our minds in the library. Do you know what I've done, Candle, for this army already? I've killed.'

'And killing makes you important?' Candle asked.

'Killing makes me dedicated,' Sasha said. She looked at the grapes in her hand. 'I've killed seven men,' she said, pulling seven grapes off the bunch. 'So, I get seven grapes.'

'I can only have grapes for the number of people I've killed?' Candle asked. She looked angrily at Sasha. Furious, even.

'Yes,' Sasha said.

'How many grapes are left?' Candle asked.

'Fourteen,' Patch said.

Candle stood and walked over to Sasha. She reached out and took the bunch from Sasha's hand.

'I can settle for only fourteen,' Candle said, her eyes burning into Sasha's. Burning with a hatred and a hurt that Sasha had never seen before.

'Now, hold on,' Sasha said, but was interrupted.

'Cadet Scholar,' Elector said. 'You set the rule. You cannot change it now that you realized you spoke too soon.'

Sasha looked at Candle, the woman's height giving her an imposing demeanor this close.

'You may revel in death,' Candle said, 'but that is your sin, not mine.' She turned to move back to her seat, ignoring Sasha as she plucked the grapes and ate them, one by one.

Sasha stood and turned and walked from the circle. No one made any effort to stop her as she disappeared into the woods.

She walked far enough into the woods she could no longer see the field and started pacing. Conflicting emotions ran through her head: anger, sadness, regret.

'What am I doing?' she asked herself. She suddenly felt very weak and sat down against a tree. It was still light enough she could see the sky through the canopy and looked up as if to see an answer above her. She started to tear up, tears turning into sobs.

What am I doing? She asked herself again. She rested her head in her hands and cried.

The Templar Project was not shaping up the way she thought it would. Nor, if she was honest with herself, was Cadet Scholar.

Cadet Scholar was not a scholar. Sasha was not sure she was even a good officer. Sasha knew she bore some of the blame for their exile to Sparta, even as she looked down on Hero and Candle for their flaws.

You forgot they were chosen by their own officers, Sasha told herself. You forgot the generals spoke with them same as they did to you. They earned their positions, same as you. You and they are in the same position. You forgot that, didn't you?

Sasha looked up and started in surprise. Mako was sitting across from her.

'What are you doing here?' she asked, wiping tears from her eyes.

'I wanted to see which path you were going to head down,' Mako said, 'and to see if I could influence you down the right way.'

Sasha looked at him. 'Why did I do that?'

'You're scared.'

'Scared?' Sasha asked.

'Scared. Scared of going back without a commission. Probably scared of losing your renaissance name. I've been with the movement long enough to know the importance officers attach to their renaissance names. To keep Scholar, you must be under a lot of pressure to prove you are one.'

'That's true,' Sasha admitted.

'That must be a lot to deal with. Being afraid you're going to go back to

Third Field Regiment without your name.'

'Yes,' Sasha admitted again, then paused. 'Wait, what?'

'The Scholar of Third Regiment,' Mako said. 'Unless I'm mistaken, that's you. Sasha Small.'

Sasha stared at him in surprise. 'How did you know that?'

'The naval and marine units are under the auspices of the Engineer Group. Marines and Pioneers both fought at the prison camp and came back with stories. You mentioned to Patch you were at the prison camp. Not too hard to figure out.'

Sasha laughed. 'Mako,' she said, 'you're right. I am worried about it. Am I too late?'

'To keep the name Scholar? I have no idea. To be a good cadet?' Mako shrugged. 'No, never too late. Remember, we're all in this together, Scholar. We've all made promises to people, all came here with expectations. If you need to spend your free time as well as your research time in the library, no one is going to think any less of you, any more than we would if Roland went out for shooting practice or Patch went for another run. We'll support you, as well as we can. But we need you to support us in return.'

'We're all in this together,' Sasha repeated. 'I feel bad about what I said to Candle.'

'Good,' Mako said.

There was a length of quiet between them. 'How many?' Sasha asked. 'How many of the cadets have seen combat?'

'Of the twelve who started, only two had not seen combat or fighting at all. Penn and Patch. Candle and Hero have been in fights, but not combat. Elector, Rose and Cardinal have seen combat, in that they watched a fight happen, but were not directly involved. That leaves you and me, Blaze, Roland and Swift as the true combat veterans.'

Sasha thought about the names, then laughed to herself.

'What is it?' Mako asked.

'The whole time I was with Third Field Regiment, I didn't think much about what else was going on,' Sasha admitted. 'I knew there was fighting in Walker County, but I didn't pay too much attention to it. There are three other field regiments out there, each fighting their own war.'

'They are,' Mako said. then he leaned forward. 'Do you know where the Second Field Regiment is?'

Sasha shook her head. 'No, why?'

'No one does. No one seems to go to it, if it does exist.'

'Did they skip it?' Sasha asked.

'Maybe,' Mako shrugged. 'Just curious.'

Night was falling in earnest now. 'We should get back,' Sasha said. They stood to walk back to their cabin.

'Should I apologize to Candle?' Sasha asked.

'Eventually, but not tonight.'

'I crossed a line with her tonight. Do you know what it was?'

'I do,' Mako said. 'It's not my story to tell, but let's just say I would stay away from her for a while.'

Sasha nodded. 'And Elector?'

'That one I don't know,' Mako said, 'although I have some guesses. All I can do is offer an encouraging word and pray to God for everyone to find their way.'

'I can't trust God to find my way for me,' Sasha said. 'God almost sent me the yeomen.'

'Did He send the yeomen?' Mako asked. 'Or did He send you the Renaissance?'

Sasha did not have an answer to that.

***

Sasha spent the next few days largely being quiet. Except for Mako, whose attention she was starting to accept as the beginning of friendship, and Hero, whose attention she still did not want, the other cadets were ignoring her. Sasha did not push it. Instead, she read, or she practiced writing with her cast-burdened hand.

On Saturday that changed.

Sasha was in the library, reading a chapter from *the War of Iron Wills*, the war that unified the Republic of Minnesota, when Patch came in.

'Scholar! Come on, we need you.'

Sasha was surprised that someone other than Mako was speaking to her. 'What?' she asked in confusion.

'It's Elector,' Patch said, turning out the door. 'He's quitting.'

Sasha leapt after Patch, stopping only when the librarian yelled 'Book!' at her. She handed it over and rushed after Patch. It was not hard; Patch was still using a cane and limping on an ankle cast.

'What do you mean quitting?' she asked.

'He wants to tell Del Oso he's quitting. We're trying to talk him down now, but he's pretty insistent.'

'If he doesn't want to be here, should we force him to stay?' Sasha asked.

Patch shrugged. 'I fail to see how that would be better, but I hope we can convince him to stay. I'd hate to see him go.'

Sasha nodded in silent agreement and followed Patch back to the cadets' barracks.

Elector was sitting on his bed, surrounded by the rest of the cadets. They all looked up nervously as the last two returned.

'You're quitting?' Sasha asked.

'I don't want to fight,' Elector said.

'If this is because Blaze –,' Candle started, but Elector cut her off.

'No, Candle. It's not about Blaze. He was my friend, yes, as light a friend as one can have. We had common experiences, and I did not wish him ill, but I don't mourn him like some of you mourn Swift.'

'Then what?' Sasha asked.

'I am not a soldier,' Elector said. 'I do not want to be a soldier, to fight and kill. I accept that someone will have to, but I do not want it to be me. So, I'm quitting the Templars and requesting a transfer to the Medical Group.'

'You want to be a doctor?' Hero asked dismissively. 'Where's the glory in that?'

'Our regimental surgeon is one of the best women I know,' Sasha said hotly.

'And doctors helped us after the accident,' Candle snapped as well.

At least we're both annoyed by Hero, Sasha thought. Despite his efforts at Sparta, Sasha still could not see Hero as trustworthy. She still caught him leering at the women from time to time.

'There's a lot of good work to do there,' Elector said in his own defense. 'And I'd rather be there than learning to fight.'

A throat cleared at the doorway. Del Oso stood there, looking at the
154

assembled cadets. He was holding a stack of papers, which disappeared behind his back as he took his stance.

'What is this?' he asked.

The cadets looked rather sheepish, none of them wanting to say anything. Then Elector stood.

'Sergeant Major, I respectfully request permission to withdraw from the Templar Project.'

'Do you?' Del Oso asked, stepping forward. 'Why?'

'I do not wish to be an infantry officer in the Renaissance Army,' Elector said. 'I would like to submit a request to transfer to the Medical Group and learn from Colonel Aristotle.'

Del Oso looked at Elector levelly. 'That is a bold request, Cadet,' he said. 'Are you sure you've thought this through?'

'I have,' Elector said. 'I want to heal people, not hurt them. Medical training is at Holiday, so I need to go there. I can't do that and be part of the Templar Project. So, I need to leave, and I don't think you're going to change my mind.'

'Oh, ye of little faith,' Del Oso said, smirking as if he had a joke in mind. He reached into his breast pocket and pulled out a folded letter, holding it out to Elector.

'What is that?' Elector asked, hesitant to take the paper.

'It is a letter from Colonel Aristotle. I wrote to him and asked him if he would be willing to sponsor and educate a cadet at Athens. That letter confirms that any cadet who wishes to become a part of the medical group may do so, and Aristotle will figure out a way to make it work.'

'What?' Elector cried, grasping for the letter. He unfolded it and read quickly. Then he looked at Del Oso. 'You knew?'

'I've been doing this for decades, son,' Del Oso said. 'You think I can't recognize a man whose heart isn't in the fight? I know the books you read, and I saw you save lives at the explosion. You're a doctor, Elector, no question.'

Elector looked like he might cry. All the effort he had put in to preparing himself for this confrontation, to discover he had allies he never knew he had.

'What about . . . ,' he paused, unsure of how to continue his question.

'Your sponsor?' Del Oso finished. Elector nodded. 'That is not your issue to deal with, Cadet. Aristotle and Carpenter will deal with that. And if necessary, the generals will get involved.'

Elector looked relieved. Sasha wondered who his sponsor was.

'While I have you all here,' Del Oso said, 'I need to speak with you, so gather around.'

The cadets all shifted so he became the focus of attention.

'I know some of you have been worried about passing the Common Phase of the training. The accident certainly took its toll on all of us, removing three cadets outright.'

'Penn's not a cadet anymore?' Roland asked.

Del Oso shook his head. 'No, he's not. He's lost a leg; he can't participate in physical training.'

Most of the cadets looked upset at that. Sasha certainly sputtered some response, but Elector got there first.

'He's still got a good mind.'

'He does, and the RAM will use it. But he's not a cadet, not anymore.'

Before any other protests came, Del Oso continued. 'For those who remain, many of you are still injured. If we tested you now, not only would you fail, but we would set back your recovery, and the generals refuse to do either.

'Luckily, the generals are not stupid, nor do they want to punish you for something that was not your fault. I've been in discussion with Colonel Carpenter, and with the generals, and we've come to a reasonable compromise that will allow all of you to continue.'

Sasha breathed a sigh of relief. She was not the only one.

'The official end of the Common Phase is next Friday, six days from today. The testing was to take up the three days ahead of that. What we will do instead is test you only on the classroom topics. Rank insignia, general orders, and such. Those will decide a pass or fail.

'For the rest, you will be tested, but not right now. During the next phase, which will last into next year, you are expected to meet and maintain certain standards. Marksmanship, strength, endurance; you will need   to maintain these, with a final test coming before the third part of training.

'During the second part, I will be holding weekly outings for marksmanship, endurance runs, and such training as we've already been doing. If you wish to conduct your own exercises, you may do so, but you are responsible for keeping yourself in shape. Monthly tests will be conducted, and it is no one's fault is you fail but your own, understood?'

The cadets all nodded.

'Good, now one last thing.' He revealed the stack of papers again. 'As Cadet Elector just showed us, you have to want to be a part of this program. Given the accident that claimed the lives of two of your number and two more have not yet returned, I would not be surprised if each of you has questioned your motives for being here. Not everyone has experience with that kind of loss.

'As such, your sponsors were each contacted, and each has provided several letters from them as well as from friends of yours from your previous life. Read them and challenge yourself. I don't want you going through this because you feel you must. Really ask yourself why you are here.'

He paused, as if inviting comment. Then he distributed the papers.

'While I have you here,' he said, handing out the papers. 'I should let you know that there will be one more change starting Monday. There will now be a position, as Cadet Captain. This is a rotating position, changing every Sunday. The cadet captain will be responsible for handling the cadet chores, training schedules, and such. I will be helping you, but this is a chance to feel at least some semblance of command in your training. Understood?' The cadets all nodded. 'Great. Then get to reading.'

Some of the cadets went to their beds to read, others stepped out to find their own place. Sasha went to the library, still empty save for the librarian, and sat down, finding several small pages.

The first was from Colonel Snow.

> *Sasha,*
>
> *I heard about the loss of your friends. I'm sorry you had to go through that again, but it is part of our life as soldiers. I hope you can understand that and continue in your studies.*
>
> *The fact is we need you. As we advance our cause in Brainerd County, I foresee challenges coming down the road. We must be prepared to attack and take towns and cities, possibly even fortified positions. Someday we will need to deal with garrisons of army regulars. All challenges I've asked Caesar to prepare you to face.*
>
> *I've also written to several other friends in Walker County, asking them to provide help if asked. By now you have met Lily; you can trust her. Do not be afraid to ask.*
>
> *Be strong, Sasha.*
>
> *LT COL Snow, 3rd MN FLD RGT*

Sasha smiled at the note, thankful for the words of support from her colonel. She opened the next. The handwriting was not as neat or measured as Snow's.

> *Sasha,*
>
> *I hope you're having a good time in Walker. I've had a devil of a time finding a decent corporal to replace you. We had a firefight with some yeomen trying to find a route up to Arrowhead and your replacement forgot what he was supposed to be doing. Master Sergeant is doing the best he can, but it's not enough.*
>
> *Don't get too lost in your books. When you get down here, we're going to have to work out how to take the towns away from the count. It's going to be hard work, exactly the kind of fighting I'll need my bobcat for.*
>
> *We need you, and soon. Snow threatened me with a warrant yesterday. I'd rather be a staff sergeant writing notes for all eternity than that. You need to come back an officer before they make me one!*
>
> *SGT Winnie*

Sasha laughed at Winnie's note. She could not imagine her friend as an officer; she was a good fighter, but she was more suited to executing the fight than planning one.

The last note she opened had Mary's well-practiced handwriting.

> *Sasha,*
>
> *I understand you are about to begin the academic portion of your training. I remember my first day in the medical school, being nervous about the classroom settings. We were all more bookish than the soldiers were, less physically capable, but united in our desire to learn. From the awkwardness of the basic training, where we were mixed in with the other types of trainees, it felt nice to be amongst friends.*
>
> *I hope you are feeling that with your companions. You're all cadets, all there for the same reason. I'm sure you'll be the thickest of siblings by the end of the training, much as I was with some of my fellow medics. Embrace it. Cherish it.*
>
> *Sasha frowned, and wondered what Mary would think of her current isolation. She continued to read.*
>
> *Regardless of the manner of your return, we all look forward to it. You've already made many of us proud, from the colonel to the*

militia. Even the civilians know you're somewhere special. One of them, the teacher (who apparently was quite impressed with the five minutes he spent with you) holds you up as an example to his students of the importance of learning, and how it can open doors. He has more children in his school than he does chairs.

I'm sorry, I don't mean to ramble. I miss my friend, and even if I know I won't see you for many more months, I do look forward to getting a letter in response, if and when you can do that.

Sincerely,

Mary, Regimental Surgeon

Sasha sat back, looking at the three letters laid out on the table. She had to repair her relationships with the other cadets, she knew that. She had to ask for help when she needed it. She needed to go back to Third Regiment ready to help them in what they needed.

She took a deep breath. Then she folded the letters and put them in her pocket.

Exiting the library, she took the paths towards the administration buildings. She looked about, worried she was committing some crime; this was where the instructors came to get away from the cadets and trainees. The only time Sasha had been there before was when Carpenter sentenced the cadets to Sparta. Sasha knew she was allowed to be here, so long as she had a good reason, but it still worried her.

She walked to a senior noncom barracks and knocked on the door. A woman, one of the older ones who led training runs, opened.

'Who are you looking for?' she asked.

'Sergeant Major Del Oso, sergeant.'

The woman disappeared, and a moment later Del Oso came through the door.

'Don't tell me you want to quit,' he said. 'I don't have any special letters for you.'

'No, Sergeant Major, but I wanted to ask if we can take extra training during the next section.'

'Extra training? I don't know that you'll have much time for it.'

'Right, but . . . ,' she paused, trying to explain herself. 'I need to know how to take a town.'

'What?' Del Oso asked.

'The letters from my regiment, two of them mentioned having to take towns. Almost no one in the regiment has any training in taking a town, so I want to learn how.'

Del Oso rubbed his chin as he thought. 'I might be able to help you,' he said. 'But it'll be on weekends. And I'll have to clear it with the generals first.'

'If you can help me, I would be indebted,' Sasha said.

'I'll look into it, but for now, you need to focus on getting into the academic life. Tomorrow is not going to be like anything you've done before.'

'Don't worry about me, Sergeant Major,' Sasha said with a grin. 'I'm not nervous.'

Chapter 18

Despite Sasha's boast, she was nervous. She made it through the tests easily enough. She doubted any of the cadets had difficulties, except maybe Hero, and all received passing marks. It was the next phase of training that worried her.

The last Sunday night, Sasha was unable to sleep. She stared up at the dark ceiling, listening to other cadets toss and turn in their own cots. When sleep finally came, it was light and filled with dreams of books written in gibberish and General Caesar renaming her Cadet Unworthy.

When the 5 a.m. bell went off, several of the cadets got out of bed and started dressing. Only five of them could run, while the rest spent their time doing lighter exercises.

They returned, cleaned and dressed, and went to get their breakfast in almost total silence. Candle, as cadet captain, was giving them commands, but in a soft voice. No one mentioned it. Afterwards they went back to their room and waited in silence.

Del Oso entered shortly after the 7 a.m. bell. 'Nervous?' he asked. No one responded. 'Deep breaths. One thing as a time. You've gone through classes with Madam Moreau, so you have the basics down. Just take them one day at a time.'

'We should get going,' Candle said. The cadets formed up and she led them out the front door. Del Oso told each of them good luck on their way out.

Candle led them to the nearby classroom. They entered, finding their seats and continued waiting. Candle, as captain, took the seat up front and to the left. The rest were at the cadet's choice. Sasha took the other front desk, next to Candle and in front of everyone.

Roland glanced about.

> *'The cadets gathered in the room, where they were told to wait.*
> *They nervously prepared for those who would decide their fate.'*

'Quiet, Roland,' Cardinal said.

Roland's response was cut off as Candle called the room to attention. Lily had entered through the teacher's door, followed by a pair of staff sergeants, each carrying a stack of satchels.

'Good morning, cadets,' she said. The sergeants moved around her, handing each of the cadets one satchel. 'I hope you are ready for this. I'm sure each of you can do well, but success will not be easy.

'Right now, you are being given your cadet satchel. Inside you will find a number of items you will need during your education. Several notebooks and loose papers; a fountain pen; pencils of various colors; some measuring instruments; and a pair of leather folders. These are yours for the next five months. Some of these items are difficult to come by, so you will take proper care of them. Understood?'

The cadets chorused in agreement.

'Good. Also, so you are aware, this classroom is now officially the Templar classroom. It is yours. Treat it with the same respect you do your barracks. Otherwise, you will lose privileges.'

She paused as the door opened again. Candle called the cadets to attention as Caesar entered the room. He waved them down.

'Good morning, cadets of the Templar Project,' he said. 'This is the first day of your advanced instruction period. Right now, I am going to give you an overview of what you can expect over the next twenty-two weeks.'

He paused. As before, he looked uncomfortable speaking in front of a group. Instead of giving in, he soldiered on.

'Your weekday mornings will be shared classes on subjects that all Templars should know, two classes each day. Monday, Wednesday and Friday, your instructions will be in history and politics. On Tuesday and Thursday, your instructions are in rhetoric and ethics. The procedures in each class will be different. Ethics will involve more back and forth discussions, while history will require more reading and memorization. Take each one as you can.

'After lunch, your instructions will be personal, decided on by your mentor officer. In some cases, you will be taking instructions with other cadets; in other cases, you will be on your own. It is up to you to meet your mentor's requirements.

'Weekends will be lighter but will not be entirely free. Some of you have requested special training that will likely happen on weekends. Presentations, speeches, special instructions will also occur largely on weekends. Where we can, these will take place on Saturday instead of Sunday.'

Caesar had gained some confidence now, and his voice had levelled off. He began to pace while he spoke to the cadets. 'Of the twenty-two weeks, we have eighteen weeks of classes prepared. The other four weeks will be used for class breaks, or to take advantage of opportunities that may present themselves. For

162

example, I expect you will spend at least one of those weeks with the Civil Council of the Liberated Counties. Another you may spend observing the siege of Walker. It is entirely dependent on the situation that develops over the course of the winter.'

He looked out over the cadets. 'Any questions?'

No one said anything.

'Very well,' Caesar said. 'Then let us begin. This week will be largely introductory, a chance to get back into the classroom setting after your sojourn to Sparta. As a rule, if it goes on the chalkboard, you should write it down. For now, take out your satchels and spread the contents across the table.'

They did so. Sasha could not help but smile at the notebooks and pencils, the wooden box containing a fountain pen and the small folder of rulers and measuring tools.

'You each should have five notebooks, one for each of the four shared classes and one for your individual instructions. The sheaf of loose papers is for mapping or drawing you may need to do. Colored pencils and measuring tools are for the same. I would suggest writing in pencil to begin with, and saving pen for formal projects, but it is up to you how to proceed.

'Now, choose one of your notebooks and write "History" on the front with your pen. That is now your history notebook. Use that for notes in this class. Once you are done, open it, and let us begin.'

Caesar spent the rest of his time discussing an overview of the history lessons. By the end of his two hours, he had become very animated, excitedly discussing the flow of history and what they would be learning. At one point he stopped and frowned. 'It is a shame,' he said. 'We are focusing on European and American history, and primarily on political, cultural and military history of those regions. We could spend years discussing just one nation, or one aspect of a nation, or other cultures. It is a shame we will not get to them, but I encourage you, if you have free time, to read about them.'

The class ended with the cadets looking at a two-page outline of history as they would cover over their course. Sasha looked it over. She was excited to learn about the historical Renaissance, and about the Age of Technology. The week on World War II she was less excited to hear about, as the thought of a whole world at war was made her sad.

There was a brief respite between their morning instructions, then they assembled back in their classroom. Again, Candle called them to attention as the teacher's door opened. This time, General Prince came in.

Sasha had not seen the general since she had breakfasted with him and Caesar

163

back with Third Regiment. He looked as handsome and confident as ever, smiling at the cadets as waved them back into their seats. She thought she saw his smile widen when he looked over her, but she was not sure.

'Cadets of the Templar Project,' Prince said. 'Congratulations. I am so pleased that you have all worked hard to make it this far, and I'm sorry for the loss of two of your friends at Sparta. I'm sure they would have passed to the second section as well. You can take at least some reassurance that Penn is doing well, and plans to continue working within the Renaissance Army, even if he cannot continue as a Templar.'

Prince sighed. 'I'll be honest,' he continued, 'I'm a little embarrassed. When I approved the Templar Project, I did not expect that my first visit would come two months after the beginning. I expected to be here more often. For that, I apologize. I will be here more during the winter months, but as a general, my schedule is not always my own.'

He smiled again. Sasha wanted to tell him the cadets forgave him, but now was not the time.

'So,' Prince said, 'why am I here today? Well, cadets, I'm here to begin your instruction on politics. What does that mean? It means I need you, as cadets, to understand a fundamental principal that I take as a commandment. The military is not meant to rule.

'Now, your first thought might be to look at the Liberated Counties and think, "But, General, you rule here!" And you're not wrong, but I see that rule as a temporary evil, and one I want to be rid of as soon as possible. I have established the Civil Council as the beginnings of government, one that will eventually take over the Liberated Counties and allow me to focus on the war. That not only requires civilians ready to lead, but a military that will let them.

'And that brings me back to this instruction. The fact is, as military officers in a fledgling movement like the Renaissance Army, you will find yourselves in situations where you can impact the development of politics in your area. I want you to be ready to understand that influence, and how best to avoid abusing it.

'In this class, you will learn about branches of government. We will discuss rights and authority. We will go over the various forms that government can take. While I am committed to the principles of democracy, I want you to understand its opposites and its dangers. When you are in the world, commissioned and working, I want you spreading that knowledge. Knowledge is power and we want everyone to be powerful.

'Now, obviously, I am not going to be here for all your instructions, but I have gone over my expectations with a suitable proxy. He understands what

164

to do, and he will be working towards the same goal, albeit with coarser language.'

He smiled again. 'Ready to get to work?'

The cadets nodded. A second notebook from each was labeled "Politics", and notes began. Again, it was a few pages of overview, writing down words to remember and diagrams of influence. Each of these would be discussed in depth, they were told.

During lunch the cadets were discussing their instructors. 'Was Caesar nervous?' Hero asked. 'Why would he be nervous?'

'Speaking in public can be difficult,' Candle said.

'We're not in public, though,' Hero responded.

'We're a group of people all paying attention to him,' Cardinal said. 'It's the same thing.'

'Prince didn't have that problem,' Hero said. 'It's obvious why he's in charge.'

'Prince is great at public speaking,' Sasha said. 'I saw him debating a mayor who had betrayed the Renaissance Army, in front of townsfolk and soldiers alike. He never once looked embarrassed or nervous about it.'

'Prince is a Dawson,' Roland said, 'he was brought up from birth to be a leader.'

'But where has he been for sixteen years?' Mako asked. The cadets all looked at the usually silent Mako, who shrugged. 'I just wonder, if he was in hiding for sixteen years, where was he staying, that he could develop the Renaissance Army in secret?'

'The Dakotas?' Roland suggested.

'The Archives?' Sasha said.

'Western Wisconsin?' Elector replied.

'Hey, Patch?' Cardinal asked the other silent cadet. 'What are you thinking about?'

Patch, staring off into space, glanced quickly at the young girl. 'I hope we get to draw,' she said, 'though I'd love to paint at some point. Maybe there will be a painting class?'

The cadets all looked at her, then laughed. 'Well,' Elector finally said. 'Anything's possible.'

***

Lunch finished, and Candle sent them all to meet with their mentors. Sasha was directed to the library. She approached, pondering who it might be.

Prince? she hoped. But he might be too busy to come train me. Maybe *Caesar, or Lily, if I'm trying to keep the name Scholar. Fox? Someone new? Who?*

She was disappointed to see no Olympians outside the library. Not Prince or Caesar, then. She hoped it would be Lily or Fox, if it was not to be a general. Then she opened the door and found herself staring at General Caesar sitting before the fireplace.

Sasha concealed her excitement. *My mentor is a general!* Not Prince, true, but that did not worry her. Caesar, after all, was the one who would decide if she kept her name. Perhaps it was best that he was her mentor.

Sasha walked to stand before Caesar. 'Sir,' she said, coming to attention. Caesar nodded, gesturing for her to sit at the chair across from him. There was a moment of silence, one Sasha felt was too awkward to let go.

'It's a shame more people don't come here,' she finally said.

'It is,' Caesar looked around, disappointment on his face. 'I am hoping to change that, but I cannot force people to read. Except, perhaps, for the cadets.'

'You won't have to force me to come here,' Sasha said. 'I come here most of my free time anyway.'

'So I hear,' Caesar said. 'That is certainly a good sign.'

Sasha nodded, unsure how to continue. If he was supposed to mentor her, he must have a plan. He probably had a dozen of them.

'I must admit,' Caesar finally said, 'that I have been having some problems coming up with a suitable plan for your education. I start with a simple plan, but I find myself getting excited about teaching you, and adding far too much information. So, I have been forced to take a different route. I have been in correspondence with Lieutenant Colonel Snow, and I have her input, but I wanted to get input from you as well.'

'From me?' Sasha asked in surprise.

'Yes,' Caesar nodded. 'Colonel Snow's message sponsoring you for this program specifically mentioned sharpening your mind. I can do that, but into what sort of instrument? My initial thought would be as a Staff Officer, much like Brigadier Lily or Officer Saxon, but then I discovered you asked Sergeant

Major Del Oso for tactical training.'

'It was in response to something Colonel Snow put in her letter,' Sasha said quickly.

'I understand. Then it is good you asked Del Oso. And as we are on the subject, I should warn you that several other cadets have made similar requests. It may be your extra training is all done together, as a team, but I digress.

'My original point, Cadet Scholar, is that I lack guidance on what you want to be. You have some say in it, obviously. Do you see yourself more as a combat commander, operating independently of Colonel Snow's control? Do you see yourself as a staff officer, assisting the colonel with her plans? What did you think you would do when you got here?'

Sasha looked at her hands, fidgeting in her lap, as she pondered his question. 'I don't know,' she said, nervously. She glanced up at Caesar, worried about his response.

Caesar simply nodded. 'Never be afraid to say, "I do not know," Cadet Scholar. Every path to knowledge starts with that sentence. Let me ask this question, then: what do you think Snow was thinking of when she asked General Prince to take you into the Templar Project? Answer simply.'

'I think she wanted me to learn to use my mind,' Sasha said.

'Just for yourself? Do you think she had a plan for you once you returned to Third Regiment?'

Sasha thought for a moment. 'Actually, I think she did.'

'What do you think that plan was?'

'I think she wants me to be her problem solver,' Sasha said. 'I think she wants me to be the officer she relies on to take care of problems she doesn't think she can. Not just to plan and think about them, but to do something about them and take care of them.'

'You believe Colonel Snow wants you to plan and execute operations to assist in Third Regiment's mission?' Caesar asked.

'I do,' Sasha said. 'I think that's why she sent me here, and why she asked me to get training on clearing villages.'

Caesar wrote down some more. 'I understand,' he said, rereading his notes before he looked up at Sasha. 'This is how I envision this working. Every Monday, I will give you an assignment. I may not be here to give it to you in person, but they will come from my hand. You will have all week to prepare, and on the weekend, you will fulfill the assignment. It may include writing a paper on a topic, giving a presentation to officers, or debating a point with another cadet. Understood so far?'

'Understood, sir,' Sasha said.

'Okay. This first week is not meant to break you but ease you into the rhythm of how a classroom environment works. Right now, what I want from you is a paper on what you think you will need to learn to help Third Field Regiment when you get back to them next summer. I want at least three topics that you want to study. You have already elected to learn how to take towns, urban combat, so that should be one of the three. For each topic, I want to know why you think it is important that you learn it.'

Sasha nodded.

'Good. Now, take this.' Caesar pulled a small book from his breast pocket and handed it to her. It was only a few inches tall, with note paper inside, and a small pencil in the binder. Nothing was written in it. 'This is your research book. Any word or topic you come across that you do not know, write it in here and look it up when you can. It is a smaller lined paper than you are used to, so it will look messy at first, but after some practice you should gain the necessary skill.'

'Okay,' Sasha said.

'Now it should be obvious that you will have to balance all of the assignments from all your classes. It may seem daunting, but I suggest you divide your time in the library into hours. You can hear the bell from here, so you should have no problem telling time.'

'Understood,' Sasha said.

Caesar looked at her, and again she thought she could hear his thoughts racing through his head. He stood, waving her down. 'I would get to work right away,' he said. 'I would also find other cadets who might be willing to help you with your writing skills, beyond what you will be instructed in. It is a skill I believe you need to know well, particularly if you are going to keep the name Scholar.'

'Yes, sir,' Sasha said.

'Good. I see you have your satchel,' he paused, as if he wanted to say something more, then shut his mouth and nodded. 'Good luck, cadet.'

He turned and left, leaving Sasha in the library with the sergeant. Sasha took out her books, titled one of the notebooks 'Caesar,' and started listing ideas, trying not to pay attention to how much her handwriting was suddenly annoying her.

***

'That was amazing!' Candle sang as she swung back into the barracks, the last cadet to return. She wore an infectious smile. 'Captain Thunder will be such a wonderful mentor and I can't wait to work with her.'

'Who's Captain Thunder?' Hero asked.

'She commands the Artillery Regiment,' Candle said. 'She's going to teach me! Ballistics, explosives, recoil. Oh, the math we talked about.' Candle giggled again.

Sasha smiled at Candle's enthusiasm along with everyone else. Internally, she was worried. *Did anyone else have a general as a mentor? Will they see me as being arrogant again?*

Candle sat on her bed and looked over at Rose. 'Who did you get?'

'Brigadier Lily,' Rose said.

'Really?' Candle asked in surprise. 'I thought you'd get General Prince, for sure.'

Rose shrugged. 'I don't think General Prince has the time to mentor me. In addition, Lily has much more experience running an army than Prince does.'

'I like Lily,' Patch said.

'Who'd you get?' Candle asked Patch.

'Archimedes,' Patch said. 'He's the head of the Engineering Group. I get to learn how to look at engineering from a military perspective. Should help me back at the Workshop.'

'I got Colonel Birch!' Hero said excitedly.

'Did you?' Elector asked in surprise.

'I did!' Hero grinned.

'I thought you were from a Field Regiment,' Roland said. 'Isn't Birch an infantry officer?'

Hero shrugged. 'Maybe he is, but Wild sent me here to learn proper soldiering, and Birch knows proper soldiering.'

'He does,' Elector agreed. 'He was the company officer Blaze and I were assigned to when we got our warrants. He's a tough task master, but I think you'll learn a lot from him.'

'I know,' Hero nodded. 'I'm going to have to catch up a lot, I know.' He

169

sighed. 'I'll probably need help to do so. Weakest link, you know.'

An uncomfortable silence followed. 'Well,' Elector said, 'I'll help you as much as I can. But I got Aristotle as my mentor and I'm going to be working a lot of catch up on my own. Being a doctor is a lot of science.'

'You'll get there,' Candle said.

Hero nodded in agreement, then turned to Roland. 'I got Birch, who'd you get?'

'Colonel Halcon,' Roland said.

'Who?' Hero did not recognize the name. 'Elector?'

'She's like Birch, a fast-rising officer,' Elector said, 'but I don't know her personally. She was assigned to a different set of companies than I was.'

'We should compare notes,' Roland said to Hero. 'We're both infantry officers, getting two different views. Might be worth it to see what the differences are.'

Hero looked like he was about to make a snide comment but bit his lip for a moment. 'Sure,' he said, 'if you'll help me catch up.'

'Deal.'

'Mako?' Elector asked.

'Commander Faro,' Mako said.

'Your former commander?' Sasha asked. 'Is that allowed?'

'Yes,' Mako said. 'I think it's going to work a little different for me than most of you. I know how to be a sailor, so he's not teaching me directly. But he's going to be guiding me to learn the aspects that he needs me to learn. He said I'll probably spend a bit of time learning logistics and administration, bigger strategies, and other things the Naval Group will need as it expands. So, Faro will set the week's assignment and find officers to help.'

'Are you okay with that?' Candle asked.

Mako nodded. 'Why not? I'm here to make the Naval Group a better formation. If that's what I need to learn, that's what I'll learn.'

'Fair enough,' Candle said.

There was a pause, then as a group all the cadets turned to look at Sasha.

'Scholar?' Roland asked.

'Yes?' Sasha dreaded responding.

'Who did you get?' Hero asked. 'We all told, so should you.'

'Brigadier Lily!' Patch said.

'No, Rose got Lily,' Roland pointed out.

'General Prince,' Elector guessed.

'Madam Moreau,' Hero guessed.

'I think the mentor has to be a military officer,' Candle said quickly.

Rose started chuckling. She looked at Sasha. 'You got General Caesar,' she said with a smile.

The cadets all looked at Sasha expectantly. Sasha gave a curt nod, and the room exploded in noise.

'Holy shit!' Hero said.

'How did you manage that?' Patch asked.

'I didn't manage it,' Sasha said. 'I have to defend my name.'

'What?' Candle asked.

Sasha sighed. 'My colonel gave me the name Scholar, but General Caesar says I have to work to keep it. I can't just say I'm a scholar – I must prove it. Since he's given me that challenge, he decided he was going to be the one to test me.'

'That's awesome!' Patch said.

Sasha looked at the cadets, looking to see who was glaring at her. To her surprise, none of them were. Even Candle smiled at her with pride.

'It makes sense,' Elector said. 'This is the brainchild of the generals. They'll want to be involved as much as they can be.'

Sasha nodded. 'Yeah. Too bad we can't all have generals as our mentors.'

'We're already getting more resources than any other group our size, save for the Olympians,' Elector said. 'We can't get too greedy.'

The cadets all nodded in agreement just as the dinner bell sounded. As they moved to put their stuff away, Sasha let out a sigh. No one hated her for having a general as her mentor. That was one less thing to worry about, at least.

Chapter 19

Sasha kept thinking over her list well into next day, when something new started to worry her.

Their first class of the day, Rhetoric, was taught by Brigadier Lily. She followed the same pattern as Caesar and Prince, introducing vocabulary and specific concepts that they were going to have to remember, outlining how most of the course would go.

'The ultimate goal,' she said, 'is to be able to get your point across to another person, or group of people, effectively. You will not win everyone over, but you will sound like a competent expert whenever you do.'

After that came Ethics, and Sasha was surprised to see Colonel Aristotle come in. The blonde man was all smiles, stopping to speak with each cadet individually. It was well after start time for that period that he began discussing the topic. Again, he went through vocabulary and topics they would have to know. It was not until just before the end of class that he began the presentation that Sasha would worry about.

'Ethics, if you have not understood by now,' he said, 'is different from the other common classes you are taking. I will not be teaching you ethics. I will be helping you to understand the ethics you already have. And as military officers, your ethics are of paramount importance. People will die because of your choices, no matter how well you make those choices. And we want you to understand your ethics and consider those things now, before you hit those options.

'As part of this particular class, on Tuesdays, I or my proxy, will be giving you an ethical question. I want you to consider, and to give your answer on Thursday. You will be giving me the answer in secret; no one, not even the generals, will know your response. There are no wrong answers; do not give me the answer you think I want to hear. Be honest.'

Sasha nodded. *I have good ethics, don't I?* she asked herself.

My father would disagree.

'The question I want you to consider and answer is: is it okay to kill? I want you to start with a yes or a no. We will discuss particulars and exceptions, but I want you to start with a yes or no answer. Understood?'

The cadets all chorused in agreement. It did not sound as strong as Sasha was used to hearing. She was not the only one worried.

That evening, Candle got the cadets to spend an hour going over their notes for their second history and political classes, then released them to their own projects. Sasha went over her list for Caesar, asking Elector to help her combine and reduce the number to three. Then she left him to study the giant books of anatomy he was focusing on. She went to work outlining what she would say on Saturday, but that ethics question stuck with her.

Wednesday's morning classes were again taught by the generals. Quick reviews of the vocabulary and concepts, then into actual classes. Caesar discussed the development of civilizations around the Mediterranean Sea. Sasha was fascinated to recognize some of the names from the Bible. Prince went into the various forms a government can take, showing relationships between branches, and between the government and various classes of people.

The cadets shared an afternoon class, where Lily began introducing them to the forces that the Renaissance Army were fighting. Sasha had learned some of this during her time with Third Regiment, but only in the vaguest sense. Seeing Lily put it in front of them in stark numbers was something else. At least Sasha was sufficiently familiar with the iconography to understand what Lily was putting on the board.

Back at the library, Sasha continued to worry about her answer to the ethics question. It got so distracting that when the cadets finished their shared review, she went to ask the librarian.

'What are you looking for?' he asked.

'Books on ethics. Right and wrong, like that.'

'But not the Bible?'

'Not religious, no,' Sasha said quickly.

'Then we're looking into philosophers.' He moved away from his desk. It was the first time Sasha had seen him do so, and she realized he walked with a crutch. 'Were you injured in battle?' she asked.

'I was one of the first to volunteer,' he said. 'I believed in Prince's message. Believing didn't save me from a grenade, though. Got commended by my officer and assigned here.'

'Your officer?' Sasha asked curiously.

'Yes. Captain Snow. She's a colonel now, fighting down south. Believe me, I'd join her if I could.' He shrugged. 'But she has no use for a lame booker. Here we go.' He pulled out several books. 'These are pretty big concepts,' he said, 'so if you don't get into them, don't worry about it. A lot of people can't get into them. I've been trying.'

'Thanks,' she said. She wanted to tell him that Snow was her former commander but was not sure if she should. She finally just turned and went to sit down. She opened the books, looking through tables of contents for chapters she wanted to read. She spread out paper, writing down words and concepts.

One by one the cadets headed off for dinner or sleep. Sasha stayed, focused on learning as much as she could. The librarian was right, it really was a complex subject, but she persisted.

'Cadet Scholar?'

Sasha looked up. Lily stood over her with a quizzical look on her face. Sasha was still unnerved by how much Lily looked like Snow, and yet was so different.

'Ma'am?' she asked.

Lily looked over the books. 'Quite the selection, Cadet. I presume you're worried about the ethical dilemma?'

'Yes, ma'am.'

'And how is your research going?'

'It's not, ma'am,' Sasha admitted. She looked at the books spread across the table and stretched. She was surprisingly sore.

'Hoping to find an answer?' Lily asked. 'Because you can't put off the burden of responsibility on –.'

'Not looking for an answer,' Sasha interrupted. 'Trying to justify one. I know what my answer is, but I'm not sure how to back up my belief. Then I think I'm wrong and I try to look at it from the other side, but that doesn't come out any better. I don't like these options.'

'It's not about liking them, Cadet,' Lily sighed. 'It's about preparing yourself for the hard decisions. You're going to have to make decisions like this. And just as we trained men and women to respond to combat situations by training them, so we're preparing you by training you.'

'It still doesn't seem fair, ma'am. I mean, how often in the field will I not have another option?'

Lily frowned. 'Consider this, Cadet. Aristotle's ethical dilemmas are about realizing that no matter how much you plan and prepare, someone under your command is going to die. Someday, someone who follows your orders is not going to return home. Maybe you made a mistake, maybe someone on the other side just had a lucky shot.'

'I understand,' Sasha said.

'Okay, then let's take it another step, and seeing as you've seen combat, I want you to imagine you are in battle. You must make a choice, and no matter what you do, someone will die. How much time do you imagine you will have to make a decision?'

Sasha thought for a moment, remembering how confusing battle was when she was just one woman carrying a rifle. She tried to imagine being the one in charge, deciding how to defend the riverbed in the night fight. How much time would she have to spend debating her choice?

'I understand,' Sasha said again.

'Do you? Or are you just repeating "I understand" when you really don't?'

Lily's voice was sharp, and Sasha winced a bit. 'I do understand, ma'am.'

'Good. Now, reading Hegel and Kant may cover many topics, but at this point, I honestly believe it's too confusing for you to read them. Did you learn anything?'

Sasha sighed. 'I was confused. And disappointed.'

'In yourself?'

'No,' Sasha shook her head. 'Well, yes, but also, they're all men. I couldn't find a single female philosopher on that bookshelf.'

'It's sad, isn't it?' Lily said. 'I've argued with the generals about it, but there's a limit to what books we could bring in. Philosophy was of low importance as it was, so when we did get a book it was "of superior importance" according to Caesar.'

'And he didn't think women philosophers were important?'

Lily grimaced. 'Not enough,' she said, and sighed. 'It's an argument I've had with numerous officers here, Cadet, and not one you should get involved with right now.'

'So right now, I should put them away and go to bed?' Sasha asked.

Lily looked at a pocket watch. 'Going to bed might not be much of an option; Candle will be rousing everyone for the morning run in about five minutes.'

'What?' Sasha exclaimed. She looked at the window, seeing the purple sky of a dawn. The librarian was asleep, head on his desk.

That's why you're so sore. You slept here all night.

'Get your stuff sorted,' Lily said. 'I'll put the books away.'

Sasha managed some quick thanks as she hurriedly packed. Then she ran to the barracks. Candle was just waking people when Sasha came in.

'Oh, good,' Candle said. 'You're not dead.'

'Sorry, Cadet Captain,' Sasha said. 'Fell asleep at the library.'

'Well, there are worse places to sleep. Want to run?'

Sasha quickly changed and ran with the other cadets. It took her some time to get up to speed, her sore muscles protesting the sudden exercise, but she worked through them. By breakfast she was feeling almost normal.

Lily's class went over how to outline arguments. Sasha took notes, already thinking about how she could improve her list for Caesar. Then came Ethics.

Aristotle had Del Oso bring out the cadets one at a time to get their responses. While in the class, the cadets worked on their notes, but were forbidden to talk.

Sasha was the fourth one called. She stepped outside, Aristotle smiling at her.

'Ah, Scholar. How goes the project?'

'The project?' Sasha asked.

'Being a cadet of the Templar Project? Is it everything you had hoped for?'

'No,' she said, 'but I think it will be. I just need to become a scholar.'

'Yes? Well, that is a good attitude. Although I must admit, it is better to learn from books by reading them, rather than by sleeping on them.'

Sasha blushed and Aristotle laughed. 'Oh, do not worry about it. I take it as a testament to how much you care about succeeding.' He smiled at her, then his face turned serious. 'And now, Cadet Scholar, I must ask. What is your answer? Is it okay to kill?'

'No, it is not,' Sasha said. She held her breath, waiting for someone to come out the door and yell at her, for Aristotle to get angry, for anything to happen.

Instead, Aristotle simply nodded. 'It isn't?'

'No,' Sasha said.

'But soldiers kill,' Aristotle pointed out. 'You have killed.'

'I have, and I expect I will kill again, but I don't kill because I want to, or because I think it is right to do so. I kill in battle, when I am fighting for my regiment and my friends. I kill to free people from those who terrorize for fun.'

'But if killing is wrong, aren't all soldiers wrong to kill? Aren't you wrong?'

Sasha chose her words carefully. 'Killing, taking another life, is a serious action, and should only be done in certain circumstances. Combat is one of those circumstances. Killing outside of those circumstances is murder, and murder is wrong.'

'Some might say that killing and murder are the same thing.'

'My father would,' Sasha admitted. 'He would say that killing is always a sin, no matter the circumstances. He doesn't understand the difference between killing and murder.'

Aristotle pushed. 'What is the difference?'

'Murder is the unjustified taking of another life, from a position of power over the victim. Killing in combat is to advance a cause. And,' Sasha said, the idea popping into her head, 'in combat there's a chance you will be killed as well. Everyone is in danger.'

'So, killing is wrong?' Aristotle asked.

'Yes.'

'Why?'

Sasha paused. 'Because it shouldn't be done. There are times when it must be done. When we executed that yeoman, that was a time it had to be done. Those involved took it seriously.'

Aristotle leaned back in his chair. 'So, killing is wrong, but allowable under certain circumstances. If that is the case, can't you justify any action by the circumstances? Maybe there are times that rape is permissible.'

'No,' Sasha said, 'rape is always wrong.'

'But you said that killing is wrong yet allowed under certain circumstances.'

'I did,' Sasha admitted. She felt her palms sweating, worrying over the course of the conversation. 'Some wrong actions can be justified, Colonel. Hero has commented several times that he's had to steal to survive. Soldiers kill on battlefields. But some things can never be justified. Rape is one of them.'

'Why?' Aristotle pushed.

Sasha mind blanked. She could not think of anything new to say. 'I don't know,' she finally said.

Aristotle nodded. 'That was very good,' he said.

'How was that good?' Sasha asked in disbelief. 'I couldn't answer your question.'

'Ethics isn't about answering questions, Cadet Scholar,' Aristotle replied. 'Ethics is about understanding the consequences of choice and how you approach them.'

'I don't know that I understand,' Sasha said. 'Officers keep saying that to me and I just don't get it.'

'That's okay,' Aristotle replied. 'We'll talk about it in class.' He wrote down a few notes. 'Thank you, Cadet Scholar. You may return to the classroom.'

Sasha went back inside, unsure of how she felt. Relieved it was over? Yes. Glad she had answered truthfully? Yes. Disappointed in her answer, as if she was worried he would think less of her for giving it? Yes.

That must be what Lily is trying to get us to do, she realized. *Teach us how to answer questions like this effectively.*

The cadet responses took more than an hour to get through, so Aristotle released them early to go to lunch. The cadets were subdued, all lost in thought as they took their food and sat around their fire pit. Sasha's mind was elsewhere, staring at the ash in the center, when someone started speaking. Sasha was so concentrating that she did not hear Candle say her name. Mako tugged on her arm, bringing her focus back to the group.

'What?' she asked.

'You have a visitor,' Candle said, gesturing to a staff sergeant standing nearby.

'Cadet Scholar?' the sergeant asked. Sasha nodded. 'This is for you,' he handed her a small item wrapped in brown paper, then disappeared.

'What is it?' Elector asked.

'Feels like a book,' Sasha said. She found writing on one side and read it.

> *The library is not the only source of books.*
> *This is a prize possession. Treat it as such.*
> *-Brigadier Lily*

Sasha nervously unwrapped the book. It was purple, a little bigger than her notepad, with no writing of any sort on the outside. She opened it to the first page to find the title.

'The Letters of Laura Cereta,' she read out loud.

'Who?' Elector asked. None of the cadets knew who that was.

'I don't know,' Sasha said. 'But I think I'm supposed to find out.'

Chapter 20

Friday passed quickly, with warnings that next week they would have new instructors and more assignments to complete. Their easy week was over.

Del Oso announced that, at the request of several cadets, they were adding a tactical training event every Saturday. Any cadet who wanted to partake should be prepared in field fatigues by seven in the morning and could expect to be out until late that afternoon.

'Looks like we only get to sleep in one day a week,' Hero said.

'Unless you go to church,' Mako replied. Hero shrugged.

Caesar found Sasha in the library that afternoon. He pulled her out and they walked to the Templar classroom.

'I am afraid I have to advance our schedule,' Caesar said. 'In the future I will send a proxy to listen to your response in my stead, but I wanted to be here for your first response.'

'Yes, sir,' Sasha replied nervously.

'You are prepared?'

'Of course, sir.'

'No more sleeping in libraries?'

Sasha blushed. 'No, sir.'

Caesar made an awkward smile, and Sasha thought he looked uncomfortable. That struck her as odd. In their interview he was direct and in charge. He could get passionate when he was teaching the classes. Yet, despite his rank, he occasionally looked scared at the prospect of interacting with others.

Is that what makes him and Prince such a good team? She asked herself. *Prince has the charisma to lead, and Caesar has the intelligence to fix problems. Together, they can deal with anything. Although, Prince is not stupid, he a smart man himself. And Caesar, when he gets comfortable, can get animated. It might not be fair to say . . . .*

Caesar cleared his throat, bringing Sasha's attention back to him. 'So, Cadet Scholar. I asked you to find three topics for study. What did you come up with?'

'Well, General, I had one problem coming up with three topics. There were so many things I thought I would have to do, so many things I had a hard time defining. In the end, I found it easier to come up with three roles I envision for myself having upon my return.

'First, as you mentioned on Monday, was the tactical training. Colonel Snow has mentioned how she needs to learn how to take towns, and after my own experience at Kimble I can understand why that is. So, I feel one role is that of teaching and leading troops to take towns.'

'I thought you did rather well at Kimble,' Caesar said.

'We did, but as I've been thinking about it, I've realized how lucky we were. We were fighting yeomen, who were disorganized and just as surprised as we were, with the bulk of their forces outside the town. If all the yeomen had been in Kimble, and Snow was forced to attack with her whole regiment, things would have turned out much differently, and probably much worse than they did.'

'You want to learn how to take towns,' Caesar said.

'Is that something you can teach?' Sasha asked. 'Or is that all Del Oso?'

'I may not be able to help with the tactical training component, but I can still teach lessons that you will find useful. Your second role?'

'Second, I feel that Colonel Snow could use someone to help plan and execute her campaign. Someone who she can rely on to develop ideas and plan battles.'

'You want to learn how to be an adjutant,' Caesar said.

'Is that what an adjutant does?' Sasha asked.

'In the Renaissance Army, an adjutant is an officer who runs a headquarters with a general or commanding officer.'

'Officer Saxon?'

'Office Saxon is my aide-de-camp. Brigadier Lily is an adjutant.'

'What is the difference, sir? They're both staff officers.'

'Officer Saxon and Officer Bellona are aides-de-camp. That means they are assistants to officers, helping us conduct our day-to-day duties. Colonel Snow could appoint an aide-de-camp, if she wanted to.

'Brigadier Lily is an adjutant. That means she works for the Renaissance Army Headquarters as Adjutant General. Her role is to keep the army moving down the path General Prince has set for her. She is authorized to send out messages under the authority of the headquarters, even if Prince is not there to give the orders.'

'Aides-de-camp work for officers; adjutants work for headquarters.'

'Correct. Coming back to your position in Third Regiment, while you would be working closely with Colonel Snow, the position I believe you want is to be the regimental adjutant, helping Snow plan and execute her strategies and running the regiment while she is away. Does that make sense?'

'It does,' Sasha said, then, 'Why are they all women?'

'Excuse me?' Caesar asked. He looked surprised at her sudden question.

'Saxon, Bellona, and Lily are all women. Are all the adjutants women?'

Caesar looked at her, blushing. 'No,' he finally said. 'Captain Saber was Colonel Snow's adjutant, among many other functions. Colonel Trumpeter's adjutant is also male.'

'Captain Tamarac is a woman,' Sasha remembered Colonel Wild's second, the only well-dressed member of the Second Field Regiment. A quick thought popped into her head. 'What about the Second Field Regiment?' Sasha asked.

'Also female,' Caesar said.

Sasha hid a smile. *There is a Second Field Regiment.*

'As we have been building the Renaissance Army,' Caesar continued, 'we have been forced to use those with previous experience in such things. Given the nature of the Iron Republic, those skills were almost exclusively taught to men. That has led to an unfortunate male dominance of the higher levels of command.

'We have found as many women as we can to fill positions, Cadet Scholar. Colonel Grace, who commands the siege at Walker, is an amazing intellectual, who can learn anything quickly. Colonel Athena was the wife of general officer, who helped him study. She will hold a prominent position next year. And of course, Lieutenant Colonel Snow, who earned her position by being a great fighter and a decent person.

'In fact, that is one of the reasons so many of the adjutants and aides-de-camp are women. They are not just doing a job; they are learning the next one. When the army begins to expand, they will be the new officers to take command and use their skills to lead.'

Caesar paused and frowned. 'Cadet, do not think that being an aide-de-camp or an adjutant is somehow beneath you. They are important jobs, and you can learn many valuable things in those positions. I am afraid I may have failed to give you a good impression of where we expect women to be in the higher echelons of the army.'

Sasha shrugged. '". . . for those women who believe that study, hard work, and vigilance will bring them sure praise, the road to attaining knowledge is broad." I'm heading down that road, maybe on a different part from others, and I won't falter. '

Caesar looked at her in surprise again. 'Where did you read that?' he asked.

'Brigadier Lily lent me a book,' Sasha said. 'When she woke me in the library, I commented that there were no women philosophers displayed. She lent me a copy of letters by Laura Cereta.'

'It is Cereta, as if it was spelled with a CH-, not a K- sound. It is an unfortunate reality that our limited space for books meant we had to choose to leave so many behind,' Caesar admitted. He looked embarrassed. 'One which I want to rectify as quickly as possible. As for that particular book, please take good care of it. It was a gift to her in the first place.'

Sasha felt something tug at her brain, the way Caesar spoke of the book. Then she realized. Caesar gave Lily that book. *That's why it is a prized possession. It was his gift to her.*

Caesar cleared his throat. 'Back to the topic at hand. You want to be Snow's adjutant, to plan and execute operations. That is something both Snow and I thought of as well. And the third?'

Sasha paused, searching for the right words. 'I want to be able to instruct other officers,' she said. She saw Caesar gesture for her to continue. 'Third Regiment started with Colonel Snow and Captain Saber. We gained Lieutenant Buck, and lost Saber. We got Officer Lynx, made Erick a Warrant Officer and Beth a Training Officer, but haven't received any new commissioned officers, as far as I know.'

'As of today, that is correct,' Caesar confirmed.

'I was sent here to improve my mind in ways Colonel Snow could not do. I feel that if I could learn how to improve minds, I could help all those other officers improve. Just because they don't have a commission doesn't mean they shouldn't be capable of their duties.'

'You want to know how to teach?' Caesar asked. His tone made it sound like he was not sure what she meant.

'I don't know if I mean in a classroom setting, but I want to know how I can pass on my lessons to others. Not every officer can be a cadet, but that doesn't mean I can't share some of my knowledge to others. Or even to enlisted and civilians, if it comes to that.'

182

'You are being instructed in rhetoric. How is what your third topic that much different from that class?'

Sasha thought. 'I don't know that it is different, sir. Maybe it is the same, but I don't know enough to know that.'

Caesar nodded. 'Rhetoric is to teach you how to relay information and arguments effectively. It should not be too much trouble to add a few aspects specific to teaching lessons.'

Caesar looked at her for a moment. Sasha saw the gears turning and wondered what he saw in her eyes. *One gear, maybe two? Slowly revolving and creaking.*

'I understand,' Caesar finally said. 'The good news, Cadet Scholar, is that all three of those roles are not only possible, but not too difficult to accomplish with what we have here. You will still need to work hard, but it can be done.'

Sasha sighed in relief, glad that her three roles had been accepted.

'I do not know if I will be back by Monday,' Caesar said. 'If I am not, you will receive next week's challenge from another officer. I trust you will take it as seriously, as if it were being delivered by me?'

'Yes, sir,' Sasha nodded.

'Good.' Caesar stood. 'This may be your last free night for a while, Cadet. Enjoy it while you can.'

Sasha nodded, and Caesar turned to leave. Then he stopped and turned to face her.

'Do you have any questions?' he asked.

'I'm sorry, sir?'

'Do you have any questions?' Caesar repeated. 'It occurs to me that you might have some questions that won't normally be answered during your training. Perhaps about where the books come from, or the nature of Snow and Lily's travels to Minnesota? Many things, you understand, I cannot answer. In some cases, I cannot tell you for safety reasons, and in other cases because it is not my story to tell. But, given your thirst for knowledge, I will answer if I can. Consider this a reward for achieving your first success as Cadet Scholar.'

Sasha looked at him, bewildered at the sudden opportunity. She struggled to find a response and asked the first question to come to mind when she looked at Caesar.

'Why is General Prince known as General Prince?' she asked. 'If he's fighting for a democratic state, why did he take a name from nobility?'

'That was not his idea,' Caesar said. 'During the time of the Republic, there was one young Dawson who was known as the Prince of the Republic. He was groomed for politics and government from a young age. Before the Commonwealth War, General Prince was that Dawson.

'When we started contacting the Old Guard and other groups agreeable to our cause, they used the name Prince to describe him. Even though many of them knew his name, they kept up the pretense to protect him. As such, when we started using renaissance names for officers, he got stuck with Prince.'

'Ah,' Sasha thought it was interesting. 'How did he survive the Commonwealth conquest?'

Caesar gave her a stern look. 'Only one question a week, Cadet.'

***

Montessori rubbed his eyes. He wanted to find an issue with the numbers before him, but there was none to find. This quartermaster had laid out everything well.

They were running out of food.

The civilians were on half rations. Soldiers on three-quarters, officers on full. Full rations were still less than Montessori was used to, leading to his shrinking beltline and growling stomach, and his irate personality. And after all that sacrifice, the garrison had bought enough time to last into December.

And what help from the outside?

Montessori did not know. None of their messengers had returned, and the count had never gotten around to installing a radio. A few planes had flown overhead, but none low enough to see any messages that might be waiting for them. Montessori's options were limited, and none of them were ideal.

Surrender?

Continue to hold out for some help that might not be coming?

Take my revenge on the population now?

He shook his head, trying to think straight. It was so hard now.

He heard knocking at his door. He launched himself out of his desk and ambled over, opening to find one of his yeomen, a former Commonwealth soldier who spoke Odessan.

'Milord, your son requests your presence downstairs. Airplanes approach.'

184

Montessori followed the man down from his office to the great hall, and out through the door. Giulio and other officers were standing in the courtyard, staring up.

'Why is this different?' Montessori asked, coming to stand next to them.

'Three of them,' Giulio said. 'Attack aircraft, flying at a thousand feet.'

'Ah,' Montessori said, seeing the trio of planes. Broad-winged aircraft, carrying bombs and rockets. 'They're to suppress the Mardurer defenses, protect the aircrafts that are coming.'

'Why do they not attack the rebels?' Giulio asked.

Montessori looked at them, then smiled. 'Transports,' he said.

'What?' Giulio asked.

'Bennabi is sending transports. He sent these planes first, so the rebels might fire on them and draw their anger in return. That will make it safe to send in the slow transports. There is an airdrop coming in.'

Montessori moved back up the stairs, followed by several officers. He climbed up past his office and bedroom to the roof. Originally decorated by his wife as a patio, he rarely came up this high. They looked, scanning the skies for any sign of other aircraft. One of the yeomen exclaimed and pointed.

There, coming at the count, was a trio of large transport aircraft. They were older planes, in keeping with the king's distrust of technology. Large engines hung between two pairs of wings, with a heavy central fuselage.

Bennabi, if you sent me a load of uniforms, I'm going to kill you!

The first aircraft dropped a pair of cargo pods. The second did as well. The third dropped six people and a smaller pod, all landing on the field between the town and the cathedral.

Montessori turned to head downstairs, back to the main hall. His son, unable to climb the stairs, had sat alone until the officers returned. 'Father?'

'An airdrop,' Montessori confirmed. He gestured to a yeoman. 'Bring the dropped men to me.'

He waited, sitting at the table until the yeomen returned with the six dropped men. They wore royal uniforms of various colors, led by a major.

'Sir,' he saluted, 'I am Major Antonio Lopez, from General Prince Stefan's staff.'

'Major,' Montessori saluted, speaking through his son. 'It is about time I saw someone. We have had no word for some months. For all we know, you had given us up for dead.'

Lopez nodded. 'That was discussed, milord,' he admitted. 'But as you have continued to survive, the consensus has shifted.'

'Explain,' Montessori said.

'There will be no campaign this year,' Lopez said, 'but General Prince Stefan will launch one in the spring. His belief is that the winter will cull the Renaissance Army's forces, draw them to the breaking point. And when he does launch his campaign, he wants the Renaissance Army to spend a lot of forces keeping you bottled up in Walker.'

'The more watching us, the less fighting him. I hope Prince Stefan, or General Bennabi, will be sending us more than prayers,' Montessori asked.

'Yes, milord. Prince Stefan and General Bennabi have convinced King Xavier to release more fuel from the reserve, enough to establish an air bridge for the continued support of you and your troops. I'm to assist in commanding the defenses. Captain Weston here is a doctor, and he's to help keep the troops in fighting shape. Lieutenant Covington is a signal officer, he jumped in with two technicians and a radio, to keep communications open. At three drops a week we can drop in enough supplies to keep the troops alive and fighting.'

'What about more troops?' Montessori asked. 'The king has a paratrooper battalion, does he not? A commando company?'

'Until the logistical situation stabilizes, we do not want to drop in too many troops.' Lopez said. 'It will be specialists and supplies only for a while.'

Montessori glared at the officers. He wanted to yell and rage, but he understood the situation all too clearly. It made sense, even as he detested his low position in the scheme of things.

'What do you need from me?' he asked.

'A place for the radio,' Lopez said, 'the bell tower would be best. Quarters for us, access to the supplies and troop positions.'

Montessori nodded. 'Very well, Major. Giulio will get you situated. Giulio,' he said to his son, 'get them settled, and make sure they understand the security arrangements of the cathedral adequately.'

Giulio turned to give the appropriate orders, leaving Montessori to sit back and think.

A banquet to welcome our guests seems appropriate. Something to celebrate, a time to eat a full meal.

He smiled. That sounded very good.

186

Chapter 21

Saturday came, along with their first tactical exercise. Only Elector stayed in the barracks, out of his desire not to fight. Some of the cadets could not participate in the exercises, but they all could start learning the lessons until they were well enough. They started with weapons familiarization, particularly with submachine guns and black carbines. Then they started drilling on entering houses and clearing rooms. It was a long day of activity, but it felt good to stretch their muscles again, even the injured ones. When Sasha did go to the library that evening, she was surprised to see another man there. About her age, wearing civilian clothes, reading in the corner. He looked up at her when she entered but said nothing.

'Who is that?' she asked the librarian.

'A militia officer,' he said. 'Came to study up on his duties. I told him the rules. He shouldn't get in the way.' True to the librarian's word, the man said nothing that Saturday.

Sunday was a day off, and even Sasha found herself staying away from the library. Some of the clerks and staff sergeants in training had organized a card tournament. Sasha watched and learned to play on the side with some of the others. Most of the cadets knew the game and participated. The winners got out of duties for the next week. None of the cadets made it into the final rounds, but it was good to socialize with the other trainees at Athens.

When Sasha and some of the other cadets did go into the library, the militia officer was there again. He looked annoyed with them, but said nothing, continuing to read. The cadets, in turn, let him be.

Monday started, with Cardinal as their new cadet captain. They went to their classroom to find neither general returned. Their duties had taken them away from Athens, leaving the cadets with their chosen substitutes.

First Madam Moreau returned, heavy cane and all, to teach them history. 'General Caesar and I are in agreement on this,' she said. 'It's not about learning dates and facts. It's about understanding the ebb and flow. It's about knowing that the historian may have a reason to lie, a reason to turn his opponents into the forces of evil, and ignore the flaws of his own side. Considering the source of information is as important as knowing the information itself.'

With that, comment she launched into the world of ancient Greece and its city states. She described several in some detail, aspects of their culture, how they fought.

'By Wednesday,' she said, 'I want you to consider three advantages and three disadvantages to fighting a war as a city-state. One page, total. Be concise.'

Their political instructor was someone new. He was built like Del Oso, not as wide, but still solid and muscled. He wore civilian clothes, well maintained but old. His hair was silvered, and his eyes were always fully open. He sat on the instructor's desk and crossed his arms.

'Cadets, my name is Scott Anthony. I was a local constabulary administer in the Iron Republic. I was conscripted as a staff officer two months before the Republic surrendered and spent a few weeks in the Commonwealth camps. Since then, I've tried to work under the kingdom, but been frustrated. Which led me to join the movement. That's my biography, don't ask any more questions. Shut up,' he said with a grin.

His attitude was relaxed and friendly. Sasha believed she would enjoy his classes.

'Now, I am going to be conducting your political instruction. I've been over the outline of what General Prince wants, and I'm going to teach you all of that, but I get to add my own knowledge, which can be summed up like this: politicians are shit. There is no system that cannot be abused, there is no individual who is beyond reproach, and there is no law that will not hurt someone. Civilizations have risen and fallen for thousands of years; no government endures. That is an important lesson when building a new movement. Nothing you build will be different.'

Scott launched into the legislative branch of government, and the various forms a legislature could take. He closed with his own assignment about organizing legislatures.

After lunch Lily appeared, handing out to each cadet their personal assignments for the week. 'I have instructions from all your mentors,' she said, 'so ask me if you have questions.'

Sasha's was a note from Caesar.

> *The librarian has set aside a book for you on a war of the Greek city-states known as the Peloponnesian War. This book is a translation from text thousands of years old, so it will take some patience getting used to how it is written. Take your time. He also has a list of other books in the library that may be helpful in your assignment.*
>
> *By this weekend: prepare to discuss how the two sides of the war*

fought to their advantages, and how they tried to overcome their disadvantages. Quotes from text that accurately support your claims will go over well.

In addition: consider how you might instruct others to remember what you have learned from this assignment. Keep your thoughts brief.

Good luck,

General Caesar

The cadets began to get into a rhythm for their afternoons. The first hour as a group was spent going over their notes for the day's classes and reviewing for the next. Then they split off into their own personal projects, each approaching the librarian for books and notes he had put aside.

Sasha's was a book titled *History of the Peloponnesian War* by a historian named Thucydides. A paper stuck inside the cover had a list of pages for her to read, and a list of other books, including a survey of ancient military history, a book of political history, and a historical atlas.

The cadets settled in. The militia officer appeared shortly after, making some comment to the librarian about the number of readers in the library, then grabbing a book and getting settled.

They all worked until dinner. When the bell rang, the cadets all started to put their books away, handing them to the librarian.

The militia officer scoffed. 'They can't put books on hold!'

'They can,' the librarian responded.

'Why is it a group of common clerks can put books on hold, but an officer cannot?' the officer responded.

The cadets all looked at him in surprise, and Sasha realized he did not know who they were. Their uniforms were grey, different from the brown the students of the Staff School wore, but he did not understand the distinction. They had no rank or other insignia on their uniforms, and there was nothing to tell him they were special students.

'They're not common clerks,' the librarian responded, 'they're cadets.'

'Cadets?' the officer asked.

'Officers in training, chosen select by the generals.'

'Why?' he asked, looking at the cadets incredulously.

'Because they're going to need capable officers in the future,' Elector responded.

'Be careful,' the librarian warned the militia officer. 'They've been through combat training, and half of them were veterans before that. In any conflict, the authority will drop on their side, not yours.'

The militia officer looked at them, red in the face from a mixture of anger and embarrassment. 'I did not intend to insult,' he said.

'And none was taken,' Mako said quickly. 'We must get to dinner.' The cadets left the militia office behind.

'Didn't want that to end in a fight?' Elector asked.

Mako nodded. 'Also, I'm hungry.'

Sasha followed, looking back at the red-faced militia officer. She almost felt bad for him.

***

Classes continued, but without the higher officers that had started their instructions. Lily took over their rhetoric instruction, riding in twice a week for class and a shared lunch with the women cadets. Scott continued as their political instructor, and Madam Moreau taught both ethics and history, which made her the only instructor they had every day.

Cardinal was growing more and more irate in her position as cadet captain. She snapped at Hero several times, and most of the other cadets at least once. By Wednesday she was anticipating the end of her position.

Alas, it was not going to be that easy.

That Thursday, Del Oso entered the barracks with Colonel Carpenter. The cadets had not seen him since he had banished them to Sparta. At least he was not angry this time.

'Cadets,' Del Oso said, 'you are only in your second week of classroom work, but it is never too early to learn about necessary diversions. Colonel?'

Carpenter nodded and looked over the cadets. 'Cadets, an army-critical opportunity has arisen, and I am required to assist. Normally there would be a training company within range, but there are none. So, I'm going to send you, as you have more field experience than any of my staff trainees.

'An agent of the Renaissance Movement has found something, and we need to secure it and transport it. You will accompany the individual to the location and await further instructions.'

190

Del Oso stepped up. 'You have ten minutes to get back to your barracks and change into field gear, then report to the armory for ammunition and equipment. This mission may be a day or two, so be prepared.'

'Cadet Captain, take your squad.'

Cardinal stood up, 'Yes, Sergeant Major. Come on, cadets.'

Twenty minutes later they were prepared, backpacks with food and sleeping gear, belt pouches with ammunition, except for Elector's, who carried medical supplies.

'Ready?' Cardinal asked. The cadets all nodded at her.

The door opened and Carpenter returned, with Del Oso and another man. He was a tall man, broad but gaunt, with greying hair. His clothes looked like he had not been out of the field in some time.

Patch bounded ahead of the group. Her ankle cast was only two days gone, and she was making up for weeks of immobility with high energy. She stopped before the gaunt man and smiled. 'Hi, Uncle Jacques!'

The man blinked. 'Libby!' she smiled. 'This is where you wound up?'

'I did. Are you the reason we're assembled?' She gasped and smiled. 'Did you find a Prize?'

'I did.' Jacques laughed. 'You know what we say?'

Patch nodded. 'There is not lost knowledge,' she began. She and Jacques finished together. 'We just haven't found it yet!' The laughed.

Carpenter cleared his throat. 'Shall we continue?'

'Oh, right,' Jacques said. 'Okay, boys and girls, I'm Uncle Jacques, and I am assigned to the Workshop. We make all the toys for the rest of the Renaissance Army. My job is to find stuff; resources, tech, whatever I can. I've been poring over old maps, looking for cities and towns lost to time, and I found something.'

'Cadets, this a highly sensitive matter,' Carpenter said, 'I want you to exercise diligence in your duties, and to not tell anyone of what you see out there.'

'That's a bit much,' Jacques said, but Carpenter ignored him.

'Any questions?' Del Oso asked.

'Why us?' Hero asked. 'I mean, is this far enough away that you couldn't ride to get someone else?'

191

Carpenter frowned at him, but Jacques responded first. 'You're not wrong, but it's also a question of discretion. As he just said, you're not supposed to speak about what you're about to see. Since I assume you're not a group of prisoners . . ..'

'Officers-to-be in advanced training, actually,' Patch said.

'Good. So, you understand. Let's go.'

'Cadet Captain,' Del Oso said.

Cardinal stepped forward. 'Scholar, want to take point? Hero take the rear.'

'Why me?' Hero whined.

'Because she said so,' Elector interrupted.

Sasha walked up to Jacques. The man was untying a mule from a nearby post. 'Where are we going?'

'Follow me,' he said, stepping off down the trail, his animal following obediently.

'Wait, I'm supposed to be on point.'

'So?' he asked. He strapped a pair of dark goggles to his head.

'It means I'm supposed to lead the squad.'

'But I know where we're going and you don't,' Jacques looked mischievous. 'That doesn't make much sense, does it?'

'But –.'

'Too late, catch up!' Jacques turned and started off and a brusque pace. Sasha hurried to catch up, the squad fanning out behind them. He moved quickly, surprisingly spry for a man with greying hair. The cadets followed closely for hours, when he led them up a ridge and stopped. 'See?' he asked, gesturing out over the view.

The view was odd. The ground was weirdly level. The trees were planted in even rows. And in the middle sat a large mound that did not look like a normal hill.

The other cadets came up. 'What is it?' Roland asked.

Patch got excited. 'It's building-fall!'

'What?' most of the cadets asked.

'Most old buildings were made of stone or brick or some other material that doesn't degrade,' Patch said quickly. 'When they fall over, they become building-fall. New settlements often use them to build to homes, but

192

sometimes they get lost or forgotten about.'

'And I've been combing through building-fall for decades,' Jacques said. 'I've got ancient maps, and I go around looking for places that might have something. You never know what survived, and some of their stuff could last a long time.'

'What did you find?' Patch asked.

'Come see,' Jacques said, then turned to Candle. 'Can you put up security around the mound, and send Libby and one other with me?'

'Scholar, go with them,' Candle said quickly, as Sasha was standing closest to the pair. Sasha fell in behind Jacques and Patch.

'What is it?' Patch asked quickly. 'It is an automobile? How would it run without fuel? Oh, is it a computational? We might be able to generate enough electricity with some river generators or chemical batteries.'

'Maybe for short periods of time, but not without difficulty,' Jacques said. 'It'd be easier to build an alcohol engine and power it with whiskey.'

'Oh!' Patch said excitedly. 'Wait, can whiskey burn correctly for an engine?'

'Maybe not whiskey,' Jacques admitted.

Jacques walked up to the mound. He gripped an exposed bar and lifted a length of stonework. 'I had to hide the entrance,' he said. 'I think it was a structure for automobiles, or at least it included a level for them.'

'An entire structure for automobiles?' Sasha asked.

'Everyone had them in the Technology Age,' Patch said.

Jacques gestured. 'Head on in. Lanterns are on the right.'

Sasha moved in and found the lanterns. She and Patch lit them as Jacques secured the cover open. 'Come on,' he said, leading them into the darkness.

Sasha swept the lantern across the scene. Much of the structure from above ground had collapsed into the lower levels, but a hallway remained, winding through the debris.

'Natural?' Patch asked.

'No,' Jacques said. 'I think it was collapsed on purpose, to keep this avenue clear for them to get out.'

'Them?' Patch asked gleefully.

'Follow.'

Sasha followed the pair silently. This was such an alien world for her. The

193

black floor was cracked and broken, but she still saw white and yellow markings, arrows pointing into what was now a wall of debris. She passed one sign, rusted but still reading 'EXIT'.

'Everyone had them?' Sasha asked.

'Pretty much,' Patch said.

'And they kept them underground?'

Jacques laughed. 'Yeah. Think about it, though. Which would you prefer outside your window, a field or automobiles or a field of flowers?'

'I don't know what an automobile looks like,' Sasha said.

'A carriage without a horse, made of metal,' Patch said, 'with . . . .'

She trailed off. Jacques had come to a stop and was busy lighting lanterns set up around the room. Sasha was about to ask him where he got so many lanterns when she finally saw what Jacques had found.

They were large, twenty feet long, maybe ten feet tall. Eight wheels, their rubber tires long shredded by small animals. Their metal bodies rusted and worn, streaked with brown. There were three of them, sitting in a row, safely parked amongst the rubble.

'Some sort of combat automobile,' Jacques said. 'See the large bulb on top? That was a turret, and it carried the main weapon, though,' he pointed the lantern to show where the gun had rusted apart, 'it usually was in one piece.' He gestured towards one end of the vehicle. 'I had to pry the door open,' he said, 'it was rusted shut.'

The inside was damp, with moldy seats lining the walls. It had been painted white, but long ago everything had rusted.

'Doesn't look like much is salvageable,' Sasha said.

'Maybe, maybe not,' Patch said. 'Won't know until we look.'

'That's not even the best part,' Jacques said. He took them behind the third vehicle.

Whoever had hidden these vehicles had left supplies and parts for their use. The original shelves had collapsed, but Jacques had constructed several tables from the debris. Some of the parts were wrapped in some type of waxy sheet, while others were exposed on the tables.

'What are they?' Sasha asked.

'Stuff wrapped in plastic,' Patch giggled.

194

'Plastic?' Sasha asked. She had never heard that word before.

'Man-made covering that protects whatever is inside from the elements. As long as it's sealed properly,' Patch said. Sasha looked at it and thought of the covering on the scroll Major Fox had given her.

'They were all sealed properly,' Jacques said, gesturing to the table, 'but something chewed into a few of them over the years.' He gestured for Sasha to walk up, unfolding a pair of spectacles. 'See?' he held up small, rusted bits. He had a tool set laid out and lifted a small metal brush, brushing off some of the rust. 'Spare parts for their engines. Still has a use, if the right mind finds it.'

'So, what are we doing?' Sasha asked.

'We're just making sure everything stays safe until the Workshop gets here,' Jacques said. 'I find stuff, but no one can do anything with it like Mobius can.'

'Who's Mobius?' Sasha asked.

'Master Mobius is the head of the Workshop. He's a genius at tech, engineering, electrics. Anything that has to do with using and learning from ancient devices, he's the one you want to take charge.' Jacques stood. 'Come, now that I have other hands, let's lift that long one there.'

He moved to the pile of rubble, pointing at one item. Wrapped in plastic, it was easily eight feet long and weighed a few hundred pounds. Sasha, her arm still in a cast, stood by with a short cart while Jacques and Patch lifted it up. Together they rolled it back towards the light.

'I think I know what you are,' Jacques said, carefully cutting into the plastic with a small blade. He gingerly removed the plastic. 'So, Libby, what are you learning?'

'Officer stuff,' Patch said, looking over the table covered in small bits. 'History, politics, ethics. Why do we do this? How do we convince people of that? I'm also learning to fight.'

'Why would you want to know how to fight?' Jacques asked.

'Oh, Uncle Jacques, you know. Yeomen, Commonwealth. Big reasons.'

Jacques chuckled. 'I'm sure they are. And you, Scalper?'

'Scholar, Uncle Jacques!' Patch said.

'Scholar, then. Do you learn books, writing and such?'

'Yes, and fighting.'

'Scholar and I are learning to clear houses!' Patch said.

195

'Oh, I know how to do that,' Jacques said, unwrapping another layer. 'I can do it with a broom, a towel and a bucket of water.'

'No, not clean,' Sasha said, 'clear. With guns.'

'Won't that just make everything messier?' Jacques asked.

'Uncle Jacques!' Patch exclaimed.

Jacques chuckled. 'War is a young man's game. Or a young woman's game, now. The old men just comment on how foolish it is afterwards.'

'Fighting the yeomen isn't foolish,' Sasha said, hotly. Jacques looked up at her, but he was not upset. If anything, he gave her a smile, as if he understood her position exactly.

'I've seen war, young Scholar,' he said. 'There is a time to fight, sure. And the blood of the young fuels those fights. The minds of the middle-aged set those fights in motion. And the tongues of the elderly comment how it will all start again in another generation. Those machines,' he gestured behind Sasha, 'are warriors of their own age, manned by the young of one side to kill the young of the other side. And now,' he finished unwrapping the item, 'our side will give them to young men and women to kill the other side's young men.'

The device he had unwrapped was a gun, to be sure. Sasha recognized it, but it was huge, much larger than even the massive gun Winnie had taken during the prison battle. Sasha glanced back at the machines, imagining the giant gun on top.

Jacques handed her a ruler. 'What is the caliber?'

Sasha measured. 'Almost an inch,' she said.

'Do you know the metric system?' Jacques asked.

'No,' Sasha shook her head.

'One more thing to learn,' Jacques chuckled. 'Well, no matter. Come take a look at this.' She went to the breech of the gun. She recognized the belt feed, where the ammunition would feed into the weapon so it could fire. The biggest one she had seen so far had been almost as long as her fingertip to thumb. This was easily larger than her hand.

'Wow,' she said.

'No wonder they needed a vehicle to carry it,' Jacques said, 'and its ammunition.' He handed her the notebook. 'Here, I'll measure, you write. If I say millimeter, write two m's. If I say centimeter, write cm.'

Sasha nodded, writing down his measurements as he made them. Patch was

196

completely involved in her own mind, humming as she cleaned and organized small parts.

Jacques finished the measurements. 'And now, we wrap her up,' he said. They wrapped the plastic back over it all. Sasha wondered if he was going to tie it up, but instead he produced a small tool from his belt. Sasha heard a sizzle and smelled something burning as he resealed the plastic.

'Okay,' he said. 'On to the next.'

***

Most of the Templars enjoyed spending a night out, even in the cooling October weather. Hero was complaining, as he always did – 'We just got our beds back, and now we're back in tents!' - while Cardinal's annoyance at being cadet captain was crossing into outright anger. Candle mentioned something about it to her, and Cardinal responded by giving Candle night watch. Sasha said nothing and was assigned to cook breakfast for everyone in the morning. She was nearly finished, the cadets, Jacques and Del Oso waiting to eat, when Mobius arrived.

He rode a large draft horse and led a pair of wagons, carrying tools and a handful of workers. Patch squealed in excitement and rushed over.

'Mobius!' she called.

'Ha, Libby. Good to see you, young one. Getting into trouble?'

'Probably.'

'Good, good,' Mobius laughed. He was a tall man, with brown hair starting to go grey underneath a wide-brimmed hat. He wore a weathered long coat, which he took off after he dismounted to reveal a vest of many pockets, a belt full of tools, and equally worn pants. He looked over at the crowd. 'Breakfast? Good. Eat up, it'll be a hard day's work, if Uncle Jacques has found what he thinks he found.'

The cadets ate, while Patch went on with Mobius about what she had been doing with the Templar Project. He seemed very interested in all of them, listening without interruption. Finally, breakfast done, Mobius stood. 'Well, let's see what we've got. Come on, all.'

'We're supposed to pull security, sir,' Del Oso reminded him.

'Don't call me sir, Sergeant.'

'You are a major, aren't you?' Hero asked.

'Only when it suits me, and now it doesn't suit me,' Mobius growled. 'Besides, we've already got security around us. Your cadets should see this.'

Jacques led the way down the hole, back through the track he had brought Sasha and Patch down the previous day. The workers brought several lanterns, illuminating the site better than the three of them had done the day before.

'Oh, my,' Mobius said when he saw them.

'What are they?' Roland asked.

'Armored Fighting Vehicles,' Mobius said. 'Mid-twenty-first century, American made.'

'American?' Cardinal asked.

'One of the empires from the Technology Age.'

'You mean the Before Time?' Hero asked.

Mobius grunted at the phrase and continued. 'These were used to carry troops into battle without exposing them to danger. The gun on top was used to support them when they got there. These must have been hidden just before the Dark Age began, maybe when Minnesota was independent of the Union.'

'What?' some of the cadets asked.

Mobius spoke as he peered into the first vehicle. 'In the Technology Age, Minnesota was one state within the Union of States. When the Union government fell, Minnesota survived for a time as an independent nation. Then it, too, fell. I would think cadets of the Templar Project should know that.'

'That will be towards the end of their lessons,' Del Oso said.

'Ah,' Mobius said. 'Anyway, it was not uncommon for military units of the time to bury or hide their equipment to keep it out of improper hands. Someone buried these beauties four hundred years ago.'

'Wow,' several people said. Sasha tried to imagine burying these things here.

What were they thinking? Did they expect to come back? Did they know it would be for a long time?

'I wonder who it was.' Sasha replied.

'One of Prince's ancestors,' Jacques said. He picked up a lantern and led them back a bit, into a side passage next to the vehicles. He shone the light on a metal plaque, fastened to the wall.

Everyone crowded around the writing.

Here sit Ares, Mars and Thor.
Our Gods of War, while we fought.
We failed them; they did not fail us.
If you find them, respect them as best you can.
But if they'll bring you victory
Allow them to roar once more.
                -Commodore Lucian Dawson
                Independent State of Minnesota

'Could be a different Dawson,' Elector said.

'Could be,' one of the workers said.

'Doesn't matter,' Jacques said. 'What matters is these machines held men and women in the heat of battle. The machines protected them, and they in turn loved these machines. We must be respectful.'

Mobius nodded. 'They'll roar again, in one fashion or another. Let's get to work.'

The workers moved back to their wagons, pulling out tools and planking and various items Sasha did not recognize. Several of them assembled carts in the lower level, while others created a rope system to pull items up to the surface. The cadets were spread out among the crews, helping where they could.

Sasha was assigned to help cart items from their hiding place to the pulleys. Some of the smaller items, such as a few boxes of ammunition or packed replacement parts, she could handle herself. The big weapons, still wrapped in plastic, needed several people to move them over to the carts.

Mobius and Jacques were working on the vehicles themselves, aided by Patch, Mako and Candle. They went into the first one, discussing the equipment and what it was used for. Sasha was annoyed at only being used only for manual labor but said nothing. Technology was not something she had any experience with, while the snippets of conversation she heard told her the four of them had some shared knowledge.

Listening to the rest of the people, Sasha realized that most of them were not Minnesotan. Many were Dakotan, like Patch, or even from Wisconsin, like Jacques. Those who were Minnesotan were younger.

'Patch,' Sasha whispered when she had a break and the fellow cadet had stepped outside of the vehicle for one reason or another.

'Hi, Scholar! Guess which one this vehicle it is. It's Ares. It was an ancient spirit of war, or something. They all were. The names, I mean, not the vehicles. Which is to say the names are thousands of years old, while the vehicles are only centuries.'

'Okay,' Sasha said, 'but I wanted to ask: is most of the Workshop made up of Dakotans and Wisconsinites?'

'Sure,' Patch said.

'Why?'

Patch blinked at her as if she had asked why water was wet. 'The best technicians come from the wilds,' she said. 'At least, these days. Originally, I like to think all communities were like this. They took what they could, and learned what they could, from the bones of the Before Time. But then some communities started to form nations, and when you do that, you lose of your communities to the nation you're now a part of.'

'Really?'

'Sure,' Patch said. 'Think about it: most civilized nations have schools. Schools teach you valuable skills, but they also teach you a curriculum, which means you're learning skills that the civilization has deemed important to learn, and not learning skills that they have decided are not important. So, technicians from civilized nations have a strong base of skills, but not as much variety.'

'Huh,' Sasha said. That was a much more reasoned answer than Sasha expected. Patch's absent-minded demeanor fooled Sasha once again.

'I mean, think about the Templar Project,' Patch continued. 'There are how many thousands of topics we could study? Science, math, language, history, whatever, but we're focusing on the projects the generals have chosen to teach us, to reach the end goal they desire.'

'Sure, I guess,' Sasha said. She had not thought about it like Patch had, but Patch made sense.

Someone called for Patch. 'If you want to talk more about it later, let me know. I've got plenty of thoughts on the subject! And on other subjects, too!'

The three vehicles were being picked apart. Sasha could not see how they were being respectful, but also could not see how they could pass up anything the find might give them. Carts of bits and pieces were carried up and put into the wagons.

'Think we'll need another hull?' Patch asked. They were all taking a break, passing around bowls of berries and nuts and canteens of water.

'No,' Mobius shook his head. 'It'll be tight, but we can do it. The rust has made most of the three unusable, and we've taken what we can.'

'What happens then?' Sasha asked.

'We'll seal the entrance,' Mobius said. 'We don't want someone else coming in a desecrating these memorials more than we already have.'

'Isn't that a bit much for a couple of vehicles?' Hero asked.

'Oh, shut up Hero,' Candle said.

'What?' Hero looked confused; even Sasha was surprised at Candle's response.

There was a moment of silence before Jacques spoke to Candle. 'Show them.'

Candle took a lantern and gestured for the other cadets to follow her into Ares. At the front was a driver's seat, and before it a wheel. On the wheel was a steel sheet.

'It's not rusted,' Mako said. 'Whatever this material was, it has survived for centuries underground without warping at all. They wanted this to survive as long as possible.'

On the sheet was a list. Ranks, names, and positions, several followed by the words KIA or WIA. Seventeen names in all.

'All three have them,' Candle said. 'Forty-one names all told. Forty-one men and women who fought inside these machines. Twenty-one of them died in them. Eleven were wounded and replaced. The rest survived and wanted the fallen to be remembered.'

'These are monuments and memorials,' Patch said. 'Necessity dictates we take from them, but we do not do so lightly.'

Hero blushed a little. Sasha read through the names, curious if their descendants were now fighting in the Renaissance Army, or in the Royal Army, or serving in the yeomanry. Would they agree with the rebellion? Would they fight for it?

The cadets marched up to the top, Jacques and Mobius following behind.

'Coming back with us?' Sasha heard Mobius ask.

'No,' Jacques said. 'I've got more maps to search.'

'We could use your expertise at the Workshop.'

Jacques shook his head. 'I've done my war. I've earned the solitude I now enjoy.'

Mobius chuckled. They climbed out of the hole. Mobius and Jacques then closed the entrance, sealing it with rocks. Soon it was unnoticeable from the rest of the rubble.

'Farewell!' Mobius called as the wagons started off, the beds filled with treasure and sleeping workers.

'How far to the Workshop?' Roland asked Patch.

'A few hours,' Patch said, 'I think.'

'Thanks for your help, cadets,' Jacques said. He was loading his packed gear onto the mule. 'Perhaps I will see you again next find.'

'Perhaps!' Patch said, excitedly.

Jacques looked over them and smiled. It was a smile of familiarity, but it was also a smile of sadness. Something about them made him remember something from his youth.

'Take care of each other,' he said. 'Goodbye.'

Jacques started off into the forest, his mule following.

Del Oso spoke. 'Cadet Captain, put us in formation and get us home.'

Cardinal motioned, and the cadets moved out. Patch kept glancing over her shoulder to follow Jacques until he was lost in the trees.

To Sasha, Patch looked mournful.

Chapter 22

The cadets returned late Friday, too late to complete any catchup work for their classes. The next day turned out to be eventful.

To start, Rose returned to the Templar Project. She walked into the barracks that morning, limping with a cane. The other cadets rose to greet her with smiles.

'How are you?' Roland asked.

'I'm fine,' Rose said. She smiled. 'I won't be running anytime soon, but I will live. What have I missed in the classes?'

The cadets filled her in, discussing the classes they have gone through so far and their Saturday tactical training. Patch got into a great explanation about their recent foray with the Workshop.

'I thought we weren't supposed to talk about that,' Elector warned.

'Not with anyone outside the Templar Project,' Patch shrugged. 'I'm sure Rose is fine.'

As soon as she was free from the group, Cardinal took Rose aside. The two sisters found a spot far enough away no one could listen and had an hour-long conversation. The cadets kept their distance, though curiosity was strong.

'They could just be catching up,' Roland said.

'That's a bit animated for catching up,' Sasha opined. Cardinal was gesturing a lot, obviously agitated about something. Rose was simply listening and responding.

'Maybe now Cardinal will calm down?' Hero asked. 'She'll stop being such a . . . ,' he looked at the others, '. . . monster.'

The cadets went off to their tactical training without the sisters or Elector. It was a day of moving through the training village, sprinting in full equipment, practicing dropping to the ground and sprinting for cover at a whistle blast. After several hours, they returned to Athens, bruised and sore and discussing how they could improve. They entered the barracks to find the rest of the cadets waiting for them.

'What's going on?' Sasha asked.

Cardinal waited for them all to file in, then spoke. 'I'm resigning from the program,' she said.

'What?' Roland asked. 'Why?'

'I don't want to be commissioned,' Cardinal said.

'I thought you were part of the Renaissance Army for a specific reason,' Candle spoke. Her eyes were full of tears.

'I was, and I'm willing to fulfill that reason,' Cardinal replied. 'But I don't want to be a commissioned officer. I don't want that responsibility. I don't want those expectations. I just want to be me. I can do my job without being commissioned. Books are fine, but I want the wind in my hair.'

'But –,' Candle began.

'I haven't slept a night since the explosion,' Cardinal interrupted. 'I barely sleep at all. I'm not happy, and I'm not well. I need to heal my soul.'

'And you're okay with this?' Candle asked Rose.

Rose shrugged. 'We promised our sponsor one of us would finish. I have promised it would be me. Cardinal can find her own path.'

Cardinal looked at the cadets. 'I'm sorry,' she said, 'I don't want to cause problems, but I'm not one of you. I will fulfill what I was brought to do, and I don't need to be in the Templar Project to do it. So, I quit.'

No one said anything. Cardinal and Rose made their way to Del Oso's office, leaving the rest of the cadets behind. They changed out of their field clothes and into their classroom kit. Sasha made her way to the library while the rest of the cadets scattered to their own places of comfort.

The militia officer was back, sitting in his corner. He looked up but said nothing as Sasha grabbed a book off the shelf and sat down to read, but try as she might, Sasha could not focus enough on her book to get more than a few words in before she was lost in thought.

'I'm sorry,' a voice interrupted her. Sasha looked up to see the militia officer before her.

'About?' she asked.

'About being a jerk before. I didn't know you were special officers-in-training.'

'Even if we weren't, it's still not okay to speak to someone like that.'

'But I'm an officer,' he protested.

'Then act like it,' Sasha replied.

'I thought I was,' he looked down at his feet.

Sasha pushed the chair opposite her away from the table. 'Sit down,' she said. He did. 'What's your name?'

'Tony Long,' he replied, 'Assistant Officer, Long Lake Militia Company.'

'What made you become an officer?' she asked.

'My town did,' Tony replied. 'I'm pretty smart, at least in Long Lake. I work with the animals, keeping them healthy. When they were voting on officers, somehow, I got brought up. I really don't know how.'

'And you didn't join the Renaissance Army when it liberated the town?'

'I thought about it,' Tony replied. 'I wanted to, but I chose not to. I sometimes regret that. Maybe the town made me an officer to punish me?'

'And are all officers in your company jerks?'

'Yes,' he said. 'At least, when they're in formation. No one does anything unless someone is yelling at them. The officers yell at the sergeants, the sergeants at the troops, the troops at each other.'

'Sounds loud,' Sasha said. 'What are you doing here?'

Tony sighed. 'The Long Lake militia gets together once a week, tries running around, marching, getting into positions, but no one seems to have any idea what to do. I volunteered to my captain to come here and learn something about tactics.' He showed her the field manual he was reading. 'Not that my company will pay any attention. I think they made me and officer so they could ignore me.'

Sasha frowned. 'Look, Tony, before I was a cadet, I was a rifle in a field regiment. I saw fights. In fights you need to yell because they're really loud. Deafening. But the officers I followed didn't yell when they didn't have to. They led by example, they showed us how to be better, they explained and taught. Yelling is something you only do when you have to.'

Tony nodded, absorbing Sasha's words. Sasha thought about them for a moment herself.

I'm not the best example of that myself, am I?

'So, what do I do there?'

'Maybe you have to yell when you're in the militia company, maybe you have to insult and berate, but here, everyone is a volunteer, and we want to be here. We're trying to better themselves and be part of the army. Don't insult us for doing so.'

Tony nodded again. Then he displayed his field manual.

'Can you explain some of this to me?' he asked.

'Pass it over.' She went over the manual with him. It was the first time she had really read it, having learned it from the noncoms in Third Regiment. She found it interesting to see where the manual said one thing, and she was taught differently.

There is no one right way, is there? She asked herself, filing that idea away for the future.

Elector came in some time later. Sasha and Tony were reading silently, each in their own heads. Elector knocked softly on the table to get their attention.

'She's gone,' he confirmed.

Sasha sighed. 'We're down four,' she said. 'Only eight left. How many, do you think, will make it all the way through?'

'Half,' Elector said. 'At most. I honestly can't say I think Hero is going to make it, and unless Rose has changed her attitude during her rest, I can't say she will either.'

'She said she promised Cardinal she would make it.'

'Promises are words,' Elector said. 'It is actions that make or break.'

He left the library. Sasha pondered the meaning of those words and wondered who had broken their promise to Elector.

Or did Elector break his word to someone?

***

'The king is his own prime minister?' Mako asked. 'That doesn't make a lot of sense.'

Scott scoffed, standing before the class. 'Sure, it does,' he said. 'King Xavier wants power; he wants control of his government. A prime minister who isn't King Xavier is a prime minister who might start thinking for himself.'

'But isn't the idea for a king and a prime minister to balance each other and keep a rein on each other's power?'

'Sure,' the instructor said with a shrug, folding his arms and sitting against the desk. 'That's why it was written that way. But in politics, the practice never lives up to the ideal.' He smirked. 'It's the common political power-play bullshit that you'll find in every government not written by some tea-sipping novelist who spends his family's money. He can get away with it, so he gets away with it. And you, get used to it.

'Think about it,' he continued after a pause. 'He gets to direct the government in every way. When you're a despot, you want to control everything. That way, you –.'

The door slammed open, startling everyone inside. A man's voice bellowed, 'What the fuck do you think you are doing?'

Sasha looked, her heart racing at the interruption. The man was tall, well built, with a bushy grey mustache and a weathered face. He wore a brown uniform, one Sasha had not seen before, with the three-circle insignia of a brigadier. He also looked vaguely familiar, but Sasha could not place him, as he immediately stomped into the room, continuing his bellowing. Behind him, two armed guards and a staff sergeant, dressed as he was, entered and stayed by the door.

Scott tried to intercept the brigadier, but he was behind the instructor's table, and the man quickly reached his target first. 'I asked you a question, boy!'

He stood in front of Elector. As cadet captain for the week, Elector sat at the front of the class, so the man had to march the entire classroom to approach him. Elector had become ashen, and shakily stood to confront the intruder. He stood, unable to form a sentence at the man who stood furiously before him.

In profile, Sasha finally got the resemblance. The man was Elector's father.

'God dammit, boy, answer me! What are you doing?' the man yelled right in Elector's face. 'I sent you here to prove to these pansies that true Minnesotans have what it takes to lead this army, and you turn into a fucking nurse?'

'Sir, I . . . ,' Elector stuttered.

Scott was now standing right next to Elector, trying to get himself between the two. 'Brigadier Senator, you and your men need to leave.' Sasha glanced to the door, seeing two guards and an aide standing at the entrance.

'Fuck you!' Senator shouted. 'I'm not leaving until my son marches into whatever office you assholes are running this project out of and puts his name in for an infantry commission. He is a man, and that is where men belong.'

'Senator, his affinity for medical services has already saved numerous lives,' Scott said, finally pulling Elector out of the way and standing between the two. 'And as a future doctor, he will save many more.'

'You've got other cadets in this class,' Senator said, 'let them be doctors; my son is a soldier!' He stood before Scott, towering over the instructor.

Scott was not intimidated. 'All the cadets in this class are capable fighters and leaders in their own right, sir, and have declared their combat commissions.'

'Oh, really?' Senator sneered. He pointed at Sasha. 'That little girl is not ready for combat!'

'Cadet Scholar has four battle under her belt already,' Scott responded.

'Bullshit! Under who?'

'Colonel Snow, Third Field Regiment,' Sasha said.

'Snow? Ha!' Senator mocked her. 'That woman earned her colonelcy on her back. I'll bet you did the same for your spot here.'

The atmosphere of the room shifted from confusion to anger. Sasha clenched her fists, as did Scott. Mako stood suddenly. Roland growled.

'That was uncalled for,' Scott said.

Senator grinned at Scott. He perceived weakness and went for the attack. 'Was it? You really think every woman of position in this army earned it by talent? It's not in their blood to fight.'

'And yet they volunteer in droves,' Scott said, 'eager to prove their worth.'

'Great! Volunteer to cook and clean, to care for the wounded and write reports. To win a war, you put army before self. Men win battles; men win wars. Stop coddling the girls and train the men! Give me men, I'll liberate territory. Give me women, and our army will melt away at the first sign of danger.'

'Really?' Scott asked with derision. 'You think Colonel Snow will melt away? Brigadier Lily?'

'They haven't seen a real fight yet!' Senator shouted. 'Once they do, they'll run.'

Scott sneered at Senator. 'Boudicea?'

The name caught Senator unawares, and he paused. He glowered at Scott. 'I said some women are capable,' he finally said, 'but not all of them. And the generals are letting too many into combat positions they aren't ready for.'

'That's not for you to decide,' Scott said. 'The generals make that decision. The generals who have gotten us this far, who have liberated so much territory, freed so many people. Does that mean nothing?'

'Defeating the yeomen is one thing, you son of a bitch,' Senator retorted. 'The Royal Army will be a different beast.'

'We've already beaten them!' Sasha interjected.

'One company is nothing, Cadet,' Senator glared at Sasha. 'An entire brigade, a division, a corps is something else. We can't win against them fielding an army whose officers are all young and inexperienced.'

'That can be said about almost anyone in this army,' Scott said. 'Half the lieutenants are less than twenty years old, most of the colonels are thirty. This is an army of improvisation, Brigadier Senator.'

'Which is why it's so important for the right men to be in charge,' Senator said. 'Like my son!'

'I don't want to fight!' Elector said.

'I don't care! Your family has defended this country for centuries, and you will not fail them.'

'Senator,' Scott said, 'you have no authority over the Templar Project.'

'Fuck you!' Senator yelled in Scott's face. Sasha admired Scott's composure. Their teacher did not even blink.

Rose stepped forward. 'This is not the behavior of an officer.'

'Shut up, you Quebecois whore!' Senator turned and backhanded Rose.

Rose fell, and the room erupted.

Scott punched Senator in the face. Senator was as strong as he looked and responded, the two men now fighting in the middle of the classroom, pounding away at each other.

Mako and Candle both turned towards the door. The staff sergeant was gone, running off somewhere, while the two guards advanced to protect their general. One pulled a baton from his belt; Candle charged him, keeping him from getting the first swing. Mako rushed at the second, clamping a hand down on the holster to keep him from drawing his weapon.

Hero and Patch were staying back, although both looked angry enough to spit fire. Elector bent over to Rose, who was bleeding profusely from her lips and nose. Sasha jumped over the table and put herself between Senator and Rose. She did not want to fight Senator, but if she had to, she was willing to. Roland appeared beside her a second later, working his arm out of the sling and grimacing at the effort.

Scott landed a punch that broke Senator's nose, but Senator was a tough man. He punched Scott so hard the instructor fell over a table. Senator turned to Rose and his son, facing Sasha, who glared at him, her arms up ready to fight. Roland was whispering something to himself at her side. Scott jumped back up, throwing a table out of his way, Hero advancing by his side, but Senator was almost upon her.

'EVERYONE STAND DOWN!'

It was Caesar, who came in through the front door, with his Olympians. The rear door opened, and Del Oso entered, several instructors behind him. Mako and Candle and the two guards they were fighting with stopped and pulled away from each other, all of them bloodied and messed. Candle's nose might have broken again.

Caesar stepped forward; his eyes focused on Senator. His face was red with anger.

'What do you think you are doing?' Caesar asked.

'Correcting my son's error,' Senator scowled. He glared at Caesar.

Caesar was unmoved. 'No error has been made, Brigadier Senator. Your son has chosen a field commensurate with his abilities. It is ideal that he made such a change early enough to matter.'

'It is not "ideal" to betray his family's trust,' Senator bellowed. 'He is from a family of soldiers, and it will remain a family of soldiers.'

'One man following his passions to help others does not equate to betraying your bloodline,' Caesar replied. 'He is still in uniform. He is still a soldier.' Sasha thought he sounded remarkably calm considering how angry he was. He should have been yelling. Instead, he spoke in a calm tone. In some ways, it was more intimidating than Senator's bluster.

'What do you fucking know?' Senator yelled. 'With your books and your ideals, you know nothing about bleeding for a cause, of getting in the mud and fighting. Well, we do, and we will not betray that knowledge. I am taking my officer back.'

'Cadet Elector is no longer under your authority, Brigadier Senator. As such, you cannot remove him from the Templar Project.'

'You dare challenge me?' Senator roared. There appeared to be no end to how loud he could be.

Order him to leave! Sasha thought at Caesar.

Caesar was quiet for a moment, then stepped forward.

'Brigadier Senator, I have tried to be reasonable, but you seem intent on pursuing this course of action. If you continue, I will have no choice but to bring you up on charges.'

Senator sneered. 'You need me,' he said. 'Prince will back me.'

'How sure are you of that statement?' Caesar asked. 'You did strike a young woman for no reason, fought with a civilian, and advanced upon another woman with the intent to do harm. After Colonel Gold's court martial, are you certain Prince will take your position?'

Caesar and Senator were staring at each other in a contest of wills. Finally, Senator scowled and dropped his gaze. 'A court martial would not be ideal for the army at this time,' he growled.

'I am glad we are in agreement,' Caesar said, 'now apologize to Cadet Rose.'

'Apologize to a cadet?' Senator's voice raised again.

'A Templar,' Rose snapped. All eyes turned to her, as she stood up. She looked defiantly at Senator. 'I am not some common cadet! I am a Templar, chosen by the generals as the next generation of officers. And you, Brigadier Senator, are only an example of how necessary we are for the Renaissance.'

Senator scowled at Rose. He took a step towards her, and found his way blocked by the cadets, including his son. He glared at all of them, fists at his side.

'I apologize,' he growled, then turned and moved to leave.

'And your son?' Caesar asked.

Senator looked at Elector. 'You're pathetic,' he said.

'There is nothing pathetic about wanting to save another's life, even my enemy's,' Elector replied. His voice wavered as he spoke, but he stood tall as he said it.

Senator spat at Elector's feet. 'I have no son,' and swept out of the room, his men following him.

There was a silence. Then Scott cleared his throat. 'Well, that was more exciting than our usual class, wasn't it?'

Some of the instructors chuckled. Caesar walked forward. 'Are you okay, Cadet Rose?'

'Templar Rose,' Elector said, still staring at the door.

'I beg your pardon?' Caesar asked.

Elector looked at him and answered. 'Our first day. You said we are the Templars of the Renaissance. Not the cadets of the Renaissance. As such, we are not cadets of the Templar Project. We are Templars, General, and we should be addressed as such.'

Caesar looked at all of them, gauging their resolution. 'Very well, Templars is it. Templar Rose, are you okay?'

'I am, General.'

'Templar Elector?' Caesar asked next.

'She's fine,' Elector said, 'just a bloody lip. Apply some pressure and it'll stop bleeding.'

'I mean you, Templar Elector. How are you doing?'

Elector sighed. 'I'll be honest, General, that was pretty much the reaction I expected from him. I'm not happy about it, but I'm not surprised.' He looked almost in tears.

'I understand,' Caesar said, and looked like he truly did. 'If you need to talk, let Sergeant Major Del Oso know and I will come.'

'Thank you, sir.'

Caesar nodded curtly. 'Scott, can you continue your lesson?'

'Yes,' Scott said. His nose was bleeding from one of Senator's punches, but otherwise he was unfazed.

'Good,' Caesar said. 'Well, then get back to your studies.'

Mako saluted, shouting 'Templars!' The others followed suit, adding their own voices. Caesar returned the salute and left, the other instructors following him.

'Well,' Del Oso said from the back. 'You realize you're going to have to do that from now on.'

'Sergeant Major?'

'That's your new unit cry,' Del Oso said. He grinned, getting into his instructor voice. 'Templars! Instead of "Yes, sir," you will now respond with "Templars," loudly and together. 'Understand?'

The Templars all smiled, 'TEMPLARS!'

'Good. Now get back to class!'

'TEMPLARS!'

Chapter 23

Brooklyn Palace was a broad, majestic building. Built to the wishes of Queen Natalie soon after her husband's coronation, designed to be the palace where great balls and galas were held. Queen Natalie entertained many guests in its grand halls and expansive rooms. It became her home while King Xavier spent his time at Highland Castle, running his kingdom.

Four years into her reign, Queen Natalie's death briefly darkened the palace. King Xavier had no desire to visit the halls that reminded him of his beloved wife. Three years later, when Charlotte Waverly of Sault Sainte Marie became the new Queen of North Mississippi, the lights came back on. Charlotte took to her hosting duties with great energy, breathing life into proper society.

With Natalie, King Xavier appeared often. With Queen Charlotte, he was rarely in attendance, except during times when decorum required him to be. Such as a celebration of her birthday.

The same rules compelled Miklos to attend. The delegation from the Commonwealth Embassy had come together, many bearing their wives on their arms while others, like Miklos, attended without escort. Not that the ball would lack for eligible young women looking for an appropriate husband, or a single night together, if Miklos was in the mood. This evening, he was not, and put on his best scowl to keep the ladies looking elsewhere.

Brooklyn Palace was immense, with miles of paths winding through acres of gardens, statues, and greenhouses. The halls were open, great doors revealing room after room of food, drink, musicians, dancing spaces, smoking parlors, and performers. Every noble family who could make time was in attendance, and hundreds of important men who wanted influence had paid their way through the doors. Thousands of guests roamed the building and its grounds, waited on by hundreds of servants.

All for one common queen, Miklos thought, looking at the royal couple on their dais.

King Xavier sat on his chair, managing not to look bored. He wore his kingly attire, the great blue uniform with numerous medals and awards, as large as they were unearned, that decked the golden sash his position allowed. His uniform was tailored to disguise his midsection, which had grown in his old age, although Miklos had to admit he was in better shape than many other kings approaching sixty.

Queen Charlotte stood before her chair, welcoming the guests as they were presented. She was a moderately tall woman, in her mid-twenties, with long brown hair washed and scented, framing a pretty face and bright blue eyes. She had a pleasant body, well accentuated by the dress her husband had procured for her. It was scandalously revealing, and more than one noblewoman looked embarrassed at the distracted attentions of their husbands.

Charlotte made no notice of it. She was eight years the queen, and during that time it was common knowledge she had never shared her husband's bed. The marriage was one of politics, bringing the Archduchy of Sault Sainte Marie close to North Mississippi and away from the Quebecois, but Xavier would only ever have one queen.

Not that he remained idle. King Xavier had an appetite, fed by young noblewomen sent by husbands or brothers or fathers looking for advancement or patronage. His bed was not often empty.

Charlotte was not so lucky, cloistered as a virgin queen. Xavier only took some pride in showing her off as a trophy, a beautiful woman he refused to treat respectfully, and whom he relegated to such a supportive role. For many it might be an insult.

But as the embassy approached her to be introduced, Charlotte did not show any insult. She smiled, bowing slightly, welcoming each introduced guest, her dress revealing a bosom that drew attention. Ambassador O'Hara, introduced two placed before Miklos in the receiving line, was proper enough to avoid being caught in the trap of staring too much, much to the pleasure of his wife.

Master Veldt, the embassy economic coordinator, was caught gazing lasciviously, and received a quiet scolding from his wife as he was led away.

'Colonel of Regiment Sir Rika Miklos, Military Attaché to the Imperial Commonwealth Embassy,' the Queen's Herald announced.

Miklos stepped forward and bowed lowly. She was royalty, and one must keep up appearances. Even if he did linger a moment on her bustline.

'Happy birthday, Your Majesty,' he said.

'Thank you, Colonel,' she replied, beaming. 'Remind me, do you dance?'

'When I can,' Miklos said. He had long ago learned that she would remember a yes answer regardless of what he said. 'Will you save a dance for me?'

'I will!' Charlotte smiled again, bouncing enough to cause her breasts to jiggle. Miklos bowed and quickly exited. Between her dress and her perfume, she had an intoxicating effect, exactly what King Xavier wanted. Everyone jealous of his trophy queen.

Miklos entered the celebration proper, already looking for a dark hole to hide in for the rest of the night. There would undoubtedly be other officers, competent members of the Royal Army, or even former Commonwealth officers, he could spend his time with. The multitude of colors of the various branches of the military, the foreign officers, the ornate civilians; it was all enough to give Miklos a headache.

He saw General Robinson, the Marshal of the Army, and went the opposite direction. If there was to be a competent officer, it would be in the opposite direction.

As if bidden, Bennabi appeared. 'Ah, Rika,' he said in Odessan. 'Five minutes and you look bored already.'

'Does it show?' Miklos replied. 'Do you know a place to hide for the rest of the night?'

'As a matter of fact, I do,' Bennabi said. Miklos followed him through the halls and crowds, wondering where Bennabi had found a room and secured it so early in the evening. It was only when they were entering the room that Miklos realized the guardsmen at the door were not from the Queen's Regiment as they should have been, but soldiers from the Field Army.

Bennabi held the curtain open. Miklos shot him an annoyed look as he passed into the room.

'Welcome, Colonel Miklos. I hope I did not cut your time at the celebration too short.'

'Not at all, Your Highness,' Miklos said with a bow.

General Prince Stefan Santiago-Locke, second son of King Xavier and Commanding General of the Field Army, sat at a table with three seats. He gestured for Miklos and Bennabi to have a seat. 'Anything to drink?'

A sergeant, appropriately adorned but from the Prince's Headquarters and not the King's regiment, stood nearby.

'A scotch,' Miklos said. Bennabi nodded as well.

Prince Stefan nodded at the sergeant, then unwrapped a small book of cigars. He offered one to each guest. Another sergeant, one with a box of matches and a cutter, appeared. The drinks followed quickly, and the sergeants stepped back, leaving the three officers at the table.

'I enjoy the field life,' Stefan said, 'living in a tent and eating common field food, but there is a time to sit back and enjoy one's position.'

'I agree,' Bennabi said. 'Though I miss the open sky.' He looked at his stump

215

of an arm.

'It is important to sit back and take time to recover after a campaign,' Miklos said. 'But not for too long.'

'True,' Stefan said. He puffed on his cigar. 'And how is your investigation going?'

'Which investigation, Your Highness?' Miklos asked.

'Into the response, or lack of one, to this Renaissance Army.'

Miklos puffed on his cigar. 'Why would you think I am running an investigation?'

'Because I, unlike General Robinson, am not an idiot. Hundreds of former Commonwealth officers work in the Royal Army. Their loyalty is to the Commonwealth, not to the kingdom. And I cannot imagine that the margrave would not be demanding answers from you. So, do not fuck with me, understood?'

Miklos nodded. 'No, of course not, Your Highness.'

'Now, from the beginning. How is the investigation going?'

Miklos measured his words. 'The investigation goes. What it is finding is . . . depressing.'

'Enlighten me,' Stefan said.

Miklos paused, and took a sip of scotch. Prince Stefan was not an officer in the Commonwealth, and as such had no authority to demand information from Miklos. On the other hand, Stefan could be a good source of information, and if he wanted some in return, so much the better.

'The fact is, Your Highness, that I have been utilizing the former officers to conduct an investigation. General Robinson's response has been inadequate.'

'I agree. What have you found?'

'I've found out many things, Your Highness. For example, I have had contacts in the Quartermaster's Corps conducting unofficial inventories of their equipment.'

'A little embezzlement and graft are not uncommon,' Stefan said. 'I presume you found something more.'

'Duluth Rifle Brigade Armory: thirty-four stands of rifles missing. That's more than two hundred weapons. North Watch, Ursa Major Fortress, sixty-thousand rounds of ammunition missing. Fargo Garrison Barracks, three field kitchens and two field mortars, missing.'

Miklos shrugged. 'Not a single armory or facility is fully stocked. You are right, of course, that some graft will always exist, so I do not believe that every single item was taken by the Renaissance Army, but if they account for a fraction of what is missing, they're much better prepared than most officers want to believe.'

'That is disturbing,' Stefan agreed. He motioned for Miklos to continue.

'The Conscription Bureau has received notice from county auditors that hundreds of young men in prime conscription age, and as many women, have disappeared from across northern Minnesota. The Inspectorate has lost track of more than a dozen highly ranked members of the Old Guard. Families under surveillance have disappeared. The Renaissance Army is not some minor uprising that is confined to Walker County; they are not all children being led by the last of the Dawson family. They are armed, and supplied, and building up.'

'Are they?' Stefan asked again, a smile on his face. He was enjoying this.

'County yeomen are pathetic as soldiers,' Miklos said, 'but it would take more than a mob of armed peasants to chase them behind the walls of Walker. And to defeat a rifle company in pitched battle, that requires a level of training and equipment that can only be obtained by careful planning. This is a serious uprising, and nothing is being done.'

'I would not say nothing,' Stefan said. 'We have plans. Ideas. Things are put in motion.'

'Slow motion,' Miklos replied.

'We have reasons for doing what we do,' Stefan replied. 'The Renaissance Army will be allowed to grow only as big as it had to be before it is nipped in the bud. You'll see that.'

'Through reports and briefings, General?'

'You want a seat at the table? Very well. You will have a seat at the table,' Stefan promised. 'All I ask in return is that you make it clear to the margrave that I, Prince Stefan, have made our victory over the Renaissance Army possible. Not Marshal Robinson. Me.'

'You haven't won yet,' Miklos cautioned.

'Do you really think I can lose?' Stefan asked with a smile.

'No, Your Highness,' Miklos said, but inside he frowned.

I think that is the exact attitude they want you to have. Arrogant, overconfident, and unprepared.

Chapter 24

Wednesday, November Twentieth, 2475

Dear LTCOL Snow,

I am finally able to write to you in response to your letters. It seems we were going to wait until we reached a correspondence section of our instruction, so we could all write our letters together. If you had told me my instruction for commissioning as an officer in the Renaissance Army would have included instruction in writing a letter, I might have laughed, but there must be a reason it's being included.

I wanted to thank you for your words after the accident at Sparta. One of the Templars who died was a friend, and I still miss her, much as I miss Sonya. I have made some friends among the rest, but no connections as strong yet. I also may have made a few enemies, through some rather stupid actions on my part. I have to admit, I have not been the best representative of Third Regiment I could have been.

Two weeks ago, we spent a Sunday travelling to Holiday to see Penn, the Templar who lost his leg at Sparta. He is doing well; still getting over the loss of his leg, which is no small thing, but he's already been given a warrant as a Staff Officer, and he's learning to function as a new role as Assistant Liaison to the Civil Council. So, he's focused on learning that, instead of feeling sorry for himself. The rest of us have healed. My cast is off, and I'm working the arm again. Soon I'll be good as new.

My instruction continues to go well. Both Scott Anthony and Madam Moreau had complimented me on how well I've improved over the last few weeks. General Caesar, though often absent, has also been favorable in his praise. I may yet keep my name.

Aristotle and Fox have been greatly helpful, balancing praise and criticism. It's gotten me through some rough patches. Lily has been invaluable, and we've taken to eating together once a week, sometimes joined by other women Templars. It's been nice to have a constant mentor, not just for me but for some of the others as well.

I am amazed, honestly, that there is so much to learn, and we learn so little of it. I could spend the rest of my life happily stuck in the library, reading.

My Saturdays continue to include training on town fighting. Oddly enough, most of the Templars are involved in the training. Only Elector, who is our Mary, refuses to come. My body and skills are improving weekly, but some of the instructors have given us warning. The winter will come eventually, and when it does such training will become more difficult. I will have to find some way to force myself to continue.

I look forward to returning to my regiment next summer and bringing what I have learned to you and applying it to our campaign. Give my best to my friends.

Sincerely

Templar Scholar

***

The library was no longer empty most of the day.

The Staff School announced that several staff warrants were available, between six and sixteen, and that any student of the school could apply. In preparation for the various exams, several challenges and requirements were posted, most of which needed books within the library. So now, eight Templars were sharing the building with more than forty clerks. More than the building could realistically hold. Carpenter had a tent put up outside, with logs pulled up to make rows for sitting and extra cadre on hand as librarians.

Carpenter also relaxed the rules to allow the Templars to take their books to their classroom, but Sasha decided to stay at the library. If anything, it gave her a chance to meet some of the students of the Staff School and interact with them. She found the experience satisfying.

'Four staff companies?' Sasha asked.

The woman, Angela, nodded. She was an Able Clerk, still without any stripes on her arm. 'One for each specialty,' she whispered. They were outside, where conversation was more acceptable, but Angela tended to whisper regardless of where she was.

'But you're all still clerks and staff sergeants,' Sasha asked.

'Know so,' Angela shrugged. 'But that's still a broad description, so each company is built around what you're good at. If you're good at drawing and taking notes, you go into Operations, and you help officers plan their battles and send their messages. If you're good at picking out details, then you're in the Intelligence Company, looking for patterns in the enemy's actions. If you're good with numbers and math, you'll probably be assigned to Logistics, counting supplies and whatnots. If you're not any of those, you go to Administration, which is the catchall, but they constantly pull test and pull Administration people for the other classes.'

'It's their reserve?' Sasha asked.

'Yes,' Angela nodded. 'Exactly.'

'And you are?'

'Operations,' she said. 'I'm good at drawing and maps. Think how much easier explaining your plan is if someone can draw out six maps in an hour. Give me a night to work and I can color them.' She beamed with pride. 'I've got a good chance of getting to a headquarters, working under a general.'

'Good luck,' another clerk scoffed. 'They're going to take sergeants who have more time in service.'

'Know so,' Angela said, 'but the sergeants will need clerks to help draw maps.'

'And you're okay with that?' Sasha asked. 'Working that hard to just be another clerk in a headquarters?'

'Know so,' Angela replied. 'Beats shoveling pig shit.'

Sasha chuckled. So did the other clerk. Soon everyone in earshot was laughing. One of the temporary librarians glared at them but did not approach.

'What are you reading?' Angela asked.

'I'm reading about the Roman Empire,' Sasha said.

'What are you learning?'

'I'm learning about defeating an enemy's plan without fighting the enemy,' Sasha said.

'But aren't you supposed to be learning how to be an officer?' another clerk asked.

'I am,' Sasha said.

'Doesn't that mean you're learning how to win fights?'

'I prefer to learn how to win the war without fighting,' Sasha said. 'Every battle I can win without fighting is a number of men and women who live to another day.'

'I like that,' Angela responded. 'That sounds like a good attitude for an officer to have.'

The bells chimed; four o'clock. 'I've got to go,' Sasha said. 'Templar review.'

'See you tomorrow?' Angela asked hopefully.

'Sure,' Sasha said. She waved to the rest of the clerks and made her way to the Templar classroom.

***

Tony held the cards. He looked at the Templars sitting around him, their attention on him. Suddenly, he turned on Candle, holding a card before him.

'Templar Candle! Describe the principle of Distinction!'

'It is the principal of Just War that states legal force in an armed conflict may only be used against enemy combatants and not against civilians or neutral parties.'

Tony laughed. 'That's correct. Wow, you Templars sure have some serious learning to do.'

'You're keeping up pretty well,' Roland said.

'Sure. Maybe I can join.' Tony smiled. 'How hard could it be?'

'It's actually not too hard,' Roland replied. 'You need intelligence, physical ability, moral strength, and professional competence.'

'Is that it?' Tony asked.

Candle crossed her arms. 'I still think Penn should be here. So what if he's lost a leg. He's still got a good mind, and as a Templar he could do his job well.'

'He could, I'll grant you that,' Rose replied. 'But Caesar does not want to lessen the requirements. He wants the best. Penn no longer is.'

'Rose,' Candle said sternly, but Rose shook her head.

'I have no less affection for Penn than you do, but I am still speaking truth.'

'So,' Tony interrupted their argument, 'just those four things. Do they test you to figure them out?'

'Not really,' Sasha said. 'They're things you usually display naturally if you have them. I showed intelligence by reading everything I could get my hands on. I displayed physical ability and professional competence by serving as a rifle and corporal for several months and doing it well.'

'How did you show moral strength?' Tony asked.

'We're not supposed to say,' Roland said, but Sasha cut him off.

'No. I'm tired of secrets, and I don't mind answering some of them. Tony, I didn't let my sergeant shoot a yeoman who had just raped and murdered a ten-year-old girl.'

Everyone looked at her in shock.

'You did?' Tony asked.

'I did. Then when he was tried by the headmen and sentenced to death, I was part of the squad that executed him.'

'Wow,' Tony said.

'The point is,' Sasha said, 'that I displayed most of those attributes by simply being myself. I didn't know about the Templars until just before I accepted their offer, so I wasn't acting like I wanted to be in.'

'If you had known about the project, would you have worked for it?' Tony asked. 'Even if it meant leaving your regiment?'

'Absolutely,' Sasha said. 'It was hard for me to leave my regiment, even though they wanted me to come here and all but pushed me into it, but I've been trying to find my limits ever since I joined them. If I had known about the Templars beforehand, I would have worked really hard to come here.'

'I did,' Roland said. 'I joined up with the Siege Corps outside of Walker. Colonel Grace had me doing all sorts of things, and at some point, told me there was the program and she wanted me to work for it. We had to come up with some things for me to study, which was difficult, but it worked out in the end, because here I am!' he smiled.

'I was assigned,' Patch said.

'I thought you had to volunteer,' Candle said.

'Well, sure, we volunteered to be assigned,' Patch replied. 'Mobius was asked to send one of us from the Workshop. He got four of us together and let us know he wanted one of us to go. The four of us talked it over for a night, and we decided I was the one who should do it.'

'How did you guys decide?' Tony asked. 'Because you're the smartest?'

'Well, at the Workshop we're all rather intelligent, so that wasn't it,' Patch said. 'The four of us were rather in shape, or at least not sedentary. In the end, we developed some challenges that determined who was most fit to go. Moral quandaries, technical challenges. Also, who didn't start crying when we fired a gun.'

The Templars laughed.

'Wait,' Roland interrupted, 'you fired your first gun just before you came to the Templars? I've seen you shoot, you're a natural!'

'Nothing to it,' Patch said, 'I just know where the trajectory of the bullet will go and can plan accordingly. I could shoot even better if I could get my heart to stop beating, but then I'd be dead, and shooting wouldn't be an issue.'

More laughter. Patch gave a lazy smile, which she did when she acknowledged she was being laughed with and not laughed at.

'Mako?' Tony asked.

Mako shrugged. 'The Naval Group is like the Workshop in that we're all rather intelligent and competent. There were rumors that someone would be selected for something, but we didn't know for what or why.'

'How did you get selected?' Roland pressed.

'The Naval Group conducted a raid on Walker shortly after the siege was beginning. We cut out the count's yacht, the *Contessa*, so they could not use it for fire support or to get troops or supplies in and out of Walker. The garrison put up a fight, and we took some losses. I kept my head, kept us organized, and finished the mission. So, I got asked by Commander Faro to represent the Naval Group in the Templars.' Mako scratched his forehead and shrugged. 'I guess it was worth it.'

The Templars nodded. Those who had not yet seen combat looked at him in wonder. Those who had were more muted.

'I'm a hero!' Hero said. 'I was wandering when I came across a young girl captured by a pair of highwaymen. I killed them and saved the girl.'

'Where was this?' Tony asked.

'Down around Fourth Regiment,' Hero said. 'Colonel Wild had his second test me. I'm actually pretty smart,' he beamed. 'I can speak four languages, and I remember things pretty well.'

'Not always,' Rose said under her breath, but loud enough for Hero to hear.

'I'm not good in classrooms,' Hero admitted. 'I've learned a lot living on my own for ten years, but it wasn't at a desk. That's a completely different type of effort.'

'It is,' Sasha admitted.

'I'm here because of family,' Elector said. 'My father is an officer, and he got me in.'

'He must be proud,' Tony said.

Elector gave a grim smile. To Sasha's knowledge, he had not communicated with his father since Senator's dramatic entrance into the Templar classroom.

'I am also here for family,' Rose said quickly, drawing attention off Elector. 'Much like Elector. Beyond that, I am afraid I cannot say. Even if we are sharing new stories.'

Tony nodded. 'It must be annoying to not know too much about your fellow Templars.'

'It can be,' Roland said, then smiled.

> *'We are few and strong and proud*
> *'We are Templars!' we proclaim.*
> *And yet for all we have done together*
> *I still don't know your name.'*

Patch barked a laugh, and the Templars chuckled as much at her as at Roland. Then Tony turned to Candle.

'Candle?'

Candle was quiet, staring out the window much like Patch had a habit of doing. 'Mine is kind of difficult to talk about,' she said. There was a seriousness to her voice that made Sasha pay attention. 'I got into a difficult situation, along with someone who was part of the movement. We got each other out, and he brought me in. Somehow, I got asked to be a Templar.'

'Somehow?' Roland questioned. 'You just became a Templar without knowing it?'

Candle sighed. 'I told them – the people who were helping me – that I wanted to be the best I could be. They gave me some tests and challenges, and eventually I spoke with a general, and I got offered to come here.'

'You were interviewed by a general?' Tony asked, an edge of wonder in his voice.

'I think we all were,' Hero said. All the Templars were nodding. 'You?'

'I've seen General Prince a few times,' Tony admitted. 'And there's that other one, the bearded one.'

224

'General Caesar,' Sasha said.

'Right. Prince's deputy. He sees the moon in the sun, doesn't he?' Tony asked.

'You think he's addled?' Sasha asked. She had warmed up to Caesar over the last few months and all but forgotten that most people did not interact with him much, if at all. Even other Templars.

'He's not odd,' Roland shot back, 'at least not in the sense you mean. He's not a talker, he's a thinker. And if we're going to win over the Royal Army, or the Commonwealth, we'll need all the thinkers we can get.'

'That's why we're here,' Elector pointed out.

'Right,' Tony said quickly. 'You guys sure are lucky.'

A moment of silence, then Patch said, 'Day's getting long. We should move on.'

'Right,' Tony said again. He pulled out the stack of cards and looked at the Templars around him. 'Ready?'

They grinned back at him.

Chapter 25

The week after Cardinal's departure, Caesar instituted learning lunches. 'These are optional lunches,' he said, 'once or twice a week, where you will be eating with an individual who is willing to impart knowledge on subjects that we cannot cover during the Templar training, but they are subjects you may wish to learn about. If you are interested, feel free to attend. If you are not interested, there is no penalty.'

Most of the Templars took the opportunities. The topics could be interesting, or at least informative. The first one was hosted by Major Cross, the chaplain, discussing different religions and the importance of tolerance. Fox had come for one, about living in the woods. The oddest was when Colonel Black, the Renaissance Army's intelligence chief, spoke. He sat behind a curtain, and none of the Templars saw his face. His talk, about the importance of information and intelligence in campaigns, was very well received.

For this lunch, only Hero and Patch were missing. Hero did not participate, as he often avoided optional assignments, and Patch was sick with a fever. The man giving their presentation was a tall, thin man with greying hair. He was a civilian, wearing a traveling kit that looked brand new. Unrolled on the table before him was a leather case, similar to the ones field medics carried around. There were various tools inside, but the ones he had pulled out for cleaning with a handkerchief looked to be a set of eating utensils.

As cadet captain, Mako brought the lunch to the guest speaker. 'Oh, thank you,' he said, then blinked as he noticed the six cadets taking their places. 'Oh, hello! I didn't see you come in.' He put the utensils down – carefully on the leather and not the tabletop – and stood, smiling at all of them.

'Ladies and gentlemen, I am Doctor John Moore, formerly of the People's Republic of Michigan. There, I was a scientist, educated to learn the secrets of the world and pass along that knowledge. Now, I'm an advisor to the Civil Council, and, when I can be, a scientist, either for the sake of science, or in the service of the Renaissance Army.'

Moore stressed the word army in such a way that Sasha realized he did not like the word. He grimaced, then looked up. 'And,' he said, moving back into his introduction, 'I've been asked by a general to introduce you to the concept of science and the scientific method. I'll be back a few times throughout the winter, so I hope to see more of you.'

'Now,' he clapped his hands and smiled, 'who here has some scientific

226

knowledge?'

None of the cadets raised their hands. Moore shook his head. 'Oh, I'm sure you do. I just don't think you know you do. So much scientific knowledge is common enough people don't realize it IS science.'

'We had some instruction,' Roland admitted, 'but it wasn't very deep. We got sidetracked to Sparta before we got too far into it.'

'Ah, okay, so a lot of you don't even know much about science in general. Okay, then, okay. Let's start with a simple question: what is science? Science is a system of knowledge gained through observation and experimentation. A scientist sees something, wonders why it happens, proposes a reason, and then tests his reason to see if he is correct.

'So, can someone give me an example of science? Something that someone has come up with after experimentation and error.'

He looked out, hopeful, but no one spoke up. His face started to fall, and Sasha felt bad for him. She raised her hand.

'Yes?' he asked.

'Cooking?' she hesitated. 'I mean, someone had to look at ingredients and work out what makes a good meal.'

He blinked at her, and she wondered if she was incorrect, but then he smiled. 'I supposed it is, isn't it? Funny, I never thought about that, but you are right. Yes, cooking is a science. It's a form of chemistry; ingredients come together and form new mixtures. Those mixtures are heated; a chemical reaction occurs that changes the mixture to a final product.'

Moore chuckled, as if this was a joke only he got. Sasha smiled in response.

Moore looked about and realized there was a chalkboard behind him. He stood and wrote down 'Baking.'

'What else?' he asked.

'What about medicine?' Elector asked. 'Medicine requires a lot of science.'

'And how! Medicine requires a significant amount of biology; knowing the systems and organs of the body, how they interact. You must understand how the body reacts to wounds, and what you can do to repair the damage. Anything else?'

Candle raised her hand. 'I'm studying artillery ballistics,' she said.

'Are you? That, my dear, is physics. The study of motion and bodies, energy and force. I presume you are learning about trajectories, arcs and gravity.'

'Yes, sir.'

'Good, good. Yes, see, those are all sciences, and I'm sure as military officers you will come across more, even if you don't think about it. This building was built with science, even if the builders didn't understand the science of it. Science is all around us.'

Moore was visibly excited about what he was speaking about, and Sasha was afraid he might knock his food over.

'Today, I want to speak about the scientific method. Have any of you heard of this?'

No one raised their hand.

'Not surprising,' he said, then blushed. 'I mean, not surprising most of you haven't heard of it. Science is one of those things that often gets lost in communities that don't have the time to learn it. Same with history or literature. When most of your time is spent on surviving, such things often get set aside. No reason to know stories if everyone starves.'

He turned to write on the board as he spoke. 'The scientific method is a process used by scientists to answer questions about our world. You start with a question or problem that you want to answer. Let's use an example, oh,' he thought, 'let's go back to cooking, since we're eating, and you all know at least something about it. Let's say I want to find the best recipe for biscuits. Biscuits are important for soldiers because they can be baked easily, in great quantities, and carried for several days before they're eaten. So, my problem is that I want to make a better biscuit, one that doesn't always taste bland.

'Second, I come up with a hypothesis. A hypothesis is a theory that I am trying to prove, something I think or believe is true, but I don't have the evidence to confirm it yet. So, my hypothesis of the biscuits is that if I add bacon or cheese to the biscuits, I can make them much more palatable, that means tasty, but what ratios? Hm, curious, I wonder how much bacon or cheese a biscuit can take before it is no longer a biscuit. If it becomes too much, what is it then, if not a biscuit?'

'A pancake?' Elector suggested.

'A roll,' Cardinal said.

Del Oso cleared his throat. 'We might be getting off track.'

'Right,' Moore said, 'I do that, you know.' He laughed, and Sasha smiled. Like Caesar, he was getting more confident, and more enjoyable, as he continued.

'Okay, then, so back to the science of biscuits.

228

'After my hypothesis, I should spend some time looking at the data available. After all, if someone else has found my answer, then my work is pretty simple, eh? So, about biscuits, I . . . ,' he paused. 'I don't know much about biscuits, I'm afraid.'

'Sometimes,' Sasha piped up, 'if we had it available, we would mix in animal grease or lard, to give it a bit of flavor.'

'Ah, excellent!' Moore said, delighted. 'Okay, so we know that adding in flavoring is something that's done already. Good. So, as scientists, we would ask around and find out what sort of things get added, and what people like best. Maybe chicken grease isn't popular, but bacon grease is? Maybe butter is best. The point is, you ask around and find out what is already known about your topic.

He took a drink of water. 'So, we have our problem, how to make a better biscuit. We have our hypothesis, add bacon or cheese. And our review of available data. Now, if we want to find out if we are right, we need to experiment.

'Now, it's important when we test that we try to account for all the variables that impact the test. After all, it does us no good to test our theory if we can't prove whether it's correct or not.

'So, let's go back to the biscuits. We want to find a couple of units that have similar duties and require similar foodstuffs. We will take note of what sorts of biscuits we give them; this group will get one piece of bacon per biscuit; this one will have a piece of bacon every two biscuits. We will note what that group does; if this group spends three days marching, while this one spends one day marching, it could have a profound impact on how our experiment turns out.'

'Once we have our data, we have to understand what it means. Part of that is understanding what constitutes success. Is it the number of biscuits being eaten versus thrown away? How well the soldiers say enjoyed the biscuits? There's a lot of data that could be collected, and it's important that you collect as much as you can. After all, if the answer is in data, and you don't collect the data, you could miss the answer. Eh?

'Finally, most of the time, you're left with a question of what to do with your answer. Sometimes, an answer has no practical use. It may lead to something else, or it may not. You don't know that before the method begins, and finding a practical use is not always the point.

'Now, with our biscuits, we would have a practical use. We could report to the generals, "We have discovered that such and such a recipe improved morale and stamina by this amount," and, hopefully, the generals will use that knowledge to make better biscuits for the army. Or they might have a reason not to, but that's not going to stop a scientist from answering the question, now is it?'

He looked at the cadets hopefully. 'No,' Elector said, 'it won't.'

'Right. Now, as military officers, it's likely that none of you will ever use this knowledge, at least not in the sense that I have explained it, in pursuit of science, but some of the principles you might already be familiar with. If something doesn't work, find a new way of doing it. If something does work, could it work better? Efficiency,' Moore clucked, 'is something all militaries love to improve, eh?'

The cadets all nodded. Sasha understood most of it, at least as long as she thought about it in biscuits.

'Can any of you think of a way you might use the scientific method?' Moore asked. 'I mean, as a military officer.'

Every Templar raised their hand, and Moore grinned at them. 'You, um … sorry, I don't know your names.'

'Templar Rose, Doctor. I was going to say camouflage. Trying different ways of hiding things to find out what works best.'

'Oh, yes,' Moore said, writing on the board again. 'Next?'

'Building boats,' Mako continued.

'Refilling ammunition,' said Candle.

'New medicines,' Elector said next.

'New tactics,' Roland said.

'And you?' Moore asked Sasha.

'How to train people,' Sasha said. 'How to find out what everyone is best at, and how to make them better.'

Moore finished writing. 'That's a good list,' he said. 'Maybe before the next lunch, you can come up with examples of how these work, using this routine I have here. Or how you applied it to your own life.'

He put down the chalk, then walked to his desk, taking a bite of his sandwich.

'Okay, let's move on to some different types of science that exist. I think some of you will be quite surprised at the world around us.'

***

'I'm sorry, sir, but you're wrong.'

'Am I?' Caesar asked. 'How so?' His voice gave her a pause, the fear that came with arguing with a general. Then she remembered her practice speeches with Lily.

You are supposed to argue with him. That's the point.

'The Fabian strategy is not just "attacking the enemy's supply lines," sir. It's about finding and exploiting his weakness; supply lines just happen to be a common weakness to most armies. If the enemy is required to defend a single location, that can be exploited to get them to react the way we want them to, to look east while we strike in the west. A strength of cavalry means we fight from forests where their mobility is weakened. It's about not fighting the war that plays to our enemy's strengths.'

'But are those not the standard maxims of guerilla warfare? What differences do you find between a guerilla campaign and a Fabian campaign?'

Sasha thought for a moment. Caesar supported stopping to think before responding, although he would not let her run out the time in silence. No one else was in their classroom, and the Olympians outside kept most people away by their presence. She had time and quiet to think.

'The difference,' she finally said, 'is that the Fabian strategy is employed by an army that could fight a normal campaign but chooses not to. Guerilla warfare is used by a movement that doesn't have the strength for a normal fight, and so must fight an unconventional campaign.'

Caesar cocked his head. Sasha learned that meant he had some issue with what she said, although he did not always say what it was. Lily told her to ignore it, so she did.

'A field regiment,' Caesar said. 'Is that an example of a Fabian strategy or a guerilla strategy?'

'At the moment, guerilla.'

'Why "at the moment"?'

'Because there's been no enemy campaign to defeat,' Sasha said. 'The field regiments are grinding through the yeomen of several counties, liberating towns and getting the people on our side, but we haven't seen a campaign by the enemy yet. When the Royal Army takes the field, I imagine we'll start seeing the field regiments fighting to support a Fabian strategy.'

Caesar looked at her and nodded. 'Very good, Templar Scholar. You are progressing quite well.' Then he smiled. He was getting more comfortable around her, and she was glad for it.

'Thank you, sir,' she responded. 'What's next?'

'Next weekend, the Templars should be doing individual presentations to the rest of the class.' Caesar started putting his notes away. 'Not only can you present what you're doing to the others, you can learn what they are doing in return.'

'Interesting,' Sasha said. She looked forward to seeing the others' progress, and to see what sort of things they were learning that she was not.

'Did you have a question?' Caesar asked.

'Oh, yes.' She thought about the list of questions she had come up with. 'Is it true you and Colonel Wild tried to kill each other the first time you met?'

Caesar looked at her, and for the first time in the dozen or so times she had met him, gave her a genuine smile and laughed. *He actually laughed.*

'Yes, in fact, that is true.' He moved back to stand opposite Sasha. 'It should come as no surprise that the Renaissance Movement has been preparing for this campaign for some time, years, in fact. A significant amount of effort was spent on keeping the preparations secret; clandestine meetings and small movements of personnel and material.

'I was attending to some matter, accompanied by Fox, Lily and Snow. Wild, at the time, was living off what he could scrounge or steal, often from criminal elements who would not be reporting his behavior to the authorities. He followed someone to our meeting place and attacked us as we left.'

'He shot at you?' Sasha asked.

'No. Shooting is noisy. He waited until we were leaving with the items we came for and came out punching. Knocked Fox out of the fight quickly by knocking him into the water, then turned to fight me, while his wolf scared Snow and Lily away.'

'Snow got scared?'

'A large animal, making predatory noises? Retreat is a viable option in those cases. In any event, Wild and I fought. Wild is strong but untrained; I have some training, though I claim no expertise. I was good enough to keep Wild from taking me out, but I doubted I would win the contest.'

Sasha realized she was sitting at the edge of her seat, eagerly listening to the story. She tried imagining the five of them – Caesar, Fox, Lily, Snow and Wild – without military ranks, just five individuals who were randomly shunted together.

'Lily and Snow ran into our erstwhile business partners, who tried to take the

232

two women prisoner. After all, our business was concluded. Why not take advantage of the situation? Snow proved to be a match for their first attempt, starting a gunfight.'

'Where were you?' Sasha asked. 'You mentioned water. Were you among trees?'

'We were in a docking area of a city along Lake Superior,' Caesar said. 'Beyond that I cannot say. We were fighting amongst buildings. The sound of gunfire caught our attention. Then came the yelling from the criminals, taunting the women and demanding their surrender.

'This angered Wild, and I managed to argue him to our side. With Fox out of the water, we closed to engage the criminals. Between us and the two women, they did not have much of a chance. They were more bullies and opportunists than professional soldiers; beating them was fairly easy.'

'And he stayed with the RAM?'

'We were not the RAM yet,' Caesar pointed out. 'All he knew was that we were smuggling things into Minnesota, and that we dealt with criminals to get what we needed. He also had some contacts we were able to use to continue smuggling. He became a contact of ours outside of Minnesota, and when things went bad on him, he smuggled himself to us. He continued to work well for us, and we brought him into the fold.'

'Wow,' Sasha said. 'That was a good story.'

'One I hope you know to keep to yourself,' Caesar said.

'Of course, General,' Sasha assured him. Then paused. 'May I ask a second question? I promise it is not one that goes into secrets.'

'You can ask,' Caesar said.

'What exactly is the Workshop? And is Doctor Moore a part of it?'

'Those are two questions.'

'They are, but I have a point I'm trying to make.'

Caesar sat back down. 'The Workshop is a facility near Training Camp Rhodes. I do not believe you have been there?'

Sasha shook her head. 'No, sir. I'm not particularly technical-minded.'

'Indeed. The Workshop is a place where the Renaissance Army brings equipment we want maintained, and where we turn to when we need to look for solutions to problems. You have met several of their personnel.'

'Sure. Patch is from the Workshop. And I met Jacques and Mobius when we found that memorial spot.'

'Then you know the type of person who works there.'

'Is it a military installation?'

'No, at least not completely. Mobius holds a commission as a major, but rarely uses it. Some technical sergeants are there, but they mostly work to facilitate communications between the Workshop and the military. They are two very different cultures, and General Prince and I want to keep the Workshop as separate as we can. If I may cut to the chase, Templar Scholar, what is your point?'

Sasha hesitated, hoping she was not about to cross a line. 'There is a militia officer who comes to Athens to study at the library.'

'Many militia officers have the option of studying, but most come once or twice. I am aware of one who has been pretty consistent.'

'Well, sir, he has been helping some of the Templars with their studies. In addition, he seems to share some familiarity with Patch and how she thinks. He also has expressed similar sentiments to what Doctor Moore was talking about at lunch yesterday, about the scientific method and using reason to solve problems.'

'Interesting,' Caesar said. 'Continue.'

'So, I was wondering if it was possible to get him into the Workshop.'

Caesar thought for a few moments. 'What is his name?'

'Militia Officer Tony Long, Long Lake Militia Company,' Sasha said.

'And he is here every weekend?'

'He is,' Sasha confirmed.

Caesar thought some more. 'It is possible,' he said. 'Have you talked to Militia Officer Long about this?'

'No, sir.'

'Please do not do so. I do not want to get his hopes up until I have a chance to investigate. In the meantime, continue to work with him. Consider if you think he would make a good Templar. If I ask for your opinion, I want it to be clear and as unbiased as you can.'

'I will try, sir,' Sasha nodded. 'Thank you.'

Caesar nodded and stood. 'Until next time, Templar Scholar. Enjoy your weekend.'

Chapter 26

The Templars lost their Sunday.

Del Oso let their morning continue as normal until after breakfast. The cadets did the weekly change of captaincy, from Mako to Patch, then Del Oso called for their attention.

'Templars,' Del Oso said. 'We've received word from General Prince that we need to temporarily relocate.'

The Templars exchanged looks. 'Sergeant Major,' Roland asked, 'is it a cavalry raid?'

'No, Templar Roland. I do not know specifics, but it is not for purposes of safety. I believe that Prince has another reason for bringing you out of Athens, but I can't say what it is.'

'Where are we going, Sergeant Major?' Rose asked. 'It's not Sparta again, is it?'

'We're spending the next week at Olympia, Templars.'

Sasha sighed some relief.

Olympia, the headquarters of the Renaissance Army. It was where Prince and Lily had their offices, where information flowed in and orders flowed out. Unlike Athens and Sparta, out in the middle of the forest, Olympia was built around a town that had been liberated, though Sasha did not know the name of the town. It was, in many respects, the capital of the movement.

'This time, we will be taking everything with us,' Del Oso continued. 'Dress in your field uniforms, full equipment, and pack both exercise and class kits, including your satchels. Each of you will be carrying some books from the library you will need for the next week. Scott Anthony and Madam Moreau will be relocating for this week as well, so you'll see them up in Olympia.'

'Just for one week, Sergeant Major?' Elector asked. 'Why?'

'I don't know,' Del Oso shrugged. 'I've been told it is of importance. General Prince will tell us when we get there. Now get to work. We have a schedule to keep.'

The Templars packed quickly. Their field packs were big enough to carry their clothes and satchels, and once the librarian brought them over, their books. The kitchen handed them some hardtack. It was a decent load once all was packed up.

A wagon would be nice, Sasha thought to herself.

Del Oso and Patch went over their route. He handed her the map, and she called Sasha and Elector to the front as guides. 'We're taking a roundabout way,' she said.

'Of course we are,' Sasha responded.

'We'll need to keep a good pace, but it shouldn't be a problem,' Patch said. 'Shall we go?'

Sasha and Elector nodded. Sasha took the compass, Elector prepped his ranging beads, and the Templars shook out into formation. Patch nodded to Sasha, and they went out into the forest.

***

The Templars marched into Olympia.

The town was still there, the people still living their lives much as they had been before they were liberated; but, in the woods around them, the Renaissance Army built the ram cabins that functioned as their headquarters and barracks. Del Oso directed them towards the guest huts, where they were intercepted by an elderly man walking about with a cane. Del Oso nodded at Patch, who walked up to the man.

'Sir? Templars from Athens, reporting for bunks,' she said.

The man blinked at her. 'Temples in Athens, what? That makes no sense. I'm waiting for cadets, what?'

Hero suppressed a laugh.

'That is us, sir,' Patch said.

'Then why didn't you say so, what?' the man shook his head. 'I'm DeWitt, and I've got you all settled in number three, what? Have any problems, find me. Then I'll yell at you until you solve your own damn problems, what?'

Del Oso led them to an assigned cabin, where it was obvious they would not be sleeping alone. Sasha counted thirty-six beds in eighteen double bunks.

'I think I just realized how blessed with space we are at Athens,' Roland said.

The other Templars agreed. They took their assigned bunks, Sasha taking a top one over Rose. They were settling in when Del Oso called them to attention.

General Prince had just arrived and entered the cabin.

'At ease, Templars,' he said. 'How are you doing?'

'Good, sir,' the Templars replied.

'Good, good,' Prince smiled. 'You might be wondering why I asked you to be relocated to Olympia for a few days. The fact is, I could use your help.'

Our help? Sasha wondered. Other Templars looked equally confused.

'I presume that as Templars, you're able to count,' Prince said, 'so you will have noticed a lack of any information regarding the Second Field Regiment. There is a reason for that. The longer they are not making a noise, the longer we can keep the roads through their territory open and flowing. Supplies flow down those roads. So does information. And, in this rare case, an interested party.'

Sasha glanced at the other Templars. They were all paying rapt attention.

'An interested party from a foreign institution has come to investigate us. We have done preliminary introductions through correspondence, and now their ambassadors are here to see us in person. Among the many things I want them to see is you; young men and women who are working to be better people and officers. Expect them to be viewing your classes, maybe even speaking with you. I want you to help them the best you can, without violating the rules you've abided by.

'That being said, do not lie. Do not fabricate. If you feel uncomfortable answering a question, say so. Can I trust you to help me?'

The Templars nodded. 'Of course, sir,' Sasha said.

'Good. Now, the ambassadors came in with some friends who are due to leave again soon, and they need some help getting ready to go. Templar Candle and Templar Scholar, I want you to go help them.'

'Templars!' Sasha and Candle said.

'Thank you, Templars.' He smiled at them, and Del Oso called them to attention again. Then Prince was gone, leaving a sergeant behind.

'I'm to show you to the wagon,' he said. Sasha and Candle followed him out into Olympia.

Olympia was the fourth official station in Walker County that Sasha had visited, and she was coming to realize how all of them followed a pattern. Ram cabins were built in the woods, in rough but recognizable rows, with one group set aside for the headquarters and cadre of the station. Paths were marched through the woods, eventually becoming the Mardurer Maze for exercise runs and training marches. Sasha was pretty sure she could find her way through it easily, even without a guide.

Sasha and Candle followed the sergeant, not speaking to each other. They saw sentries ahead of them, civilian guards. At first, Sasha thought they were the Council Guards, but as they got closer, she recognized them as Hollander Caravan guards. In fact, she recognized one of them from the Madero wagons.

Mariposa might be around.

Sasha worried about seeing her friend again. Mariposa was Sasha's only friend in Penelope's Haven, the daughter of a caravan leader who stopped by once a month. It was Mariposa who had originally put the idea of the Renaissance Army in Sasha's head. Back when Mariposa only knew of it as the Mardurers. Would she be happy to see Sasha? Angry?

Come to think of it, what was the Hollander Caravan doing here? They haven't been allowed inside the Liberated Counties for months.

'Here,' the sergeant said. 'Report back to your barracks when you're done.' And he left.

The two turned a corner and saw a single massive Hollander wagon, laden with goods destined for various towns across northern Minnesota. She did not see anyone around.

Then Mariposa stepped out from behind the wagon, looking over the materials and making notes on a clipboard. Sasha decided to smile, to be optimistic about the meeting. She was not sure what to do about Candle; hopefully Mariposa would know not to say her name in front of a stranger.

Mariposa turned to the two women approaching, her eyes widened, and her mouth dropped. 'Oh my god!' she gasped. 'You're here!'

Sasha's smile faded when she realized Mariposa was staring at Candle.

Candle looked nervous, glancing at Sasha, eyes wide.

'I thought you might be here,' Mariposa said, stepping forward. 'I just didn't think I'd . . . ,' she glanced over at Sasha, and gasped again. 'BOTH OF YOU?'

Mariposa knows both of us, Sasha thought, realizing she should not be surprised. Mariposa did travel extensively; she must have many friends across the kingdom.

Mariposa stepped forward and hugged Candle, then hugged Sasha. 'I wondered if I would ever see either of you again,' she said.

238

'I did, too,' Candle said, stuttering in confusion. 'I'm sure Scholar did as well.'

Mariposa looked at Sasha. 'Scholar?'

'It's my Renaissance name,' Sasha said. 'Hers is Candle.'

'Scholar and Candle,' Mariposa said. She laughed. 'Okay. Can I still be Mariposa?'

'Of course,' Candle said.

'We were told to come and help you,' Sasha said, 'but it looks like you're done.'

'We were just going to eat before we go,' Mariposa said. 'But I know why you're here.' She gestured for the women to stay and went towards the rear of the wagon.

Sasha looked at Candle, who stared after Mariposa with anticipation.

Mariposa returned carrying a small bundle. An arm was waving, grasping at a lock of her hair. Mariposa had a huge smile.

A baby? Why? Is it Mariposa's?

Sasha looked over with a confused look on her face and saw Candle crying.

'Is that . . . ?'Candle hesitated.

'Yes,' Mariposa said, smiling as she handed the infant to Candle. 'He's doing well, growing fast.'

Candle smiled and the boy, who looked up and let out a big laugh. Candle walked over to a log nearby and sat down, singing softly.

Sasha looked after them, then it hit her. 'That's her son.'

Mariposa nodded. 'Yes. I've been keeping him for the last few months. I didn't know where she had gone; in the RAM, sure, but not as an officer. That's a surprise.'

Sasha looked at Mariposa in confusion. 'We're officers in training. How did you know?'

'You have Renaissance names,' Mariposa said. 'All officers of the Renaissance Army have them.'

'You knew that?' Sasha wondered. Was that common knowledge outside the Renaissance Movement?

Mariposa gave her a grin. 'Come on, Scholar, you should be able to figure this out.'

239

Sasha thought for a moment, then sighed. 'You're a part of the Renaissance Army.'

Mariposa nodded. 'Well, the Renaissance Movement, anyway. One of the reasons I tried to steer you towards them, but I didn't know you'd become an officer; I just figured you would do well in the RAM.' She gestured to the wagon. 'Mind if we eat?'

Sasha nodded, and Mariposa went to grab a basket. As usual, she had more than enough food, which she shared.

'So, you're officer cadets?' Mariposa asked.

'Templars,' Sasha responded.

'What is a Templar?'

'The Templar Project is a special program the generals set up, to train exceptional young men and women as officers of the future.'

'And you somehow managed to get yourself selected to the program?'

Sasha shrugged. 'When I left with my regiment, I had to catch up and learn as much as I could. Apparently, I exceeded expectations, and they asked me to join.' She paused. 'Did you hear about Penelope's Haven?'

Mariposa sighed and nodded. 'I saw it after it burned. The yeomen were burning a lot before they got bottled up in Walker. They even menaced our caravan when we tried to leave Walker for Brainerd.'

'Really?' Sasha was surprised. Hollander Caravans were protected by a king's decree, which not only extended to granting them armed guards, but the personal protection of the king's government. Yeomen who threatened the caravans were usually not yeomen for long.

'They did,' Mariposa said. 'We almost got into a firefight with them. Dad managed to yell his way out, but it was a close thing. I can't imagine being in a firefight. Can you?'

'I've been in several,' Sasha admitted.

'Several?' Mariposa asked. 'Wow. Quite the change from Penelope's Haven.'

'Indeed,' Sasha said. Mariposa laughed. 'What?'

'You speak differently,' Mariposa said, 'and it's not just confidence, Templar Scholar. By the way, how did you get that name?'

'When I left with the people who rescued me, I was behind all of them on how to be part of the regiment. I learned all I could from everyone I could,

240

including a few books available. There weren't a lot to choose from, but I read them over and over again. I got called the Scholar of Third Regiment, so when I was asked to come to the Templars, my colonel asked me to take the name.'

'It's not a bad name,' Mariposa said.

'No,' Sasha admitted. She thought back to the conversation with Fox prior to the prison battle that spring. *Better to be called a scholar than a killer.*

'How does one become a Templar, anyway?' Mariposa asked.

'You prove you can be a good fighter, prove you want to learn, and prove you're a good person,' Sasha said.

'How do you prove you're a good person?' Mariposa wondered.

'A lot of different ways. For me, I kept my sergeant from shooting a surrendered yeoman.'

'Well that's good,' Mariposa smiled. 'I'm sure the yeoman was glad you did that.'

'I was in the firing squad that executed him a few hours later.'

Mariposa looked at her friend in surprise. 'What?' she whispered.

Sasha shrugged. 'He raped and murdered a ten-year-old girl. He was tried by headmen and sentenced to death.'

'You killed someone?' Mariposa asked.

'I've killed at least seven people,' Sasha said with a grimace. *Why does this keep coming up?*

And why do I keep answering?

'Does that upset you?'

Sasha paused. 'Sort of,' she said. 'It upsets me that I constantly have to tell people that, as if the number of people I've killed is somehow important. I've killed when I had to, when my friend's lives were threatened. Even then, I've lost friends.'

Sasha sighed. 'The man who gave me the scroll, Major Fox, called me a killer. He didn't mean it as an insult, but a compliment. He said there are some people who fight well, and I'm one of them. I understand what he meant, but I'm not happy about it. I'd rather be a scholar than a killer.'

'So, it doesn't bug you?' Mariposa asked. 'Killing people?'

Sasha thought for a moment. 'It does bug me, killing people. I don't like it. But I don't kill because I like it. I kill because I'm a part of the Renaissance

Army, and I want to see it win. And if that means I have to kill, so be it.' She looked at Mariposa. 'Does that make me a bad person?'

Mariposa shook her head. 'No. I think if you were a bad person, you wouldn't feel guilty about not feeling guilty. Besides, Debor-, I mean, Candle has killed more than that, and she's a good person.'

'I know,' Sasha said. She thought about questioning Mariposa about Candle's history but decided against it. She chose instead to change the subject. 'I'm surprised your caravan is out here.'

'According to our logs, I'm not here. I'm stuck in Virginia County. I'm certainly not hauling a pair of men and a large printing press into the Liberated Counties.'

'Printing press?' Sasha asked.

Mariposa shrugged. 'I don't know, it wasn't my choice. The men I brought in had to bring it. They said it was their fee to talk with the generals.'

Sasha smiled at that. *A printing press.*

'Anyway, this is the last run for a while,' Mariposa continued. 'The king is taking a harder look at our timetables, and it's getting harder and harder to sneak in. Rumor has it he's hoping winter takes a heavy toll on the rebels before the spring offensive. Luckily there are some avenues that haven't closed yet.'

'A spring offensive?' Sasha asked.

Mariposa nodded. 'That's what I've heard. Field Army officers have been moving around the Red River Valley and along the railways, surveying for offensives. Troop placements, supply needs, that sort of thing. They've been contracting with our western offices for the finer goods officers enjoy. Anyway, I imagine they'll put up a different fight than the yeomen.'

'They did when I fought them,' Sasha said, absently thinking about the entire Field Army taking the field. The prison camp was one rifle company; there were one hundred and forty-four such companies in the Field Army, in addition to artillery, cavalry, and heavy weapons. The idea of more than fifty thousand soldiers marching into Walker County made Sasha shiver.

Mariposa was shocked again. 'You've fought Royal Army?'

Sasha nodded again.

'Well,' Mariposa said after a moment, 'your life sure has changed since the last time I saw you.'

'Yes,' Sasha admitted. 'For the better.'

242

'Good,' Mariposa smiled. 'Good.' The food was largely gone, and Mariposa began to tidy up. 'We should get moving. After all,' she grinned, 'there are rebels about.'

They made their way back to Candle. The baby boy was smiling and laughing with his mother, who was singing a song to him in a language Sasha had never heard before. She looked up as the two women approached, her face pained.

'I don't want to say goodbye again,' she said.

'I know,' Mariposa replied. 'You could come with us.'

Candle thought for a moment, staring down at her son. 'No, I can't. As much as I'd like to, I can't.' She raised her son up and kissed his forehead, whispering to him in the language again. Then she hugged him, and quietly sang.

> *'You are my sunshine, my only sunshine,*
> *You make me happy, when skies are grey.*
> *You'll never know, dear, how much I love you,*
> *So please don't take my sunshine away.'*

Candle looked up and handed him up to Mariposa.

'Thank you,' she said.

Mariposa nodded. 'Of course, Candle.'

The two Templars helped Mariposa secure the child. Mariposa hugged each of them and climbed up to the driver's bench. She started the wagon down the track, the mounted riders falling into formation.

Candle looked on the verge of bawling. Sasha waited for the wagon to move out of site before she turned and pulled Candle into a tight embrace.

Candle cried for several minutes, her head awkwardly sitting on Sasha's shoulder. Finally, she took some deep breaths and stood up.

'Thank you, Scholar.'

'I'm sorry,' Sasha said.

'For what?'

'For being rude. For the grapes.'

Candle laughed. 'I was so angry with you about that. Everyone else had to keep us apart for days.'

'Well, I'm sorry,' Sasha repeated. 'I was not living up to my own expectations. I was not being the officer I thought I should be. And I saw you, all cheery and happy, even on the edge of failure, and I got angry.'

'I've always been bright and cheerful,' Candle said. 'Most people don't mind. But you were under a lot of pressure, what with the generals tapping you.'

Sasha frowned. 'What does that mean?'

Candle looked down at Sasha. 'You know. Being called upon by one to help destroy a mayor during a town debate or having a late-night discussion with General Prince and Colonel Aristotle when you're just a rifle. You were marked long ago, Templar Scholar.'

Sasha went white. 'How do you know about that?'

'I listen,' Candle said. 'You're the Scholar of Third Regiment, aren't you? Sarah Little, or something?'

'Or something,' Sasha said.

'The woman who fights while screaming like the devil. Who kept her sergeant from murdering a man, and held a riverbed against an entire rifle company for ten minutes?'

'I was alone in that riverbed for a less than a minute,' Sasha said. 'How do you know all this? Have you been talking to Mako?'

'I make it a point to learn all I can about people. If you knew my story, you'd know why. Am I right about who you are?'

'Yes,' Sasha admitted. 'I didn't know I was that well known.'

'Lots of stories travel about,' Candle said. 'Does Fourth Regiment really run about naked?'

'No,' Sasha said. 'But they are a very wild-looking bunch. Lots of bare arms and tattooed stripes.'

Candle smiled. 'The point is, Scholar, that twelve Templars came to Olympia, all carefully chosen, all tested, but only one had reputation before all this.'

'Weren't you all interviewed by a general?' Sasha asked.

'Yes, but that was the first time most of us had met one.'

Sasha looked at Candle, thinking about what she said. All the members of the RAM knew General Prince and saw him as he toured the Liberated Counties. He was a public leader. It never occurred to her that most of the soldiers of the RAM would not have fireside chats with a general. At least, it never occurred to her exactly what that meant.

244

'Can I ask one question, before we get back?' Sasha asked, hoping to change the subject.

'Sure.'

'About the grapes, I've been curious how many –.'

'Thirty-eight.'

'Thirty-eight?' Sasha's jaw dropped and she stopped. Candle advanced a few steps then turned back.

'In one night.'

Sasha was speechless, staring at Candle in shock. Candle shrugged.

'I'm not happy about that number any more than I think you are about yours, Scholar, but it came down to me and my unborn child, or a boat full of scoundrels. I made my choice.'

Sasha closed her jaw, looking at the taller woman. She finally managed a curt nod. 'That kid has an amazing mother.'

'Damn right he does,' Candle smiled. 'Now let's get back to work, shall we?'

Sasha agreed, and followed Candle back to the other Templars.

Chapter 27

The morning routine was the same. Awake early, light exercises and a mile run. Olympia had showers, and the Templars made use of them. When they returned to their barracks, they found a surprise waiting for them.

'New uniforms?' Roland asked. 'But we haven't worn out the old ones.'

'They're not just new,' Rose said, pointing to the jacket Roland had just unfolded.

The jacket was the same dull grey jacket the cadets were used to wearing, but now it had some color on it. The shoulder had a badge sewn on, an open yellow book beneath the blue diamond of the RAM, and a large red T overlaying both.

'The badge of the Templars,' Sasha said.

Nor was that all. The left topmost pocket now sported two small square ribbons, and above those was a red badge with a golden wreath and a pair of crossed rifles in silver.

'What are these?' Roland asked.

'That top one is the Combat Badge for Infantry Service,' Elector said, pointing to the wreath, 'the rifles mean you saw combat with an infantry unit. The gold ribbon is the Ribbon of Merit, which your previous commander awarded you for your service. And the yellow and gold ribbon is for service in Walker County.'

'The same colors as the yeomanry?' Sasha asked. Elector nodded.

'How do you know all that?' Candle asked Elector.

'My father wanted the RAM to use the Republic's award system. General Prince agreed to an award system but wanted to avoid the huge fields of ribbons some officers had in the old army. There were a lot of compromises.'

'I'm surprised we didn't know about the awards,' Candle said.

'We might have learned it if we weren't shunted off to Sparta,' Sasha pointed out, unfolding hers.

They all unfolded their new jackets. Sasha saw the Combat Badge, with two crossed axes instead of rifles, and one ribbon she recognized as the colors of the Brainerd yeomanry – blueish grey and crimson – with a gold star.

Rose was the only one whose jacket lacked anything other than the Templar badge. Patch had one ribbon. Hero, Elector and Candle had two, and Mako had three.

'What's with the gold star?' Mako asked Elector. He had the Walker ribbon, with the gold star on it.

'Mentioned in Dispatches,' Elector said. 'Your unit commander mentioned you by name in an official report.'

Four of them had combat badges. Sasha and Hero with the crossed axes of a field unit, Roland with the crossed rifles of an infantry unit, and Mako with the silver anchor of a naval unit. Candle and Hero both had a medal that Elector identified as the Badge of Heroism, for heroic actions taken outside of combat.

'From when I saved that girl,' Hero beamed. He looked at Candle. 'What's yours for?'

'Heroism,' Candle said blandly as someone started calling for breakfast.

As at Athens, food at Olympia came from a common kitchen, but there were no fire pits to eat around. Instead, numerous tables and benches stood in the town square. Civilians and military alike ate similar food, which Sasha thought tasted better than the food at Athens.

'I agree,' Candle said.

'It certainly tastes better than the food at Sparta,' Hero replied.

'Because you kept screwing it up,' Roland joked. Hero made a rude gesture but laughed.

Del Oso appeared as the Templars finished their meal.

'How do they fit?' he asked. The Templars all commented on how nice the new jackets were, then Patch raised her hand.

'Why do I have a ribbon?' she asked. 'I'm not military.'

'Your unit commander gave it to you,' Roland pointed out.

'The Workshop isn't a unit, Roland, and I'm not military!' Patch said again.

'Awards are given by commanders,' Del Oso said, quickly interrupting their debate, 'following criteria that General Prince chose. If you want to know why you got an award, you must ask the officer who gave it to you, or perhaps General Prince. He might know. Now, if there's nothing else, we have class.'

The Templars followed Del Oso to a ram cabin that was set up as two smaller rooms, connected by a door. Their half had been converted into a rather cramped classroom with seats for twelve people.

Templar Scholar

After a short time, Patch called them to attention. General Prince came in through the door, followed by two men in civilian clothes and Officer Bellona. Prince waved them to sit down.

'Templars,' Prince said. 'These are our guests. This is Michael Shaw, and this is Antonio Germaine. Gentlemen, these are the Templars. Eight of our best and brightest. Not all from Minnesota, not all destined for fighting, but still our best.'

Shaw looked at the Templars and smiled. He was a handsome man, Sasha thought, with soft blond hair and a strong chin. He stood with a confidence that Sasha liked. His clothes were of high quality but worn from constant travel.

Germaine looked to be Shaw's opposite. He scowled at the Templars and did not stand tall and straight. He was pudgy. The top of his head was bald, the black hair only appearing on the sides.

Prince dressed in a well-cared-for uniform as usual, but what Sasha noticed today was the lack of any ribbons or medals on his chest. He had the flag of the Renaissance Army on his shoulder for a unit badge, but nothing else. Come to think of it, Sasha recalled seeing very few members of the RAM with ribbons on their uniforms.

Why are we different?

'These men are going to observe you for some time today,' Prince said, interrupting her thoughts. 'Please do not worry. Continue as normal.'

He led them to the back, where they took their seats. Shortly thereafter, the thump of Madam Moreau's cane heralded her approach. Madam Moreau came in, settling herself into her position at the front. When she saw the ambassadors in the back, she gave them a long, hard look.

'Class,' she said, shifting her attention to the students. 'Last week we discussed the Roman Empire. This week, we shall discuss the fall of that state, and the beginning of the Middle Ages. Before we begin, I want to make one point.

'History is a story. It is the story of people, of leaders, of countries and armies. It is a story that we learn from books, or from listening to our elders. It is a song, a poem, a painting of an event. All important to remember and learn from.

'Yet, it is also important to recognize that as a story, it will include the particulars of he who writes it. When we spoke of Rome, we learned of Hannibal Barca, and we read some of what was written by the Romans about him. Did the Romans do him justice?'

The Templars shook their heads.

'No, they did not. No matter how hard you try, any history you learn or write will never include everything that happened. We read through the campaigns of the Punic Wars in one day. That covers a century of time, thousands of days in which hundreds of people made decisions. Think of how that all is worked into, or ignored, in the history we studied. Think of all that was missed. You cannot study history without acknowledging that it does not tell the whole story.

'I'm sure you all remember Scott Anthony's speech when he first instructed you at Athens, when he said he would teach you how politics can be manipulated. I say the same thing about history. The story that is recorded cannot be the whole story, and often is written to promote or disparage a version of the truth. "Our enemies are barbarians and we are the chosen people" is a theme you will read about often enough.'

She paused. Sasha realized this was not planned. Madam Moreau was speaking completely on her own, in reaction to the visitors behind her.

'Why am I telling you this?' she asked. 'I have two reasons.

'First, as officers of the army and leaders of the Renaissance Movement, you will have a voice in shaping how the story of the Renaissance Army is remembered. What will you choose to record? What will you emphasize? What will you ignore? Ask yourself this now.

'Second, if history is indeed a story, then learning about the misdirection of history will help you with the misdirection of life. Perhaps it will even let you understand when someone is feeding you bullshit.'

With her last word Moreau glared at the pair of ambassadors. Sasha glanced back at them. Shaw was completely stone faced, maybe even amused, but Germaine glared right back at Moreau. Prince was frowning, obviously concerned with Moreau's speech.

Sasha jumped when Moreau's cane slapped the desk. 'Attention front! Pencils ready. We begin with the division of Rome into two empires.'

Moreau's instructions involved more interactions with the Templars, asking them to remember facts from previous classes. The Templars stumbled a few times, but Sasha thought they came off as attentive. Either Moreau was showing off for the ambassadors, or she was trusting the Templars to respond to a more interactive experience.

From history they went into politics, and Prince stood this time.

'We have discussed the forms and organs of government,' he said. 'Now we must discuss the relationship between government and people. And to do so, we must understand rights.

'A right is a freedom that every person has. You have the right to decide whom to marry. You have the freedom to decide what future you want to fight for. It is a basic and fundamental principle of democracy. And it is a principle that many of you did not grow up experiencing.

'The relationship between government and its people is largely about rights. Oppressive government limit the rights to many of their population; free governments limit their own abilities to circumvent those rights. The debate over what constitutes a right and what does not has been going on for millennia. We will not be able to answer that here, and if we were to have a debate on the subject, I'm sure we would find a number of differences in opinions. That's fine, but you will leave with a better understanding of rights before we move on.'

Sasha thought she heard one of their guests scoff but said nothing. No one else took any notice of it either.

***

Olympia, at least, had a sizable library. The Templars had access to it and the books they brought from Athens, giving them more than enough to work with. The library itself was never completely empty, always a few officers researching something. They paid little attention to the Templars who took over a corner of their building. The Templars found the books they needed and settled in.

After an hour of work, the two ambassadors came in. They went to the books, speaking to each other in yet another language Sasha did not recognize. At least, most of it she did not recognize. Some of it sounded like Spanish, some of it like Quebecois.

Shaw glanced over and saw the Templars and waved at them. He came over, Germaine begrudgingly following.

'Hello, Templars,' he said. For the first time Sasha heard him speaking English, and she hid a smile.

'Hello, sir,' Roland welcomed them. 'Come to see our humble library?'

'Humble to some, but impressive considering where you are,' Shaw said. 'Isn't that right, Mister Germaine?'

Germaine shrugged without answering.

'Have you enjoyed your time with us so far?' Roland continued. 'I can't imagine watching officers learn to fill out paperwork is all that exciting.'

'It isn't, Germaine confirmed.

'But no system is every fully exciting,' Shaw finished quickly. 'It must be a commandment. "Thou shalt learn four boring things for every exciting thing thou learnst."'

Shaw beamed, and the Templars laughed. He was displaying none of the formality he carried in the classroom, and Sasha felt the tensions ease from everyone but Germaine.

'So, where are you coming from?' Candle asked.

'Oh, someplace far away,' Shaw waved his hand. 'It doesn't really matter where.'

'You're from Boston,' Sasha said.

The table went silent and everyone looked at her. Germaine scowled, and Shaw looked surprised.

'What makes you say that?' he asked.

'There's someone else in the movement from Boston,' Sasha replied. 'You sound exactly like her.'

'Oh,' Shaw said and smiled. 'Well, that's a relief. I hope you can understand that we'd rather not let people know who we are. Can we trust your discretion?'

'What?' Hero asked.

'He wants us not to tell anyone they're from Boston,' Elector answered.

'Oh, okay,' Hero nodded. 'Sure.'

'And most of you are from here,' Shaw said, 'but not everyone. Quite the diverse group you've got here.'

'We're a capable bunch,' Roland admitted.

'And so young,' Shaw said. 'The oldest of you is, what twenty at most? And the youngest?'

'We're old enough,' Sasha replied.

'Are you? I mean, many nations won't even recruit soldiers into their ranks until at eighteen, and many of you are under that.'

'We were forced by circumstances,' Candle said.

'And how many of those circumstances were created by the Renaissance

Army?' Germaine asked suddenly. 'Tell me, if General Prince hadn't riled up the yeomen, would you still have been forced out of your homes?'

'Yes,' Sasha said.

'Really?' Germaine did not sound convinced. 'Can that be said for every soldier in your army?'

'What is your point?' Elector asked.

'My point is that the Renaissance Army has brought war to this land,' Germaine said. 'People are displaced, lives have been lost, all for the vanity of one man.'

'Vanity?' Roland asked. 'That's a harsh statement!'

'It's also true!' Germaine said. 'Prince wants revenge, so he starts a war.'

Roland slapped the table. 'Take that back!'

'I will not!'

Many of the Templars looked at him angrily, but Sasha was not looking at Germane. She was looking at Shaw. Shaw was sitting back, watching the exchange with anticipation.

'The Renaissance Army is not about revenge,' Elector said, motioning Roland to sit back. 'It is about a rebirth of civilization, of the science and culture that brought the old world to rise.'

'The old world fell, young man, and left billions dead in its wake.'

'And we'll learn from that,' Elector continued.

'Do you think so?' Germaine snorted. 'The Renaissance Army. You focus on the Renaissance all you want, but this is still an army. It still is an instrument of death and destruction, and you still answer to one man. What happens when you finally capture a city of any size? Do you think there will be elections? Will General Prince sit down and listen to the people? Or will he impose a government and tell them how it will work.'

'Any liberation must come with a military governor,' Rose said. 'It's common sense, to use an officer who understands the Renaissance Army and can guide the liberated city into the workings of the movement.'

'Oh, common sense, is it? Here's a military governor, please speak with him while we hang the count and his cronies from the walls, and don't ask if we won't do the same to you.' Germaine spat the words out. Shaw still said nothing.

This is a strategy, Sasha thought. Germaine pokes, Shaw watches.

'We don't execute nobles for being noble,' Mako said.

'You haven't captured a noble yet,' Germaine pointed out, 'or a general. A company of riflemen or a troop of yeomen? Do you really think the same will hold true if someone of substance ends up in your hands? Worse, do you think if the people demand executions, Prince will be able to avoid it? Much easier to give the people a little blood than argue them out of their hysteria.'

'The Renaissance Army will not do that!' Roland snapped.

'The Renaissance Army is not the white knight you expect it to be, boy,' Germaine scowled. 'It's already brought death and destruction. Do you think so many people are happy their lives are being uprooted for the purposes of Prince's private war? They'd be much happier under the boot of the yeomen than free to start fighting for Prince.'

Sasha finally spoke, loud enough to cut off Roland and Candle.

'If I did not know from your accent that you were from Boston,' Sasha said, 'I might have guessed with that statement.'

'What do you mean?' Germaine asked.

'Boston does not suffer from yeomen,' Sasha said. 'You have no idea of what it's like to live under their oppression. You cannot guess how much better it is to be liberated.'

'Peace is better than war,' Germaine said.

'Is it?' Sasha asked. She closed her book and laid it on the table. 'When I was twelve, a man rode into town, escorted by the yeomen. He called every girl between ten and eighteen to the mayor's house and interviewed us one by one. I was young enough I was just asked questions, but some of the older girls had to disrobe for him. In the end he offered one of the girls a large sum of money to go and work in a brothel. She declined, but it was a significant amount of money, enough that she was tempted to take it just to help her family.'

'As if they yeoman wouldn't have taken it back next week,' Roland interjected.

'So, she had a choice,' Germaine said. 'She was not forced.'

'A choice between a brothel bed and a yeoman's is no choice any woman should have to make!' Candle snapped. 'She had a choice between a wolf in sheepskin or a pack of wildcats, all demanding the same thing.'

'Is her choice better now?' Germaine asked. 'Join the local uprising, or leave?'

'There are plenty of men and women in the Liberated Counties that have nothing to do with the Renaissance Army,' Elector said.

'Yes, and I'm sure the Royal Army will ask each individual what they did before they bring the torches to bear.'

'Assuming the Royal Army will ever get into the Liberated Counties,' Sasha said.

'EXCUSE ME!' a voice cut them off. The staff sergeant librarian was standing over them, looking at all of them sternly.

'You are making a scene and disrupting the studies of everyone else in the building. Please quiet your conversation, or leave, or I shall contact the provost if you insist on being difficult.'

'You can't do that!' Germaine protested.

'He can,' Sasha said. 'Librarians have authority in a library. He could press charges on a general, if he wanted to.'

Sasha was not actually sure that was right, but it got the guests' attention. Shaw whispered something and the two stood.

'Thank you for your time,' Shaw said, bowing. Germaine stood straight until they left.

'Oh, lord, what could they possibly give us, or what would they want to give us, if that's what they think of us,' Candle asked.

'Who brings a printing press to a group they hate?' Sasha asked quietly. She looked down at her book and forced herself back into a mood for reading. The ambassadors were a mystery, but this chapter was her responsibility. The mystery could wait.

***

As headquarters for the Renaissance Army of Minnesota, Olympia was assigned a fair number of horses. From riders with dispatches, to forays by officers to the various camps of the army, there was a great need for them.

This meant that the Templars were able to take them out for rides. Not all of them could ride, and some had little interest in learning, but Sasha and Rose both enjoyed the sensation, and even raced. Rose won, handily.

Rose returned to the stables and Sasha went to ride through the maze, just enjoying the scenery. The leaves were turning red, and the hue of the forest was following suit. The wind was turning chilly but was still warm enough to be enjoyable.

She paused when she heard her name. Looking behind her, she saw Shaw riding up on another mount.

'Mister Shaw,' she said guardedly.

'Templar Scholar,' Shaw replied. 'I hoped I might run into someone. I appear to be lost.'

Sasha was skeptical but nodded. 'The Mardurer's Maze can do that,' she said.

'The what?' Shaw asked.

Sasha turned her horse down the path and Shaw fell in beside her.

'The rings of paths around RAM facilities are known as Mardurer's Mazes. Have you heard the word Mardurer before?'

'It's a common, and sometimes insulting, name for the Renaissance Army,' Shaw replied.

'Insulting?' Sasha laughed. 'Maybe to some people. It was the name I learned them by first.'

'And now?' Shaw asked.

'Now that I'm a Templar, I think of it as the Renaissance Army. I know what the Renaissance is and why it is important, but the name Mardurer will never be an insult.'

Shaw chuckled. The cantered down the path, and he cleared his throat.

'I wanted to take a chance to apologize for Mister Germaine,' he said. 'He lost a number of family members in the Commonwealth War, so he tends to hate conflict.'

'He hates conflict, so he sows it?' Sasha asked. 'Odd, to say the least.'

'I shall speak with him,' Shaw continued, 'remind him why we are here.'

'Why are you here?' Sasha asked, pulling her horse to a stop. 'I understand the need for security, but why does Boston care what happens this far west?'

'I'm from Boston, I never said I was here on behalf of the city,' Shaw pointed out.

Sasha shook her head. 'No, you didn't, but my question stands. Why are you here?'

'To see what's happening,' Shaw said. He shrugged. 'Do you know how difficult life is for so many people, across the world? And now, here's a

255

resistance group, fighting a war against an oppressor, that's making greater headway than any other group in memory. And there are a lot of groups in my memory. So, consider my curiosity piqued.'

'You came to see if the Renaissance Army is legitimate?' Sasha asked.

'Legitimate may be the wrong word. Moral and righteous would be better.'

'So, you want to see if the Renaissance Army is good.'

Shaw nodded. 'Better way to say it,' he agreed.

'Well,' Sasha said, 'you must be impressed so far.'

'What makes you say that?' Shaw asked.

'How many resistance groups fighting a war against an oppressor demand a printing press as the price?' Sasha asked.

Shaw laughed. 'I will admit,' he said, 'that did catch me off guard. When we made our first contact, I was expecting weapons or ammunition. A request for soldiers or some demand for technology that I couldn't give. When the message came for a printing press, I was relieved. It is a lot easier to get a press than a machine gun, though a press could do a lot more damage.'

Sasha pulled her horse to the side and dismounted, reaching into her saddlebags. 'I have some treats for the horses,' she explained, 'and I've been riding for some time.'

Shaw dismounted as well. 'I didn't bring any.'

Sasha gave him some. After a few moments, she spoke.

'My personal instruction is under the direction of General Caesar. Have you met him?' Shaw shook his head. 'We have developed an understanding. As I do well, and as I prove I am worthy of the name Scholar, I get to ask questions from him about things beyond our discussion. I propose an understanding here. A question for a question, with the understanding that security of our groups must come first.'

Shaw nodded, petting his horse's neck. 'Sounds good. Me first. Prince says you were with a field regiment that liberated several towns in another county. How can you honestly tell me they're living a better life now than they were under the yeomen?'

'Because I came from a similar place,' Sasha replied. 'All of us did. The soldiers of the army are the sons and daughters of the farmers we liberate.'

'Not everyone in the RAM is from Minnesota,' Shaw pointed out.

'No, but most of them are. We know how our actions impact the towns. Our medical officer makes her services available to the civilians, so they have a doctor to help them if something goes wrong. Solutions to problems come from themselves, not imposed upon them by the count and his yeomen. The harvest is evenly distributed, so no one starves. We have several soldiers who were trained in basic engineering, so they're helping repair and build homes.'

'The calm before the storm. The Royal Army is coming; you know that.'

I know,' Sasha said. 'Those who want to leave can. The ones who stay want us to win, Mister Shaw. They obviously think the risk is worth it.' She patted her mount on the head.

'Your question?' Shaw asked.

'How does the world see this movement?'

Shaw mused on the question for a moment. 'The kingdom has you branded as traitors and brigands who've managed a few small victories. Most governments I'm aware of have noticed you but consider you a minor problem for King Xavier to deal with.'

'I'm not too interested in the governments of the world, Mister Shaw,' Sasha said.

'The people then? Most of them offer you sympathy. They don't think much of your chances.'

'They'd help if they could?' Sasha said.

'If it wasn't for consequences, a lot of people would help you if they could. Alas, such things carry heavy penalties.'

A pause. Then Shaw spoke. 'What do you think the end goal of General Prince is?' he asked.

'To bring about a new Renaissance,' Sasha replied.

'But what does that mean?' Shaw pressed. 'Does he mean to overthrow King Xavier and find himself a position within the Commonwealth? Does he mean to free Minnesota? Atlantic America? The whole Commonwealth? Will he impose a government, or will he build one? He wants me to believe this is a great philosophical movement, fine, but he's a general in an army, and armies fight wars. When does this war end?'

Sasha thought for a moment. 'I don't know,' she admitted.

Shaw gave her some time. 'That's it?'

'Anything else I can say is guessing,' Sasha said. 'I'm a Templar, Mister Shaw. Selected for important training, but still a student. I haven't had a lot of discussions with generals about how to end the war. All I can say is that they won't stop fighting, and I won't stop fighting, as long as there's no place in the world for free people to go.'

Shaw nodded. Without speaking they both started walking their mounts down the path. 'Your turn,' Shaw finally said.

'Are you going to help?' Sasha asked.

'You know I can't answer that,' Shaw said, 'so let me tell you how I can help if we decide to. The Renaissance Army needs an avenue to send messages out into the world. We can provide that. If they need to get people to safety, we can do that. We may be able to give them some supplies such as medicine or printing presses, things like that. But that will be conditional on the Renaissance Army remaining as good as you say they are.'

Sasha nodded. Her stomach growled. She was getting hungry. 'One last question,' she said.

'Do you fight for Prince or the movement?'

'What?' Sasha asked.

'Do you fight for General Prince or the Renaissance Movement? If Prince does something that threatens the movement, and you had to fight him to keep the movement alive, would you?'

Sasha stared ahead. The idea of fighting Prince was preposterous. He was the leader of the movement; it was his vision.

But he's had to compromise his vision before. Senator has demanded concessions. Maybe Caesar has done so, or Aristotle. If they compromised themselves out of the movement? If Senator took over, would you support him the way you do Prince?

'I support the movement,' Sasha said.

'Not Prince?'

'Prince is building the movement to be bigger than he is,' Sasha replied. 'He's expecting us to support the movement over him. I cannot imagine him being in opposition to the movement, but if it did come to it, I would support the movement.'

'I hope it doesn't come to that,' Shaw said. 'Your last question.'

'Why is Boston still independent?' she asked. Shaw looked at her and she shrugged. 'Almost two dozen city-states and regional associations fought the Commonwealth. All of them except Boston were folded into the Atlantic Dominion under a Commonwealth consul or absorbed into one kingdom or another. Boston avoided that. They also avoided being taken over by Quebec, and Quebec has wanted Boston for centuries. How?'

'It's a long story,' Shaw said.

'But you know why?'

'I know some of it,' Shaw admitted.

'So, Boston does something, avoiding being conquered, and now wants to be let into the deepest secrets of the Renaissance Army?'

'I don't represent Boston,' Shaw said.

'So you say,' Sasha replied. 'Mister Shaw, before the Renaissance Army came, I lived in a town not far from here. I worked with my family to grow crops and care for animals. I watched the yeomen take my brother and brother-in-law for their armies, watched them take our produce as taxes. I fed their yeomen and felt their hands on me without my permission. I had few men willing to marry me, and even fewer I wanted to marry in return.

'The Renaissance Army gave me, and a lot of young men and women, a new path forward. One in which we have say over what we do and how we do it.'

'A way into war,' Shaw pointed out.

'The Renaissance Army doesn't conscript,' Sasha said.

'Yet,' Shaw replied. 'What happens after your first defeat? What happens if there's not enough men and women to plant and tend crops? So far the Renaissance Army has attracted support but that won't last.'

'I know,' Sasha admitted. She put away the rest of the food, patting her mount's head. 'But that's several bridges down the road.'

They remounted.

'You have brothers in the army?' Shaw asked.

'Yes. They serve in the wagons, down south.'

'Are you afraid you'll have to fight them?'

Sasha nodded. 'I am, but there are many other things I fear more.'

They started down the path.

'What I'm here for,' Shaw replied, 'is to look at how this movement impacts the people. Anger is one thing, and any demagogue can harness it for his purposes. Even in Boston, we've heard the rhetoric, but do actions match words?'

'Do they?' Sasha asked.

'Much more than I'd feared,' Shaw said, 'much less than I'd love. Tell me, is your town liberated?'

'Burned, by the count's son, some months ago,' Sasha said.

'Oh,' Shaw replied.

'Meanwhile,' Sasha continued, 'the Mayor of Pelican Point decided to gather his family and leave; they were allowed to do so without incident. Yeomen have been ambushed repeatedly, with no executions, but when a medical officer spent twelve hours as a prisoner of the enemy, she was repeatedly threatened by yeomen and had to be guarded by the Royal Army.'

'Your army does make great pains to be good, Templar Scholar,' Shaw agreed. 'The Civil Council, the teachers. I've seen far worse attempts at rebellion. I want to believe, but a golden path often leads to the devil's door.'

Sasha chuckled. 'We seem to have gotten away from one question for one question.'

Shaw laughed. 'We did, didn't we? I hope the conversation was enjoyable?'

'I thought so,' Sasha said. She started down the path, forking to the left.

'I thought Olympia was this way,' Shaw pointed to the right.

'I thought you were lost,' Sasha replied. She turned around and trotted back to Shaw.

Shaw grinned. 'Sorry,' he said. 'I wanted to get some alone time with you. I figured you were a local, and you'd have a more natural view of the army than someone who came in from the outside.'

'I just figured you went with me because I was the only one riding alone,' Sasha said. She started down the path to the right, getting closer to Olympia.

'In my line of work,' Shaw said, 'there is little that is done by accident.'

'Including Germaine?' Sasha asked.

Shaw smiled. 'Attacking the cause gets the supporters riled up. How they defend it is significant.'

'I'll have to remember that,' Sasha said.

'Will that do you any good?' Shaw asked.

'I'd like to know how to get things done without violence. If I can win a war without a single drop of blood, I'd do it.'

Shaw laughed. 'Well, that's good.' He swiped a branch out of his way. 'And if you can't?'

'Then I'll fight,' Sasha said. 'And I'll win.'

***

The ambassadors stayed in a few more classes that week, then disappeared on Thursday. The Templars finished their week at Olympia with no further interruptions. Del Oso secured them a group of horses, and they rode back to Athens that Sunday. Sasha was glad to be back. Olympia was nice, but there was too much of a feeling that she was on display there, between the generals and officers. Here, they could just be students. Different from the clerks, yes, but still students.

They got back into their barrack. Del Oso asked them to stay for a while until he checked with Colonel Carpenter. The Templars nodded, laying down on their beds. It was a warmer November day, and the windows and doors were left open. With the breeze, Sasha soon fell asleep.

Del Oso returned and woke everyone up. 'Templars,' he said, 'I've got good news. Gather around.' He waited for them to do so before he continued. 'The Renaissance Army has been working to build up their infrastructure, which is a long-worded way of letting you know that correspondence will be coming more regularly.'

Some of the Templars smiled at that. Others looked less impressed.

'From now on, on Saturdays, the cadet captain will stop by the Commandant's Office and pick up any letters for the Templars. The staff sergeant on duty will have them tucked away. It is your responsibility to hand them out to the Templars. If you wish to write a letter, secure it as you were taught, and give it to your cadet captain. Any questions?'

None of them said anything.

'Okay then,' Del Oso said. He handed out the letters, Sasha receiving three. Two were sealed with the sigil of Third Regiment, but one was simply a folded piece of paper with her name on it.

One of the Third Regiment messages was from Colonel Snow. It was a short one, responded to her letter, and asking her to spend time keeping up with her exercises. We will need you next summer, she wrote. Be ready.

The other was from Mary. It mentioned the others, giving her their best wishes and letting her know how they were doing. Third Regiment was spreading across the north of the county, and their group of friends was spread out with them. They were all busy, and eager for her to get back. Sasha was glad to read it. She missed her old friends, even if she was enjoying her new ones.

The last one was the unsealed note. Sasha opened it with curiosity.

> *Templar Scholar,*
>
> *I wish you would have spoken to me first before you went to the generals. When I was asked to stay a few extra days, I thought I was in trouble!*
>
> *I met with General Caesar and Master Mobius, who is from the Workshop. They spoke with me at length, especially Mobius. It was odd, but enjoyable.*
>
> *In the end, I think it has all worked out. By the time you read this, I will have returned home, gathered my belongings, and moved to the Workshop.*
>
> *Thank you for interfering. I don't know when we will meet again, but I look forward to it.*
>
> *Be safe,*
>
> *Tony*

Sasha smiled. Tony had made it out of the militia company he hated and was working for something he wanted.

And she had made it possible.

Chapter 28

December began, and the weather turned cold. Many of the men around Athens stopped shaving their beards, allowing them to grow as protection against the change in temperature. Some kept them nicely trimmed, but a few, including Roland, were having a competition to grow the grizzliest beard they could.

Not everyone was adjusting well. Candle began complaining about the weather often, and even the stoic Mako moaned a few times about it. All the Templars were issued thick underclothes, and a few of the Templars bartered for extra layers.

Sasha continued to mingle with the clerks at the library. Though the warrants had been given out, the challenge had awakened an interest in reading among several clerks, and the library was rarely empty anymore. And though Sasha read the *Tribune* as often as anyone else, she was constantly surprised by the additional information she could pick up from the clerks.

'War games?' Sasha asked.

Angela nodded. 'To get headquarters ready for campaigns. It's a way of challenging the officers that doesn't require a lot of resources. You make them generals or colonels in an army, split them up, and have each of them tell a group of umpires what they're doing. The umpires then decide what happens, and it goes on from there.'

'How do you know all this?' Sasha asked.

'Staff clerks learn all about these, because much of our training is like war games. We need to know how to write efficiently, so we do these type of games where an officer writes and order and you have to write it on down the line, to see how it changes. Other times we do these big mock battles. I hope we do one of those soon, it'll be fun to do one at a higher position.'

Angela looked excited at this. She had not been selected for one of the warrants, but had been advanced to staff corporal, a fact she was very proud of. Sasha returned her smile.

Sasha did not think much about the war games until that Saturday, after their tactical training. Prince invited them to eat with him in their classroom, where he and his aide-de-camp were waiting. After some small talk, he moved into his reason for being here.

Templar Scholar

'This last week, Olympia hosted war games for some officers who will have important roles in the future of our campaign. It went well enough that I want you all to experience something similar. Therefore, tomorrow, instead of being your day off, will be a war game.'

Some of the Templars smiled, probably because of the word 'game.'

'Now, here is how it will work. The game will be composed of two teams, red and blue. Each team will consist of one general headquarters and three division headquarters. Each headquarters will include one officer from the war game, one Templar as an adjutant, and selected clerks from Athens. The headquarters will be separated from one another. General Caesar and I will be the umpires.

'Once you are all in place, you will be read into the scenario. One team will be attacking, one will be defending. The general headquarters will develop a plan and send orders to their divisions. The division headquarters will then write orders for their regiments. Those orders will come to the umpires. The umpires will decide what happens and send messages back to the divisions. They report to the generals. And the process starts again.

'The purpose, Templars, is not to "win" the game by winning the battle. The purpose is to understand the importance of communication between headquarters, and the friction that can come from men and women misreading or miswriting orders. Even though I know some of you will not be pursuing tracks that might lead you to serve in a headquarters like this, I want you all to have that understanding. It is a lesson that goes far beyond military concerns.'

The Templars spent the rest of Saturday pondering what was going to happen the next day. The anticipation was making most of them oddly nervous. It would be a true test of so many things they had learned but had not yet put into practice, much more so than the ambassadors they met in Olympia. That was showing off with words; this was showing off with actions.

'Using words,' Roland said.

'Think you can write orders without making them rhyme?' Sasha asked.

'Where's the fun in that?' Roland laughed.

> *'Templar Scholar, I write you to say,*
> *There's a hill not too far away*
> *Please take it by fight*
> *And last until night*
> *And this army may yet win the day.'*

After the Sunday services the Templars assembled in front of Carpenter's office. Caesar and Prince were there, along with two groups of officers that

264

caught Sasha's attention.

The first was a group of women, two colonels and two majors. They wore matching olive-green uniforms, with blackened insignia on them instead of the shiny brass Sasha had come to expect in Walker County. They looked tough, like this was not a game for them, but an actual war.

The other group were Royal Army.

Sasha had to stare at them to understand them. They were wearing Royal Army uniforms, she was not wrong about that, but they had been changed to fit the Renaissance Army's standards. One was a Lieutenant Colonel, three of them majors. Their uniforms looked worn, and Sasha could see where sergeant's stripes had been removed from one of them. Sasha wondered who they were, when Prince spoke.

'Ladies and gentlemen,' he began, 'welcome to the Athens war games. I hope you're all ready. Gentlemen Templars, please follow Colonel Moses. Lady Templars, please follow Colonel Athena.'

The women moved off to one side.

'Were those men wearing Royal Army uniforms?' Candle asked.

'I think so,' Rose said.

'Yes,' Sasha confirmed.

'How do you know?' one of the colonels turned and looked at Sasha. She was an older woman, with greying hair and a stern look, and spoke with an Iowan accent.

'I fought the Royal Army last spring,' Sasha said.

'With what unit?' the woman asked.

'Third Field Regiment.'

'Colonel Snow?' the woman asked. 'I remember her. Aggressive. Good instinct. A little lacking in education.'

Sasha frowned and the woman chuckled.

'Dear, don't get upset. No one is perfect, especially our idols.'

They reached their destination, some of the clerk barracks near the library. The older woman turned back. 'I am Colonel Athena,' she said, 'and I will be acting as the general for the red team. I do not know the scenario involved, but I trust we will deal with it as officers, won't we?'

The Templars and other officers all nodded.

'Well, now we wait,' Athena said. She started asking questions about the Templar Project, about their training and exercises. The conversation flowed until a staff sergeant arrived and handed her a letter. 'Ready?' she asked. The officers and Templars all nodded, and then opened the paper.

'We are the Red Team,' she said, 'and our mission is to capture the town of Liberty.'

'Oh, the names,' the other colonel said. Everyone laughed. Athena continued.

'Our army is composed of three divisions. Each division consists of three battalions of infantry and one battery of artillery. The headquarters will by manned by myself and Templar Rose. First Division is Colonel Halcon and Templar Scholar; Second Division is Major Root and Templar Candle, and Third Division is Major Lanza and Templar Patch.

'Commissioned officers are the unit commanders; they will make the decisions. Templars are their aides-de-camp; they will write the orders and read the responses.

'Our enemy is the Blue Team, consisting of a headquarters and three divisions. The exact composition of those divisions is currently unknown, but intelligence estimates them to be of at least six and no more than ten battalions of infantry, at least one battery of artillery, and possibly a squadron of cavalry.

'It is eight o'clock in the morning. Weather is fair and the sun is up. Each round will take up one-half hour of time within the game. Game ends at eight o'clock that evening. So that give us . . . ?' she paused, looking at the Templars.

'Twenty-four rounds,' Candle said quickly.

Well done,' Athena said. 'Each round will consist of four phases. Phase One, Army command will issue orders to Division commands. Phase Two, Division commands will write orders to their subordinate units. Three, the generals will inform the Division commands what happens. Four, Division commands report to Army commands. One, two, three, four, and we begin again. Like a dance.'

She folded up the paper and looked at the assembled. 'These games should take no more than six hours; less, if we move quickly with our orders. The only communication between commands will be by letter. Food and drink will be brought to us, privy breaks will be limited to ensure we cannot speak with each other. Remember, as much as I want to win, this is an exercise to improve all of our skills. Understood?'

'Yes, ma'am,' they chorused.

'Good. Follow your officers, and good luck.'

Rose left with Athena, and Sasha met the other colonel. A dark-haired woman who reminded Sasha of Mariposa.

'I'm Colonel Halcon,' she introduced herself.

'Yes, ma'am. You teach Templar Roland, don't you?'

'I do,' Halcon grinned. 'A good head on his shoulders. Good soldier. Sings too much. Too poetic in words. Orders in battle have to be short and concise. Save the poetry for the after-battle letters.'

'Yes, ma'am,' Sasha agreed.

'And you? Scholar, eh?' she asked, her Iowan accent weak but noticeable. 'Why Scholar?'

'I read everything, and I like to think,' Sasha said. 'What is a Halcon?'

'It is Spanish for Falcon,' Halcon said. 'I have an affinity for that bird. Will you have any problem working with an Iowan?'

'No, ma'am,' Sasha said. 'If I may ask, do you have any problem serving under your mother?'

Halcon chuckled. 'I do not. How did you know?'

'You look alike and have similar accents,' Sasha shrugged. 'It is curious, I think.'

'Maybe.' Halcon turned and started walking to one of the clerk barracks. 'My father was a general in the Iowan army; he imparted to our family a sum of knowledge and a sense of duty. And, somehow, that brought us here.'

Sasha smiled. 'My father is a committed Alvanist. He imparted on me a respect for life that brought me here.'

'Aren't Alvanists severely pacifistic?'

'I didn't learn everything he tried to teach me,' Sasha said.

Halcon laughed and opened the door. 'After you.'

The bunks of the barracks were pushed to the back half of the room. A table was set up with a map on it. Two clerks, including Staff Corporal Angela, came to attention.

'Names?' Halcon asked.

'Staff Corporal Angela, ma'am.'

'Able Clerk Romero, Colonel.'

Halcon shook their hands. 'I'm Colonel Halcon, acting as commander for First Division. This is Templar Scholar, acting aide-de-camp. She will be writing the orders. You are moving blocks on the map and couriering letters, correct?'

The two clerks nodded.

'Good,' Halcon said. 'Then let us get to work.'

***

The game lasted five hours.

It was quite the experience for Sasha. Halcon was a much more aggressive officer than Sasha was, but was willing to listen to Sasha's council. Several times she followed Sasha's advice, scouting ahead with skirmishers or marching a specific way. It paid off, as the scouting detected a formation digging in along a ridge line that Halcon almost advanced right into. Sasha smiled as she wrote the report to Colonel Athena.

But the experience started to sour. First Division was ordered to hold and scout, keeping contact with the enemy pinning them to their positions. Sasha expressed disappointment at being held to a supporting role.

'It happens,' Halcon said, though Sasha thought she secretly agreed with her.

Second Division started a rough fight crossing a river, and Third Division was moving into a position in the middle. Then Sasha started receiving reports of the enemy moving to their flanks.

'Let them know,' Halcon said.

Sasha did, writing that the enemy was scouting them out.

The rounds continued. The scouting was a prelude to an attack. First Division was bending back, forming an L-shape.

'You told them about our battle?' Halcon asked.

'I did,' Sasha said. Somehow, Athena did not seem to be appreciative of their situation. Or maybe, Rose was not being appreciative.

The reports from their regiments were getting worse; at least four regiments advanced on their position. Second Division continued their fight to hold onto the river crossing. Third Division advanced to a position between First and Second but did not seem to be engaged.

'Let the general know we are outnumbered, will need to pull back if not reinforced,' Halcon said.

Sasha nodded and wrote: '*We are hard pressed. Reinforce or we must retire.*'

The orders came back, to pull back to a line next to Third Division. Halcon and Sasha worked out the orders for their regiments to pull back, but it was too late. The enemy assaulted that round. One regiment ran. Sasha and Halcon tried to rally, but the enemy struck hard and their division fell apart.

The game ended shortly after that. Blue Team managed to keep Liberty in their grasp, and thoroughly wrecked First and Second Divisions in the process. Third Division was never significantly engaged. Neither Halcon nor Sasha were happy with their performance.

The officers and Templars convened in the General's room. Moses, the victor, looked pleased with himself. Athena looked decidedly grim.

'Well,' General Prince said, 'that was a bit of an embarrassment, wasn't it? But that's what we're here for; to learn from these mistakes in a game, and not on the field. Be upset with yourself but learn from it.'

'What went wrong?' Halcon asked.

'We did not realize the extent of the fight First Division was getting into,' Athena answered her daughter.

'We did tell you, ma'am,' Sasha said.

'You said you were in a fight, but failed to disclose how serious it was,' Rose replied.

'We told you we were being pressed,' Sasha retorted.

'Pressed, not overrun,' Rose said. She pointed at the general's map, which showed both units truthfully. 'Nothing you wrote indicated you were facing half the enemy army.'

'Ladies,' Athena said sternly, but neither woman heard her.

'We needed help and we asked for it,' Sasha said. She was getting hot, the pair getting far too close to each other. 'I shouldn't have to spell it out word by word.'

'If you're not getting your message across, maybe you do,' Rose replied. 'I mean, if you had been able to tell us, we could have actually done something with Third Division, instead of having them sitting in the middle doing nothing, because we didn't know where the real fight was! For someone who claims to be a scholar, you were obliviously stupid during this game.'

Sasha punched Rose, a fist right at the other woman's check.

She regretted it as soon as she did it. It was an act of naked aggression, the act of a bully, not an officer.

Like Senator.

Sasha started to apologize, but Rose responded much quicker than Sasha expected. Rose rushed her, the pair falling into the table. Blocks scattered across the floor, fists flying and legs lashing out to find purchase. Rough arms grabbed Rose, pulling her off Sasha, then pulling Sasha up. The Templars kept the two combatants away from each other as Athena's voice filled the room.

'Is this what the Templars are?' she asked. There was something dangerous about her calm and cool demeanor. 'You brawl? The point of this exercise, ladies, was to learn our weaknesses. Both of you should have learned what you need to work on. Instead, you insult each other like children. All of you made mistakes. All of you can get better, but this,' she said, 'is not better.'

Athena directed Rose to one of the other cabins; Halcon took Sasha back to the cabin they just spent five hours in.

'Ma'am,' Sasha began, but Halcon hissed and snapped her fingers.

'Grow up, Cadet,' she said. She set Angela to guard the door and left.

Sasha paced the room. The map they had fought over still sat there, the block arrogantly displaying her loss. She wanted to flip the table over but forced herself back. She was in enough trouble as it was. She paced, thinking to herself, trying to justify her actions.

She had not thought of anything reasonable when Caesar came in. He had a grim look on his face. Sasha came to attention, saluting.

'How is your face?' he asked.

'Fine, General,' Sasha replied. *Is he on my side?*

'And your hand?'

'Sore, sir.'

'And your ego?'

Sasha blushed and said nothing.

'It is a simple question, is it not? Why else would you fight another Templar during a training mission?'

Sasha swallowed. 'Bruised, sir,' she admitted.

Caesar nodded. 'I understand,' he said. 'What was the casualty numbers for First Division?'

'Well over half,' Sasha said.

270

'Over a thousand men and women,' Caesar confirmed. 'If this had been a real battle, those men and women would be truly dead. Lucky for you, it was a training exercise. You will work on your correspondence.'

'But Rose didn't read my notes right!' Sasha protested. 'And what she said to me was –.'

Caesar slapped his hand down on the table and she jumped. He glared at her, much as he had Brigadier Senator when the man had struck Rose. 'I am not excusing Templar Rose's behavior, Templar Scholar. I am holding you accountable for your own,' he said, sternly.

Sasha looked at him. That was something her father had said several times, after her fights with Samuel Cartier. For a moment she was a little girl again, being chided for fighting, hoping to regain the respect of her father.

'Do you wish to learn?' Caesar asked. 'Or do you wish to give up?'

'I wish to learn,' Sasha said.

'Good. As a result of your poor showing during this exercise, we will begin a series of weekly order tests. The Templars, all of them, will have to learn these skills. I expect you to focus on this and learn.'

Sasha nodded. That was not a bad punishment.

'As a result of your fight with Templar Rose,' Caesar continued, and Sasha cringed, 'you are to prepare an oral report on the influence that a rivalry between officers can have on the outcome of battles and campaigns. I want you specifically to look at the Union Generals of the Battle of Gettysburg, American Civil War, 1863; the Russian Generals during the Battle of Tannenberg, First World War, 1914; and the Iron Generals in the Corridor Campaign, War of the Saints, 2180 to 2181.'

'Yes, sir. When am I to give this report?'

Caesar looked at his pocket watch. 'At about three in the morning. In the library, I think.'

Sasha blinked. 'But when will I sleep?'

'Tomorrow night,' Caesar said. 'Tonight is given up for restitution. Or would you prefer an alternative punishment?'

'No, General,' Sasha shook her head. 'I will learn from my mistakes.'

'Good,' Caesar said. 'And I would avoid Templar Rose whenever you can.'

'We live in pretty close quarters, sir,' Sasha said.

'I know,' Caesar replied. 'One more thing you should have thought about.'

Chapter 29

December passed slowly. Once again, Sasha found herself ostracized from most of the Templars. Although they all agreed Rose had made errors, none of them thought she deserved to get punched. Sasha agreed. Instead, she kept her head down, worked hard, and tried to learn from her mistakes. By Christmas, she was speaking to everyone except Rose herself. The two had not shared one word in almost a month. The other cadets had noticed and were subtly trying to get the two to talk.

'If I knew what to do about it, I would do it,' she snapped at Mako halfway through December.

On Christmas Eve, as snow fell and the temperature plummeted, Sasha sat in the library, and for the first time in a while, thought about her family.

She had not seen them since the previous April, almost eight months ago. And they had been stuck in Walker Town, under siege, for more than six. Michelle, her sister would have had her child in May. *Did she have it before or after Penelope's Haven was burned?*

The wind howled and Sasha felt the chill cutting into the building. The windows were winterized, as Angela called it, the thin paper materiel removed and replaced with straw and cloth, boarded on both sides. It was better than the paper, but not perfect, and the fireplace could not heat the entire library by itself. She buried herself in her blanket and thought about warmth.

She was just starting to feel warm when the door opened. A figure stepped in, laying a bag down below the coat pegs and securing the door quickly. Sasha watched the figure take off a large coat, revealing Rose, wearing her thick pants and her valuable sweater. Again, Sasha became angry at the woman's obvious wealth.

Now what are you here for? she asked silently.

Rose hung up her coat, hat and scarf, then picked up the bag and approached Sasha.

'May I sit?' she asked.

Sasha nodded, still watching Rose carefully.

Rose pulled a chair up to the fire, pulling one of the smaller tables over to sit between the two women. Rose then reached into her bag and pulled out two small metal cups, and finally a small glass bottle filled with a deep red liquid.

'I propose peace,' Rose said. Her voice sounded odd, and Sasha realized she was nervous.

'Peace?' Sasha asked.

Rose nodded. 'I have not been a proper lady, not a proper officer,' she continued, setting the cups down. She frowned and started rummaging through her bag, finally finding her corkscrew. 'I have not been happy here, and I have not been happy with you. And it is not your fault. So, I ask for peace.'

Sasha nodded. 'I want peace as well,' she said.

Rose worked the corkscrew, succeeding with a resounding pop. The silence was unnerving, so Sasha spoke.

'Why are you unhappy?'

'I am the smartest person here,' Rose said, beginning to pour. Sasha started to speak but Rose interrupted her. 'It is not a bad thing to know one's strengths. I am the smartest person here, and yet I do not belong. I do not want to be here, but I must be here. It is required. And you, all of you, all want to be here. You are all so . . .,' she paused, looking for the right words. Finally, she shrugged. 'I am the smartest person here, smart enough to know I am the worst.' She handed Sasha one of the cups.

'Not the worst,' Sasha said, taking the cup. 'Hero, I think, might be the worst,' she continued. Rose chuckled and Sasha sniffed the cup. 'What is this?'

'Brunswick Port,' Rose said. 'A sweet wine, one I am particularly fond of. I was supposed to drink it tonight with my sister, but she is no longer here. And as a rule, I do not drink alone.' She raised the glass in a toast. 'To peace among Templars.'

'Peace among Templars,' Sasha agreed. She drank. It was sweet, and thick, and it burned. 'Wow.'

'Lovely, no?'

Sasha decided to sip from now on. 'I'm sorry,' she said, staring at her drink. 'I was not acting like an officer either.'

'You know, there are some who think that being an officer means always being right?' Rose asked. 'I know officers who say that is wrong. There cannot be common officers, only the exceptional are fit to lead, but being exceptional is not a trait; it is a choice. You choose to be better, or you choose to be bitter. I had realized some time ago that I must make peace. After our conflict in the war game, though, Candle pressed the issue. She said many things to me, used many harsh words, but she was the final weight to make me see what was right.'

'Mako pressed me the same, only without the profanity,' Sasha said. She sipped again, wondering what the rest of the Templar Project would be like if she and Rose made peace.

For a minute there was simply silence, then Rose spoke. 'Is it true you had two names?'

'What do you mean?' Sasha asked, confused.

'I heard that in your previous unit, you were called Scholar, but also Bobcat.'

Sasha laughed. 'It's been a while since I was called that. Yes, I was called both names in my old regiment.'

'Why did you choose Scholar and not Bobcat?'

'Because I'm prouder of my learning than I am my fighting. I'm good at fighting, and I'm fine with that. I'm proud to be fighting for the Renaissance Army. It's a good army that fights the good fight.

'However, the good fight still costs me friends. Even in the three months I was with them, I buried friends. Good people.' Sasha took a sip. 'I first thought of taking Bobcat, but my colonel recommended the name Scholar to me, as I like to read, and she wanted that to be my focus here. And I agreed.

'I want to know how to win without fighting. If it comes to fighting, I'll be there, in the thick of it, pulling my weight; but if I can win without the fight, I'd prefer that. If anything, it means I'll be burying fewer friends.'

'Admirable,' Rose said. 'I'm here because my family has obligations. And one of those fell on me.'

'What about Cardinal?'

'Cardinal escaped the accident at Sparta physically, but she cries when she sleeps now. I think it scared her more than she wants to admit.'

'What's she doing now?'

'Healing,' Rose said. 'There are ways to heal the soul and the mind. Some use faith, other science. She's finding her way.'

'And you're staying here.'

Rose nodded. 'One of us has to succeed. I will fulfill the obligation. For my sister, I will do this.' She did not sound happy about it. Indeed, she looked as if she was about to cry.

'I've always been a bit jealous of you,' Rose finally said. Sasha stared at her. 'I am the smartest person here, but you want to be. And you work hard to be. You're working to get what comes naturally to me, and you're building

274

yourself up far more than I am. It is intimidating to think how many others like you there are.'

'Hopefully enough to win the war,' Sasha said.

Rose chuckled, then reached into her pack. She pulled out two boxes. One she unclasped and unfolded into a board, a grid eight squares by eight squares. The other she opened, revealing numerous pieces. She began placing the pieces on the board. 'This is chess,' she said. 'It is a game all members of my family must learn, and it is a game worth knowing. When you were upset that I knew how to lead an army better than you, this is one of the ways I learned how.'

'Where did it come from?' Sasha asked.

'This set? It was given to me by my uncle. As for where the game came from, no one knows. My uncle said, "Chess has existed forever, and will exist forever. It has been and always shall be." He was exaggerating, of course, but it was nice to hear at the time. Come, I will teach you. And we will play twice a week, until you can beat me. Then, we will play three times a week.'

'Okay,' Sasha said. She looked at the pieces. 'What sort of game is it?'

'One that will teach you how to move pieces about, to impact the flow of battle by movement, not just fighting. To anticipate and counter without violence.'

'Sounds good,' Sasha said leaning forward. 'Show me.'

***

Christmas day at Athens was pleasant. It was cold, but not unbearable. All the Templars chose to go to a Christmas service, hosted by the facility chaplain. It was such a different experience from her father's stern Christmas lectures that Sasha wondered if she should have attended a service sooner.

Breakfast was a treat, with hot chocolate and ham steaks. Afterwards, the Templars and clerks divided into several teams and waged a snowball fight across Athens. Even Elector got into it, everyone laughing through the action. The only time the cadre of trainers yelled at them was to inform them hand-to-hand combat was not allowed, and surrenders must be accepted.

There was a large, early dinner. The cooks of Athens had put in tremendous effort to make a memorable meal for more than two hundred souls, and they succeeded admirably. There was even a caramel peanut dessert. After dinner, there was a huge bonfire where hundreds of men and women sang Christmas carols and mingled about.

Sasha noted several times that people would pair off and disappear together, returning after varying lengths of time. Candle disappeared with one of the cooks, and a short time later Hero made off with Angela, the clerk. Sasha watched them leave, then turned her attention to the bonfire.

Let them celebrate as they see fit, Sasha told herself. She was having fun where she was, singing and interacting with everyone else.

There was a decent snowfall that night, and the next day the camp went to work digging paths between the various buildings. It was too cold for the showers to work, and running was impossible with the icy ground as it was. The kitchen had a hard time getting their fires started, so breakfast was late, but no one complained.

Colonel Carpenter issued orders that the cabins were all to be prepared for blizzards. Each barrack brought in several days' worth of firewood and buckets of water. The cooks asked for volunteers to cook up breads for storage. Oats and cured meats were sent to each barrack. The librarians even allowed them to stockpile books in their barracks, taking careful accounting of the books taken and threatening court martial if they were not returned.

'I hope the trainees at Sparta will be okay,' Candle said at one point.

'Oh,' Sasha said, 'I didn't think of that. They must be. The generals wouldn't let them freeze, would they?'

They asked Del Oso, who nodded. 'They should be fine,' he said. 'Lance built a number of ram cabins over the last few months. Most of the troops moved on to their units, but those who are left will have a bed. They'll be crowded, but they'll survive the winter.'

New Year's approached and talks of another large celebration went through the camp. The weather turned bitter cold and being outside was not ideal. Instead, several of the staff clerks took charge. Soon, each building at Athens was designated for a function during the party. Several became dance halls, the cots stacked against the wall and homemade instruments strumming. Others became drinking and dining halls. The Templar barracks became a debate hall, where small conversations and debates could be held. Several barracks were set aside as sleeping halls, and, informally, one became what Candle described as the 'Love Barracks,' which she said with a wink and a grin. Elector laughed when Sasha described what she thought went on there.

'It won't be an orgy,' he said.

I would hope not, Sasha thought. Elector guessed her thoughts.

'So what if it was? Would you think less of anyone for it?'

'No,' Sasha said. 'I swear it.'

Elector gave her a look of disbelief, and Sasha shook her head.

'Friends of mine in Third Regiment were open about their . . . intimacy. I learned not to judge them.' She paused again. 'Maybe I need to work on it more.'

Elector nodded. 'My dad would approve of it.'

'Really?' Sasha asked.

He nodded. 'He hated sending young men out to war as virgins. He thought everyone should know intimacy before they face the horrors of war.'

'Huh,' Sasha said, considering the words. Elector rarely spoke of his father. 'Have you . . . ?' she asked, trailing off, surprised she was about to ask that question.

'Spoken to my father recently, or known intimacy?'

'Uh, the latter,' Sasha said. She felt committed now.

'That is, respectfully, none of your business.'

Sasha nodded. Elector changed the subject. 'What do you think your old unit is doing now?'

'The Third Regiment? I know the plan was to build some winter cabins, try to avoid moving everyone into liberated towns. Hopefully they're all warm and safe.'

'Miss them?' Elector asked.

'Sometimes,' Sasha said.

'That must be nice,' Elector said quietly. 'I wrote my father a letter. It was returned unopened. I guess I have no connection to who I used to be.'

'My father is a pacifist and I'm a soldier. I understand the conflict.' And she did. The pair of them left their families behind to follow their own nature. It took strength to do that, and the ordeal tested that strength. Elector was recovering from his struggle; Sasha had finished hers long ago.

'But you're glad you came?' Elector asked. 'You're glad you made the trip to the Templars?'

'I am,' Sasha nodded. 'The lessons, and the books. Back in Third I had so few books to read.'

'Anything good?'

'The one I was halfway through before I came here was the biography of

Rudolph Imperian. Fascinating read.'

Elector laughed, a loud and natural sound. Sasha smiled even though she did not get the joke.

'Sorry,' Elector finally said.

'What is so funny?' Sasha asked.

'My family follows me everywhere,' Elector chuckled. 'Rudolph Imperian is my ancestor. I'm his direct descendent.'

'Really?' Sasha asked. 'Wasn't he descendant from the last governor of Minnesota, from the Before Time?'

Elector nodded. 'My family has been involved in the independence of this land for hundreds of years. You can understand why my father was upset with me for shirking that responsibility.'

'You aren't shirking anything,' Sasha said quickly. 'An army needs soldiers, but it also needs doctors, and clerks, and cooks. You're still defending this land; you're just doing with a different set of skills.'

Elector smiled, another natural smile, and Sasha replied in kind.

The party began after dinner, and despite the cold and light snow it was a fair success. While the officers and senior cadre members were in their own cabins, celebrating their own way, the clerks and Templars and junior cadre spent the night as they wished. The topic often turned to differing experiences in celebrating New Year's. Some, like Sasha, had never passed the night with any big celebration. For others it was a big party. With a dozen cabins open, it was not hard to find a place where one could celebrate as they saw fit.

Sasha was in the Templar barracks as midnight approached. She had consumed some alcohol, feeling warm but not drunk. Some of the clerks were trying to teach a song to celebrate the event, but they had different lyrics in mind and were providing much entertainment to the rest of the people arguing over who was right. The Athens bell, normally silent after nine, range out a quarter to midnight. Word spread that it would count down to the actual event.

Mako appeared next to her, carrying a bottle of cider. 'In my family, we share a bottle to celebrate. Will you share with me?'

Sasha nodded, just as the bell rang and someone started counting. Soon the whole cabin was shouting the numbers down to midnight. Then they cheered, sang whatever version of the song they knew, hugged and kissed each other, drank whatever was in their hand or just shouted to high heaven.

Sasha and Mako took a drink from their bottle. She smiled, looking out over

278

the crowd. Then her smile faltered.

'Unhappy?' he asked.

'No, just thinking.'

'What's that?'

'How the kingdom doesn't allow for celebrations like this,' she gestured.

'It's not illegal, is it?' Mako asked.

'No, but it's difficult to do something like this when your stomach is empty and your laughter stolen,' Sasha said. 'I mean, if the yeomen walked in here, they'd expect to be the center of attention, to get all the food and drink, and the Love Barracks would not be voluntary.'

'Sounds like a good enough reason to fight them,' Mako replied.

'It does, doesn't it?' Sasha smiled. 'Happy New Year, Mako.' She hugged him.

'Happy New Year to you as well.'

Sasha looked back at the cabin full of celebrations. There were a few more days until their instruction began again, and while Sasha was looking forward to it, she also wanted to see more events like this.

I want more of these celebrations, she thought to herself. *Everyone should have time to enjoy their life like this.*

Chapter 30

Colonel Miklos was ushered into the King's Hall at Fort Snelling, the large review room where King Xavier would come for briefings. Inside, dozens of officers awaited their monarch. Miklos made his way to General Bennabi, who struggled to find a comfortable position in his chair.

'The chairs have shrunk,' he complained as Miklos sat down. It was an old joke Bennabi made at the expense of his ever-growing belt.

'At least it's warm in here,' Miklos said.

'And a good thing, too. Word is coming in from Fargo that we're looking at a major blizzard in a few days.'

Miklos cursed in his native tongue. He had never had a great love of cold, but he would tolerate it for the sake of his duty. This posting would often try his resolve. He hated how cold it would get in winter and did not care if the layers he wore caused whispers. He was damned well going to be warm.

Bennabi glanced at him and guessed his thoughts. 'You know, I heard from some friends in the margrave's office that there is a running debate about what posting is the coldest. Some of them say northern Quebec, up near the Hudson, but I'd like them to come out here for a few days and see for themselves, and we could send someone out there to test their claims.'

'I'd rather not find out, personally,' Miklos said.

Bennabi chuckled, then turned back to his aide. Miklos settled in and looked out over the chamber.

The room was built as a throne room, with the king's seat on a raised dais at one end. On the opposite side was a large map of his kingdom, with the projector screen lowered for this presentation.

Between the king and his map were six large tables, three on each side, for the six principal officers of the kingdom. Behind them were chairs for their aides, then above them viewing galleries for other officers. Miklos was in the gallery, above and behind Prince Stefan.

All six of the principal officers, the highest ranking and positioned men in the kingdom's military, were already present on the chamber floor. Through some design, the three sitting on either side were political allies, and opponents of those across the divide.

Prince Stefan sat on the side Miklos called the professional faction. With the quartermaster general and the admiral of the Royal Navy, the three of them served their king and kingdom respectfully, concerned more with executing their duties than enriching themselves.

Across from them sat Marshal Robinson and his faction, one that Miklos labeled the patronage faction. The inspector general and the adjutant general were both capable enough to run their departments sufficiently, but they played favorites and promoted discord among their subordinates.

Professionalism and patronage, Miklos thought to himself. He knew which side he fell on.

A door in the wall behind the throne opened and several of the king's guards stepped out, followed by the king's herald. He stamped his heavy staff on the floor, signaling the king was about to enter. He waited for the officers to find their places and settle down.

'Rise for His Majesty, King Xavier, First of his Name, of the Family of Santiago-Locke, King of North Mississippi and Prime Minister of the Same.'

Robinson, as the highest-ranking officer, stood. 'Chamber! Attention!' The officers rose as King Xavier came in.

The king wore his blue military uniform, complete with golden sash and medals. He climbed the steps to his throne and nodded. 'Be seated,' he said, with a nod to his son.

Prince Stefan walked to the front, near the projector.

'Gentlemen,' he began, 'this presentation is classified. It is not to be disseminated to civilians or subordinate officers until such time as I deem fit.'

He gestured to an aide, who dimmed the lights and lit the projector. A slide shifted into place, with the counties of northern Minnesota marked.

'The Renaissance Army is a threat to our kingdom; not necessarily to the throne, but to our system of government. By attacking the counts, they promote lawlessness, disrupt taxation efforts, and sow discontent. They've managed some surprises last year, but this spring they're going to find themselves up against an entirely different animal.

'Before winter fell, the RAM spread to four counties. In Walker, where they originated, they've wrested control of the entire county, save for Walker Town itself. Smaller forces have taken control of parts of Bemidji, Brainerd and Wadena Counties, as shown here. As of yet, we have not heard of any influence by the RAM in Menahga or Grand Rapids County, but I doubt those counties have been forgotten. We assume the enemy has influence there but are not actively resisting yet.

'As for the size of the enemy forces, we lack much information that we consider to be accurate. What we do have comes from reports that yeomen have submitted, from our own officers now on the ground in Walker Town, and some information gathered by the Royal Air Corps' recon flights.

'We do know that Walker Town is under siege from an enemy force that is estimated to be between four and six hundred at arms. We estimate the field regiments found outside Walker County to be between one and four hundred each, with the First and Third on the higher end of that estimate, and the Fourth on the lower end. Please note, we do not know where the Second Field Regiment is, or if it even exists.'

He advanced to a slide of Walker County, with icons splashed across the countryside. 'The Royal Air Corps has identified a number of locations that appear to be facilities built or taken over by the RAM. We estimate these facilities could be used to train, arm, and maintain about two thousand people. And we probably have missed some of them.'

Stefan looked out across the officers. 'In short, we have an enemy that has engaged us in four counties and put a significant amount of effort into keeping us blind to their true numbers and capabilities.

'Nevertheless, we will bring them to justice.'

Stefan paused for a moment before continuing. 'My father has asked me to prepare a campaign for the springtime. The directive is to destroy the RAM as a military force and relieve the siege of Walker Town. The king has also directed that this be done without reducing the ability of any component of the military below the minimum necessary to deal with their standing duties.'

Some of the officers shifted at that. Bennabi barely suppressed a groan.

Miklos understood their discontent. The military forces in North Mississippi were mostly used for garrison duty, watching large population centers for signs of riots or unrest. King Xavier wanted the RAM defeated, but not while risking the stability of his cities.

'Unless the RAM has managed to assemble ten thousand armed men and women in Walker County, we have the resources available to win against them,' Stefan said. 'And we have a plan to do it. Generals, Father; Operation Tempest.'

The slide clicked over. It was the same map, but now augmented by army icons and movement arrows.

'Simply put, Tempest is a hammer-and-anvil operation. The anvil is in the east, north and south, the hammer coming from the west.

'First, the anvil. The North Watch will deploy a force of three to four thousand men to Grand Rapids County. They will have a significant amount of territory to cover, but so far there has been no sign of RAM activity in their sector. That will probably change once they the first troops arrive on station. If the Second Field Regiment does exist, I believe it would be there.

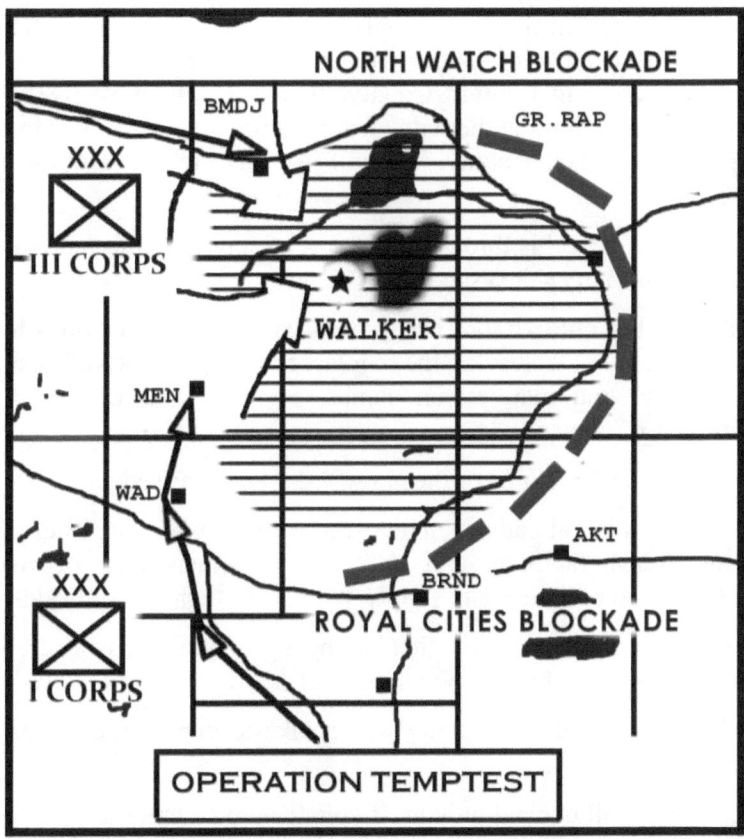

'To the south is a force from the Royal Cities Garrison, around three thousand, which will deploy to Brainerd and Aitkin Counties. They will continue the anvil in the south, with the added objective that they are to keep the Third Field Regiment from falling back into Walker.

'And now the hammer,' Stefan said, 'consisting of two corps from the Field Army. III Corps will deploy to the north, via the Red River Valley and along the northern railway to Bemidji. I Corps will deploy from the south, marching up through Wadena and Menahga Counties.

'The objective of the hammer is twofold; to relieve the city of Walker Town, and to destroy the RAM forces in Walker. Which corps manages which objective will be decided by the situation as it develops. Both offensives will have to go through contested counties before they get to Walker, and we don't know what is in Walker itself.'

'Are you seriously suggesting that a rebel field regiment can stop an entire Royal Army corps?' Inspector General Lavern interrupted.

'Not stop,' Stefan responded, 'but they could delay and divide. Both field regiments can threaten the corps' logistical support, harass their flanks, and will need to be dealt with. The First Field Regiment seems to have made significant progress in Bemidji County. III Corps will most likely have to spend some energy hunting them down and burning them out, leaving I Corps to campaign in Walker County. We will just have to see how the situation develops.'

King Xavier cleared his throat. 'What sort of support will you require from the rest of the military?' he asked.

'Significant, but not extraordinarily burdensome. District troops to protect supply lines and depots, leaving the regulars to engage the RAM. Inspectorate troops to build and man prison camps. Supplies and wagons from the quartermaster, of course.'

'What about the Air Corps or the Navy?' the king pressed.

'The Air Corps has already been involved with the planning,' Stefan replied. 'Attacking RAM facilities and defenses, reconnaissance of roads and fortifications, and continuing to supply Walker through the air bridge.

'As for the Navy, it is possible that having a group of boats and crew for the lakes will be required, but my planners and I don't feel that's likely.'

King Xavier nodded. 'How long will it take to deploy the troops to their starting positions?'

'That, Father, will depend on you. If you declare an emergency, we can run eight trains a day. If you do not, we're limited to three.'

'How long?' Xavier repeated his question.

Stefan stifled a sigh. 'To transport the III Corps to the closest uncontested train depot in Bemidji is three days per unit; one day by train from Saint Cloud to Fargo; one day by river boat from Fargo to Grand Forks; one day by train from Grand Forks along the railway. That movement will take 64 trains, to transport every unit and one week's worth of combat supplies. Eight trains a day puts III Corps concentrated in the north in ten days, from the time the first train leaves to the time the last train arrives. At three trains a day, the same movement takes 24 days.'

'Not counting any trains needed to transport district or inspectorate troops, or quartermaster trains with more supplies,' Aguilar, the quartermaster general, said. 'Or, frankly, returning trains with prisoners and wounded.'

'Correct,' Stefan said. 'North Watch to Grand Rapids will take two days for one unit to move by rail via Duluth and Virginia, sixteen to twenty-four trains depending on the exact units designated for their force. The troops from the Royal Cities will likewise take two days by rail, via Duluth to Brainerd.'

'So, III Corps through the Red River Valley is the largest issue? Not I Corps marching?' Xavier asked.

'I Corps will be marching to Menahga, via Wadena. Approximately 120 miles, so an eight-day march. They can be in position when III Corps is ready.'

A hand raised, drawing attention to Adjutant General Olson, who looked embarrassed to be speaking at all. 'My Lord Prince, I wonder if the anvils you are building are too weak. Even without district or Inspectorate troops, your seven thousand men will have to cover nearly 150 miles of territory. Certainly, some of the Renaissance Army will escape.'

'I'm sure they will,' Prince Stefan said. 'But, General Olson, my task is not to punish every single member of the Renaissance Army. My task is to destroy the Renaissance Army as a movement. I don't care if ten men and women escape. Quite frankly, I don't care if a hundred, or a thousand, men and women escape. Let them go home and remember that their great start against Walker County failed dramatically. Let them see the Old Guard die, the last Dawson hang. Let them know the Renaissance Army failed and let them spread the word.'

The words hung in the air. Miklos avoided smiling. Prince Stefan certainly had a flair for the dramatic.

'Your plan sounds like a good start, General. Keep at it,' King Xavier ordered. 'I cannot tell you yet whether I shall call an emergency. Be prepared for both.'

Stefan was stoic as he replied. 'Yes, Father.'

Chapter 31

Stockpiling supplies was a smart move. A blizzard came suddenly one morning and lasted well into the next day, and the biscuits and jerky became their only food. The Templars spent the time clustered around the oven. They discussed and debated the class before, told stories. Rose showed them her chess board and taught them all to play.

Evening was almost upon them when someone knocked at the door. Elector went to open it and two men came in, dressed in heavy winter furs. Both were tall, one carrying a Verendrye long rifle, the other a large crossbow.

'Major Fox?' Sasha asked the first man. She did not know how she knew it was him, but as he pulled off his hat and smile, her suspicion was confirmed.

'Ah, Templars. Everyone alive? Have all your toes? No cannibalism yet, eh?'

His companion chortled. 'This many youths stuck in a room, I'm surprised it hasn't turned into an orgy. It would help keep everyone warm.'

He laughed, as did Hero. Everyone else managed an awkward chuckle. They looked at the newcomers.

'What are you doing here?' Candle asked.

'Immediately, we are checking on you on behalf of Colonel Carpenter. Is everyone alive and well?'

'We are,' Rose said.

'Good,' the other man said. He had his massive backpack in his hand. 'Is that stove up?'

'It is,' Sasha confirmed.

'Good,' he ambled over towards the stove, producing a large skillet. He centered it on top, pulling wrapped chunks of meat. 'Anyone here not had moose before?'

Sasha looked at Fox. Fox grinned.

'That's Fitz,' he said.

'What's his rank?' Roland asked.

'He's not in the Renaissance,' Fox said. 'He's an independent individual.'

'Not that I won't kill a yeoman in passing,' Fitz said, 'but I'm not one to take

286

orders.'

'But you help?' Rose asked.

'When it's convenient. See, lass, in the forest it doesn't matter who's head of the capital. It doesn't matter where the capital is. It's you against nature. Eventually nature will win, but until then, you live the good life.'

'Fitz came into Olympia yesterday,' Fox said. 'Bringing dispatched from out east. Doing a favor for a friend.'

Fitz sang a short tune.

> *'Sweet Eileen, Pretty Eileen,*
> *Finest girl I've ever seen*
> *Ask me once, I'll say no twice,*
> *But Eileen knows how to ask me nice.'*

'If everyone is out of immediate danger,' Fox said, 'the generals had an idea for you to learn from the dispatches.'

'You came out in a blizzard to give us a class?' Roland asked.

'You have something better to do?' Fox asked.

Fitz laughed loudly. 'Not much of a blizzard, boy. Barely worth the name.' He tossed spices onto the meat and lay them on the skillet. 'This'll be fine. Now, who wants to wrestle?'

'Fitz, just watch the food,' Fox said, 'I've got to get these Templars focused.' He gestured for the Templars to all sit about him.

'Each of you gets to be part of this. Three possible scenarios for the Royal Army to conduct come the thaw. As Templars, you get to take a look, and work out how to defeat the plans. You will give a presentation on the plans sometime soon. How that presentation goes, and who presents what, is entirely up to you.'

He pulled three bound stacks of paper from his pack. 'First is Operation Tempest. The plan is simple. Regulars from North Watch and Royal Cities will deploy as an anvil to the east. Two corps from the field army will deploy to the west as a hammer. They will march in, relieve the siege of Walker, and destroy the Renaissance Army.

'Second is Operation Constellation. Deploying from the four corners of Walker, regular and district troops will establish a grid of fire bases, no more than two miles apart. Each fire base will house one company of infantry and their support.'

'Ha!' Fitz called. 'The forest will eat them.'

'Third is Operation Red Wall. Regular and district troops will besiege Walker County, cutting off all external support. They will slowly constrict, slashing and burning the entire county and killing everyone in it.'

'Oh, Jesus,' Mako said.

'Not subtle,' Fox agreed. 'So, your assignment is to look at these plans, determine what flaws can be exploited, what we can do to disrupt or stop them.'

'What should we plan to fight back with?' Sasha asked.

'For now, don't worry about that. Just find things to exploit and determine what we would need to be able to exploit them.'

'Better to run!' Fitz called. 'No use fighting what can't be beat.'

'Also,' Fox said, 'I want all of you to think about what you would do if you were in charge of the Royal Army. What plan would you come up with?'

'But first, food!' Fitz called. The pan sizzled, not only with meat but some miscellaneous vegetables Fitz must have carried in with him. The Templars grabbed their field plates and each took a helping.

Fitz removed several layers of fur, and Sasha noticed a large knife and pistol on his belt.

'Did you kill the moose with your crossbow?' Roland asked.

'Aye. See, outside of the Verendrye, gunshots get you killed. Yeomen don't take kind to people who can shoot and aren't in a uniform, so I got to be quiet when I hunt.'

'Must be difficult,' Sasha said.

'Sure,' Fitz beamed. 'Got to get the right shot at the right time. My first attempt I only managed to piss the devil off. Climbed so high to save my hide. Lost my bow, too. Had to build a new one, stronger one.'

'And you kill yeomen?' Roland asked.

'Sometimes.' Fitz shrugged 'Some yeomen aren't too bad, just normal folks trying to get by, but some are scum. I hear about one of them enough from friends of mine, I take him out.'

'Doesn't anyone get in trouble?' Sasha asked. 'Don't they punish the farmers?'

'Hell, no! See, very few crossbows these days. They see my bolt, they know it was me that killed 'em. No reason to punish common folk for my sins. More often they tack up wanted posters and start scary stories about me stealing

288

babies and whatnot. Now eat!'

The food was good, particularly after more than a day of jerky and read. They all ate quickly and quietly, eager to fill themselves up. Fitz scrubbed his skillet with snow, then lay down on Hero's cot to sleep.

The Templars went to work. Without desks they laid out maps and papers on their beds, rearranging them to fit the project. Fox sat back and watched, whittling something.

'Tempest is the best written,' Rose mused.

'I wonder who came up with them.' Roland pondered. 'Maybe Caesar came up with Tempest, if it's best written?'

'Maybe,' Rose said.

'The king's men came up with them,' Sasha said, looking at Fox. 'Isn't that right? The dispatches were the plans, from spies in the Royal Cities?'

Fox shrugged. 'Maybe,' he said, but he smiled at her with a knowing wink.

'These are the enemy's own plans?' Hero exclaimed. 'What, is the king himself our spy?'

The Templars chuckled, then went back to work.

'Constellation requires too many troops,' Mako said. 'They'd need about six hundred companies to put one firebase every two miles.'

'Five hundred and seventy-five companies,' Candle said.

'Does the Royal Army even have that many?' Mako asked.

'No,' Sasha said. 'Not even close.'

'Even with all their non-rifle companies?'

'No,' Sasha repeated herself. 'If they took every troop they had, they might be able to pull it off, and I mean every other troop.'

'Red Wall isn't an operation,' Patch said, squinting at the meager supply of papers laid out across her bunk. 'It's not detailed enough and isn't particularly well thought out.'

'You sure?' Elector asked.

'They have four companies deployed in the middle of lakes,' Patch said.

'Ah,' Sasha said. 'So, it looked like Tempest is their best option?'

'Appears so,' Elector said. 'If only by volume of paper.'

Tempest took three of their bunks. The other two operations only took up one.

'So, we ignore the other two?' Hero asked.

'No,' Rose shook her head.

'The assignment was to plan for all three,' Sasha said. 'We have to do all three.'

'Should we get to work?' Elector said.

'Can the crossbow launch grenades?' Patch asked.

'Patch! Focus,' Candle scolded.

'What? It could be helpful.'

'Maybe later,' Sasha said. 'For now, let's pick apart the enemy's plans, shall we?'

Patch sighed and joined them at the beds.

***

Athens spent two days digging itself out of the snow. After being stuck inside for three, it was a good chance to stretch some muscles, and the Templars found themselves appointed leaders of groups armed with shovels and buckets. Paths opened; the kitchens rekindled. Warm food flowed again.

Lily rode in a few days after, the first contact with the outside world since Fox and Fitz snuck in almost a week earlier.

'I sure hope Sparta was ready for winter,' Roland said as Lily warmed her hands by the barracks fire.

'Most of the companies at Sparta had been dispersed to their company depots,' Lily said. 'Those still at Sparta were not left in the cold, don't worry. It is not the policy of the RAM to let anyone freeze to death. It reflects poorly on us.'

Candle set water to boil. Several staff from the kitchens came in, bearing sandwiches and a pot of soup.

'Bear with me, Templars,' Lily said. 'I'm hungry, so I hope you don't mind if we eat while we talk.'

'Of course not,' Sasha said quickly.

'Does it always get this cold for this long?' Mako asked. He and Candle sat on beds, wrapped in extra blankets.

290

'Often,' Sasha said. 'Getting snowed in for a few days is a fairly common occurrence. Once, we had a blizzard so bad, the smaller families spent two weeks living with the larger families. It gave us fewer buildings to heat, and the bodies helped keep the homes warm.'

'It's nice to spend the nights sleeping with someone else,' Hero pointed out. 'Body warmth and extra blankets.'

'It is,' Sasha admitted, remembering when she was sleeping in an alcove packed with her and two other young girls, all wrapped in three family's worth of quilts.

'So,' Lily said, spooning herself a bowl of soup from the pot. 'You've looked over the documents Fitz brought with him. What do you think?'

Candle and Mako stood and discussed Constellation. They discussed the sheer impossibility of the math needed for the plan to work, and how long it would take to implement such a plan.

'So how do you defeat it?' Lily asked.

'Technically, it's already been defeated,' Candle said. 'The field regiments are already operating outside of the area of operations that Constellation encompasses.'

'The amount of supplies it would need to support all those troops in the field would make the army significantly vulnerable to attacks on their supply lanes,' Mako said.

Next came Red Wall. Patch and Roland spoke. 'It's hard to take this plan seriously,' Roland said.

'It has no staff support, no sense for how it would actually work,' Patch agreed.

'Not to mention how it plays right into the Renaissance Army's hands, as far as propaganda goes,' Roland says. 'Think of how many people would rise up if they tried to punish an entire county.'

'Some might argue such a response might deter future rebellions,' Lily pointed out. 'Massacre an entire county.'

'If there was only one voice talking about it, maybe,' Roland agreed. 'But with our people calling out our version of the events, we can whip up fervor elsewhere.'

Then came Tempest. Elector went first, describing the plan and the importance of logistics and how vulnerable the forces would be to it. Rose and Hero discussed the plans for I and III Corps, respectively, and how they would be defeated.

'So, the key to both is to attack their supplies, separate them, and attack their parts?' Lily asked.

'Without knowing what we CAN hit them with,' Rose said, 'we can only come up with vague generalities.'

'Fair enough. What about you, Scholar? What is your contribution to the presentation?'

Sasha discussed the Third and Second Regiments, and how important it was for them to stay active, even if their areas were secondary to the main enemy advances.

'Why?' Lily asked.

'Because every troop dispatched to protect railways and villages against them is one less sent to aid either of the army corps,' Sasha said, continuing with her presentation.

'Not bad,' Lily replied when all was done. 'If vague.'

'We don't know the Renaissance Army's strength,' Sasha said. 'We have to be vague.'

'No, I agree,' Lily nodded. 'So, someone tell me, what other things can we do to distract and disperse the king's forces?'

There was quiet for some time as the Templars all thought. Then Sasha spoke.

'Threaten the cities?' she ventured.

'What do you mean?' Lily asked.

'Count Walker never let enough of his force go into the field to weaken Walker Town itself. It had the most people, and he wanted to keep it under control. The Royal Army has its second largest concentration in the Royal Cities, where they can watch the greatest number of people. If the cities were threatened, it might scare them into sending troops to the cities instead of against us.'

'Okay,' Lily said. 'What else?'

She moved on, but she smiled at Sasha, and Sasha sat back. *Did I give her an idea, or did I figure something out they're already working on?*

Sasha pushed the thought aside and listened to Patch discuss firing grenades from crossbows.

292

Chapter 32

Just after the blizzard, Athens lost two-thirds of its clerks. They were assigned, given positions in whatever formation the generals were building with all the troops they were training. Sasha found the clerks she had formed friendships with heavily hit by the assignment, as they were the clerks pushing themselves harder than the rest. Sasha missed Angela, but the young woman had been so excited to get a posting that Sasha could not help but celebrate with her, even if neither of them knew where it was.

The latest edition of the *Renaissance Tribune* brought news of several promotions, including Colonel Trumpeter to Brigadier, and both Saxon and Bellona promoted to Master Warrant Officers. Another article announced that the Renaissance Army had acquired a printing press and would begin printing its own books. The same broadsheet announced that the February meeting of the Civic Council would be held in Olympia.

Correspondence with their sponsors had slowed during the blizzard but came back quickly. Sasha received letters from Third Regiment that told her Winnie was promoted to First Sergeant, and Buck was now a captain. Another blizzard came through, once again cutting off Athens. With most of the clerks dispersed, recovery was both easier and harder. At least the kitchens were willing to provide better food for the days stuck inside.

Classes continued as best they could, with Scott Anthony and Madam Moreau conducting their classes huddled around fireplaces. The library became the social center for those who remained. Exercises such as running and field practice were impossible, so the Templars made do with shoveling and clearing the now empty cabins of snow so they would not collapse.

February began with an announcement. The Templars were having a surprise week off, not for any special military training, but for the Templars to see the Civil Council in action while they were at Olympia. An important political event for the Templars to watch, assuming the early year blizzard season did not come back to trap them all again.

Sasha became the cadet captain that Sunday morning. She went to work getting everyone packed and supplied for their trip, then guided them through the woods to Olympia. The weather was cold, but bearable. At least someone had managed to carve out a route through the forests for them to follow.

When they arrived, Olympia looked different from their previous visit. It was obvious the Civil Council was already set up by the tents. Like the tents used by the civilian hospital, they were strung up a short way out of town, near the ram cabins where guests to Olympia normally stayed. The cadets suffered through DeWitt's welcome, then found their cabin. Scott Anthony was already there, laying on one of the beds as they entered.

'Here we are,' Scott said as they entered their cabin. 'You're in the back,' he said. Sasha noticed that clothes and bags were present in some of the other bunks.

'We're sharing?' Hero said sternly. 'We can't get our own space?'

'If you think it's crowded during normal operations, you can't imagine how it'll get during the council meetings.' Del Oso said. 'The council sits sixteen people. Then there are the council functionaries, clerks, bailiffs, and such, another dozen or so. They deliberately try to keep it small, usually end up asking a bunch of locals to fill in where needed, get them involved in the council.'

'That would still only be two cabins,' Hero said, 'and Olympia has four.'

'Some military people come, but many of the bunks are taken up by civilians,' Scott said, his voice straining to contain his annoyance at Hero's attitude. 'The council represents many different towns and villages, and not every grievance can wait for the council to cycle back through their area. Some people spend days traveling to get here.'

'Is it really a big enough area for that to be a problem?' Roland asked. 'I mean, Walker County, some parts of Brainerd and Bemidji, maybe a few villages from some other counties. That's not a significant amount of people.'

'Or territory,' Rose continued. 'Are there any liberated towns that are more than one hundred miles from each other?'

'Maybe not,' Del Oso said, 'but the invitation still goes out.'

'So, we're here to observe the council,' Sasha said.

'Right. The council meets Monday through Friday, and we're going to see it.'

'Why?' Hero asked, still sounding petulant.

'And why wait until now?' Patch asked.

Scott replied. 'In the last few weeks, your historical classes have covered various democratic revolutions and the development of democratic institutions across the world, along with the development of dictatorships and autocratic governments. Your political classes have followed a similar track. We waited until you had that information in your heads, until you could understand what is going on, before we brought you to the council.

'As for why, well, it should become clear to you by now, if it has not already, that the Renaissance Army is, for all intents and purposes, a dictatorship.' He cut off several protests from the Templars, 'I don't want to argue, Templars, but it is. The council can advise and suggest, but General Prince has the final say. They meet because he wants them to; if he decided to disband them, there is little they can do.

'This is something Prince wants to change. Prince is pushing for the council to take more responsibility, moving towards a government that is independent of the military. After all, what good is a government if the military can remove it at will?'

'General Prince would never do that!' Roland exclaimed.

'No, but Senator might,' Rose and Sasha both spoke at the same time. They glanced at Elector, whose grim face confirmed their words.

'It is important that you understand the necessity of civilian control of the military,' Scott said. 'It is important you understand how much trust is necessary for that control to work, on both sides.' He paused, letting them all think about it for a moment. 'Get settled in,' he continued, 'I'm going to check in on the schedule for this week.'

'It's not separated by gender,' Del Oso said, nodding at the bunks. 'Pair up. Scott and I are in this set. You have these four. Store your gear, sit down and wait. This isn't a military camp; the rules are different here. Cadet Captain, get everyone settled.'

Scott and Del Oso turned and left. Sasha climbed a bunk and looked down over the rest.

'Put your stuff away,' she said. 'Settle in.'

***

The cabin filled up quickly, and by the end of the day it was packed with thirty-two men and women. The sky dropped sleet on Olympia that evening, so they spent the night inside, eating chicken and talking. Sasha found that evening particularly satisfying. She had only a limited idea of what civilian life in the Liberated Counties was like, mostly from Arrowhead in Brainerd County.

The civilians who joined them were a sampling of people who had active interests in the Renaissance Movement: a father and son who wanted to discuss a system to improve animal husbandry; a woman who was petitioning for the establishment of a civilian mail system; others just had business opportunities or ideas to improve the council.

There was even an Alvanist man. Sasha recognized him as the leader of another Alvanist community in Walker County, though she had long forgotten his name or where he was from. He, in turn, did not recognize her. He was not as overbearing as her father might be, commenting positively on some of the ideas being bandied about the room. He even spoke with the Templars without preaching at them.

They talked about the war, or the politics of the counties, of this problem and that solution. They passed around broadsheets and discussed the events described, taking sides civilly and without rancor. Sasha participated in a dozen conversations, fierce but civil debates, ending each one with a smile and a handshake. Sasha was rarely so happy; she smiled the whole evening.

They all slept soundly that night, the rain on the roof providing a gentle alternative to sound of more than thirty snoring men and women.

The next morning was Monday, the first day of the council, a day set aside for petitions. The council set up four different boards, each to listen to their own topics. The Templars went to watch the Military Petition Board. They entered the tent and sat in the back, watching the seats and sides fill until the four council members entered.

'Good morning,' said one of them, an older gentleman Sasha did not know. The man gestured to a note taker, who pulled out a pen and started taking notes. 'This is the Civil Council's Military Petition Board, meeting for Monday, February tenth, 2476. And we begin.'

It was an oddly informal way to start a meeting, but that was not what tugged Sasha's attention. 'It's February tenth,' she muttered.

'Yes,' Candle said. 'What of it?'

'It's my birthday,' Sasha whispered.

Candle's face lit up, but Scott shushed them from the side, and she said nothing.

The petitions went quickly, Sasha thought. Petitioners gave their names to a council official. They were called up in order of their appearance, so as not to show favoritism, and each one was given five minutes to state their petition, followed by a few minutes of questions from the board members.

The Templars watched for two hours until the first break and saw over a dozen petitioners. The first was the Alvanist pastor, who gave a short speech and a simple request that they cease their war against the king for the sake of peace. He spoke well, without the fire and brimstone of Sasha's father, but with a measured voice. He ended his speech with an acknowledgement that the petition would go nowhere, but he believed that 'during a time of war, someone should always be calling for peace.'

The petition was acknowledged and recorded, and the pastor sat down.

Most of them were people advising the council on how they thought something should be run. Sasha agreed with some of them, like the woman who argued that the military should be required to train civilian engineers. Some Sasha hated, like the man who demanded all women leave the uniform and the council, because it was God's will that they be subservient to men and had no place in places of authority. The Templars glared at him as he left. He glared back.

The petition boards, for their part, did not vote on anyone's petition. They listened, and asked questions, but did not disregard anyone who spoke. Some of them even took notes.

During the break, Candle broke the news to the rest of the Templars about Sasha's birthday. Some of them did not seem to care; others were excited.

'Did you celebrate your birthday at home?' Candle asked.

'Birthday celebration was a special mass for another year of piousness, then special sweet bread after dinner,' Sasha said.

'No gifts?' Rose asked.

'We didn't have enough for gifts,' Sasha said. 'Things were replaced as they needed to be replaced, and we did not have many luxuries.'

This news brought frowns to most of the Templars, but they were ushered into the second session before they could continue their conversation. This session ran the same as the first, except they ran out of petitioners before the first hour was up. With an hour left to go, the Templars came up to the council members and spoke with them about the petition process.

'Will every petition you hear be presented to the council?' Elector asked.

The elder gentleman who led the Military Petition Board shook his head. 'No. Each petition will be voted on by the four of us afterwards. If all of us reject it, it is recorded but not sent to the council. If anyone does vote for it, it is forwarded, but those with four votes will be considered long before those with one vote.'

'If only one person votes for it, it will go forward?' Elector pressed.

'It can, but it will not get too far. The council only has so much time to discuss anything, so something with four votes gets more attention than something with one vote. The Alvanist's message, for example. His message may be read to the council, but that's it. No vote will be taken on it. The man who demanded all women return home, his won't even make it past the board. Even if it somehow did make it to the general session, it's too far down the list of importance the council would run out of time before they got to it.'

'Well, that's good,' Sasha said. The other Templars agreed.

They had lunch with some of the council members, learning about how the council was formed and what it had done so far. Some of the council members were more affable than others; Sasha saw Elder Templeton, the woman who came and spoke in Arrowhead, but she did not share a meal with the Templars.

That afternoon was a social gathering of sorts, where everyone was mixing together, discussing politics and movements and the war's progress. Sasha, along with most of the Templars, was asked her thoughts on the campaigns, on what might happen when the spring came, and the Royal Army began its expected campaign. Sasha answered as best she could, trying not to reveal what she knew about Operation Tempest.

Another topic that evening was the king's speech. Sasha shared a birthday with the Kingdom of North Mississippi, and every year on February tenth the king gave a speech, describing the previous year and advancing plans for the next. It would be several days before the text was expected in the Liberated Counties, but everyone had an opinion on how he would address the Renaissance Army.

The schedule allowed for some free time before dinner. Sasha took the opportunity to walk about the town. It was a cold February day, but after the sleet of the previous day people took the chance to stretch their legs and move about. Some congregated in discussion groups. Sasha avoided most until she saw a decent sized crowd, standing about a woman. The woman was on a box, elevated above all, and most strangely, she was singing.

'Who is that?' she asked one of the bailiffs who happened to be passing by.

'That's Aquillon Madrillon,' he said. 'She showed up late last year, out of the Dakota Plains. Comes to the council meetings, sings her songs.'

'She sings songs?' Sasha asked, wondering what songs she could be sing at council meetings.

'Aye, sounds odd, right? But listen to the words.'

Sasha stepped to the back of the crowd, the bailiff next to her, so she could listen to the words.

Michael Bernabo

Four score and seven years ago,
The fathers of our nation did show
A nation conceived in liberty,
That all are equal, both you and me.

But now we fight this horrid war
To see if liberty can endure
And on this bloodied battlefield
We justly say we shall not yield.

But there is little that our words can add
On a battleground that bled many a lad.
This hallowed ground shall long remain
As a testament to the soldier's pain.

So, to the living we say instead
We will do what we must to honor the dead,
That their last full measure was not in vain.
This is not the end of liberty's reign.

In the view of God's just might,
We shall fight to make this right,
There is no limit to what we'll do
To rebirth our nation, to say anew

That government of the people,
By the people, for the people,
On this earth, we will cherish
And from this earth, never shall it perish.

She finished her song. The people clapped, but she stared, oblivious to their presence. One or two stepped forward to talk to her, and she responded, staring off into space as she spoke. Sasha was reminded of Patch.

'Do you get it?' the bailiff asked.

'She's talking about war and liberty,' Sasha replied.

'No, she's singing about it. See, she sings about a topic, and the song sticks with you, and you think about it. I've heard people discussing the topics weeks after the council.'

'Is she part of the Renaissance Movement?'

'No,' the bailiff shook his head. 'At least, not in any official capacity. There were some questions asked when she first showed up. I spoke with her myself. She seems harmless; not too focused, sure, but harmless.'

Sasha watched the woman begin again, switching now to a new song.

The first of them is in respect to the power of your speech;
You always see more benefit, the more minds you can reach.
So, when a lord demands that you must censor your thought,
He wants you screaming silently when you're taken out and shot.

The second has to do with all the arms a man can bear;
For it is wrong to think your lord will ever be just and fair.
So, when a lord demands you must give him all of your arms,
He wants you weak and powerless, when he comes to do you harm.

The third is that a family's home is theirs and not their lord's,
He cannot force an open door for men to hang their swords.
So, when a lord demands you give his men a place to settle down,
He wants you tired and wary, should trouble come to town.

'She sings about rights?' Sasha said as Aquillon continued singing.

'Yeah, but I don't know where she gets her songs from. The generals know about her and haven't done anything to stop her from showing up. They must be okay with her message.'

'Have they ever listened to her?' Sasha asked.

The bailiff shrugged. 'Don't know.'

They listened for a few more verses before Sasha continued her way. She found her classmates in the central square, where a few tables were cleared off and set about. They had somehow procured a honey cake, with a small candle lit in the middle.

'Happy birthday!' they called. Several starting singing birthday songs, the various tunes and words mixing together in a terrible cacophony that made Sasha, and many surrounding individuals, laugh out loud.

'Make a wish and blow out the candle,' Candle said, chuckling at herself.

Sasha smiled and leaned forward, blowing out the candle in one quick blow. 'Did I do it right?'

'You've never had a birthday candle before?' Candle asked.

'No,' Sasha shook her head. 'Just prayer and sweet cakes.'

'We had a whole meal planned around our birthdays,' Candle said. 'Three or four hours, several courses, small gifts from everyone.'

'We had the same,' Roland said. Mako nodded.

'Ours was a whole day,' Rose said, 'but it was not as fun as you might think. My family had obligations, so it wasn't MY day. It was a reason for guests to come and obligations to be met, but I did get a lot of gifts.'

'I don't really celebrate a birthday,' Patch said. 'I don't know when I was born. Sometime in the spring, I think, but we don't know the date. No one did. So, we always celebrated everyone's birthday on the summer solstice. One big party for everyone.'

'I've never really had one either,' Hero said. 'I don't know the date myself; winter, sometime. My family wasn't much into celebrating it, anyways.'

They divided up the cake and ate it, talking about how they used to celebrate various holidays during the year. Sasha was amused by the common holidays they all shared, and the unique holidays no one else knew about.

'You know what is happening right now?' Rose asked as the sun went down.

'What?' Hero asked.

'The nobles of the kingdom are assembling for the king's speech.'

'Wait,' Patch said, 'you were born on Founding Day?'

'Yes,' Sasha said, 'on the same day the king was crowned. I am as old as the Kingdom of North Mississippi.'

Rose raised her glass. 'Then may you outlive the kingdom.'

The Templars toasted. 'To outliving the kingdom.'

***

The Council of Nobility met in the Great Hall, a large meeting room constructed for the business of legislating a kingdom. Positions for the one hundred nobles, each consisting of a fine desk and comfortable chair, ringed a raised dais where the current speaker could hold the attention of the gathered decision makers. A chandelier of electric lights filled the hall with a yellowish light.

This evening was the King's Founding Speech, the one time a year when the hall would become full. Of the one hundred nobles, only four were missing. Two were sick or dying, their places taken by their heirs apparent. A third was in Denver for the winter, negotiating deals for resources collected from the mountains, and likewise his son was in his place. Only one seat was filled by a man not of noble blood, as the family that hired him was besieged in Walker County.

Above them, in the gallery, every seat was taken, a rarity indeed. Ambassadors and their staffs, families of the noblemen, generals and captains of industry, all gathered for the speech, to see how their next year might go.

'Ready?' Ambassador O'Hare whispered to Miklos in Odessan.

'I hope so,' Miklos whispered.

'At least he's gotten better,' O'Hare replied.

Miklos smirked. O'Hare had been the first military attaché to North Mississippi and had been to seventeen of these speeches. He often told stories of the first ones, when the king would read numbers and charts in a monotone voice, but that soon changed, and King Xavier had become a proficient if uninspiring orator. Miklos, having only been to five, had not seen any growth in his time.

The sergeant-at-arms of the council knocked his heavy staff on the floor, calling the viewers to their seats. He waited for the bustled to subside before he called.

'Ladies and Gentlemen here assembled, 'Rise for His Majesty, King Xavier, First of his Name, of the Family of Santiago-Locke, King of North Mississippi and Prime Minister of the Same.'

The crowd rose and clapped as King Xavier and his family entered. Xavier led, dressed in his blue and gold uniform. Behind him came General Prince Stefan, in a medal-bedecked brown uniform. Last came Queen Charlotte, again dressed as a trophy in a silver dress, and the king's daughter, Princess Samantha, who was dressed much more modestly in red. Samantha was thirteen, old enough that ambassadors were discussing her name for marriage.

The king began speaking, and Miklos sat back, eyes roaming the crowd to see who else was paying attention and who, like him, was already bored. He noticed the ambassador from Charleston had snuck in a small book and was reading it in his lap. A general of the district troops was napping, and two young gentlemen were having a whispered discussion of some import.

Miklos smiled. Xavier may have become a better speaker than he had been, but his subject matter was still the minutiae of a kingdom. He spoke of agriculture and industry, of wealth and infrastructure. A lot of numbers.

After some time, he finally reached the portion of the speech where he discussed Walker County.

'And it is known, my Lords of the Council, that we are short our full number, because one of our own is locked away, besieged within the walls of his city, by a rebellious group. This group calls itself the Renaissance Army of Minnesota. And while the word Renaissance, when its meaning is looked up, may invite images of books and art, of an expanse of knowledge, it is still an army, which invites death and destruction. It claims to be of Minnesota, which promoted discord within our unified kingdom. And their leader is a Dawson, the family that brought the former republic to a fiery and fatal end.

'No, my lords, this is no movement to better the lives of the men and women of our kingdom. This is the last petulant wail of a family that failed in its obligations to its country. There is no doubt in my mind when we crush this army and view its ranks, we will find the final gasp of the Old Guard behind their leaders.

'This winter, that army has weathered the cold in whatever homes they could force themselves into. They've been forced to huddle and starve, while we prepare our grand offensive. The operation has been planned and gamed, the men prepared, the generals eager. I have no doubt that by the end of this summer, law and order will return to Walker, and the Dawson family will finally be finished.

'Two months from now, the grand offensive will begin. Between now and then, any member of the Renaissance Army who surrenders himself to us will be granted amnesty. They will not be punished for their actions. We will interrogate, yes, but not punish. After two months, after April tenth, the amnesty expires, and the campaign commences. I urge the men and women in Walker to think of this, and to not oppose the might of the forces that will soon be making their way towards your land.

'And as we look to our neighbors, and the threats they may pose to our kingdom, we should recognize that . . . .'

Miklos let the king's speech fade back into the background. He had not proclaimed an emergency. Whatever else he said, that was the one thing they needed to hear.

With no emergency declared, Stefan will have a hard time getting his forces in place quickly.

Miklos waited for the speech to end and the appropriately long applause to die down. He maneuvered through the crowded halls of the kingdom, eventually finding Bennabi standing outside a conference room, waiting for him. The pair moved inside; there, Prince Stefan and several other officers

303

stood, speaking.

'No emergency,' Prince Stefan confirmed. 'I think he doesn't want to appear panicked to the world.'

'Does this disrupt you?' Miklos asked.

'No. Delay, yes, but we planned for this eventuality. We will begin moving supplies early. It will be worked around.'

'It could have been worse,' Bennabi said.

'How so?' Miklos asked.

'You should have seen the plans Robinson came up with,' Stefan said. 'Operation Constellation. Ha! Absolute shit. Spreading out the entire Royal Army across one county. My father also came up with a plan, by which I mean a raw idea without any merit to it. At least he's smart enough to recognize a bad idea; we burned all the copies of it.'

'Am I still at the table?' Miklos asked.

'Oh, yes,' Stefan nodded. 'So long as you mention to the margrave who won this little war.'

I will mention it, when it is won, Miklos thought to him. Outwardly, he bowed.

Chapter 33

'Penn!'

The former Templar beamed at his comrades as he intercepted them short of the tent. He moved about on his own now, his missing leg replaced with a wooden one, and supported by a pair of crutches. Along with his new leg was the insignia of an able warrant officer and the red aiguillette of a staff officer.

'Nice leg,' Hero said.

'Nice uniform,' Rose continued.

'Thanks!' Penn said. 'How are you doing? Still at it?'

'We are,' Sasha said with a smile. 'And you?'

'I'm keeping busy,' Penn said. He continued towards the tent. 'Major Scribe, the liaison officer for the Civic Council, has been relying on me to handle a lot of responsibilities. Can you believe they only had him and two staff sergeants before I came along?'

'Do you really need much more than that?' Roland asked. 'It's a pretty simple thing, isn't it, to liaise between a general and a council that doesn't have any real power?'

'It would be, if the generals treated it like it has no power,' Penn said sharply. 'But General Prince takes this council seriously. Yes, he has no real reason to follow them, since there's no constitution, but he still pays attention to them. And it can take a lot of time to gather information and formulate responses, Roland. We don't give one-word answers here.'

Roland nodded. 'Okay, then.'

'So,' Penn said, 'what did you guys see yesterday?'

'We watched petitioners,' Rose replied.

'Anything good?'

'One man demanded all women return to their wifely duties,' Sasha said.

Penn chuckled. 'Oh, lord. He's a persistent fool, isn't he? At least he hasn't tried anything more than a petition. There were a few more aggressive men at some of the earlier meetings.'

'What are we seeing today?' Candle asked.

'Debates. Monday is petitioners, Tuesday is debates and hearings. The rest of the week is devoted to the Civic Council as a whole, with committee meetings in the afternoons.'

'And you'll be debating?' Sasha asked.

Penn grinned. 'I am.'

Roland held the tent flap open for them. It was the same tent they had watched petitions at the day before, but now the podium had a table with chairs on either side of it. The room was filling with people there to watch the debates. One table was empty. At the other sat a young man, calmly looking at papers. From behind, all Sasha saw was a head of brown hair and a well-washed white shirt.

'Who's that?' she asked.

'Zac Holden, the Constitutionalist,' Penn replied.

'The what?'

Penn chuckled. 'He showed up last fall, an exile from Michigan. He's been working to get a constitutional convention going, wants to build a real government instead of depending on the generals. Gives a lot of speeches but doesn't have a lot of support.'

'And the generals let him?' Roland asked.

'Why wouldn't they?' Sasha asked.

Roland looked as if he were about to respond but Penn cut him off. 'In addition to his speeches, Mister Holden spends a lot of time helping people. He's genuinely interested in the people, and he's genuinely worried about how much power the generals wield.'

'That makes sense,' Rose said, 'if he's an exile from Michigan.'

Everyone nodded at that. The People's Republic of Michigan was a topic they went over in the political class a few weeks earlier. Once the most democratic and progressive of nations in Atlantic America, it had fallen into despotism and eventually monarchy. People from Michigan who tried to hold to the old democratic beliefs were often persecuted or exiled.

A bailiff called for everyone to take their seats. The Templars had a row up front, right behind Penn, who took his spot at the empty table. Sasha glanced over at Holden, who looked over and nodded a welcome to Penn. He was maybe twenty years old, with a pleasant face and big brown eyes. His clean shirt did show smudges of ink on the sleeves, and she realized he had been writing something while waiting for the debate to start. Sasha smiled at that.

The chairs filled up, but people continued to enter, with extra men and women standing along the edge. The Council Members sat, looking out over the crowd. Templeton took the lead.

'The Military Petition Board is convened today, Tuesday, February eleventh, for the purpose of a positional debate. The petitioner is Mister Holden, civilian. In opposition is Staff Officer Penn, Renaissance Army. Are we ready, gentlemen?'

Both men nodded. 'Very well. Mister Holden, you may begin.'

Zac Holden stood up. When he spoke, he did so with a loud voice, powerful enough everyone in the tent could hear him.

'"The Stairway to Hell begins with a Step towards God". That is a quote from the Reverend John Meyers, when he was a senator in the Michigan Legislature in 2380. The nation had just finished the War of the Three Fools and was looking to rebuild some prestige by annexing a few communities in Wisconsin. Of course, they didn't call it annexation. They were extending their security to aide communities that were suffering from vague and largely fictitious threats. The result was an expensive and bloody occupation that spread west over Wisconsin, and ultimately led to the fall of democracy within Michigan.

'The Renaissance Army has begun a movement to reshape our corner of the world, and the first steps have been taken with the right intentions in mind. But these things have a way of getting out of hand. The needs of the army will soon clash with the needs of the civilians it protects. The promises made to two different groups that cannot all be kept, the mass of decisions that must be made without the time to properly dwell on what's going on. That means the steps will get trickier.

'Now, we all want this movement to succeed. It's a breath of fresh air in a world dominated by the Commonwealth and their puppet kings, but it is still a fragile thing. Those steps may yet lead down instead of up, all dependent on General Prince keeping his focus on the movement. It follows, then, that anything we can do to build structures of governance and ease the pressure of General Prince's position is ultimately beneficial to the movement as a whole.

'To that end, I petition the council to pass a resolution, creating an independent and civilian judiciary, an independent and civilian constabulary, and our own rules of law and punishment.'

Sasha heard a few voices around her murmuring. Penn was taking notes. One of the councilors, the older gentleman, glared at Zac.

'It seems like a lot, I'm sure,' Holden continued, 'but I believe this is for the betterment of the movement. Consider this: we are currently dependent on the

307

provost to act as the arm of law and order in the Liberated Counties. They have taken over the role of the yeomen, and I much prefer them to the count's lackeys. But the provost is a military formation, and when the necessity of the war draws the army away, what will we be left with? Should the army go without their provost squadron because we need them? They were raised and trained for a reason, and it would be naïve to expect them to do otherwise. By establishing, a civilian constabulary now, we can free up the provost for the duties they are being raised to complete.

'Second, by establishing our own courts, we free up the time of many military officers who have better things to do. Under General Order Eleven, any civilian who believes they cannot get a fair decision from their headman may ask for a military trial, which requires at least three officers to act as a panel of judges. It takes time to listen to the arguments and make a decision, at least a day if not more, and that doesn't include the time it takes to find three officers.

'Look at the trial of James Vest. His judges were a combat officer, who should have been training her soldiers; a logistical officer, who should have been tending to his workshops; and a medical officer, who should have been practicing his surgeon's skills. The time it took for them to come out, read up on the rules of a court, and then put them into practice, was far too long. By establishing a civilian judiciary, we take the need for such courts out of the hands of military officers who have too much to do.

'Finally, I argue that such an independence is ultimately beneficial to the movement. For far too long, the concept of law and power have come from military units. First those of the occupation, then the yeomen, who carry a military bearing about them, and now by the Renaissance Army. The disconnection of authority from military power is an ultimate goal of the movement; General Prince said it himself when he addressed this body in January. I argue that the time can never be too soon.

'The goal, for everyone here, is success for the movement. A civilian government with strong institutions that hold the trust and respect of the people, one that governs the Liberated Counties and allows Prince and the Renaissance Army to focus on the war is a part of that, and it isn't a part that can simply be thrown together at a moment's notice. It must be built. This will help us to do that.

'Thank you,' Zac said, sitting down.

'Thank you, Mister Holden,' Templeton said. 'Mister Penn?'

***

The board voted to approve Mister Holden's petition, three to one.

'Sorry you lost,' Candle said. Penn joined his former classmates for lunch. Scott Anthony managed to get them a classroom for a private meal, so the classmates could speak without interruption.

Penn chuckled. 'I don't look at it as win or lose, Candle. I look at it as influencing the process to see that we don't go too far, too fast. Besides, I think Mister Holden has some good ideas, overall.'

'Even though he's a Constitutionalist?' Roland asked.

'Even though,' Penn said. 'I mean, what does that mean? It means he wants a formal civil government, and not a military dictatorship.'

'Prince isn't a dictator,' Candle said.

'Yes, he is,' Sasha replied.

'How can you say that?' Roland asked, frowning.

'Because he is. He knows it. Did you read the broadsheet from last month? He said as much. Hell, Scott Anthony said as much when we arrived.'

'I did,' Scott Anthony said, arriving with a tray of fruit. 'Eat up, this stuff isn't going to last too much longer.'

'Hey, Scholar,' Candle pointed to the tray. 'Grapes!'

'All yours,' Sasha said. The Templars chuckled.

'Look,' Penn said, 'I like Mister Holden, and I like what he's trying to do. So do the generals. They're glad to have someone making the movements towards a constitution who isn't a military officer or hasn't been given power by the generals.'

'How can you say that?' Candle asked.

'What did I say I was here to do, Candle?' Penn said. 'I joined the movement to keep it on the right track. The best way to do that is to build a system based on rules. That's what a constitution does. Now, Mister Holden is jumping too fast, but he's jumping in the right direction. I'm not debating him to make him stop, I'm debating him so that the people listening know the consequences of how and when to jump with him.'

'Good,' Sasha said. Elector nodded next to her.

'Okay,' Scott Anthony said quickly. 'How about a quick poll. Consider that the debate you just saw indicated that there are two political parties forming in the Liberated Counties. On the one hand, you have Mister Holden and other Constitutionalists. One the other, you have the generals and their party, let's call it the Renaissance Party. Who here supports the Constitutionalists?'

Sasha raised her hand. So did Scott Anthony, Patch, Elector and, to some shock, Penn.

'Really?' Roland asked.

'Yes,' Penn said. 'Really.'

'And who supports the Renaissance Party?'

Del Oso, Roland, Mako, Rose and Candle raised their hands.

Everyone looked at Hero. He shrugged. 'I don't know. I agree with both and disagree with both.'

'Fair enough,' Scott Anthony said. 'Second question. Who here is going to let that impact you as officers?'

No one raised their hand.

'Good,' Scott Anthony said.

Penn chuckled. 'Can we switch topics? I want to know everything about what you've all been doing. Spare no details, Templars. None at all.'

***

As much fun as petitions and debates were, the last three days turned out to be boring.

The three days had all sixteen members of the council together, discussing the petitions and resolutions that had made it to that point. As Penn explained it, the resolution was read out loud. Each member had five minutes to speak on it, then there was a period of questions. Finally, the council voted.

It sounded good in theory, but in execution, Sasha found it slow. It took eighty minutes for each councilor to have their time, and while some yielded their time when they had nothing to say, most took their full five minutes. Some spoke passionately on the topic, either for or against, but several councilors seemed to think they had to ramble on for as long as they could, sometimes straying far from the purpose of the resolution. A lot of them could also use some time in Scott Anthony's rhetoric class. *Natural orators, they are not.*

'The rules were set when the council was elected,' Penn said at Wednesday lunch. 'When a new council is elected, the first thing they'll do is vote on rule changes.'

310

'When is the next election?' Roland asked.

'Next March,' Penn said.

It could take as long as two hours for the council to vote on something. Each session was three hours, each day had two sessions, and in three days of watching Sasha saw the council deal with only eight issues.

Holden's civil law system was voted down, but not killed. The council said they were not prepared to support it at this time but directed Holden to continue planning. Holden, sitting near the Templars in the viewing area, shook his head but did not look surprised. A resolution calling for mandatory school for children was likewise pushed down to a future meeting. Resolutions to provide more draft animals to Charity, the civilian hospital, and to send an ambassador to King Xavier for some undefined purpose were totally defeated.

The council did pass four of their topics. They asked the RAM to begin training civilians in engineering roles, so that the Liberated Counties could plan and build their own infrastructure. Major Scribe, the RAM liaison to the Civil Council, gave a short response accepting the resolution and promising an answer by the next meeting.

'Will they do it?' Sasha asked Penn later.

'Probably,' Penn said. 'Then Holden will probably ask for civilians to begin training with the provost.'

'Which he should have done this time,' Elector said.

'True,' Penn replied, 'but I can't tell him that.'

The council passed a petition to ask for access to the RAM's small printers, to establish and produce their own newspaper. They passed a resolution for the migration of workers during the farming season, columns of men and women who would move from town to town to increase their crops. And finally, they passed a resolution that one whole day of the next session would be devoted to the process of the next election, even though it was more than a year away.

'It'll take time for them to agree to anything,' Penn pointed out. 'How recently liberated does a town need to be to vote? How many councilors does each county get? A lot of questions to consider.'

'Is that why elections will be in March?' Elector asked. 'So recently liberated counties have time to get adjusted to being liberated?'

'Something like that,' Penn said.

'Still,' Sasha said, 'it was nice to see things being discussed.'

'You think that group will rule better than Prince?' Roland asked.

Sasha sighed. 'It's not about ruling better, Roland. It's about keeping abuses from happening. We all trust Prince to command the RAM and rule the Liberated Counties because he's Prince, but what if he were to fall? Would people trust Caesar to command in the same way? Or Senator? Or anyone other than Prince?'

'You keep saying that,' Roland scowled.

Sasha shook her head. 'Think about all the societies we've studied where the government was built around one ruler, and what happened when that ruler fell. What made the empires of the previous world great were the institutions that allowed the nation to grow and endure regardless of who was running it.'

'The previous world died,' Candle said.

'I know,' Sasha replied, 'and it's our duty to learn from them and do better.'

***

The last act of the council was to vote on their next session, one month from then. They voted to hold it in Bemidji County, to show newly liberated towns the system that was evolving. Sasha was glad to see the vote was unanimous. The Renaissance Army was not the only part of the movement that faced danger.

The people crowding at Olympia began to disperse. Aquillon, the singing woman, was there for much of the day, as caravans left to take people back to their homes. Sasha hoped to see Mister Holden, but he seemed to disappear when he was not watching the council, the same as many of the council members, who disappeared as soon as they could. Others stayed long enough to bid people farewell.

The Templars said their goodbyes. The Alvanist minister wished them luck. Penn and Scribe both took their time before riding off to wherever they were meeting with General Prince.

'Huh,' Roland said. 'Where was the headquarters?'

'What?' Rose asked.

'Olympia is the RAM headquarters. Where was General Prince or Brigadier Lily?'

They looked at Scott Anthony, who chuckled.

'They temporarily removed themselves to another location,' he said.

'Why?' Candle asked.

'Two reasons,' Scott Anthony said. 'One reason is military.'

'Mobility,' Del Oso continued. 'They wanted to exercise their headquarters' ability to relocate. To keep running the war when not in comfortable surroundings.'

'The second is political,' Scott Anthony finished. 'They did not want the council to be overshadowed by General Prince. Prince holds all the power. He had enough trouble with petitioners coming to him and not the council.'

'Even though the council holds no power,' Roland said.

'For now,' Sasha pointed out.

Sasha hoped to see either Prince or Lily before they left, but Del Oso managed to get them a ride back to Athens, a horse-drawn sleigh that was leaving early Saturday and not much later than that. The Templars, bundled up and covered in blankets, enjoyed the ride through the February cold.

'You know why we got this?' Roland said.

'Why?' Rose asked.

'Because this period of the Templars ends next month,' he said. 'Then come the exams.'

'Shit,' Hero said. 'I'd almost forgotten. Thanks for reminding me.'

'You're welcome.'

'I wasn't being serious,' Hero said. 'What if we fail?'

'Warrants for all,' Patch replied.

'And if we succeed, commissions and war,' Roland said.

Hero looked sick to his stomach. Sasha almost felt sorry for him.

Chapter 34

A few more blizzards fell across them during February, followed by a warm March. The snow started to melt. Some of the insulated windows were removed and replaced with the paper panes. Letters resumed, and Sasha got word from Third Regiment about their winter interactions with the northeastern towns of Brainerd County and into neighboring Aitkin County, adding a score of villages and towns to their territory. Snow's letter in particular stressed how difficult the rest of the county was going to be, and how important it was for Sasha to come back ready to work.

The threads of their training were coming together. Their history class just finished discussing the Iron Republic and was now onto the Commonwealth Wars. Their politics class was full of lively debates. In one ethics class, Madam Moreau simply wrote a challenge on the board. The Templars debated themselves into three factions, arguing passionately about the topic. Moreau said nothing the entire class.

Sasha's reviews with Caesar continued, discussing lessons from history that she could use in the current campaign, or discussing how she might teach those lessons to others. Every meal was a chance to sit down with an officer or a civilian and discuss something or other. Doctor Moore, Brigadier Lily, Colonel Carpenter, even Elder Templeton stopped by for a meal and a conversation.

There was anxiety about the tests. They were supposed to take up the entire week. Rose, who had a formal education, told them all about how such things worked at other institutions. They pondered what they would have to do.

'It's got to be difficult, right?' Hero asked nervously.

'Sure, but not so difficult we all fail out,' Elector replied.

'But it lasts a whole week! What sort of test lasts a whole week?' Hero whined.

'It won't be one test,' Candle said. 'It'll be several tests.'

'Will it?' Sasha asked.

'Sure,' Candle replied with a grin. 'If it was one test, what would it cover? Politics or ethics? Then why spend so much time teaching us history? Why allow tactical training? It's more likely a bunch of different tests.'

'Candle's right,' Rose interrupted.

'Oh, so I can fail multiple tests instead of one,' Hero muttered. He was spending almost as much time in the library as Sasha these days, often with another Templar helping him study one topic or another. Even Sasha spent time helping him, finding him too focused on the tests to annoy her.

The class assignments lessened in their intensity, and at Rose's urging, they began reviewing. The dedicated notebooks proved invaluable as they reviewed, reminding them of lessons months earlier.

'Look at how my handwriting has improved,' Sasha said, looking at her first pages of notes.

Candle leaned over. 'Spelling, too. Nice to know that Templar Scholar can properly spell Templar.'

'It was the first time I'd ever tried spelling it,' Sasha scowled. 'It was only ever spoken before.'

'Hey, I don't judge,' Candle said. 'See? F-A-L-A-N-K-S.'

Elector glanced up. 'Phalanx?'

'Yeah. No one's perfect.'

Tuesday and Wednesday, they found time to discuss the exams with their instructors. Scott Anthony and Madam Moreau both gave them important information, but also spent a lot of time asking them, over and over, how they were feeling.

'Exams can be very stressful,' Scott said, 'particularly if it's for an elite institution.'

'I don't think we've been around long enough to be an elite institution,' Elector responded.

'Fair enough,' Scott said. Sasha thought he was leading up to something, but he moved on.

Thursday after breakfast, they had a visit from Caesar.

'How are you all doing?' he asked.

The Templars were silent, afraid to admit to their general how they were faring. Caesar was not fooled.

'It has been brought to my attention that many of you are showing signs of pressure. While this is inevitable in any setting, it is also important that stress be managed, and you have not had time off from your studies since the January blizzard.'

'What about the Civic Council?' Sasha asked. She thought that might have counted as a week off, as it did not involve studies or classes.

'You were still operating as Templars and learning from the experiences. What I am talking about is a short period of time where you are under no obligations. Does anyone know what day it is?' he asked.

'March nineteenth,' Rose said.

'That is the date. I am asking what is special about today.'

The Templars looked about in confusion. Then Sasha chuckled.

'It's the spring equinox,' she said.

'Exactly. Can you explain to the other Templars the importance of this evening?'

'It's used as a celebration by farming communities,' Sasha said quickly. 'They usually have a festival, a way of celebrating the end of winter and the beginning of spring.'

'Usually?' Rose asked.

Sasha shrugged. 'Some celebrations are more raucous than others. My family prayed a lot. The other side of the town ate everything they could.'

'In any event,' Caesar said, 'Olympia will be hosting a festival, and many people are making their way there for it. The Templars will be attending.'

'In what capacity?' Elector asked.

'As guests,' Caesar said. 'Sergeant Major Del Oso will be providing you with mounts and directions. You will be entirely on your own; though there will be military personnel there, not all of them will be on duty. You may fraternize and act as you see fit. "Eat, drink and be merry," for next week you have exams.'

Sasha chuckled, as did the other Templars who understood the joke. Sasha was happy that Caesar felt comfortable enough with them to make one.

He's grown along with us, Sasha thought. He's more comfortable as a general now.

Del Oso found them a short time later. He gave instructions to Cadet Captain Patch and spoke to them all.

'You all deserve a week off,' he said. 'We can only manage one night. You'll have the chance to eat, to drink, to dance, even to pray, if you so choose. Get out there, shake off some of your stress, and come back ready to test.'

'What will you be doing?' Sasha asked.

'With my Templars gone? I'll sleep in until five or so, then take a mild ten-mile run without any children slowing me down.'

'And then eat a few rocks for breakfast,' Roland continued.

They laughed, Del Oso the loudest of them all.

'In all seriousness,' he said, 'this is your last chance for some true rest for some time. Stay out of the libraries. Celebrate, relax. Take advantage of the opportunity.'

'We will,' Hero grinned. Sasha could easily guess what he wanted to do.

Del Oso led them to the Athens stable, where they were given six horses. Candle rode with Sasha, and Mako with Roland. Del Oso waved them off, and they set out to Olympia.

'Excited?' Candle asked Sasha.

'I guess,' Sasha replied. 'I'm not sure I'll find this as relaxing as other people will.'

'Sure,' Candle nodded. 'But, try? No one will think less of you if it's not your type of party.'

'I'll try,' Sasha confirmed. 'I actually am excited, you know.'

'Are you?'

'The only festival where I wasn't praying, I was working a stand. The only part of it I got to enjoy was the fireworks, and that was followed quickly by . . .,' Sasha paused. She was not sure how to put it into words.

'What is it?' Candle asked.

'A memory I'm not fond of,' Sasha said, 'and yet, it occurs to me that if the event had gone differently, I wouldn't be where I am. It was in Duluth; I was enjoying the fireworks with a man who was to become my husband, and we were attacked by a drunk. I defended us, successfully, but in doing so broke our betrothal. Alvanism dictates against violence, even in self-defense. It is a horrible memory, but if it had gone better, I would be in Duluth, married, probably with a child.'

'Feelings are so odd, aren't they?' Candle asked. 'If my husband hadn't died, I'd be at home taking care of our child, with no thought of being a Templar. I both love being here and hate the path my life took to bring me here.'

'Does that make us strange, to have such conflicting emotions about our pasts?'

Candle chuckled. 'I think everyone has those conflicts, but I think most people don't recognize them, or they trivialize them, or ignore them. I think acknowledging them makes us strong.'

'Templar strong,' Sasha said.

Candle laughed. 'Yes, Templar strong.'

***

Olympia looked ready for the festival. The snow was almost all gone, and though the wind was cold it was well above freezing. Colorful flags flitted in the breeze, and dozens of tables and benches stood about the town. The inhabitants and the staff were washing the walls and hanging vibrant decorations.

'Is this normal?' Rose asked as the Templars rode into town.

'Only half of my hometown celebrated, but they never got this elaborate.'

'It's like something you'd see in a city,' Mako added.

'Yes,' Sasha agreed, thinking of the festival she went to during her short stay in Duluth several years earlier. 'Something like that.'

Patch followed the directions Del Oso gave them and found the wooded area north of town. Instead of RAM cabins, someone had built several rows of wooden stands, each one now holding a single tent.

'Hello, Mister DeWitt!' Candle called as they approached. He scowled at them and began his prepared speech.

'I'm Mister DeWitt, and if you've come for tents, you're not getting them like that, what? Horses go in that field over there! Then come back to me and I'll get you settled, what?'

The Templars moved over to the field. Ropes strung from tree to tree turned the field into a large pasture for the horses to graze. Dozens were already milling about. They registered their horses, stored their saddles and gear in a tent, and walked back to DeWitt.

'Finally. Names?'

'Templars Candle, Scholar, Mako –.'

'Temples, ah, yes. Some sort of junior officer's club, what? Come with me, and I'll get you settled, what?'

DeWitt hobbled through the rows of tents, the Templars following them. He never checked a page or book or anything but led them right to their spot.

318

'Here!' he exclaimed. 'Eight tents for eight Temples, what?' He walked to each tent, exclaiming a name and pointing at it. Sasha's was third, between Elector and Candle.

'Tents got stuff inside, too, for y'all. We were told to put it in there when we put the tents up, what?'

'Yes, sir,' Roland replied. DeWitt coughed then hobbled away.

The tents were big enough for one person and not much else. Sasha glanced inside hers. A couple of thick blankets, a pillow, and a wrapped package.

'What's this?' Rose asked nearby. 'Clothes?'

Sasha looked up as Rose unrolled her bundle, the Templars gathering around. It appeared to be a set of simple civilian clothes: a thick shirt, pants, socks and heavy slippers, and undergarments.

'Huh,' Candle said.

'I get it,' Elector said. 'This is our night to celebrate, not as soldiers or Templars, but as men and women. They don't want our uniforms to distract us; they want us to celebrate amongst the people.'

The Templars all realized he was right. The clothes had no rank or other insignia. Civilians might know them as being military but would not know in what capacity.

'Okay,' Rose said. She started unbuttoning her shirt.

'Rose!' Candle said.

'What, I'm not going to be able to change in that tiny tent, so why bother trying.' She was down to her undergarments when she looked up. 'Boys, turn around.'

They all changed like that. Sasha pondered for a moment if this was a sign of growth: that the Templars were comfortable enough with each other not to be diving into tiny tents to avoid a little immodesty. She was certainly more comfortable undressing in front of the boys, though she did have them turn around for the last bit as well.

The civilian clothes fit well but were not uniform in color. Some were khaki, some brown, some shade of green or another. Pants and shirts had been mixed, so no one was wearing one color, but the cut and style of the clothes were uniform.

'I feel more comfortable,' Rose said. Sasha agreed, they were comfortable clothes.

'We should find food,' Elector said. 'Do they have food at festivals?'

'Of course,' Sasha said. 'Part of the reason for the festival is to celebrate food. Winters usually require rationing, so it's a chance to eat as much as you can, especially as much of it is about to go bad.'

'Ah, gluttony, my favorite sin,' Roland said.

'I prefer lust,' Hero said.

'Good luck with that,' Rose said, but Candle piped up.

'Oh, Hero, we could probably find some willing participants tonight. Hunt together?'

'Sure,' Hero blinked in surprise, along with the rest of the Templars. They all looked at Candle.

'What?' she asked. 'It's been a while, and if I can find someone willing, why shouldn't I?'

'Just be careful,' Rose said.

'I always am,' Candle said. 'And if anyone else wants to, there's no reason to be shy about it. Even a one-night love is still a wonderful thing.'

'Anyway,' Elector interrupted, 'Food?'

'Sure,' Sasha continued the conversation away from Candle and Hero.

The Templars made their way down into the town itself. A lunch was being handed out in the main square; a bowl of soup, with some bread and cheese. It was a simple meal, but one that left the Templars wondering about seconds.

The square filled with civilians, with military personnel dressed much like the Templars, and with vendors. The crowd grew, the noise growing in accordance.

'Roland,' Candle said, grabbing at Roland's shoulder and gesturing over to the side. Sasha saw the two wagons of the Hamline Family Theater rolling through the town.

Roland grinned in delight.

Chapter 35

The festival was indeed made up of people from numerous villages, and the whole town was involved. The main square was going to be for food and music. A second square, formed by the ram cabins of the Renaissance Army on one side and the town on the other, was for dancing. The Hamline family set up on the opposite side of the town. Signs were hung over door frames; a quiet house, a house for children, a house for naps. The church was the house of prayer, while the mayor's house would be the aid station.

Several volunteers arrived to provide safety and security measures, followed quickly by a group of riders protected by civil and Olympian guards. Sasha saw several of the councilors, followed by General Caesar and his entourage. Brigadier Lily stopped by to say hello. General Prince, it seemed, was off somewhere, and would not be here for the event.

Music began to play, and the crowds grew. If there was an official start to the festival, Sasha missed it, but the crowd seemed to know.

'I'm going to the theater,' Roland finally said. 'Anyone want to come with me?'

'Sure,' Patch said. The pair wandered off.

Then Candle stood. 'Come on, Hero. Let's see what the dance looks like.' Hero followed her into the crowd.

'Are you going with them?' Mako asked.

Sasha laughed. 'No. I'm not ready for that. Maybe I never will be.'

'Maybe not,' Mako said. 'I'm going to spend some time in the church. I'll find you later, if you want.'

'Sure,' Sasha said. Then Mako was gone. She looked at Elector and Rose. 'Want to just wander about for a bit?'

'How long do these normally go?' Rose asked as the three of them stood.

'The one in my home would last until after midnight, but I wasn't allowed to stay up for that,' Sasha said. 'I've heard the one in Walker Town could last into the next morning, but I never got to participate in that one either. The one in Duluth lasted quite a while, until dawn, if I'm not mistaken.'

'So,' Elector said. 'Can I ask about your hometown? Was it liberated?'

'No, my town was burned, and its folk sent to Walker's dungeons.'

'Oh,' Elector said. 'I'm sorry to hear that.'

'Me too, but until I can do something about it, I have to keep it at arm's length. There's only so much I can worry about at any one time.'

The three walked through the town. A voice was sounding from the south of town, and Sasha recognized Aquillon Madrillon, the musical orator she heard at the council meeting. Aquillon stood on a platform, surrounded by a crowd. Some looked at her with amusement, others with disdain, but others listened to her words with a serious intent.

> *'It is a sad thing indeed for a man to say*
> *"I'll only vote if I get I my way."*
> *The ballot box is not for one.*
> *It is for all, or all are done.*
>
> *Thus, when Election Day draws near,*
> *You must go out, you show no fear,*
> *This your God-given right;*
> *This is your political might.'*

Rose shrugged. 'I think Roland is right,' she said. 'Aquillon sings truths so people will remember them with the tune.'

They spent some time in the library, looking through the small but expanding selection. Sasha considered spending the night reading through the books to her heart's content, but she felt she should listen to Del Oso. He was right. They needed a break from their routine.

The three made their way towards the dance. People were dancing in groups, circles closing in and spreading apart, dissolving and reforming, as instructed to by one of the musicians.

'Is this normal farmer's dancing?' Rose asked.

Sasha shrugged. 'I don't know, I've never seen a dance this big, but it looks similar to what I've done before.'

The dance came to an end, and the singer called out for the groups to go find more people to bring in. Candle appeared out of the crowd in front of them.

'Come on, Templars.'

'What?' Sasha was surprised by the sudden exuberance in Candle's face.

'No, we can't!' Rose protested.

'Nonsense, you two! Dancing is knowledge, knowledge is power, so dancing is power. Now come on!'

The music began again, and Sasha was thrown into a group. She started next to Candle, and as the dance progressed, she ended up with strangers, which appeared to be the point. The singer's instructions were simple enough – once Sasha got over her initial embarrassment – and the partners, military and civilian alike, all offered encouragement. Sasha completed the last sequence without stepping on anyone's toes.

The song ended and Sasha slipped away before the next. She enjoyed herself, but she was not ready for another round just yet. She drifted over towards the Hamline family. Their stage set up, costumes on, they were already deep into a performance. Sasha saw Roland sitting in the front row. Patch was not with him.

Bill was on stage again, wearing the brown robes this time. His daughter was a princess again, her hands bound before her. His wife wore the same grey uniform she had on before, but instead of a monocle she had a large staff, making her look like some sort of witch. The uncle stood, wearing silver clothes with black armor and a slender sword. Sasha did not catch the dialogue, but three of them left, leaving the uncle standing alone.

After a moment, the son jumped on stage, wearing black clothes with silver armor, a sword at his hip. He skidded to a stop before his uncle, grasping for his sword. He was breathing harshly, as if he had been running.

'No, no,' his uncle said in a strong Quebecois accent. 'Take a breath. I give you my word, I shall not begin a fight until you are ready.'

'Grateful,' the son said. He stretched, always keeping his eyes to his uncle.

'I do not wish to be forward,' his uncle began, 'but you are a pirate.'

'I am,' the youngster confirmed.

'The silver pirate?

'The dread pirate.'

'Not silver? Do you have the black mark?'

The boy shook his head and raised his blank hand.

'What do you have?'

'The black mustache,' he twisted his around, comically. Some of the audience laughed.

'Oh, I do not mean to pry.' He pulled his sword and tossed it to his nephew, momentarily unarmed. 'This sword was the masterwork of my father, commissioned by the silver pirate. When it was done, the pirate tried to steal it, and they dueled. My father took his death blow, but not before he relieved the silver pirate of his leg. Since then, the silver pirate has had the black mark upon his hand, as sin for his betrayal.'

The son looked confused. 'You see I have two legs. Why ask to see the mark?'

'It is his feature.'

'But you said your father cut off his leg.'

'Aye, clean off.'

'Then why ask to see my hand, if you can see I have two legs?' the son asked, bewildered. Some in the audience chuckled.

'You talk in circles,' the uncle chuckled. 'Are you right in the head? The silver pirate is known by the black mark, and by the black mark is he known. What use is the counting of legs?' He held out his hand, and his nephew threw him his sword.

'It is a marvelous weapon.'

'It is. Are you rested?'

'I am. It is a shame, I think, to fight.'

'I agree. You seem like a decent pirate. I hate to kill you.'

'I am a decent pirate, and I hate to die.'

They started dueling, the fantastic dueling of the stage. It looked odder than usual, before Sasha realized they were holding their swords in their left hands. They bantered back and forth, making the crowd laugh. First the uncle switched his fighting hand, announcing he had tricked his nephew, then the nephew announced he had tricked the uncle. Sasha found it amusing but wanted to move on. She waited for the nephew to win the fight, leaving his uncle unconscious as he ran off the stage, before she continued.

The crowd around Olympia enjoyed themselves, and Sasha smiled. After so long in the Templars, with the books and exercises and pressure, it was nice to have a night off from the classes.

Aquillon was still on her box, singing another song. It was the song about rights that Sasha had heard during the Civic Council. Sasha listened, catching the verses she missed before.

> *"Number seven plainly states a man may be tried by his peers,*
> *For only those who live alike may share some common fears*
> *So, when a lord demands you submit to judgement from his throne*
> *He wants you kneeling silently, believing you are alone."*

324

'It's fascinating,' a voice said next to her. She turned to see a familiar young man standing next to her. 'When she first showed up, we thought she was just one of those odd people, but she's had an impact on the people. They have debates and conversations over what her songs mean. For example, do you know what she's singing about right now?'

'She's singing the Bill of Rights,' Sasha said.

He looked at her sharply. 'You know about them?'

'I do, Mister Holden.'

Zac blinked in surprise. 'You have me at a disadvantage.'

'Templar Scholar,' she reached out her hand to shake his.

'Oh, a Templar,' Zac said. 'Right. You were at the council meeting.'

'Yes. I saw you debate with Officer Penn.'

'Not a lot of sympathy in that audience,' Zac said. 'I'm surprised one of the Templars agreed with me.'

'Then you'd be very surprised to learn half of them agreed with you, Mister Holden.'

'Please, call me Zac, and yes, I am surprised. The Templars are a part of the Renaissance Army, are they not?'

'We are, but we're also the future of the movement. It would not be a true renaissance if we all shared the same views.'

'True,' Zac said with a smile.

Sasha smiled back. She did not want to disrupt the crowd watching the singer, so she gestured for Zac to follow her. 'The March council meeting was last week. I haven't heard any news on it. Can you tell me?'

'Sure,' Zac said. 'A lot of the usual stuff. The Alvanists prayer, for example.'

'What about the guy who wanted all the women to return home? Did he show up again?'

'Not this time. Not sure what happened to him, but he didn't come. There was a lot of annoyance at how long it was taking to get wagons and sleighs up and running after a blizzard.'

Sasha chuckled at that. 'What about your independent law and order resolution?'

'Failed again,' Zac confirmed, 'but got three more votes this time. Another session or two and it might pass.'

'Tell me, Zac, what do you do when you're not arguing in front of the Civil Council?'

'I do a lot of things,' Zac replied. 'I'm helping set up the civilian newspaper, for one. It'll be larger than the army's broadsheets, more civil minded, which I think will be good for the people. I also spend a lot of time coordinating movements of people and supplies.'

'Like a quartermaster?' Sasha asked.

'Kind of. There are a lot of people to move about the Liberated Counties, and I help find where they need to go. Like, if a village needs another dozen or so farmhands, I can help find them and move them over.'

'So, you're building a government from the bottom up?' Sasha asked.

'Sort of,' Zac blushed. 'I'm not trying to pull something over the generals' eyes, but there are things that need to get done and I'm not the type to sit around and not do them. And if someone lets the generals know what I'm doing, I'll gladly stand before them and tell them why.'

'Trust me, Zac. The generals know what you're doing and why.'

'How can they?' he asked.

'Because they're the generals,' Sasha replied with a grin.

They approached the dancing field, having circled the town. A slower song was beginning, and couples began forming while portions of the crowd stepped off to the side. Zac looked at her with a blush on his cheeks. 'Would you like to dance?'

Sasha started. 'I don't know how to dance to this,' she protested.

'Neither do I,' Zac admitted. 'But it could be fun.'

Sasha blushed. *But why not*? She asked herself. *Try something new.*

She took his hand, suddenly aware that her palms were sweaty.

They stepped out onto the field. 'What do we do?' she whispered.

'Whatever they're doing,' Zac suggested. The couples that knew the steps were stepping two steps in one direction and turning. Two steps and turning.

'Two steps and turning,' she said.

'Right.'

They turned to face each other and placed their hands; one pair cupped together, his other hand on her waist, her hand on his shoulder. It was an intimate feeling for Sasha. She was sure her cheeks were deep scarlet by now.

Hours ago, you were partially undressed around the Templars and you were fine; now you have a man's hand in yours and you are embarrassed.

'Ready?' Zac asked. She nodded. They then proceeded to take a forward step and run into each other.

'I think you're supposed to follow my lead,' he said.

'How?'

'I don't know.'

'Okay, tell me what you're doing.'

Zac nodded and started speaking slowly. 'Back, back,' he said, and they took steps. Sasha's first step was too short, her second too long. 'Don't stop, keep going,' he chuckled, and Sasha laughed.

They managed to get into a rhythm where they did not step on each other's toes. By the end of the dance they managed a few turns without looking at their feet. Sasha looked at Zac, or over his shoulder, looking for other Templars, or at other dancers. It was a little awkward.

The song ended and they drifted to the side of the field. 'So, what now?' Zac asked.

'You could find someone else to dance with, if you want,' Sasha replied. 'I'm not ready to try again.'

'Or we could continue on,' Zac said. He looked a little nervous, and Sasha wondered why.

He kind of reminds me of Horace, she thought. *When he would mention marriage.*

'Are you courting me?' she asked suddenly.

Zac turned beet red, and people around them turned and looked at them. 'Uh, not courting. I was just hoping to spend the night with someone.'

'You mean in bed?'

'What? No!' Zac looked panicked. Some of those around him were laughing, others glaring. 'Can we move somewhere more private?' he asked.

They left the crowd for some space. 'I didn't mean like that,' Zac said. 'I just meant that these things can be fun when you're experiencing them with someone. If you're the kind of person who has problems with crowds, having someone to focus on can help.'

'Oh,' Sasha said. She blushed. 'I'm sorry, I didn't mean to embarrass you.

I'm not very good with that.'

'That?'

'Romance,' Sasha shrugged.

'I said I wasn't —. '

'No, but I didn't know that.' Sasha sighed. 'There was little chance for romance in my life before the Renaissance Army. Since I joined, I've seen romantic relationships, but I haven't really tried to experience it myself. I'm not sure I want it, but I'm not sure I don't, either.'

Zac nodded. 'Okay,' he said. 'I can't say I have a lot of experience with that.' He looked nervously at his feet. 'Do you want to get back to the festival?' he asked.

Sasha looked back. 'I think I want to walk about by myself for a bit,' she said.

'Of course,' Zac said, bowing slightly. 'Good night, Templar Scholar.'

Sasha smiled at him as he turned and left. Then she turned and started walking around the festival, lost in thought.

Growing up, the people of Penelope's Haven had always considered a woman growing up alone to be the worst thing that could happen to her. Women were supposed to marry men and raise families. Sure, they could spend time working in a factory, or work as nurses and caretakers and maids if they had the skills, but they were still expected to be part of a family, with a husband and children and all those family duties.

That was not true in the Renaissance Army. Sasha thought of all the women she knew in uniform, women who did not have any romantic relationships.

Is it not true? Sasha asked herself. *Beth loved Rick before his death. Sonja was experienced with men. Candle has a son and had a husband. And just because you haven't seen a ring on a woman's finger doesn't mean she's alone. Lily could have a lover. So could Snow. Only I don't know, because it's not important for me to know.*

She skirted the theater group, seeing the family of travelers on stage, making the crowd laugh. Aquillon was not at her perch anymore, and Sasha wondered where she was. Was she eating? That was an oddly normal thing for the woman to do, but she must eat sometimes.

She wandered at the edge of the dancing field. Candle, she saw, was off to the side, drinking with a young man. Hero was sharing kettled corn with a girl near the band. Mako was there as well, dancing with a young woman. They were having fun, at least.

What do I find fun? Is it something I could share with a man? Do I need a man to have fun? Or am I married to books?

Sasha was approaching the forest, lost in thought, and did not notice the figure before her until she was within arm's reach.

'Lost?' the voice asked.

Sasha started. 'Who's there?' She was just far enough from the festival lights she could see the figure, but not identify it.

'It's Officer Saxon. Is that Templar Scholar I hear?'

'It is, ma'am.'

'Shouldn't you be dancing with some young politician?'

'What?' Sasha stuttered. 'You saw that?'

'I went around the perimeter, saw a few things. You two seemed to get along well enough. Did he say something stupid?'

'No, I did. He wasn't courting, I just didn't recognize he wasn't.'

'Ah,' Saxon said in understanding. 'Was it embarrassing?'

'I asked him if he wanted to bed me in the middle of a crowd.'

Saxon laughed. 'Well, at least you got your message across. And now you walk the darkness?'

'Lost in thought,' Sasha admitted. 'Pondering the questions of a Templar.'

'Ah, how appropriate for walking through the darkness,' Saxon chuckled.

'What are you doing out here?' Sasha asked.

'Security,' Saxon said.

'For the festival?'

Saxon did not reply for a moment. 'Come with me.'

Saxon walked into the forest, Sasha in tow. She was heading towards a dim light, a campfire, built out of sight from the town. They passed one Olympian on their way in. Sasha was very curious now.

'Be quiet,' Saxon whispered. She moved around the fire, with Sasha following close behind.

It was a campfire, with a ready supply of firewood and a single tent. Sitting close by was Lily. She was not wearing her uniform, instead wearing what looked to Sasha to be flannel night clothes. Her long hair was unbraided.

What is she doing here? Sasha wondered.

The tent flap opened, and Caesar crawled out. He was wearing a similar set of clothes, and Sasha was suddenly struck by the intimacy of the setting. The two were alone in the forest, no longer in uniform. Protected from intrusion, free to be themselves. Not general and adjutant, not Caesar and Lily, but whomever they were before the Renaissance Army.

Caesar sat down next to Lily; their hands intertwined. Lily laid her head on Caesar's shoulder, whispering something to him as they stared into the fire. Both chuckled, a sound that Sasha found odd considering how reserved they were most of the time. Caesar put his arm around Lily's shoulder and kissed her forehead.

Saxon tugged on Sasha's sleeve. Sasha followed her away from the fire and back out of the forest.

'I didn't know,' Sasha said.

'No reason you should have,' Saxon said. 'They don't make a point of telling everyone.'

'Why did you show me that?' Sasha asked. She felt guilty, seeing two of her mentors relaxed, as if she had seen them naked.

'You're an Alvanist,' Saxon said, and Sasha stopped suddenly. 'Yes, I know your background. I imagine like most farm girls, you were expected to marry, and your parents had someone in mind?'

'A few possibilities,' Sasha admitted.

'So, it wasn't about romance, but about culture,' Saxon said. 'I can't tell you too much about their backgrounds, you understand, but I want to tell you one thing in the strictest of confidence. Lily spent several years working in brothels. You know what those are?'

'I do,' Sasha scowled. 'Their agents came through my hometown once, looking to buy girls.'

'Fuckers,' Saxon said. 'Anyway, she was indentured to them for some time, never given a choice about who to be with. When she escaped, she ran into Caesar. Caesar was the first man to treat her properly, and the two developed a relationship, but it didn't come quickly. It took years to develop.'

'Okay,' Sasha said. She was not sure why Saxon was telling her this and wondered what part Snow had in Lily's story. The two had to have come to the Renaissance Army together, right? It was too strange to think they might have come to it separately.

'The point, Templar, is that she was a bit like you are. Suddenly having the freedom of choice, it took her a while to find what she wanted. So, take the time you have, and figure it out for yourself. Maybe it'll be with a politician, maybe it won't. Don't rush it, you know?'

Sasha nodded in the darkness. 'Right,' she said.

'Good. Now, go on.'

Sasha walked back to the town. The crowds were noticeably smaller. Either people were beginning to head to their beds, or maybe the colder night air was chasing more people inside. Sasha thought about going inside, but she was tired, and she figured that getting a good night's sleep was as good a way to be on vacation as anything.

When she got back, she saw feet sticking out of Elector's tent, and heard Patch gently snoring in hers. The rest must still be out, and Sasha hoped they were all enjoying their time.

She crawled inside her tent and slept.

Chapter 36

Sasha was up early; she was so used to it she did not need Del Oso to wake her up. She stretched and crawled out of her tent.

The sky was the light blue of pre-dawn, good enough to walk about. The noises of sleeping folk sounded through the forest alongside morning insects. It was a strangely peaceful setting.

Sasha walked about, noticing that Candle and Hero's tents were still vacant. Sasha was making for the fields around town, when she spotted someone coming up the path. She recognized the woman first.

'Candle?' she asked.

Candle stopped and looked up. 'Oh, Scholar. Early to rise or late to bed?'

'Early to rise. Yourself?'

'Late to bed,' Candle giggled. 'Sorry, I just had a good night.'

'With the young man you were dancing with last night?'

'Him? No, he was a bit immature for my taste. It was with one of the lieutenants from the militia company. The redhead.'

'The woman?'

'Yes. And don't you go off on some high horse, Scholar!' Candle's voice turned serious. 'You can make the choice of whom, if anyone, to take to your bed, but you get no say about mine.'

'I know,' Sasha said quickly. 'I'm sorry. I don't mean to be judgmental.'

'And yet, you are. You spent your whole life being judged by your family and town for being different, you do the same to others. Let go, Scholar. If you're going to be a leader of the future, be more open minded!'

'I'm trying, Candle, I swear I am. But I'm fighting fifteen years of Alvanist teachings. Until I joined the Renaissance Army, the only time sex ever came up was either as the duty of a wife or a threat by the bully who wanted to take me,' Sasha said. 'It was bought in brothels or demanded by the yeomen. It was never something fun, to be enjoyed. Even my father taught me it was a duty, something to be endured for children.'

'What did your mother teach you about it?' Candle asked.

'Not much different. That it could be pleasant, if the couple were in love, but
332

otherwise just a necessary act.'

Candle shook her head and chuckled. 'Well, that's stupid. Sex is a wonderful, beautiful act, when everyone involved is ready for it, but it's not for everyone. Maybe you're just not interested in it. Not everyone is.'

'A friend of mine from Third Regiment said something similar, once. She told me I inherited my religions prudishness, even if I rejected its pacifism.'

'Sounds smart. What else did she say?'

'That I can't be anyone else but myself.'

'Even smarter. But that also means that I can't be anyone else but myself, even if that makes you uncomfortable.' Candle looked over Sasha's shoulder. 'Everyone else back?'

'Hero is still out.'

'Good for him,' Candle said, and Sasha could see the smile even in the limited light. 'I was hoping he might have some luck last night. He's been far too hard on himself lately.'

'It appears he did,' Sasha said. She looked at Candle. 'Candle, I am glad you had a good night.'

Candle smiled, but her eyes turned serious. 'It was my first time since my husband.' Her smile dropped and she looked at her feet. 'Since he died, I mean.'

Sasha blinked. 'But you go on about –.'

'I've always been flirty,' Candle said. 'Even when I was married. Just who I am. I've kissed a few since I came to the Templars, trying to move on, but never felt ready until now. It feels freeing to be ready, you know? I'll always love and miss him, but now I get to be me again.' She smiled again, with tears in her eyes.

Sasha stepped forward and hugged her. They embraced for a few moments before Candle stepped back, wiping the tears from her eyes.

'Well, I'm going to get a few hours' sleep,' Candle said. 'Go walk about. If you're up, you're up.'

Sasha nodded and continued through the maze. She varied her speed, jogging, walking, sprinting across a field, letting her body decide how fast to go. She felt good after a few laps around.

People were moving about as she finished; sentries coming in or going out, and the townsfolk who volunteered to make the breakfast meal. Sasha smelled coffee and made her way in.

'Hungry?' an old woman said as she sighted Sasha. 'Lots of people sleeping in, so you get first crack, eh?'

'Yes, ma'am.'

The old woman poured coffee and arranged a plate for her. 'So, early riser? Or still awake?'

'Early riser,' Sasha said.

'Well, that's good. So many will sleep in today, up late dancing or chatting or whatever,' she winked at Sasha. 'Personally, I would have stayed up for whatever when I was young, but that was quite before your time.'

This topic comes up far too often lately.

'I'm not much for whatever,' Sasha said.

'Well, to each their own, but if I were off to war, I might want to know what it's like.' The woman handed her plate off to Sasha. 'Enjoy.'

Sasha had her pick of tables and sat down to eat. She had forgotten to bring a book, so she watched the town slowly wake up.

People trickled in as the sun rose and dull blue sky became bright. Whispers of conversation grew to a dull hum, then a constant sound. Tables filled up.

The redheaded officer sat across from Sasha.

'Morning, Templar,' she said. She looked nervous, as if Sasha scared her.

'Morning, Lieutenant,' Sasha replied. 'Have a good night?'

The redhead blushed. 'Um, I did. Yourself?'

'Quite enjoyable,' Sasha said. She wondered if she should say something else but could not fathom what.

'Is it true you're trained to take a town?' the other woman asked.

'I've had some training, yes,' Sasha admitted. 'It's going to be needed when I get back to my unit.'

'After you're commissioned?'

'Right. My colonel wanted me to know how to clear towns, since she lacks anyone with that knowledge.'

'Does that mean you know how to defend them?'

'I know a bit,' Sasha said. 'You worried about something?'

The redhead nodded. 'My hometown got burned by the yeomen, and we moved here. More defensible, sure, but I'd still like to prepare some surprises if we're attacked again. Unfortunately, the captain of the town doesn't seem to want to do more than just talk about it.'

Sasha frowned, and they started talking. Roland and Elector appeared shortly after, along with two other officers who heard the conversation. Within an hour, more than a dozen officers – militia and regular and Templar – were sitting about, having discussions about various topics. Only Candle and Hero were missing the conversation, still asleep after the night's celebrations.

Candle appeared shortly after Sasha's third cup of coffee, having had at most two hours of sleep. 'Have any of you seen Hero?' she asked, concerned.

'No,' Sasha said. The others shook their heads. 'Why?'

'He hasn't been to his tent; all his Templar clothes are there. And I ran into the girl he was dancing with. She said she hasn't seen him since about midnight.'

'He didn't go back with her?' Elector asked.

'No, she says he tried but she declined, and he left. She doesn't know where he went after that.'

The Templars detached themselves from the conversation and gathered out of earshot.

'Where else could he have gone?' Elector asked.

'There were plenty of homes open for common sleeping last night, and the church, the meeting hall,' Candle replied. 'Maybe he went back with another girl?'

'Okay,' Sasha said, 'let's try to find him. Mako and Rose, look about the church and the meeting hall. Elector and Patch, you look through the tent park. Roland and I will circle the town.'

'What do I do?' Candle asked.

'Stay here and have breakfast. If Hero wakes up, he'll be hungry. We'll come back to report to you.'

The Templars separated. Roland fell into step with Sasha.

'What do you think?'

'I'm hoping Hero found a willing townswoman and spent the night with her.'

'I hope that too, but that's not what I asked. What do you think?'

Sasha could not answer that question. She had never quite liked Hero, and she could imagine him doing so much stupid stuff, but he was a Templar, and if he did do something stupid, it would reflect poorly on all of them.

They circled the town, ducking into houses and watching the people ambling about. They found the Hamline family, sharing their own early breakfast.

'Roland!' Bill Hamline called out.

'He knows your name?' Sasha asked.

'We spoke last night,' Roland said. 'Fair morning, Master Hamline. How breaks your fast?'

'Bread well baked, coffee heated to perfection. A fine culinary sunrise. How fares you and your lady-friend?'

'We fare poorly, Master Hamline. Have you seen Templar Hero about?'

'What does a Templar Hero look like?' Bill asked.

'Dressed like us, about our age, a little shorter than me, brown hair.'

'I cannot say I have seen a man by that description, but I can keep an eagle eye open. What did he do?'

'Probably something stupid,' Sasha said. They thanked Hamline and continued around. They searched the town before returning to Candle at the town square.

'Anything?' she asked.

'No,' Sasha said. The others returned shortly, also having found nothing.

'Shit,' Elector said.

'We have to tell someone,' Rose said. 'Who's in charge?'

'Caesar and Lily are here,' Sasha said. 'We should tell them.'

***

Saxon was less than thrilled to see the entire Templar class approaching the Olympians.

'I hope you have good reason for coming out like this,' she scowled. She glared particularly hard at Sasha, and Sasha frowned in response.

'Templar Hero is missing,' Sasha reported. 'We need to tell General Caesar and Brigadier Lily.'

Saxon stared at Sasha, the implications of what she said running through her mind. 'Shit,' she said. 'Stay here.' Saxon disappeared into the forest, two Olympians watching over the Templars while they waited. After some time, Saxon returned. 'They're coming.'

Caesar and Lily exited the forest a short time later. Both looked grim, and Sasha swallowed back a pang of regret at disrupting their time together.

'What do you mean, missing?' Lily asked.

'Ma'am,' Sasha began, 'Templar Hero did not return to his tent last night. We searched the tent park, church, town, every place we thought he could have ended up, short of entering every house.'

'Did he go home with someone?' Lily pressed.

'Not that we can tell,' Sasha reported.

Lily looked at Caesar, who was staring at the town, as if he was trying to find Hero through the walls and crowds. Finally, he looked back at the Templars. 'Go back to your tents,' he said, 'change into your fatigues, pack everything. Then report back to me at the mayor's residence.'

The Templars moved back to the tents and changed; all sense of decorum gone in the race to find Hero. They packed everything and returned.

Caesar had assembled some of the militia officers; they were discussing the terrain and how best to find someone.

'We are sending word out and conducting a search,' Caesar said. The Templars were divided up, some to carry messages, some to lead search groups. Sasha found herself a messenger, escorted by two riders. She rode to Athens, to Sparta, to Holiday. She carried a simple letter from Caesar, informing them of the situation and asking them to keep their eyes out.

It took her all day to ride her route and return to Olympia. Several others had returned by that point, and the rest would be back early the next morning. They all reported the same thing.

Hero was gone.

***

The Templars returned to Athens in silence. Whatever joy or peace they had found at the festival was endangered by Hero's disappearance. They returned their mounts, received their instructions for the rest of the weekend, and went back to their barracks.

Roland finally broke the silence standing over Hero's bunk. 'What the hell?'

'I don't know,' Candle said. She looked miserable.

'He didn't say anything to you?' Elector asked.

'No,' Candle said. 'We talked about our worries for the test, what we wanted to focus on before they happened. We talked over how to approach the women, how to dance, how to have a good night, but he never said anything about running.'

'Maybe he just lost his faith,' Mako said.

'Hero was never religious,' Candle replied, but Mako shook his head.

'I don't mean religion; I mean faith in himself. Hero always struck me as a man of opportunity. He had the chance to save that girl, and he took it, and he took the opportunity to come here, but he's struggled this entire time. When he did talk about his past, he was never in one place for long. I think this experience was so different for him, he stopped believing he could do it.'

'I think he was a coward,' Rose said.

'Hey!' Candle snapped. 'He was my friend.'

'Was he? Or was he just trying to bed you?' Rose asked. 'I never had a conversation with him where he didn't make some comment or innuendo, and I imagine the other women here will say the same thing.'

Candle rejoined. 'Yeah, he started out as an annoyance, sure, but he was working on getting better. He was learning. I mean, he took that clerk to bed on New Year's, and she went willingly. He was persistent and trying to get better; how is that cowardice?'

'Because he refused to learn,' Rose shrugged. 'To learn from our interactions is to admit he was wrong, and he couldn't do that. When he made a mistake in class, he would explain it away. He couldn't shoot because his rifle was misadjusted. He couldn't run fast because of a stone in his shoe. If he couldn't bed a woman, it was her fault, not his. Nothing was his responsibility, because responsibility scared him.'

Candle glared at Rose but said nothing.

'How long was he planning it?' Sasha asked. The Templars looked at her. 'Well, look at what he brought with him to Olympia. His boots, nondescript clothing, a compass. He could have taken food from the festival, and he knew how to tie a blanket into a bag. He could have been waiting for a chance for some time.'

Another moment of silence before Roland broke it.

'He's really gone?'

338

'Unless he's got a good excuse for disappearing,' Elector replied.

They all looked up as Del Oso entered the barracks.

'Templars don't make excuses,' Roland said, staring at their sergeant. 'If he returns, it'll mean a court martial.'

'It will,' Del Oso confirmed. 'Still no sign of him.'

'I don't recall him being that great of a woodsman,' Elector said.

'We don't have an unlimited supply of trackers,' Sasha said, 'and he has a full night's start.'

'I wonder where he's going.' Patch said.

'If we're lucky, he's going to disappear into the Dakotas,' Roland said. 'If we're not, he's going to be selling information for gold.'

'That's a disturbing thought,' Sasha said.

'It is,' Del Oso said, 'but it's one you all need to put behind you. You all have a week of tests ahead of you, and you need to be prepared. I don't mean books or body, but psychology. You cannot let a companion take you out of the mindset you need to be in to do well. A friend's death, departure, or even betrayal, cannot be the end of your story here.'

The Templars nodded.

'Sergeant Major,' Candle started. 'Why do you think he ran?'

'What did I just say?' Del Oso asked.

Candle shook her head. 'No, I must know. I trust you, Sergeant Major. Did we fail him?'

Del Oso looked at the earnest expression on her face. 'No,' he finally said. 'You did not fail him. No one failed him but him.'

Del Oso took a seat on what had been Hero's bed. 'The Michigan Marine Corps requires every officer to come from their enlisted ranks for this reason. After three years, a marine has been given enough responsibility that the corps has a sense for how he handles it. Think, for a moment, how many of the Templars had prior service with the Renaissance Army. Only four of you did not: Rose, Cardinal, Candle, and Hero.'

'I thought Hero fought with Wild's regiment?' Sasha asked.

Del Oso shook his head. 'I think Wild might have stretched Hero's responsibilities a bit. I'm confirming that through my own means.

'In any event, of the four who did not, Hero was the only one we were worried about. Candle had proven herself capable before she joined, in fact it's why she was invited. Rose and Cardinal come from a family where responsibility was considered a birthright, and we had every expectation they would continue to do so. Only Hero lacked any reason to believe that he could handle it.'

'Then how did he get in?' Roland asked. 'If we all proved ourselves, how did he slip in?'

'He did save that girl,' Candle pointed out. 'And he rushed in to get Sasha out of the magazine explosion and was ready to fight Senator if he had to.'

'Hero can be very good at talking when he wants to be,' Mako said. 'Charming, even.'

'That is true,' Del Oso said. 'Enough that he convinced Colonel Wild to endorse him. The generals both had their doubts, but ultimately they wanted an even dozen and took a chance.'

'A chance that failed,' Elector said.

Del Oso stood. 'Templars, I'm not going to lie to you. Each of you will face some self-doubt about what happened with Hero, but don't let that get to you. As of right now, it doesn't matter why he left. He left. Stop asking yourself why, stop asking yourself how you could have changed it. What happens to him now is the concern of the court martial that would be convened. You must put it behind you and move on. You did so after the magazine explosion, and you did so after Cardinal quit. Before this war is over, you may have to get over more Templar deaths.'

The thought chilled Sasha. She tried to imagine standing at a grave, with Patch or Elector carved into a wooden cross. She imagined her name on the cross.

'Stay focused on the exams,' Del Oso counselled. 'This is why you are here. Every class and test, every victory and loss, was all for this.'

The Templars nodded in silence. Finally, Elector stood. 'I'm going to the library,' he said. 'If I can't figure out why Hero did it, I'll not figure it out while studying for next week.'

'Me too,' Sasha said, standing. The rest of the Templars followed suit.

Behind them Del Oso watched them leave, then set about removing Hero's things.

Chapter 37

Hero's absence was a topic of conversation for the weekend. The cadets debated whether he was worried he was too weak or too stupid to succeed at the test. Was he worthy to become a Templar or should he never have been chosen? Did he always plan on leaving? Where was he going?

Sasha argued that his name was too much. 'I've had to worry about losing Scholar,' she said. 'Perhaps being called Hero brought too many expectations?' The other cadets debated that for a while, ultimately concluding that none of them knew for sure.

It was good they spent the time talking Hero out of their immediate attention, for the next five days they had their examinations.

Monday morning started with their physical tests – running, strength exercises, obstacle courses. Everything Del Oso had been preparing them for showed up on this test. Even a swimming portion, in uniform. Sasha regretted not working out more during the winter, but she endured. It was tiring but in the end everyone passed.

Monday afternoon had them in a classroom, answering several ethics questions. Much like the weekly questions they had been subjected to, each question put them in a difficult situation with no good answers. Unlike their weekly questions, they were not presented with two options; they had to write and explain their answers by hand.

'Only four more days!' Candle tried to motivate the Templars that evening. Most of them cheered weakly.

Tuesday was all classroom. Prince's test on their political education was a series of essay questions on rights and governments, ending with a long-form response in which each Templar had to explain their ideal government. Sasha was surprised at that, and after several false starts decided on a federated republic, with each region responsible for their own local needs, but unified together for their mutual benefit.

That afternoon the tests were individualized, and the first tests that week Sasha actually enjoyed. Except for Elector, the cadets assembled in a room, each one given their own packet. The first page told her she was advising Lieutenant Colonel Snow of Third Field Regiment and gave her a list of the squads and equipment that made up the regiment. Then came three situations she had to write plans for, including maps and timetables.

The first was an operation to cut the supply lines to a firebase. The second was an operation to disrupt and curtail enemy patrols across the region. And finally, a plan to defend a town from a possible enemy attack.

Sasha answered the best she could, keeping the plans simple and trusting the officers on the spot to understand the ultimate objectives. She only had an hour, but she felt confident of the one-page plans she wrote out.

After a short break, the six Templars came back and took their seats. Now, instead of her own packet, she received Patch's. They now had an hour to review, critique and question the plans in front of them.

Patch had been given different scenarios; breaking through a trench line, cutting off river traffic, and an operation to deceive the enemy about their true strength. Sasha read through Patch's responses and smiled to herself. Where Sasha would have recommended constant, low-level harassment, Patch recommended a single overwhelming strike, followed by downtime, then another overwhelming strike.

Taking on the role of another officer, Sasha questioned the tactics and recommended her own, utilizing smaller groups instead of larger. She liked her responses.

The Templars were asked not to speak to each other during the next break, a request that was followed with some difficulty. The reason why became apparent when they sat back down to write a response to their reviewer's critique.

Sasha's had been reviewed by Roland, and again Sasha was struck by how different his methodology was to hers. Roland preferred to create situations where the enemy forces were eliminated, or at least devastated by defeat. Sasha was perfectly fine with getting the other side to stop doing what they were doing. Sasha wrote her responses, in some cases accepting Roland's critique and offering a solution the blended both their styles.

Dinner was active, with the Templars talking over each other discussing their situations. The conversation went on so long the cooks had to came out to chase them off, yelling at the Templars to continue their discussion in their barracks. Sasha had never seen Del Oso look so proud.

Wednesday started with their tactical test; shooting, squad movement, clearing structures. The Templars completed the goals; they were challenging, but nothing the Templars had not gone over a dozen times. Roland started singing another song about the Templars, and by lunch everyone knew it.

Caesar's history test was that afternoon; some important dates and concepts, followed by a few essay questions. Sasha thought Caesar had planned the test to sound like they were having conversations with interested civilians rather than him. Sasha noticed that the questions were simpler than the ones he had been giving her all year, but then again, they had no books from which to draw information. It was all by memory.

Thursday started with tests on the Royal Army and the Commonwealth, describing uniforms, insignia and badges. That afternoon were smaller tests on medical knowledge, logistics and what Prince had titled 'military knowledge,' a test that certainly got the Templars' attention. Some of the questions included 'what do you say to a woman whose son died under your command?' or the page that asked her to write a letter as if she knew she was going to die shortly after it was completed.

The talk that dinner was more subdued.

'We were having too much fun,' Roland said.

'Don't say that,' Candle replied, but Roland continued.

'No, I don't mean it's a punishment. I mean they want us to remember why we are here. This is a serious thing, after all.'

On Friday, they assembled in their classroom, wondering what the last test was going to be. When Lily entered, the Templars all looked up.

'The last day of tests. Excited?'

The Templars all nodded.

'Good. Because this is an all-day test.'

The Templars looked at each other. All day?

'Each of you will receive a topic. You will research and prepare an oral presentation on that topic, to be given this evening. You should plan for a presentation of no less than seven and no more than ten minutes. You will have access to a blackboard, so if you want to draw a map or write anything down, you can.

'With your topic, there will be several suggested events, people, or ideas to research. Feel free to use them, or not to use them, as you see fit. Do not share your topic with others.'

'After dinner this evening, you will all give your presentations. Your audience will be your fellow Templars, your instructors, and other officers who are available to watch. After your presentation, there will be a question-and-answer period. Each of you is expected to ask questions, so be prepared. If I think you're not paying attention, I will call on you.'

With that, she pulled several slips of paper from her pocket, handing them out to each Templar. Sasha received hers and opened it up.

> *Discuss three lessons the Renaissance Army must keep in mind when conducting field, light or guerrilla warfare against the Kingdom of North Mississippi. Use historical examples to make your point.*
>
> *Campaigns to consider:*
>
> *Boer Wars, 1880 – 1902*
>
> *Partisan operations in Yugoslavia during the Second World War, 1941 – 1945*
>
> *Wisconsin Resistance to the Michigan Occupation, 2382 to now.*

'Any questions?' Lily asked.

'Will we get any time to practice our presentations, or are we giving them cold?' Candle asked.

'Good question,' Lily said. 'I'll see about dispersing you an hour before dinner, so you have time to practice on your own. Now, go to the library,' Lily said, 'and good luck.'

The Templars took over the library, each sitting at their table with books spread out before them. Sasha looked over everything.

What do I want the RAM to remember? Sasha looked at her assignment. She knew she could talk about tactics and strategies, but the RAM knew how to do that. She would not be saying anything knew.

So, what bothers me? What do I worry about?

She jotted down a few thoughts. She read them to herself and started organizing them. Thoughts became ideas; ideas became excitement and nervousness.

Not everyone will agree with me.

Lunch was quick and quiet, the Templars too caught up in their thoughts. The afternoon wore on, many of the Templars now whispering their speeches under their breaths.

An hour before dinner, Lily reappeared and dispersed the Templars. What few trainees remaining at Athens could fit in one barrack, leaving many of cabins open for each Templar to practice their speeches. The trainees, and some of their instructors, listened and gave advice. Sasha got some good advice on her speech, and a glare or two from some of her audience. The criticism was worked into her speech; the glares steeled her for similar looks from her friends and teachers.

Dinner came, and the Templars were too nervous to chat much. After dinner, Del Oso brought them to the Templar classroom. The normally spacious classroom was full of extra tables and chairs as the audience was already sitting. The generals and their aides-de-camp were there, as were Carpenter and some of the officers of Athens. Aristotle had made his way from Holiday, and Mobius had come over from the Workshop. Fox was there, grinning. Scott Anthony and Madam Moreau sat at one table, and several officers Sasha did not recognize filled out the rest of the seats.

Lily stood at the front, gesturing for the cadets to take their seats. Their spots were assigned, with a table just behind them for Del Oso and Lily. The Templars sat down.

'Welcome,' Lily said to the assembled men and women. 'And thank you for coming. This is the presentation night of the Templar class. Each Templar will have one minute of preparation time on the blackboard, seven minutes of presentation, with a question-and-answer period afterwards of three to seven minutes. We anticipate this whole process will take at most two hours, with a ten-minute break between the fourth and fifth presenters. During the presentation, we ask that you pay attention and keep your questions for the end. Do not interrupt. Any questions for me?'

No one said anything.

'Good. The Templars will be giving their presentations in alphabetical order. Templar Candle, you are first.'

Sasha watched her classmates give their speeches. They were all better speakers than their first week, less prone to fidgeting, louder voices and less mumbling. They were also all much more confident in their interests.

Candle spoke on sieges, but instead of tactics or planning, she stressed the importance of building infrastructure to support the troops conducting sieges, which provoke an intense discussion with Mobius about the Workshop sending their projects to sieges. Elector followed with a speech on health and hygiene, important but a little dull.

Mako discussed the use of boats on lakes and rivers for tactical and logistical purposes. This prompted a round of back-and-forth between Mobius and Patch about how to build smaller boats for easy transport across land that went so long Lily had to cut them off.

Templar Scholar

Patch went forth, discussing small tricks from the Workshop that could help a unit function, things like battery powered lights and crossbow grenade launchers. That piqued Sasha's interest; she asked about mobility, using the technology without getting bogged down by equipment. Patch was enthusiastic, sure that it could be done.

Lily extended their break to fifteen minutes. The Templars drank some water, most still lost in their own thoughts. Then the final three were up.

Sasha was disappointed in Roland's speech; he discussed the concept of risk in fighting battles but spent too much time listing examples, rather than delving into his theory. Aristotle tried to draw some more thoughts out of him, but Roland did not seem to rise to the challenge.

Rose spoke on alliances and the importance of acknowledging the value of every member. She gave a nice speech, Sasha thought. Certainly, better than the speech Sasha was about to give.

It was Sasha's turn. She stood and walked to the podium. She remembered her first speech, and how nervous she had been. Now, it had turned from fear into a healthy caution. Like entering battle, she knew more of what to expect, and while she was uncomfortable, she used that as an expression of how important this moment was. She set her notes down and looked at her audience.

'Ladies and gentlemen, my name is Templar Scholar, and I was asked to give a presentation on lessons the Renaissance Army should remember when conducting its light warfare against the Kingdom of North Mississippi.

'The Renaissance Army has campaigned against the king for more than a year, using field regiments to liberate counties from the yeomen and challenge the government of the king. I cannot talk about tactics and strategies, because the RAM has proven it knows how to wage this sort of campaign. Instead, I shall talk about an important aspect that I've found is often overlooked. I will talk about civilians, and their need for protection. Protection for our enemies, protection from themselves, and protection from us.'

Sasha was watching the crowd when she said that. No one glared at her, but there were more than a few questioning faces.

'First, from our enemies. Field warfare is highly dependent on civilians as a source of supplies and recruits. The enemy knows this. I could bring up any number of examples from history of civilians being punished for the actions of light units in their area, or I could simply point to last year. Count Walker destroyed a dozen towns and villages, executing civilians and forcing the survivors into the walls of Walker. Count Brainerd started by arresting the leaders and their families, before Third Field Regiment put a stop to it.

'The RAM has done much towards the protection of townspeople; concentrating civilians in the more defensible towns, raising and arming a militia, keeping the enemy unclear on our true strength. These are all sensible precautions against the yeomen. But I hope that there is some plan in place for when the Royal Army takes the field. They will, I think, not be so easily dissuaded.

'Second, protecting people from themselves.

'The RAM has a policy of letting prisoners go. This is not just to solve problems of feeding all those prisoners, but also keeps them out of the hands of the civilians they had power over for so long. I am from one of the towns that Giulio Montessori burned, and if he fell into my hands, I might be tempted to vengeance. And I doubt I'm the only one, which is why we need to be wary of it. Vengeance harms communities, reducing conflict to violence without rule of law or process.

'Going from under the boot to over can be exhilarating and dangerous. While the RAM has avoided letting such passions go, other organizations have not. For example, during the Commonwealth War, several resistance groups in Wisconsin managed to defeat the occupying forces from Michigan, while that nation was focused on fighting the Quebecois. The stories of what they did to captured civil-servants and compliant civilians is enough to give you nightmares, only rivaled by what the Commonwealth did to them when they swept through the region after Michigan's capitulation.

'The point, ultimately, is that any liberated population is going to stretch their muscles, so to speak, after spending so long under an occupation force. Their desires for justice must not extend into revenge. That is on us to keep those passions from exploding.'

Sasha took a deep breath before continuing.

'Third, we must protect the people from ourselves.

'The Renaissance Army revealed itself sixteen months ago; in that time, we have liberated thousands of people in at least four different counties. That is impressive, even if we acknowledge that most fights have been against county yeomen, and not royal soldiers.

'Yet, how often have we heard concern? Last November, we were paraded before a group of ambassadors. "What is the end goal?" one asked. "What do you bring other than war?" A few months ago, we watched our former classmate debate a man who ultimately wants a codified constitution. "We trust General Prince; it's the next general we're worried about," he said. These are not the words of men who want us to lose to the Royal Army; these are the positions of men who worry about us losing ourselves.

347

Templar Scholar

'The Renaissance Army commands the Liberated Counties. We control the flow of supplies and people. We arm the militia; we patrol the roads. So far, we've avoided any major conflict with the civilians of the Liberated Counties, but what happens when it occurs? How often has idealism lost itself to the pressures of command? We declare the Renaissance is for everyone, but what happens if there's a weak harvest and not enough food to feed the army and the people?'

'The Renaissance is a fragile thing. Many people are still coming to terms with its goals. They expect us to act on the necessities of war, to prove ourselves to be no other than the next resistance group clawing for power, with sweet words but selfish action. They don't want us to be. Mister Shaw does not want us to fail, he wants us to succeed, but he knows how difficult it can be. Mister Holden is not a prophet of doom, but someone who survived the fall of Michigan, when they forgot their purpose as the People's Republic and started acting the tyrant. He comes with warnings we must pay attention to.'

Sasha realized she was excited, passionate even, about her speech. Her nerves were long gone, replaced with a confidence she did not realize she had. She paused, looking at the audience. No one looked bored, all stared at her, listening to her every word.

'There will be hardship in the future,' Sasha said. 'Hardships that will strain the Renaissance Army and the Liberated Counties. When that happens, the Renaissance Army must sacrifice what it can to prove to the people, both here and beyond our borders, that we are a true rebirth.'

Sasha looked at her last paragraph, the words suddenly boring and formulaic.

'That, ladies in gentlemen, is the purpose of the Renaissance Army,' she said, ignoring what she had written. 'We protect the Renaissance. Not the generals who named their army thus, but the people. We protect them from our enemies by winning battles. We protect them from their worst instincts by removing the temptation. And we protect them from ourselves by remembering that they are what's important – serving the people is why we are all here.

'Thank you.'

She looked up. Now was the time for questions.

Roland's hand snapped up. He looked sternly at her. 'If it comes down to winning the war or placating civilians, you would choose winning the war?'

'Of course.'

'Then don't you think the civilians would understand sacrificing for victory?'

'Sacrificing for victory is one thing, Roland. What I'm talking about is

348

sacrificing their comfort for ours. Leaving civilians cold and hungry while our soldiers are warm and fed.'

Roland's response was cut off by Scott Anthony. 'Templar Scholar, would you support a stronger civilian government to counter the power of the generals?'

'Eventually,' Sasha said. 'I do support civilian departments to take over aspects of governance, but I think that a government would be premature at this point.'

'So, you're a Constitutionalist?' he asked.

Sasha shrugged. 'I don't know if I can answer that, Scott.'

Aristotle raised his hand. 'In a scenario where the civilians under your authority are demanding you release yeomen, or even a nobleman, into their hands for revenge, how far would you go to protect the accused?'

Sasha blinked at the question. 'I . . . ,' she paused. 'I wouldn't fight them, Colonel, if that's what you're asking, but I would be firm and point out why they're wrong.'

'Mob justice does not respond well to reason, Templar. If the men responsible for destroying your hometown were in our custody, imagine how you and other survivors might demand their heads. How much would you pay attention to what their guardians were saying.'

Sasha felt that Aristotle was asking one of his ethical questions, the ones with no good answer, only which bad answer you wanted to take. 'I would protect the accused, Colonel. I believe that, ultimately, the respect for the rules would overcome the passions of the mob. Although I fully admit it would not be an easy exchange.'

Another pause. Sasha hoped she was done, then Caesar raised his hand.

'Templar Scholar,' he said, 'you mentioned that Mister Shaw asked you what the end goal of the Renaissance Movement is. In your words, what is the end goal?'

What does that have to do with my speech? Sasha asked herself. But Caesar was a general.

'The end goal, sir, is a better world.'

'That's it?' Prince asked.

'That's what everyone's fighting for,' Sasha said. 'It might mean different things to different people, but we all want something better. What other answer is there?'

Prince looked at her, then nodded at Lily. She motioned for Sasha to sit, and Prince stood and walked to the front.

'Templars,' he said, 'I must say, I am impressed. When we looked over the lists of topics for tonight, I made a mental note of what I expected each speech to be about. In no case was I correct. Templar Mako did not discuss the supremacy of the navy, but the importance of its integration. Templar Scholar did not discuss the tactics of guerrilla warfare but the politics of it. This is the type of thinking I was hoping the Templars would produce. You've made me very proud today,' he said.

There was clapping. The Templars were both embarrassed and relieved. Then Del Oso bellowed them to attention.

'Templar Candle, with me,' one of the officers called. One by one, each Templars was called out by an officer until only Sasha and Rose remained. Lily directed them to take their chairs and pull them up front, now sitting behind the podium facing their audience. The officers had thinned out; Mobius was gone with Patch, and Aristotle with Elector, and some of the other officers with their Templars.

Several faces still stared up at them, including both generals.

Rose leaned over. 'Surprise test?' she asked.

Sasha nodded. *I guess so.*

Chapter 38

Sasha and Rose waited. Before them sat two generals, their aides, the adjutant of the army, both their instructors, and the officer who had changed Sasha's life.

'Templar Scholar, Templar Rose,' Lily began, 'this is a last-second challenge. Over the last few months, we have tried to improve your minds, giving you challenges to broaden your views and sharpen your wits. The two of you are, by the consensus of the officers who had interacted with you, the two brightest Templars – Rose by way of her education before coming to the Templars, Scholar by way of her efforts after enlisting.

'Tonight, we find out what progress you have made. Each of you is going to be giving a presentation. The topic: The Renaissance Army. I want you to tell me something about this army you have come to suspect, that you have figured out on your own, that you were not told, but you reasoned. It does not have to be profound or major; any minor issue will do. I expect three reasons that led you to this belief. This is an impromptu presentation, with no prep time. Be brief.'

She held out her hands, balled into fists. 'Templar Scholar pick a hand. If it has a stone in it, you are going first.'

'Right,' Sasha said.

Lily opened her hand to show an empty palm. 'Templar Rose, you are going first. Templar Scholar, have a seat.'

Sasha sat down, glancing up at Rose, who was showing a rare grimace, staring at her feet as she thought. After a few moments, she stepped up to the podium.

'In January, the Templars spent some time analyzing plans drawn up by various commands of the Royal Army. We spent hours poring over maps and tables and routes, discussing the officers and options available. All of this was done with the knowledge that one of these plans was going to be executed come springtime. When Operation Tempest was chosen, we focused on that operation exclusively, gaming out scenarios.

'What we were not told is that the Royal Army is marching into a trap. The Renaissance Army is fully prepared to defeat Operation Tempest.

'First: during our discussions in January, there was an underlying belief that garrison forces would not be as involved in the final campaign as the king originally envisioned. When pressed, it was argued that the garrisons might not leave the urban centers they were assigned to if there was a worry of large-scale rioting or unrest. I believe this is something the Renaissance Army is capable of orchestrating, and something we will do once significant portions of the field army have been committed, depriving the offensive of important support and further weakening it.

'My second argument has to do with the field regiments. They are more than strong enough to take their assigned counties away from the yeoman. Strong enough, even that any army corps that came into the county would have to spend men and resources on garrisoning supply lines, but not enough to defeat said army corps. No, the reason the field regiments are so small is that they are meant to draw off the units of the army corps, making the main offensive smaller and smaller.

'Lastly, regarding the training program that Lieutenant Colonel Carpenter maintains. Instructors have mentioned how many hundreds, sometimes thousands, of men and women have passed through their program, and yet a survey of the forces we know about revealed only about fifteen hundred in service. Where did those other thousands go? I believe they have been assigned to a field army of some strength, one powerful enough to defeat at least a division of the Royal Army, if not a completed army corps.

'All of this leads me to believe that Operation Tempest is doomed to fail. Renaissance Movement operations in the cities will force units back to their garrisons, depriving the operation of troops. The field regiments will draw offensive troops away to protect their lines. And the remainder will be destroyed by the assembled force of trained soldiers.'

Rose paused, thinking for a moment. 'Thank you for your time,' she said. She turned and sat down at the other chair, glancing at Sasha nervously.

For a moment no one spoke, then Prince stood. 'Templar Rose,' he began, 'that was surprising, and fairly accurate.'

'The assembled force, sir?' Rose asked.

'It is called the Army of the Lakes. When it is activated, it will assemble almost five thousand men and women, as well armed, trained and supplied as we can make it. Good job.'

Rose smiled. 'Thank you, sir.'

'Templar Scholar?' Prince said.

Sasha wiped her sweaty palms of her hands on her pants and stood, taking her place at the podium. She took a deep breath.

'General Prince,' she said, 'you are the commanding officer of the Renaissance Army of Minnesota. You have assembled Old Guard forces with New Guard volunteers, organized and armed regiments of soldiers, and are fighting to begin a new Renaissance. You've given me a chance to become more than just another farmer, and for that I will always be thankful.'

Another deep breath. 'General Prince, you command the RAM, and you report to General Caesar.'

From their reaction, Sasha knew she was right. Saxon audibly gasped, Bellona's eyes widened in shock. Fox barked a laugh and Scott Anthony looked surprised. Lily smiled, and Madam Moreau gave Sasha the biggest grin the teacher had ever worn.

The generals both looked stoically at her, like children caught in the act of mischief.

'My first argument is about General Caesar's official position. It has never been defined. When I was in Third Regiment, I asked several people about him, but many people did not know anything about him, sometimes not even his name. Colonel Snow only said Caesar was right where he needed to be. Throughout the Templar Project, no one knew, or if they did know they would not tell us. He was just a general, many assumed Prince's assistant or executive, but it was never official. The ambiguity of his position was meant to mask his true position.

'Second, I point out that several times during the Templar Project, we have been shown that General Caesar does not lie in the normal chain of command. His advice has been accepted as just that, advice, without the force of a general's position. For example, when Brigadier Senator forced his way into the Templar classroom, Caesar did not give him a direct order to leave; I think it was because he couldn't. Senator would not ignore words from a superior officer unless he believed he had sufficient cause to ignore them, and Caesar not being between him and General Prince, who he considers to be the leader of the movement, is enough for him to feel confident in ignoring Caesar's orders.

'For my third argument, I would bring up the number of officers, or even just the number of individuals, who are not from Minnesota. Just in this room: Rose, Saxon, Fox, Lily, and Caesar. Two of your field regiments are commanded by non-Minnesotans, Snow and Wild. The Templars started with twelve cadets, six of whom were not from Minnesota. Even amongst the civilians: Doctor Moore, Doctor Adams, both educated in foreign lands, but now here. Why? Because the Renaissance Movement has designs beyond the borders of Minnesota. And those designs would be better served if the leader of the movement itself was not a Minnesotan, but someone who can claim to be above such nationalist concerns.

'And that, generals, is my surprise. Prince commands in Minnesota, but the Renaissance Movement is looking far beyond one set of boarders. This movement is looking to have an impact far across Atlantic America, and possibly even beyond. And I stand ready to help.'

She nodded at the officers and turned to sit down. Rose, looking up at her, smiled and winked.

Prince looked over at Caesar. 'Do you want to take this one,' he grinned, 'sir?'

The officers chuckled as Caesar looked at Sasha. He looked proudly at her. 'Good job, Templar Scholar. You are correct. General Prince commands the Renaissance Army of Minnesota. I command the Renaissance Movement, such as it exists, both in Minnesota and beyond.'

'Including the army from Quebec?' Sasha asked.

Everyone froze. 'Quebec?' Caesar asked.

'Templars Rose and Cardinal are not just Quebecois who happened to come into the Renaissance Movement, are they? They're obviously from well-off families, probably even nobility. Rose, at least, was forced to come here. Because there is a Quebecois army, and they wanted to be represented in the Templars.'

Prince looked at her, then at Caesar. 'She is just like you; she can't turn her brain off.'

Sasha blushed. 'I'm sorry –.'

'Don't be,' Prince said. 'If more people followed Caesar's path, the world would be a much different place. You are, again, correct. Rose?'

'The Army of the True Queen,' Rose said, looking at Sasha with a mix of astonishment and pride. 'Small, but important, happily ensconced in the Verendrye woods, and awaiting the right time to strike and take back the throne from the Commonwealth puppet who sits on it.'

Sasha sighed. 'Good. I was worried I might be wrong about that one.'

'Were you?' Rose asked.

Sasha shrugged. 'I don't know. I knew it, but I wasn't sure.'

'Ladies,' Lily said, stepping up to them, gesturing for them to follow her. They moved, but Sasha stopped.

'General Caesar?' she asked.

354

Caesar looked at her. 'Yes, Templar Scholar?'

'Normally, at the end of a test, I get to ask one question. Is that still the case?'

'As always, it depends on the question.'

'How many generals are there? At least three, you two and the Quebecois general. How many in total?'

Caesar glanced over at Prince. Prince held his gaze for a moment, then shrugged.

Caesar looked back at Sasha. 'Five,' he said.

Sasha nodded. 'Thank you, sir,' and followed Lily out the door.

Rose stopped just outside. 'Five,' she said, 'wow.'

'You didn't know that?' Sasha asked.

'I did not. I knew of three.'

'Who are the other two?' Sasha pondered out loud. 'Iowa and Wisconsin, I'd bet.'

'Or maybe a Dakota?' Rose asked. 'Someone who gets support of the factions on the plains?'

'Could be,' Sasha answered. She looked at Lily, standing there watching them. 'Can you tell us if we're right?'

'Yes, I can,' Lily said.

'And?' Rose pressed.

'Just because I can answer your question, doesn't mean I will,' Lily responded. Then she smiled. 'Perhaps you should get to bed. Tomorrow is going to be a big day.'

'It is, isn't it?' Rose replied.

Sasha smiled.

Chapter 39

That Saturday morning, the Templars slept in. All their tests were done, all of their challenges finished. When they finally emerged for breakfast, elation was mixed with nervousness.

'What happens if we failed the tests?' Roland finally asked during breakfast.

'Warrants for all,' Sasha said. 'Even failing as a Templar, you can still become an officer.'

'It would be a shame to come all this way and not make it,' Rose said.

'Doesn't mean it won't happen,' Candle said. She was not eating much that morning.

'If it does, it does,' Mako said. 'We've done everything we can and cannot change it now. Let's focus on what is before us.'

'At the moment, we have nothing before us,' Roland pointed out.

'Except a lot of food,' Patch quipped.

They finished breakfast and made their way back to their barracks. Del Oso was approaching at the same time they were. 'Fill yourselves up?' he asked.

'Some more than others, Sergeant Major,' Elector said. Candle stuck her tongue out at him.

'Good. We're assembling at the Templar classroom at 10. You've got about half an hour.'

'We passed?' Candle asked.

'Just get ready, Templars.'

'Templars!'

Getting ready consisted of changing into their classroom clothes and sitting about waiting. Sasha risked a glance over at Hero's cot. It had not yet been removed, although all his stuff was missing.

'I wonder where he is,' she pondered out loud.

'Nowhere he should be,' Roland growled.

'Amen,' Candle said. She had taken Hero's flight the hardest. She had spent so much effort trying to even him out, she had taken it as a personal failure that he left.

356

Del Oso came in and bellowed them to attention. They silently assembled, following him down the path they had taken so many times before.

Once again, the Templar classroom was filled. General Prince stood up front. Each table had one mentor sitting down, with a small binding of papers on the desk. The Templars took their spots, Sasha sitting next to Caesar. Rose sat at her table alone.

'Templars,' Prince said, 'I know it's been a long and rough week for you. It was supposed to be. But you are Templars, and you handled it well. I am pleased to state that you all have passed the second phase. Congratulations.'

The Templars all sighed. Several whispered prayers.

'The bindings before you are your tests. We made copies for our own records, but we wanted you to see how you did. What did you get right? What did you get wrong? What can you improve? What did we think of your essays? Feel free to take a look, but don't worry too much about the minor details. You passed; that's the important thing. And that means we transition to the third phase of the Templar training: apprenticeship.'

Sasha smiled. She glanced at Caesar, who returned his own smile.

'For the next ten weeks, you will be apprenticed to a mentor, possibly the same one you have been working with all year, perhaps a new officer, as the situation dictates. Your mentor will have individual details. You will be learning directly from them, and they will decide themselves if you pass the third phase or not. I will have no say in the matter; you must impress them and them alone.

'But this isn't just a test of you as a student, but a test of you as an officer. So, for the length of this apprenticeship, you are all temporarily commissioned as Second Lieutenants, with all the rights and responsibilities thereof.'

Sasha grinned. *Not just a student anymore. An officer, and apprentice to a general!*

Prince looked at a pocket watch. 'Templars, at 11 o'clock, Sergeant Major Del Oso will begin calling you out to proceed to your assignment. Until then, pack up. Your uniforms, your tools, your weapons, everything. Then spend your time saying goodbye. It will be some time before you see each other again.' He paused for emphasis. 'Good luck, Templars.'

His speech done, Prince walked forward and sat next to Rose.

We both get generals for mentors.

Sasha looked at Caesar. He tilted his head.

'Nervous?'

'A commission and an apprenticeship on the same day? Yes. Nervous, but confident.'

'Good. That means you are taking this seriously.' He slid the papers over to her. 'You do not have time to review these now, but I do want to go over them later. For now, as Prince said, go pack and say your goodbyes.'

Sasha nodded, standing to head back to the barracks. The other mentors were similarly brief in their instructions and the Templars were soon all back, packing their belongings.

'Anyone surprised by their mentor?' Candle asked. Her nervousness about failure was gone, and she smiled broadly again.

'I am,' Elector grimaced. 'I was hoping to go to Aristotle, but it looks like I'm going to Major Huron.'

'From the siege corps?' Sasha asked.

'Yeah, I wonder why.' Elector shrugged. 'Roland? I doubt you'd stay with Colonel Halcon.'

'Captain Pine,' Roland replied. 'Anyone know who that is?'

They all shook their heads. 'What unit?'

'None given,' Roland frowned.

'Maybe it's a secret formation?' Patch asked. 'Something to fight Operation Tempest?'

Sasha and Rose traded looks while the rest nodded.

'Makes sense,' Sasha said.

'So,' Candle said. 'This is it?'

They were all quiet again. Then Patch piped up. 'Well, we can write letters, can't we? If they're really making post a constant thing, we should write letters.'

'Good idea, Patch,' Elector said.

'Libby!' Patch said. 'Until we leave, I'm Libby, not Patch. I know we're not supposed to exchange names, but you are my friends, and I want you to know who I am.'

There was a seriousness to her voice that was rarely there, and the Templars all looked at each other.

'Okay, Libby,' Elector said. He stuck out his hand. 'Edmund.'

358

They shook, but before they could let go Candle stepped forward and put her hand on top of theirs.

'Deborah,' she said. She smiled at them.

Sasha stepped forward. 'Sasha.'

Mako stepped beside her. 'Gideon.'

Rose was next. 'Lorelai.'

Roland was last. 'Santiago.'

The seven stood with their hands in the middle of their circle.

'Huh,' Mako said. 'It's been so long since I told anyone my name, it feels weird saying it out loud.'

'I agree,' Candle said.

'Well,' Sasha said. 'I guess we should pack.'

They turned to get their things. After a moment, Patch yelled over. 'Gideon, where are you from? I've always wanted to know.'

'Carolina,' Mako said, 'along the Albemarle. Spent most of my time on the Atlantic Ocean.'

'Really?' Patch squealed. 'That's amazing.'

'Atlantic beats Lake Superior?' Sasha asked.

'It does indeed. Libby, where are you from?'

'Colorado,' Patch replied. 'Out west. Know the Princedom of Denver? I grew up in one of the baronies; Boulder, in the rail yards.'

'How'd you end up all the way in Minnesota?' Sasha asked.

'Long story. Let's see: Lorelai is from Quebec, we all know that. Santiago, Edmund and Sasha are Minnesotan. Deborah, where are you from?'

'Tennessee,' Candle said, 'Memphis, to be exact.'

'You're from the Empire of Mississippi?' Elector asked in surprise. 'You don't sound it.'

'Well, I do have a knack for accents,' Candle said, her voice shifting to a southern drawl Sasha remembered from some of the yeomen who used to patrol her hometown. 'I used to speak like this more often, but once I got onto river boats, I had to change how I sounded to a more neutral tone.'

'And now you fight them?' Mako asked.

'Fight who?' Candle returned to her normal accent. 'Memphis was part of the Empire; then the Commonwealth came, and the Empire got split up, and Memphis became part of Ohio. And we all know what Ohio is.'

'Heavy on the religion,' Rose said. 'You're Hebrew.'

'I am, and not one that conforms to a king's ridiculous theology.' Candle shook her head. 'It is a shame how far a despot can go.'

The Athens bell chimed eleven, and Del Oso bellowed Elector's name.

'Speaking of going,' Elector said, standing. 'Good luck everyone. Stay safe.'

Elector took his leave. The rest of the cadets stood about, absorbing his absence. Then Roland's name sounded out.

'Roland,' Rose said. 'Do try to be careful.'

'Why do you single me out?' he asked.

'Because you are the only infantry Templar left. Be heroic, but don't be stupid.'

Roland laughed. 'Oh, I'll write my own song with my deeds, and it will be sung for centuries.'

'Just so long as you're the one singing it,' Rose said.

Roland smiled and left.

'Many of us are in dangerous professions,' Mako pointed out. 'Patch plays with explosives.'

'Yes, but he runs into machine guns,' Rose said.

Del Oso called out the next name.

Rose looked back last Templars. 'I hope to see you all again.'

'We hope that too,' Patch said.

Rose bowed and exited. The last three sat in silence until Mako's name was called.

'Ladies,' Mako said. 'Go with God.'

'You too, Mako,' Sasha replied. And then there were two.

'Libby?' Sasha asked.

'Yes, Sasha?' Patch replied.

'Will you be safe?'

'I'll be playing with explosives, so there's no good way to answer that. You?'
360

'I'll try.'

'Good,' Patch said. She picked up her bag and handed Sasha hers.

'We haven't been called,' Sasha pointed out.

'Why should there be a last Templar?' Patch asked. Sasha smiled, took her bag, and followed Patch out the door.

Del Oso stood with General Caesar and some of his Olympians, and one man in civilian clothes who waved at the two young women.

'Uncle Jacques!' Patch exclaimed.

'Libby!' Jacques smiled.

'What are you doing here?' she asked. 'Shouldn't you be under some building-fall, poking about for anything you can find?'

'I spent three weeks trapped in one,' Jacques said. 'Blizzards are a pain.'

'Was it worth it?' Patch asked.

'Once I show you what I brought back to the Workshop, you'll be able to tell me. Let's go!'

He turned, Patch following quickly, Sasha forgotten. She watched them walking away, Patch rapidly guessing what he found, Uncle Jacques laughing and providing clues.

'The Workshop is full of interesting people,' Caesar said behind her, startling her.

'I sometimes try to imagine what it might be like to live there,' Sasha said.

'For you, it might get boring. Although, to be fair, we have not spent any time testing your technological skills. It could be that you are a genius at mechanical or electrical engineering, and we would not know it.'

'Should we?' Sasha asked.

Caesar cocked his head. 'Best not to risk it, I think,' he said. 'Besides, I like the idea of having someone following in my footsteps.'

The group walked to the stables, where Saxon waited with several horses. They left Athens, following out into the woods of Walker County. It was a cool day, and they were riding through some difficult terrain.

'Where are we going?' she finally managed to ask Saxon.

'You'll see,' she said with a smile.

Another hour of riding. Sasha knew they were now northeast of Olympia.

Where could we be going? she asked herself, picturing her mental map of Walker County. Olympia was in the eastern part of the county. Athens was southwest of Olympia while Sparta was to the west. Charity, the civilian hospital, was north of Sparta at the time of the accident but could have moved. Holiday, the military hospital, was south of Olympia. Sasha knew of Rhodes, the technical school, which was southeast of Olympia, though she had never been there. She had no idea where the Workshop was, but she was sure that was not their destination.

She continued thinking on the question. She understood that there were facilities in Walker County she did not know of. Mako came from one. The trained troops who came out of Sparta had to go somewhere, and the quartermasters had to have their own facilities. But again, she knew little. Finally, she had to admit defeat.

I have no idea where we are going.

Sasha's stomach was missing its lunch when they came to a stop and dismounted. Two Olympians took the extra reins and rode off into the forest, leaving the three officers and four guards alone.

Sasha was confused but said nothing. Caesar led them through the trees on foot. They crested a hill, and Caesar gestured Sasha forward.

'Welcome to Avalon,' he said.

Sasha looked down the hill, and after a moment of surprise, laughed.

Chapter 40

Avalon. The secret castle of the Iron Republic. The Templars had discussed it at length. Some believed it never existed, others that it was real but superbly hidden. The Republic had never confirmed its existence. Neither the Commonwealth nor the Kingdom had been able to find it. Sasha had come to believe it did not exist.

Now Sasha understood perfectly. The Commonwealth and the Kingdom had both combed through these woods several times, and probably had marched right over it.

The entrance was built into the side of a rocky hill face; a rather large rock that was currently swung out, revealing a descending staircase. A squad of Olympians stood guard as their group arrived and dismounted.

A figure came up the stairs, an older man with grey hair who walked with a cane. He had dark skin, and greying hair that was well maintained. He wore a uniform, but it was one Sasha had only seen before in history books: the uniform of the Republic of Minnesota.

'Sir,' he said, coming to a crisp salute. 'Welcome back to Avalon.'

'General,' Caesar said in response. 'May I introduce Templar Scholar, my apprentice for the next two months? Templar Scholar, this is General Emilio Payne, former general in the Iron Army of Minnesota.'

'The general who commanded the Expeditionary Corps in New York?' Sasha asked.

Payne smiled. 'Indeed. It was a good fight, lost unfairly.' He held out his hand. 'Pleased to meet you, Templar Scholar. Both Caesar and Prince have made numerous mentions of your project over the last year.'

'Pleased to meet you as well, General,' Sasha said, taking the hand. 'If I may ask, what is your role in this?'

'Unofficial. I was a prisoner until recently, and I'm lending my experience as a general to the Renaissance Army, without lending them my name or rank. Many people think I'm dead; I want them to continue to do so.'

'Prisoner?' Sasha asked.

'General Payne was a prisoner at the Brainerd Prison Camp,' Caesar said.

'Really?' Sasha exclaimed. 'I fought there! Third Regiment, to the south.'

363

'In the creek bed?' Payne asked. 'I heard about that afterwards. That was a tough fight.' There was a tone in his voice that told Sasha he had been in tough fights himself.

'It was,' Sasha agreed.

Caesar cleared his throat. 'Avalon is the headquarters of the Renaissance Movement, as a whole. Olympia is for Prince and the RAM, who need a public and official headquarters for the sake of legitimacy. We need to continue to be a secret for now.'

'And part of that secrecy is trust,' Payne said. 'Most people do not know that Avalon exists. Our location and existence are both of the utmost secrecy. Not to mention, within those walls, you will hear many things you cannot speak of.'

'Like the Army of the True Queen?' Sasha asked.

Payne stepped back in surprise, then looked over at Caesar. Caesar gave him a proud smile.

'She was told nothing. She was challenged to a display of reasoning and deduction. She argued that there was a Quebecois army allied with us and explained her reasoning. She was right on most of the details, so we filled her in.'

'Outstanding,' Payne said. 'You will do well here.' He turned gesturing for her to follow them down the stairs.

'And what do we do here?' Sasha asked.

'Planning,' Payne replied. 'Information is funneled to us every day. We accumulate, evaluate, and plan. What happens if the king sends troops here, evacuates there? Then we report to the generals what we think will work and what we think won't.'

They were descending now, and Sasha realized Avalon had electric lighting. It was dim, enough to see where she was going, but not enough to read.

'I'm amazed that the Republic could build this place.'

'They didn't, at least not alone. They got the Duluth Archive to help. Four stories, underground, powered by an underground river. The top level has radios for command and communications. There is an armory, conference rooms, and a kitchen.' Payne waved his hand. 'An emergency headquarters that was never activated.'

'Until recently,' Sasha said.

'Until recently,' Payne agreed. He turned and beckoned her to follow him.

364

Caesar brought up the rear.

'The top level is for the guards, radio room, and some outdoor gear. Cold weather coats, rain slicks, and some desks and chairs if you want to sit outside. Just be prepared to run inside if told to. It's a standing order that Avalon must be able to hide itself within three minutes of a warning.'

He started down the stairs, Sasha in tow. The next landing was only a short flight down. Out of the sunlight, Sasha had to get used to the low light.

'The second level is the conference level. It's got the offices and conference rooms where the work at Avalon is done. Third level is the residential and cafeteria level, where you'll live. The fourth is the mechanics level. There's no reason for you to go down there.'

He led her out on the second level, to another hallway. This one had seven doors leading off its length, three on each side, with a final large double set at the end. Payne led them down to the big doors and opened them.

Inside was a large room, the walls covered in maps, small desks and shelves full of files surrounding them. In the middle was a large map, ten feet to a side, of northern Minnesota. Grid lines crossed the map, and Sasha recognized the blue and red blocks of military units. Extra lights and lanterns brought up the light levels to a readable level.

'The War Room,' Payne said. 'Here, we collect and analyze all the intelligence and reports, separate from General Prince's command. We can game, calculate, and plan for any number of contingencies.'

Two staff sergeants were in the room, one adjusting units on the map, the other filing paperwork. Both looked up and came to attention.

'Staff Sergeants Jane and John Pressman, may I introduce Templar Scholar, General Prince's temporary second aide-de-camp. Templar Scholar, these two oversee filing, keeping the paperwork in order, checking the maps. It's a shame they're so good at it, because they'd make fine staff officers in their own right.'

'Maybe later, sir,' Jane responded. 'We're happy to be where we are.' She smiled at Sasha. 'Welcome, Lieutenant.'

Sasha nodded at them. 'Hello.'

'There are a handful of junior enlisted,' Payne said, 'who handle the food, help with clerical duties, various odds and bits that a facility like this has. Two radio techs are here to operate the radio. The facilities technician lives on the bottom level with his family; you'll get to know them pretty well.'

'Good,' Sasha said, surprised as she was to find a family living at Avalon.

'Which room will be her workroom?' Caesar asked.

'Conference Two, General. Is the room ready, Jane?'

'Yes, sir,' Jane said, putting her papers down and moving out the door. 'Let me show you.'

She led them to another room, opening it and turning on the electric lights to full. Sasha blinked at the sudden brightness.

'You're allocated an hour of full light a day in here, but most of your work will be by lantern light or done up top in the daylight. I really wouldn't read in this dimness,' Jane said, gesturing at the table.

Someone had built a meticulously detailed relief map of Walker Town and its surroundings. The trenches, the trees, the buildings, all constructed to as much detail as they could have been.

Sasha blinked at it in surprise. 'My workroom?'

'You are going to plan the capture of Walker,' Caesar said.

'Me?' Sasha said in surprise.

'You have trained with the Olympians and the Marines on clearing towns, have you not?' Payne asked. 'You've learned about planning battles from Caesar.'

'I have,' Sasha admitted. 'But to plan this by myself.'

'Oh, you won't be alone,' Payne continued to speak. 'You will plan, and report to us. We will offer you criticisms and critiques. You will return here, modify, and return. It will be a back and forth, a dialogue of sorts.'

'When you are not working here,' Caesar said, 'you will help with the normal duties at Avalon. Assessing intelligence, compiling information, gaming out scenarios.'

Sasha nodded. 'Okay,' she said nervously.

'Templar Scholar,' Caesar said. 'You are more than capable of this.'

'But if Colonel Grace hasn't managed to take the town in a year, why would I do any better?'

'Because you have access to more resources,' Payne said. 'Jane?'

Jane gestured to one wall, where a makeshift series of shelves now stood, some with folders,   many of them empty. 'These shelves,' the young woman pointed to a column, 'are all from Colonel Grace and the siege group. Status reports, ideas, enemy intelligence, all arranged.' Then she stepped to the next column. 'These shelves are a number of reports from other units who have spent the winter preparing for this.'

'I suggest you read those first,' Payne said.

'Your first briefing is next Saturday,' Caesar said. 'I want three possible plans. Even if you prefer one, I want three.'

'Yes, sir,' Sasha said.

'Jane here is an excellent sounding board, and she's been assigned to assist you,' Payne said, 'when other duties do not preclude her from helping.'

Jane smiled. Sasha nodded nervously.

'Good,' Payne said. 'Jane, take Templar Scholar down to her room and let her get settled. Dinner is in an hour; you can meet the rest of the personnel then.'

Jane waved for Sasha to follow. Sasha did so, descending to the third level behind the sergeant. This was another hallway, long, with a dozen doors leading off.

'It's not much,' Jane said, opening the door that now had 'Scholar' written in chalk on it. 'But it's yours for the time being.' She flicked a switch and a dim light turned on.

Sasha took a moment to survey her room. A single bed, a small desk and chair. There was no dresser, just some drawers underneath the bed. A small washroom with a basin and a toilet, and, Sasha saw, another door opposite.

'You're sharing the facilities with Saxon,' Jane said. She showed how to lock the door. 'Just make sure to unlock it when you're done.'

'Right,' Sasha said.

'Well,' Jane replied. 'Get settled. Dinner will be up top, tonight. Should be fun!'

Sasha nodded and the sergeant disappeared. Sasha went into the washroom and tried the faucet. Water flowed out. She used some to splash on her face then shut it off.

Caesar told me, told all of us, this was going to be a test of our abilities, she told herself while staring at the face in the mirror. To her, it still did not look like the face of an officer.

Someday, it will, she told herself.

Someday.

***

Miklos spent several days in the headquarters of Prince Stefan's field army.

Saint Cloud Military City was Stefan's own domain, an expanse of depots, barracks and armories that covered a hundred square miles, and housed eighty thousand troops. It was the brainchild of Prince Stefan, a study in efficiency. There were no grandiose palaces for headquarters, but common-looking brick buildings. The barracks were cleaner than most Miklos had seen, and paved roads led from one structure to another.

Stefan had included all the important officers of the Field Army in this meeting, even those who would not be heading out for Operation Tempest. All four corps commanders, all eight division commanders. General Coronado, General Bennabi. Representatives of the North Watch and the Army of the Cities. Three dozen officers all told, including Miklos.

'Tomorrow,' Stefan said, 'we begin.' He looked at the officers assembled. 'Are we ready?'

He nodded at Lieutenant General Vega, the I Corps commander.

'I Corps is ready,' Vega replied. 'The first troops will march out in the morning. We've already positioned supplies, and we will be moving the artillery by train. We'll be in position to invade the Liberated Counties within three days.'

'And III Corps?' Stefan turned his attention to another officer at the table.

Major General Van Kalvin cleared his throat. 'It will take three days for any one detachment to move to Bemidji via the Red River Valley. Three or four detachments per day, it will take at least a week before I'm comfortable moving out of Bemidji in any force.'

None of the officers there were happy with that.

'North Watch?' Stefan asked.

A major from the North Watch stood. 'My Lord, our heavy equipment is ready to be moved by train, along with an advanced guard. The rest will march out early in the morning.'

'And the Royal Cities?'

Another major. 'III Corps troop movements will take up most of the available trains for some time. Our initial companies will march out in the morning. The rest will be ready to move by rail as the opportunities present themselves.'

Stefan glared at the officer, and he was not the only one. But the Army of the Royal Cities answered to the king himself. If King Xavier was okay with such a delay, there was little anyone could do about it.

'District troops?'

'All appropriate companies are ready. They will begin moving, some by rail, some by road. They'll be on position as soon as they can be.'

'Inspectorate?'

'Our companies are in position,' the representative said. 'We'll be waiting for you.'

'Quartermaster?'

Coronado spoke. 'We've moved enough forward supplies for two weeks of activity. We will continue to send supplies forward, particularly once we know what is needed.'

'Air Corps?'

Bennabi spoke. 'We are prepared to begin daily reconnaissance flights and bombing missions against the Renaissance Army infrastructure within the Liberated Counties. Once the campaign begins in earnest, we are prepared to provide close support if requested.'

'Good,' Stefan said. He looked at all the officers again.

'Well, gentlemen. It's getting late, and many of you have to travel in the morning.' He stood and saluted them.

'Good luck.'

And with that, Tempest began.

Chapter 41

Sasha threw herself into her new duties with a fervor born of a fear of failure, but soon became enjoyment. Sasha realized she liked this work. Reading, writing, planning, all of it. She took to it quickly and looked forward to it every morning.

'Is that weird?' she asked Saxon.

Saxon shook her head. 'I don't see why it should be. I'm the same way.'

Sasha's appreciation for her position was not her only surprise at Avalon.

On her first day, Sasha was looking through the organization list for the siege group. It was specific, down to every rifle and engineer. For a formation that had grown up haphazardly in response to the siege, it was a surprisingly strong formation, with a core of capable officers and noncoms, and a strong militia backing.

It was one of those officers that surprised Sasha, the officer in command of the southern trenches, and therefore the largest formation under Grace's command.

'Captain Saber?' she asked Saxon with a grin. Saber had been Snow's executive when Third Regiment left Walker. He was the experienced officer who supported Snow. He lost his arm during a skirmish with the yeomen and taken a fever, evacuating with Aristotle's field hospital after the Brainerd Prison Camp.

'Yes,' Saxon said, 'the same man who marched south with Third Regiment last year.'

'I can't believe I forgot about him,' Sasha said, her face suddenly dropping.

'He asked for an assignment after he recovered from his wounds,' Saxon said, 'but didn't want to go back to Snow. I don't know the particulars, but he was assigned to Walker to command the trenches.'

'Huh,' Sasha said, wondering if Saber was angry at Snow for something.

Would that mean he's angry at me, too? I did help cut his arm off.

The second surprise came on Thursday, when Sasha got her first look at the Army of the Lakes.

Payne showed it to her that morning, the large hand-drawn table of their organization, then watched as she read the boxes, followed the lines, and put

370

together the formation in her head.

Unlike the field regiments, which were built around the commander's own personal preferences and the resources at hand, this army was built to a strict structure, based on threes.

The army had three divisions; each division had three regiments, each regiment had three companies, each company three platoons of three squads. And at every level, additional boxes showed where support was being added. Machine guns at the platoon level. Mortars at the regimental. A cavalry regiment attached to the headquarters for screening and reconnaissance.

'We've added in as much support as we can,' Payne said.

'I see,' Sasha said. 'How many people total?'

'On paper, about five thousand, five hundred, but in reality, it's just shy of forty-eight hundred.'

'How many do I know?' she wondered out loud.

Saxon responded. 'You know Brigadier Senator, of course, the commanding officer, and Colonel Athena, the Third Division commander. Captain Thunder is the chief of artillery, and you know her assistant, and, of course, one of the platoon officers in the Second Regiment.'

'Candle and Roland?' Sasha asked.

Saxon nodded. 'You know a few other officers here or there, some of the enlisted personnel you met at Athens and Sparta. Training officers have transferred, or will transfer, when the order goes out.'

'At the moment,' Payne said, 'the army is divided up into company-sized camps. When the order goes out, a few promotions go through, and the army consolidates.'

'Companies of Old Guard,' Saxon said, 'companies of defectors from the Royal Army, companies of volunteers from the Liberated or soon-to-be Liberated Counties. I was worried we wouldn't get more than four thousand last summer. We got considerably more. '

'And we have enough supplies for this?' Sasha asked.

'Maybe,' Payne said. Sasha looked at Saxon.

'We have ammunition for one good fight, maybe two,' she said. 'We also have to worry about planting season; otherwise we'll be out of food by the end of the year.'

'And we must worry about horses,' Caesar said, entering the room and the conversation. 'And medical supplies, uniforms, tools to keep the equipment functioning. Supplying an army is as strenuous a job as getting it to fight.'

'Have you ever met Colonel Gold?' Payne asked.

'No,' Sasha said, suddenly surprised by that fact. 'I have not.'

'There's a reason for that,' Saxon grumbled. She had a stern look on her face.

'Gold is particularly good at organizing our logistics,' Payne said. 'He's done wonders in clothing, feeding, and arming this whole rebellion.'

'Just so long as you give him a good watcher,' Saxon muttered.

'Saxon!' Payne snapped, but Saxon looked up defiantly.

'Don't,' she warned.

Caesar cleared his throat. 'If we can get back to the matter at hand?'

The two nodded, leaving Sasha wondering what that was about.

***

If there was one advantage Sasha appreciated at Avalon, it was the information about Operation Tempest that flowed through the headquarters. It came in slowly, filtering through local operatives, through the network of informants, and up to Olympia, then on to Avalon.

III Corps moved by trains through the Red River Valley. I Corps started marching out of Saint Cloud. The Royal Air Corps started air raids on the facilities they knew about. Sparta was heavily damaged, as were a few company camps and the village the Naval Group had just rowed their boats out of. Slowly, the enemy troops moved into position.

Alongside that information came news about the Renaissance Movement's own counter, and it proved how close Sasha had hit the mark in January. The cities were under threat, but not by military units.

'Renaissance Councils?' Sasha asked.

'The Renaissance Army was not grown overnight,' Payne said. 'The infrastructure in the cities forwards people and materials to us. Did you think we make all these rifles and ammunition ourselves? You can't just mold a mortar in the middle of the woods.'

With Tempest underway, the councils moved to active agitation. Each council had autonomy, working to help the movement without taking orders. Which was why the Red River Council opted to sink a riverboat full of ammunition, while Royal Cities Council went as far as assassinating two officers outside Snelling Castle.

The strength of the activities sparked debates at Avalon. Caesar and Sasha were of the mind that targeted assassinations were excessive, making the Renaissance Movement seem more like a criminal organization than an intellectual movement. Payne and Saxon disagreed, mentioning that the use of targeted strikes against military personnel, as opposed to attacks that could put innocent civilians in danger, showed that they were not engaging in violence for violence's sake.

'But it doesn't matter,' Payne said. 'We have no authority over them.'

'Is that true?' Sasha asked, looking at Caesar.

'Officially, no,' Caesar replied. 'They do take orders from me and General Prince. However, as we are too far removed from the particulars of the cities or regions involved, we have kept from issuing direct commands to them. We give them desires or objectives. "Please develop contacts within this installation," and such requests. Then we let them complete those objectives as they see fit.'

'Unfortunately,' Saxon said, 'that also means we have to deal with the differences between them. Red River is more subtle, while Royal Cities is more aggressive. But they all get the job done.'

'Usually,' Payne said.

The impact on Tempest was immediate, though it took some time for that to become apparent to Avalon.

The actions upset and unnerved the nobles. The rebellion of the Renaissance Army was a nuisance when it was confined to a few rural counties, but the sudden violence in their own streets made the threat all too real for the nobles. That turned into a flood of messages to the Royal Cities, demanding Royal Army assistance. King Xavier and Marshal Robinson could have easily dispatched troops from their garrisons, or even from the half of the Field Army still stuck in Saint Cloud, but they seemed even more unnerved by the councils than the nobles were. And they started to make mistakes.

First, they cancelled the troops earmarked for Tempest from the Royal Cities, citing worries of a general uprising. Those troops were supposed to secure the railways that Third and Fourth Field Regiments were threatening. That in turn forced General Vega to dispatch one of his brigades to fill that role.

That was a huge victory for the Renaissance Army. A field army corps had two divisions, each with two brigades. I Corps had just lost a quarter of its strength.

III Corps suffered more. Van Kalvan lost his Sixth Division, a full half of his force, to reinforce the garrisons along the Red River Valley. His Fifth Division was moving into Bemidji when the First Field Regiment started an aggressive campaign against the supply lines. They cut the Grand Forks – Bemidji Railway and ambushed the wagon trains and engineers. Van Kalvan had to turn back and move troops west, away from Walker, just to keep his troops fed.

'Consider the numbers,' Payne said. 'The Army of the Lakes fields forty-eight hundred men and women. A whole Royal Army Corps fields twelve thousand. If they're allowed to concentrate, it would be over quickly. But they're hemorrhaging units trying to keep their supply lines open. III Corps is already all but spent, and I Corps will suffer more as it goes through Colonel Wild's territory. Imagine if General Senator could bring the whole of his force on one brigade.'

'He'd outnumber it by two to one,' Sasha said. She had figured that out already but enjoyed hearing him confirm her thoughts on the subject.

'Exactly. And we're pretty certain they don't know about the Army of the Lakes. They must suspect, but they can't know. So, Senator waits for his opportunity to strike.'

'Will he move north or south?' Sasha asked.

'South,' Saxon replied.

'How do you know?' Payne asked. 'It makes sense to move north and strike III Corps while its ridiculously weak.'

'III Corps is spent,' Saxon said. 'It's not much of a threat. I Corps is a threat, and Senator will believe it is his mission to end that threat.'

'That would be a hell of a battle,' Sasha said, looking at the map and frowning.

'What's wrong?' Payne asked. 'Is it the troops?'

'No,' Sasha said. She pointed at the map itself, the small towns labelled along the roads, and the farms not shown at all. 'Any civilians in the area are going to suffer.'

'They will,' Saxon agreed.

'Then why don't we find another way?'

'You know the answer,' Payne said, calmly.

Sasha sighed. 'Because this is the best way, not the perfect way.'

'Exactly,' Payne said. 'These are the kinds of decisions your ethics training was about. Understanding and accepting the consequences of your actions.'

'Templars are trained to make the hard choices,' Saxon said.

Sasha sighed. 'I'd still much rather find a way to win without killing anyone.'

'There are worse things to say as an officer,' Payne said. 'Much worse.'

***

When she had time, Sasha turned her attention to the siege of Walker.

Avalon certainly had enough intelligence on the matter. They had numbers on the defenders, their officers, and equipment. They had maps of the defenses and the routes planned to respond to one attack or another.

The more Sasha looked at it, the more she understood why no plan had been finished yet.

Walker Town was small. To a young girl it had always seemed like a large city, but she was used to thinking in miles now. Walker Town was less than a single square mile, which gave the defenders a tremendous advantage in responding to any attack.

Secondly, Count Walker was using the terrain to his advantage. The western marsh was nearly uncrossable to begin with. Now, the bridges were burned, and every footpath up from the marsh to the streets was blocked, watched by an armed guard.

The southern front was not much better. An initial line crossed the entire isthmus, anchored by a redoubt on each end and with three bunkers built into its system, all under the guard of the castle's heights. A second trench followed the castle walls, wrapping around to the Golden Crown Inn on the west and the Cathedral Gate on the east.

The lakefront was the longest front they had to guard, but Walker had even planned for that. The lakefront buildings formed their own obstacles to a landing, made more difficult by prepared defenses. Walker built no defenses on the open beach between the town and the cathedral, but more than enough machine guns covered the landing to make it a dangerous landing. Finally, the cathedral's lakefront was steep and covered by its own array of guns.

'Not easy way to get in,' Sasha said.

'No,' Jane said. 'Count Walker's no fool when it comes to this stuff. Much as I hate to give him any due, he's good at this.'

'Right,' Sasha agreed. 'What are the current plans?'

'Is that where you want to start?' Jane asked.

'I do,' Sasha said. 'I want to know the plans as they developed. From the beginning.'

'Okay,' Jane said. She went to one alcove and pulled out the papers.

'So,' she began, 'Major Grace came and took over the siege of Walker in early June of last year. At that time, there was no real plan. Prince has called a few conferences, one before winter, when the air bridge started, and one in March, to look at the situation again. A lot of plans have been floated in one form or another.

'The first plan was, technically, General Prince's plan. He simply wanted to leave the siege in place and starve them out. The only other plan brought up last summer was Brigadier Lily's plan to use our assets in Walker to assassinate their leadership.'

Sasha looked up from the map in surprise. 'Assassinations?' she asked with disdain.

'Not a lot of people supported that one,' Jane admitted. 'Once the air bridge started, Prince knew that starving them out was no longer an option. He asked the Workshop to look into ways of cutting it but had to admit we might have to take Walker away from them. So, he asked a lot of officers their opinions, independently of each other, to get a diverse set of plans.'

'How diverse?' Sasha asked.

'Well, Payne supported Caesar's starve-them-out plan. Colonel Black supported Lily's assassination plan. Other than those two, every other officer supported one of three options.

'The first option,' Jane pointed to the trenches, 'was to cut through the trenches to the south. Senator, Birch and Moses supported this idea. They argued that it was possible to find a path through the no man's land to get to the trenches, or at least close enough they could start the assault before the alarm went off.'

'Sounds dangerous,' Sasha said, looking at the map. 'Walker's got, what, seven machine guns overlooking the route? Assault troops get discovered, that's a lot of firepower to face.'

'And look at the castle and the redoubts,' Jane pointed out.

Sasha nodded. 'You take a trench and the castle can turn it into a kill zone.' She shook her head. 'Dangerous.'

'Well,' Jane shrugged, 'there aren't a lot of good options.'

'What about the marsh?' Sasha asked.

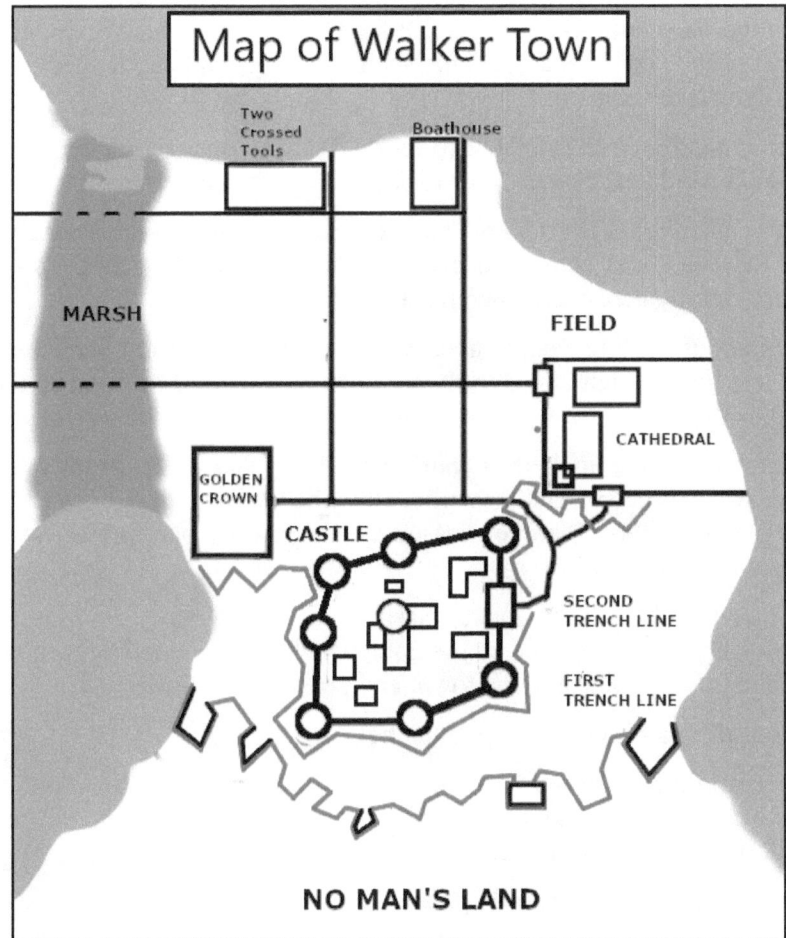

'That's what Colonel Grace suggested, along with Colonel Archimedes and Colonel Athena. They believe that a path can be tracked through the marsh right up to the edge of town. Grace supposedly has sent couriers in and out of the town that way before. Then, they could blast their way in and fight house to house.'

Sasha looked at that part of the map. 'That doesn't look good, either,' she said. 'How many rifles does Grace think she can get through her path?'

'It would be a single file,' Jane said. 'So, all of them, one at a time.'

'They get caught, it would be a slaughter,' Sasha said. 'At least one gun in the inn,' she pointed at the Golden Crown Inn, overlooking the marshlands. 'One or two more in the town, moved daily. That just seems too risky.'

Jane nodded. 'The third plan is to land troops using the naval regiment. Caesar and Faro both like this plan. It lands sixty troops in Walker, either in the town itself, or on the field between the town and the cathedral. Then successive waves come in.'

Sasha moved around the table to look. 'Sixty troops isn't a lot,' she said. 'How long would each wave have to wait before the next one arrives?'

'Forty-five minutes to an hour,' Jane replied. 'The issue is marshaling troops where the boats and come and get them without exposing them to danger. Moving laterally across the town front is too risky.'

'What about landing troops directly into the town, moving back and forth across this little stretch of water? It would be quicker than moving all the way around, isn't it?'

'Commander Faro looked at that idea,' Jane said. 'The problem is that landing area has been heavily fortified, and the water around it isn't great for moving boats across. There's a reason the dock was place further east along the shoreline than that.'

'So, then they land at the docks,' Sasha said, 'which puts them immediately into a city fight. Or, they land on the field, which has them under machine guns from the Bishop's Gate and the town, and possibly the castle.

'The castle is a bit far,' Jane pointed out.

'The castle guns are the big ones,' Sasha pointed out, 'the water-cooled machine guns with a range of more than a mile. Aiming will be poor, but they can still hurt the landing force.'

Sasha looked at the map, then stepped around to the east side.

'No one wants to land here?' she asked.

Sasha was looking at the cathedral's terraces. A short one at the cathedral's main level, a larger patio below, then a gentle garden leading to a steep decline to the waterline.

'No,' Jane said. 'It's a very small landing area, with defenders sighted immediately in their way. One machine gun,' she pointed to the marker on the top terrace, 'on the cathedral itself. Troops in the cathedral, maybe even on the cathedral. And the redoubt can fire on any boats moving across the lake.

'Hm,' Sasha said, still staring at the cathedral.

Jane looked at her. 'What are you thinking?'

378

Sasha looked up. 'All the plans you told me about; all of them require the troops to attack at night?'

Jane nodded. 'How did you know?'

'All of them require stealth until the moment of attack. The trench and marsh plans require a final act of violence to break through the last defenses. The naval plan you could, conceivably, land several waves before being noticed, but that's unlikely if they're watching for it.'

Jane nodded. 'So?' she prodded.

'So, when you're conducting an ambush, you don't use a whistle to begin it. A whistle gives up surprise without harming the enemy. I don't want the first sign of battle to be that we are coming. I want the first sign of battle to be that we are already here.'

She gestured at the cathedral's landing. 'Land there, under darkness, and take the cathedral before anyone can respond. If they counterattack, it'll be against prepared defenses, not against troops out in the open or clinging to a small beachhead.'

Jane looked at the map alongside her. 'Sounds like a good place to start,' she opined.

Sasha rubbed her hands together, imagining attacking at night.

'If this happens,' she said, 'I have to be there.'

'Do you?' Jane asked.

Sasha nodded. 'If I'm involved in planning, I have to be involved in the execution.'

Jane nodded. 'Can I stay here?'

Sasha chuckled. 'Yes. Is there paper?'

Jane turned and pulled some from an alcove. 'What are we doing?'

'I want to write to Colonel Grace; ask her what sort of distractions she can conduct at the trenches and the marsh. I also want to write to Commander Faro and ask him about distractions and landing at the cathedral. If the water works for him, I might have my own plan.'

Jane handed her the papers. Sasha went to the writing desk in the corner and sat down.

'Also,' Sasha said. 'I'm going to need a gun.'

Chapter 42

Colonel Athena,

This letter is the official order activating the Army of the Lakes and all subordinate units.

You are hereby promoted to the rank of Brigadier, and directed to take command of the Third Division, Army of the Lakes, also known as the Renaissance Division. Your command will consist of the Second Minnesota Infantry Regiment, 'Renaissance Guards,' the Fifth Minnesota Infantry Regiment, and the Eighth Minnesota Infantry Regiment; Battery C of the Minnesota Artillery Regiment; and other subordinate units as prepared for your division by group officers.

Your point of assembly is Athens. All subordinate officers will expect to find your headquarters there as soon as is practical.

You will report to Major General Senator, Commanding Officer of the Army of the Lakes, at Camp Congress no later than Wednesday, April 8th, with status of your command.

Good luck,

General Prince

Sasha looked at the letter she had just written. She smiled at the Renaissance Guard and the Renaissance Division, though she was annoyed that Athena was being given the last of the three divisions. She glanced at Rose, finishing her letter to Colonel Moses announcing him as the commander of the Second Division, the Volunteer Division, and Bellona, finishing her letter to Colonel Birch as commander of the First Division, the Iron Division.

Apparently, Senator was exercising his influence to impact the assignments. He and Athena did not get along, so he posted her and the regiments most likely to follow her as his third division, as some sort of insult.

'He's a fool,' Rose scoffed when they were discussing it. 'Good thing Athena doesn't care. The insults Senator can give aren't severe enough to worry her. And the insults that are severe, Senator can't give without overstepping his bounds.'

'Not after Gold,' Saxon added.

'What happened with Colonel Gold?' Sasha asked. Every time the colonel had been mentioned, it had not been about his work as the officer in charge of the supplies for the Renaissance Army, but about some incident that for which he had been punished.

'Colonel Gold is an Old Guard, in the vein of Brigadier Senator,' Bellona said, choosing to not use Senator's new rank until she had to. 'He was much more vocal about his displeasure with allowing women in uniform and combat positions. He was rude and condescending to every one of them he met.'

'And a bit harassing,' Saxon grimaced. 'He made more than a few jokes at the expense of women in his command, even in their presence.'

'Shortly after the siege of Walker began,' Bellona continued, 'there was an incident at a depot. The officer in charge raped and murdered a junior officer who was a woman. There was an attempt to cover it up, but –.'

'Allegedly,' Saxon interrupted.

'Saxon,' Bellona cautioned, but Saxon continued.

'No, Bellona, we must be fair. There may have been an effort to cover it up. Hell, there probably was, but we don't know for sure.'

'In any event,' Bellona said, continuing through gritted teeth, 'the officer in question, another member of the Old Guard, was tried and executed for the crime. Then Colonel Gold was brought on charges that he had cultivated an atmosphere toxic to the running of the army.'

'That's a crime?' Sasha asked.

'It should be,' Rose replied.

'It was more nuanced than that,' Saxon said.

'The charges didn't stick,' Bellona continued, 'but the debate between Lieutenant Colonel Cicero, the Provost Marshal of the Army, and Colonel Gold was legendary. In the end, Gold was not censured or punished, but new rules were put in place anyway.'

'You have to understand,' Saxon said, 'Gold is exceptionally good at his job, but now he's watched by officers who are loyal to Prince, not to Senator.'

Sasha frowned. 'Someone from the Renaissance Army raped and murdered a woman?'

'No army is without its villains,' Rose said.

'I know, but still,' Sasha shook her head.

They moved on to more letters, now to the regimental colonels. Sasha wrote to Colonel Halcon, commander of the Renaissance Guard, and now Colonel Lanza, of the Eighth Regiment. Riders stood ready to move out and deliver their orders.

'Senator is moving south?' Rose asked, breaking the silence and changing the subject.

'He is,' Sasha confirmed. 'He feels the threat from there is bigger than from the north.'

'Is it?' Bellona asked.

Sasha mused for a second. Rose and Bellona had access to the same intelligence she did. They were not asking her for news, they were asking for her opinion.

'III Corps has managed to assemble less than twenty-five hundred men at Bemidji, thirty miles away. Most of his troops are fighting to keep his supply lines open, and First Field Regiment has them dancing to their tune.

'I Corps, however, has managed to pull the entire First Division to Park Rapids, plus some of their support units. That's five thousand men, twenty-five miles away. I'd have to agree, that is the bigger threat.'

'I'm surprised Colonel Wild hasn't had as big an impact,' Bellona said.

'I'm not,' Rose replied. 'Wild hasn't had as much time to interact with his county. He doesn't have the support Trumpeter has managed around Bemidji.'

'Not to mention his personality,' Saxon muttered. The women chuckled.

'He did threaten them enough to pull another brigade to supply-line duty,' Sasha pointed out. 'The other Second Division brigade is at Menahga now, protecting wagon trains. That puts Park Rapids at five thousand men, not eight thousand.'

'True,' Rose said.

'Maybe Wild will force General Vega to leave another brigade in Park Rapids,' Saxon said, pulling out another form letter. 'Then Senator will only have to fight one brigade.'

'That would be nice,' Sasha agreed.

**

All the officers shared dinner that evening. Even Lily joined them. Sasha watched her and Caesar out of the corner of her eyes. They were completely proper, no indication that they shared a romance at all.

'How goes the plan for Walker?' Prince asked.

'Lot of plans and augmentations,' Caesar responded. 'It is likely any campaign we execute will include aspects from several different operations, as the situation demands.'

'And Lieutenant Scholar has been updating those plans?' Prince asked, looking at the Templar.

'And adding her own,' Caesar said.

'Really?' Lily replied. She looked at Sasha. 'And what plan do you recommend?'

'Landing at the cathedral,' Sasha said.

'Why there?' Prince asked.

'Because the cathedral is one of our objectives, should the Renaissance Army breach the walls of Walker,' Sasha answered.

'So, you assault it first?' Lily continued the questions.

'I think we land by stealth,' Sasha said, 'at night. If we can get past, or even close to, the initial defenses before we're noticed, we have a decent chance of seizing the cathedral before they can assemble the troops to stop us. And that's assuming we don't toss in feints from the other directions to distract them.'

Prince sat back. 'Interesting concept. I must say, I'm not a huge fan of landing a force in the cathedral's shoreline. Limited amount of room to maneuver.'

'No, sir,' Sasha admitted. 'But I remember thinking the same thing about the prison camp, and you brought some toys to get around those defenses.'

Prince chuckled, followed by most of the table. 'True,' Prince admitted. Then he looked at Caesar. 'How long from Order to Execution?'

Caesar looked at Sasha. 'Seven to ten days,' she replied.

'Why the discrepancy?' Bellona asked.

'Regardless of what plan we use, it will take some time to assemble the forces we have,' Sasha replied. 'Then we have to determine our course of action, make our final preparations, and execute.'

'We have been in contact with every officer who might be involved,' Caesar said. 'They are all prepared to move within twelve hours of activation. Everything we can do to cut down the time needed is being done.'

'Do you have everything you need?' Rose asked.

'I'm using everything I have,' Sasha said. 'Give me more, and I'll use it.'

'We are departing for Bemidji County tomorrow morning,' Prince said. 'I trust you to oversee the rest of it?'

'Of course,' Caesar replied.

The dinner broke up. Bellona and Saxon moved off, talking about one thing or another. Prince left for bed, while Caesar and Lily walked towards the officer's cabins, lost in silent conversation. Sasha watched them go and hoped they had a nice night together.

Rose appeared by her side. 'I have a small bottle of wine, if you'll share this night with me.'

Sasha smiled. 'Lead the way.'

They found a spot, a small hill overlooking the fields where horses grazed. Rose opened the bottle.

'To the Templars,' she said and drank. She handed it over to Sasha.

'To the Templars,' Sasha agreed She drank. 'How is Cardinal?'

'Good,' Rose said. 'She thought about going home but decided to stay. She's found herself a good place here. She still can't sleep a full night, but she says she's getting better.'

'I hope so,' Sasha said. 'I wonder how busy Penn usually is. I mean, is he only busy for the council meetings, or does he have something to do all the time?'

'If he's not busy with council stuff, he's probably working to better himself,' Rose replied. 'He was a Templar. He may have lost his leg, but his mind is still eager to learn.'

Sasha nodded. 'Ever think about how Blaze and Swift would be doing if they were still here?'

Rose shrugged. 'Very little. The two of them were not good people, and I think they might have washed out if they hadn't found the capacity to change.'

Sasha frowned at Rose. 'Not good people? I know Blaze was an ass, but if it meant losing his commission, I think he would've changed.'

'He would have acted like he'd changed,' Rose cautioned. 'Blaze was too sure of himself to change as easily as you think. And from what we know from Elector, he was firmly in Senator's camp. He'd say what he needed to in order to graduate, then go back to a place where he could go back to who he was.'

'And,' Sasha said, 'he probably would have kept Elector from changing his

384

course to medical.'

'Probably,' Rose nodded.

'But what about Swift? You think she wasn't a good person? She was my only friend to start with.'

Rose chuckled and handed over the bottle. 'She made fun of Candle and Cardinal, called them the petty princesses? And she probably had a name for me as well.'

'She called you queen bitch, once,' Sasha admitted.

Rose nodded, unsurprised. 'To me, she called you the flailing farmer.'

'What?'

Rose continued. 'Swift was not a good person, Scholar. She may have met the four pillars of the Templars as the officers understood them, but as a Templar she spent more time tearing down her peers than she did building herself up. She tried to be everyone's friend by insulting everyone else, as the moment dictated.'

Sasha thought on that. Swift had been highly critical of the other Templars, that was true. But had it really been as bad as all that?

'You can ask the others,' Rose said, guessing her thoughts. 'She tried it with everyone.'

'Did anyone else fall for it?'

'To start with, but as the Templars continued on her attitude started to wear thin. Only Hero displayed any continued interest, but his interest wasn't in her words.'

'Hero,' Sasha scowled. 'Any idea where he went?'

'Nothing for sure,' Rose said. 'He either went west, into the Dakotas, where he can disappear, or . . .,' she stopped.

'Or he's heading south to betray us,' Sasha finished.

'He may not have had much luck within the Templars, but Hero is a fairly charismatic individual. He could easily persuade someone of importance he had information, and as a Templar he does have a lot of information to trade.'

'How do we protect against that?' Sasha asked. 'How can we protect the movement from traitors.'

'We can't,' Rose said. 'Any individual given authority is a leap of faith. We trust in the intuition of those in power, but ultimately it's all trust.'

'Fantastic,' Sasha said. She looked at the bottle. 'Only one drink left.'

'Finish it,' Rose said. She watched Sasha finish the wine. 'Maybe you're right,' she said when Sasha was done. 'Maybe Swift could have changed. Maybe Blaze could have. Hero tried and failed, but so many of us succeeded. Many of us were not at our best when we arrived at the Templars, but here we are, apprentices to generals.'

Sasha smiled. 'I'm going to miss the books when I go back to Third Regiment,' she said. 'I'll have to get used to working and not learning.'

'You'll find time for both, I think,' Rose said.

'And you? What awaits you in the Army of the True Queen?'

Rose looked at the ground, a little embarrassed. 'A letter signed by the queen. "Upon successful completion of the Templar Project, Lorelai Durant is to be released from her commission as a military officer and returned to civilian life, if she so chooses." I made them sign if before I agreed to come here.'

'You'll be released?'

Rose chuckled. 'My father is an officer for the queen. He wrote the letter and made sure to add "if she so chooses". He hoped, I think, that I might enjoy my commission. I never had any brothers, and I think that weighed on him.'

'Well,' Sasha said, 'I hope you stick around. The Army of the True Queen could sure use a Templar Officer.'

'I agree,' Rose said, 'but I have not made up my mind. Perhaps I shall stick around. Perhaps I shall not. I do not have to decide now, so why should I?'

A bell rang out across Olympia. 'Ten,' Rose said. 'We should turn in, I think.'

Sasha nodded. They started their way down the hill when recognition struck her.

'Lorelai Durant?'

Rose looked at her. 'Yes?'

'Of the Montreal Durant family? The one we've read about in class?'

If Rose blushed it was hidden by nightfall. 'Yes. Those Durants.'

'You're in line for the Throne of Quebec?'

Rose waved it off. 'Eighth, maybe. I don't pay attention to such things.'

'And your father, then? The Duke?'

'Duke, and commander of the Army of the True Queen.'
386

Sasha chuckled. 'How far we've come.'

'Yes,' Rose laughed with her. 'Stay safe?'

'As safe as I can be running right into danger.'

'To the surprise of no one. What was the other name? Bobcat?'

'Yeah,' Sasha admitted.

'Well, Bobcat-Scholar. Fight well.'

'You too, Rose. You too.'

***

'Nice shooting, L.T.,' Sergeant Pierce exclaimed. Sasha had just struck down five targets with five bursts, the first time she had taken down all the targets without needing a second shot at any of them. 'I guess you were right. The suppressor does help with the balance.'

'For me it does,' Sasha agreed. She was learning to shoot the black carbines, the weapons of the Olympians. They were ridiculously light, hard for her to get used to. Then she learned about the suppressors; they deadened the sound a little bit, but the weight made the weapon more manageable.

Pierce was the Olympian that was now in charge of her tactical training. An older veteran, he was in prime shape. They were joined by Collins, a young enthusiastic man, and Locke, a grim-faced woman who did not seem to laugh at much. The four of them were one team, to join with three other teams as the hostage platoon. Assembling and training those teams was someone else's responsibility.

Pierce had the team's equipment worked out. Each was armed with a black carbine and various tools and grenades. Locke carried a short shotgun for breaching doors – 'Get it? Locke opens doors!' Pierce laughed – and Collins a dedicated grenade launcher.

'Who knows how much fighting we will have to do to get to the hostages,' Pierce said about the grenade launcher. 'I'd rather have it and not need it than need it and not have it.'

Sasha nodded, deferring to his experience.

Caesar gave them permission to run clearing drills through Avalon, without firing their guns. Pierce tried to build comparable shooting range outside and was somewhat successful. Other times they just put on all their equipment and ran around Avalon, or up and down the stairs, getting used to the weight of it all.

'We'll get a chance to train as a whole platoon before it goes up, won't we, L.T.?' he asked.

'We will,' Sasha said. 'I don't know how much, but I'll make sure we get enough.'

'Good,' Pierce said. 'Now, let's try pistols.'

Sasha let her carbine fall, the sling catching it and holding it in front of her. She drew her pistol.

***

In Walker Town, in a small home not far from the Inn of the Two Crossed Tools, two men were conversing. One, an older man, sat at a table and watched. The other, a younger man in the jacket of a yeoman lieutenant, paced the room angrily. Finally, he turned to his elder.

'Are they joking?' Douglas Wells asked his uncle.

David shook his head. 'No.'

Douglas turned away and paced the room several times more. His uncle's calm eyes followed him back and forth.

'No,' Douglas finally said.

'No?' David asked with an amused tone. 'Really?'

'Uncle David, this is no joking matter.'

'I know, which is why I'm wondering why you're acting like a child.'

Douglas turned and rushed at the older man. 'A child! How?'

'By not looking at the bigger picture,' David said.

Douglas looked at David, and for a moment entertained the thought of punching his elder. Then he turned around. 'What did you get me into?'

'I've never gotten you into anything, Douglas.'

'Really? Enlisting before the Commonwealth War?'

'If you'll remember, I advised you to keep your government job pushing papers. You enlisted on your own.'

Douglas opened his mouth to protest but stopped. It was true. He was six months into a desk job at a government office when the Commonwealth War began, and he enlisted three months later. Two years at the front in New York with the Minnesota Expeditionary Corps, another two in a Commonwealth prison camp due to his family connections. Since then, odd jobs he could find. He even spent a few months as a yeoman, before his integrity drove him from their ranks.

It was in this desperate state that his uncle offered him money in exchange for a few odd jobs here and there. Nothing major, nothing too difficult. Carry a message here, obtain a package there. It was not until recently Douglas had realized he was secretly helping the RAM. Help that continued even after the count's yeomen conscripted him to count their supplies. Over the last year, Douglas gave the Renaissance Army important information. Now they wanted more.

'Uncle, you told me that when you are in uniform, you have to consider the morality of your actions. What they're asking me to do is wrong.'

'Is it?' David asked.

'How is it not?' Douglas demanded. 'Walker has barely survived this siege, and the fact that we've managed to get this far without losing more people than we have is amazing. If I destroy those supplies, the lives of everyone in this city is in danger.'

'The lives of everyone in this city are already in danger. We're under siege.'

'Then what am I missing, Uncle?'

'The bigger . . . .'

'. . . picture, right. Here's what I see. If I destroy the supplies, Walker will have to call for more to be airlifted in, so the siege will continue, but he'll know someone sabotaged his supplies, and a witch hunt will take place. Many people will die, perhaps the entire civilian population. Nothing will change except the number of mouths to feed. How is that not the big picture?'

'Because you're missing one question. Why now? Why would they order you to do it now?'

Douglas could not think of an answer.

'And why wait for a signal?' David continued. 'If the idea was to simply destroy the supplies, why would they tell you to wait for a final signal?'

Douglas continued to look at his uncle. 'Why?' he finally asked.

'There's a plan, something that you are an integral part of. Something that involves cutting Walker's air bridge, probably involves an attack on Walker. Something with multiple teams working together.'

'So?' Douglas asked. He was no longer defiant, but curious.

'So, your job is the start. What are you going to do? If you refused to complete your mission, the siege could continue. Perhaps hundreds of men and women will die assaulting Walker's walls, thinking you've burned their ammunition. Perhaps it will last long enough for the Royal Army to break the siege.'

'An assault on a city is a terrible waste of manpower,' Douglas said. 'I saw that at Auburn and Syracuse. An assault on Walker could kill hundreds. A thousand, maybe.'

'And if the siege continues, will that be better?' David asked. 'You mentioned how few people died this winter, but you know as well as I do how close that was to being different. How thin our medicine has been stretched; how little food is given out. The children survive because their parents sacrifice their own food. The sick survive because their loved ones pool their rations. We're on the edge of a knife, Douglas. Perhaps ending the battle now with an assault will save more lives than another three months of siege.'

'You don't know that,' Douglas growled.

'No, but I do know that there is a plan. The generals didn't send you these orders for fun. They have a plan, and you have a duty to carry it out.'

'What about morality, Uncle? I think this plan is wrong.'

'Think it's wrong all you want, but understand why you have to do this. No, you should not follow orders that require you to shoot a child or burn down a church, but there are thousands of outcomes to this action, and the generals have decided that some of them are ideal to end the campaign.'

'Shit,' Douglas said.

'I know. You've heard my stories from the Rangers, Douglas. You know some of the stuff we did against the Quebecois north of the lake. We had some shit shows, but we learned quickly which officers knew what they were doing, and which ones were just bullshitting. The generals know what they're doing.'

Douglas threw up his hands. 'Fine, but when this is done, I'm going to find whatever officer came up with this plan and give him a piece of my mind.'

Chapter 43

By Sasha's estimate, Avalon was only about two miles from Olympia, but travelling between the two directly was forbidden. Instead, she followed a six-mile route, which ended with Sasha and her escort arriving in Olympia from the far side.

She reported to Lily's headquarters, where she found the adjutant looking over a map similar to the one she saw every day in Athens.

'Any updates from General Prince?' Sasha asked.

'Nothing new,' Lily replied. 'Nor from General Senator.' She gestured to the map. 'There are only so many moves they can make before a fight will break out.'

Sasha looked at the map. Senator's army was south and east of them. Two of his divisions were just east of Park Rapids. The Third Division was further to the south, near Menahga, about six miles away from the other two. If the troops in either garrison tried to attack, Senator could move to counter.

'I know,' Sasha agreed with Lily's statement. 'We just need to wait.'

'Agreed,' Lily nodded. 'But you're not here for this.' She directed Sasha to an office, one of the small ones kept available for when it was needed. A staff sergeant was assigned as her aide for the day, and they discussed what she needed. Soon after, she found herself alone in the room, waiting for her first guest.

This is so odd, she thought to herself. She felt so important, and yet still a child. At some point, do I just turn into an adult and become used to this?

Before she could continue her thought, her first guest arrived, coming to attention before her.

'At ease, Sergeant Major,' Sasha said. Del Oso, her previous instructor, relaxed. 'Have a seat, if you will.'

'Thank you, ma'am,' Del Oso said, sitting down. 'I trust everything is going well?'

'As well as it can be, Sergeant Major. Do you know why you are here?'

'No, ma'am, I do not.'

'I'm involved in the planning of taking Walker Town,' Sasha said. 'There are lots of moving parts, but we will need someone to find and secure the

391

hostages. I have requested, and General Caesar has agreed, that I shall command that platoon.'

Del Oso nodded, following attentively.

'My duties preclude me from doing any extensive training of an entire platoon, so I need someone to build, train, and equip said platoon in my absence.'

'I see,' Del Oso said.

'Sergeant Major, I will not force you to do this. If you feel that serving under me, given that I have been under your instruction for most of my time in the Templars, would be unwise or embarrassing, say so and I will find another. I will not think less of you for it.'

Del Oso smirked. 'You are learning to speak like General Caesar does,' he said, quickly adding, 'ma'am.' Then he shook his head. 'I have no issue with it, Lieutenant.'

'Good, I'm glad to hear. Now, I'm training with some Olympians, who will be my team. You will build the rest of the platoon, three teams of four each. That's sixteen total. During the attack, our mission will be to help secure the cathedral and the hostages within. Once that is done, we may be asked to help with the rest of the assault, but our primary goal is the hostages.'

'Understood,' Del Oso said.

Sasha nodded, then handed him a folder. 'Here are some of the various plans we might be asked to conduct. Major Lance has assembled some men and women for you at Sparta, people with previous training and experience. Get your twelve together, communicate with me by correspondence through Olympia, and I will send any changes to you the same way. We will have a few days to train together before the battle begins, but for now, you'll be on your own.'

Del Oso smiled. 'Will do, Lieutenant' He stood and saluted. Sasha did as well. And she was alone again.

She spent ten minutes reading before her next meeting.

'I see you've survived so far.'

'I see you remember me, Doctor Adams,' Sasha replied.

The Bostonian doctor laughed. 'Hard to forget a youth who speaks like a veteran. And please, call me Carissa. How is everyone holding up?'

'The Templars are down to seven,' Sasha said. 'One quit, and one ran away.'

'Oh, dear,' Carissa shook her head. She sat down. 'Still, I'm not entirely surprised.'

'We were,' Sasha said. 'We thought we were all better than that.'

'For students, you are all exceptional. But you are still young,' Carissa said. 'So, what brings me to your office?'

'Some time in the next few weeks, or possibly months, we are going to forcibly end the siege of Walker.'

Carissa shook her head. 'Forcibly,' she repeated disdain.

'Yes. We hope to do so with a minimum of casualties, but the fact is we can't guarantee that. We may be looking at significantly more casualties that the siege group's medical staff can handle.'

'Right,' Carissa shook her head. 'So, you need us to be ready in case more people get hurt than you can handle.'

'Yes,' Sasha admitted.

'I can prepare a group to move to Walker, when the time comes,' Carissa said. 'If things go terribly, even that might not be enough.'

'I know,' Sasha said. 'When we receive word to start our operation, we will send you a notice. You will have forty-eight hours to move to Walker.'

'Then I should get going and prep my doctors,' Carissa said. She turned at the door. 'Where are you going to be during all this?'

'Leading the attack on Walker, most likely,' Sasha said.

'Why?'

'My entire family is in Walker,' Sasha replied. 'And if I'm going to put lives on the line to save them, it's only fitting that I put my own on the line as well.'

Carissa nodded. They spoke of details for a time before Carissa left. Sasha did not have time to open her book before the next guest came through.

'Hi,' Zac said, nervously.

'Hello, Zac. How have you been?'

'Good. Yourself?'

'Decent,' Sasha replied. 'One of the Templars ran off that evening.'

'I heard. Any idea where he ended up?'

'No, not yet, but I wonder if he'll make himself known sometime. I hope your morning was better.'

Zac turned red, and Sasha laughed. 'Don't take offense. I've been informed I am a bit prudish when it comes to romance in any form.'

'To each their own,' Zac said. 'But I take it I'm not here to get into an embarrassing conversation?'

'No. I'm here to inform you and the Civic Council, officially, that in the next few weeks we will be conducting an operation to end the siege of Walker.'

'I see,' Zac said quietly. 'I hope there's a plan in place?'

'I cannot say,' Sasha said, 'due to secrecy issues, but regardless, after we take Walker, we will need to deal with the ramifications. A significant portion of the population will ask to leave, and we will let them, but if even a small part of the population elects to stay, that could be several hundred additional civilians adding to the population. Not to mention there is the question of Walker Town itself.'

'I see,' Zac said. 'You know, some of the council wonder if it might be possible to move into Walker once it falls. Have a stable, set government in a capital.'

'That's a discussion for another time,' Sasha said. 'What I'm doing now is informing you that we may need to relocate several hundred individuals out through the liberated towns.'

Now Zac whistled. 'Several hundred? Can't they stay in Walker?'

'I hope they do, but we need to be prepared.'

'I see,' Zac repeated. 'How much time do we have?'

'I don't anticipate us starting the operation for a month, maybe more. Once it starts, though, we have ten days to finish.'

'Okay,' Zac said. 'We do have agreements with the towns and villages to accept more refugees as they come in. I'll have to start letting them know more might be expected.'

'Good.'

'Will we be hearing details of this plan?'

'Officer Penn will be acting as a liaison during the campaign. He will be briefed on the plan and, when the time comes, will be coordinating with you.'

'I see,' Zac repeated. 'Anything else?'

'Were you really trying to take me to bed that evening?'

Zac shrugged. 'I just asked you to dance. If it went further, I wasn't against the idea, but I don't talk to women only with that endgame in mind.'

'But you thought about it?'

'I did,' Zac admitted. 'Why?'

'I'm trying to open myself to the idea,' Sasha said. 'Or, at least, not completely close myself off from it. It seems something that so many people just accept as a part of life. Somehow, I missed it.'

Zac nodded. 'Well, good luck, Templar Scholar. And be careful.'

'With the war or the romance?'

'Both.'

The next guest came in, saluting.

'I don't think you have to do that,' Sasha said.

'Actually, I do,' Penn said. 'As a Warrant Office, I am one-half step below you, as a Second Lieutenant, on the officer scale. As such, you are my superior officer, even though I have been a warrant officer for seven months, and you a commissioned officer for seven days.'

'Ha,' Sasha said. 'It's been more than three weeks.' She gestured for him to sit. 'We're going to take Walker.'

'Oh, my,' Penn said.

'We don't know when or how, exactly, but sometime during the coming campaigns, Prince will give his order. When the operations begin, we're going to need you to act as liaison between the siege group and the Civil Council.'

'Sure thing.' Penn said. 'How likely is it that this operation going will occur while the Civic Council is meeting?'

'The schedule is dependent on orders from General Prince. When he gives the go-ahead, we have ten days to complete the operation. So, to answer your question, I have no clue.'

'Fair enough,' Penn said.

They spent twenty minutes discussing some of the possible plans and outcomes. Penn, though long removed from the Templar Project, had continued his education separately from the rest of them. Even as a pacifist, he grasped the military aspects quickly.

'Any questions?' Sasha asked.

'What's it like being Caesar's apprentice?' Penn asked. 'I don't know him too well, and all the people who do either love him or hate him.'

'Intense,' Sasha said with a smile. 'He's always thinking, and he's always trying to get me to think.'

'Is he succeeding?' Penn asked.

'I hope so. You tell me.'

'I say yes,' Penn smiled. He stood and saluted. 'Lieutenant Scholar.'

The next guest brought lunch.

'So,' Scott Anthony asked, 'why the hell am I here?'

'We're going to take Walker Town,' Sasha said. She went over the quick details.

'I'm not a fighter,' Scott said.

'Tell that to General Senator.'

'Okay, that was about defending my students, and,' Scott grinned, 'about punching that sanctimonious prick in the face. That's always fun. But, seriously, why am I here?'

'Once the town falls, we'll want to get things moving quickly. We don't know how many will want to stay, how many will want to leave, or even what the status of Walker will be.'

'Status of Walker? You mean you don't know how much of it will burn before you're done?' Scott shook his head. 'Don't get into the language game, Scholar. Say what you mean and mean it.'

'Okay,' Sasha said. 'When Walker falls, we want you to take over as governor of the town.'

'Me?' Scott asked.

'Yes. Anyone currently in authority in Walker is there because of the count, so we need to impose someone temporarily. The generals don't want a military officer, as they don't want to set a precedent for large population centers. Members of the Civic Council or their functionaries might get too caught up in politics, and we need someone who will cut through the bull and get things done. And once Walker falls, we will need to move a lot of moving parts very fast.'

Scott nodded. 'Can I say no?'

'Why?'

'Maybe I don't want to be a governor.'

'The appointment is only for three months,' Sasha said. She pulled the

396

appropriate document from her folders. 'One of your responsibilities would be to cultivate a replacement. How would be up to you.'

Scott looked at the document, reading every word. 'When?' he asked.

'Soon,' Sasha said.

'That's the best you can do?' Scott laughed.

'There are a lot of moving parts,' Sasha replied with a smile. 'We just don't know yet.'

'Fair enough,' Scott said, standing. 'Well, I should go practice my elocution. Also, can I get a gavel?'

Next were two young women.

'I'm not saluting,' Patch said as she came in, sticking her tongue out at Sasha.

'I will!' Cardinal said. Sasha had not seen the woman in six months, but the former Templar looked a lot less haggard than she had when she left. She was now a warrant officer, in a deep blue uniform with a pair of wings on her sleeve.

'Until Caesar told me,' Sasha said, 'I didn't even know we had an Air Group.'

'Without any planes, it's just a bunch of people sitting around, planning,' Cardinal said. 'But if and when we capture planes, we'll be ready.'

'So that's the skill you had? Piloting?' Sasha asked.

'It is. Our uncle is a man of some means, and he taught me. Never officially, of course, because of my age and gender, but I know how to fly.' Cardinal beamed.

'Good,' Sasha said. 'I'm glad to hear it.'

'You know it's not much of a surprise,' Patch said, looking up at the small office window. 'A lot of people would say it is odd for an army in a landlocked area to put resources into a navy or marine force, but the generals have done it. Planning for the long campaign. It makes sense that they would have similar forces preparing for air combat, and possibly other aspects of warfare.'

'It does, doesn't it,' Sasha agreed. 'So, both of you know why you're here?'

'We're to discuss cutting the air bridge,' Patch said. Cardinal nodded.

'Right. Cardinal, have you been paying attention to their operations?'

'I have,' Cardinal nodded. 'General Bennabi, the commander of the Royal Air Corps, is one of the most competent officers in their ranks. He had kept his planes from falling into patterns. Their approach varies in direction, speed, and grouping. The only place we know they'll be is right over Walker.'

'I was kind of hoping we could shoot them down prior to getting to Walker,' Sasha said.

'Well, that would depend on the system shooting them down,' Cardinal replied. She looked at Patch.

'We've used the guns Uncle Jacques found to build a decent anti-aircraft battery,' Patch said, now staring at a blank wall while her hands were toying with a string of beads she was pulling slowly from her pocket. 'While we lack the technology to make efficient use of the weapons, we have managed to build mounts to hold and aim them and lay out a few hundred rounds of exploding shells. When the time comes, they will be able to lay explosive rounds within a fifty-meter area at close to two kilometers.'

Sasha wrote that down, trying to remember the conversions. Cardinal leaned forward. 'One-hundred- and fifty-foot area, and up to a mile and a quarter.'

'Thanks,' Sasha said.

'The thing is,' Patch continued, 'as Cardinal said, the pilots have been varying their drops significantly. So, we cannot plan for anything except the transports being over Walker itself.'

'Which puts Walker in danger,' Sasha replied.

'Any aircraft that is shot down will not simply fall,' Patch said. 'The debris will come down in a trajectory. Depending on their direction, speed and altitude, they could fall harmlessly in the lake, or they could land in the woods.'

'Or they could land on Walker itself,' Sasha said.

'Always a possibility,' Patch said.

'But not one anyone can account for,' Cardinal continued. 'But you need to cut the air bridge, and that means Walker will be in danger.'

'So, we have to shoot at them over the town itself,' Patch finished.

'Right,' Sasha said, resigned. 'How will this work?'

'According to your correspondence, we have forty-eight hours from the go order to get to Walker,' Patch said. 'We can move and be set up within twenty-four hours of that.'

'And the air bridge itself?'

'We will have to adjust our weapons and fuses once we see what they're doing, so the first aircraft might be through unscathed while we do so, but we can hit the rest of them.'

'Great,' Sasha said. 'What would you need from the siege group?'

'Machine guns,' Patch said.

'What?' Sasha asked.

'Every transport aircraft has come escorted,' Cardinal answered.

'The battery is going to be attacked as soon as it opens fire,' Patch continued.

'Some machine guns to defend it would be nice,' Cardinal said.

'Six to twelve,' Patch finished.

'I'll see what I can do,' Sasha said. 'After outfitting the Army of the Lakes, the number of weapons remaining is low.'

'Do what you can,' Patch said, 'we'll put it to good use.'

'Right,' Sasha said. She handed them each a sheet. 'Here are notes. Correspondence can reach me through Olympia.'

'Got it,' Cardinal said. She saluted and left. Patch was still sitting there, now looking up at the ceiling.

'Is something wrong?' Sasha asked.

'I was told to wait here after Cardinal left,' Patch said.

Sasha's next question was cut short when Brigadier Lily entered the room, followed by the woodsman who brought them the plans back in January.

'Fitz?' Sasha asked.

'Aye,' Fitz said. 'Have we met?'

'Back in January,' Sasha replied. 'You braved a storm with Major Fox to bring us intelligence, then made us moose while we worked.'

'It was undercooked and over salted,' Patch said.

'Right,' Fitz said. He had a serious look on his face, much different from the boisterous grin he had worn several months earlier.

'Tell them exactly what you told Prince,' Lily said.

'I came across a fellow a few weeks ago,' Fitz said, 'named Johnny Coal. Your generals know him, had a bit o' dealin' with him before they got all rebellious. We got to talking about your Renaissance, and he mentions how he doesn't want to be around Walker if you all try to take it.

'That pricks my interest as an odd thing to say, so I get him some whiskey and press on the story. See, Johnny Coal is a smuggler, gets things for people what shouldn't have them but are willing to pay for them. So, I'm guessing he got Count Walker something he wasn't supposed to have.'

'Like what?' Sasha asked. 'Artillery? Flame throwers?'

'Chemical weapons of some sort,' Fitz said grimly.

'Oh, fuck,' Patch said, suddenly focused on Fitz.

'I went and told Prince as soon as I could,' Fitz said, 'up near Bemidji. He gave me this letter and asked me to come here.'

'Did he say how much?' Patch asked. 'What's their quality? Delivery system?'

'Didn't say much. Just that it was enough to make taking Walker painful.'

'Patch,' Lily said, 'when you get back to the Workshop, let Mobius and Doctor Moore know. They can start preparing to deal with it.'

'Right,' Patch said.

'Scholar,' Lily turned to her, holding up a letter, 'take this to General Caesar. Inside is Fitz's recounting of the conversation, and instructions from Prince.'

Sasha nodded. How will this impact the battle? she asked herself. Then she shook her head. How does this endanger the innocents inside the city?

'Get going,' Lily urged her. 'Quickly.'

***

Sasha returned to Avalon, following the circuitous route but at a faster pace. When she arrived, she found Saxon waiting for her.

'I have news,' Sasha said as Saxon led her down the stairs into Avalon.

'So do I,' Saxon replied. 'Radio message from General Senator. Enemy garrison in Menahga has thrown out a column to the east, towards where Athena and Third Division are waiting. He has given her permission to engage them tomorrow.'

'What size is the enemy column?'

'Don't know,' Saxon said. 'A battalion, about' She sighed. 'The first true battle of the Renaissance Army.'

'It won't be the last,' Sasha replied as they opened the doors into the War Room. Caesar, Payne and the sergeants stood at the map, watching the moving pieces.

400

'This is what General Senator has prepared for,' Caesar said, responding to Sasha's comment 'He has the temperament and the army to win this battle.'

I certainly hope so, Sasha thought.

'And your news?' Saxon asked.

'Count Walker may have chemical weapons,' Sasha replied. She filled them in on her conversations at Olympia.

Saxon gasped, then spat. 'Fantastic.'

'You will factor that into your plans,' Caesar said.

Sasha nodded. 'Of course.'

'Good. Then that is all we can do for now. When the battle begins, I want everyone in the War Room. We will all watch it together.'

Sasha nodded. 'As if I would be anywhere else, sir.'

Chapter 44

For a day and a half, Sasha observed a battle from afar.

The Army of the Lakes had four radios; one with General Senator and his army headquarters, and one with each of the three divisional headquarters. The regiments of each division reported to their leaders through voice and letter, and the division decided what to transmit.

In Olympia and Avalon, radio techs would listen, write the note, and run it to their superiors. Both locations were not transmitting, not giving Senator any orders at all. They were simply watching.

At Avalon, the radio techs handed their notes to one of the Olympians, who carried it to the War Room, where the officers, staff sergeants and Payne waited, moving blocks around a map of the area where the Army of the Lakes operated.

Sasha watched, listened, and most of all, chafed at not being able to do anything to help.

The battle began that morning. Athena reported the enemy's strength at one infantry battalion and an artillery battery, some eight hundred soldiers. Her division was twice that size, and Athena had chosen her plan carefully. The Royal Army advanced, unaware of the trap Athena lay before it.

Third Division met the enemy later that afternoon, laying a regiment across the road and throwing back the column's lead company. The column commander believed he was facing only a strong spoiling position and launched his first attack without artillery, relying on his battalion's heavy weapons to support his lead company. The attack lasted an hour and gained no headway, even as his artillery and other companies got involved.

An hour later, Third Division reported a flanking maneuver, using another regiment from the north to force the column south and away from its base. The column fled thirty minutes later, leaving many weapons and three howitzers behind them. Though still more than five hundred strong, the column was forced south, not west, away from its supply depot.

In Menahga, the senior officer panicked. Between dispersion companies to protect supply lines and the column Athena just shattered, his command was at a third of its nominal strength. He pulled his forces out of the city that afternoon, surrendering it without a fight and marching south. Athena quickly took the city, grabbing a significant amount of supplies and cutting the supply line to the Royal Army First Division to the north.

'A good first day's work,' Payne said.

The final report of the day listed casualties. Third Division had lost thirty-four dead, fifty-one wounded, most from their second regiment's flanking attack. They rounded up almost two hundred prisoners, many of them wounded, and counted about a hundred dead. The weapons and supplies were too numerous to mention, but Athena was already preparing them to be taken into the army's logistical pipelines.

'What will Senator do tomorrow?' Sasha asked.

Caesar gestured at the map. 'By cutting the I Corps supply line, Senator is forcing the troops in Park Rapids to march south into battle. They cannot survive for long without a stable line of support, and their general knows this.'

'He's forcing the enemy to come to him,' Sasha said.

'I hope he chose his ground carefully,' Payne said. 'He's giving up the initiative.'

'But he gains the defensive ground,' Saxon said.

'Which is more important?' Sasha asked.

No one had an answer.

***

Sasha had a hard time sleeping that night. She knew several people in the Army of the Lakes; Candle and Roland, Provost Isabelle. Elector's father. Colonel – well now Brigadier – Athena. Halcon. Sergeants from Sparta. Clerks from Athens. Some friends, some passing acquaintances.

Sasha got out of bed to find Senator made one report during the night, informing Olympia, and by extension Avalon, of his plan.

Senator's two divisions were set four miles south of Park Rapids, just east of the first lake the Royal Army would encounter when it moved south. The terrain north of him was mostly open ground, and any attacker would have limited cover. If forced to retreat, he could head east, into Hunter's Forest, or south into the lakes north of Menahga. He set the Second Division on the road, their right flank anchored on a small lake, with one regiment in reserve. His First Division was dug in on the left, along higher but more exposed terrain.

Athena's division was still at Menahga, seven miles south, watching for an attack from the south. Cavalry was scouting north, both through the fields and the few roads that led through Hunter's Forest.

Nothing was transmitted until well after dawn. A single brigade, marching in force down the main road. Scouts between the two forces fought each other for intelligence and position.

Sasha watched the blocks move and did the math in her head.

A royal infantry brigade marched with eighteen hundred men in three battalions, with forty mortars and more than a hundred machine guns of various sizes. The soldiers trained for years and were well equipped and well led. They could draw other troops from the division and corps levels, artillery and cavalry, but Senator did not mention whether they marched with any such support. He probably did not know.

The two Renaissance divisions Senator led against them held the best ground Senator could find. They were more than three thousand strong, as well trained and well equipped as the Renaissance Army could make them. They had fewer mortars and machine guns, but every soldier was in place and dug in. All they had to do was hold their ground.

The Royal Army has the training and equipment. The Army of the Lakes has the numbers and the terrain. It's going to be a real battle.

There was no word for some time, and Sasha wondered if someone had forgotten to transmit, or worse, if the radio operator had been killed, but just before 10 a.m., the First Division operator reported in. Saxon took the message and read.

'Bombardment commenced against western and central regiments. Field artillery included.'

'So, they have brought guns south,' Sasha said.

'Yes, now it's a question of how many,' Payne said. He sat on his stool, his eyes closed, imagining the battle playing out as he heard it. 'Templar Scholar, what is the complement of a Royal Army Divisional Artillery Battalion?'

'Four batteries, six guns each. Twenty-four guns total,' Sasha replied quickly.

'I think it's likely that two of their batteries came down with this brigade, and the other two are in Park Rapids,' Saxon said.

'I would amend that,' Caesar said.

'To what?' Saxon replied.

Caesar looked at Payne. 'General Payne?'

'It is likely any other artillery not currently engaged is with the other brigade,' he said.

'What's the difference?' Saxon asked.

'You presume the other brigade is still in Park Rapids,' Sasha replied quickly. Wild was watching the city, and without a radio he would not be able to warn Senator if the other troops were moving. Unless they had worked something else out. A semaphore, perhaps.

Saxon nodded in understanding. 'Well,' she said, 'Senator has his cavalry out probing the flanks. They can't get too close without being detected.'

'We hope,' Payne said.

Jane accepted another note from the radio operators. 'Second Division reports light bombardment along their line, mortars only.'

'They're going to hit the First Division in strength,' Payne said.

'Good luck,' Saxon responded, and Sasha hid a smile. Two of First Divisions' regiments were made of Old Guard, veterans of the old republic who had reason to hate the kingdom with a passion. They were not going to move easily.

'Second Division reports again, states their cavalry screen has found a lot of enemy horsemen to the east.'

'Are they screening the other brigade?' Sasha asked.

'Or trying to get us to think they are,' Saxon replied.

'Which do you think it is?' Payne asked.

Sasha looked at the map, thinking not about the situation, but about who might be leading the other side.

Lieutenant General Vega, the I Corps commander, was an aggressive and straight-forward man. If he were trying to flank with a second brigade, he would give it an adequate screen to keep Senator from finding out about it.

Major General Medina, the First Division commander, was young and known for his attempts at finesse in military exercises. He was more likely to use the cavalry as a feint, to attempt to draw off a reserve.

'If only we knew who was in charge,' Saxon said.

'But we do not know,' Caesar grimaced. 'We know Vega was in Park Rapids, but we do not know if he stayed there. We also do not know what instructions or plans he left for Medina if he left.'

'I am of the mind that Vega left Medina some specific instructions, but is leaving the execution to him,' Payne said. 'If they win, the plan was his and so goes the glory. If the plan failed, Medina executed it wrong.'

Saxon growled. 'How stupid, to play politics with responsibility.'

Payne shrugged. 'They still think the internal politics of the Royal Army are more dangerous than battle with the Renaissance Army. They'll lose that belief soon enough.'

Another report.

'First Division reporting a general attack on their line. Second Division reporting an attack on their Third Regiment at the road.'

Sasha looked up in surprise, then chuckled.

'What is it?' Saxon asked. 'Something wrong?'

'No,' Sasha said. 'Not really. I started with the Third Field Regiment. For a moment I forgot the radio was talking about the Third Infantry Regiment.'

'Confusing, eh?' Saxon managed a smile. 'I know. That's why I say all the regiments should have their own names. Keep the numbers but use named to avoid confusion.'

'I like that idea,' Sasha said. 'Snow's Liberators.'

'The Blizzard,' Saxon chuckled.

'Field regiments were not supposed to be field regiments,' Caesar said. The women looked at him. 'When we developed the concept, they were County Renaissance Groups; the cadre of officers and enlisted personnel who went into a county and slowly turned it against the nobility. We wanted the name to be nebulous, so it was not obvious what they were doing.'

'So, what happened?' Sasha asked.

'General Senator happened,' he replied. 'He took issue with using the term "group". He wanted to use a recognizable military unit. I argued against it; particularly that the word "regiment" calls to mind a homogeneous formation, and not the elastic and reactive unit that I wanted them to be. However, General Prince decided to follow General Senator's recommendation.'

'Why?' Payne asked.

'General Senator had lost a few debates against me and was growing increasingly agitated. General Prince felt that giving him a victory would placate him.'

'Okay,' Payne said. He paused, then, 'If I can ask, since you're here, how is

406

it the word "field" became synonymous with light infantry warfare?'

'That was not a decision on our part,' Caesar answered. 'When a sergeant was trying to gather recruits from a village, someone asked him about the difference between light and standard infantry. I do not know exactly what he said, but it became parlance among the population to describe light formations as "Field Infantry," and standard infantry as "Battle Infantry". The name stuck for field regiments, but we have managed to avoid calling our infantry formations battle infantry.'

Another report. Sasha read this one. 'Senator's command reports an air raid just struck near where his radios were operating from.'

'They triangulated the position,' Caesar mused. 'I wonder if they approached slowly for that purpose, to give themselves a chance to bomb our transmitters.'

'Good thing they're ordered to move every hour,' Saxon said.

'We may have to change that in the future,' Payne said.

Saxon took the next note. 'Second Division reports an enemy formation is in fact moving via side roads to the east of the highway, near Webley's Crossing. Infantry and artillery sighted.'

'Shit,' Payne said. A staff sergeant placed a red block on the map.

'Eighteen hundred men,' Saxon said. 'Probably more.'

'If they scraped every soldier out of Park Rapids, yes,' Payne said.

Sasha stared at the map. Webley's Crossing was a farmhouse set on the shores of the long lake. Three roads ran from the crossing; north towards Park Rapids, south towards Menahga, and west back to the highway through Hunter's Forest. If the Royal Army seized the crossing, they could flank Senator out of his position, or move south and retake Menahga. Or both, if they brought enough soldiers.

'It was always his plan to disengage if he had to, right?' Sasha asked.

'Yes. But disengaging from an enemy assault can result in a rout,' Payne replied. 'His best bet is to push back what he's already facing and use the first lull to move south, into the trees and the lakes.'

'Shit,' Saxon said. Another note came in. 'Senator is ordering Athena to move her division north in support of Second Division.'

'She's seven miles away,' Sasha said. 'They're two and a half. She's got better roads than the enemy brigade, but I doubt that'll make up for the distance.'

'Shit,' Saxon said again. Sasha understood. Caesar had said it himself; this battle could make or break the rebellion. Up until today, the Royal Army had been content to follow the Renaissance Army's plans. And now it could all fall apart in one day.

'What happens if the Army of the Lakes fails?' Sasha asked.

'They fall back into Walker and we try to pull the same stunt on I Corps we did on Montessori,' Payne said. 'Split it up, smash its parts as they separate.'

'Not ideal, to fight across the liberated territory,' Saxon said. 'Prince promised to keep the war as far away from them as he could.'

'It may be closer than he'd like,' Payne said.

Caesar said nothing, staring at the map. Sasha wondered if he could find a solution. She certainly could not see one.

Another note. Sasha found herself closest to the door. When the sergeant handed it to her, he smiled.

Sasha took the note and read it. Too excited to be embarrassed, Sasha giggled.

'What?' Payne said. Saxon and Caesar looked at her.

'Report from Brigadier Athena; she started her advanced north with her Second and Fifth Regiments two hours ago and is currently one mile south of the crossing.'

The officers looked at her in stunned silence. The staff sergeants hurriedly moved the blocks: two regiments now sat just south of the crossing, almost as close as the Royal Army was.

'Holy shit,' Saxon said with a grin.

'Athena's still outnumbered,' Payne said, 'two to one.'

'But she has excellent defensive terrain, and possibly the element of surprise,' Caesar said. The farmhouse set at the crossroads, surrounded by a few hundred yards of farmlands cut into the forest. If Athena could make it there first, she'd have the advantage.

'It will still be a hard fight,' Saxon said. Sasha knew the aide was doing her duty in keeping the generals grounded, but she heard how hard it was for Saxon to avoid her excitement. She wanted to be optimistic.

'It will we be a hard fight,' Sasha agreed. 'But it is far from decided.'

They anxiously awaited the next note. This one from Athena. 'A company of Renaissance Guards has advanced and occupied the Webley farm. The rest

408

are moving up to support,' Saxon read.

'How long would it take for the flanking brigade to move to another route?' Sasha asked.

'Two or three hours,' Payne said, 'if they stick to roads. If they give up their artillery and heavy machine guns, they could turn east and head through the forest. But that'll even the odds a lot.'

'So, they'll have to take the farm,' Saxon said.

'And that'll take time. Enough for Senator to win at the road,' Sasha finished.

Another note. Saxon took this one. 'Senator sent a message to Athena asking how it is that she expects to defeat a brigade that outnumbers her. Athena replied she's,' Saxon paused, then whistled, 'she's loaded the Renaissance Guards with every heavy weapon she took from the fight yesterday.'

'That's a lot of weapons,' Payne said. 'Where's the rest of the guard?'

'We don't know,' Sasha said. 'Athena hasn't transmitted their position.'

'Can't fit all of them in the farmstead,' Saxon said.

'No, nor would we want them to go there,' Caesar commented. 'The rest of Athena's division needs to be in position to move if the brigade shifts. They are most likely in the forest, staying hidden until they can be effective.'

Saxon stayed by the door to read the reports. 'Athena reports the enemy is attacking the farmhouse with two companies.'

'No bombardment?' asked Caesar.

'Maybe they don't think they need to? Maybe they're in a hurry?' Payne replied.

'If so, they're about to get bloodied,' Sasha said. She looked at the spot on the map where less than one hundred Renaissance Army soldiers were currently being attacked by almost four times their numbers. The hastily painted spot represented a farmstead that now acted as a fort. The inches of blank parchment represented hundreds of yards of open fields. If Athena had given that company as many weapons as she could, it was going to cut that first attack to pieces.

There were no more reports for half an hour. Sasha looked at the map, trying to imagine what was going on. *Were the lines holding? Was the farmhouse?*

Finally, two notes were delivered. 'First Division reports it has repulsed enemy attack; they're falling back and skirmishing. Second Division still skirmishing,' Sasha read. Then she switched to the second note. 'Third Division reports enemy is bombarding the farmhouse.'

'That farmhouse is empty, isn't it?' Payne asked.

'General Senator was ordered to warn the civilians something was coming, but I don't know that they were informed. Or, if they were informed, that they

left.' Saxon shrugged.

'Pretty cavalier attitude about civilians in danger,' Payne said.

'We can't stop every campaign every time we put someone in danger who shouldn't be,' Saxon retorted. 'We can do everything we can to minimize such things, and we should, but there is still a limit.'

Payne frowned. 'I know,' he said after a moment, 'and I agree.'

For an hour they watched and waited, listening to more communiques. Another attack on the farmhouse was repulsed, and an attempt to turn Birch's western flank was thwarted by the First Division.

'They've got to be low on ordnance and ammo,' Saxon said.

'So is Senator,' Payne replied.

'So, what now?' Sasha asked.

'Senator attacks, probably,' Payne said.

'Really?' Sasha asked.

'The main thrust has worn itself out on his defenses,' Caesar said. 'General Senator is an aggressive general; he is going to attack to clear the battlefield and destroy as much of their combat power as he can. The question is where.'

'He'll use his First Division,' Payne said. 'His best troops are there.'

'Moses' division is full of defected regulars,' Saxon said, 'they're capable of fighting, and they have one regiment in reserve.'

'And if he turns them with Second Division,' Sasha added, 'he'll push the two brigades away from each other.'

'I know, but Senator wants the glory for his First Division,' Payne said.

'So, is Senator the type of man to do what's best for the army as a whole? Or will he select another course just to give the glory to who he wants it to go to?' Saxon asked.

Caesar said nothing, but Sasha thought he looked worried. It was hard to believe the father of Elector could be so selfish as to risk defeat for glory, but she had to admit, she was worried too. Elector had never said much to make
410

her think he was not that kind of general.

There was another stretch with no communications. Finally, another message came down. 'Athena reports she's holding, requests update from Senator. He replies he's pushing the enemy off the field,' Saxon read.

'But not how?' Sasha asked, unnecessarily.

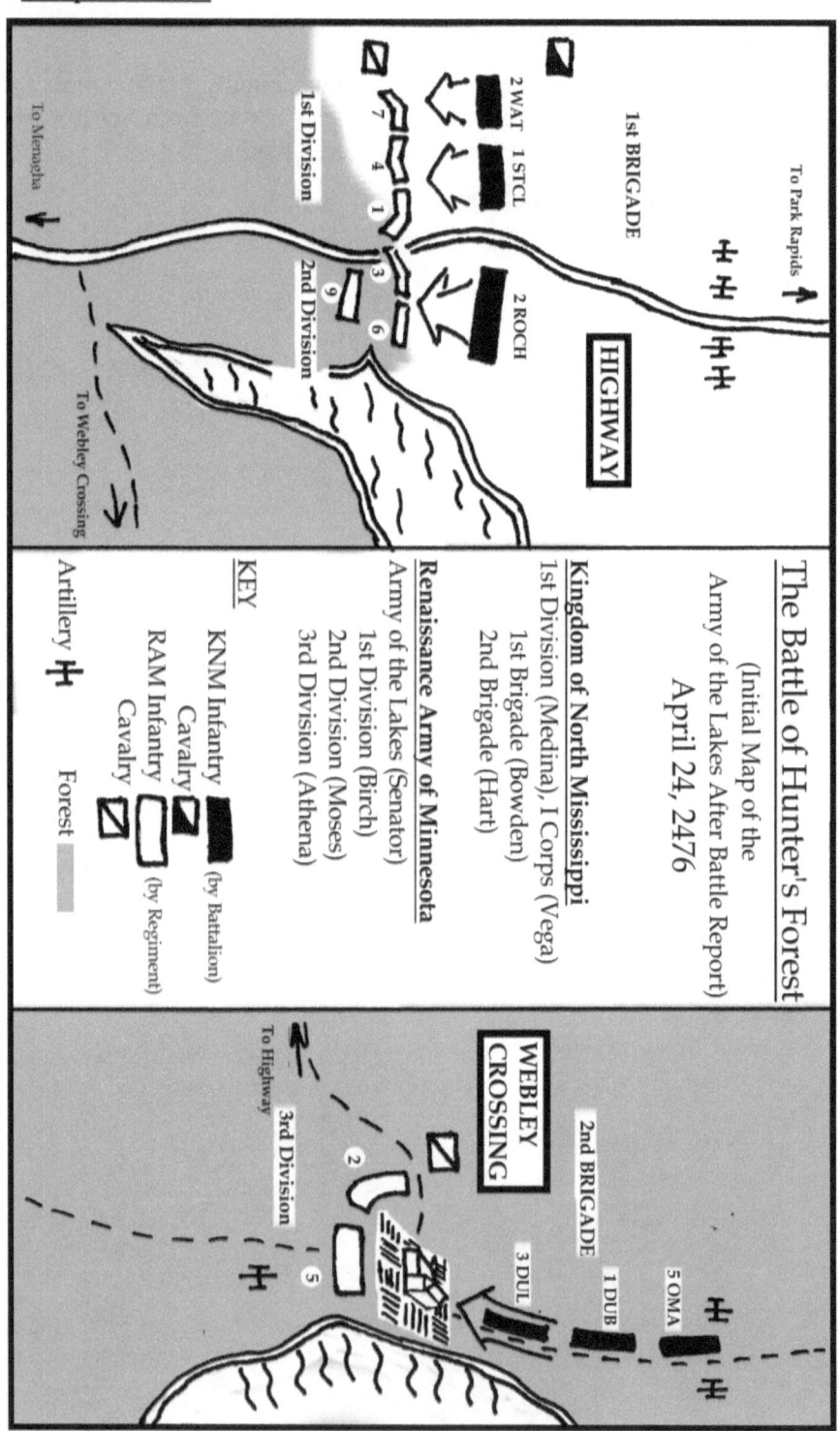

The Battle of Hunter's Forest
(Initial Map of the
Army of the Lakes After Battle Report)
April 24, 2476

Kingdom of North Mississippi
1st Division (Medina), I Corps (Vega)
1st Brigade (Bowden)
2nd Brigade (Hart)

Renaissance Army of Minnesota
Army of the Lakes (Senator)
1st Division (Birch)
2nd Division (Moses)
3rd Division (Athena)

KEY

KNM Infantry
Cavalry
(by Battalion)
RAM Infantry
Cavalry
(by Regiment)

Artillery   Forest

1st BRIGADE
2 WAT
1 STCL
2 ROCH
HIGHWAY
1st Division
2nd Division
7
4
1
3
9
6
To Park Rapids
To Menagha
To Webley Crossing

WEBLEY
CROSSING
2nd BRIGADE
3 DUL
1 DUB
5 OMA
3rd Division
2
5
To Highway

'No,' Saxon confirmed.

Sasha examined the map and the blocks. If Senator attacked with his right, he could force his opposition west into the open grounds and away from the other brigade. She could see it, and she was a seventeen-year-old trainee.

Another message. 'Second Division has swept their opponent west.'

There was a sigh of relief. Senator had made the right choice, using the Second Division for his attack and pushing the two royal brigades apart.

Reports came more frequently for a while. Senator's success was pushing his brigade north and west had started to crumble the opposition's morale, and their gradual retreat turned into a rout. Senator kept the pressure up until his enemy was running back to Park Rapids but did not allow them to get too far ahead, instead keeping them close to their defensive positions.

Athena reported one last attack on her position, then reported that the enemy was falling back. She positioned her troops to defend the crossroads and sent scouts to monitor the enemy but did not pursue.

'A win,' Payne said.

'A win,' Caesar agreed.

'Thank God,' Sasha said.

'Saxon, Scholar,' Caesar said. 'Go eat something. Take a nap. Take a few hours off. Payne and I must discuss some things in private.'

The two women nodded and left.

'That was close,' Sasha said to Saxon.

'It was,' Saxon agreed.

'I was frustrated that I couldn't do anything to influence the battle,' Sasha said.

'I know, I was, too.' Saxon shrugged. 'We can't all be generals, yet.'

Sasha nodded, suddenly realizing how hungry she was. 'Sandwiches?'

'God, yes,' Saxon said.

***

The last footnote to the battle occurred a few days later, when the courier from Olympia brought the casualty lists from the Army of the Lakes. Senator included the list with his official report, the detailed entries an example that Senator, for all his faults, understood the sacrifices his soldiers made.

413

Templar Scholar

Almost three hundred men and women of the Renaissance Army died that day, and another five hundred were wounded to one degree or another. A tremendous number that stressed the significance of their victory.

The list was a book in and of itself. Two days of fighting cost the Army of the Lakes a quarter of its troops. Sasha knew many of the wounded would be back with their units soon. There was a reason Aristotle received so many recruits; the Renaissance Army wanted to keep its troops healthy.

Sasha was hesitant to check, but she made herself look through, read every name, hoping to find no one familiar. She thought of everyone she knew in the Army of the Lakes. Senator and Moses. Athena and Halcon. Her fellow Templars, Candle and Roland. Angela and the other clerks from Athens. Kayla, Maxwell and the other instructors from Sparta. So many times, she stopped, looking at a name and wondering if it was someone she knew, someone half remembered from a chance encounter or a single meal.

She only found one she was sure of.

Second Lieutenant Roland, Second Minnesota Infantry Regiment 'Renaissance Guard', Killed in Action at Webley Farm, Thursday, 23 April 2476.

Chapter 45

'Defeat?'

The word hung in the silence of Prince Stefan's office. Even Miklos, standing in the back, cringed at the word.

Prince Stefan turned and looked at the assembled officers. His face was grim but resolved.

'Not defeat,' Stefan said. 'We are set back, to be sure. But Tempest is not defeated. No plan survives contact with the enemy. This plan is no different.'

One of the officers cleared his throat. It was a colonel attached to King Xavier's staff. 'My Lord, King Xavier does not want platitudes. He asked me for details, sir, and I must ask you.'

It said something of Prince Stefan's professionalism that he did not crush the man before him. Miklos thought he might, being his superior in both rank and social position, but such a move could prove devastating to the cohesion of his staff. An officer who lashes out loses effectiveness.

'Tell my father that I am unsurprised the Renaissance Army has conducted their operations in cities where soft District Officers cower in barracks and refuse to take the field. If those . . . gentlemen had taken their orders seriously, I Corps would have been strong enough to defeat this Army of the Lakes. And I intend to take full accounting of their failures once this campaign is concluded.'

The officer opened his mouth to speak, but Prince Stefan talked over him.

'I Corps is regrouping, as it must after the last few days. So must the Army of the Lakes. Each formation must be wary of each other and cannot leave the other behind. If the Army of the Lakes retreats to deal with another threat, I Corps will advance. Which is why Tempest had two hammers aimed at Walker.'

'III Corps is not faring too greatly,' one of Stefan's staff officers said.

'Not at the moment, no,' Stefan agreed. 'Losing half its strength to guard supply lines that should be the responsibility of District Troops has hurt the offensive, and III Corps is conducting aggressive operations against the enemy regardless. Tell my father the RAM forces around Bemidji cannot sustain the offensive as long as III Corps can.'

'Is that true?' someone asked.

Stefan shrugged. 'The evidence isn't conclusive at the moment, so we're putting a gilded cloak on it to get the king's support. Politics,' he said with disdain.

Another officer spoke. 'My Lord, could we not also point out that the troops diverted to protect supply lines are largely untouched, and if District Troops can make it to their assigned positions, represent a significant increase in combat power for both corps involved?'

Stefan snapped his fingers. 'Good idea, George. I'm stealing it.'

The officers laughed. Miklos hid a smile. He'd seen commands run themselves down after such defeats, too focused on what happened and not on what happens next. Stefan would not let his command suffer that face.

'Can we get any further troops released?' another officer asked.

'Not likely,' Stefan said. 'The King was very firm on that point. II and IV Corps are to remain in Saint Cloud for the time being.'

'Sir,' Stefan's chief of staff said, 'we can't just send King Xavier a list of people we want him to kick in the ass and get moving. He's expecting the colonel here to return with grand plans.'

'This is not a time for grand plans,' Stefan said.

'But will the king know that?'

Stefan chuckled. 'Good point.' He cleared his throat and looked at the desk for a moment.

'Colonel, tell King Xavier that Tempest is still in operation. Any District Troops he can kick out of their warm barracks and into the field will greatly increase its chances to succeed, particularly if we can send I Corps reinforcements that the Army of the Lakes cannot hope to match.

'In the meantime, we are sending supplies and personnel to I Corps to bolster it for future battles. So long as it remains a viable threat to the Army of the Lakes, that army cannot move from its position to threaten III Corps.'

'And what about III Corps, My Lord?' the colonel asked.

'As we stated, III Corps was much more impacted by the failure of the District Troops than I Corps was. III Corps has been conducting aggressive operations against RAM field forces and is in a good position to strike towards Walker and relieve the siege. With the Army of the Lakes tied up against I Corps, they have a good chance of succeeding. In fact, George, put that in a letter to Van Kalvin. A flying column could make it in two days.'

'Bemidji is about as far away from Walker as the Army of the Lakes is,' someone pointed out.

Stefan nodded. 'Prepare a note for Vega. I want him prepared to launch an attack if necessary, to keep the Army of the Lakes from moving back to Walker.'

'Without reinforcements to back it up, General Vega won't like that.'

'He's a lieutenant general, he'll figure it out,' Stefan said. He looked at the map before him, the blocks placed about it. 'That's all for now, gentlemen. If everyone except Colonel Miklos will clear the room, please.'

As ordered, everyone else left. Miklos, under no authority to stay, chose to do so. He sat before Stefan, expecting him to outline his reasons why he was not responsible for the campaign so far, with the expectation that Miklos would forward those reasons to the margrave.

Instead . . . .

'Is the Imperial Commonwealth fermenting rebellion in my father's kingdom?' Stefan asked.

Miklos was momentarily stunned. 'No,' he finally said.

'Is it not?' Stefan asked. He looked at Miklos levelling across the desk. 'An army, three thousand strong, supplied and equipped, trained and led, far beyond what peasants in the woods should be capable of. Encoded radio communications. Precision strikes in a dozen cities that intimidate nobles and generals to stay at home. Correct me if I'm wrong, but didn't the Imperial Commonwealth conquer a dozen nations like that.'

'We did,' Miklos said, 'and yes, I was a part of several of those campaigns. But this is not our doing.'

Stefan considered him for a moment. 'The Old Guard lost too much during the Range Riot to put this together. They must have outside help. If not the Commonwealth, then who?'

Miklos said nothing. There was not much he could say. The Commonwealth system kept the peace by keeping neighbors wary of each other, lest one get more powerful than the others. North Mississippi was known to be smuggling weapons to Wisconsin independence movements and Ohio Valley rebels, to keep their neighbors from consolidating those areas. Undoubtedly, those neighbors were returning the favor.

'I do not know, My Lord,' Miklos finally answered.

'And if you did know, you wouldn't tell me,' Stefan continued. 'I didn't

417

expect you would. I understand how this works, but I tend to believe you honestly don't know. Otherwise, you wouldn't have been making such a big show last year of investigating what Robinson wasn't asking.'

Miklos inclined his head in a nod.

'They knew how to hit Tempest,' Stefan said. 'They knew how to derail it without too much effort on their part. That's not a coincidence, Colonel. They have to have an intelligence network operating in the Royal Cities.'

'Undoubtedly, My Lord,' Miklos agreed.

'Lavern is working on it,' Stefan continued, 'but I hope that you'll let me know what you find, if you find anything that you are allowed to turn over to us.'

Miklos thought for a moment. General Lavern was the inspector general of the kingdom, the man responsible for security operations, intelligence matters, and various high-level prisons across the kingdom. He was a competent man, if a sadist. He was also firmly in Marshal Robinsons' camp, and a political enemy of Prince Stefan.

'If I find anything,' Miklos said. 'And what will you do?'

'Issue orders,' Stefan said. 'Tour the front. Give inspirational speeches. Maybe I can kick Van Kalvin into relieving Walker, or Vega into taking on the Army of the Lakes again. Or maybe even convince my father to release what's left of the Field Army. That would end this right quick.'

'It would,' Miklos agreed. 'Is it likely?'

Stefan looked at him, signed and shook his head.

'No,' he finally said. 'Speeches it is.'

Chapter 46

After the battle of Hunter's Forest, the focus of Avalon became Walker Town. The officers still read the reports and moved the models for the various units deployed in the field, but they all knew that taking Walker was the next step. With the warning of the chemical weapons, a potentially very dangerous step.

Word came from Patch that the Workshop was sending a team to deal with the chemical weapons. Even Caesar paused to think about what sort of team they might have assembled, but he knew of nothing. 'We gave them the Workshop because they can answer questions no one else can. It would be unfair to question them now, after all they have done.'

'But we still don't have a plan!' Sasha groaned.

The officers stood around the map of Walker. It was unchanged, despite the violence happening elsewhere in their war.

'You still think the cathedral is the way to go?' Payne asked.

'I do,' Sasha said.

'Through stealth?'

Sasha nodded. 'I think it's the best way. The cathedral allows us to land without –.'

'I know your arguments, Lieutenant,' Payne cut her off, 'and to be frank, I'm not entirely against them. It's not a great place to land, but then again, none of them are. Given what little we have to work with, there aren't a lot of good options. Landing by stealth, and taking the hostages first thing, is growing on me as an option. And it's growing on him, too,' Payne finished, nodding at Caesar.

'Sir?' Sasha asked.

Caesar looked at her levelly. 'I am not convinced' he said, 'but I feel that you are making better progress on this plan than others are making on theirs. That being said, there are many factors that we do not yet know. Will the Army of the Lakes be in the area when we are tasked to take Walker? Will more reinforcements be dropped in to man the defenses?' Caesar shrugged.

'Not to mention the big question,' Saxon said. She gestured at the map. 'Where are the chemical weapons? If they exist, taking them out might be first priority. Maybe even before securing the hostages.'

'Do we have any intelligence on that?' Caesar asked.

'We sent a letter to Colonel Grace,' Sasha replied, 'asking her to look into it. If her contacts within Walker can find out where the weapons are, that will help immensely.'

'Good,' Caesar said. 'Have you been keeping up all the alternative plans?'

'Yes, sir,' Sasha said, though she still found all of them to be inferior to her own.

'Give them to me,' Caesar said. 'I want to give them all a thorough inspection this evening. Tomorrow, we should plan on gaming out a few scenarios.'

The other officers around the table nodded. Jane pulled the files and handed them off. Caesar left the room, carrying all the files with him.

Payne looked at the map, then up at Sasha.

'You still want to lead a platoon into this?' he asked. 'You could easily use your position to get out of it.'

'I'm a Templar, General Payne. It's my nature to run into danger.'

Payne chuckled. 'Okay, then,' he said, and left.

Saxon and Jane both stepped forward. The three women stared at the map.

'You ready for this?' Saxon asked.

'Me? Why wouldn't I be?' Sasha responded.

'There's a lot that can go wrong,' Saxon said. 'And if it goes too wrong, you'll be stuck there.'

Sasha nodded. 'That's why I have to be there,' she said.

'Because you're a Templar?' Jane asked.

'Because I'm responsible,' Sasha replied. 'One way or another, it's on me.'

'Assuming they go with your plan,' Saxon pointed out.

They will, Sasha thought. It was clear to her. Soon it would be clear to them all.

***

The letter came.

It was in Rose's handwriting, but Prince's words. It described the campaign
420

of the First Field Regiment and the uprising that was spreading across Bemidji County. Having lost half its strength to garrison the Red River Valley, the remaining division was forced to spend much of its strength defending the railroad and the supplies. The possibility of an offensive from the north dwindled.

Prince ended it with the sentence Sasha had been anticipating.

'Move on Walker and capture with all haste.'

The orders were already written; Caesar simply put his signature to them and sent them out. Payne hosted one last meal before they left, trying to avoid the worry in the eyes of those who would be staying in Avalon.

Caesar led Saxon, Sasha, and a handful of Olympians out of Avalon early in the morning, reaching Walker by mid-afternoon. A warrant officer and escort waited for them just outside the siege camp.

'General Caesar?' the young man asked. 'I'm Staff Officer Atlas, Colonel Grace's adjutant. She requested I meet you and direct you to your headquarters.'

'I have a headquarters here?' Caesar asked.

'After General Prince's last visit, Colonel Grace had a second headquarters established to allow a general and his staff to be a part of the organization without interfering with her own staff's work.' Atlas turned and led them on their way, the general and his entourage following.

During their ride, cresting a hill, Sasha instinctually looked right and caught her first sight of Walker Town, with the cathedral's bell tower and the castle's high keep visible through the trees. They stood more than a mile away, but Sasha suddenly became nervous.

My family is still in there, she thought.

They approached the headquarters, nestled in the forests south of Walker Town. Several lean-tos and tents were up, along with small wood cabins, built within the trees. The rifles standing guard wore a mixture of clothes, with only a green sash across their bodies to signify they were on duty.

'What's with the sashes?' Saxon asked.

'Colonel Grace likes to rotate headquarter guards every two weeks. Those on duty wear the sash,' Atlas said. 'That way, they can keep the uniforms they're comfortable in, and get away from their trenches for a short time.'

'Interesting,' Saxon said. Sasha made a note of that.

The riders dismounted, handing off their horses to be cared for, then they followed Atlas to an open hut. 'This is your HQ,' he said. It was a simple roof, fifteen feet by ten feet, with two small tables and some chairs. Though there were no walls, there were some heavy curtains they could drop for some privacy.

Atlas gestured to a small cabin nearby, only ten feet to a side. 'That's for the general. The staff will have to sleep under tents.'

'Wouldn't be the first time,' Sasha said. Saxon looked less than pleased.

'If you want to leave your bags here,' Atlas suggested, 'Colonel Grace would like to officially welcome you.'

Caesar nodded, and Atlas led them through the encampment. Several of the Olympians followed; the rest took up guard at the cabin and the hut.

Grace's headquarters were a similar hut, with curtains swept to the side to show a pair of people standing around a table. Atlas cleared his throat. 'General Caesar, ma'am.'

The two figures turned and came to attention. One was Colonel Grace, a woman who Sasha realized was easily still in her twenties, with raven-black curly hair swept back into a ponytail, wearing a simple but clean dark brown uniform. She stepped forward and saluted, and Sasha turned her eyes quickly to the other figure, the taller man with one arm.

Captain Saber.

'General Caesar,' Grace began, 'welcome to the Walker Siege Group. You've met my adjutant, Officer Atlas. And this is Captain Saber, commander of my infantry battalion.'

Caesar nodded. 'This is Officer Saxon, my aide-de-camp, and this is Lieutenant Scholar, my apprentice.'

Sasha watched the three officers opposite the table look at her, but she was only interested in Saber's response. When his eyes reached her, they widened in surprise, and he smiled.

A friend, I think.

'Thank you for hosting us,' Caesar said.

Grace shrugged. 'I must say, while I like the idea of ending the siege, I worry that we're rushing things.'

'Normally I would agree, but if Prince's warning is accurate, we can't stand to wait.'

'What warning is that?' Saber asked. Grace nodded at Caesar, who faced

Saber.

'General Prince came into intelligence in Brainerd County that someone transported to Count Walker some form of chemical munitions.'

'What?' Atlas exclaimed. Saber grimaced but was silent.

'As such, under the direction of General Prince, we've come to end the siege,' Caesar finished.

'Any thoughts on how?' Grace asked. She shrugged. 'I'm not against ending the siege, but with hostages and now chemical weapons in play, I'm even more hesitant to push anything. My siege group has the defenders tied up and can apply pressure, but I doubt they can assault the town as it is. A position I've mentioned in several letters over the last few months.'

'Believe me, Colonel Grace, it is not our intention to force a confrontation without being prepared.' Caesar turned to Sasha. 'Lieutenant?'

'Prior to leaving Olympia, we sent out letters directing reinforcements to converge on Walker, somewhat in excess of two hundred souls.'

Grace and her officers blinked in surprise.

'Anything special?' Grace asked.

'The Naval Group and its Marine Company will be making their way towards Agency Bay. The Workshop is sending an air battery and a team who can work with the chemical weapons. A squad of Chosen Rifles, a team to secure the hostage, and a company left over from the Army of the Lakes will all be here within two days.'

'And then we figure out what to do with them?' Grace asked.

'We have a number of plans,' Caesar said. 'But there are many questions we will need answered before we can make a decision.'

'Well, I do have one answer for you,' Grace said. She nodded at Atlas, who moved around the hut, letting the curtains down. Once they were all down, she continued.

'We got word to our contacts within Walker, asked them about the chemicals. Got a reply back yesterday.'

'Took them long enough,' Saxon said, but Grace shook her head.

'Getting messages in and out of the town isn't easy, Officer Saxon. They had to wait for the timing to be right, to avoid getting captured and killed. But it was worth the wait.' Grace turned to Caesar. 'General, our sources in Walker believe that there are some two dozen chemical munitions and Count Walker has them stored in the cathedral, with the intent of harming the hostages should it come to that.'

Caesar looked at Grace levelly, considering what she said. Then he looked down at the table, with the map spread out. Sasha watched him thinking. *Is that what I look like? I hope so.*

'Do we have a plan?' Atlas finally asked.

'We do,' Caesar replied. 'We are going to cut the air bridge and ask for a surrender. Failing that, we shall take the cathedral by force via a naval landing.'

Sasha realized she was holding her breath and let it out. Saxon failed to hide a smile.

'I thought a cathedral landing had been ruled out,' Grace said.

'It had been, for us. But Lieutenant Scholar here came at it from a new angle, believing that landing covertly and taking the cathedral before the enemy can react would remove the hostages from their control. With the added threat of chemical weapons, the value of the cathedral, and therefore her plan, has increased.'

'Lieutenant Scholar?' Grace asked, looking at Sasha. Sasha met her gaze and saw the same whirlwind of thoughts in her eyes that she found in Caesar's.

What can I do to think like that? she asked herself.

Grace make a clucking sound. 'A Templar,' she finally said.

'Indeed,' Caesar confirmed.

'Then you knew Roland?' she asked sadly.

Sasha nodded. 'Yes, ma'am. I heard him compose many poems over our months as classmates.'

'I really did like him,' Grace said. 'I expected he would do great things as a Templar.'

'He did do great things, Colonel,' Sasha said.

'You know details of his death?' Grace asked. 'I would like to know more. After dinner, can you enlighten me?'

Sasha nodded. She had penned a letter to Candle asking for details, but before she could send it, a long and detailed series of letters came in from General Senator and other officers involved in the battle. Lily forwarded them to her attention, and she read through all of them to learn as much as she could about the Templar's death.

'We should also start going over the plan,' Saxon said.

'Yes, of course,' Grace said. 'But first, out of curiosity, who was your sponsor, Templar Scholar?'

'Lieutenant Colonel Snow, Third Field Regiment.'

Grace smiled and turned to Saber. 'Does that mean you know her?' she asked.

'I do. She was the first civilian to join Colonel Snow and become a rifle. Then she cut off my arm.'

'Really?' Grace asked with an evil grin. Atlas looked shocked, while Saxon barked a laugh.

'I did not!' Sasha protested. 'I simply immobilized the limb. Mary cut it off.'

'Likely story,' Saber said with a smirk. The officers all laughed. Even Caesar broke a smile.

'But you are right, Officer Saxon,' Grace said. 'We should go over the basics. When can I brief my officers?'

'Tomorrow morning,' Caesar said.

'That quickly?' Atlas asked.

'General Prince was very specific,' Caesar said. 'We have ten days from our arrival to end the siege. Tomorrow will be day two.'

'Oh, my,' Atlas said. He looked at Sasha. 'I hope your plan is a good one.'

'Me too,' Sasha admitted. 'Me too.'

***

The Army of the Lakes was built to a plan. Every squad, every staff sergeant, every officer was selected months ago and trained to be the best at their role as they could be. The instrument that General Senator took over was the best that the RAM could build.

The Walker Siege Group was completely different. It was a mix of whatever could be spared, and whatever was cobbled together to meet a need. When Major Grace took command, it was less than one hundred troops trying to deal with the yeomen in Walker Town. Slowly, she assembled her troops, cut off the enemy's avenues, and bottled up the riders in their town.

It was Grace who had burned the bridges to limit the garrison's ability to sortie. She constructed the initial siege lines, welcomed the militia into her ranks, developed the infrastructure that kept her troops fed and warm throughout the winter. She received some support from the generals; a trio of mortars, a platoon of infantry, some supplies, but much of her force she built herself, convincing the locals to join her cause.

Most of the officers in the siege group came from the militia, those eager to fight after the burning of a half dozen towns. Grace had organized them, found their strengths, and positioned them appropriately. An aged veteran commanded one company, a young Renaissance officer another. The group chaplains were priests from nearby towns, and the supply officer was a wizened grandmother who chuckled when people saluted her. The lack of any commonality in their dress was even more extreme than Fourth Regiment's. Only a few from Grace's command wore anything that resembled a military uniform, including Captain Saber and Lieutenant Elector.

Grace assembled the officers in her amphitheater, a specially modified hillside that allowed dozens to watch a central platform. Sasha stood with Caesar, Grace and their staffs, behind the platform. Officers filled in the benches.

The siege group's officer sat mixed with officers coming from the reinforcements. Commander Faro of the Naval Group arrived with Ensign Mako right behind him. The Workshop sent two teams; Lieutenant Patch, with her Air Battery, and Tony, who now wore a warrant officer's insignia. Sasha also saw Major Fox, who still looked at her with pride as he came to the siege group's amphitheater. Penn sat in the back, ready to take notes for the Civic Council.

When the officers were all seated, Grace finally stood. She nodded to the group chaplain, who intoned a short prayer. He finished, and Grace stepped forward. 'Ladies and gentlemen, I will be brief. The siege of Walker must end and end soon. For details, I present to you General Caesar.'

Caesar stood, and the group Sergeant Major bellowed everyone to attention. Caesar waved them back to their seats.

'Officers of the siege group, and those recently arrived. Intelligence has fallen into our hands that Count Walker has been provided with chemical weapons. Weapons enough to kill the population of the town, and possibly more.'

'What proof do you have?' one man yelled out. He wore civilian clothes with a sash Sasha had learned meant he was a militia captain. 'What proof is there that we should risk our lives to take this town? We've held them for a year. We can hold them for another.'

'Captain Granger, is it?' Caesar asked.

426

The captain blushed. 'It is,' he said, surprised the general knew his name.

'The proof, Captain Granger, is too imperfect to count as absolute truth, but the sources are too trusted to dismiss as fiction. both inside and out of Walker. We must take the threat as real. Regardless, we have ample reason to want to end the siege, anyway. So long as Walker is besieged, the Royal Army will continue to campaign for its relief. And this army has better things to do than sit still.'

'And you're the one to end it?' Granger asked.

'I am General Caesar, Captain. I am General Prince's problem solver. He directs me to find a solution to something, I find the solution. He directed me several weeks ago, before the Royal Army began their campaign, to plan for this eventuality. It was his belief that Count Walker would surrender after the Royal Army was turned back. The count has not done so. And we cannot allow this distraction to continue. So, here we are.'

Some of the officers grumbled. Caesar shook his head. 'Do not, any of you, think that this is an insult. Despite being outnumbered by the garrison, you have kept them in their walls for a year. You survived a Minnesota winter with less than a dozen deaths. You have performed the mission given to you wonderfully. Take pride in that.'

Some of the siege group's officers were nodding. At least the grumbling stopped.

'Now, to brief you on the plan, Lieutenant Scholar.'

Caesar moved back to his seat and Sasha took the space in the middle. She looked up at more than two dozen officers and, to her surprise, began speaking with a confident voice.

'Ladies and gentlemen,' she began, 'with the Royal Army attempting to reach Walker County, the Air Corps' involvement in the siege, the danger to the hostages and civilians within its walls, and now the threat of chemical weapons, it is important we end this siege as soon as we can.

'First, let me catch everyone up to speed. Walker Town has been under siege for almost a year now. Their garrison consists of hired yeomen, veteran farmers Count Walker brought with him to tend nearby lands, and an assortment of volunteers and conscripts, ranging between two and three hundred men.

'Most of their defenses are concentrated in the south, where a series of trenches have been dug to keep the siege group from attacking. The western marshes are all but impossible to approach, since you burned the bridges last summer, and are watched only by a few fortified houses. The castle itself, and the cathedral, are both garrisoned. Patrols of the town and the shore are sporadic.

'The enemy does have a number of machine guns and light mortars, which they've placed at various spots. Most armaments are rifle carbines and submachine guns, with some long rifles and shotguns in the mix. Expect a variety in any firefight.'

Some of the officers of the siege group were rolling their eyes at her. They knew the enemy they faced for a year. She ignored them and continued.

'The siege group consists of two companies of regular infantry and three of militia, with a single battery of heavy mortars. Other troops assigned are non-combat. To this order of battle, General Caesar is bringing a number of reinforcements: the Naval Group, under Commander Faro, consisting of four armed boats and eighty sailors; the Marine Company, thirty-six strong, under Lieutenant Mars; Sparrow Company, eighty-seven strong, under Able Infantry Officer Sparrow; a sixteen-strong team to secure the hostages, under myself; a six man squad to secure the chemical weapons, under . . . ,' she looked at Tony.

'Officer Roach,' he said triumphantly.

Some of the officers chuckled. Sasha spoke over them.

'Officer Roach, a team of sharpshooters under Major Fox, and one battery of anti-aircraft guns, under Lieutenant Patch. Well over two hundred troops.'

Some of the officers whistled at that.

'We will have no other forces available,' Sasha said. 'Some extra militia may turn up, but they will most likely not be involved in this. General Caesar will assume command of the forces during the operation, with Colonel Grace as his second. Any questions so far?' she asked.

Another militia captain raised his hand. 'What's this one called?' he asked.

'I'm sorry?' Sasha asked.

'I know the Renaissance Army likes to give names to things. Hell, it'd rename half of us if we gave it a chance. So, what's the name of this little operation?'

Sasha paused for a moment. No one had ever discussed names of operations, at least not officially. She could easily just say it did not have one and move on. That would certainly be the easiest way to answer.

'Operation Blaze-Swift,' she said.

Elector smiled at her. Mako nodded. Patch chuckled. If Caesar or anyone behind her made any motion, she did not see it.

'Blaze-Swift?' the captain asked.

'It is a two-part operation, intended to force a surrender by making the position of the garrison untenable, or, if that fails, to end it by assault.

'The first phase, Blaze, will commence soon after the next air lift to Walker, sometime tomorrow or the day after. Assets of ours inside Walker are prepared to blow the supply cache, destroying not only their ammunition but their food as well.'

A wave of murmurs swept the officers. The idea of blowing up part of Walker Town was not well received.

'With the destruction of their supplies, it is our belief that the Air Corps will conduct one significant drop to immediately resupply them with a full airdrop, using every aircraft at their disposal.

'The anti-air battery, under Lieutenant Patch, will then cut the air bridge.'

'Can they do that?' someone asked.

Patch stood up. 'We can. We've been working with tech salvaged from a centuries old site. Our battery should be able to shoot down their aircraft.'

'Should?' Grace asked. 'I don't wish to sound rude, but I don't like that this plan hinges on a system that should work.'

'We're going to be setting up the basics tonight,' Patch said, 'testing it out, making sure it's ready for the main event.'

'Even if it doesn't work one-hundred percent,' Sasha continued, 'we will still be able to put pressure on their aircraft. With only nine transports, even shooting down one significantly reduce their capacity to reinforce Walker and makes the Air Corps hesitant to commit resources against prepared air defenses.

'Regardless, with the destruction of their supplies and the loss or significant reduction of their air bridge, pressure will be on Count Walker to surrender. We will make the demand.'

'And if he doesn't?' Captain Granger asked.

'Then we commence with Operation Swift,' Sasha continued. 'Swift is a nighttime amphibious landing on the eastern side of Walker, under the cathedral walls, with feints by the siege group against the trenches and the marshlands. The Naval Group has assembled four boats, capable of landing eighty troops per wave. The first wave will consist of the Marines, hostage rescue team, chemical team, and several squads of Sparrow's company to secure the landing area.

'The teams will infiltrate the cathedral. Ideally, they can secure the building before the garrison can react. The Naval Group will bring the balance of Sparrow's company over, giving us more than one hundred rifles in and around the cathedral.'

'Will one hundred be enough?' someone asked.

'The cathedral is surrounded by a wall,' Granger replied before Sasha could, 'with two gates. You capture those gates and you won't need a hundred men to hold it.'

Sasha continued. 'With the cathedral secured, we will have a commanding position over the siege lines and be in a position to threaten Walker Town and Walker Castle. The Naval Group will be on hand to ferry troops as needed, and if the siege lines are abandoned, we can free up both those companies to take Walker Town. The castle will then be under close siege. With the hostages and civilians freed, we can choose to ignore Count Walker and his yeomen, bottle them up and let them starve.'

She looked out over the crowd. 'The next airdrop is Day Zero, the beginning of our timetable. Demolition will occur by Day Two. The air bridge cut is expected Day Four or Five, with surrender demanded the next day and the assault that day or the next, depending on weather conditions. At most, we expect this operation to take eight days.'

She stepped back. 'Any questions?'

Several raised their hands. She gestured to one. 'What is the Naval Group bringing to the battle and how many troops can they land at once?'

Faro elbowed Mako, who stood up. 'The Naval Group is bringing a squadron of four boats to the battle. The biggest is the *Contessa*, now re-christened the *Prince Dawson,* with two machine guns and carrying about forty troops. Two fishing boats we've taken from other lakefront villas, named *Minnesota* and *Renaissance*, each with one machine gun and about twenty troops. The smallest is the *Winter*, no troops, but two machine guns, one of them a heavy weapon, and a heavy mortar. They will be making their way to an anchorage this evening, and we will be testing our loadout with the assault troops as soon as we can.'

Mako sat. More hands in the air. 'Will the air battery be able to support the assault at all?'

Patch stood, her head cocked to the side as she thought. 'I suppose,' she said. 'Depending on where you need it to hit. It's not an indirect weapon, so it needs to be able to its target, but in the right circumstances, it can be useful. However, I wouldn't depend on it.'

More questions. Sasha answered as best she could, getting support from others as needed. For the most part it was going well. Then one last hand.

'Lieutenant Scholar,' he said, 'it looks like a fine plan, sure, but it still puts a lot of people in danger; not only us, but the civilians in Walker and the hostages as well. If it goes well, you gain glory in designing the plan. If it doesn't go well, what do you lose?' His voice was full of disdain, and several other officers nodded in support.

'I lose two parents, two siblings and a niece or nephew I've never met,' Sasha replied. The officers assembled and looked at her in surprise. 'Assuming,' she continued,' that I survive the assault.' She grinned at them all.

'I am from Walker County, from a town that was burned by Giulio Montessori last spring. My family have been held for a year. I want them to be free and safe, but to do that, I must put them in danger, more than they've already been in.

'As such, we are prepared to jump on the plan,' Sasha continued. 'The assets supporting this operation are moving to their staging points. As early as tomorrow night, we can launch Swift without waiting for Blaze. The only significant difference would be the supplies available for the sustained fight.'

'If that's true,' someone else asked, 'why not launch Swift now? After Blaze, aren't they going to be expecting an attack?'

'Because we want the garrison to surrender without a firefight,' Sasha said. 'Unless the garrison up and surrenders tomorrow, someone is going to have to die to finish this siege. They will die when the supply depot explodes. They will die when the air bridge is cut, and as the Air Corps sends attack planes along with the transports, all the dead will not be on their side.' She glanced at Patch, who was staring up into the canopy.

'If those deaths and the loss of supplies doesn't force the garrison to surrender, it will have to be by assault. It will be a bloody affair, and I don't want to do it, but if we have to, we will.'

'Is that why you're going in with the first wave?' one of Grace's officers asked. It was an elderly woman with a major's insignia on her dress.

'The responsibility is mine, so should be the danger,' Sasha said.

The faces staring at her showed mixes of emotions. Some looked at her with pity, others with pride. Some still looked angry, others embarrassed. Mako smiled at her. Elector looked sad. Patch was still staring at nothing.

'Is that all?' Grace asked, standing beside Sasha. 'Any other questions?'

Silence.

'Captain Saber and all company officers will stay behind so we can go over our own contribution. Major Willow,' she gestured to the elderly woman, 'will meet with Lieutenant Patch and Commander Faro to integrate them into our supply needs. Sign and countersign will be announced before the battle begins. General Caesar?' she glanced over her shoulder. He shook his head. 'Dismissed,' she said to the officers.

Sasha turned back to Caesar and Saxon. 'How did I do?' she asked.

'Good,' Saxon said, 'very good.'

'You should work on your projection,' Caesar said, lost in thought.

Saxon and Sasha shared a smile. 'What do we do now?' Sasha asked.

'We are splitting up,' Saxon said.

'Officer Saxon will be returning to the HQ to coordinate messages. I will be taking a brief tour of the southern trenches. You will be heading with Ensign Mako back to the naval staging area.'

'Why there?' Sasha asked.

'Your team is assembling there,' Saxon said. 'Take your three from our entourage, and the other twelve will meet you there.'

'Am I coming back?' Sasha asked.

Saxon glanced at Caesar. 'Lieutenant Scholar, you were correct when you decided that Swift needs to be ready to launch on a moment's notice. As such, you should be prepared to stay with your team until such time as Swift is launched. We will be in regular communication by riders; it is not even eight miles from here to there.'

Sasha nodded. Saxon snapped her fingers. 'Hey, Templar. Do not think of this as any sort of demotion. You will be where we need you. It's more important than double-checking incoming paperwork with me.'

Sasha nodded again, forcing a smile. 'I understand, I truly do.'

'Good,' Caesar said. 'Now get going. It is important you and your squad spend some time going through some exercises before committing to Walker.'

'Right,' she said. She saluted. 'Good luck, sir.'

'You too,' Caesar returned it.

Saxon walked her out. Five horses waited; her three squad members, a guide, and one for her, her kit packed and sitting on the back of the saddle.

'Let's go,' Sasha said. They mounted and started out, connecting with another squad making their way towards the same place. Mako rode with them.

'Ensign,' Sasha said as they formed into a column with the two officers riding next to each other.

'Lieutenant,' Mako said. 'Good briefing.'

'I hope so,' she said.

'Good plan.'

'I really hope so.'

Mako nodded. 'We're going to save your family.'

'We're going to save all of them,' Sasha said.

Mako smiled. 'By the Grace of God, so we are.'

'By the Grace of God and the actions of Templars,' Sasha said, 'so we are.'

Chapter 47

Mako called their destination Port Jonah, after the Biblical character. It was a small lake that connected to Agency Bay through a tiny channel. Several places were prepared for the incoming boats, with small channels dredged and netting hung to hide them from airplanes flying overhead.

Port Jonah was home to a small village, with a dozen men and women left living in it, the rest having moved to other towns or enlisted in the Renaissance Army. The visitors pitched tents south of the town, under the cover of trees, in rough rows. Mako led Sasha to the west side.

'Your squad,' he said, gesturing to a dozen men and women sitting around a campfire eating a late lunch. Sasha approached, being noticed by a young woman who called everyone to a quick attention.

I'm still getting used to that, she thought. Saluting was not common at Avalon. She waved them down while Del Oso approached.

'Lieutenant Scholar, welcome to your team.'

Sasha smiled at the man. 'Thank you, Sergeant Major. I hope the training has been going well?'

Del Oso smiled. 'For the most part, ma'am. It's been rough with only three-quarters of the squad here.'

'Well, we're all here now,' Sasha said, 'and I'm eager to run through some exercises. May we speak in private?'

Del Oso nodded and gestured down a track. Sasha started to follow, then stopped and addressed the sitting soldiers.

'I look forward to getting to know each of you,' she said. 'If the Sergeant Major says you're good, that's enough for me. I just hope he'll say the same about me when we're done.'

'Couldn't you just order him to say it?' a young corporal asked.

'One lesson of being an officer,' Sasha said, 'never give an order you know won't be followed.'

The squad chuckled. Sasha gestured for Del Oso to follow her out of earshot of the rest.

'Your tent is closest to the town; I'm next to you, and the rest of the squad down into the forest.'

434

'Good to know,' Sasha said. She turned to her former instructor and sighed. 'Have you heard about Roland?' she asked.

Del Oso nodded. 'I did. It was a soldier's death.'

'He was too young,' Sasha said.

'All soldiers are too young. It's one of the commandments.'

Sasha looked back towards the squad. Sergeant Pierce was introducing her squad to the others. 'How are they doing, really?'

'Decently,' Del Oso said. 'Not as good as a dedicated team might be, but we've had two weeks to prepare, and I got the cream of what was left in Walker County. Master Sergeant Kravitz is an instructor at Sparta, and First Sergeant Ibrahim is out of Olympia. Both of them know the game.'

'And now we get to introduce my own team into the group,' Sasha said. 'We have been practicing, I swear, Sergeant Major, but our facilities were limited.'

'Well, we'll get everyone through some weapons familiarization, and some exercises this afternoon,' Del Oso said. 'Worse comes to worst, you put other squads at point and follow them.'

'Shouldn't officers lead from the front?' Sasha asked.

'When this goes down and you're on our side of the water, you are leading from the front,' Del Oso replied.

***

The Naval Group moved in that night, sailing from their normal anchorage – wherever that was – around the large peninsula to the east of Walker, down through the narrows into Agency Bay. They waited for early morning light to pass into Port Jonah, not trusting the tiny channel in the darkness. Their crews worked quickly to get the boats moored and hidden.

'We're just over three miles from Walker, in a straight line,' Mako said. 'We don't want them to know we're here.'

Sasha understood completely. The aircraft could fly right overhead on their way to drop on Walker, and the boats might give away everything. She glanced to the west. She thought she could see the top of the cathedral tower over the trees.

The Naval Group brought with them Lieutenant Mars and the Marine Company. Some of them Sasha recognized from the fight at the prison camp, but none of them appeared to recognize her.

Fox and his Chosen Rifles walked in later that morning, followed quickly by Sparrow's company and Roach's team that afternoon. Sasha was busy bustling through Del Oso's training, proving herself to be fitter than she expected, and so missed everyone getting settled. It was not until a runner from Commander Faro brought an invitation for all officers to meet for dinner that she realized she was going to meet everyone.

Thought you were done with the socializing, didn't you? She chided herself as she changed into her class uniform. It worked better for formal occasions and was not dirty.

Commander Faro was a tall Hispanic man, whose name was Spanish for lighthouse. He wore a meticulous black uniform with gold lace and insignia and spoke with a crisp Minnesotan accent. He had a calming presence that flowed over the room the officers assembled in.

When Sasha arrived, the naval officers were already there. Faro, Mako, and a gruff-looking woman who introduced herself as Senior Lieutenant Sage. 'Good to see another woman,' she said in a raspy voice. She had thinning hair and skin pocked by one childhood disease or another. She asked questions about the Templars, listening in earnest, until she was called over by Faro to discuss something having to do with the boats.

First Lieutenant Mars came next. Though the Marine Company had been present during the prison camp battle, Sasha had only interacted with a few of their enlisted folk, and never saw their commander in person. He was a particularly handsome man, blonde hair and blue eyed, with a strong jaw and another meticulous uniform, black with red trim. He glanced about the room with an arrogant look, passing over Sasha as quickly as he could and walking over to the naval officers.

Tony arrived and came to sit next to Sasha. 'Tell me, do you think Mars is handsome?'

Sasha looked up in surprise. 'What? Maybe, I guess.'

'You guess?' Tony smiled.

'Sure, he's handsome. But as Candle would say, he knows he's handsome. Do you think Sage is pretty?'

'No,' Tony said. 'She's a survivor, though. Looks a lot like my friend before a sickness took him two winters ago. If she could beat that, she could do anything.'

Sasha nodded. 'Did you think I was pretty when we first met?'

'Sure, but mostly I was too busy looking down on you for thinking you were a common clerk.'

'Ha!' Sasha laughed. 'I had almost forgotten about that.'

The company's two warrant officers arrived, cutting off Tony's response. Able Officer Sparrow, the company commander, was a short Hmong woman who was a few years older than Sasha. She carried herself with an air of confidence like Mars did but smiled at Sasha when she entered. Behind her was her second, Officer Goliath. He was an African man who, like Del Oso and Scott Anthony, was thick with muscles. They both wore green fatigues that showed signs of ageing and patching. Sasha thought she heard Mars scoff at them as Sparrow sat in a chair, Goliath standing to her side.

Finally, Fox made his way in. The taller man towered over everyone else, but ignored the open chair, leaning against the wall.

Faro said something to the officers around him, who moved to find their own seats. Mako sat by Sasha, on a stool. Mars stood next to Faro, and Sage took the last chair.

'Ladies and gentlemen,' Faro said, 'we are the assault force for Operation Swift. You all have, independently, been working on your part of the plan. Now, we must implement it together.

'Lieutenant Scholar,' he said, looking at Sasha, 'it is a fine plan, I think. I believe the Naval Group can pull its weight in this operation, and I mean it to.'

Sasha nodded. The man was the equivalent to a lieutenant colonel, the highest ranked officer in the room and the one in charge of the landing, even if it was her idea.

'So, let us go over our plan then, shall we? The Naval Group can land approximately eighty troops in each wave. The Marine Company is thirty-six. Your teams are sixteen and six?' he asked.

Sasha and Tony nodded.

'Then that leaves us with twenty-two positions in the first wave. Officer Sparrow, you have one undersized company. What exactly is your strength?'

Sparrow spoke. 'Out company is significantly off book. We don't have a third platoon, our second doesn't have an officer assigned, and have one staff sergeant instead of three on my staff. However, we did pull in two extra medics and a spare weapons team, so I can add an additional pair of medium machine guns to the mix. Eighty-seven total.'

'You don't have a platoon officer?' Mars asked. There was something about his voice that made Sasha think he blamed Sparrow for her situation and thought less of her for it.

'My company is made up of spares, Lieutenant,' Sparrow said sternly. 'I make use of what I can get.'

Mars sneered but said nothing. He was a step above Sparrow in the rank hierarchy, but both were company commanders about to go into battle next to each other. There was a limit to how far he was going to push, and how far Faro would let him.

'What would you do with twenty-two slots, Officer Sparrow?' Faro cut off any further discussion.

'I would send Goliath with two squads and two LAMB teams, along with one medic,' Sparrow said. 'I will follow with the balance of my company in the next wave.'

Faro nodded. 'Major? What are you bringing?'

'Including myself, I have eight sharpshooters,' Fox said.

'How many do you want in the first wave?'

'None,' Fox said. 'The first wave is only to take the cathedral, and the plan depends on stealth. Our rifles aren't quiet weapons.'

'And if I pushed?' Faro asked. 'Once we do some test loads on the boats, we can probably fit in some more people.'

'If you want me to go in the first wave, I'll take as many as I can, but we're sharpshooters. We can't be leading charges.'

'I understand,' Faro said. 'Lieutenant Scholar, as the architect of this plan, perhaps you should brief the assault portion?'

Sasha nodded, standing and unrolling a map. She gestured to Tony, who held one end as she held the other.

'The Naval Group will be landing the first and second waves in the gardens to the east of Walker Cathedral. This location puts us out of the direct line of fire from most of the garrison's weapons, save for the easternmost redoubt of their trench line and whoever is guarding the cathedral itself.

'While stealth is important, it is also imperative that we get up to the eastern veranda quickly. It is a commanding position and could threaten the landing zone if the enemy gets weapons there.'

'Why conduct a landing under such a position?' Mars interrupted. 'Why not land elsewhere?'

'There is no better place to land,' Sasha said. 'The field is covered by half a dozen machine guns, and the city has been blocked and boarded up. In addition, the concept of Swift is to take the cathedral, with the hostages and the chemical weapons, before the defenders can react and threaten them.'

Mars said nothing, then gave a curt nod.

'Now, the cathedral landing will be among the gardens, then up to the veranda. From there we have three routes: the front route to the front gate and main entrance to the cathedral; the second heads up to the priest's quarters and the Bishop's Gate; and finally, the entrance to the substructure of the cathedral, with the reliquary and storerooms.

'The defenders should be light. Each gate has a defensive trench and a standing guard, but they can't fire onto the landing beach behind the cathedral. There are firing positions on the veranda and patrols in and around the cathedral.'

'Fantastic,' Goliath said grimly. Mars chuckled.

'We land and take the veranda,' Sasha said, 'ideally without alerting anyone to our presence. The hostage and chemical teams move into the substructure. Our goal is to secure the hostages and the chemical weapons. The Marines will move into the priest's quarters, to secure them and the Bishop's Gate. The company will move to the front, to take front gate and the entrance to the cathedral.'

'Why split our forces?' Sparrow asked.

'Seizing the two gates into the cathedral area allows us to stop reinforcements from coming in,' Sasha said. 'It gives Officer Roach and me time to complete our missions.'

'And this is in conjunction with feints at the trenches and the marshland?' Fox asked.

Sasha nodded. 'We want them distracted.'

'Okay then,' Faro said. He turned around, moving several cups from a table behind him and setting them on a shelf. Then he and Sage moved the table into the middle of the room. 'Put down the map, and let's take a look at this up close. I want us to all know this by memory, flawlessly. The entire siege may depend on it.'

***

The next day Sasha saw the first stage. She and several others rode to a position where they could watch the airdrop over Walker. It just so happened that this day, the aircraft flew over her on their way to the drop.

The first planes to fly overhead were six fighters, small biplanes that flew in threes. The only planes Sasha had ever seen before were high and slow moving, but these were lower and faster. She could see in individual pilot's heads as they flew over the lake towards Walker.

'They'll spend some time flying over Walker Town,' Faro said. 'See if they can goad the defenders into attacking.'

'Why don't they attack anything they see?' Sasha asked.

'If they attack, they get shot at, and might get shot down.'

Next came a trio of attack planes. These had one set of wings but were significantly larger than the fighters. She saw rockets and bombs slung underneath the wings.

'They don't always come this way, do they?' Sparrow asked.

Sasha spoke, remembering her conversations with Cardinal. 'Walker is close enough to Saint Cloud they can take an indirect route. Since there was always the possibility we could set up a warning system or endanger the planes if they take the same route, they vary it. They head towards the Iron Range, turn west towards Walker, then turn south and back home, or they fly west and north and east. They have so many options, we can't guess.'

Finally came the transports, another trio of them. They were larger than Sasha had expected, far larger than the smaller aircraft that had come through earlier. They looked like a giant metal cigar, with an engine on each side suspended between two wings. They also looked incredibly slow. Sasha imagined she could shoot the engine out with her carbine from here.

'Each plane drops four pods,' Sasha said. 'Each pod carries eight hundred pounds of supplies.'

'Almost five tons a drop,' Tony said.

'Enough food to last five days, in basic forms such as crackers and canned food. Some more ammunition and extra equipment. Sometimes a person.'

'I'm surprised they can only carry five tons between all of them,' Tony continued.

'They're not great aircraft,' Sasha replied. 'King Xavier doesn't think much of airplanes, and there are limits on what the Air Corps can spend money on. Someone who knows mentioned to me that many of their aircraft are obsolete by normal standards of Commonwealth nations, but they're cheap to maintain so he keeps them.'

'Ah, Tony said. 'When do we get airplanes?'

440

'As soon as we learn how to build them,' Sasha said.

'Really?'

Sasha grinned.

'Oh,' Tony was crestfallen. 'That wasn't very nice, Lieutenant.'

'Sorry, Tony.'

'Roach,' he said. 'Officer Roach,' he stressed his Renaissance name.

'Right,' Sasha said quickly. 'I'll remember that.'

'Please do.'

The group rode back. They took a late nap, adjusting their sleep schedules to be awake all night. They did some land navigation in the dark, getting used to moving at night, returning to their camp just before midnight. They were having a round of tea when a loud sound emanated from the west. They caught a glimpse of a large fireball rising over the trees.

'Guess he did it,' Sasha said.

'Who?' Mako asked.

'Whoever was tasked with blowing up the supplies,' Sasha sighed. 'I hope he's okay.'

Chapter 48

Major Lopez wore a dirty uniform. He had rushed to the scene of the explosion, digging men out and salvaging what he could.

He should have cleaned up for this meeting, Montessori thought.

'How bad?' he growled.

'Bad,' Lopez said through Giulio. 'Except for what was distributed to the front lines, we've lost our entire cache of reserve ammunition and spare weapons. The food supplies have been reduced from ten days to two. Medical supplies were not affected as they were kept at the hospital.

'Both the warehouse and the granary are completely gone. The damage to the castle could have been worse if the ammunition wasn't stored in an underground magazine. Most of the damage is superficial; broken windows and the like.

'By our reckoning, eleven men were killed in the blast, and twenty-four wounded to one degree or another.'

'What happened?' Montessori asked. 'Sabotage?'

'Possibly,' Lopez said. 'No, probably, but with a blast that size, it is doubtful we could ever determine how it was caused, so we can't tell if it was sabotage or accident.'

'It was sabotage!' Montessori pounded the table.

Lopez nodded. 'Nevertheless, we have a supply problem.'

'Cut the civilians off from food!' Montessori growled.

'Many of those civilians are family members of the garrison, including those who followed you from the imperial service,' Lopez said. 'They may turn if their families starve.'

'Not all of them,' Montessori said. 'Starve the rest.'

'No, sir, I will not,' Lopez said. He spoke over Montessori's protest. 'If we starve the civilians, we will push more people into the ranks of the Renaissance Army, and I will not allow that to happen.'

Montessori glared at him, imagining all sorts of tortures he could inflict. 'Very well then, Major. How do you propose we solve this problem?'

Lopez paused and sighed. 'The Air Corps is prepared to increase their drops from three to nine aircraft, with a corresponding increase in escort. They can be here in two days with enough supplies to rebuild our reserves.'

'That makes you nervous?' Montessori asked.

'Sir, this could have been an accident, but it most likely is sabotage. And if it is sabotage, why now?'

'You think the Mardurers can break the air bridge?' Montessori laughed at him.

'They've defeated the plans of two different army corps,' Lopez said. 'I expect they believe they can try.'

'And what do you recommend?'

'I think we need to seriously consider negotiating for surrender,' Lopez said without hesitation.

Montessori stared at him, then picked up his goblet and threw it at the major. 'Get out! Order the increase of planes to Air bridge. And don't come to me until you have found your spine!'

The major saluted and retreated, leaving Montessori with his son.

'The chemicals?' he asked.

'Ready,' Giulio said, 'but why not threaten to use them if the siege isn't lifted?'

'Because that wouldn't lift the siege, only change its nature,' Montessori told his son. 'They would pull back from the siege lines, but they would harass supply lines. Besides, no matter the true nature of this General Prince, I do not believe he would give up so easily. For him, to lose is to die, and he therefore will risk anything to win.'

'And if we use the weapons, it'll be a propaganda coup for them,' Giulio said.

Montessori shrugged. 'I don't give a rat's ass about propaganda for peasants. If the Mardurers are closing the noose around us, they'll find themselves grasping a dying city. Maybe that will scare them into surrender. Maybe inflame them enough to punish those cowards who left us to rot for a year. I don't care.'

Giulio paled, but nodded. 'I understand.'

***

Word came that the Air Corps was responding to the loss of supplies as predicted.

Sasha and other officers went to watch the drop. It seemed odd to make a picnic of it, but she, Tony and Mako, along with an escort, made their way to a position between Port Jonah and Walker, with the town visible across the lake.

'That's where we land?'

'Yes,' Sasha answered Tony's – *no, Roach's*, Sasha told herself – question.

'Doesn't look too bad from here,' he said. Then he shrugged. 'I'm sure it'll look different at night.'

'It certainly will,' Sasha said. They positioned themselves in the trees, watching the cathedral a mile and a half away. The castle and siege lines were visible as well.

Pierce appeared. 'Security perimeter set, ma'am,' he said.

'Do any of them want to watch the attack?' Sasha asked.

'Those who do are set to do so, L.T.' Pierce said.

'Sergeant Pierce,' Mako asked, 'how many Olympians are there?'

'More than one,' Pierce responded.

'That's how they always answer the question,' Sasha said.

'I'm just curious, Sergeant, if you have any problem spending your time guarding one man, or in this case, woman.'

'I don't,' Pierce answered. 'The Olympians are divided into squads and spend six weeks at a time on rotation. My squad is currently assigned to General Caesar's headquarters, including Lieutenant Scholar here. In a few weeks we will rotate to Olympia, and one of the squads there will take over for us.'

'I'm glad you get some down time,' Mako said. 'Will you ever stop being Olympians?'

'End of June,' Pierce said, 'we have the option of transferring if we want. I know a few who do, but not because we hate being Olympians, but there is fighting going on, and some of us hate not being in it.'

'I get that,' Sasha said, remembering how helpless she had felt during the battle around Menahga.

'You'll get your chance soon enough,' Mako said.

444

'Tell me something I don't know,' Sasha replied. It was one of Payne's favorite responses, and she had started using it.

'You're named after your father,' Mako replied.

Sasha looked at him in surprise. 'My father's name is Alexander, my name is – starts with an S. I was named after the woman who helped my mother birth me after two stillbirths.'

'Maybe, but Sasha is still a nickname for Alexander. Don't ask me how you get one from the other, but apparently it's true.'

'I'll have to ask Caesar about that,' Sasha said, looking at Mako as if he was playing a joke on her. 'Wait, how the hell do you know my father's name?'

'You really haven't spent any time learning about the other Templars, have you?'

'Only from other Templars,' Sasha replied.

'There!' Roach said, pointing to the sky and ending the discussion.

A single plane, high in the air. 'One of the patrol planes out of Duluth,' Mako said. 'Scholar, remember the first time we saw one?'

'Swift and Blaze,' Sasha nodded.

Then came fighters. Twelve of them, double the previous amount, followed by nine attack aircraft.

'They're really worried, aren't they?' Roach asked.

'Patch will handle it,' Mako said confidently.

Sasha nodded. Not that she had any doubt that Patch could handle it; the woman was competent at whatever she put her mind to, even when she was staring off into space, thinking of something else. But those aircraft were here to suppress anything the siege had to threaten the bombers, which meant Patch was going to be shot at.

Mako muttered a prayer. Sasha found herself whispering one as well.

Now came the transports. Nine huge biplanes, turning towards Walker.

'They're not shaking out into a line,' Roach said.

'I wonder why?' Mako pondered.

'They expect a trap,' Sasha said. 'They're worried the explosion was meant to cause this scenario, and they want to spend as little time over Walker as possible. So, they're going to do mass drops as quickly as they can and head back fast.'

'Is Patch ready for that?' Roach asked.

'Yes,' Scholar and Mako said in unison.

'Then why isn't she shooting?'

'She's worried about debris landing on Walker,' Sasha said. 'She's holding her fire until the best possible moment.'

'So, Walker gets their supplies,' Roach pointed out.

'They do, but no more, and since the Air Corps can vary their route over Walker, the only place Patch knows the aircraft will be is over the city.'

'There's still a danger,' Mako said, 'but Patch is trying to minimize it.'

The first trio was right over Walker now. Sasha pulled out her field glasses and stared through them, watching them fly away. *What if Patch isn't ready?'* she wondered. *What if something went wrong?*

The second trio was beginning to drop. Roach said, 'I don't understand, did she forget or –.'

The air around the first trio, over the marshland, filled with black puffs, and the dull drumming of the autocannon sounded from several miles away. Through her glasses, Sasha saw debris fall off the aircraft, smoke billowing from one aircraft's engine. Another suddenly rolled over and fell out of the sky.

'One down!' she said, looking at the other officers. None of them were smiling. They were all aware of how many people were in those planes.

The first trio was turning in a tight circle. The second trio was starting to take fire now, while the last trio was starting to drop. Sasha started to raise her glasses when the horizon lit up with a flash.

No one would know until later, but the planes were each loaded for two drops, not one. One of the plans in the first trio still carried several hundred pounds of explosives when a shell struck the fuselage. The resulting explosion sent a shockwave across Walker, and through the other planes.

'Oh, my God,' Mako said.

None of the first trio was still flying, both shredded in the explosion. Several of the rest trailed smoke, damaged by shrapnel or shock.

One transport from the third trio was over Walker when it shuddered, turning over as its wing gave way. The plane, filled with supplies and hundreds of pounds of aviation fuel, fell into Walker Town.

'Oh, no,' Roach said.

Sasha looked out with her glasses. Just between the cathedral and the castle she could see the town, see the flame beginning to rise. The sounds of bells tolling alarm sounded from the cathedral.

'Oh, my God,' Mako said again.

The smaller aircraft were attacking Patch's battery now, swooping on the far side of the town. Tracers from machine guns flew up to meet them. More air bursts as Patch defended herself. The remaining transports were flying away as fast as they could, but Sasha felt little elation.

'The town's burning,' Mako said.

'Yes,' Sasha replied. She pulled a notepad from her pocket and wrote something quickly. 'Mako,' she said, 'take Roach and the escort and make your way back to Port Jonah. Give that to Commander Faro.'

'Where are you going?' he asked.

'To see the general,' Sasha said. She leapt backward. 'Sergeant Pierce?'

'Ma'am?'

'You and I are taking the fastest horses to the headquarters.'

Pierce grabbed the two fastest and they galloped down the path south. Pierce did not ask any questions, although he certainly had them. When they arrived, they found Caesar, along with Saxon and Grace and other officers, reading a message from Patch. She left Pierce to get new horses and approached the officers.

'Lieutenant Scholar?' Grace asked in surprise.

Sasha saluted. 'Ma'am, I need to speak with General Caesar.'

'In private, or can is be discussed with all of us?'

'With everyone is preferable, ma'am,' Sasha said. 'We need to launch Swift tonight.'

The officers all stared at her. 'Tonight?' Grace asked, looking at her hotly. 'Do you have any idea what just happened?'

'The town is burning,' Sasha said, then spoke over Grace's protest, 'and in the event of a fire, the civilians not involved in fighting it are evacuated to the cathedral. Everyone would be in one place, and the garrison would be busy fighting the fire to defend against us. We could rescue not only the hostages but a vast majority of the civilians of Walker in one action.'

Grace stopped talking and was staring at the map. 'The original plan,' she said, 'was to demand a surrender before resorting to an assault.'

'I know, ma'am,' Sasha said. 'I know what was planned. But this is an opportunity I feel we must strongly consider.'

Caesar looked at Sasha, his mind working fast. He glanced at the officers around him.

'She makes sense,' Saxon said.

'It's too risky,' Atlas said quickly. 'We should stick with the plan as it is.'

'Can we launch early?' Caesar asked.

'Of course,' Atlas said. 'We're ready to go on any say so.'

Sasha watched Grace. The woman had held this siege for a year, with limited support and supplies from anyone else. Caesar may have been the superior officer, but this was Grace's territory, and her voice carried that extra weight. She looked at the map, thinking, her mind working as fast as Caesar's. Finally, she looked up at Sasha.

'General Caesar,' she said, 'I find myself in agreement with Lieutenant Scholar.'

'You do?' Caesar asked. 'It is a risky move.'

Grace nodded, then frowned. 'Sir, expecting Walker to surrender is a dream. Ideal, but it's not going to happen. You don't smuggle chemical weapons into your town if you aren't planning to kill as many people as possible. No, sir. As much as I want the count to surrender, he won't. He's in it to the end. The lieutenant is right; we have an opportunity we cannot ignore. We need to move now.'

'Would the assault wave be ready in time?' Saxon asked.

'I sent Mako back with a message indicating I was going to propose this course of action and to prepare the wave on the assumption I would be correct. Nightfall will be in a few hours, and by midnight we can be on the ground.'

Caesar looked at the officers around him. Grace gave him a nod.

'So ordered,' Caesar said.

'Atlas, get the orders out. Challenge is Needle, response is Thimble. Go!' To his credit, Atlas did not protest. He had given his opinion, but now that the decision was made, he was doing his duty. Sasha admired him for that.

'Lieutenant Scholar,' Caesar said. 'Get back to your command. And good luck.'

Sasha nodded. 'To us all, sir. Good luck to us all.'

Chapter 49

Sasha was no coward. She felt the fear of fighting before, from bullies to bandits to the Royal Army, and it had never kept her from the fight.

Sitting at the bow of the *Renaissance*, being carried into battle, made her face her fear of battle in a different light. She had nothing to do but wait, listening to the fears of her part in the battle, her plan of the battle. Was it wrong to jump the plan? Should she have waited? If this did not work, would they forgive her? Could she still be a Templar? An officer? A part of the Renaissance Army?

So many fears, and she had to sit perfectly still.

The *Renaissance* carried both Sasha's and Ibrahim's squads, three members of Roach's team, and a squad of Sparrow's company. The sailors rowing were the only ones allowed to move. They were rowing as quietly as they could, which was still much louder than Sasha would have preferred.

Just to her south was the *Prince Dawson*, the re-named yacht of Count Walker, filled with Mars' Marines and Major Fox's shooters. South of them was the *Minnesota*, with Del Oso, Roach, Goliath and the rest of their squads. Elsewhere, Faro and the *Winter* were moving about.

Sasha peered over the lip of the boat. Low clouds moved over Walker during the evening, and now they reflected the fire from the town, becoming a dark orange carpet against which the black shadow of the cathedral stood in sharp contrast, growing slowly closer.

In planning for this, Sasha read through books on amphibious assaults. She thought the soldiers and marines, stuck on boats much stronger than this one, heading towards defenses that knew they were coming. She hoped she never had to do that, hoped the gunners at the cathedral were not paying attention to the boats approaching their beach.

She slowly moved her hands over her gear, checking her pouches. They were all there, as they were the last six times she checked. But she had nothing else to do.

She focused on her breathing, forcing herself into a normal rhythm. She fidgeted with her carbine. She patted her pouches. And she waited.

The rowers stopped rowing. The boat drifted forward and shuddered as it reached the shoreline and came to a rough stop.

Here we go.

She jumped off, landing on the solid ground and moving up the hill. She heard the others behind her, moving as quietly as they could. She looked ahead, looking for any sign of a sentry, any sign this was a trap. She saw nothing in the darkness.

The fear was quiet now. She had things to do.

She followed the plan, moving up. The same light clouds that outlined the cathedral now outlined the top of the cathedral's wall, allowing Sasha to move without keeping one hand on the wall.

She paused. She heard something to her left, about where the veranda should be. She heard no second sound, no alarm or gunshot.

Someone was next to her, a member of her team. She started moving again. *I'm glad we practiced at night.* She thought of the confusion during the battle at the prison camp a year earlier, when the regiment had marched at night without much experience. So much could have gone wrong. So much almost did.

She reached the sharp inclined from the lower to the upper veranda. She heard the light taps of boots on stone, but still no alarm.

She turned, following the wall that separated the lower and upper veranda to stairs down. There were small windows in that wall, anyone inside would see her, sound an alarm or open fire before she could react. No one did. She almost fell down the stairs but caught herself.

'Needle,' she whispered.

No answer. She was the first one there.

Sasha headed down the stairs, to the door leading into the interior. She sensed someone behind her, other boots on the stairs. 'Needle,' another woman whispered. It was Locke.

'Thimble,' Sasha replied. She felt her way to the door's handle. Behind her, Locke challenged someone else, then let them move forward.

It was Pierce.

'L.T.?' he asked.

Sasha found the handle, gripping it and feeling for the latch. Word was it was always left unlocked, so patrollers could get in and out quickly. And now?

Sasha pressed down on her thumb, and the door clicked open. She sighed and opened the door all the way.

450

Michael Bernabo

She rushed into the cafe. A single lantern burned on the far side. She made her way towards it, hearing others following her inside. *I hope the other squads are moving just as well.*

The lantern was hung at the doorway into the storerooms and basement of the cathedral. She leaned and looked down the hallway, seeing a few more lanterns and doors.

Pierce was by her side. 'L.T., we're all here. So is Roach,' he whispered. Sasha glanced back into the room, now filled with armed soldiers.

'Let's go,' Sasha said, heading down the hallway.

They cleared each room as they went. The first was an empty storage room. The next filled with chairs and tables for events on the veranda.

The third was not a common-looking door, but ornate, with a painted facade. In the dim light, it looked like a garden, with animals and a shining sun. Sasha checked the handle, knowing it was locked. Only two people had a key to this door, Count Walker and the bishop, because it was a special plot for the count and his family.

The Montessori family crypt, she thought.

They continued down the hallway, heading for the stairs. They were below the small hallway between the priest's quarters and the cathedral itself. So far, no sound of fighting. No sound of violence. By now, the boats were on their way back to pick up the second wave. Goliath should be approaching the main gate, and Mars was inside the quarters, making his way to the Bishop's Gate.

My plan is working. Everyone is moving, no shots fired. I'll have to find out what happened to the defenders, there should have been someone on the terraces.

Sasha looked back. Everyone was there. Del Oso and Pierce, and the rest of her platoon. Roach was in the back, with his team. All of them looked forward to her.

Okay.

She moved up the stairs, carbine ready. The stairs spun around and up. She looked left and right, Pierce at her side. No one was seen. Not even a single guard.

I'm surprised we haven't found anyone yet.

Right, towards the cathedral. That door was unlocked, and in they went.

This was the last hallway before the cathedral. A set of stairs to the left, heading up into the choir area. To the right, the two main doors for the priests, then a side door at the far end.

Sasha moved to the main door with her team and Ibrahim's team. Del Oso made his way to the far door, while Kravitz went up to the choir balcony. Roach set his team behind hers.

'Take the door, Pierce,' she said.

'L.T., I should go first.'

'No,' Sasha said. 'I need to –.'

A firefight erupted at the Bishop's Gate. Gunfire and a grenade, shouting and yelling.

'Shit,' Pierce said. He moved to go through the door.

'Sergeant!' Sasha snapped.

Pierce looked at her, and for a second, she thought he was going to rush in himself. But he swore again and pulled the door open for her to head in.

Sasha rushed through.

For my family!

Chapter 50

A man was approaching the door when Sasha came through. A yeoman officer, from the looks of him. Sasha had only a glimpse of a uniform and a surprised face when she shot him down with her carbine.

The suppressed gunshots alerted the entire cathedral. Sasha rushed forward, her platoon following her, as civilians erupted in panic at the fight in their midst.

'Stay down!' Del Oso was yelling. Other sergeants followed suit, bellowing for the civilians to stay down. Most civilians were already ducking for cover.

Sasha ran.

She had to. The front gate and the bell tower were both at the front of the building, each with armed troops stationed there. Armed troops who most likely would fire indiscriminately at civilians and RAM soldiers alike inside the cathedral.

The door was beginning to open when Sasha reached it. She fired without aiming, a completely wild burst that peppered the door and frightened whoever was opening it. They slammed it shut again.

Sasha reached the door, with Pierce right behind her. She paused to listen when Pierce grabbed her by the collar and pulled her back. Her protest was drowned out by someone firing through the door, right where she had been.

'Don't ever do that, L.T.,' Pierce said.

'Right,' Sasha agreed.

More gunfire outside. Goliath was making his attack on the door guard. 'Keep that door shut,' she said to Ibrahim, turning towards the door to the bell tower.

Roach made his way through the chaos to the door, his squad strung out behind him. Del Oso was busy getting the civilians under control, but the noise was ridiculously loud.

'Locked!' Roach shouted.

Locke appeared carrying her shotgun. She loaded a solid round, aimed it at the lock, and fired, ripping the lock to pieces. The door swung open, and a burst of gunfire struck at them from inside. Locke fell backwards, on top of Sasha, while Roach and his squad pressed themselves against the wall.

'You okay?' she asked Locke.

'Hit in the leg,' she said, grimacing. 'Not bad. Ricochet. No blood.'

The defender fired again, and again. Sasha wondered what he was shooting at, as no one was standing in the doorway, but he kept firing, until she heard the harsh click of an empty magazine.

Sasha rushed the door. Her eyes over her gunsight, she tracked up the stairs, finding the man on the second landing, fumbling to reload his submachine gun. She killed him quickly, continuing to run up the stairs.

Speed was of the essence, and Sasha ran. She did not know if there were chemical weapons in the tower or not. She did know the radio was up there, and that meant armed men. She had to get up there. Her team followed her up.

The upper levels were dark, the lanterns extinguished to aid the defenders. A rifle shot fired at Sasha, and Sasha shot back at the muzzle flash. She continued up, slowing in case she ran right into a defender.

A pop sounded from below and a red flare shot up into the bell tower. The projectile illuminated quickly, showing Sasha half a flight of stairs from a pair of defenders whose guns were aimed the wrong way. Both died under a hail of gunfire from Sasha and her team.

The stairs terminated at the belfry, a solid wooden ceiling blocking most of their view. Sasha slowed, waiting to listen. A lantern illuminated the room, reflecting off the stonework Sasha could see, but if anyone was up there, Sasha could not tell. She took a deep breath, ready to rush.

'We surrender!' a voice called. 'Don't shoot, we surrender!'

Sasha glanced at Pierce, who shrugged. 'Hands up!' Sasha called. 'If anyone does not have your hands up, you will be shot!'

'Okay,' the voice wavered. Sasha rushed up the last few steps.

Two men stood, arms raised, weapons on the floor. Both were radio technicians, one of the Royal Army, one from the Royal Air Corps. The radio transmitter and equipment were set about the belfry. The shutters were closed, and the tower was rather hot.

Sasha covered them with her rifle as Pierce kicked their guns away from them. She glanced around, looking to see anything that resembled a barrel or cylinder, but did not see anything.

'What do you two know about chemical weapons?' she asked quickly.

Both men looked confused. 'Nothing, ma'am,' one of them said.

'Are you sure?'

'We're just radio techs, ma'am,' the second said. 'Jumped in to maintain the radios.'

'I'm told the Mardurers don't shoot prisoners,' the first said nervously.

'We don't,' Sasha confirmed. 'Sergeant Pierce, take them and the radio downstairs.'

Part of her was relieved not to find the gas canisters up here. On the other hand, that meant the munitions were still somewhere else.

She opened the shutters slightly. It was too dark to see individuals below her, but from the muzzle flashes and bursts of tracers it looked like the marines had pushed the yeomen off the Bishop's Gate and were settling in. The castle to the west showed some lights, but the cathedral tower was not tall enough to see completely over the wall. The town was still burning, the flames casting light over the field. She saw figures running about, some of them firing at the Bishop's Gate. The return fire was limited.

Mars doesn't want to hurt civilians, Sasha thought. Good.

A flash from the castle gate caught Sasha's attention, and she saw a solid yellow bolt arc through the air and slam into the tower below her. The shell detonated, and the belfry wobbled.

'Cannon! We got to go, L.T.!' Pierce called.

Sasha followed him down the stairs, several at a time. They leapt over a missing landing, the air thick with dust and smoke. They just reached the bottom when another shot struck. The tower collapsed behind Sasha, the door breaking under the falling masonry as she collapsed outside the rubble.

'You okay?' Pierce asked.

'I am,' Sasha said. She looked about. 'Where's Roach?'

'No idea,' Pierce said.

The dust in the air was thick, and Sasha found herself covered in it. She coughed, trying to get out of the cloud. Her ears were ringing.

A medic appeared and pulled her forward. She did not know his name but was glad for someone to take charge of her for a minute while she reoriented herself. The medic checked her head, asked her about her limbs. Sasha coughed, shaking her head to clear the fog and for the first time looked at the crowd of civilians.

There were too few people there.

Sasha did some math. The yeoman burned a dozen towns and villages before they got bottled up. Penelope's Haven was by far the largest, at just over two hundred. Even accounting for those who fled or were executed by the yeoman, there should have been five hundred hostages in the cathedral. The families who followed Count Walker here were holed up in the Golden Crown Inn, just east of the castle. The town, counted separately from those who lived in the cathedral or castle, was about eight hundred. If every able-bodied male not conscripted to arms was left to fight the fire while the women and children came in, there should be a thousand people at least crammed into this building, many of whom Sasha should have known.

There were maybe four hundred.

Sasha stood and walked into the crowd. 'Is Mrs. Gifford here?' she asked the closest civilians.

'Somewhere,' a man responded.

'Can she come forward, please?'

The question went through the crowd. Sasha waited for several minutes until two women approached. One was Mrs. Gifford, and the other her daughter, Annabelle.

'Yes,' Mrs. Gifford asked cautiously. Her daughter looked over her shoulder, nervously.

'Where are the hostages?' Sasha asked.

'I don't know,' Mrs. Gifford said. 'We thought they would be in here when we came here after the fire started, but they weren't.'

'We didn't deserve this!' Annabelle said harshly. 'To have our homes burned.'

'That was an accident,' Sasha said.

'One which you took advantage of,' Mrs. Gifford said. 'I get that war is cruel and callous, but your apathy for families you've never met is astounding.'

Sasha blinked in surprise, then realization set in. *She doesn't recognize me.* In addition to a uniform and weapon, she was covered head to toe in dust from the bell tower.

'Mrs. Gifford, I would never intentionally harm the woman who nursed me back to health after my first taste of whisky.'

Now Mrs. Gifford looked surprise. 'Sasha Small?' she asked after a moment.

Sasha took her helmet off. Mrs. Gifford gasped, and Annabelle's mouth

456

dropped in shock.

'I swear, Mrs. Gifford, we are trying to hurt as few people as possible, but there were supposed to be hundreds of hostages in here. My family, my townsfolk. And yet they're not here!'

Mrs. Gifford shrugged. 'I'm afraid I don't know. I visited your family several times when they were here, but the last time I saw them was a month ago. When the herded us in there after the fire started, I was surprised to see them missing. We were told they were still in here.'

Sasha grimaced. She looked back at the front door, where a sergeant was talking with Pierce. Pierce pointed out Sasha in the crowd, and the sergeant approached.

'Now you're in trouble,' Annabelle said sternly. The sergeant's stripes on his shoulder were the same as the ones the yeomen used, so the townsfolk knew he had some authority, but they did not recognize Sasha's rank. They thought Sasha was a common soldier.

The sergeant stepped up and snapped to attention. 'Lieutenant,' he said.

Sasha saluted back, hearing Annabelle gasp. Mrs. Gifford chuckled.

'Report, sergeant.'

'We've secured the front door and the trenches outside. No counterattack to speak of; too distracted to make a go of it. Some of the Chosen Rifles are on the roof, and Officer Goliath is securing his position.'

'Good,' Sasha said. 'Any word from Lieutenant Mars and the Bishop's Gate?'

'No, ma'am.'

Sasha frowned. It was unlikely Mars had too much trouble, as she had seen him defending the gate, but this was not the time to have communication problems.

'Report to Lieutenant Mars,' she said, 'tell him the hostages were removed from the cathedral somehow and we're trying to figure out what happened. If he has any information, let me know.'

The sergeant nodded and disappeared through the crowd. Sasha looked around. Del Oso had one of the front doors open, enough to talk with Goliath's defenders but not enough to invite attention. Roach was gone, hopefully looking for his goal.

'What do we do?' Mrs. Gifford asked.

'Everyone!' Sasha called. 'Please stay in your spots and keep this area clear. There's a fight going on and everyone is in danger. Stay low and we will do everything we can to keep you safe.'

Presuming those chemicals don't go off and kill us all.

***

Sasha moved back to the hallway with Ibrahim's squad, looking for anything they might have missed their first time through. There she found Mars, with two of his marines and three priests, coming to find her.

'There are some civilians in the priest's quarters,' Mars said. 'They appear to be families loyal to the count.'

'Have they said anything about the hostages?'

'No,' Mars said, glaring at the three. The older man, the bishop, stared defiantly back at them. The two younger ones looked at their feet, nervous at their sudden change of position.

'Where are the hostages?' Sasha asked. Mars rolled his eyes, and the bishop sneered.

'Rebels have no standing in God's eye,' he said.

'"Blessed are the meek, for they shall inherit the earth" means you're wrong,' Sasha said.

The bishop sneered at them. 'The count protects,' he said. 'He protects the innocent from your lies.'

'He executed two families and burned my town to ashes,' Sasha said.

'Because you rebelled against his lawful authority,' the bishop snapped.

'The yeomen take women, girls, for their beds,' Sasha said harshly. 'They take their food, their work, everything.'

'That is the way of the world,' the bishop said. 'There is always a hierarchy, always someone on the top and someone on the bottom.'

'Yes,' Sasha said, 'but being on the bottom does not mean you have to be a victim to the ones on top.'

'Suffering is part of life,' the bishop said.

'You bring war,' one of the younger priests said, 'and death and destruction. We brought them back here to protect them from all you threaten.'

'You have a poor definition of protection,' a voice called out.

458

It was Roach, descending the stairs from the choral balcony, holding something gently. It looked like an artillery shell, but it was colored yellow.

'What's that?' Mars asked, suddenly nervous.

'One of a dozen chemical shells,' Roach said, 'set and primed to explode and fill the cathedral.' He turned the shell in his hands to show off the side. Stenciled in bright white letters was one word.

MUSTARD.

'Mustard gas!' Sasha exclaimed. 'That's what they chose? MUSTARD GAS!' She was angry now. Sasha studied chemical weapons after Fitz's warning, and mustard gas was one of the ones she feared.

'This is protection?' Mars asked, looking back at the three men.

The bishop glared at Roach. The vocal priest looked shocked, while the youngest priest glared at the bishop.

Sasha stepped forward, facing the youngest priest. 'Do you know what that is?' she asked him. He glanced at her, trying to look defiant, but she saw the anger in his eyes. 'Do you want Officer Roach to explain to you what would have happened to the people you were trying to protect if those had detonated?' She stepped right up, face to face with the priest. 'To the children?'

The priest's face fell. 'They're gone,' he said. The bishop turned to shout but the marine behind him pulled him back. 'Most of them, the ones who were just caught up in things, were moved to the Golden Crown Inn. The influential families, and those who had members in the Mardurers, got moved into the castle.'

Sasha sighed. 'Thank you,' she said. Mars motioned to the marines and they pulled the priests back and out of the hallway.

'Shit,' Sasha said.

'Indeed,' Mars said. He looked at Sasha. 'We have to finish what we started. There will be time to pick everything apart later.'

It was an oddly comforting thing to hear from the marine officer, and Sasha nodded. 'You're right.'

'Goliath is holding the front,' Mars continued. 'I've got the Bishop's Gate. Scholar, take care of the civilians and act as a general reserve. Roach,' he said, glancing nervously at the munition in his hand, 'put those someplace safe.'

Roach nodded and went back to work. Sasha moved back into the cathedral, stopping for a moment at the altar.

I don't know if you can hear me, or if you care, she prayed, *Maybe I am a sinner and you've shunned me. But if you can help me save my family, please do so.*

Please.

***

Outside of the cathedral, the battle raged.

Goliath's assault on the front gate signaled the southern forces to begin their diversion. Weapons sighted for long-range opened fire, taking the defenders by surprise even as they turned to deal with the fight at the cathedral. Troops who might have pushed Goliath off took cover. But long-range fire was all Captain Sabre would allow. The height of Walker Castle made any foray into no man's land too dangerous to risk.

That did not hold true to the west. Several grenadiers, rifles and a pair of LAMB guns worked their way into the swamp during the night. Unsure of who was a defender and who was a civilian, the chosen troopers fired over the houses, provoking responses from the dangerous ones and scattering the innocents into cover. The firefight was rather one-sided, there being too few defenders watching the swamp and too many troopers hiding in it. The troopers came closer and closer, sensing an opportunity to break the overstretched defenders.

The defenders did counterattack at the cathedral. Shooting down the church tower took out the best observation post the RAM had, but even then, the attacks against both gates fell flat. Goliath's position at the front was supported by long range fire from Saber's lines, and Walker had dug excellent trenches. Against the Bishop's Gate, the open field, illuminated by the city fire, was too difficult to cross against determined rifle fire, and impossible once the Naval Group's *Winter* positioned herself to sweep the field clear of anyone advancing across it.

The second wave of boats returned. Without needing to move stealthily, the rowers emphasized speed, cutting several minutes off the best estimate. Sparrow and the bulk of her company, plus a few extra men and women tacked on here and there, landed at the cathedral, moving to defend the gates and other points along the wall. The boats then split up, the *Prince Dawson* moving to the north, the *Renaissance* and the *Minnesota* moving south, all with the intent of grabbing more troops.

Between all the defenses and now the fire, the defenders were spread too thin. Even as they succeeded in containing the fire behind a series of fire breaks, the RAM troops in the swamp captured the western defenses. Word spread and soon every armed defender was running for the castle. Officers trying to form defenses in the town itself were ignored as panic swept through their ranks. The civilians hid, waiting for the fighting to die down around them.

By the time the *Prince Dawson* landed reinforcements to secure their foothold in the city itself, every defender had withdrawn to the castle and the Golden Cross Inn. The gates were closed and secured; the defenders repositioned to cover the approaches. Anyone not inside by then surrendered to the RAM rather than fight a hopeless cause.

Vittorio Montessori lost his city.

Chapter 51

'Hey, Scholar?' Roach's voice called from the top of the stairs.

Sasha sat with two of her squads in the hallway as a reserve, the other two helping the medics check out the civilians. She had been quiet for the last fifteen minutes, trying not to obsess about the situation and largely failing. His voice pulled her back.

'Yes, Roach?' she asked.

'Can you see a wire coming through the ceiling about ten paces from the stairway? By the wall?'

Sasha grabbed a lantern and lifted it, peering up at the ceiling. A quick jerk of movement caught her attention. 'I see it,' she said.

'Okay,' Roach called, 'I'm coming down.'

Sasha waved Pierce over. He was several inches taller and could reach the wire. It had been laid between the bricks and painted over. As he pulled it free, she followed it to a tapestry. It then turned downward towards a drain just below the floor, where it disappeared down below.

'What is it?' she asked Roach as he descended from the stairs.

'It's the wire connected to the chemical charges. It went off a few minutes ago.'

'What?' Sasha gasped.

'We removed everything first chance we got. All it did was singe the pews.'

'So, everything is fine?' she asked.

'Yes, and no. Yes, in that we removed the threat to the civilians. No, in that it looks like someone removed several of the shells from this wire, so some of the shells are missing. Also, I want to know who set off the detonator.'

Sasha blinked at him, then looked at the wire. 'We secured everyone we could,' she said.

'Right. So, I'm following the wire. Want to come?'

Sasha grabbed a lantern and motioned for Pierce to follow her.

Down in the basement they found the wire coming out of the drain, right where it was supposed to be. 'Is it odd that this would be built like this?' Roach asked. 'Shouldn't there be pipes instead of a small hole in the floor? Aren't pipes what big buildings have?'

'No idea,' Sasha said. The wire ran along the ceiling until it reached the entrance to the crypt.

'Of course,' Pierce muttered.

'We need the key,' Roach said.

Pierce ran to get it. It took several minutes until he returned with the key and several other armed troops. 'Just in case,' he said.

The unlocked door swung open, heavily clanging into the stone wall. Sasha handed the lantern to Roach and drew her carbine to her shoulder. They entered.

Sasha was nervous. Penelope's Haven had a small graveyard outside of town, as did most communities. But a crypt – an underground cave filled with dead – struck Sasha as horrifying. Even if only one person was interred so far.

The crypt was built with twelve alcoves, each large enough for a stone tomb. Eleven of them sat empty. The twelfth held the countess. It was a beautifully ornate stone tomb, with painted scenes of the woman's life.

'He really did love her,' one of the troopers said quietly.

'He did,' Sasha said. It was about the only kind words she could ever say about Count Walker.

'My father told me,' Roach said, 'that she was quite the influence on him. That while he was never going to be a great nobleman, a lot of the excesses of his yeomen did not start until after her death.'

'So, if she had lived,' Pierce asked, 'things might not have gotten so bad?'

'That's what my father says,' Roach shrugged.

'Let's find the wire,' Sasha said quietly. The countess had never done anything to her, and she had no intention of disturbing her rest.

'Here,' Roach said. The wire ran along the ceiling to the back panel. It was a small altar of some sort, with an ornate cross on the wall, a cushioned bench for knees, and a box of candles and matches. The wire ran off to the side and into the wall.

'Huh?' Sasha asked.

'The wall's crooked,' Pierce said. He pointed, and Sasha realized there was a door in the wall. It looked like it was normally flush with the wall, but was left slightly ajar to allow the wire to run in.

Roach reached and tugged on the door, but it did not open. He looked through the opening. 'Do we have a long sword or bayonet? And some rope?'

The requested tools were produced. Sasha watched Roach use the bayonet to feed the rope in, then fish it out several feet lower. With the rope in two hands, he lifted. Sasha heard harsh scraping, then the door swung open.

The lantern light revealed a short hallway, then stairs leading down and to the right. Sasha recalled the maps she had studied so long.

'This leads to the castle,' she said.

'Or at least in that direction,' Roach agreed.

Sasha stepped in, to the top of the stairs. The hallway was bare stone, with support columns every few feet.

How did we not know about this? she wondered.

Sasha turned to Roach. 'Roach, go up and find Mars. Tell him what's going on. The rest of you, with me.'

'Hey,' Roach reached out and grabbed her elbow. He leaned in and whispered. 'You're not going to do anything stupid because you're upset your plan didn't work?'

Sasha looked at him, and a dozen answers flashes across her mind. Anger at being questioned like this. Surprise he would doubt her judgment. Concern that he was right. Fear that she was doing the wrong thing by heading down this hallway. Fear that staying was the wrong choice. Fear that it was too late to do anything at all.

Templars are trained to make the hard choices.

'No,' she said. 'I swear, Roach. Nothing stupid.'

Roach looked at her reproachfully. 'Be careful,' he said, and he left.

Pierce took the lantern and stepped into the tunnel. He stood to the far left, holding the lantern towards the middle of the hallway, while Sasha stood on the far right. If anyone shot at the light, they would not be shooting directly at anyone. Her troops fell in behind them.

I wish Del Oso were here. Sasha thought of waiting, but this was an opportunity that she had to investigate now.

'Let's go,' she said.

***

The tunnel went on for some time, ending at a stairwell leading up. *We must be under the castle*, Sasha thought.

They ascended to a doorway. This one was locked by a simple mechanical lock. Sasha pulled and found it secured. She turned and looked at the squad, motioning to Locke to come up with her shotgun.

'It'll be loud,' Pierce whispered.

'I know,' Sasha replied, 'but I want in. The doors go, and we rush in.'

Pierce frowned but nodded. Sasha took a breath and tapped Locke's back.

Locke's shotgun charge blew the lock out of the door and it swung open. The noise was deafening, but Sasha forced herself through the door, carbine up.

Light followed Sasha into the darkened room, revealing tables. Pierce found wall lanterns and started lighting them, revealing the room as more troops pushed their way in.

'A shrine to himself,' Pierce said.

That is what it looked like to Sasha. Some of the objects were tailor dummies with old Commonwealth uniforms on them. Others were long display tables with glass tops, holding mementos and trophies. Everything was covered in a fine layer of dust.

'No one's been here in a while,' someone said.

'We're underneath the Count's Tower,' Sasha said. 'We must be. This is the storage basement no one else has access to.' She grinned. If she was right, and she was sure she was, they were well inside the castle walls.

'What's up there?' Pierce asked.

'Next level up is the ground floor, with the county offices and the Main Hall. Above that is his personal office, and above that his sleeping quarters.' Sasha thought for a moment, trying to remember the internal construction of the Count's Tower. 'This door should lead up to a landing behind the office. No one else but him and his most trusted staff are allowed to use it.'

'So, we can get all the way up to the roof?' Pierce asked.

Sasha nodded. 'Indeed. I want security on that landing, Pierce. I want to keep this way open for as long as we can. If you have to fall back, fall back down here.'

Pierce nodded and Sasha moved to the door.

The stairway gently circled up, curving to her right. She moved slowly but steadily, passing the first landing with two doors. She heard voices on the far side of one door but continued upward.

The next level was the count's personal office. It took up most of the level. Bookshelves, only half full, lined the wall. A massive desk sat in the middle. Behind it, on the wall, was a huge painting of the countess. The windows were shuttered, and glass strewn about the floor.

The depot detonation, she thought.

She continued up to the bedroom. She saw open windows, so she gestured to the trooper following her with the lantern to stay back. She did not want anyone to see her up there.

The room itself was huge, larger than her family's house in Penelope's Haven. A massive bed sat to one side, with several dressers and another desk. A plush carpet, also covered in broken glass, stretched across the floor. A wind blew through the windows, billowing the curtains. Sasha approached slowly and looked out.

Walker Town still burned, though a portion looked to be done already, and Noble Boulevard kept the fire from jumping too far to the south. The Golden Crown Inn still stood, so far unaffected by the battle.

The cathedral looked to have taken a few more hits from that cannon but was otherwise intact. Not much gunfire was coming to or from the building. The trench works were still inhabited, but Sasha could not tell by whom.

The view was surprisingly calm. She heard few gunshots from her vantage point, saw no attacks. The battle was in a lull.

Sasha turned her mind to other things. *Where are the hostages?* She wondered. *Where could they be?*

Below the tower, the main hall stretched out to the south, with the squat servants' quarters angled to the east. Further east, next to the main gate, sat the stables and the yeoman barracks. To the west was the darkness where the supply depot had been, and the granary ruins that half-stood next to it. To the north were what had been gardens, and the castle chapel.

Sasha looked at the chapel. It had always struck her as odd that the count had a chapel built within the castle in addition to the cathedral. The reason, she had been told, was that the countess wanted the cathedral to be for all the faiths of Walker, while the chapel was Iberian Catholicism for those who practiced that specifically, such as the count and some of his followers.

Sasha started to step away from the window but stopped.

The chapel was lit up, which was no surprise, but it was also guarded, which was. Two men stood at either door, armed with automatics. In addition, each door had been barred from the outside. Which meant they were there to keep people inside, not out.

They're in the chapel, Sasha thought. They're right there.

***

'You sure, L.T.?' Pierce asked.

Sasha nodded. 'It's guarded and locked to keep people inside. It's the only place that makes sense. The barracks and stables are too close to the front gate, and the granary and warehouse were demolished in the explosion.'

'I'm not saying it sounds wrong,' Peirce replied, 'but you don't know.'

'No,' Sasha admitted, 'I don't.' She looked down the stairs. 'Stay here, keep that tunnel open.'

'Right,' Pierce said. He did not look happy, but he did not try to stop her.

Sasha slowly opened the door into the servants' building. A short hallway led to an outside door. A door to the side led to the sleeping rooms. Sasha had no idea if any servants were left in there, and she did not have time, or personnel, to find out. She only had three with her; Locke, Collins and a third soldier she did not know.

The next door was opened just as slowly. The main entrance to the chapel was to her left. To the right was the back entrance, for the priest. The front was well lit, while the back was darker. There was a dull roar from the burning village, and a few gunshots in the air, but the lull in the battle continued.

Sasha gestured, then sprinted from the door, running to the middle of the chapel wall, hiding in the darkness. The other three followed.

Okay, how do we get in?

She jumped as a loud bang sounded. Her team froze.

'God damn it, Jim!' someone yelled. 'I told you to secure that door.' Someone from up front yelled.

'I did!' Someone from the back door responded. She saw the figure appear at the edge of the light. He could not see the team standing close to the wall, hidden in the darkness.

'Well, do it again, dumbass!'

Jim cursed and walked towards the door in the darkness. Another figure stepped to the edge of the light. It was the other guard. Sasha aimed at him, barely ten paces away, completely oblivious.

'Approaching the door, Sergeant!' Jim called. 'At the door, Sergeant! Now I'm . . . OH, SHI–.'

Gunfire erupted behind her, and Sasha acted. She shot the second guard, rushing forward to get inside before the garrison realized she was there. Cries of alarm sounded above her, from the wall. She grasped the wooden bar and lifted it off the door just as a rifle bullet buried itself in the doorframe. She threw open the door and rushed inside.

And found three yeomen in there.

Sasha's momentum through the door carried her into the first yeoman, who grabbed her rifle and pulled her off balance. She socked him in the nose, trying to wrestle control of the weapon. Locke came in right behind her, sweeping to the right, and shot the second yeomen. The third yeoman fired a pistol and Locke went down with a cry. Collins came in third, shooting the third yeoman at close range.

The yeomen Sasha was fighting with was bigger than she, and the initial force of her body slam had spent itself. He was starting to gain the upper hand when another figure slammed into them.

It was Del Oso, of all people, and his bulk and muscles pushed the three of them back and through the priest's door. The flimsy wood burst apart and the three tumbled into the chapel proper.

The yeoman succeeded in pulling the carbine from Sasha's hand and clubbed Del Oso in the side of the head with it as they fell. Sasha sprung and dropped her body weight on his arm, pinning the weapon to his chest, while her hand grabbed for her knife. He awkwardly punched at her. She swayed out of the way and drove the knife into his throat. He punched again, but all he succeeded in doing was cutting his own throat open. Sasha was sprayed in blood and he convulsed.

Sasha was momentarily shocked by the violence of it, until a familiar voice brought her back to the present.

'Whoever you are, you just murdered a man in cold blood!'

Chapter 52

Sasha did not say anything at first. Of all the ways she imagined seeing her family again, doing so immediately after cutting a man's throat was not one of them. She wiped the blade of the knife on the man's sleeve and slid it back into its sheath.

'You are a murderer,' Alexander Small protested again.

'I heard you the first time, Father,' Sasha said, standing up and looking her father in the eye.

Her words took a moment to register, and a look of shock crossed Alexander's face. 'SASHA!' he exclaimed. Sasha heard gasps around her. Many people here knew her.

'You okay, Sergeant Major?' Sasha asked, lending a hand to Del Oso.

'Just fine, Lieutenant,' Del Oso replied. Pierce appeared behind him, picking up Sasha's carbine and returning it to her.

'How's Locke?' Sasha asked.

'Grazing wound to the ribs. She'll be fine,' Pierce said.

'Good. Now what are you doing here?'

'Not ten seconds after you left, Goliath came through with a platoon and the rest of your squads. We were just steps behind you when you went out that door.'

Sasha sighed. *Ten seconds.* She turned to make her way to the front entrance.

Alexander Small still stood there, staring at her in disbelief.

'Sasha,' he said. 'You killed a man.'

'Not my first,' Sasha said.

'Sasha!' he exclaimed. Her mother appeared at her side, the smile on her face disappearing as she took in her daughter drenched in blood. Behind her, Sasha saw her sister, holding a baby, starting wide eyed at the scene before her. Next to her, Mayor Cartier looked sick. Samuel, her bully, was nowhere to be seen. Neither was her brother, Thomas.

'Sasha,' Abigail Small said, still staring at her daughter's blood-streaked face. 'What are you doing here?

'Saving you,' Sasha said.

A window shattered from a bullet strike. Pierce appeared again, hauling Locke through the door.

'The troops at the gates know we're here,' he said. 'They're shooting back.'

'Everyone, stay down,' Sasha bellowed, trying to sound like Del Oso. 'We're going to get you out of here, we just need to –.'

A machine gun opened fire, peppering the chapel. Windows shattered and wood splintered, but the lower stonework held.

'We can't stay here,' she said to Del Oso.

'That machine gun can't hit us here, Lieutenant,' he said.

'No, but they do have the cannon that took out the bell tower.'

'Oh, shit,' Del Oso replied. 'Forgot about that.'

Sasha stayed low and moved over to the closest window. She peaked out, hoping to see the machine gun. She could not. She turned to crawl into the priest's office when she saw the wire. The same wire that Roach had found, coming from a hole drilled in the wooden wall. She followed the wire up to the ceiling, where she spied a wooden box snuggled in the rafters.

Roach said some were missing.

'Sergeant Major!' she called. Del Oso looked at her, and she gestured up. 'We found Roach's missing munitions.'

Del Oso cursed. 'We can't say here,' he agreed.

'Get smoke grenades ready,' Sasha said, moving over to the front door. The glass panes next to the heavy wooden door were missing and boarded up. Damage from the supply explosion.

'Needle,' she said loudly.

'Thimble,' a voice on the other side answered. The door unlocked and a corporal from Sparrow's company pulled the door open.

'Ma'am,' he said.

'We have to evacuate the civilians to the main building,' Sasha said.

Tracers shot through the gap between chapel and hall. 'Bit dangerous, that,' the corporal said.

'Can't be helped,' Sasha replied. 'They've got explosives planted.'

'Great,' the corporal muttered.

470

Sasha glanced around the corner. Del Oso had tossed the smoke grenades into the gap between the castle and the chapel. The machine gun spat tracers through the gap, but it was blind fire. Too high.

'Corporal, who's got the guns in the tower?'

'Officer Goliath,' he replied.

'Tell him to keep the wall tops clear, but not to engage anyone on the ground unless they're shot at. Go!' The corporal disappeared and Del Oso appeared next to her.

'Get ready to run,' she said to Del Oso.

'What?' Del Oso asked, but Sasha was already running towards the castle wall.

It was thirty yards to the wall. From the outside it looked to be of solid stone twenty feet tall, but it was less impressive on this side. It was only a ten-foot wall, not of stone but wood and earthworks. A trick of construction to make the castle look bigger than it was.

She advanced towards the front of the castle, staying in the darkness, until she reached a support pillar that offered some cover from the gun. To her right was a garden, between her and the chapel.

She brought her carbine up and waited. Goliath's troops in the tower started shooting at figures on the wall, clearing men that could threaten Sasha or the civilians. Unfortunately, the windows of the tower did not overlook the stables, so the tower could not directly help fighting the machine gun. On the other hand, neither could the gun threaten them.

The gun fired into the smoke, and Sasha responded, firing several bursts at it. Then she ducked back as it turned to fire on her. The bullets chipped stone.

Now's your chance, Del Oso. Get them moving.

A carbine fired to her right; someone else was in the garden, firing at the machine gun. It turned on them, the bullets cutting down stalks of whatever was growing there. Sasha stood and fired, dropping to the ground after two bursts. Her unseen friend fired again, the pair alternating to keep the gun's attention.

This is working, she thought. *We're going to* –.

The chapel exploded.

The explosion demolished the wooden superstructure of the chapel. The stone foundation stood proud, but debris rained down over the entire area. The shock of the explosion left Sasha breathless for several moments; when she did start breathing again, the smell of garlic permeated the air.

'Shit,' she whispered. She could not hear herself talk. She crawled forward, trying to get away from where the machine gun thought she was.

A figure moved about in the garden. It was Collins, her grenadier, holding his head and stumbling about. Sasha wanted to shout to him to get down, but it was too late. A burst of fire cut him down right before her eyes.

The machine gun swept across the field, cutting into the chapel, the garden, and towards the building. Anywhere there might be an enemy they could not see.

But they revealed themselves to Sasha. The gun was set into the upper level of the stables, firing out of a window, protected by stone walls.

Someone fired on the machine gun from the servants' quarters to Sasha's right. It was in a better position to hit the machine gun than the tower was, but it was made of wood not stone. The machine gun tracers swept across the structure, and Sasha heard someone scream. A second later the roar of a cannon grabbed her attention, the solid yellow shot arched overhead and glanced off the tower.

Sasha took a moment to think. So long as Goliath held the tower, he could keep the walls clear of the enemy and threaten their remaining positions. The cannon could take out the tower, collapsing it and possibly trapping everyone inside the walls if the debris fell deep enough into the basement, but at the very least removing Goliath from the fight. As much as she wanted to retreat, Sasha was in a position to take out the cannon before it did too much damage. And the enemy did not know she where she was.

She crawled slowly forward towards Collin's body. The grenade launcher and the shells were still in his backpack. She pulled them off. She heard the report of the cannon and ducked as the shell exploded on the tower. There was the sound of falling stonework.

Sasha crawled forward to where a beam from the chapel landed and loaded the launcher. It was still dark, and she could not see. *Where?*

The cannon fired again, and Sasha saw it perched at the corner of the stables. The shell flew overhead and missed the tower, streaking off into the distance. Sasha returned fire with the launcher, a weapon she had little training in. The grenade went off behind the cannon. The machine gun opened up at her again, bullets striking the beam and around her.

Another gun fired to her left; someone had carried a LAMB gun up and was shooting at the machine gun. Other rifles went off, fire pouring into the stables. She obviously was not alone, and now the machine gun was distracted.

Sasha reloaded. She crawled forward, into the garden. *The cannon threatens the tower. The tower is our key to taking the castle.* She had to take it out.

She saw a glimmer of light; a lantern, being used to reload the cannon. She aimed, taking a deep breath. *Take it easy.*

She fired.

There was a flash as the grenade exploded amongst the cannon's crew. Sasha smiled, then a second explosion went off, followed by a larger third detonation. The window with the machine gun lit up and the gun flew outwards. Half the building collapsed.

I must have hit the shells, Sasha thought.

'Lieutenant?' Del Oso said behind her.

'Sergeant Major,' she said, crawling backwards. Del Oso was at the beam.

'You're still alive,' he sounded relieved.

'I am,' she nodded. 'Did you get the civilians out?'

'Yes. A couple of them got knocked over when the chapel went off, but they're being checked out now.'

'What's the situation inside?' Sasha asked.

'Goliath has armed the tower, taken the Great Hall and the secondary quarters, and removed everyone from the guest hall. By the way, the Great Hall? Their headquarters. Captured Giulio Montessori and a Royal Army major.'

'Fantastic,' Sasha said.

'He wants us to hold this line,' Del Oso said. 'Goliath, I mean. I've brought you two LAMB guns and a dozen rifles.'

'Right,' Sasha said. She looked up at the sky. 'I hope this all finished by dawn, otherwise we'll be rather exposed.'

'So, we're digging in,' Del Oso said.

Sasha nodded. 'We're digging in.'

***

Vittorio Montessori stood in the barracks. He had come out here to breathe fighting spirit into his yeomen to retake the chapel. Then the rebels had taken his tower behind him, captured or killed his son, and swept his men from the walls. He cursed them loudly, his anger as a count not enough to keep his experienced general's mind from recognizing the truth.

It was over.

General Montessori knew it. Count Walker came to know it too. Those Mardurers had taken his town, his cathedral, and his great hall. If the hostages were not in fact dead, then they were free and out of his reach. Only the gatehouse, yeoman barracks and half the stables remained in his control, and that was not enough territory to defend, even if the yeomen left were of a mind to defend it. He saw the defeat in their eyes.

It was over.

He moved up the stairs, ignoring the last few officers and sergeants planning their defense, entering the room of a yeoman officer. He did not know whose it was, nor did he care. He locked the door behind him and set his automatic on the bed. From one of his pouches he pulled his special item.

An infantry mine.

One of his men, experienced with explosives, had modified it. It no longer responded to a trigger but had a fuse like a grenade. He sat down at the desk and spread the stand, setting it facing him. From another pouch he pulled an eight-inch book. Inside was a picture, faded and old, of his wife, shortly after they first met.

He smiled at it, setting it in front of him. He reached over and pulled the pin out of the mine. He did not know the length of the fuse, nor did he care. He picked up the book and stared at his long-dead wife.

I only ever saw beauty through your eyes. I only ever knew peace in your arms. You, alone, thought to make these ungrateful peasants' lives worth something. If you had lived, if you had continued your great works, perhaps they would have been more grateful. Perhaps, then, we could have avoided this rebellion. Perhaps –.

Chapter 53

Sasha stood on the top of the Count's Tower, the tallest point in Walker Town, now that the bell tower had been toppled. She looked out over the burned-out ruins of the town; the cathedral she had fought for, and the inn she had stayed in so many times. She saw the trenches to the south and the marshes to the west. It was quite the view.

Someone was behind her. She turned to see General Caesar climb up the stairs. *He looks out of place on a battlefield,* she thought. *He's not a soldier.* For a moment she wondered if Prince would look any better but could not decide. *Maybe generals don't belong on battlefields.*

'Templar Scholar,' Caesar said, coming to stand next to her.

'General,' she said.

'Your plan worked, Sasha. Walker has fallen.'

'Yes,' she said, 'but it was a close thing.'

'Battles often are,' Caesar replied. He looked out over the town. 'You remember listening to the battle reports from the Army of the Lakes?'

'I do,' Sasha said. 'I was so scared Senator was going to lose, and with the Army destroyed, I Corps would just march into Walker County unopposed.'

'I was too,' Caesar admitted. 'It has been a while since you have asked a question,' he said, 'so let me answer one you might have asked one week or another. This war was not meant to start for another few years. We had many more preparations planned; much more we were going to do.'

'What happened to change it?' Sasha asked.

'We were forced to accelerate our schedule when we were almost found out. It was not entirely unforeseen, but neither was it ideal.'

'I would be more sympathetic,' Sasha responded, 'but if you had waited a few more years, I'd probably be married to Samuel Cartier, bearing his children, or whored to the yeoman for punishment for some slight or another.'

'True,' Caesar said. 'It is odd, I think, to consider how misfortune and fortune are intertwined. While I cannot claim any belief in a supernatural being, there is an artistry to the universe that I find . . . poetic.'

Sasha nodded, then yawned.

'You have been awake for about a day?' Caesar asked.

'About.'

'Seen a doctor yet?'

'No, sir. My wounds were minor; they had more pressing matters to tend to.'

Caesar nodded. 'Many of the seriously wounded have been seen to. The doctors are viewing the minor cases now.'

'Then I should go see them,' Sasha said. She turned and stopped when Caesar cleared his throat.

'Are you upset?' Caesar asked.

'I am,' Sasha admitted, 'but not at you. More than a year with the RAM, Third Regiment, the Templars, all my friends, my learning, my advancement, and one small conversation with my father and I feel like a child again, being scolded for not sharing my bread with my brother.'

Caesar was quiet for a moment. 'I understand,' he said, 'more than you might expect. The only advice I can give you is to learn to accept that they will not accept you. You each have chosen your own course for your life. It cannot be expected that those pathways will always run alongside each other.'

'I understand,' Sasha replied, and went down the stairs. Saxon and the rest of Caesar's entourage were in Count Walker's suite, looking through the papers and items.

'He lived quite the life,' Saxon said, looking about the decorations.

'At the expense of the lives of the farmers,' Sasha said, walking through the room. She was too tired, and frankly, too sore, to help go through papers.

She entered the hallway. Everything was being systematically stripped from the castle; uniforms and civilians alike rushing about, carrying armloads of anything to wagons to be sorted through and distributed later.

Sasha entered the main hall and saw four older men sitting around a table in the middle. Sasha hid a smile as she approached while their attention was focused on a pair of men carrying out a large box.

'I'm surprised one of you didn't bring a deck of cards,' she said.

The four turned and looked at her, first in surprise, then they beamed. 'The butterfly's friend!' they cheered.

'Well,' David Wells said sternly. 'Now it is Lieutenant the butterfly's friend.'

'I see you were involved,' Dellwood said, gesturing as Sasha's stained uniform.

'I was,' she admitted. 'I'm glad you all made it through unharmed.'

'Unharmed?' Le Croix shook his head. 'We haven't had a proper drink in a year.'

'Well, I'll see what I can do,' Sasha said.

'Uncle!' a man called, slipping into the room. He was wearing a yeoman's jacket, with the insignia torn off.

'Douglas!' Wells said. 'Come on in, take a look at what the inside of the castle looks like.'

'I've seen it,' Douglas snapped. Sasha looked at the man, who noticed her and glared at her. 'Who're you?' he asked.

'Lieutenant Scholar,' she said.

'Well, Lieutenant,' he stressed her rank, as if he did not believe her, 'excuse me if I have words with my uncle.' He turned to David. 'Where is he?'

'Who?'

'Who! The guy who ordered me to blow up the supplies, that's who. The guy who planned this whole attack, who is responsible for the deaths of every civilian, for the burning of the town, for all of it!'

'That would be me,' Sasha said. Douglas looked up, startled. The four sergeants all turned and looked up at her.

'What?' Douglas said.

'Lieutenant Scholar, junior aide-de-camp to General Caesar.'

'And you planned this attack?' Douglas asked incredulously.

'Planned it. Revised it. Led it,' Sasha said. She was not at all willing to listen to yet another person critique her plan.

'Did it even occur to you people live here?'

'Of course. Just as it occurred to me that my family were hostages, and that innocent men had been pressed into service in defense of the town, but we had to end the siege, and we did.'

Douglas looked at her, ready to argue, but no words came. Finally, he shook his head. 'You did what you had to.' Any defiance in his spirit evaporated. Now he just sounded tired. 'At least it's over. I just wish I still had a home to go to.'

'I can understand that,' Sasha said, heading for the door.

The castle was still abuzz with soldiers moving about, wagons carting loads of supplies and weapons and material out. She walked through the castle gate, too wrapped up in her own thoughts to acknowledge the armed men saluting her as she left.

Walker was in chaos, people rushing about here or there. The town was full of people packing up to leave or looking for those who might have been trapped in rubble. The cathedral was still a prison camp, now housing the yeomen and soldiers who had defended the town for so long. And in the field between them, the hospital, surrounded by crowds of people waiting for their chance to get aid, or get out.

Sasha asked an orderly where lightly injured were being treated. He gestured towards a row of benches and pews set out, and there Sasha saw the hostages from Penelope's Haven. She could not see her family, but if they were anywhere, that was a good place to start.

Sasha approached, seeing a few familiar faces, then came to a sudden halt. Samuel Cartier stood before her. The boy who had tormented her and bullied her for years, who threatened her with violence and abuse. He no longer looked a threat to her. Indeed, he looked skinny and hollow after a year as a hostage. He obviously had not taken to the experience.

'Sasha,' he said, quietly.

'Samuel,' Sasha replied.

'A lieutenant,' he said, 'and a soldier?'

'Yes,' Sasha said, 'thanks to you.'

'Me?' Samuel asked.

'Your bullying and harassment taught me to stand up for myself. And now I stand up for the whole county.'

Samuel looked at her, and he teared up. 'I'm sorry,' he whispered.

'Why?' Sasha asked, her anger rising. 'You had plenty of opportunities to apologize before. Why change now? Did sitting in Walker County bore you? Did you find the yeomen not to your liking?'

Samuel stared for a second, then lifted his shirt. His torso showed scars, welts and bruises.

'The yeomen knew I fancied you,' he said, 'so they broke me for answers. I had none, but they broke me anyway. I cried and screamed and fought, and it did nothing. And if I did that to you . . .,' he trailed off.

Sasha stared at him, and the anger that had grown inside her fell away. She

478

hated him, and always would, but he was no longer a demon. He was a man, one who fell far short of the quality she was now used to. He had no power over her, unless she gave it to him. And she was not going to do that.

'Go tend to your family, Samuel,' she said.

She walked past him and through the survivors of Penelope's Haven. They looked up as Sasha approached. Many of them knew her, and looked at her with a mixture of horror, wonder, and relief. Mrs. Neilson, one of the elders of the Alvanists, stood and turned to her.

'A fighting Alvanist?' she scolded Sasha.

'I make no claim to being an Alvanist,' Sasha said. 'At this moment I just want to see my family.'

'They're not here,' Mrs. Neilson said. 'All the civilians with children went down to that tent,' she gestured at one set up in the shadow of the cathedral. 'Your mother took most of your family there. Your father is helping search the city for anyone else who might need help.'

'Good,' Sasha said. She looked forward to seeing her family without her father present.

She spotted them outside the tent. They sat around a table, eating some bread, watching the hospital. Abigail sat with Thomas next to her. Michelle and her nephew were opposite. Sasha approached them from behind.

'Excuse me,' she said, finding her voice wavering.

Her family turned and looked at her. Before anything else could happen, her mother leapt from her seat and dragged Sasha into an embrace.

'Oh, my daughter!' she said, crushing Sasha in her arms. 'Oh, you are safe and alive. Praise the Lord.'

Sasha gripped her mother back. 'I'm glad you all are safe.'

Her mother finally released, and Michelle was there, taking her place. Sasha hugged her sister and felt her sob. 'Oh, I've been so worried.'

'You saw me a few hours ago,' Sasha said.

'You looked busy. Besides, seeing you once in a year and a bit is not enough,' Michelle scolded her. She finally pulled Sasha out to look at her. 'You're bleeding?' she said.

'Some scrapes, nothing warranting a surgeon,' Sasha replied.

'And not the first time,' Michelle brushed the scar on Sasha's lip. 'When was this?'

'Fighting the Royal Army, last spring,' Sasha said.

Michelle turned to Thomas, who was holding the baby. Thomas looked at her angrily, as if she should not be welcomed warmly, and yet happy, as if he wanted to jump up next.

'Here,' Michelle said, taking the baby from their brother. 'This is Noah. Noah, this is your aunt, Sasha.'

The baby was close to a year old, old enough to look at Sasha as she took him. He laughed and caressed her face. 'He's beautiful,' Sasha said.

'He is,' Abigail Small said of her grandchild.

Michelle took him back, and Sasha turned to her brother. Thomas stood up, his face still conflicted.

'You killed someone,' he finally said.

'Yes,' Sasha agreed.

'That is a sin,' he said. 'You can't go to heaven.'

'I know, but I will sin and sin again to keep you all safe.'

Thomas opened his mouth but said nothing. He finally stepped forward and hugged Sasha around her waist. He was a few inches taller than last she had seen him, and his hair was longer. Sasha hugged him back.

'What happened to you after you were taken?' Abigail asked.

'I was not taken, Mother, I left of my own will,' Sasha said.

'I know, but your father –.'

Sasha cut her off. 'My father took it too far. He let the yeomen take me for their pleasure.'

'He did it because –. '

'After sixteen years under his roof I know why he did it, and I do not care. Mother, I love you all, but I am not an Alvanist, and I do not think I ever will be. You live as you wish, and I will fight to protect you while you do.'

Abigail looked at her daughter sadly, then reached out and stroked her chin. 'Okay, Sasha. Okay.'

'So,' Michelle said. 'You left?'

'I left with the Third Minnesota Field Regiment,' Sasha said, 'under Lieutenant Colonel Snow. We moved out of Walker County, and I was inducted into their ranks as a rifle, a common soldier. I read everything I could and studied warfare under them. We got into some fights, and I made a name as a decent fighter.'

'I'm sure you did,' Michelle said. Her sister smiled at her.

'You're happy for me?' Sasha asked, amazed.

'I said to you before that I prayed for you to learn to accept yourself.' Michelle responded. 'I'm glad you finally have.'

Sasha smiled in return. 'Anyway, I read so much I attracted the attention of the generals. They gave me the opportunity to join the Templars, a training program to produce officers and leader for the new renaissance. And I excelled. Mother, you would not believe the books I have been reading. So much knowledge, so much.'

Abigail smiled at her daughter, tears in her eyes. 'So much knowledge, but last night you fought.'

'I had to fight. It was my plan, Mother,' Sasha said.

'What?' Abigail's mouth fell open. Michelle looked up in shock, and Thomas just stared.

'The attack on Walker was my plan; I had to be involved in the operation. I had to lead. Otherwise, I wouldn't deserve to have my voice heard by the generals; I wouldn't deserve to have others follow me.'

Her family looked at her in shock. 'You gained knowledge and wisdom,' Abigail finally said.

'I did,' Sasha nodded. She was going to say more but Elector appeared from the tent. He saw her and came over.

'Templar Scholar,' he greeted her.

'Templar Elector,' she said. 'This is most of my family. Abigail Small, my sister Michelle and her son Noah, and my brother Thomas. This is Templar Elector, our class's doctor.'

'We've met,' Michelle said, smiling up at him. 'He's the one who gave Noah a look over. You know my sister from the Templars?'

'I do,' Elector said. 'A fine woman, quite the scholar,' He smiled at them, then turned to Sasha. 'Scholar, I've run into some issues trying to get civilians out of the city. I think there's been some mix up somewhere; I was told we should remove them, but Captain Saber is under the impression we need to keep them here. Can you check with General Caesar when you get back to headquarters?'

'Will do,' Sasha said, 'but I can't guarantee he'll be able to help. Colonel

Grace is in command, now that the operation is over.'

'I know, but you'll ask?'

'I'll ask,' Sasha promised.

Elector smiled again, bowed to the family and turned back to his tent.

'Scholar?' Michelle asked.

'It's my Renaissance name,' Sasha said. 'Because I read so much.'

'That's a good name,' Abigail said. She looked at her daughter. 'I wish you would come home.'

'You are my family, but not my home,' Sasha said. Her mother teared up, but Sasha shook her head. 'Don't, Mother. I don't wish to be cruel, but I must be honest. I love you, all of you, even Father, but I am not an Alvanist. I am meant for a different life than you. You taught me many lessons I have used to better myself, but this army is my home.'

Abigail opened her mouth to speak but said nothing. She stepped forward and hugged her daughter again. Sasha hugged her back, not hearing that someone was calling out her name.

'I love you,' Abigail said.

'I do, too,' Michelle said.

'Lieutenant Scholar!'

Sasha still did not hear. The civilians will be given the option of leaving the county,' she said. 'You can move back to Duluth, or elsewhere. Do you know your thoughts?'

'We haven't had a chance to discuss it,' Abigail said, 'but I suppose –.'

'Lieutenant Scholar!'

Sasha finally heard her name and turned to see Sergeant Pierce approaching quickly. 'Ma'am,' he said with a quick salute, 'sorry to intrude, but I was asked to find you and bring you back to the headquarters.'

'What?' Sasha asked. 'Why?'

Pierce looked at the civilians around them and stepped in to whisper in her ear.

'III Corps is coming.'

Sasha blinked, suddenly blind, her mind focusing on the state of the siege group and the forces assembled, her mind racing around the possibilities that her entire operation had been too late. *Where was First Field Regiment? Does*

482

III Corps know Walker has fallen? How many troops are approaching?

'Okay,' she said. She looked at her family. 'I'm sorry, I have something I must attend to.'

'No!' Thomas stood up suddenly. 'No killing. Killing is a sin, and you shouldn't do it. Even if you already have, you shouldn't do it again!' It was not the accusatory tone her father used; the tears in his eyes, the edge to his voice told Sasha that Thomas was genuinely worried for her soul.

Sasha looked at Thomas and smiled. She stepped up to him and placed a hand on his shoulder.

'It is wrong, Thomas. And you're right, I shouldn't, but I'm not fighting because I like it. I'm fighting because you deserve to grow up in a world where you can live at peace.'

'I didn't ask you to fight for me,' Thomas said.

'I know,' Sasha replied. 'And you never will.'

She hugged him, smiled at her mother and sister, and then turned to Pierce.

'Let's go, Sergeant.'

***

Sasha found the temporary headquarters to be filled and then some. Junior officers and sergeants, eager to do something but lacking orders, stood on the outside, anxiously awaiting a plan. There was a solid tension in the air at the news.

Sasha pusher her way into the center. Caesar and Grace stood by the table at which they had spent so much time, moved from its normal place to this temporary tent. The table was now covered with a larger map of Walker and its surroundings, with new red blocks. Sasha looked and read the situation: five companies of infantry, two troops of cavalry, and at least two batteries of artillery were now on the map, west of Walker. Sasha did some quick math in her head.

'A thousand strong?' she asked Saxon.

'Thereabouts,' Saxon said. 'All estimates.'

'How did they get so far away from Bemidji?'

'That is a question for later,' Saxon cut off all the questions and side conversations with a loud voice. 'For now, we need to decide what to do about it.'

Sasha nodded. The siege forces, even with the extra units attached to finally take the city, were well under a thousand, with a significant percentage of them support troops not trained for combat. How many rifles could they put in the field right now? Four hundred would be a generous estimate.

'If we get them to attack the walls of the city,' someone was saying, 'we can use that to our advantage.'

'But there's no guarantee they will,' Grace said. 'It's just as likely they'll besiege us, and the supply situation here was tenuous before we blew up Walker's stockpiles.'

'We can't defeat them in the field,' Saber said.

'The report said at least two of the companies were district foot troops,' Atlas said.

'Two companies of district troops are easy to defeat; but if the other three companies are army regulars, we are outmanned, even without the district troops. In addition, they have field artillery, not just mortars,' Caesar said. Sasha recognized his tone; part of his mind was listening to the conversation, while the rest was cycling through the available information to formulate a plan.

'Maybe we should have kept one regiment from General Senator,' Saxon said softly.

'His battle was a close thing, and every regiment was involved. One less might have tipped it a different way,' Patch said, arriving suddenly.

'You're not a soldier, you're a technician,' one of the militia officers said.

'I can still read a battle report, Captain.'

Sasha looked at the map, thinking of the reports from Senator, the flow of the battle as he and his subordinates had reported it. *What had he seen?*

'How quickly could they get here?' someone asked. Sasha was beginning to tune out the conversation, listening only enough to hear the words, without paying attention to who was speaking.

'Two days, once they get word to move.'

'You'd think they'd want to move quickly to strike this group and get back south before I Corps had a chance to react.'

The Army of the Lakes thrashed I Corps back behind their fortifications, but what's left could still do a lot of damage. If Senator did leave them, how quickly would they recognize it? How quickly could I Corps begin their own offensive in support of III Corps?

484

'Hell, this force is probably hoping to get to Walker and back to Bemidji before Senator has a chance to react.'

'Then they won't besiege us; they'll go for an assault.'

'Yeah, but they're better equipped for it than we were. No offense to those present, but they are.'

I Corps has scouts and patrols keeping an eye on the Army of the Lakes. Also, aircraft flying reconnaissance. And they were tracking radio signals, enough to know where the headquarters were.

'Besides, how can we defeat this force AND guard our prisoners AND evacuate the wounded AND –.'

'We get the point, Captain.'

'Can we abandon the city?'

'We might have to.'

But the Army doesn't use radios unless they have to, and the RAC did try bombing them. Luckily, the signal crews knew what they were doing and avoided getting caught, but still. Imagine the surprise if the radios suddenly popped up so far away from where they had been.

Sasha's eyes snapped away from the map. She stepped out of the circle and swung around to Patch. She leaned in to whisper in Patch's ear.

'How easy is it to mimic a radio transmitter?'

'What do you mean?' Patch asked.

'I mean, if you detect a radio transmission using a call sign, can you tell it is a different transmitter than the last one?'

'Depends,' Patch whispered back. 'A lot of it depends on transmission strength.'

'How so?' Sasha asked, then a voice cut across their conversation.

'Unless the Templars have something to add,' Grace said. Sasha and Patch looked up to see all the officers looking at each other.

'Well, Templars?' Saxon asked.

'I think Templar Scholar has an idea,' Patch said, 'or at least the beginning of one.'

The officers all looked at Sasha now. Sasha looked across the table at Caesar. 'Sir, I was wondering if we could trick the force to retreat by trapping it with the Army of the Lakes.'

'The Army of the Lakes is outside of Menahga,' Grace pointed out. 'They can't get here in time.'

'Right, and the Royal Army knows that because they've been listening to radio transmission from the headquarter radios,' Sasha pointed out.

'Usually,' Saxon said, 'but the Army's gone dark the past few days, to make their positions harder to find.'

'Right!' Sasha said. 'So, if we used radios to simulate the traffic of the Army and its divisions, what would III Corps assume?'

Everyone staring at Sasha showed a look of surprise at her suggestion, then slowly turned to look at Caesar. Caesar stared at her, an odd look on his face. It took her a moment to realize what it meant.

I thought of something he hadn't. I've never done that before.

'Yes,' Caesar said. 'It is possible. Colonel Grace, how many radios do we have access to?'

'Gloria?' Grace turned to a technical sergeant standing behind her.

'Two with the siege group, one with the Naval Group. We captured three field radios being used by Walker.'

'Similar to the ones we already use,' Patch said.

'So, we have more than enough,' Saber put in.

'Or do we?' Mako asked. 'If all our transmitters go offline at the same time new transmissions appear, it might seem suspicious. We need to maintain the current level of transmissions.'

'What level of transmission?' Gloria said. 'Other than a few tests, none of them have ever been used operationally. The idea was to allow southern and western defenders to coordinate if the garrison tried to break out, but they never did. We have more than enough radios to simulate the Army of the Lakes.'

'But do we have the personnel for it?' Grace asked. She looked at Caesar. 'How well trained are the personnel Senator has in the Army of the Lakes? Can they produce the necessary transmissions?'

'Your signal squad listened to the transmissions, did they not? They can at least produce a fair approximation.'

'But none of that means anything if we're overrun before the radios are in place,' Saber said. 'That force was ten miles away an hour ago; they're closer now.

There was a pause in the conversation. Sasha had to admit he was right. For the plan to work, the radios had to be in the field, where units from the army would most likely be. The could not all come from the same place, and it would take time to spread them out appropriately.

'Then we need to stop them short,' she said. 'Bloody them, make them think they're fighting the Army of the Lakes when the radio starts up.'

'But we can't give up Walker,' Grace said. 'If we take too many troops out, the garrison could rise up.'

Someone cursed. Caesar was still staring at the map. 'Are they sticking to roads?' he asked.

'So far.'

'Then they will be traveling down the highway. What is the closest settlement up the highway?'

'Hazel's Well,' Grace said. 'Two plus miles.'

'We set a defense there,' Caesar said. 'Enough to delay them long enough to get the radios in position.'

'I'll go,' Sasha said.

'Why you?' Atlas asked.

'My brother-in-law is from Hazel's Well,' Sasha said. 'I've been there half a dozen times. I know how to defend it.'

'Very well,' Caesar said. 'Gather your platoon and rearm. By the time you have gathered, we will have figured out the allotment of horses.'

Sasha turned and left the tent. Pierce and Del Oso fell into step next to her.

'I'm taking a rifle,' Sasha said. 'For this fight, I want a full rifle, not a carbine.'

'Right,' Del Oso said. 'If I may suggest, we should get some LAMB guns if we can.'

'Agreed,' Sasha said. 'And as much ammunition as our mounts can carry.'

'It'll be one hell of a fight, L.T.,' Pierce said.

'That it will,' Sasha agreed.

'Do you really know how to defend Hazel's Well?' Pierce asked. There was no accusation in his voice, just curiosity.

Sasha nodded. 'I know exactly how to defend Hazel's Well, Sergeant, but we have to get moving. Now.'

Chapter 54

Thirteen men and women rode with Sasha out of Walker Town. Two of them would take the horses back to Walker, but the other eleven were Sasha's initial force to defend Hazel's Well.

A Templar can hold of a thousand soldiers with only twelve, right? she asked herself sarcastically.

They reached the former village after a hard ride. Sasha was nervously leading her group when someone opened fire on her.

Sasha's horse died underneath her. She fell off, hitting the ground with a hard thud. Yells and screams erupted behind her as she scrambled for cover behind her horse.

Someone got here first.

She wrested her rifle from the saddle of the dead animal. Safe from danger, she took a moment to see what was happening.

Another horse lay dead. Another human was slowly crawling for safety in the long grass. The rest had scattered. Sasha looked about, trying to see if they had run or taken to the grass. At least some were fighting back, as a LAMB gun started chattering to her right.

She peeked over the horse and looked at the town. Only two structures faced them, and both were being peppered with bullets. She heard her troopers advancing, calling out and coordinating. She had yet to give an order, and they were doing what she would have wanted.

One of the buildings jumped and the windows expelled dust. Her grenadier has landed a grenade right through the roof. She brought her carbine up to her shoulder and fire at the next window. She wanted them distracted as Del Oso and Pierce were making the last few feet into the village proper.

Sasha rolled out from behind the horse and into the tall grass to the side of the road. She advanced through the grass, hearing the gunfire diminish. By the time she reached the edge of the grass, the firing stopped.

'Village clear!' Del Oso bellowed. 'Assemble on me!'

Sasha jumped up and hustled into the village. Del Oso sighed when he saw her. 'Glad you're okay, Lieutenant.'

'I am, my mount is not. Anyone else hurt?'

488

'A sprained ankle, but no casualties. And we got a prisoner.'

'Okay,' Sasha said. 'Secure him in a hut. I'm getting everyone in position before we have another surprise.'

Sasha had visited Hazel's Well several times over the last few years. Her brother-in-law was from here; her sister's wedding took place here and the two of them had lived here for the short period of time between their wedding and his conscription. It was only a day's ride from Penelope's Haven. That was how she knew it had two qualities that aided any defenders, both on the north side of town.

The first were the two large stone buildings. One was a barn for animals and the farming equipment, the other was a sizable granary, both solidly built, probably sturdier than the bunkers at the prison camp. Great defensive positions.

The second were the rice paddies.

Hazel's Well did not grow grain, but rice. Long ago, the inhabitants had expanded the river northeast between two lakes into several rice paddies, allowing the natural flow of water from one body to another to irrigate their crops. The result was a huge expanse of open terrain, five hundred yards wide and half a mile deep with lakes on both sides. The only structure in the field was the bridge over the river, just about in the middle of the field.

'I can see why you chose it,' Del Oso said with approval.

'It's not perfect,' she said. 'The paddies go down about three feet from the top. They're irregularly shaped and different sizes. You could easily fit several hundred rifles in them and hide from us.'

'So long as they're not moving forward, that's fine,' Del Oso said. 'We can make this work. What about flanking around the lakes?'

'To flank to the east, they'd have to cross the entire Leech Lake; that'd take a few days. West is much smaller, only a few miles to circle it, but they aren't good roads. It's all side paths and hunting trails. This is their likely avenue of approach.'

The defenders sighted the machine guns, one in each stone building. Two rifles took debris from some of the fallen buildings and made small walls between the two buildings, and from the barn into the forest. The defenders would have some cover when they moved around.

Soldiers pulled the extra ammunition off the saddles and let the guides move back for their next load. Sasha was now alone.

'Where is the prisoner?' she asked.

'That cabin,' Del Oso pointed, and Sasha hid a sigh.

Michelle's cabin.

It was indeed the same cabin her sister had lived in when she was a resident of Hazel's Well. A simple, single-room building, one that had burned but had not fallen. One rifle stood at the door, an automatic in her hand.

She stepped into the hut. Sasha had no idea what happened to it after her sister moved back to Penelope's Haven, but she remembered sleeping on the floor next to the bed. The same bed that now held a man wearing a yeoman's uniform. It was a red and yellow dressing, dirtied from hard riding. He grimaced, sitting up and showing pain when she entered. He noted his guardian coming to attention when Sasha entered, and she saw his eyes search her uniform for recognizable insignia.

'An officer?' he asked.

'I am. Second Lieutenant Scholar, Renaissance Army of Minnesota.'

'Yeoman Corporal Leo, Mahnomen County Yeomanry.'

'What are you doing here, Yeoman Corporal?'

'Call me Leo,' he said. Then he shrugged. 'I'm here to stop the war you've brought to this kingdom.'

'Are you?' Sasha asked. Then she shook her head. 'You really think we are responsible?'

'You are in rebellion against your rightful lords,' Leo said. 'I'm sure you have legitimate grievances against Count Walker and his people, but there must be other ways of dealing with them, rather than resorting to open warfare.'

Sasha blinked at him. 'You're educated,' she said. 'An educated yeoman.'

'Count Mahnomen has high requirements for his men.'

'Much higher than Walker has for his.'

'COUNT Walker,' Leo stressed his title, 'can run his county as he sees fit. And if his yeomen act improperly, you have ways of demanding accountability.'

'By complaining to the count?' Sasha laughed. 'You really cannot see why that does not work? I lived with the fear of yeomen taking an interest in me for too long, Leo. When they finally did, it was one of the most terrifying moments of my life. If it wasn't for the Renaissance Army, I would have become just another girl taken, used, and discarded.'

Leo frowned. 'We don't do that in Mahnomen County,' he said.

'You've never taken a woman to your bed?'

'I have, but she was always agreeable.'

'Was she?' Sasha asked. ''Did you give her a chance to say no?'

'What?' Leo looked at her in surprise.

'I mean, Leo, if you try to take her to bed, and she believes she has to or she will be punished, she will probably try to do everything she can to convince you she wants to. She doesn't want you to punish her for being less than enthusiastic.'

Leo looked concerned. 'We don't –.'

Sasha interrupted. 'You've never stopped at a village on patrol and been provided with food and drink, brought to you by pretty young girls who giggle? You've never gotten a discount from a hard-working merchant who doesn't want you to take his wares or imprison him?'

'I've never asked for any of that,' Leo snapped.

'You don't have to. As long as you enjoy the benefits of the authority your position gives you, you are responsible for them.'

Leo shook his head. 'And that gives you the right to start a rebellion? Leading men and women to war for your personal grievances?'

'The Renaissance Army started the war,' Sasha nodded, 'but everyone who fights for it volunteered. I've seen them, reading books and learning skills and working for a better future than the one the nobility can offer. One that won't demand such extravagances from all of us.'

Leo scowled. 'Civil war is never the answer.'

'Says someone who rode a hundred miles with guns in his hand. How big is the III Corps column?' she asked.

Leo smirked. 'Big enough to break the siege of Walker.'

'The siege is already broken. Walker fell last night.'

Leo's smirk vanished. 'What?'

'The count had smuggled in chemical weapons,' Sasha said. Leo's face turned ashen. 'We had to move in and remove them before he used them. Very interesting devices, a chemical munitions. I saw the ones he had positioned in the cathedral, to smother the hostages, men, women and children, in pain and death if he was in danger of losing. It was a hard fight, but in the end, we won.'

'The count?' Leo asked.

'There is a new one. He is now a prisoner.'

Leo's shoulders sagged. 'There is no government,' he finally said, 'that can represent everyone. Someone will always suffer, but forcing more to suffer just because you happen to be that small portion that falls at the bottom? How arrogant.'

Sasha shook her head. 'I agree with you in principle,' she said. 'But you are looking at it as someone who doesn't suffer under it. You don't see how many people it hurts, but we're not here to debate government. How big is the III Corps column?'

'Big enough,' Leo said stubbornly.

'How much artillery is it bringing?'

'More than enough.'

'Who leads it?'

'Someone experienced.'

Leo was smirking again. He was expecting to see the column tear through Sasha and move straight to Walker. He did not expect to be a prisoner for long.

His prediction might not be too far from the truth.

'Well,' she said. 'We'll see if that's all true soon enough.'

He laid back down. Sasha went back to her line.

She was down to eleven, leaving one behind to watch Leo. There was no sign of the column yet, but Sasha thought they had to be close. With nothing to do, Sasha went into the forest, using chalk to mark positions for her troopers to move to if they had to pull back. Then she went back and spoke with each rifle and gunner individually.

'What happens if we have to pull back?' asked the guard. He frowned. 'Do I . . . shoot him?'

'No,' Sasha said. 'Let him be freed.'

The guard looked relieved at that.

Riders appeared from the south. Eight mounted horses, one a rider to bring them all back. Two Chosen Rifles with their long guns and several rifles. Bringing up the rear was a large draft horse, carrying a medium machine gun, the gunner of the weapon, and a girl holding on to him tightly.

'My daughter,' he said when he dismounted. 'She has nowhere else to go, so she stays with me.'

'This won't be safe,' Sasha cautioned.

'I know,' he replied with a scowl. 'But she's here. She can help.'

Sasha looked at the girl. She was a tiny thing, stick thin arms and legs. 'Name?'

'Lupe,' she said.

'How old are you, Lupe?'

'Twelve, ma'am.'

Sasha would have guessed eight. 'Can you run?'

The girl nodded.

'Then you're my runner. Stick close to me and stay out of trouble.'

She set the new machine gun in the woods, with a good field of fire. The three gunners assigned to it dug in, reinforcing their position. The Chosen Rifles went into the trees. She trusted that Fox had told them what to do.

Where is everyone else? Sasha asked herself. The III Corps column had to be close, but so were any troops coming from Walker on foot. The lake to the west could be a great spot for the Naval Group to sail around, if they could get into it. But no matter which direction she looked, she saw no one.

Sasha waited and scanned the far trees with her binoculars.

Five minutes later, she saw someone.

It was a scout, wearing the long blue trench coat of a district soldier. He was holding one of the Galveston rifles with the long bayonet and was scanning the far side of the paddies. Others appeared on either side, spread out across the tree line.

'Lupe,' Sasha said, 'stay low, let everyone know the enemy skirmishers are here.'

***

Ten minutes passed. Sasha had spotted six more district soldiers on the far side, but they remained in the trees, half a mile away.

Sasha wished she knew the composition of the enemy forces. The note said they had brought artillery with them. *Where was it? Was it setting up now? Did they bring mortars or heavy machine guns? Autocannons? How many companies? Has their cavalry found another route around Hazel's Well?*

Lupe returned, moving silently. Sasha scanned the far trees again, then turned and looked southeast.

Troops were coming up the road. They looked like Sparrow's company, only smaller.

'Lupe,' Sasha said, 'run out to those troops, tell them the enemy is on the far side of the fields, and they should approach without being seen. I recommend the troops go into the trees and Sparrow come see me.'

Lupe was off again. Sasha forced herself to wait patiently until Lupe returned with Officer Sparrow in tow.

'Lieutenant,' she acknowledged. 'Where are they?'

'Across the paddies. Looks like some skirmishers from a garrison company.'

'I guess a few companies did leave their depots after all. No regulars yet?'

'No,' Sasha said. 'I've deployed my troops in the town, at the stone buildings. A medium gun is in the forest, along with a pair of Chosen Rifles.'

Sparrow nodded. 'I agree. Deploy in the trees.'

'Aren't you missing a few people?' Sasha asked.

'We've had some stragglers. We did assault Walker last night.'

Sasha nodded. It felt like a lifetime ago, but it was only half a day. 'Yeah,' she said.

'I'll put my troops in line and have the sergeants place stragglers in as they come,' Sparrow said.

'Wait,' Sasha interrupted. 'Lupe, go with Officer Sparrow. When she establishes where she'll be putting her post, remember and come back to me. I don't want you getting lost the first time we need to pass a message.'

'Good idea,' Sparrow said, motioning for the young girl to follow.

'I don't think your mother would approve, L.T.' Pierce said.

'Are you going to tell her?'

Pierce shook his head. 'No. I just think she's too young.'

'I think we're all too young.'

'Truth,' Pierce said. 'Well, if she's going to be here, at least,' he stopped. 'Here they come.'

Sasha looked out. The skirmish line of garrison troops, more than a hundred strong, moved out of the trees, spaced a dozen paces apart. They moved across the field into the paddies, forming into lines where they could follow the footpaths through the paddies. They did not jump into the water, but they were being cautious. The platoon moving up the highway stayed off the road itself, walking in a staggered column. Sasha could hear voices. The sounds of sergeants yelling for their men to keep their distance.

The defenders waited. The range was too far to give their position away, and they knew it. Sasha looked to see Sparrow's company still getting into the woods on her left.

The skirmishers reached the river, a broad and shallow feature that lost much of its water to the irrigated paddies. The company crossed, the central platoon crossing at the bridge, the platoons on either side wading across. They advanced another few yards when they stopped. The skirmishers knelt, some stepping into the paddies to lower themselves. Sasha examined their formation.

Three platoons in a district company, four squads per platoon. Looks like three platoons abreast, each with one squad in reserve. NCOs and officers in the middle of their commands.

For a minute the skirmishers did not move, except for a few runners for the company captain. Then, a squad from the center platoon started running straight up the road into Hazel's Well.

Here we go.

They were a hundred yards away when Sasha told the gunner next to her to fire. His tracers reached out and knocked the lead trooper from his feet. The rest of her team started, Sasha adding two shots of her own to the barrage. Sparrow's troops remained quiet.

Four men were left lying on the roadway, the rest having dived into paddies. The skirmish line behind them had similarly disappeared into the depressions, where they were beginning to fire back. Several automatic rifles opened fire, and two rifle grenades detonated before the stone buildings.

Sasha walked down the stable. 'Conserve your ammunition,' she said. 'Sparingly. Don't waste, but don't stop.' She reached the double doors on the highway, facing the double doors in the warehouse. Del Oso was there. 'Conserve,' she said across the road.

'I'm with you, Lieutenant,' he said. He looked concerned. 'I'm expecting artillery.'

'So am I,' Sasha admitted. 'Stay safe.'

Lupe came back. 'I know where she is now,' she said.

'Good. Go tell her I expect a barrage any second. And don't come back until

495

after it stops.'

Lupe disappeared, and Sasha took a deep breath. She had been under a bombardment before, when the mortars at the prison camp struck at them in the creek bed. It was not a pleasant experience. And though the stone buildings were tough, they would also be standing against actual artillery, much more powerful than what she had faced.

Sasha glanced out the window, observing the district troops in fight, and heard the droning of a shell just in time to duck back.

The entire building shuddered as the first shell struck nearby. Sasha heard shrapnel glancing off the stonework. Then silence. 'Was that it?' she asked.

'Ranging shot,' Pierce said.

More droning, and Sasha cringed.

The shells were coming in every two or three seconds, exploding around what had been Hazel's Well. Many were high explosive, while others burned and produced smoke. One of the ceiling beams collapsed, and stones fell.

'L.T., this building might not be too safe,' Pierce called from his corner. 'We might want to think about –.'

A shell exploded right outside Pierce's corner. It cut through the stonework and shredded the sergeant mid-word. Sasha covered her head with her hands as stones pummeled her. Then came the crashing as the building gave way and collapsed.

Chapter 55

'Lieutenant!'

Sasha coughed. She was pinned underneath rubble and felt the heat of a fire. Her leg hurt, and her arm was awkwardly stuck beneath her body.

'Lieutenant!' the voice called again. At first, she hoped it was Pierce, but the image of the man being torn apart by stone and shrapnel was still fresh in her mind.

'Del Oso!' she said as loud as she could. She found the air thick with smoke and coughed.

'There she is!' The debris shifted around her as someone was standing above her. The beam pinning her lifted, and someone grabbed her collar, pulling her out from beneath the stones. Del Oso was all but carrying her from the rubble into the woods just next to it.

'You scared the hell out of me,' Del Oso said. 'We've already lost one Templar.'

'And Sergeant Pierce,' Sasha coughed harshly. She could hear now, a roar of gunfire as the royalists pressed their attack and Sparrow's company responded. 'What's going on?'

'They've added a company of rifles to their attack, and Hazel's Well is pretty much gone,' Del Oso said. 'The other stone building is still standing, but everything else got knocked over.'

Sasha shook her head, trying to clear the last of the confusion away. 'Let's get on the line,' she said.

They moved into the forest between the machine gun and the rubble. Sasha looked out over the field to see what had changed.

A rifle company had joined the enemy's attack, adding more than a hundred soldiers hopping down the paddies towards Sasha's position. Several enemy machine guns were set into the far tree line, firing into the forest and engaging Sparrow's company. Sparrow ignored the fire coming from the forest, concentrating on the infantry crossing the paddies.

Sasha limped into position behind a tree. 'I've lost my rifle,' she said.

'I'm sure there's an extra one somewhere,' Del Oso said grimly.

Sasha nodded in understanding. She could not think of anything to do. The

497

two lakes forced their battle into a small, confined corridor, and the open terrain put the burden of tactics on the other side. She had put the defenders in place, her only options limited to how often to move individual troops from one position to another. Other than that, all she and her troops could do was hold out until the plan went into effect.

What if the plan has taken place already? What if it has been done, and the enemy didn't fall for it?

That thought chilled her. She knew the answer.

The sound of artillery filled the air, and Sasha cringed, but the barrage fell far behind them, in the trees, and stopped after only a few rounds.

'Well, that's good,' one of her rifles said.

Sasha nodded. 'And now they readjust.'

Three streaks of light flew from the enemy line. Sasha watched them arc up and over, wondering if they were some weapon of the Royal Army she was not aware of. Just over the defender's position, each one exploded into a flare. Three red flares, over their positions.

'Now, what do you suppose that means?' Del Oso asked.

Sasha watched. The volume of fire died down as the flares hung overhead. She saw several enemy troops falling back, crawling or jumping over the paddy sides. 'I think they're pulling out,' she said.

A mortar shell landed between her line and the advancing troops. It did not explode but started burning and spewing smoke, creating a small cloud. Another landed nearby. The drone of artillery heralded another barrage, but this too fell between the lines, adding smoke. Soon it was a murky wall through which Sasha could not see.

'Stay ready!' Sparrow's voice called. 'Eyes open!' Sasha pulled out her pistol. It was the only thing she had left.

There was an eerie silence now. Not a gunshot, not an explosion. After all that, there was nothing. Sasha saw smoke, and only smoke.

She breathed. Stay focused. Do not give in yet.

A shadow in the smoke. Sasha watched, hoping it was a figment of her imagination. Then it was real. A soldier, bayonet forward, charging out of the smoke, others following behind him. They let out a fierce war cry.

The forest opened fire in response, every weapon unloading into the charge. Sasha aimed and fired, the range long for a pistol but the only thing she could do.

The soldiers pressed on, too many left dead or dying behind them. The few that did reach the trees fired back, some tossing grenades at the defenders. The defenders responded in kind, and their positions were more prepared and higher up the hillside than the attackers'.

Sasha heard Sparrow demand their surrender, added her own voice to the call, but they refused. They charged again, straight at the machine gun position Lupe's father was manning. They were cut down to a man, their last grenades finding the machine gun nest and making Lupe an orphan.

The charge lasted less than three minutes. Sasha's ears rang from the noise.

'What the hell was that?' she asked.

Del Oso shrugged.

The smoke was dissipating, and Sasha pulled out her field glasses to find the lenses were shattered. She discarded the broken equipment and stared across the field, trying to see the next wave, but all she saw was the enemy reforming on the far side of the expanse. No more covering fire, no artillery came their way.

Sasha looked at the carpet of dead lying just before their line and asked herself the same question she had asked Del Oso.

What the hell was that?

＊＊＊

That, Sasha would learn, was Company B, Fourth Rochester Rifle Battalion.

The company that, a year earlier, had marched into Brainerd County to evacuate a prison camp. The company that had met resistance and been forced to surrender. The company that had marched out with their heads held high, their Captain Lewis speaking highly of them and the honor they had brought to the battlefield.

The company that marched back to an army that met them with scorn and derision. Their surviving officers drummed out of the army, their sergeants demoted, their character mocked by soldiers who had not been there. For a year, they had been insulted, their pride tarnished, and their anger swelled. They had done nothing wrong. They had fought and lost honorably. Yet, they became scapegoats.

When the prearranged signal to withdraw was sent up, they ignored it. They would not suffer that derision again. It did not occur to them that there was blame enough to go around the whole of the army. Their wounded pride had suffered more than anyone's, and they would not suffer it again.

Their charge was made with the expectation of death, as only a soldier can expect it.

After the battle, by order of the battalion commander, Company B was officially disbanded and removed from the rolls of that battalion. The new company would be Company D, and the battalion would never hold a Company B within its ranks again.

***

More reinforcements came in, boosting their defensive line to over a hundred. By then, Sasha noticed a dull pain in her leg. When she looked down, she noticed the boot was blackened and burned.

'Sergeant, send a medic over when you can.'

When a medic did arrive, the dull ache had grown to a sharp pain. With Del Oso standing by, the medic cut off her boot.

'From the collapsing building?' Sasha asked Del Oso. 'The building burned me?'

'Phosphorus shells,' Del Oso said, and for once he looked scared. Sasha did not blame him. Aristotle once taught them what phosphorus could do and how to treat it.

'It can't be that bad,' Sasha said, 'if I didn't feel it for so long.'

The medic removed her boot, then her socks. 'It's not bad,' he said, 'but it's not nothing,'

Sasha looked. The skin on her calf looked red and boiled. The medic touched it, and she winced. 'Why does it hurt now?'

'Adrenaline,' the medic said. 'You were too focused on the battle to notice. And the phosphorus wasted most of its energy on the leather boot.' He looked at her calf for a moment, before pulling out a salve and some bandages. 'I'm afraid I don't have an extra boot for you. You'll have to put that one back on.'

'Better than nothing,' Sasha said. The salve did feel good, and she looked up at Del Oso. 'I'll be fine.'

'I hope so,' he said. 'Mustard gas, then phosphorus. You brush with death too many times, Templar.'

Sasha smiled at him. 'Better me than someone else.'

Lupe appeared. 'Officer Sparrow says she sees no sign of the enemy,' the young girl said through tears.

'Your father?' Sasha asked. 'Did he make it?'

Lupe shook her head. 'Officer Sparrow,' she choked out the words, 'wants you to get her a status of your platoon.'

'I've got that,' Del Oso said. 'Lead the way, Lupe.'

The two disappeared. The medic worked on her leg, and the survivors of her team reordered themselves. Soon Sasha was re-armed with another carbine, and the one working LAMB gun was positioned, but the enemy did not come back.

An hour later, a rider from Walker came, bearing a message.

The ruse had worked. The radios had scared the column into retreating. III Corps was falling back.

The battle was won.

Chapter 56

The Naval Group arrived shortly thereafter, dropping off the marines and more reinforcements and supplies, and picking up wounded and prisoners. Sasha was one that Sparrow told to board the boats. She tried to protest, but Sparrow would not hear of it.

'You are magnificent!' Sparrow said. 'I will not risk you further. Go back and bring your talents to the generals.'

Sasha limped to the boats. *Renaissance* and *Minnesota* were unloading their weapons to bolster Sparrow's line in case III Corps came back. She found Lupe, sitting nearby, watching the wounded being loaded onto the *Minnesota*. The young girl's eyes were red with tears. With all the work done, she had stopped being busy, and the impact of her father's death finally fell home.

'What do I do now?' Lupe asked of Sasha.

'We'll take care of you,' Sasha promised. 'I'm sure Grace will have a role for you.'

The walking wounded and prisoners were loaded onto the *Renaissance*. Sasha took a position near the rear, consenting to carry an automatic and helping watch the prisoners. Lupe sat beside her, staring at the men in uniforms that she knew were enemy troops Most of them were lightly wounded district soldiers, with a few army regulars, and Leo as the lone yeoman.

'Big enough?' she asked him when he saw her.

Leo gave her a miserable look. 'You weren't supposed to win.'

'Famous last words of many vanquished generals,' Sasha replied.

Leo said nothing the rest of the ride.

By daylight, Sasha quite enjoyed sailing. A warm breeze blew across the lake, and the gentle rocking made the passengers sleepy. Sasha stayed awake, but Lupe soon dropped off. Most of the prisoners dozed as well.

Without worrying about stealth, Mako made good time back to Walker. The city was in full swing of evacuation. Hospital tents were being taken down. Carts of all kinds were lined up, being loaded with wounded, food, supplies, and weapons, anything that could be carried.

Mako landed them at the burned wharf. The prisoners were removed first, then the wounded.

'Want to go to the hospital?' Sasha asked Lupe.

'Can I stay with you?' she replied.

'Maybe,' Sasha said. 'I have to check in, see what I need to do now.'

'We don't get to rest?' Lupe asked. She was not whining, Sasha noticed, just asking.

'Not yet,' Sasha said. 'Too much to do.'

Sasha led the way into the castle, where a tent was set up just inside the front gate, with Olympians at the guard.

'Officer in charge?' Sasha asked.

'Officer Saxon, at the moment, ma'am,' one said.

Sasha paused. 'Sergeant Pierce is dead,' she said.

The Olympian nodded. 'We heard. We also heard he died bravely.'

'You won't hear different from me,' Sasha said. 'I'm sorry.'

The Olympian nodded again. 'We'll mourn when we can, ma'am.'

'Right,' Sasha said and entered the tent. Officer Saxon looked up from a table of reports.

'Lieutenant Scholar, you okay?'

'Sore and stiff,' Sasha said. 'I lost some good men and women out there today.'

'Well, your plan worked, that's for sure. III Corps couldn't fall back fast enough once the radios started up.'

'So, we bought some time?' Sasha asked.

'Not as much as we'd like,' Saxon replied. 'The major we captured had notes. King Xavier has ordered that, in the event Walker Town falls, the Royal Air Corps is to destroy the town. Now, we're rushing the evacuation.'

So much for Scott Anthony's governorship.

'What about Patch's AA Battery?' Sasha asked.

'The bombers can fly higher than it can reach,' Saxon said.

'Okay, we evacuate,' Sasha agreed. 'What can I do to help?'

'You can help me coordinate at the command tent. Fill in at an odd job if it comes up.'

'Yes, ma'am,' Sasha followed along behind Saxon. Lupe sat down nearby, waiting for something to do.

It was a busy day. Sasha compiled reports and assigned routes for evacuations. Caesar came back from meeting with local elders, staying long enough to get a status update from Saxon and Sasha. Then he handed Sasha a letter – 'Do not misplace this, Templar Scholar!' – and took Saxon to meet with delegates from the Civil Council, leaving Sasha the task of coordinating.

In truth, it was not as difficult as Sasha might have expected. Everyone already had their orders, they were either sending updates on their progress, or requesting advice on problems. Sasha answered every question quickly, keeping the people moving.

The only thing that bothered her was her arm. At first, she dismissed it, then wondered if it might have been sprained or broken again. Finally, she noticed it was turning bright red.

'Lupe,' she said. The young girl hopped up. 'Can you find Officer Roach and bring him here? He should be in the cathedral.'

Lupe nodded and disappeared. A minute later Penn appeared.

'Having fun?' he asked.

'Tired, sore, and in a bit of pain. You?' Sasha replied.

'You managed to finish the siege before the next council session begins. I'm less of a liaison, more of a storyteller.'

Sasha thought about the date. 'The council begins in two days?' she asked.

Penn nodded. 'If you had followed the original plan, you'd have struck at Walker while the council was in session.' He shrugged. 'As it is, enough of them were close by that Caesar's already spoken with them.'

Sasha nodded. 'Sorry.'

'Oh, it's not your fault. I understand the expediency. So will they, even if they won't admit it.'

Lupe came back through the tent with Roach in tow.

'Yes, Lieutenant?' he asked.

She showed him her hand. 'Is this what I think it is?'

Roach inspected her arm and cringed. 'Lupe, go to the hospitals set up on the field; find Lieutenant Elector or Doctor Adams. Tell them I have a mustard burn at the HQ. Now, please.' Lupe nodded and disappeared.

'It is what I think it is,' Sasha confirmed.

'It looks like a mustard gas burn. Where you near the chapel when it exploded?'

'I was, but I don't recall getting splashed. It was mostly just wood and bits.'

'Well,' Roach said, 'if it's any consolation, the mustard gas wasn't the best quality. Doctor Moore said it hadn't been stored properly.'

'It wouldn't have hurt anyone?' Sasha asked.

'No, it would have hurt everyone in the cathedral, but it wouldn't have been the giant cloud of death Count Walker wanted. And this burn has been baking for quite some time.'

Elector appeared. 'Not too bad,' he said after inspecting it. 'If you had come to me sooner, you might have escaped scarring.'

'I didn't know,' Sasha said. 'I was so sore from last night I didn't think anything of it. And then with III Corps coming, I got too busy. And pummeled with artillery. You should see my leg.'

'Maybe later,' Elector said. He spread a salve over her skin and wrapped it gently. 'This'll need good changing,' he said. 'Once the evacuation is over, I'll go over it with you.'

Sasha nodded, but could not respond for a sergeant came up. 'Lieutenant? There's a civilian man outside who wishes to speak with someone.'

'Anyone in particular or asking for any officer?' Sasha absently asked.

'He's looking for someone named Sasha Small, ma'am.'

Sasha looked up at the sergeant. 'Tall man, long nose, looks like he's upset about everything?'

'Yes, ma'am,' the sergeant said, confused. 'Do you know him?'

'I do,' Sasha admitted. 'Penn, I'm stepping out for a minute; shout if you need me.'

Elector cocked his head. 'Want me to go with? I know how fathers can be.'

'No,' Sasha shook her head. 'Thank you, though.'

Sasha stepped out of the tent. Several rifles and Olympians stood guard, some standing and others sitting, as wagons and people shuffled down the road into the forest. Anyone heading to Bemidji with the garrison was marching west, across a hastily repaired bridge. Everyone going with the Renaissance Army was marching south, through a corridor cleared in the minefield.

Alexander Small stood before the entrance, watching the people moving into the forest. Sasha cleared her throat, and he turned.

'Father,' she said. The guards, who had spent some time wondering who this man was and who he was looking for, looked up in surprise. One of them shifted awkwardly.

'Sasha,' Alexander said. He looked at her, saw the cane and the wrapped arm, and chose to ignore them. 'I shall call you by the name I gave you when you were born, not the name you take as a killer of men.'

Sasha said nothing. She looked at him, unsurprised to find him hostile even after she had saved him and the rest of their family.

'Mrs. Gifford even congratulated me. Can you believe it? That someone thought I would take pride in my daughter being a killer?'

'What you take pride in is no business of mine, Father,' Sasha said. 'I for one, am very proud of myself.'

'No doubt, finally being allowed to fight,' Alexander scowled.

'Father,' Sasha sighed and rubbed her eyes. She had been up for so long, her patience drained quickly. She took a deep breath.

'I do not take pride in killing. I take pride in winning, in getting the job done, with as few deaths as possible. I take pride in knowing that hundreds of people have the chance to live free, and not under threat from the yeomen.'

'Sasha . . . ,' Alexander started, but Sasha cut him off.

'Father, I planned the assault on Walker,' she said. 'I did. And when I planned it, I did so with the expectation that I would be involved, that I would be sharing the dangers. And this morning, when a column of a thousand men was close to destroying everything we'd done here, I came up with the plan that deceived them into retreating. So instead of massive bloodshed, there was only a minor skirmish. I was there, because I felt I had to be.'

'Sasha, they've made you a killer!' Alexander exclaimed.

'No, Father, they did not. Samuel Cartier made me a fighter. Colonel Snow made me a soldier. And General Prince has made me an officer. I don't like killing people, but I do so when I must, in the service of the army and movement that made me a leader.'

'Men would not follow a woman into battle,' Alexander said.

'Yes, we would,' one of the guards said. The others nodded their agreement.

'Father, you have seen it yourself. I rescued the hostages with some of the most well-trained troops in the Renaissance Army, and they followed me. I listened to their experience, but I made the decisions. The responsibility fell on me.'

Alexander looked at her, and for once she thought his resolution slipped, but he shook his head.

'Why are you so stubborn?'

'You gave me your stubbornness, along with your name,' Sasha said.

Alexander blinked in surprise. 'What?'

'Sasha is a shortened form of Alexander, Father. By accident, you gave me your name. And with it, you gave me your stubbornness and your intellect.'

Alexander shook his head. 'Too bad I did not give you my capacity for love.'

'On the contrary, you did.'

'You kill because you love?'

'I do,' Sasha said. 'I know you don't understand; I know you cannot believe it, but I do. I kill because I love my friends and family so much, I want to protect them.'

'We didn't ask you to.'

'No, and you'll never have to.'

Several riders came towards the tent; Colonel Grace and her staff dismounted. Sasha turned slightly and saluted as Grace approached.

'Ma'am,' she said. Alexander took a step back as the dirty men and women filed past.

'Lieutenant Scholar,' Grace said, pausing to look at her arm. 'You are well?'

'Mustard burn from last night,' she raised her hand. Then gestured to her leg. 'Phosphorus burns from this morning. Elector is here checking on me.'

'Oh, dear,' Grace said. 'Well, good work at Hazel's Well. And with the plan to use the radios. This army was surely blessed when you joined its ranks.'

'Thank you, ma'am.'

'Anyone else home?' Grace nodded at the tent.

'No, ma'am. General Caesar said he would be back shortly after midday. I'm watching the table; nothing to report beyond general status updates.'

'Okay,' Grace said. She turned slightly to see Alexander. 'And this is?'

'My father, Colonel Grace. Father, this is Colonel Grace, who has prosecuted the siege since last summer.'

Alexander glared at the woman, keeping his hands resolutely at his side. Grace looked him up and down, then crossed her arms. 'I'd offer my congratulations on your daughter's success, but I doubt an Alvanist would appreciate it.'

'No one should fight,' Alexander said, 'ever.'

'I would agree,' Grace replied, 'but that's not the world we live in. When one is constantly attacked, it is good that one learns to defend oneself. If the king ever comes in peace, I shall respond in kind. Until then, I fight.' She turned to Sasha. 'Join us inside when you are done.'

Grace entered the tent. Alexander glared. Sasha was about to speak when another group of riders approached: Caesar and Saxon and their entourage. Sasha saluted again when they walked up.

'Colonel Grace is here?' Caesar asked.

'Yes, General.'

'Good,' he said. He looked at Alexander, who glared back at him.

'I remember you,' Alexander said.

'I am sure you do,' Caesar replied coolly.

'You stole my daughter and turned her into this!' Alexander shouted. Several of the Olympians stepped forward but stopped at Saxon's glance.

'I did nothing of the sort,' Caesar said. 'I gave her tools and opportunity to fashion herself into the best she could be. The woman you see before you is simply your daughter unbound.' He looked at Sasha. 'Do not take too much longer, Templar Scholar.'

Saxon was a step behind, stopping beside Sasha. She glanced at Alexander, then back at Sasha. 'You have an unworthy father,' she said, and continued on her way.

'I see you have companions who share your hatred of your family's ideals.'

Sasha watched the officers disappear into the tent. 'My family's ideals are not attacking me, only my father,' Sasha looked back to Alexander. 'Father, why are you here?'

'I am trying to save your soul!'

'Are you? You have done nothing but tear me down, to insult who I am and belittle what I've done. You keep saying you want to save my soul, but I'm already a killer, Father. You ignore that fact and attack me. You say you are here to save me, but all you do is try to make me small.'

508

Alexander stared at her, his face red. 'Sasha, this is your last chance! Reject these men and their evil ways! Our family has followed Alvanism for generations. Do not betray that now!'

He shouted. He went so far as to step forward, grabbing for her arm. She stepped back, quickly gesturing for the guards behind her to stop advancing. Alexander looked up at them, realizing the danger he had just incurred.

Sasha looked at him. He was taller than she, yes, but no longer imposing. He had changed from the strong man who faced the world with the power of his conviction to a weak man who hid behind them rather than admit he could be wrong. And something else, the way he spoke about their family, reminded her of a fight from months ago.

'You're Senator,' she said.

'What?' Alexander asked in confusion.

Sasha stared at him. 'You are worried about what my actions say about you. You think if I'm not an Alvanist, people won't think of you as the perfect Alvanist.'

'I care for your soul.'

'Thomas cares for my soul, Father. That's why he's conflicted; he sees how much better I am without your faith, as much as he wishes it weren't true, and he can't bring himself to make more than a token request. He's glad to be free, and he's thankful I did it, even if he believes I've forever tainted my soul.

'But you, Father, you don't care about any of that. Oh, you're okay with suffering, okay with pain and punishment, because that makes you the perfect Alvanist. If your family accepts that, then you've raised the perfect Alvanist family. But if I reject it, if I reject your faith for my own, then your family isn't perfect, and that means neither are you.'

She was right. She knew it with certainty. Just like when she stood before the generals and expose their true relationship, she saw it in his eyes. He wasn't driven by love, but by fear. He did love her, she had no doubt, but not enough to overcome that fear. That fear that his access to heaven was dependent on his perfection of faith as he saw it, and how she blemished that.

Suddenly, Sasha had no more desire to continue this fight. Alexander Small would not let himself be convinced of anything, and she had better things to do than argue with a rock.

'Father,' Sasha began, 'you are taking the family west to Bemidji. From there, I imagine you will make your way to Duluth, to the Lester River Community. Go in peace. Give my best to Christian Proctor and his family;

509

and the twins, if they are still there. Know that I fight for your peace and your happiness, even if you cannot understand the truth of it.' He looked at him. 'I love you, Father. Now go.'

Before he could respond, she turned and made her way back into the tent. She took her place at the table and did not see him move away.

One of Grace's officers was speaking. 'With most of our wagons and animals busy, it'll be awhile before we can move the bulk of our forces to Bemidji. For the moment, we're simply getting them out of Walker and under the trees.'

'Presuming we go to Bemidji,' Saber said.

'Trumpeter and Prince have managed to sway much of the county,' Saxon said. 'A siege of Bemidji is more of a formality at this point.'

'I wasn't talking about Trumpeter, I was talking about Senator,' Saber replied. 'With the siege lifted, he may start making demands of our personnel. The Army of the Lakes is still hundreds short of its paper strength.'

'Your point was anticipated,' Caesar said. 'Templar Scholar, the letter I gave you, please read it.'

Sasha nodded and pulled the letter from her breast pocket. Opening and unfolding it, she read.

'"As Commanding General of the Renaissance Army of Minnesota, I order that all units that have been involved in the siege of Walker Town, previously known as the Walker Siege Group, are hereby assembled as the Renaissance Siege Corps, independent of the Army of the Lakes. Furthermore, Colonel Grace, as commander of the Walker Siege Group, is promoted to the rank of Brigadier General, with all the rights and responsibilities thereof, and may make such changes, promotions, and reorganizations to her command as she sees fit. Signed this day, Thursday, April Thirtieth, 2476. General Prince, Renaissance Army of Minnesota, Commanding."'

Sasha stopped reading and beamed at the table. Many of them were smiling, even Grace.

'Congratulations, General,' Caesar said. Grace took his hand.

'Thank you, General. This is a surprise. A siege corps?'

'We will need the expertise you've gained over the last year in the future; I wrote to General Prince and he agreed. I am hoping to add the AA Battery and some more infantry to your order of battle before you get to Bemidji, but I cannot promise anything. We are stretched thin as it is.'

'We'll make do, as we always have,' Grace replied.

'So, who will be in command at Bemidji?' one of the militia officers asked. 'She outranks Brigadier Trumpeter, but he's been fighting there longer.'

'We're both adults, Captain. We'll figure it out.'

'First,' Caesar said, 'let us go over exactly where everyone is going. Templar Scholar, please report.'

Sasha nodded and started reporting on everything they had missed.

Chapter 57

Sasha managed a small nap that afternoon, but was up that evening to watch the Royal Air Corps destroy Walker Town. She found a spot on a hill outside town, next to several officers and civilians, including, she was surprised to see, Scott Anthony.

'I'm sorry your governorship begins with destruction,' Sasha said.

'Did you really think it would start any other way?' Scott chuckled. 'Look, I knew everyone was going to do everything they could to avoid it, but war is war. It would take a pretty hefty miracle to take a city without a major fight. I was hoping, but this is more realistic.'

'How many are staying to rebuild?' Sasha asked.

'Maybe a hundred,' Scott shrugged. 'Again, I'm not surprised. Walker'll be pretty ugly for a while.'

Someone called their attention. The sky was clear of clouds, but in the darkness, there was little chance to see the bombers themselves. They heard the drone of engines, followed by the whistling of falling ordnance, then the thunder and lightning of explosions marching across Walker. The cathedral, the castle, and the town exploded and burned, the smoke plumes rising into the air. After the Royal Air Corps bombers left, their smaller attack aircraft flew in, leveling anything left standing.

No gunfire met them.

'Per General Caesar's orders,' Saxon said. 'Too many people have died already, and we can't stop them. The bombers fly too high to be shot down.'

'Right,' Sasha said.

Walker burned into the next day as the columns continued to march away. Zac Holden had done his work well, sending families to their new homes with little delay. Only around forty stayed with Scott Anthony to rebuild Walker after the fire died.

The column Sasha watched was the one leaving the Liberated Counties. Except for Giulio Montessori, who was now a prisoner of the RAM in a secure location, every yeoman and army regular captured in Walker was being sent to Bemidji, along with the civilians who wanted to leave. The column was huge, but Sasha still saw her family, along with the Giffords, leaving town. She did not wave or call out to them, and they either did not see her or purposely ignored her.

All that remained were the military units themselves.

Grace assembled them in a clearing south of Walker. Except for those watching the column moving to Bemidji, every unit was there, including Patch's battery and Roach's chemical team. A group of civilians, including the retired sergeants of the sergeant's game, stood to one side. Hundreds of men and women in a dozen different uniforms, gathered around a wagon with a flat stage built across it.

Sasha took her place with Caesar, behind him and next to Saxon.

'The column is in its way?' Saxon asked.

Sasha nodded. 'They'll make it to Bemidji, no problem. Scott Anthony has the few who are staying, and Zac Holden is distributing those who are joining up amongst the liberated towns.'

Saxon sighed. 'Less than half wanted to join us.'

'It makes sense to me,' Sasha replied. 'Many of them were veterans who came with their families following Count Walker. They had no reason to believe we would leave them alone, no matter how much he promised them. The yeomen and count functionaries aren't going to stay amongst the people they used to terrorize. And a lot of them just lost their homes because of what we did. They have no reason to love us.'

Saxon looked at Sasha. 'I know,' she agreed. 'That doesn't mean I have to like it.'

'No,' Sasha nodded, 'it doesn't.'

Talking died down as Grace took her stand. 'Ladies and gentlemen of the Siege Corps,' she called, shouting a bit to make sure everyone could hear here, 'honored guests, fellow warriors and supporters all. Here ends the siege of Walker Town. When we took this mission, who among us thought it would be a year? A year in which we kept a superior force cooped up in their defenses. A year in which we would grow from a mix of whatever could be spared to a finely tuned orchestra of units. Before the Army of the Lakes, we were here. And don't ever let them forget that.'

Someone cheered, and the group followed suit. Grace waved for them to settle down.

'If you haven't figured it out by now,' Grace said, 'with the siege of Walker ended, we no longer need to be here. We are moving north to Bemidji. Some of you will not be following us. To those of the Workshop, the Marine Company and the Naval Group, I say, thank you for your efforts, and feel free to come by anytime.'

Another round of cheers. Sasha liked Grace as a speaker. She was entertaining, keeping the attention of her audience while she said what she had to say.

'Some of you,' Grace continued, 'will not be joining us. You enlisted for the term of the siege and have no expectations of continuing. To you, I say thank you. We would not have been as successful without every individual working together. You, also, are welcome back any time.'

Saxon tensed at this. Sasha wondered if she had a problem with letting some of the militia go when the siege corps was so small.

'This siege ended with a battle, and after a battle, it is important to reflect. Ladies and gentlemen, a moment of silence for the fallen.'

Sasha bowed her head. She thought of Collins and Pierce, who died under her command. She thought of Lupe's father, and the rifle company that fought to the death rather than retreat again.

Do not forget.

'And now, ' Grace called, 'a moment of excitement. It is also important when a battle is over to mention those who did so much to make it happen, who went above and beyond the ordinary in the course of their duties. There will be more coming in the future, but right now we can honor four men and women who did so much to make this happen.'

Sasha listened with one ear. Her attention was divided between the awards ceremony and thoughts about what they were going to do next. Walker was now entirely liberated. The Army of the Lakes was active in the south, and General Prince was disrupting III Corps to the north. There were still a few weeks before the apprenticeships were done. What was she going to focus on now?

Sasha clapped when necessary. Douglas Wells, the man responsible for intelligence gathering and blowing up the supplies in Walker Town, was awarded an intelligence medal. A corporal received a life-saving medal for rescuing people from a burning building, and a sergeant received the Colonel's Cross for clearing the Golden Cross Inn. Sasha clapped each time.

Then Grace called out. 'Second Lieutenant Scholar!'

Sasha blinked in surprise. Saxon elbowed her and nodded towards the wagon. 'You heard the general, Lieutenant. Get going.'

Sasha made her way out from behind Caesar and up the stairs to the wagon. Grace stood before her, trying not to smile.

514

'Lieutenant Scholar, apprentice to General Prince, member of the Templar Project. You stand here not because of your actions in combat, but your actions as a member of the general's staff. Your plan for capturing Walker worked. You identified the need to accelerate our timetable. And when the crisis of III Corps came, you thought up a creative solution that avoided a pitched battle.

'Awarding soldiers for actions in combat is good. It is important to share stories of heroism and valor. It's also important to share stories of intelligence and planning. To let our soldiers, our civilians, and our enemies know that we are more than just the number of weapons at our command, but the sum of our thoughts.

'That you put yourself in harm's way, that you led the landing in Walker and the defense of Hazel's Well, is exactly what this army expects from a Templar. But the mind that you brought to the battle, to identify opportunities, is exactly what this army needs from the Templars. And so, I, Brigadier General Grace, seconded by Commander Faro and approved by General Caesar, award to you the Renaissance Cross, for your contributions to the victory of the Siege Corps over both Walker Town and the III Corps.'

Grace turned and took the medal from Atlas. It was similar to the Colonel's Cross, but with blue lacquer instead of black, and a blue ribbon. Grace moved to pin the cross on Sasha's uniform. Sasha stared over Grace's shoulder, aware of hundreds of eyes watching this moment. Patch and Elector and Mako were there. How would they react to seeing her win an award?

Grace finished and stepped back, saluting Sasha. 'Congratulations, Lieutenant.'

Sasha saluted, and the crowd erupted into cheers. Sasha stepped back and down the stairs to return to her spot. Caesar looked at her with an oddly neutral expression, but Saxon welcomed her with a smile and a handshake.

'Good job, Templar.'

'I don't know that I deserve this,' Sasha said.

'You probably don't,' Saxon teased.

Sasha stifled a laugh.

***

When Grace was done, the units began to leave. The boats and marines left straight away, wanting to get back to their haven before the RAC sent planes in to find and sink them. Sparrow left, leading an advanced company up to Bemidji. Elector and Patch were both busy helping to pack up their own groups for transport, again looking to avoid the attention of the RAC.

That night was a late dinner for the officers, and a few guests who remained. Sasha spent some time talking with the sergeant who won the Colonel's Cross, trading battle stories while they sat on the edge of the crowd.

Saber appeared. 'Congratulations, Lieutenant,' he said, holding out his hand.

'You too, Major,' Sasha replied with a smile.

He chuckled. 'Once Grace was sure we were keeping Sparrow and her company, my position became too big for a mere captain. Commanding the Trencher's Battalion is worthy of a major.'

'I'm sorry you didn't get your promotion before the whole crowd.'

Saber shrugged. 'Nothing is perfect. Are you heading back to Third Field Regiment?'

'Eventually.'

'Give my best to everyone there.'

Sasha nodded. 'I will, sir.'

Saber left. The sergeant was summoned to Grace's side, leaving Sasha alone for a few moments until Lupe appeared.

'Lieutenant,' the young girl said.

'Lupe,' Sasha said. She gestured for her to sit down. 'How have you been?'

'When I finally went to sleep, I slept for almost a full day,' Lupe admitted. 'The doctors said I needed it.'

'Lucky you,' Sasha replied. 'I've managed a few hours here and there.'

Lupe smiled. Sasha saw it was a shallow smile, with only a shadow of mirth behind it, but it was a start. 'How are you doing?' Sasha pressed.

Lupe shrugged. 'I cry, sometimes. Other times I'm numb. I'm an orphan, now. Never expected that.'

Sasha put her arm around Lupe and hugged her. 'I'm sorry.'

'I know, but it's not your fault. The yeomen killed Mom, and Dad fought for me until they killed him. Now I'm going to fight them.'

There was a fire in her voice that made Sasha cringe to hear in someone so young. 'Are you sure? You could find a place in a town, stay away from the war.'

Lupe shook her head. 'No, I have a place here. Grace is putting me on her

516

staff. Junior clerk or aide or something. She wants me to learn from her.'

'Grace is a fine mentor,' Sasha said.

'She wants me to be a Templar,' Lupe said, 'like you.'

Sasha blinked in surprise, then smiled. 'I think you could make a fine Templar, Lupe. But it is lots of hard work. Learn to fight, learn to think, and always be a good person.'

'I will,' Lupe said. They both looked up as someone appeared before them.

'Sorry to interrupt,' Saxon said, 'but we're leaving first thing in the morning. Might want to say your goodbyes now.'

'Goodbye, Templar Scholar!' Lupe said, grasping Sasha in a fierce hug. 'I will see you again.'

'Of course,' Sasha promised. The officers all mixed together for several minutes, shaking hands, embracing, saying their goodbyes. Grace offered Sasha her hand. 'Congratulations on that cross, Templar. And thank you.'

***

True to their word, Caesar and his entourage left early the next morning, before much of the siege corps was awake.

'We want to slip out without being noticed,' Saxon explained. 'Ridiculous theatrics, but Caesar insists.'

'Not existing must be exhausting,' Sasha said. Saxon stifled a loud laugh.

They rode through the forests, heading east towards Avalon. The sun rose up, bringing some heat to the day. Sasha wondered if they would stop for food or continue all the way to Avalon when Caesar motioned for her to ride up alongside him.

Sasha kicked her mount forward. It occurred to her that they had not spoken much since the awards ceremony, and she wondered if she had somehow upset him.

'Sir?' she asked.

'What do you think of your award?' Caesar asked.

Sasha glanced at the cross hanging off her tunic. 'I'm proud of it, but I'm not sure I deserve it.'

'I agree,' Caesar said. He was speaking formally, as he had often done earlier in her training, before they had become comfortable with one another. Sasha worried if something had changed between them.

'In what way do you agree, sir?' Sasha asked nervously.

'You are an apprentice to a general,' Caesar said, 'and the award could seem like patronage, giving you the medal because you are close to me. You are also a Templar; great things are always expected of you. Not all of them will come with awards and ribbons.'

'I understand, sir,' Sasha said. 'Then why did you approve it?'

Caesar did not answer for a moment. Sasha was about to move away and avoid the painful silence when he finally spoke.

'I sought advice,' he said. 'I spoke with General Grace. She said that the Renaissance Cross is meant to acknowledge those who find intelligent solutions to problems. Everyone knows that it was you who came up with the plan, both for Walker and for III Corps. In her mind, if we ignored your efforts, if may seem that we were saying what you did was not as impressive as so many are saying it was.'

'Ah,' Sasha said.

'Officer Saxon likewise came to your defense. She argued that not giving you the award because you are a Templar may make sense to us but might not make sense to the rest of the army. They may start to wonder if we are serious about appreciating intelligence and knowledge over violence and bloodshed.'

Sasha did not have a response. That rationale had not crossed her mind.

'And finally, I was approached by Scott Anthony. I do not know how he heard about the discussion – I suspect General Grace may had approached him – but he made his way to speak to me. He told me I would be a damned fool if I ignored the opportunity to prove the Templar Project makes good officers. He also questioned whether I was considering denying you that medal out of shame.'

'Shame?' Sasha asked.

'That you came up with a plan and I did not,' Caesar said.

'I can't believe that, sir.'

'He may not have been too far off the mark,' Caesar admitted. He looked at Sasha, and she saw some disappointment in his eyes. 'You proved to be exactly what I wanted the Templars to produce. I should have considered that you would find solutions beyond what I could. It is a failing of myself that I was momentarily blinded by ego.'

They continued in silence for a minute before Sasha asked. 'Why did you follow their advice?'

'You do not appoint people to be your advisors if you are going to ignore their advice,' Caesar said. 'I could argue with any one of them. All three I must pay attention to.'

Sasha nodded. 'Right,' she said.

'I would make clear to you,' Caesar said, 'that I am proud of what you did. But you will notice that I am not wearing a ribbon or medal of any kind. I am not doing this for the awards. My goal is to win the war, and I want that to be your goal as well. Not to amass medals, not to pepper your uniform with ribbons, but to end the war in our victory.'

'That is my goal, sir,' Sasha said.

'Even if you were to never get another award again?'

'Even so, sir,' Sasha said.

Caesar looked at her levelly. 'Good,' he said. 'That cross means you did well yesterday. But I want you thinking of what you are going to do tomorrow.'

Sasha nodded, then changed the subject.

'Lupe said something to me that caught me off guard. She said Grace was going to groom her for a Templar. Sir, are you planning other Templar classes?'

Caesar nodded. 'We are,' he admitted. 'Similar in size, with a few more dedicated instructors and a better idea of what we are doing. I imagine we will be looking at new recruits in a few weeks. Why? Did you think you would be the only ones?'

Sasha shrugged. 'It never occurred to me one way or the other. When Lupe mentioned it, it was the first time I thought of other Templar classes.

'Lupe is too young for the next one,' Caesar said, 'but a year under Grace's tutelage will more than prepare her. Grace is a talented woman.'

'She is,' Sasha said. 'But she's no Lily.'

Caesar turned red.

***

They arrived at Avalon, finding the inhabitants thankful at their survival. 'You didn't know?' Sasha asked.

'Oh, we knew, but we're still happy to see you,' Payne said.

Sasha grinned. She went down to her room, still decorated as it had been when she left with Caesar . . . *less than two weeks ago? Time does certainly fly.* She looked at the calendar. *Three weeks left here as it is.*

Sasha changed into her general work clothes and went to the War Room, surprised to find everyone there. 'What's going on?'

'Minor engagement outside Menahga,' Payne said. 'Looks like someone convinced I Corps that the Army of the Lakes had moved north entirely, threw out a few companies to raid the local towns. Nothing Senator couldn't smash.'

'Any more casualties?' Sasha asked.

'A few, but the royalists didn't have much fight in them. They fell back as soon as they met resistance. Senator still exacted a toll.'

Jane called attention as Caesar entered. He waved everyone back. 'You were saying Senator exacted a toll?'

Payne gave a formal report on the events of the previous day. Sasha stepped back and listened, looking at the large map and mentally moving the blocks around to match Payne's report.

'So now they know III Corps wasn't facing the Army of the Lakes,' Saxon said.

'Yes, but I doubt they'll advance south yet,' Payne said. 'Trumpeter and First Field are playing hell with their lifeline. And with Walker fallen, there's no reason to rush. Van Kalvin will work to secure Bemidji and keep his supply lines open.'

'As he should,' Caesar said. 'And what of the other matter I wrote to you about?'

'Jane?' Payne directed the staff sergeant, who gestured for the officers to follow her. She led them down the hallway towards the conference room Sasha had used to plan the attack on Walker and ushered them in.

The room had been redone in Sasha's absence. The maps and models of the city, the pages of documents and letters about its status, all had been removed and replaced. Now, instead of Walker and its surrounding area, it was a broad map that stretched from one wall to the next. Sasha recognized a tract of road and its towns in the upper middle of the map.

'It's Third Regiment!' she exclaimed.

'It's Wadena, Brainerd and Aitkin Counties,' Payne said. 'Our southern front.'

'When you're not performing your duties in the main room,' Saxon

520

continued, 'you can work on a campaign for when you return to your regiment.'

Sasha beamed. The shelves had more reports on them, the maps had unit pins. 'Can I get to work?' she asked.

'You don't want the rest of the day off? The guards are planning a cookout this evening.'

'I'll be there, but I want to get into this,' she gestured.

'I understand,' Caesar said. 'We will let you know when you need to start getting ready.'

They left, only Jane remaining.

'Where do we start, ma'am?' Jane asked.

'As with Walker,' Sasha said, 'we read.'

***

The last three weeks at Avalon were rather uneventful, mostly accepting and filing reports.

General Senator sent a personal letter congratulating Caesar and his staff on a successful plan for Walker, particularly singling out Sasha for praise. He admitted he was angry when he heard the radio transmissions simulating his headquarters, but chose not to reveal his location, in the hope he could lure I Corps into another fight. He did so, describing the battle in some detail. He discussed how the weapons captured from the Royal Army were distributed. He also asked the generals to promote Athena to Brigadier General and second in command of the Army of the Lakes.

'I would have guessed he would go with Brigadier Birch, his protégé,' Saxon said.

Payne shook his head. 'Senator isn't as big a jackass as you think. He knows who his best officer is, even if he hates her.'

I Corps fell back to the west, not south, leaving one brigade in Park Rapids and establishing new supply lines through the Smoky Hills. The Army of the Lakes let them, though Wild was causing havoc and raiding the wagon trains for badly needed supplies.

III Corps was successfully stuck in Bemidji County, fighting to secure their supply lines back to the Red River Valley. The Siege Corps was moving into position around the city itself, slowly closing the siege Colonel Trumpeter had started, but other than skirmishes, nothing happened. Neither side had the stomach for a full fight.

Third Regiment was reporting on the army units moving in to secure the railway through their county. Though Snow had yet to engage them in combat, she took copious notes on their new fortifications. Sasha was eager to get back and lend her talents to her former regiment.

Second Field Regiment's mission to keep an open passage to the outside world ended. A letter from Colonel Boudicea described a chance battle with a troop of yeomen, revealing their existence. Their secret revealed, the regiment moved into open rebellion across Grand Rapids County.

'I'd like to meet her,' Sasha said.

'Boudicea?' Payne asked. 'Why?'

'When Senator interrupted our class, Boudicea was the only woman he thought deserved to lead a combat unit. She must be something.'

'She is,' Payne said with a smile. 'Something indeed.'

Sasha helped write the announcement confirming Grace and Athena as Brigadier Generals. The same announcement promoted Lily to Major General, and Aristotle and Gold to Brigadier Generals. Three combat generals balanced by three supporting generals.

Not all of the news was good, or at least did not reflect well on the RAM. First Field Regiment was engaging III Corps across Bemidji County, leading to some lawlessness as old grudges reignited. Murders had occurred, and Trumpeter's command was too widely dispersed to contain every conflict. Prince and Trumpeter were in some ways fighting two enemies, not just the royalists.

Similar acts occurred around I Corps in the south. Some individuals took revenge on civilians left behind when I Corps withdrew, including harm coming to women and children. Caesar was angry at that; even if the RAM did not participate, they were the authority in the liberated areas, and stopping such violence was one of their duties.

'Perhaps Senator is turning a blind eye?' Saxon asked.

'That is a dangerous accusation,' Payne replied.

Sasha agreed. She wanted to avoid that particular line of thought.

Sasha continued her role, helping Caesar plan, going over operations for Third Regiment, gaming royal responses. As her days wound down, she started to worry.

'About what?' Payne asked.

'Here, I'm one officer, helping others make the decisions. Between all of us, we have come up with some good solutions. There . . .,' she trailed off.

'There, you will be the only officer advising Snow,' he continued, 'and she may not be smart enough to challenge you.'

Sasha looked at him sternly.

Payne shrugged. 'I met her, you forget. After the prison camp. She is a capable woman, absolutely. And the reports from Third Regiment tend to indicate she continues to be a good colonel, but she's not an intelligent woman in the sense that you or Saxon are. There's nothing wrong with that.'

'I know,' Sasha said.

'Then don't feel guilty because you will be smarter than she is. That's the whole reason you're here, isn't it?'

'I guess,' Sasha admitted.

'She'll be better at something else,' Payne said. 'She wants you to be better at this. That's why she wanted you here.'

'Right,' Sasha finally agreed. 'That's why I'm here.'

Chapter 58

Sasha awakened on her last morning at Avalon and did not want to get out of bed. She had been assigned to Caesar's staff for ten weeks, spending most of that time at Avalon. She was used to the beds, the filtered water and steady food. She was used to knowing what was happening across the entire theater of war.

You could always ask to stay, she thought to herself.

But Snow needs you back with Third Regiment. She asked you to become a Templar to help her. How can you abandon her now? And Winnie and Mary? Everyone else who supported you?

She sighed and thought about her last morning with her friends in Third Regiment. How fearful she had been to leave. And now here she was, so glad she had done so, so glad she had come here. Content even with the bad things, the lost friends, the battles. All of them had shaped who she was so much more than any other period of her life.

'I am a Templar,' she said out loud. 'I am not the girl I was before.'

Sasha got out of bed and went through her normal routine. She bathed and dressed, then made her way to the cafeteria.

Everyone stationed at Avalon, except for Caesar and Saxon, was there. The soldiers with whom she had trained, the radio operators and facility technicians, the staff sergeants and General Payne. Everyone was having breakfast, talking with her, remembering their experiences at the camp.

'I'm surprised you didn't ask to stay,' Jane said.

'I have to get back to my regiment,' Sasha said. 'They sent me to the Templars for a purpose.'

'They're your unit,' Payne said.

'They are,' Sasha agreed, but she wondered if they really were, or if the Templars were now her unit.

She spent an hour with them before Payne finally stood. 'Ladies and gentlemen,' he said, 'I am not one for long speeches, particularly when there is nothing in my hand but coffee, but I wish to raise a glass in toast to Templar Scholar. Young lady, I'll admit I know little about you except what you've shown here these last few months, which is that you are a smart, courageous, and fierce young woman. God help whomever you face in battle.'

'Hear, hear!' someone called, the rest of the room chorusing after him.

'To Templar Scholar,' Payne said. They all raised their glasses at Sasha.

'I don't rightly know how to respond,' she said, wiping a tear from her eye, 'except to say I will miss you all terribly. I do hope to see all of your again someday.'

They all agreed.

Sasha went back to her room and packed her things. Not that she had much, but what she possessed had made this room her own for a time. It looked sad when she took down her small ornaments and cleared out her papers. Her room now felt like a piece of artwork that had the paint scraped off, waiting for the next artist to come along.

Caesar and Saxon were waiting with their mounted guard on the surface. Sasha tied her pack to her horse, bid a final farewell to the people, and left Avalon.

They rode the circuitous route to Olympia in quiet. They were almost into the town when Saxon signaled a stop. She looked at Caesar.

'Sir, might I take Templar Scholar on a ride with me?' she asked.

Caesar nodded, and Saxon gestured for Sasha to follow. Two Olympians followed close behind, out of earshot.

Saxon was quiet as they rode down a path. Finally, Sasha spoke.

'This path circles the town,' she said. 'Every town or village has a path that circles it. Why is that?'

'I don't know,' Saxon said.

'How odd,' Sasha said. 'I wonder if anyone would know, or –.'

'Sasha,' Saxon said. Sasha stopped in surprise at hearing her true name. She looked at Saxon, waiting for her to begin.

'I want to know if you're going to run.'

'What?' Sasha asked. She started to protest, but Saxon raised her hand.

'Bellona and I came to the RAM from Duluth. We were both educated enough to read and write, and the generals took us and made us their aides-de-camp. It was exhilarating, learning everything they wanted us to, challenging ourselves to grow. Much like you have experienced as a Templar.

'But we also realized something; knowing more means you can see further.

Experienced farmers can read the weather better than city folk; a sailor can read the sea better than a farmer. And a general, or any educated officer, can see the difficulties of the campaign better than the common soldier.'

'I don't understand,' Sasha said.

'Don't you?' Saxon asked. 'Sasha, how had we gotten this far in the campaign?'

'By staying one step ahead of the king. By learning his plans and using our forces to disrupt them. By surprising him and his generals.'

'Correct, but Sasha, the Army of the True Queen is the last true surprise we have. They've already shut down most of our conduits from their supply depots and the caravans that carried them to us. They must know by now we have intelligence organs operating in the Royal Cities, and they're aware of our resistance groups in the Red River Valley and the cities, which means they're looking for similar groups elsewhere. So, what does that mean for the future of the Renaissance Army?'

Sasha thought for a moment. 'If we don't have any more surprises for the Royal Army, we're going to be fighting a harder war from now on.'

'Right. Which means?'

'That the Renaissance Army needs officers willing to take the initiative, willing to change the course of the fight, not just follow orders from the generals.'

'That's right,' Saxon said, with a look of surprise on her face. 'I didn't think you'd jump ahead that far.'

'The Templars were told we were the future of the movement,' Sasha said. 'We've had almost a year to consider what that means.'

'Indeed,' Saxon said. 'Sasha, I'm not trying to get you to run, far from it, but I want you to be ready. The fight is going to get much more difficult from here on. Other people may not be aware of that, they might be expecting more surprises, more hidden troops or fancy toys. But you know, now, that most of those are used. Now, it's going to be tough going.''

'I understand, Saxon,' Sasha said.

'Good. Now, let's get you to your bed for the night.'

'A tent?' Sasha asked.

'Nope, not even close.'

Sasha followed Saxon. 'I wonder.'

'What's that?' Saxon asked.

'I wonder if this is the line of reasoning that led Hero to run away,' Sasha said. 'He was getting scared and he ran because he was smart enough to get scared.'

'Maybe,' Saxon said. 'Too late to do anything about it now.'

***

Saxon led Sasha to the far side of Olympia. Several new ram cabins waited for them, nestled in the trees. One had a large chalk T on the door.

'We just built these for groups of officers, visiting civilians, and such,' Saxon said. 'And now it's going to be for the Templars for a few days.'

'Who else is here?' Sasha asked, excited to see her friends again.

'No one. You're the first.' She looked at Caesar, waiting patiently. 'We have to go. I will see you in a few days.'

'Thank you, Officer Saxon.'

Sasha watched them ride away. For the first time in a long time, she had nothing to do. She rode to the stable and turned in her horse, then returned to the cabin.

It was noticeably longer than every other ram cabin, and the layout was completely new to Sasha. Before her was a common area, with two tables and chairs and the stove, moved out of its normal position in the middle of the building. A shelf held several of the Renaissance Army's new books, and a few paintings hung as artwork. A hallway ran down one edge of the cabin, with six doors spread out along its length.

Sasha checked the rooms. Each one had a single bed, a chest, and shelves on the wall, along with a chair and a desk that folded down from the wall. It was roughly the size of the room she stayed in at Avalon.

On each bed was a package, one that reminded her of the festival. Inside was another set of the off-color clothes officers wore during their off times.

Sasha found the washroom and cleaned up, changing into her new clothes. It was still early afternoon, and a warm breeze was blowing through the open windows. Fatigue overtook her, and she soon fell asleep on the reading chair in the sitting room.

She was awakened by a kick to the chair. Patch stood over her.

'Morning, Templar Sleepy.'

'It's afternoon,' Sasha stretched.

'I know!' Patch sat down across from her. 'I'm so tired,' she said. 'We had to get the battery ready to join the Siege Corps.'

'Really?' Sasha asked. 'It got approved?'

'It seems most likely that the Air Corps is going to fly in support of sieges than anything else, so it makes sense to leave the guns with the people prosecuting the sieges, but it also means giving up some personnel, and Mobius wasn't too keen on that. You know how much he likes to keep people close.'

'Sure,' Sasha said.

'Anyway, that's what I've been doing since Walker. Figuring out what the battery needed to fight, and what could go back to the Workshop. How about you?' Patch asked.

Sasha considered for a moment, then answered truthfully. 'I spoke to my father for possibly the last time in my life.'

'What?' Patch sat upright. 'What do you mean?'

'I found my family after the fall of Walker. I spoke with my mother and siblings right afterwards. They were glad I was alive and doing well, though unhappy with my place in the army,' Sasha said. 'After III Corps, my father found me. He was less happy all around. Wanted me to give up my position and meekly come back to the family. I told him no, then I told him goodbye.'

'How could your father not like who you've become?' Patch asked incredulously.

'Do you know what an Alvanist is?' Sasha asked.

'No. Wait, yes. The pacifists? Why would they . . . YOU'RE A PACIFIST!?'

'No, but my family is.'

'And they saw you in uniform?'

'Worse, they saw me kill someone. With a knife.'

'Oh, dear. That could not have sat well with them.'

'No,' Sasha admitted. She leaned forward. 'I wish things had gone differently, but I can't imagine how. We're just two completely different types of people. And I can't be a part of their lives, and they can't be a part of mine. I just have to live with that. The Renaissance Army is my family now.'

She looked at Patch, who had an odd look on her face, her hand flipping a pencil around absent-mindedly. Finally, she shrugged. 'I don't know what to make of it. Would you say it worked out?'

'About as well as I could expect,' Sasha said.

'Good. Hungry? I could eat a lot.'

'I suppose I could, too.' Sasha stood. 'Do you want to change?'

'Why, my clothes are still clean.'

'But you've been wearing them all day.'

'If there's no mud on them, they're clean. Let's go.'

***

Mako and Elector arrived the next morning, Rose a few hours later, her arm in a sling.

'What happened?' Elector asked.

'Got too close to an artillery barrage outside Bemidji,' Rose responded. She unbuttoned her shirt, exposing a shoulder swathed in bandages. Elector removed them, inspecting the wound. 'Shrapnel cut up my shoulder.'

'Looks painful,' he said.

'It is,' Rose said. 'And it needs a cleaning. Can you?'

'Aye,' Elector said.

Sasha watched Elector work. Rose's skin showed a dozen gashes where metal had cut into her. Rose hissed as Elector started cleaning.

Sasha broached a painful subject. 'I don't know how much you learned up in Bemidji, but did you hear?'

'About Roland?' Rose asked. She nodded. 'Prince told me. We were too busy for me to mourn much, but I did cry a few times. Do you know details?'

'I have some reports from officers above him, but it's all very technical. I'm hoping Candle can give a much better accounting.'

Candle arrived just after lunch, weary from a long ride. Covered in dust and grime, she smiled at the rest of the Templars.

'We're all here,' she said, a hint of pain in her voice. 'I need a shower.'

'Of course,' Rose said, 'but. . ..'

'. . . but you want to know about Roland.' Candle nodded. 'Get me some water.'

She took a seat in the sitting room, taking her shoes off and rubbing her feet.

'When Third Division swept that column out of Menahga, Roland's platoon did well. Roland was so proud of himself. I met with him when I rode down to take control of the field artillery they captured, and he was ecstatic at what he was doing. He was also disappointed that Third Division was stuck in the south while the next fight looked to be coming from the north.

'The next day, when Senator's fight was warming up, Athena got worried that Senator didn't have enough troops to fight. She sent two of her regiments north, not telling anyone she was doing so. Roland's company was the lead one, loaded with as many machine guns and mortars as they could carry.

'When word came that a second brigade was flanking, Athena's division moved eastward. Roland ran forward to fortify that plantation, getting most of the company in before the royal troops showed up. Their first attack was mostly infantry, and Roland chewed it up badly. He forced them to pause and redeploy, which gave the rest of Athena's division enough time to get into position to support his defense.

'I saw the battlefield afterwards. Roland's plantation had hundreds of yards of open terrain around it. The royal troops couldn't close in without being shot at from the forest, but neither could Roland get reinforcements. He was on his own with two platoons.'

'He was in charge?' Rose asked.

'The other platoon lieutenant got thrown from her horse and missed the battle. She was pretty upset about it afterwards; afraid people would think she was a coward. She's not, if anyone asks.

'Anyway, Roland was stuck out there with two platoons, fifty troops give or take, with lots of machine guns and ammunition. The royal troops bombarded him with artillery, doused his walls with machine gun fire, and tried three times to take the plantation. Roland held on tenaciously, knowing how important that position was.'

'Also sounds like he couldn't withdraw even if he wanted to,' Elector said.

'That, too,' Candle confirmed. 'Roland was wounded early on; some survivors said he was wounded two or three times, but he did not pull himself out of duty or turn command over. He moved about, repositioning, carrying ammo, shouting encouragement. The plantation was reduced to rubble and he defended it still. He kept that whole brigade from moving forward.'

'What killed him?' Sasha asked.

'A bullet. Someone firing from the tree line, probably not even aiming just trying to put fire on the position. Caught Roland in the chest, finished him quickly. The battle was almost over, too. Roland almost survived, but it just was not to be.'

'He took his name from a hero who died saving an army,' Elector said. 'He would have been proud.'

'More than half the troops who came with him died there, most of the rest were wounded. When the royal troops retreated, the survivors carried Roland's body out in reverence, presenting it to Athena and requesting a special burial for him.'

'Did she?' Mako asked.

'Athena buried the dead of the plantation at the edge of the fields, in a platoon formation. The troops lined up in three lines, with Roland buried at their head as their officer. Even Senator came to watch, respectfully, knowing full well it was a Templar who died.'

'Did you cry?' Rose asked. 'Scream and yell? I might have.'

'I was angry,' Candle admitted. 'Even before I knew he was dead, but I didn't have to be loud. I had cannon to roar for me.'

The sitting room fell to silence. Finally, Candle looked up. 'What about you?'

'My time with Prince was not boring, but it was nothing exciting,' Rose said. 'Many small skirmishes, many speeches, many plans and deceptions. A chance shrapnel in the shoulder during one of the fights along the roadway, but nothing compared to most of you.'

'I shot down five bombers,' Patch said.

'Over Walker?' Candle asked.

'Yeah,' Patch said. 'Just before Mako landed Scholar on the beach so she could storm the castle by herself.'

'I was not by myself,' Sasha said, 'I had my platoon with me.'

'I'm surprised Caesar let you lead your assault on the castle,' Candle said.

'I planned the whole assault on Walker,' Sasha admitted. The Templars all looked at her.

'Really?' Rose asked.

'It's true!' Patch said. 'Even convinced them to jump ahead of schedule. And she was right to do it.'

'But why lead?' Candle said. 'We already lost one Templar to battle, I'd hate to lose two.'

Sasha shook her head. 'We didn't train to stay out of danger. My training in town fighting made me one of the few officers who could lead the rescue team. And I had a personal reason for being there.'

'Her family was among the hostages,' Patch said.

'Patch!' Sasha exclaimed.

'What? I didn't do it!'

'I think most of us already knew that,' Mako said. They paused for a moment, an all burst out laughing.

Elector sighed. 'Well, we should let Candle wash up. We have a lot of waiting to do.'

'Until tomorrow,' Candle said. 'Major Thunder rode up with me, and she says we've got until tomorrow.'

'Tomorrow,' Sasha said, nervously.

Chapter 59

A pair of sergeants brought them breakfast early the next morning. Then a woman named Nicole appeared with new dress uniforms. She went to work, dressing each of them, measuring for adjustment and then undressing them. 'You won't ruin them by sitting around in them before they're needed,' she said, tailoring the uniforms.

Morning dragged on. The Templars tried to read, or play chess, or think, but everyone was nervous, even Patch. Nicole finished her work, the uniforms now hanging from pegs on the wall, awaiting the ceremony.

The Olympian bell rang noon. 'Here we go,' Nicole said with a smile, and with the help of the sergeants got the Templars dressed.

The six Templars stood in their dress uniforms. They all had ribbons, and most had medals now, earned during their apprenticeships. Sasha beamed with pride, seeing them in the uniforms they might only wear once. She looked at their faces and knew they were feeling the same thing.

Nicole was meticulous in her attention to detail, taking each uniform and conforming it quickly and efficiently. She pronounced all six Templars done. 'And with twenty minutes to spare,' Nicole announced.

'How long do we wait?' Candle asked. 'Are we supposed to go somewhere?'

'Someone will come and get you,' Nicole said. 'Have a seat and relax.'

Sitting was fine for some, but relaxation was not coming for anyone. Mako closed his eyes and prayed. Elector stared at the clock, lost in thought. Patch examined a painting in detail, while Candle stared at her shoes. Rose paced back and forth, and Sasha repeatedly read the first page of a book on the history of Quebec.

Several minutes before one o'clock, someone knocked on the door. Nicole opened it, and a young woman in a blue uniform walked in, a warrant officer's rank on her lapel and a huge smile on her face.

'Cardinal!' Candle exclaimed. The Templars jumped up as a former member entered the room. 'What are you doing here?'

'I was sent to get you,' Cardinal said. She smiled at everyone, showing surprise when Rose stepped forward and gave her a hug.

'What have you been up to?' Elector asked.

Templar Scholar

'I actually can't say,' Cardinal said, 'except to let you know the Templars are not the only secret project the Renaissance Army has going.' She did tap her finger gently on a patch on her uniform. A sword with wings.

'Ah,' Rose said, beaming. Sasha smiled too.

'Well, Templars,' Cardinal began. 'Are you ready?'

'Are we?' Elector asked Nicole.

Nicole checked the uniforms of everyone who sat, then nodded. 'Ready,' she said, moving to open the door for them.

Cardinal led the Templars through Olympia, avoiding as much dirt as she could. Nicole followed behind, muttering about the pants getting dirty. What few people who saw them stopped to look, some probably unaware of what was going on.

They approached the building; a new, large hall for gatherings. Olympian guards stood at the front door. Cardinal led them to a side door, opened it, and gestured for them to walk in. They stood in the hallway between the office and the hall, waiting for something.

Cardinal disappeared inside, leaving them alone for a short time. Then Del Oso appeared, wearing a surprising uniform: the formal dress of a Michigan Marine. 'Ready?' he asked.

'Templars, Sergeant Major,' Candle said.

Del Oso called them to attention, then turned and marched them inside.

At the front of the hall stood Prince, with Caesar and the other mentor officers – Aristotle, Lily, Thunder, Faro and Archimedes – standing behind him, all wearing formal uniforms. Among the benches were people, many of whom the Templars had interacted with. She saw Scott Anthony and Madam Moreau; Colonel Carpenter and Major Lance, the head officers of Athens and Sparta. Some in the crowd Sasha was surprised to see, such as Doctor Moore, the scientist from the Workshop, and Doctor Adams, the surgeon from Charity. She saw a contingent from the Civil Council, including Elder Templeton, and several drill instructors. She saw Mobius and Uncle Jacques, also from the Workshop. Major Fox and Major Scribe. Penn and Cardinal. Many unknown officers. They all looked up as the Templars were marched into the room.

Del Oso stopped the Templars in front of Prince and turned them to face the general. Then he stepped back.

Prince looked at the six of them. 'Templars,' he said. 'Welcome, and congratulations. You started this project nine months ago. Some of you came from within our ranks, some from without, but all of you volunteered to be the best you could be. And now, here you are. Six capable, enthusiastic officers, ready to lead the Renaissance, both the army and the movement, into the future.

'When Caesar first explained the project to me, I understood it, but did not support it. We would be too busy fighting, raising an army to spend resources on such a small group of people, I said. We needed officers immediately, not down the road. And every man and woman we asked said the same thing.

'But he argued for it anyway. "This project will not create officers, it will create leaders," he said. Repeatedly. Then, one by one, the voices that had sided with me against the Templars changed to support Caesar. "Her mind will waste," said one. "He will become bored," said another. Soon, I became the minority opinion, and I acquiesced. The Templar Project began.

'I know Caesar's words, Templars. "Learning is your faith, the library your temple." But there is more to it than just books. It's passion. Your passion brought you not only to the Templars but through it. Your dream to rebuild ancient glories, your desire to heal the sick, even your love of books, has brought you to this ceremony. It defines your role in our army. Your passion has become your art, and that is a feeling some people never have.'

Prince paused, looking at each one in the eyes.

'This movement is not just about warfare. It is about the future. The rebirth of civilization, of science and art and knowledge. If there's one regret I have, it's that you are trained for war. I do not want this renaissance to be a rebirth of war. I want it to be one of learning, of civilization and enlightenment. And I pray, with all my heart, that all of you will find a life beyond warfare.

'But before that dream must come the fighting. Fighting that is hard, fighting that is dangerous. Fighting that brings with it a cost.

'Twelve Templars started the program. Twelve extraordinary people, men and women both, but only six stand before us. One lost his leg but retains his love of knowledge. One accepted her limits and continues to work elsewhere. One failed and ran. Two died in an accident, and one died in battle.

'Templars, before we continue, I feel I must inform you that in the official dispatches of Major General Senator, Templar Roland was singled out as an exceptional officer, who held his position with extreme courage. So great was his accomplishment, that at the nomination of several generals, it is my honor to award him the General's Cross, posthumously. Templar Roland, Hero of the Renaissance Army.'

The crowd clapped behind them. Sasha broke her stance to clap as well, followed quickly by the others. Roland would not be forgotten by the army.

When the clapping subsided, Prince looked at the six of them and spoke softly. 'Templars, you are aware of what lies before this army, and this movement. You know the fights we will face. If any of you wish to leave, if any of you wish to go back to your original standing, make it known now.'

None of the six moved. None of them spoke. Prince smiled, a sad but proud smile.

'Raise your right hand and repeat after me.

'I am a Templar of the Renaissance Movement, and I solemnly swear that I will support and further the movement, that I will defend the people from all enemies, and that I will do so to the best of my abilities, so help me God.'

The Templars repeated the phrase. When Prince lowered his hand, so did they. He glanced to Caesar and nodded.

'Templar Candle, front and center,' Caesar said.

Candle walked forward, coming to stand before Caesar. Prince stood to her left, while Major Thunder marched forward and stood to her right.

'Templar Candle,' Caesar asked, 'do you accept the responsibilities of a commission in the Renaissance Army?'

'I do,' Candle said.

Prince and Thunder stepped forward and attached metal insignia to Candle's lapels. Sasha's eyes widened as she saw two bars on the insignia, not one.

Caesar stepped forward and attached something to Candle's chest. The three stepped back and saluted, Candle following suit.

'Congratulations, First Lieutenant Candle, Minnesota Artillery Regiment, Army of the Lakes.'

Candle saluted, then turned to make her way back to the line. Sasha saw the front of her jacket.

A Templar badge. Not an embroidered patch, but a metal badge, colored to match the patch exactly.

'We're jumping to First Lieutenant!' Rose whispered.

Elector was next, with Aristotle pinning his officer's pin. 'First Lieutenant Elector, Second Field Hospital, Minnesota Siege Corps.'

Mako, with Commander Faro. 'Lieutenant Junior Grade Mako, Naval Group.'

Patch, with Master Mobius and Colonel Archimedes. 'First Lieutenant Patch,

Renaissance Workshop.'

Rose finally stepped up. Sasha smiled as Cardinal walked up to take Prince's place, pinning her insignia alongside Major General Lily. 'First Lieutenant Rose, Renaissance Movement.'

Sasha smiled again at the vagueness of her assignment. *How many people in the room know about the Quebecois army?*

She did not have time to ponder. Her name was called, and Sasha walked forward to stand before Caesar.

'Templar Scholar,' Caesar asked, 'do you accept the responsibilities of a commission in the Renaissance Army?'

'I do,' Sasha said.

Caesar nodded then stepped around. Sasha realized both generals were pinning her insignia on her. Then Caesar stepped back to stand before her and pinned the last Templar badge on her.

'Congratulations, First Lieutenant Scholar, Third Minnesota Field Regiment,' Caesar and Prince saluted. Sasha returned it and turned back to stand in line.

'Ladies and gentlemen,' Prince said, 'I give you the first class of Templars.' He saluted, and every man and woman in uniform followed. Del Oso and Cardinal, Saxon and Bellona, every single one was saluting the six young men and women in the middle.

The Templars saluted back.

'Huzzah!' someone called out from the back of the room, and the crowd erupted in claps and cheers. All decorum fell as officers rushed forward to congratulate the Templars.

Fox was first in front of Sasha. 'Not bad for a pacifist's daughter,' he whispered. She smiled and agreed. Bellona came by with a cursory 'Good job,' while Saxon beamed a smile at her and hugged her like a sister. Aristotle clasped her hand and shook it hard. She glanced up and saw the generals had taken some steps back, allowing the Templars to bask in their attention.

It took some time for the congratulations to end. As the guests finished, they would move back to their positions, and the crowd thinned around the Templars. Finally, Prince stepped forward and motioned for everyone's attention.

'I am very proud of all of you,' he said, 'and I'm sure General Caesar is as well.'

'Absolutely,' Caesar said.

'As this is a night of celebration, we leave the Templars with several gifts.'

Saxon and Bellona stepped forward, each carrying a small stack of books. Each general took a book, opening it to read the front page before handing it to a Templar.

Both books had the look of freshly printed books from the Workshop. Sasha opened the first, from Caesar. The title was printed in bold. *Memoirs of Ulysses S Grant.* Below, Sasha read the inscription.

> *Templar Scholar,*
> *Find wisdom from his words*
> *And consider sharing the wisdom you possess.*
> *Welcome to our ranks.*
> *-General Caesar*

Sasha smiled at that, wondering for a moment what she should write. Then she shifted to the second book, this one with a red cover. She opened it to read its title, *Red Badge of Courage*, noting it was authored by someone named Stephen Crane. There followed by an inscription from Prince.

> *Templar Scholar,*
> *You are the first to follow in Caesar's footsteps.*
> *It is a good path to pursue.*
> *I wish you the best.*
> *-General Prince*

Sasha smiled again, tearing up a little.

'Now,' Prince said, 'I'm afraid duty calls. For those who can stay, please do so, but when the Templars are ready to go back to their quarters, they will find their final gift waiting for them. A gift they have more than earned, so do not keep them from it long.'

The generals bid their goodbyes, then they quickly left, leaving the Templars with their admirers.

Chapter 60

The last gift had been prepared at their cabin while they were going through the ceremony. One of the tables was covered in food and drink, and the Templars were informed that any vendor would give them more if they asked. As it was, they spent the first hour in the sitting room, drinking a sweet wine and laughing around the ample table.

'No!' Patch exclaimed, 'I do not believe it.'

'A whole army?' Candle asked.

Rose nodded. 'A whole army. Only three thousand at arms and in support, but it will be enough to swing the tide when they become necessary.'

'Should you even be telling us this?' Mako asked.

Rose shrugged. 'I don't see why not. We are all Templars.'

'And you're going back there?' Sasha asked.

Rose nodded. 'A Templar in the Army of the True Queen; that was the point of my coming here.'

'Just so long as you write,' Sasha said. The Templars around the table looked at her. 'Oh, surely I wasn't the only one to think it. If we can correspond regularly with our sponsors, we can correspond regularly with each other.'

'That does sound nice,' Patch said.

'It might not be terribly consistent,' Candle said.

'But it'll be something,' Elector smiled.

Mako stood. 'I say we should. If we are to be the future of the Renaissance, we must be able to coordinate.'

Candle laughed and stood as well, moving towards the window. 'It's getting hot, let's get some breeze going.'

She opened the front door, and a familiar voice came through.

'Is that the Hamline family again?' Rose asked.

'Looks like,' Candle said. 'Looks like they're burying someone.'

Bill Hamline's voice broke over the crowd, loud and clear in its oratory.

Templar Scholar

'Friends, elf and dwarf, lend me your ears
I've come to bury this knight, if not to praise him.
What good a man is, what bad a man does,
All buried with him, so let it be with our friend.
For what actions should a life be judged?
He did greedily grasp for the ring,
The same artifact he did swear to destroy.
Does this erase the years in the White City?
Fighting the dark shadows of evil?
What is the balance? What is fair?

He died nobly protecting the fellowship.
Does that clear the strife between us?
Where is the final dart?
To what afterlife has he gone?
Friend, I know not. So, it comes to what I choose.
He was a captain in life, he fought and led
Against villains such as most men never know.
From the ivory walls of his home
to this dread end, he marched,
ready to do his duty, to fight the fight.
That I will honor; that will I remember.

Did Sir Knight falter?
Did he attack the ring-bearer?
He did; he broke this fellowship.
That I cannot forget, but I can forgive.
For what would a man not do to save his home?
If his ivory walls would burn, what would he do?
He faltered, but I do not pity him.
He broke the fellowship, but I do not blame him.

Our charge and his friend have continued on,
The artifact in their hand.
For us, there are two others of our fellowship,
Taken by dark forces to an uncertain fate.
Let us carry after them, my friends.
Let us rescue those two from death and worse.
Friends, elf and dwarf, let us hunt!'

Sasha laughed suddenly.

'What is it?' Mako asked.

'Hamline, the entertainer. The first time I heard him, I was with my friends back in Third Regiment, the night before I left for the Templars. He was giving a play then, too. We listened to some of it.'

'And now you're hearing him on the last night with the Templars,' Rose said.

There was another somber moment. Patch teared up a little, then coughed. 'You know who would have liked that? Roland.'

'Yeah, he would have,' Candle said. 'He probably would have bugged the entertainer for stories and tips.'

'Again,' Sasha said.

'He was persistent, wasn't he?' Rose said.

'Yeah,' Sasha agreed. 'He certainly was.'

Mako barked a laugh. 'If he were here, he's probably be reciting some poem about us.'

The Templars all laughed.

'It would probably have been particularly good,' Rose said. 'He would not have wasted effort on it without it being perfect.'

'He'd probably be orating it to us now,' Patch said.

Candle walked to the serving table and poured herself some wine. On the way back she stopped at the table's end and spoke in a voice like Roland used to do.

> *'When the Renaissance was born*
> *As Prince led a nation to war,*
> *There gathered here in Walker*
> *Twelve young who wanted more.*
>
> *Six men who demanded to be*
> *Much more than one more rifle;*
> *Six women who declared that*
> *They were more than just a trifle.*
>
> *These twelve young men and women*
> *Boldly took the Templar name!*
> *And by book and by rifle they proved*
> *They will set the world aflame.'*

Candle had dropped her voice to sound more like the departed Templar, even accenting the T's the way he had done. The five others looked up at her, beaming as she finished her rendition.

'Something like that,' Mako said with a raised glass.

Elector stood, clearing his throat, and looked around at the Templars.

> *'And of those twelve young heroes,*
> *We find just six remain*
> *Lest we forget the obvious*
> *That war is not a game.*
>
> *Let us remember the soldier Blaze,*
> *A model officer for all to see.*
> *Let us remember the noble Swift,*
> *As fine a woman as could be.'*

The table clapped, Candle rapping her knuckles on the table as she held her glass high. Then Rose stood.

> *'Let's sing out the name of Penn,*
> *He lost his leg but not his might.*
> *Let's sing out the name of Cardinal,*
> *She battles her demons in the night.*
>
> *We mourn the death of Roland,*
> *Who on the field bled.*
> *We lament the existence of Hero,*
> *Who from the field fled.'*

Patch leapt up and continued.

> *'A moment given to Mako, the sailor,*
> *On his boat he is at home.*
> *Another for Scholar, the learned,*
> *Never is she without her bo....'*

Patch paused, and Rose cleared her throat. 'Say tome. It's a kind of book.'

'Thanks!' Patch said.

> *'Another for Scholar, the learned,*
> *Never is she without her tome.*
>
> *We toast to Rose, the Duchess,*
> *As natural a Templar as was ever made.*
> *And finally, brave Elector,*
> *Who gave up his rifle for a surgeon's blade.'*

The five standing Templars had their wine glasses hoisted over the middle of the table. They looked at Sasha. She took a deep breath and stood up, lifting hers as well. She started slowly.

'General Caesar had a dream, an idea
That burned fiercely in his mind,
To mold the future of the Renaissance
Out of the best men and women he could find.

"Learning is your faith, the library your temple."
Oh, Templars took the words to heart.
Each of them forged their own future,
Turned their passions into art.

We are brothers and sisters, forged by generals.
Our mettle is tried and true.
We are the Templars of the Renaissance Army
There is nothing we cannot do.'

They all looked at each other and drank the wine. After the laughing and cheering and poetry, the silence was deafening. Every one of them had tears in their eyes.

'Well,' Rose finally said, 'that may be the shittiest poem ever to make people cry.'

They all laughed. Sasha looked about and wished that this moment could last. The six of them, here, in this room, together, Templars all.

'I say,' Elector broke her thoughts, 'that we make our way to the stage, and see the entertainer provide some real poetry.'

'Tonight, we celebrate,' Patch exclaimed. 'Tomorrow, the war.'

'Tomorrow, the war,' Candle shouted, and led the Templars out of the room. Sasha slowly followed, letting them all leave, absorbing the last ounce of contentment in the room before closing the door behind her.

'Tomorrow, the war.'

Epilogue

The wagon bumped over the roads from Snelling Castle. Miklos sat inside, stuck in a gloom.

Operation Tempest had proven less a thunderstorm and more a light rain. Even the most optimistic officer on Prince Stefan's staff had to admit the RAM had countered every advantage Tempest brought. A few well-placed operations in the cities and the district troops were recalled. The forces in the field stretched to cover supply lines that were constantly attacked. And then this sudden Army of the Lakes completely surprised the generals and their troops.

This Renaissance Army sure does know their enemy, Miklos thought.

Not that Stefan's troops had not managed a few small victories – some prisoners from this Army of the Lakes. A failed ambush outside Bemidji cost the Renaissance Army two dozen casualties. And more than a few fat officers resigned their commissions rather than leaving the comfort of their depots, giving more aggressive, younger men a chance to shine.

Small victories indeed. King Xavier was not happy. He was not at the point of publicly dressing down his own son, but Stefan's star was not rising as fast anymore. After all Stefan's attacks on Marshal Robinson, the silence from the prince was deafening.

Bennabi was likewise frustrated. The Renaissance Army's weapons not only destroyed most of his transports, they killed what little support King Xavier had for his whole corps. All his planes were grounded now, and Bennabi was fighting for their continued existence, instead of using them to burn the Renaissance Army out of the forest.

The wagon rode through the gates into the embassy. Miklos exited to find his aide standing before him.

'What is it?' he asked, harshly. It was late and he wanted to sleep.

'Sir, I think you should come with me,' the aide said.

'Captain, if ever I need you to be sure that this is important, it's now.'

'It's important, sir.'

'What's going on?' Miklos asked.

His aide waved him silent and led him towards the military building. Once

544

they passed the front door, the captain stopped him in the hallway.

'Sir, an individual presented himself this morning to the gate guards. He indicated that he was a former member of the Renaissance Army, and he requested asylum.'

'The Royal Army gets ten of these a week from people seeking attention and rewards. Why come to us?'

'He said, given the losses the Royal Army has received, he did not think they would treat him with respect.'

Miklos sighed. The captain pressed on. 'I'm not an expert, sir. He sounds genuine, but he also sounds like a smooth talker. If he does have another motive, I can't figure it out.'

'Very well,' Miklos said. 'Let's see if we can figure out what his game is. If he is genuine, he may be a source of information.'

'And if he's not?'

'He'll be dead by dawn.'

***

The young man sat in an interrogation room. He looked nervous, glancing about his surroundings with unease, but far from panicked. He dressed in a simple smock, a peasant's jacket over the back of his chair.

When Miklos entered, he stood and came to attention. Miklos found that a curious response.

'Do you know who I am?' Miklos asked.

'Imperial Commonwealth officer. Colonel of Regiment in the Scouts, sir.'

You've studied the Commonwealth? That was odd. Commonwealth ranks were not secret, but they were different enough from the insignia common in Atlantic America that most people did not know them.

'How did you know that?'

'We spent a week learning about your military in the Templars, sir. Rank and uniform recognition was one of the things we had to know.'

Miklos gestured for the young man to sit, then took the seat opposite him. 'I am Colonel of Regiment Sir Rika Miklos, Military Attaché to the Commonwealth Embassy.' He pulled out a notebook and a pen. 'And you are?'

'My name is Neil Washington, sir.'

Templar Scholar

'And you were a member of the Renaissance Army?'

'Yes, sir.'

'In what capacity?'

'I was a Templar, sir. An office in training, the future of the Renaissance, I was told. I even had a Renaissance name; Templar Hero, future infantry officer.'

Miklos' fatigue disappeared, replaced with curiosity.

'How did you join the Renaissance Army?'

'I was with a pair of ruffians out in Menahga county. They took a girl, but we got cornered. The girl didn't know about me and I had the drop on the pair, so I killed them and became a hero. That's how I got the name Hero, see? Joined their Fourth Field Regiment. It was a nice change of pace. A lot of the women were willing, and I had a sweet spot with the colonel, helping him get on the good side of the people there.

'Then I got an offer for the Templars. It was this special program, the generals' own, training the future leaders of the Renaissance. Lots of books, classes on history and politics, speaking, and ethics. Training on shooting and attacking towns and all that. It was a lot of fun, but it was also difficult. The generals paid us a lot of attention.'

'You left because it was getting hard?' Miklos asked.

'I can deal with hard, sir. I may not be as perfect as some of the other Templars, but I can hold my own in a fight, and while I suck at books, I can speak four languages. No, it just wasn't what I was looking to get into. The girls in the program weren't as willing, and the benefits of being an officer weren't as big as I was hoping for. Plus, I can't imagine that the Renaissance Army is going to win against the might of the Commonwealth. They're actively promoting democracy in the Liberated Counties. For everyone, like they didn't learn anything from the fallen empires.'

'So, you left them,' Miklos said, 'and made your way here.'

'Yeah. I wanted to get here sooner, try to warn the Royal Army what it was about to get into with Tempest, but it took me a bit to get out of the Liberated Counties without getting caught, then had to make my way down here without attracting attention. I figured by now the king's government must be pretty pissed off at getting embarrassed, and I wasn't likely to get a warm reception, you know?'

Miklos stared at him. 'Warn them about Tempest?'

546

'I knew the generals had troops in the cities, the special kind that don't get parades,' Washington shrugged. 'My pa was one of them, way back when. He had stories. But it figures the generals would wait to use them for maximum impact. And what's more maximum when the nobles sending their troops off to fight suddenly stop feeling safe in their own homes.'

'And you knew about this?'

'Well,' Washington sighed, 'I wasn't told directly, not really. But one of the officers implied it. See, we spent a few days going over the plans to try and pick them apart, and Templar Scholar – one of the other Templars, pretty enough to plow once or twice –mentioned threatening the cities as a way of drawing off Tempest's forces. The officer didn't disregard it outright.'

'Plans?' Miklos asked.

'Sure. The one where the army builds a wall around Walker and slowly burns down the whole thing. Or the other one, with the hundreds of fire bases across the county. The ones that weren't really thought out.'

'When was this?'

'During the big January blizzard, when we got snowed in.'

Miklos sat back and thought for a moment.

Until he spoke of Tempest, the man before him had said little to pique Miklos' interest. A few articles in newspapers and rumors around the pub would bring anyone up to speed on Tempest.

But Prince Stefan mentioned ridiculous plans brought forth by General Robinson and King Xavier. And the blizzard in question happened days after the briefing where Stefan revealed Tempest to the king.

The realization stunned Miklos. The Renaissance Army had intelligence organs in the cities, that much was certain, but every investigation so far focused on low-level clerks and secretaries, the kind of people who process papers when planning and orders start taking shape.

If they had these plans only days after they were revealed, then the Renaissance Army has at least one highly placed asset in the Royal Army. A general or highly valued colonel.

That shouldn't be possible.

Miklos looked at the man before him. He was a mercenary, someone out for himself. He rode the Renaissance Army for as long as it benefited him, and now rides the winds into the arms of the Commonwealth.

Miklos detested such men. They had no allegiance to anything or anyone.

But he also appreciated how easy they were to control.

'We will grant you asylum,' Miklos said, 'conditionally. You will be provided a room and food –.'

'And women?' Washington asked hopefully.

'And women. So long as you provide intelligence on the Renaissance Army, you will be taken care of. But if you falter –.'

'Don't worry, sir. I'll take the candy over the rock, anytime.' Washington smiled. 'Oh, it's been too long.'

Miklos feigned a smile.

It was good this Templar Hero was so easy to control. Miklos was going to have much to do, and the less work Hero was, the more time Miklos could spend on other things.

Such as his own personal war against the Renaissance Army.

Michael Bernabo

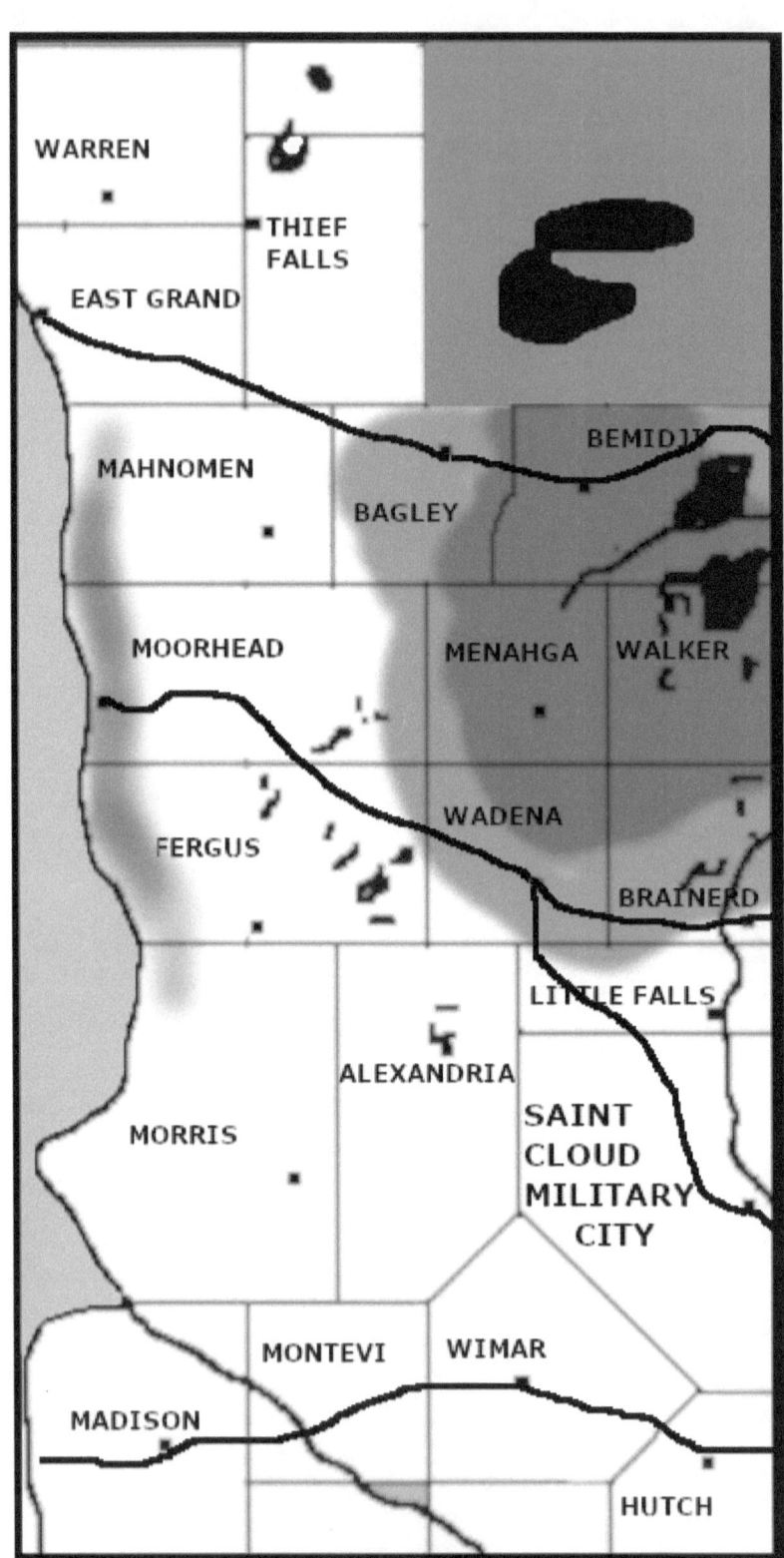

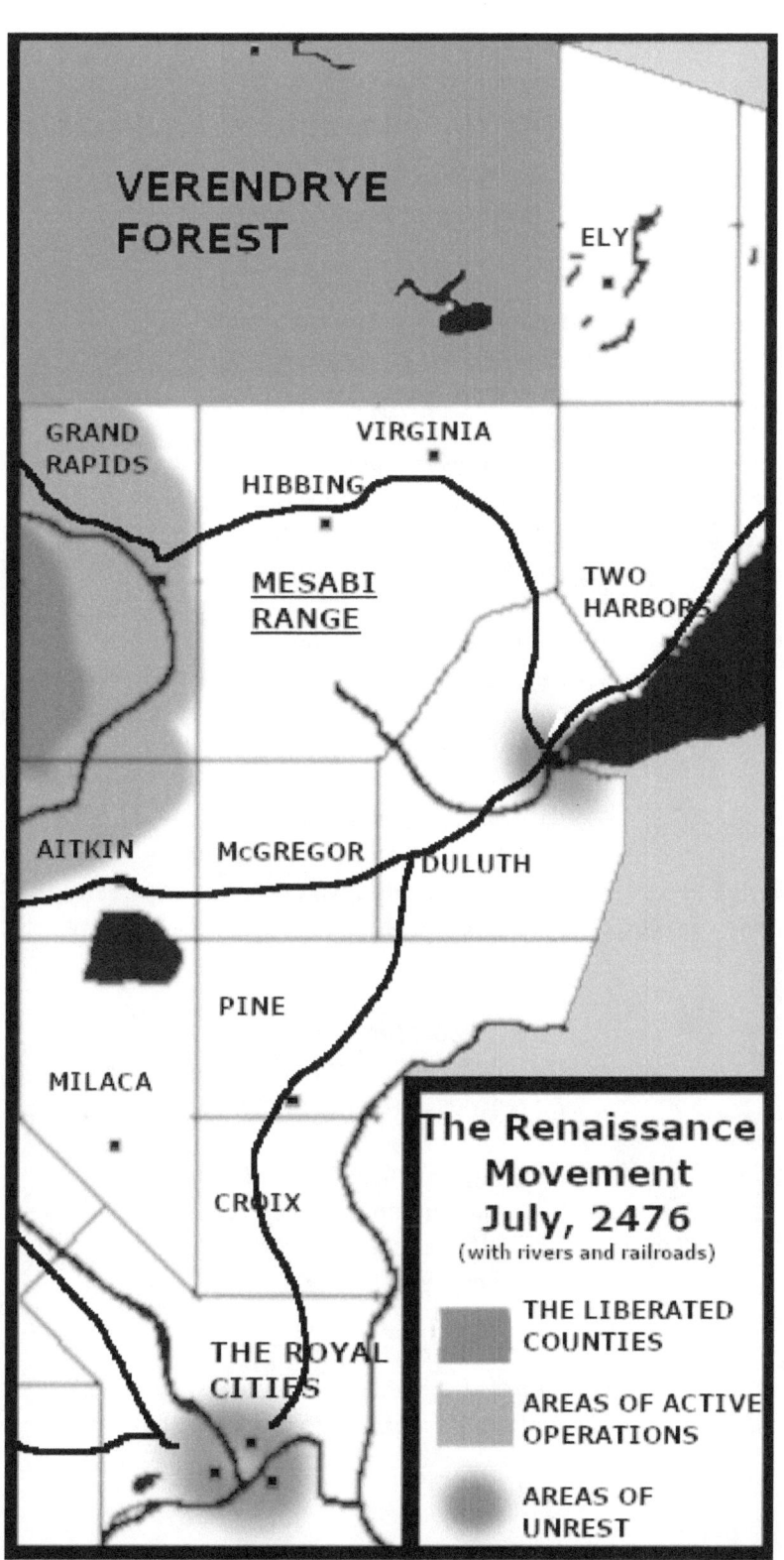

Thank you for the characters, Kickstarter Backers!
(In Order of Appearance)

Bill Hamline
Hamline Family Traveling Theater
A character with skills who you wouldn't think to find in a post-apocalyptic setting.

Libby, Templar Patch
Templar, Renaissance Workshop
'Quirky, brilliant, logical (ultimately), but scattered. I can hear her taking about rules for weaponry.'

Madam Moreau
Instructor in Grammar, History and Ethics, Templar Project
Someone who teaches the character about how history is written by those who benefit from writing it.

Doctor Carissa Adams
Senior Doctor, Civilian Hospital at Charity
'Someone with a medical background who also has engineering skills. Someone who can contribute to the reincarnation of the tools we have now such as CT scans and MRI's.'

Scott Anthony
Instructor in Politics and Rhetoric, Templar Project
'Someone who teaches Sasha the dark side of politics.'

Tony Long, Chemical Officer Roach
Long Lake Militia; Renaissance Workshop
'Officer Candidate, Rough on the outside, but soft on the inside, with a great sense of humor.'

Uncle Jacque
Surveyor for the Renaissance Workshop
Someone who has spent his life learning to work with old technologies.

Doctor John Moore
Renaissance Workshop; Advisor to the Civil Council
'A character who is a skeptic and wants to bring back the scientific process. . . .'

Lawrence Shaw
Ambassador from the Bishop of Boston
'I'd like to suggest a character that represents the intrigues that might be going on pushed by the Catholic Church.'

Fitzpatrick 'Fitz' O'Cloud
Independent Woodsman
A hunter who respects the RAM, but is not part of it.

Aquillon Madrillon
Singer of Ancient Lore
'Musically inclined and hides the old stories in music.'

Zac Holden
Liberation Outreach, Civil Council
'Civilian. Very friendly and always willing to help. Strives to do the right thing.'

Douglas
Renaissance Agent in Walker Town
'I like the idea of someone who ultimately wants the same end result but doesn't agree with the same methods as everyone else'.

Yeoman Leo Cross
Yeoman in the Bemidji Yeomanry
'Mostly what I want . . . is an account of the position of "bad guys' . . . the goes a little deeper than avarice, and a total lack of moral character.

Michael Bernabo has been creative his entire life,
writing and illustrating a fantasy picture book in kindergarten,
and a sixty-page epic science fiction story in middle school.

Michael's first book, *Renaissance Calling*, was published in 2017.

Michael currently lives in Minnesota, where he spends
much of his time writing and enjoying stories.